The glitter, the glamour,
the sex, the sin.
Hollywood, where they lived other
people's dreams in shadows on the silver screen—
and acted out private nightmares when
the camera stopped.

Mary Loos's
THE BARSTOW LEGEND

A novel of Hollywood. Where Belinda Barstow
is coming of age. Hollywood. Where a world is
in turmoil with the advent of television.

The Barstow Legend

****

by Mary Loos

THE BARSTOW LEGEND
A Bantam Book / September 1978

ISBN 0-553-12036-0

Published simultaneously in the United States and Canada

Bantam Books are published by Bantam Books, Inc. Its trade-
mark, consisting of the words "Bantam Books" and the por-
trayal of a bantam, is registered in the United States Patent
Office and in other countries. Marca Registrada. Bantam
Books, Inc., 666 Fifth Avenue, New York, New York 10019.

PRINTED IN THE UNITED STATES OF AMERICA

To Grace with love

"God Almighty, look!" said Claudia Barstow, "Michelangelo's *David* has just been let loose on the beach."

She stood with her niece, Belinda, peering through the tall clumps of salt cedar that had been planted against the bulkhead to conceal the stout wire fencing and padlocked gates. Now the public could not gape so easily into the front garden and swimming pool of her beach house. Such fenced-in privacy was one of the penalties of having Belinda become the top box office star of the past year.

Claudia was certain that most of the handsome young men on the beach would have given anything for a chance to be inside her garden. And no doubt Belinda would have given anything to be just one of the young people outside on the shore this glorious afternoon. But of course it was impossible. Too bad. When Claudia herself was a young film star—one of the first residents of this strand, much narrower and less populated then—there hadn't been such a crowd. Swimming, running along the beach, and visiting back and forth had been casual, and easy.

Now was the time of afternoon when Santa Monica beach society was gathering surfboards, snorkels, towels, and beach bags, heading for the state parking lot up the way.

Claudia, back in America after being abroad, was startled by the change in freedoms of the young. There was open talk of "making it with chicks." The mid-fifties rebellion had engendered cycle gangs, girls perforce wearing tight jeans to ride with their men. It was an era of black leather jackets worn to divert switchblade rumble wounds. The revving up of cycles which roared along the coast highway sometimes punctuated the late hours as boppers on their peripatetic sashay to jukebox hangouts often carried tone-deafening portable radios that screeched out the latest rock and roll.

Claudia was bewildered by it; she felt she should have known there would be great changes when she saw the freedom of sexuality during the war when she served in England with the Entertainment National Service Association (ENSA). Then, in moments of dramatic confrontation on battlefront, labor laden farms, shiveringly cold coal mines, and blitzed cities under duress of bombings, she had seen passions and couplings she had never believed could have existed outside closed doors.

Even though she herself had not been young at the time, she remembered the clinging embrace of her young protégé, John Graves, in a crowded air raid shelter. John Graves—now a star, her niece's first crush in the picture she had just finished in Europe. But a romantic yearning was different, a relationship built of a myriad of associations. God knows, Claudia was no prude, and her own life, freewheeling and arrogant in her stardom, had pursued a path she hoped her niece would never know. But these madcap youngsters, apparently accepting sex on its own terms, were different.

Some of these young people were no doubt born during the massive moral turnabout of World War II which had shuffled myriad and alien bodies into juxtapositions never before known in the world.

Claudia suddenly realized how she feared for Belinda.

Her main concern now was how Belinda would adjust to this new world. Right now, within a pebble toss, were at least a dozen youths, bronzed, muscles glistening with salt water and oil in the rosy glow of the late sun. They were as handsome as any lads she had ever seen. And in her salad days in theater and on movie set, she had plucked many a flower, and was an expert.

But there was one young man, who must have been in his early twenties, on the beach who was different from the rest. In the group of fraternizing, shouting young people, he was alone. No girl screaming and laughing, no companion rushing for the first beer up Santa Monica canyon where they gathered at Doc Law's.

He had just stepped out of the surf, and he slowly approached the cedars and the wire fence, too often the repository of the public's towels and gear. His short dark hair curled tightly to his head. His wet face seemed sculptured, the full lips and the firm chin promising sensuality. Claudia, taken with his almost pagan handsomeness, thought his ears should have been pointed like a faun's.

Being a connoisseur in her later years of the advantages of well-built men of medium height, she noted that his body had rare beauty of bone structure, muscular legs like columns, solid and forceful, arms with strength between wrist and elbow. A full chest and strong back, curving down to a slender waist, firm, slim hips and buttocks, and a stomach almost concave. As he paused to pluck a fringe of seaweed from his shoulder, his overlarge hands bent at the wrist like the great statue of David in the Piazza Signoria in Florence.

In motion, she noted, scanning his almost illegally brief shorts, there was the promise of a larger penis than that on many a larger, taller man.

The young man, seemingly lost in thought, approached the fence. He sat on the sand a few yards away and picked up a large sketchbook. He opened it, dusted flecks of sand from it, studied a page, closed it carefully, and put it in a flat canvas pouch. He added a packet of charcoal pencils and a wisp of cloth. He arose, Claudia felt, with as much grace as if he were doing yoga, and he walked away.

Claudia knew Belinda would be a setup for the first man who romanced her under the right circumstances if he could manage to get her alone. It had to happen; her innate sexuality, which had been triggered too early by glamor and fame, was apt to explode again at any moment. And she was stepping into a world of predators.

Claudia remembered the last time Belinda had tried to walk on the beach in the afternoon.

"There's Belinda Barstow!" the word had exploded like Fourth of July fireworks on the beach. In a moment, she was surrounded by a mob; that same freakish beach alert which occurs almost before a lifeguard rushes out to rescue someone drowning. But this time the victim was a young girl on the beach, pressed and pushed on all sides. Someone started snatching buttons off her little terry coverup. Her beach bag was stolen. A pimply, arrogant boy forced her into his arms and kissed her, thrusting his tongue into her mouth; another started snapping pictures. While she fought him off, two girls snipped locks of her hair with manicure scissors quickly dug out of their purses.

As she broke away screaming, guards came running from the private beach club down the way. Claudia had rushed out and started beating against the oily backs of the boys who gathered around her. Someone had alerted the police, and sirens and patrol cars roaring onto the public parking lot increased the onlookers.

Police had broken up the crowd and escorted Belinda back to her garden, where the gates were hastily padlocked. Cops tried to get the names of offenders, but suddenly everyone was anonymous and innocent. Belinda, with a bleeding lip and a fingernail scratch across her back, was sobbing, and Claudia had called a doctor to sedate her.

Since then, on weekends and holidays the studio had sent a guard to break up the crowds that gathered at the fence. A direct line was installed to the beach patrol and the Santa Monica Police.

Yards away was the glistening ocean, which Belinda henceforth could not enjoy, save at dawn hours and warm evenings after dark, when Claudia patrolled with the little Yorkshire, Atlas, who would bark at a footstep on the sand a block away. Or Effie, stark in her white uniform, with her dark face dissolving in the dark, would stand by, as she had when Belinda was a little girl, cavorting in the waves, the child of Jeffrey Barstow, the aging matinee idol and film star.

Claudia hoped Belinda's first real love affair would be with a young man, not too worldly or ego driven by success. She hoped Belinda would find one simple springtime romance, at least for starters. She must find out more about the boy on the beach. He had to be an artist. She'd maneuver around and see if his sketches were any good. Someone eligible to be invited inside that fence for some normal boy-girl companionship might be the answer to Belinda's problems.

Claudia, the wise, the worldly, had managed to select a man who could give her beloved niece more unhappiness than she had ever known, even in the checkered and tragic start of her own life as an adult.

"Wasn't that young man's physique something!" she said.

4

"I noticed him before," said Belinda. "He comes here early in the morning, and sometimes he runs with a black whippet when it's too early for him to be tagged for having a dog on the beach. But anyway, when I saw them, I grabbed Atlas. No use for a Yorkie to tangle with a whippet."

"You didn't tell me about this," said Claudia. "Did you talk to him?"

"Of course not," said Belinda. "It was the day I had to rush to the studio for tests. I think he smiled at me, but I don't think he knew who I was. He just went his way."

Claudia looked at Belinda. Her profile was so clean-cut it seemed to knife against the darkening seascape like a fine newly minted coin. There was a dignified sadness about her, which somehow ennobled her youth. How true what had always been said about the Barstows: their physiognomy evoked classical comparisons.

This was the time of the evening, she recalled, when a young woman who had no plans for the evening began to fear the shadows and the loneliness of nighttime. And Claudia knew what it was like to be a film star, how many nights no one called, when the whole world thought her life was one gay affair after another.

Claudia realized that most young men of Belinda's age didn't have the funds or the know-how to take out a major celebrity, and the girl had had more than her share of older men courting her in ways she had not been prepared to handle, and which had caused her great tragedy.

As she thought about Belinda's plight, Claudia felt as ancient in her place on the long parade of Barstows as if her history were written on parchment. She found herself, after her uninhibited career, being a pseudo mother-grandmother image, seemingly looking upon a filmic parade of clones, made up of fragments of her own memories.

And now, living in California again, she found too many changes. How could she cope with them! How could she help Belinda, when she didn't even know this world herself anymore? She had been away from America and the changing scene too long, and she was too cozily in love with her husband, Max Ziska, to assess the reality of the new society.

Disturbed by her own flashing thoughts, she arose and

looked up the beach. The first lights were going on in all the houses with their private fences along the sands. Way down the beach, illumination flashed on the old building that held the carousel, concessions, and cafés of the ramshackle, charming old Santa Monica Pier. But between that hurdy-gurdy world and the place where she stood, millions of dollars of ocean frontage had held and enshrined the nucleus of the film world in her day. She had been the first to move here, having come west in, my God, was it 1913! Could it be? And now she was the doyen of this precious stretch of beach.

She thought of all the powerful and glamorous citizens who had lived alongside her during the lush days when this area, referred to as the Gold Coast, had been home of the film elite.

Gone far away or dead, all of them, Norma Shearer and Irving Thalberg, Douglas Fairbanks, Bebe Daniels and Ben Lyons, Paulette Goddard and Burgess Meredith, Randolph Scott, Louis B. Mayer, Mervyn Leroy, Virginia and Darryl Zanuck, Joe Schenck, Anita Loos, Al Lewyn, and, crowning the millionaire fringe of beach, the fabulous Marion Davies–William Randolph Hearst mansion, even that great edifice with rich panelings and furnishings imported from Europe and worth a ransom when they were purchased, pulled apart by a milling horde of screaming decorators and do-it-yourselfers like the death scene of Madame Hortense in Zorba the Greek.

It was appalling how many once-great names, friends and rivals alike, were under the sod. Tyrone Power, Clark Gable, Gary Cooper, Dick Powell, Humphrey Bogart, Lionel, John, and Ethel Barrymore, Cecil B. de Mille, Harry Cohn, Jerry Wald, Erich Von Stroheim, her brother Jeffrey, long gone, and of course, her longtime protector, Simon Moses, who had built a studio around her success as a dazzling young film star.

Those early times had been filled with work and excitement. Everyone knew each other; the town had been a village, the name Hollywood synonymous with glamor. Now, in 1960, it was fragmented. Studio talent pools were obsolete; the greatest collection of filmic glamor met in Italy, now that the United States was involved for the first time in the international film festival.

What had happened to Hollywood? The exciting recent pictures were Cocteau's *Le Testament d'Orphee*; Renais's *Hiroshima, Mon Amour*; Fellini's *La Dolce Vita*—a film so intense in its freedom from cliché that it had startled the whole "they lived happily ever after" school of film makers; and even *Ben Hur*, a film with American producer, production staff, Willy Wyler directing, and an American cast, was shot in Italy. The most startling film made in the United States was a drag farce, *Some Like It Hot*.

It was a time, thought Claudia, when the old tigers were beginning to lick their wounds and stop baring their fangs. Eisenhower, Khrushchev, de Gaulle, and Macmillan had met in Paris, and summit talks to divide the world had failed.

The same disturbances of the old order were happening in the world of celluloid. Television, the ugly sister, had somehow shoved its foot into Cinderella's glass slipper and was saving the studios. The princes from New York who handled the purse strings were enchanted. Rentals of empty stages were saving Titan, the studio she had helped found.

Claudia was overwhelmed at the great dose of common sense being thrust into her brain by her situation: Max's responsibilities with production, her own personal duties as dialogue director for Belinda, and above all the secret in this house which had been locked up against the world.

Claudia, who until recently had never even thought of running a household, now found herself involved in everything from Dr. Spock to kiddie clothes at Bullock's Westwood store.

As if on signal, the french doors from the dining room opened, and Effie walked out on the porch with the little boy, Alex.

Effie's dark face was alight with pleasure as he toddled beside her, balancing delicately by holding her hand. She had done the same for his mother, and she guided him forward.

The child, golden curls brushed back from his forehead, his eyes the same startling blue as those of his mother, Belinda, and his grandfather, Jeffrey, smiled and toddled toward Belinda.

"That's right," said Effie. "Go to your mama."

Alex held out his hands, and Belinda grasped them, smiling.

"Effie!" said Claudia. "You've just got to stop it. You say that in front of somebody, and it'll be the worst thing you could do for Belinda."

Effie put her hand over her mouth. She was a loving woman, and the most difficult thing in her life was to stifle truth, for she loved Belinda as her own family, just as she had loved Belinda's father, Jeffrey. This child was the crowning triumph of her three generations of service to the Barstow family, even though his birth was a secret.

"Oh, oh, I'm sorry," she said. "It's just so natural that he belongs to B'linda."

"You've just got to remember to say," said Claudia, "that I'm his stepmother; Max is daddy, Belinda his stepsister, and that's it."

"Yes," said Belinda. She picked him up and hugged him. Then she set him down and turned to Claudia.

"Just because of a movie company, I can't tell the truth. Why can't I say he's my baby! I think it's rotten. Why shouldn't Alex have millions in his own name? His father was the richest of all the golden Greeks. And most of all, why can't the world know he's a Barstow? Why does my lousy, mean old mother in Italy have to pretend to be his mother? It's all just because of Titan studio's old money madness."

"Now, now," said Effie, "I'm sorry I started this. I'll be more careful." She put her hand on Belinda's shoulder. "I'm sorry, honeybun. I'm so sorry. We all are. It really isn't fair. It isn't."

Belinda's eyes brimmed with tears. "I haven't got any life!" she said. "The only one is on the set when Max makes me be somebody else. I can't do anything. I can't go out. I can't have any fun."

"You're going to," said Claudia. "I know it isn't fair, but the studio has millions invested in your star image. Anyway, I'm going to look around, and I'm going to find someone nice for you to be with. Don't worry, honey. At least we've made it possible for the baby to live with us. Everybody thinks your mother and Max had the baby. God knows, it was rough enough at the beginning. But at least I was lucky enough to marry Max after we unloaded your mother.

And we love you. We're a family, and the three Barstows are together. Isn't that something?"

"Yes," whispered Belinda.

Claudia reached in her pocket and brought out a handkerchief. "Here, wipe your eyes," she said. "How would you like it if the baby were in Italy, living with your mother, who was annoyed at pretending he was hers, and her new Italian prince for a proxy daddy?"

"I'd hate it!" said Belinda. Her anger erased her tears, and she picked up the baby. "Alex," she said, "your father may have been the greatest Greek hero of them all, and one of the richest men in the world, and you'd be worth millions if he'd lived, but most of all, you're a Barstow, and someday you're going to let the whole world know it."

"Amen," said Effie.

"Come the day, that'll be a nice scandal," said Claudia. "I agree with you, honey, but for the sake of all of us, and Max upstairs who's knocking his brains out getting that script ready to save dear old Titan again, let's let it sleep for now. My God, I sound like one of those lousy soap operas Effie likes so much."

"No way!" said Effie. "They wouldn't let the writers get away with this plot. Come on, Alex, time for your supper."

"Well," said Claudia, "Alex, say good night to your so-called stepmother who is really your great-aunt, and your half sister who is really your mother. My God, I'd better stop this chatter myself, he'll be getting onto it pretty soon."

She kissed the little boy, who was ready for his supper. Effie took him away, turning to give them a winning smile.

"Times like this I could use a drink," said Claudia. "Poor Max, upstairs writing about his Borgia family, couldn't in his wildest hallucinations dream up what we've been through." She stood up. "It's getting too cold out here. I wish Max would come down. Let's go inside, light a fire, and talk about the script. It'll get our minds off our problems."

Belinda stood up and stretched. Claudia admired the curve of her arms, the flawless shoulders and breasts, the slender waist. Even a cotton shirt and slacks could not disguise the fluidity of her body. Her blonde hair was tied

in a mane behind her shoulders. Her level eyebrows, with
the upward curve like her father, Jeffrey's, suggesting a
diabolical possibility behind the curved angel wings, the
bright blue double dark-lashed eyes, the smooth porcelain
nose, and the full lips all bespoke the classic formation
that had made her face the perfect vehicle for emotion,
along with the fluid beauty of a divine sort.

This time of day was usually a gathering time. Max was
at work revising a few last scenes for his new production,
Young Lucretia. When he worked, Claudia had learned
to pretend he was away at an office, and she waited for
him to step out of his sanctum.

Sometimes when she was in the garden she would see him
as he stood staring out at the ocean, his eyes half-closed,
his white hair ruffled, his mind on the story seething in his
head, as he nervously chewed on the flesh between his
forefinger and thumb.

She understood Max so well, and his creative process,
that she feared for him in this new world of computerized
film making. Sometimes she felt that he was as vulnerable
as the last prehistoric animal walking through a forest
of dreams into the world of reality; he was a nineteenth-
century poet coping with the plastic medium of the
twentieth century.

Max had told her Gordon Craig, the brilliant son of
Ellen Terry, had believed that any theater should be the
production of one expert, instead of a group of contribu-
tors. He, too, believed in the artist-director; he had told
Claudia that Craig would have hated motion pictures; so
he did, in a way, when he had to battle Fergus Austin.

To him, his production must be the total expression of
the poet. To fashion his fantasy into reality it would be
sharpened, formalized, and perfected by the critical essence
of his mind; he envisioned his work as the elixir of some
inner instinctive source. What seemed minutiae and repetition in film he knew would come magically alive in the
mosaic he assembled from chaos; he knew he was master
of organizing his raw materials into artistic emotion.

He had overwhelmed her sometimes with the vitality of
his mind, the simultaneous unfolding and exploding of
feelings and images. He had a mystic view of art; he was

Narcissus, reflecting not only his own face, but also the faces of his characters, the earth, and the sky.

At this moment, Claudia knew, he was braindeep in the story of the Borgias, and for the hundredth time she wondered if Lucretia Borgia was the right vehicle for Belinda.

It seemed incredible to Claudia that Max had written this years before he even knew Belinda, or that he had never seen the possibility that the two lives in many ways were akin. Although she loved Max, she sometimes felt that he was so engrossed with his own characters, and they seemed so alive to him, that life was the shadow, and they the reality.

In making his beloved Belinda the beautiful puppet of the Borgia family, it had not entered his mind that the story in a way paralleled her own tragedy. And Claudia was not going to tell him. For to disturb his creative fires would have been the worst fate that could happen to him. He could not accept any diversion from his preplanned rhythm. God knows he was nervous enough as it was, his hands were often palsied, and he never seemed to know what he wore or what food was put in front of him.

Only when the last lights were out and he touched her in the dark and found her body did she know that he was back from the Renaissance and the bloodbath of the Borgias, to be her husband. They forgot age and time in the oneness of their bodies and their affection. Their love had come late to them, thus they cherished it all the more.

Sometimes, half-dreaming after a session of fulfilling sex, as Max slept and she lay awake, marveling at the turn her life had taken, she felt as if she and Max had borne Belinda, which in a way they had.

But now, Max did not come downstairs. Instead, his soft lead pencils were dropped helter-skelter and his meticulous script lay scattered on the desk.

Max could not help himself; he was born to use the private emotions of his star to create his fantasies, and the finished product of *The Oracle* had again proved his instinct true. Belinda's youthful beauty and innocence had been a writer-director's dream. Blank paper on which he could write his script.

On location, when Belinda had fallen in love with the sensual actor, John Graves, who played opposite her in *The Oracle*, Max had used her naïveté and her drive to belong to the adult world to give her a depth of emotion on the screen which she did not possess in her own personal experience.

In *Young Lucretia*, he planned using her wistful, unresolved experience and her smothered sexuality in the same way, to show the tragic manipulation of Lucretia Borgia by the Italian Renaissance society.

Belinda likewise, at the age of fifteen, had given birth to a child under the most secret circumstances. Her only night of sex had followed the most expensive party the modern world had known, in the villa of the man who bedded her, Pericles Niadas, who worshipped her image in the film he financed.

Lucretia Borgia, also a beautiful child, was ambitiously used by such infamous characters as her father, Rodrigo (Pope Alexander VI), and her murderous, conniving brother, Cesare. The very fact that two papal bulls had recognized her illegitimate child, Gennaro, the Infans Romanus, as possibly the son, first, of her father, and then her brother, had triggered Max's fertile mind into searching for the dramatic possibilities in this beautiful young woman, adrift in a sea of Renaissance power and intrigue. Flame had been kindled when he saw her portrait by Pinturicchio in the Vatican.

And later, in his creative mind, Belinda was related to the golden-haired, soft-faced girl, swathed in flowers, velvets, and brocades, who had been forced to parade her naked beauty in orgies at the Vatican.

Max had seen the unspoken flicker of concern in Claudia's eyes as the story unfolded from his script. He had written it in Europe, when he was captive in the war, and had scribbled his dreams to keep alive, incarcerated in rat-infested cells. At one time he had to sleep on his manuscript, protecting it with his body from the teeth of rodents who were after the paper.

Since Belinda was a star, now that she had made her debut in *The Oracle*, literature of all sorts had been rushed to her; writers with scripts of every degree of prominence, book club selections and successful plays were shoved temptingly in her direction. But so far, Max had held a tight rein on her services, and the choice was *Young Lucretia*.

Claudia had finally agreed to Belinda playing the role, as production designs by Lyle Wheeler, multi–Academy Award winner, and costume sketches by the gifted Janos proved the beauty that would be on screen. She also immediately began blocking out the scene in her mind where young Lucretia gives her first dinner, and, without her knowledge, poison is passed to one young suitor who adores her, much to her despair. The character of Lucretia could be a tour de force, and Claudia knew how important that second role would be after Belinda's stunning rise to stardom in one film. So she had joined with Max in approval of the new production.

She realized too well the turmoil he was going through.

Thinking of the vicious times of the Borgias, and knowing of the horrors he would put on the screen, she knew Max disliked himself for what he was doing. But he could not help himself. His drama and his story were so powerful, and most of the writing of it had been done under such painful conditions in a prison hospital after the war, that his first dedication was to his work.

Even in his later years, married happily to Claudia, and protecting both Belinda and the infant Alex in the shelter of his own home and work, he had to divorce his personal self from his creative being, and the nervous anxieties were beginning to eat at his heart.

The script was now being polished, and he was satisfied with it at last. Together they had deliberately chosen Leslie Charles to play the diabolical Rodrigo, her father. Leslie had been close to Belinda, almost a cicerone to her at times in Rome, and Claudia knew Belinda felt comfortable with him in her scenes.

As a young man, Leslie had played in Claudia's films, he had grown into a socially prominent figure in Beverly Hills; an aesthete of good taste, he had collected a society about him which was witty and bright. An offshoot of the London–New York–Paris more conservative homosexual set, he never pushed forward young studs or hustlers at social affairs, never forced anyone to employ a protégé, privately helped young men, and publicly only had the most attractive and important homosexuals and bisexuals mixed in with his heterosexual acquaintances. The only door into Leslie's rambling Spanish house above Sunset in Beverly Hills was the one opened by talent, charm, and good behavior, all of which were getting rarer as the film business was beginning to fragment while the vulgarians moved in with television and rock music.

Claudia smiled to herself; it was a long jump from Tyrone Power to Elvis Presley. Tyrone had held his hand on his heart as he made love, and Elvis beat a tattoo on his guitar over his penis as he excited young America. The focus had changed.

No one else but Claudia knew that Max was overwhelmed as he faced the new Hollywood; he retreated comfortably in films of a classic, period background, and decided to stay there as long as he could.

But these problems were not easily eliminated from his perimeter, for Titan had involved him in a mesh of business puzzles which she feared were destructive to his creative efforts.

He understood the sere, scrapping, sometimes bitter moods of Fergus Austin, who had fought every foot of the way to be in charge of West Coast operations of the studio.

Fretting over the tumble of thoughts, as the darkness fell on the sea, Claudia switched on the lights and lit the fireplace gas jet, setting the logs afire against the California chill. She peered into the wide hall and the stairwell. It was past time for Max to descend and join them. Had there been another hassle with Fergus Austin on his business phone?

Max was not ready to come downstairs.

It was not Fergus Austin who bothered him, although the phone as usual had jangled, disturbing his work.

He remembered Fergus as a sprightly, redheaded, bustling person when he first came to America before World War II. Even then he knew Fergus had respected his talent, realizing that you don't fool around with genius.

Max was not a complete dreamer; he had knocked around sets too many years, hearing the vulgarities of the staff, not to be aware of what was said about him.

The so-called forces of the studio hierarchy were proud that Max, like the old-time C. B. de Mille, clothed classicism with more than secondary sex characteristics. The audience felt it was getting educated while it was being aroused.

As a gaffer had said, "Mr. Ziska, you give Titan studio real class. The front office gets off its so called intellectual rocks with your pictures."

Max smiled wryly at this in his lone hours when he slaved over his scripts and his own cross-plotting of productions. Like all men who created films, he knew well that every thought had to be reduced to the visual scene and the precise word was the jewel. There was no room for flowing prose. But he kept his long labors of research, writing, editing, and cutting away from the eyes of the studio. His work seemed to flow from a great fountain of inspiration, but in reality it was the result of endless labor, as precise as that of a master stonemason building a castle. To protect his necessary charisma, his hours of travail were concealed from everyone, even Claudia, whom he loved, and most of all, from the studio personnel, for his fire must come from his own banked coals, ready to be stoked when the time came.

The new production was being birthed, sometimes painfully. They were going to have to cross-collateralize profits from *The Oracle*. What difference did economic sacrifice make to him? Achievement, not money, was the keystone of his existence.

More than Claudia realized, he understood the parallel of Belinda's life and that of his beautiful heroine, Lucretia.

Max had been accused and criticized for using a child in a woman's place, and sometimes he felt guilty. But he argued with himself that he must never allow personal feelings to interfere with the total experience of creativity.

Belinda had been aloof at times lately, and the growing excitement and publicity about her had brought a barrage of interviews and requests that would have been too much for a grown woman to face, much less a girl with Belinda's problems. But it was too late to put her in the Mary Jane pumps and pleated skirt and soft sweater she had worn as a junior high school girl when he had first met her. She had had the mantle of Barstow panache and genius thrown across her beautiful shoulders since her birth. Thank God he was the one who had discovered her, and by a strange twist of fate had her in his house where he could protect her.

Young Lucretia had again, like *The Oracle*, taxed the resources of Titan studio. Now there was no rich Greek to play indulgent Croesus for the production, and, unfortunately, a great part of the profits of the picture went into the coffers of the dead Greek's corporation, for the vast amount of money in the production had come from the generosity of Pericles Niadas, who had wanted with his life (which he gave unwittingly) to have the glories of his ancient Greece brought into being. That dream had been accomplished, and it was a pity he had not lived to see it. It was also a pity that Titan only owned a minor percentage of the profits, and the millions which the film made after production, distribution, and advertising costs were a small trickle compared to the vast empire the Greek shipper had left.

But at last Titan was in a position to continue with another blockbuster, and Max was again embarking on a picture of classic proportions.

So far, Fergus Austin, as vice-president in charge of production, had handled his needs carefully, considering his constant battle with New York bankers, and changing business methods, which involved the problems of Titan's lessening empire.

Fergus had made it plain to Max that a corporation, when it falls on bad times, is nothing.

At any time there could be a statute for bringing action against management for malfeasance. There were times in the sacrosanct meetings in boardrooms in New York when even the creative elders were barred while they were voted out. Adios. No banquet, no gold watch, just clear out; and leave the furniture and trappings, they belong to the studio.

Lock up the files of your life and leave us the key.

These personal problems were the machinations of fate that a creative person should never know. It could affect his whole artistic output. It was a necessity for the creative individual never to allow an outside influence to color his work.

Fergus's world might be business and budgets, cross-plots and production, but if Fergus said the picture could be filmed in California, then that's the way it should be, as long as he didn't interfere with artistic effort. It had taken several weeks of location scouting to convince Max.

In California, especially around Santa Barbara, Montecito, along the Seventeen-Mile Drive near Monterey, some of the stately mansions and gardens of Pasadena, the lush grounds of the Huntington Museum, and various estates in Pacific Palisades, were edifices and endless gardens where wealthy merchants in the early part of the century had spent millions recreating memories of Italy. Even streets sentimentally carried Italian names. If Fergus said second units with doubles could cover establishing shots and exteriors in Rome, then Max would accept it. And especially Fergus' most satisfactory cop-out to save money, it was necessary to film in California, for Twentieth Century Fox's *Cleopatra* had glutted Rome's facilities.

"One of the best films ever made about Paris," said Fergus, clinching the argument about location, "is *An American in Paris*, which was made on the MGM back lot in Culver City. It was the spirit that mattered. Maybe this *Cleopatra* situation is a break."

Max agreed, for most of his sets were in banquet halls, bedrooms, private meeting rooms, behind-the-scenes machinations of the court of Alexander VI. Second location units could do the establishing shots.

If Fergus had thrown Max a curve and insisted that his own private company would have to cross-collateralize funds, which meant siphoning profits from *The Oracle* and its success right into the new production, that was alright with Max, too. His salary, aside from ownership, was sufficient to give him more than enough wealth to sustain this house, and give Claudia everything she wanted. Making the film was what mattered.

But all these problems, ironed out by months of conferences, were as nothing to the letter that lay on his desk. It was the one correspondence he had hidden from Claudia, for he knew how it would disturb her. And he had not yet decided what to do about it.

It was written on fine vellum pages in a precise handwriting, the envelope was postmarked *Roma*, and it bore the crest of the Bonavente family, much older and more aristocratic than the lineage of the *principessa* who wrote it.

Although Max had cast it aside at least six times, and in his first fury almost torn it up, now, as he looked out and, blinded by his thoughts, gazed unseeingly at the golden lights of the pier snaking out into the black sea,

Max thought of the poem of ravishment limned by Pope's "Rape of the Lock"—so amazingly Belinda:

> Rather let earth, air, sea to chaos fall
> Men, monkeys, lapdogs, parrots perish all—

So it would be if the terrible letter he held secretly in his possession would interfere with this—his life.

He tried to toss the reality out of his mind. But this one piece of paper might destroy Titan studio. He sat down at his desk and looked at the letter again, trying to control himself. He knew he must think about it impersonally and forget the poison that dripped from the lines. He put on his bifocals and read it again.

Dear Max:

I find it necessary to write this to you and have you face the facts as I see them.

As you know, it was very humiliating to me to have to pretend to be the mother of Belinda's bastard child. It almost ruined my relationship with Carlo *and* with Roman society. I had a great deal of legal trouble when Carlo and I finally did decide to marry, proving that I had not been married in the church in my short and unconsummated marriage to you to protect both my daughter's name and, I may add, our partnership and the legal investment of our corporation with Titan studio.

As you know, you and I shared equally in the corporate funds which I worked out on our contract for *The Oracle*.

I was coerced into signing over my part of the production funds when Fergus insisted on cross-collateralization of your new picture, *Young Lucretia*. If I had been on hand to protect your interests, I would have made a much better deal. I am shocked at your lack of consideration of my economic needs.

As it is, I am not certain I approve of your next production. If it turns out not to be such a blockbuster, I have lost a great deal of money. After all, I was the one responsible for your return to Titan films.

I must remind you again, Belinda is my daughter, still a minor, and legally under my jurisdiction. Only my personal problems with my new marriage keep me from having her with me. However, I might decide that she should leave films and come here to take a dignified place in Roman society. Although I would accept her, I could not stomach having the baby, Alex, here. Since the world believes you are his father, he could remain with you and Claudia.

(I must say, you certainly wasted little time marrying *her* when we dissolved our marriage. I am surprised you did not select a younger companion, but I suppose she and Belinda ganged up on you. I know only too well how stubborn Barstows can be.)

It is much more expensive to live in Rome than I expected. Carlo is a charming companion, but the Bonavente fortunes are not what they once were; and maintaining, staffing, and restoring our villa in Tivoli and our apartment in Rome is quite costly.

If you insist on using Belinda in this new film (and I cannot say how well the subject will be received by Italian society), I will have to insist that to protect myself I must be included in participation in the corporation you are setting up. That would amount to 50 percent of your share.

Most importantly, I am in need of fifty thousand dollars for the time being. I shall allow Belinda to remain with you if you see your way to having Titan or yourself send me that sum immediately. Otherwise, I shall be forced to ask that Belinda join me in Rome at once.

I know this will be disturbing to you, and I do not care to have you discuss this with Claudia, as it is none of her affair. She is bound to be biased, since Belinda is the meal ticket for both of you. To be blunt about it, I do not wish to get into any transcontinental telephone arguments. There is to be no compromise.

You may convey this information to either Fergus or David Austin at your convenience, and I shall expect to hear from you at once.

I have no apologies to make. I have worked very hard to achieve my social position in Rome, against the odds you and Titan put in my way by forcing me to pretend to be pregnant, and I refuse to be sabotaged again by a self-interested film company or your ambitions. I think I am being more than fair to allow Belinda to be under your roof and to further your career, when she could be in Rome with her mother, taking part in a very attractive social scene. In the long run, it might do her a great deal more good than the tinsel career you are offering her. I had hoped she would not follow the Barstow legend, but what could I expect of Jeffrey Barstow's child?

And as a last reminder, Max, remember that I put your feet back on your current path, and I feel you owe me.

Most sincerely,
Jessica

Max tucked the letter under his desk blotter as he had since this time bomb had shattered his creative world. He knew the scenes he had been rewriting did not reach the core of his creativity; he was too disturbed. He must resolve this problem. It was like a dead elephant on his doorstep. He wanted to walk around it and ignore it, but it was not possible.

He would have chosen to talk to David Austin, for David's creative attitude toward Max had put him head and shoulders above any studio executive Max had ever known in guiding and supporting talent, including the great days in the twenties when as a very young man he had seen Eric Pommer and the UFA geniuses Lubitsch, Pabst, Murnau, and Dupont at work in Germany.

However, David Austin, as owner of Titan, was one of the new breed. Smooth, impeccable of manner, apparently most at home on airplanes and in conference rooms, in any place he called home for the moment in his international dealings. He was as usual away, constantly on the move. At the moment, in Wardour Street in London, setting up a massive television series on Mary Queen of Scots, which would hopefully bring a healthy trickle of money into the stagnant banking pools of Titan studio. David's whole life focused on structuring the new world of studio finance. He was a magnificent gambler, his stakes his world of celluloid, and so far he had won, drawing to an inside straight in making *The Oracle* eventually pay off against great odds.

There was only one person to see, and that was Fergus

Austin. Max had made an appointment to go to the studio the next day to check set models. He would have to see Fergus privately. There was nothing to do but show him the letter. How ironic that Fergus's ex-mistress, whom he hated, held the trump card.

Claudia and Belinda were to go with him to check wardrobe. He would settle them down for lunch in the commissary, where the inner circle of old studio personnel would greet Claudia warmly. She was a fragrant breath of the glories they remembered in the golden days of the studio. She enjoyed these rap sessions; God knows she was tied down enough with her responsibilities in this house, thought Max. And as for Belinda! Thank God the girl didn't realize what a pawn she was in this international game—"beat the bankers: movie star gets the dealer a hundred extra points."

Poor child, she must be protected at all costs. And she enjoyed hearing stories about her father, Jeffrey Barstow. It was fun and games for her to be part of the Barstow legend. It made her feel mature. Such family memories might help her gain the serenity to step into the role of Lucretia Borgia.

To soothe his nerves, Max walked into his bathroom; with all its glistening accoutrements, thick carpeting, and Claudia's faultlessly arranged luxuries, the only comfort it gave him was the bottle of Valium in the medicine cabinet. He took one and decided to give himself a few moments for it to start to work before he went downstairs wearing his pasted smile. But his hands still shook. He started out of the french doors onto the balcony, listening to the sob of the surf in a receding tide. Sometimes he felt it was depressing to be at the edge of this overwhelming stretch of water, the waves restless and mournful to match his mood. He waited for the Valium to enter his system, and give him tranquillity. Sometimes love was a powerful burden to bear.

2

The early-morning sun presaged a hot day. Claudia, sleepless, had awakened Max twice from nightmares, in which he cried out in some inner agony. She had found him sweating, sponged off his face, and once gave him a tranquilizer and heated milk for him in Alex's upstairs diet kitchen.

She decided to take Atlas for a walk; it was early enough to ignore the leash laws. Belinda was asleep in her bed, her blonde hair disarrayed, the ruffled canopy of her four-poster bed caught the pool reflection, casting a bright light on her face. Claudia always marveled that she wanted windows open; faint breeze and sunlight didn't disturb her, it just seemed to make her beauty glow. Claudia was grateful that her niece had the peace of mind to sleep curled up like a baby.

She gathered up the Yorkshire and slipped out of the house quietly. Even Effie was not yet in the kitchen, stirring about as usual, with the familiar hum of juice maker, the soft click of the double refrigerator doors, and squeak of oven hinges marking the first rhythm of her days of service.

Claudia kicked off her sandals, enjoying the feeling of sand between her toes. She pulled her pedal pushers above her knees. As she and the dog ran along the shoreline, she remembered how many years, it was over forty, she had run along these shores.

In the distance, the kids from Paradise Cove were floating over a drift, pulling in the nets of the fishing boat, *Fury*, catching bait for the day's fishing. Soon they would drop their catch in the bait tanks and chug up the coast a few miles, where at seven o'clock, the first gang of eager fishermen would board. She felt as if she knew the crew of two towheaded kids, she had watched them so many times. They were bending their bare browned torsos over the edge of the boat. She could see the flash of wriggling silver as they hauled their nets aboard and began bailing their catch into the bait tanks. She heard the faint chug of the motor as the tanks aerated. It was all so familiar, part of the water ballet of the seascape, and she loved them for being part of the young scene.

She noted that one of them was waving at someone on the beach. Then she saw the young man jogging along the sand with his black whippet. He waved a hand in salute to the boys on the *Fury*. It was the young man with the magnificent body she had admired the day before. For a moment he stood, immobile, and then dashed on up the beach, his dog cavorting and springing in the air. They were both joyous together, young and in tune with the fine morning.

She smiled to herself, remembering that she had run along these shores at the same age. Oh, how many years ago!

After she reached the pilings of the Santa Monica Pier and saw the early-rising young athletes of muscle beach already beginning to do their handstands, lifting barbells, and starting their endless volleyball game, she walked back to the house, sometimes wading, enjoying the slippery strands of seaweed that wrapped around her ankles. It was delightful to pull away from them, and be only concerned with the tactile problems of the moment, trying to free her mind of concern about Max, Belinda, the baby Alex, the character of Lucretia, and the horrors of the script which seemed to obsess Max so much. No wonder he had nightmares. Was it right to put these scenes on film? One scene she loathed the most. The bloodbath of the dying ox, on its back in Cesare Borgia's bedroom, its great legs tied to posts, degutted, so Cesare could lie in its pulsing body, in a bath of blood as it was slowly disemboweled, the hot flowing blood pulling the poison from his body, so he could recover from the accident of drinking his own poisoned wine. It was a horror beyond horrors, but Max insisted it was true history, and a magnificent counterpart to the legend of the beautiful pawn, Lucretia—Cesare's sister, his mistress, and mother to the child of her own father.

But Claudia attempted to remove this scene from her mind. She wanted to find a little peace before the scramble of the day began.

She was relieved in one way that at last Belinda was starting a picture after a long hiatus from acting. For almost a year after her return from Europe, she had been busy with the usual star-building. She had run the gamut that Claudia remembered so well from past years, in personal appearances throughout the country to bolster up her new image as *The Oracle*, practically saving Titan studio from the doldrums.

Her appearances at preview parties, openings, radio and television talk shows from city to city, grinding out local publicity, had undoubtedly made millions, as her image became more and more important to the mother studio. The old star system being gone, a new sex image, with a multimillion-dollar production behind her, was plasma.

It had taken the power of Max Ziska, and the arguments of Claudia, sometimes even threats, to keep Fergus Austin from pushing Belinda into a quick new film. But since she was not of age, the family controlled the decision. It had been a chance to help her to grow into her craft, and Claudia had worked incessantly to teach her.

Too many times in the years she had been part of Hollywood, Claudia had seen promising young stars blossom and fade rapidly, unprepared for the needed skills of their craft.

This must not happen to her niece.

She and her brother Jeffrey knew the dangers of changes in a lively acting career, so she had cautiously led Belinda into the wonders of the playwright's world—and her heart had leaped with joy when she found Belinda's respect for the written word.

Sometimes, as she saw the eager facility with which Belinda pursued a new role, she choked back the thought that she herself was a big fake. She had never studied so thoroughly when she should have; now she was making a surrogate apology for her own youthful capers by her rigid discipline.

As she walked along the shore, pushing the sand reflectively with her feet, she thought wryly that indeed she was much more a taskmaster now in her mature years than anyone had ever been to her.

Claudia had literally deluged Belinda with a variety of roles, more than she could possibly have played if she had been in one of the grand old stock companies.

Belinda had studied every role from Juliet to Laura in *The Glass Menagerie*. She had suffered with *Saint Joan*, nibbled at *Hedda Gabbler*, played the hapless Alma in *Summer and Smoke*, even reverted back to Shaw, as Raina in *Arms and the Man*, and then jumped to Laurie in *The Time of Your Life*.

From Shakespeare to Saroyan and Tennessee Williams. Claudia marveled that Belinda, a film star, a box office pet, had been able to be intrigued, and to play them all in readings, absorbed, amenable. It delighted her to see the actress, the seeker of truth in a role, her niece. Sometimes she thought that the child was so incarcerated by life that these shadow people were her playmates.

It was time for Belinda to find some sort of life of her own. And Claudia knew how difficult it could be. At the same age she had been under the protective wing of Simon Moses, who had adored her, built Titan company around her brash young talents, and in the years that followed, even though her life as his mistress had been unorthodox, she had in her way been protected and loved, and her life had certainly not been constrained in any nursery atmosphere.

She had worked hard—but God knows, she had played hard.

It was time for the nestling to try her wings. And how that was going to be achieved was a problem. For she was too famous, a target for the sophisticated world's growing focus on sexuality, and, strangely, in spite of the fact that she had borne a child, too innocent to be set adrift under such conditions.

Down the beach she saw the dot and apostrophe of the boy and his dog. She turned into the gate, and as she did, she paused. The young man had left his knapsack by the fence. The page of a large artist's notebook was open. At first she paused; even without her glasses, she could see that the composition was elegant, drawn with a firm hand

and a strong definition. Her glasses, always in her pocket, were put on quickly. Not that she was eavesdropping, but she wanted to see what talent this interesting young person might have.

And then she stood in shock. For every sketch was Belinda. One was of her running on the beach. One, her face, poignant and in thought; he must have peeked at her as she sat dreaming by the pool. Another, her hair turbaned in a bath towel.

There were dozens of Belinda. He had sketched her in bathing suits in the early morning, in slacks in the garden, and had invaded her privacy of mood and thought as if he had been her lover.

She looked up the beach. He was still far away; this sorcerer who had spied on them while seeming so casual. Feeling guilty but impelled by her curiosity, she flipped back pages.

The next sketches were startling. This young man had sketched Belinda in the full trappings of the Renaissance, hair crimped, flowered, and ribboned, gowns of stiff fabrics, brocades and silks, all folded line, revealing the beauty of her breasts and slender waist, hands moving in the special way that Belinda had, making arcs of her verbal expressions; the young Lucretia, poised for flight, a sad girl, a laughing girl. It was as if this young man had penetrated the soul of a filmic creature not yet born.

Claudia, staring at the double spread of sketches, shuddered. This man must be a warlock! What had led to this invasion of Belinda and the character she had yet to play?

Claudia saw him turn back by the channel that filtered the Santa Monica canyon stream into the sea, so she quickly turned the pages back to the one he had left open. In a panic, she was not ready to face him; she had to collect her thoughts. So she picked up Atlas, blew away a few grains of sand that had spilled on the paper, and fled for the house.

Once inside, she stopped, her breath drawing in quickly, her heart beating fast. She could hardly believe what she had seen. She felt almost ill, as if she had seen Belinda and Max and Lucretia exposed somehow to a rape of the inner essence of themselves.

The door to the kitchen was ajar. Effie was turning on

the juicer. Coffee was perking. Sometimes in the morning she would sit at the kitchen table, and she and Effie would plan the day.

Hoping her agitation wouldn't show, she sat facing the beach with the doors open to the dining room and the glassed terrace beyond.

"Morning," said Effie. "You're up earlier than Alex, and he's the original early bird."

She gave Claudia her warm, handsome, toothy smile; then it faded.

"You all right?" she said. "You look like you've seen a ghost."

"I did," said Claudia. "Only it wasn't born yet."

Effie glanced at her, puzzled. But practicality was her banner.

"Well, here's juice and coffee to chase it away," she said, "and since you've been exercising, after I give Atlas his breakfast, I'll fry you an egg. It'll do you good."

As Claudia sipped the juice, she peered out at the beach. Sure enough, between the fronds of salt cedar, she could see the gleam of tan flesh. The young man gathered his sketches together, and she saw the quick black flash of the dog as the two moved up the beach to the parking lot.

She looked at the kitchen clock. It was not even eight o'clock yet. She had been startled into shock. There had to be an answer to those sketches. She must tell Max.

On second thought, she decided to keep it to herself. There was no use to disturb him with this enigma. The only thing to do was to talk to the young man herself and try to discover some logical reason for this artistic invasion.

It would be a busy day. Max had told them they should be at Titan studio for an early lunch. They could visit the art department, the production designer's lofts, and see the magic that was being created. Belinda could begin to see fantasy coming alive. On this production he would share with her more, help her to know the labyrinth of creativity that surrounded the concrete production that presented her image to millions of viewers throughout the world. It was a fascinating macrocosm.

Anything that made Max happy made Claudia happy. She plotted the day with Effie; the laundress would come today. There wouldn't be any family lunch. Dinner, why not

fish and some artichokes with dill butter? Check vitamins
and yogurt. Think about Belinda having lunches sent into
the studio sometimes, the commissary could get dull, and
besides, it wasn't the place it used to be when Simon Moses
had his double chicken soup with homemade noodles and
great chunks of chicken breast in it. Everything was becoming an assembly line; they'd have to work out nutrition and
flavor to go together.

"I'll spoil her with breakfast in bed today," said Effie.

"I don't call breakfast in bed spoiling her," said Claudia.
"She's working hard on her readings, and she deserves it."

"Does she ever," said Effie. "That girl's got to have a
little fun and companionship."

"I'm trying for that," said Claudia.

The memory of the boy on the beach loomed in her
mind. To focus on other matters, Claudia opened the
Times. The news took her away from personal concerns.
Headlines and pictures revealed terrified policemen battling
several hundred young people. Students at Berkeley had
become enraged at the House Committee on Un-American
Activities, which had violated what the students had felt
was their right and the right of their teachers to follow personal political beliefs. Claudia looked at the angry faces
of the students. They were so young, many of them
Belinda's age, that they tugged at her heart.

She remembered the McCarthy days, when so many
of her friends had been pinioned by the slur against human
freedom, and she was aghast that this group of frenzied
young people had pitted their very flesh and blood against
a club-wielding police force.

The scene on the steps of San Francisco's City Hall was
a turning point in the lives of the youth of America. They
were tired of conforming; tired of the lies and deceit their
elders had handed them.

Small wonder. They had faced a war that none had
wanted; and, in steaming jungles, in ghettos, in outposts
of Peace Corps camps, in college campuses and city streets,
young Americans were beginning to wonder what reality
was, not what it was supposed to be.

As usual, the *Times* editorial page was attempting to
slap their hands and put them to bed without supper. But
for once these youngsters had tired of being docile. They
weren't going to be put to bed without food. They were

going to get the hell out of the house and find their own
way in the dark. They were ready to go hungry.

Analyzing all these problems of the young, Claudia
thought of. Belinda peacefully asleep in her bed upstairs.
She might have her problems, but she had a brilliant career
going very well, and most of all, she thanked God that
her niece was not one of the mob of Medusa-headed girls
in the newspaper. At least Belinda was not on the steps of
the San Francisco City Hall, kicking policemen in the
balls.

Later on, from upstairs, came the proof that Belinda
had awakened. Like a million elders in the land, Claudia
silently cursed the day that Elvis Presley had been let out
of the army; for the hundredth time she heard Mr. Swivel-
hips blurting out his petulant, explosive sexuality. He was
singing his new release, "Teddy Bear," and this meant
that Belinda was arising, no doubt doing her own imitation
of him as she headed for the bathroom and her shower.

"I'd better hurry," said Effie, carrying a tray on the
way to the hall stairs, "or I'll get stuck with 'O Solo Mio,'
which somehow he calls 'It's Now or Never.' "

"I wish it was never," said Claudia. "I'm looking forward to the next on her disc; it's usually calmer—the
Everly Brothers with 'When Will I Be Loved?' "

"That always goes on when she's drying her hair," said
Effie. "Good thing Mr. Max's study is on the other side
of the house."

Fergus Austin was already in his late sixties. He carried
one more resentment in his plagued mind while attempting to keep the crumbling fragments of Titan studio together in one corporate mass.

He had just returned from an emergency visit to Las
Cruces Sanatorium. His wife, Esther, had refused to eat,
and Dr. Lindstrom had finally called him, thinking his
familiar voice would help her.

He had listened to her insane prattling, and she had
smiled at him vacantly, called him Jeffrey, and then had
her breakfast, thinking it was the long-dead Jeffrey Barstow
coaxing her to eat her Wheaties.

Now Fergus instinctively knew he was going to face
another crisis. Max had some trouble smoldering within

him, and Fergus wondered what it could be. Titan had poured hundreds of thousands into preproduction for *Young Lucretia*; there could hardly be problems.

Taking time off to lunch with Claudia and Belinda was a sop to the necessity to keep things on an even keel. Claudia was like family to Fergus, but he still veered away from Belinda. Not only because she was the child of his nemesis, Jeffrey (how long could you hate a dead man?), but Belinda was an unknown quantity, although he had to respect her talent and her charisma, which even at her young age had pulled her out of her frightening first year in films.

Like many other young stars, this last year she had filled in time; she had finished with the pressures of the Los Angeles Board of Education, with a cap-and-gown one-woman high school graduation, devoid of schoolmates, the event cautiously kept out of the papers because of her sex image.

Grace Boomer, who had handled her publicity in Europe, had been at Titan so long that time and tide was her security blanket. Even Fergus, who had known her since she was a young "spinner" on the town, was afraid to let her go to pasture. She knew so many secrets about the stars and executives of Titan studio that it would be a disaster if she decided to write her memoirs.

So instead, with new wig and teeth, and bourbon rationed during working hours, she was carefully protected, to show the new young publicists what to do, and most of all what not to do. She guided a new generation of publicists over an old road, and Belinda was her special charge.

Belinda had also been kept busy with the standard routine of French lessons, fencing, ballet, singing, and of course, Claudia taught her diction, manners, and voice placement.

From time to time she had carefully protected interviews, wardrobe fittings, many photographic sessions in the still gallery, personal appearances for prestigious charities; she had launched a ship, two airplanes, and a Greek art exhibit at the Los Angeles County Art Museum, and an International Trade Center in New York. Publicly she had been made into a sacred personality.

In preparation for the new picture, her eyebrows had been shaved, and penciled variations tried out; they were grown back in again as suitable on their own. Wigs had given her headaches, costumes had been fitted, the possibility of corseting her so that her natural waist would be half an inch less than eighteen inches was attempted. In other words, she had been a captive, pulled and pummeled, regimented, tortured, and most of all, in the thrall of people mostly old or older than even her parents, bored.

Fergus was wary of her instability, which he observed more clearly than Claudia who lived with her, and saw her through the veils of familial love.

He noted Belinda's excesses, excess of tears over small things like a dress or wig that did not function smoothly for her. She sometimes performed a charming little act, a fake euphoria, which even Max accepted as youthful exuberance. She had sudden immature passions for people, be they wardrobe, publicity, personnel, interviewers, make-up men, dress designers, or visiting celebrities. Her whims of the moment usually ended in an unearned dependency. There were more crises than the family realized, which either he or David managed to circumnavigate without being obvious about it.

It was almost a game, he thought, jettisoning young men who were after the sex symbol, so ripe, so hopefully to be plucked. And one by one, they had been blocked in an unseen game. God knows how many would have their lives and their ambitions altered by the force of Belinda's magic person, added to the power of the Titan publicity department, with its adjunct of international advertising, which had more influence around the world than most religions. It was ironic that Belinda had started her career as the virgin of the sacred shrine of the ancient Greek oracle at Delphi, for indeed she had become a symbol to hundreds of thousands of people—a sex-child, as Titan had promoted her. In ancient times, she would have been enshrined in another way: desired, yet untouchable.

Fergus thought of the blood sacrifice of several men, which even Claudia didn't know about.

There was Si Merkle, the sharp young agent on the way up who had bombarded Belinda with flowers and perfume and was barred from the studio lot. Now he was third man on the totem pole at the monopolistic Star Lists Agency, a candidate to be fourth, and, no doubt, soon to resign and join a less prestigious firm.

There was the manic-depressive writer, Vernon Miles, who had his option dropped after going over Max's head and trying to talk Belinda into doing his play, falling in love with her, and then picketing her dressing room with a sign that read: BELINDA UNFAIR TO YOUNG AUTHOR. He conveniently retreated to New York; his play was produced successfully; and his well-publicized refrain was a hate song of the headless stupidities of Hollywood.

Fergus was irritated that one young girl's body could bring about such a torrent of abuse of the film industry.

Then there was the choreographer, Homer Case, who had been teaching Belinda the intricate manners and dances of the Renaissance court. He sent her his poetry daily, and it became a little too inflamed for Fergus's prying eyes. Naturally, all her private correspondence was examined before she received it. Hundreds of smutty letters had to be destroyed. Homer Case was sent on a sudden mission for Titan to choreograph a film in India, where he would remain for at least six months.

There was the Western star, Tex Arthur, with the facade of a Remington bronze and the brain of a frontier cowpoke, who had fallen for Belinda at a highly publicized rodeo on the old studio ranch. By a ridiculous coincidence, Fergus recalled, the cowboy had tried to lure Belinda into the same little adobe cottage near the lake that Claudia and Simon Moses, original owner of the studio, had kept as a love nest.

Fortunately, Whitey, the studio cop, had been trailing Belinda as ordered, and he got her to the phone on a fake call.

Tex Arthur had been dropped by the studio and was now doing Westerns in Italy.

Now, as Fergus looked at Belinda, he realized that she was reaching the age where supervision would not be possible.

He glanced at Claudia, so happy, so seemingly in control, and he wondered what was going to happen when she realized that Belinda would not remain under submissive surveillance forever. He knew there was no reason to discuss it; Claudia was too engrossed in the girl's career, and Max too in love with his picture.

Fergus thought of Antonio Valli, the young actor who had been selected to play Cesare Borgia. A brilliant actor fresh from London repertory, Valli was a northern Italian raised in Lucca, and he had told Fergus the stories of his countryside, home of Puccini, and of how passionately the composer had fallen in love with the characters he created. His wife Elvira suffered every time he started a new opera, for his dream-host took over his affection as his leading lady took form in his mind. Eventually, the woman who played the role would become his incarnate passion. So it was with Max, only he fell in love with a whole production.

Fergus knew, although he would never admit it, that he also had to be deeply involved in the production at hand, emotionally tied to it (romanticists would say in love with it), in order to sign the daring documents that transferred a fortune into the reality of a picture. Each time he was risking Titan's future and his own. He trusted Max's genius. Of course, the production was backed up by the most solid craftsmen the picture business could offer; each man knew his work, and each was aware that in the hard days of the sixties the blockbuster would have to earn sixty million dollars to keep the stockholders happy.

It was time for the big drive, the start of production, when thousands of dollars were ticked off each minute. Fergus glanced at Belinda, idly pushing her salad around, and his palms sweated.

The Titan commissary was bustling with the new wave of television activity. Actors dressed as gamblers, dance hall girls, cops and robbers, nurses and interns rushed for their fast-food lunch, the dragon of television waiting to quickly can their afternoon's work so other episodes could be filmed. Theirs was a peripatetic business. There was no future beyond contracts for thirteen segments. The studio rental space could rise and fall on Nielsen ratings.

Max was at a meeting in the production department and would join them later. Claudia noted the smothered anger on Fergus's face as he glanced at the crowds from the television companies. She felt he was not protean enough to ride with the punches of this new industry within his sacred walls, which had produced so many epic films.

As vice president in charge of production, which he had been for over a third of a century, he seemed a ripe candidate for apoplexy.

Claudia, having known him as a friend, and sometimes but rarely, a lover, since he was a kid of seventeen in the Bronx, gave him a fond pat on the hand. The affection of a long business relationship through sorrow and success had taken the place of the tumescence of youth.

"Easy, Fergie," she said, "having a stroke isn't worth it."

He crushed out his cigarette nervously between his nicotine-yellowed fingers. His once-red hair, now peppered white, seemed to bristle.

"You can say that," he said. "You're out of the rat race."

"Hardly," she said. "I'm still girl guide to Belinda; and if it weren't for her I think that water tower would topple. How about that? After my brother, Jeffrey, and myself leading you out of the wilderness, you're still depending on Barstows."

She flushed, realizing she'd been unnecessarily tactless. She knew the heartbreak of Fergus's life. He had married Simon Moses' daughter, Esther, his girl from the Bronx. Unprepared for wealth and position after her father became a tycoon, Esther had been desperately unhappy in her life with busy, ambitious Fergus. In a moment of despair, she had fled for one night into the arms of Jeffrey Barstow, and the result had been the child, David, whom Fergus had raised, believing him his own son.

Fergus had learned the truth when David was twenty-one. In spite of the shock, he had still accepted David as a major stockholder through his mother's family, a bright young man who would save Titan from financial disaster. David had expanded his picture making to international success, and Fergus, now under his aegis, was attempting desperately to keep the old Hollywood headquarters afloat.

The best thing to do, thought Claudia, was to change the subject.

She gestured at the Titan water tower. There was the old relic with the angry fist of Prometheus holding a bolt of fire in a clenched fist, defying Zeus. How long ago Fergus had designed the logo of Titan Films!

"Remember when that water tower went up?" she asked

him. "What a celebration! Cold chicken—orange juice and gin. What a hangover!"

"I don't even like to think about it," said Fergus. "We were nervous then, when we were just starting a film company. I'm still skating on thin ice, Claudia, and I'm damned sick of it."

"Well, why don't you quit?" said Claudia.

"For what?" said Fergus. "To sit on the oceanfront, count sea gulls, and get out my binoculars to see what you and Belinda and Max are up to down the beach? By the way, that baby is toddling a lot. I see Effie taking care of him, but she's getting old. You'd better fence the pool."

"I don't know what we'd do without her," said Claudia. "We are fencing the pool. We've got to break in a Chinese cook and get a proper nanny for Alex when the picture starts. Effie's got to be with Belinda. There's so damned much organizing to do between running a house and being a dialogue director. Holy Mother, Fergus, I never thought I'd be a den mother."

"It agrees with you," said Fergus. "You're not even a good drinking partner anymore." He grinned at her.

Well, anyway, thought Claudia, I wrenched a smile out of the bastard. Nervous, chain-smoking Fergus, his studio in jeopardy, but he still fights on.

She patted his hand again. "I love you, Fergus," she said.

Max came toward them. How glad she was to see him.

"I've arranged for Janos to show you wardrobe and take you through the art department," said Max. Then he turned to Fergus.

"I would like to see you in your office."

"At least have your usual pastrami sandwich," said Claudia. "You're keyed up, dear."

As he smiled, the waitress brought him the sandwich, flanked with coleslaw. They knew him well.

Janos came to the table. He was a slender man, his impeccable clothes, cashmere turtleneck sweater, suede jacket, Gucci shoes, his casual manner and his very thin mask of "man tan" makeup revealed his preplanned desire to be the apogee of elegant nonchalance.

"Wait!" he said. "Just wait until you see the wardrobe I designed for you."

"Run along," said Max. "Show her the Kevin Frazier

sketches. They're brilliant. I want to talk to Fergus. I'll meet you in his office later."

Claudia was used to these long sessions; Max left such practical problems as promotion, distribution, and exhibition to others, and Fergus carried the load.

Max wolfed his sandwich; he wasted no time when something was on his mind.

Janos led them down the narrow studio street into the vast wardrobe loft, where long tables of seamstresses were busy beading, embroidering, and cutting patterns for the upcoming picture. Belinda saw one little Latin seamstress delicately stitching innumerable beads on a small cap. Janos took it from her and set it on Belinda's head.

"This one you wear in the first scene in the Vatican," he said, his eyes sparkling. "You look like pure Renaissance! Even without makeup or hairdressing—but wait! Now you'll really see how you will look!"

They followed him across the street to the production art department. At the end of a corridor was a large room, an active fantasy factory. Drafting boards and long trestle tables were scattered about.

Miniatures of sets, like dollhouses, were arranged, some with replicas of furnishings, others with tiny figures establishing the production schemata. At the end of the room was a large easel.

"And now!" said Janos, switching on an overhead light. There, in an elaborate sketch, was Belinda, or rather, Lucretia Borgia with the face of Belinda. Gowned in the high-waisted, embroidered fashion of the time, her fingers flashing with jewels and one hand holding a golden goblet, stood the flaxen-haired vixen; the young girl to whom marriage meant death and family meant incest. Out of the garlanded neck, her face arose like an evil flower, her expression sly and pseudoinnocent; her lips parted, the tip of a darting tongue revealed as if in contemplation of a sensuous passion; her eyes half closed.

Claudia felt a prickle on the back of her neck. How could she know the work of this artist? Yet she had seen this, or part of it, before.

She wondered what her niece's reaction was. She saw that Belinda was staring at the doorway.

Claudia followed her eyes.

It was the boy on the beach. He wore a beige crew neck cashmere sweater, and his tight, tan trousers fitted his firm legs so that his whole body was a unity, only apostrophized by a golden belt buckle, modeled after the lion on the column of the Piazza San Marco. A stripe of sunlight flashed on his black curls and gilded his tanned skin. Where Janos pretended elegance, this young man, in a natural way, had it. Claudia thought she had never seen such a put-together casual look on a man in her life. As he moved forward, he seemed to glide on his moccasined feet.

"This is Kevin Frazier; he's doing portraits of the Borgias for the film. That is Belinda Barstow, Leslie Charles, and Antonio Valli," said Janos. "Miss Barstow, and Mrs. Ziska."

Claudia stared at him a moment and then burst into laughter.

The young man looked at her quizzically.

"Oh! I'm so relieved!" she said. "By accident I saw your sketches in front of our house at the beach. You had captured my niece so well that I thought you were a warlock."

The young man smiled. She thought his teeth were too small, almost feral, but then she checked herself from more imagining.

"I am a warlock," he said. "But my sketching in front of your house was premeditated. You see, I had to be most Machiavellian. And also, I knew—"

He paused for a moment and stared at Belinda. "I knew I had found the perfect model. No other would do."

Belinda smiled easily. She was used to compliments. No one said anything. Claudia stared at the portrait; Belinda looked at the face and tried to think of what to say. Kevin Frazier stared at Belinda as if he were devouring her features.

Janos finally broke the silence. "We've very fortunate to have Kevin. He was supposed to be doing portraits of the royal family of Iran, but Mr. Austin called him in to do special production work."

"It's new to me," said Kevin. "I never worked as a member of a production line before. I must say, it's almost like the craft guilds of the Renaissance. Sometimes I feel as if Michelangelo or da Vinci might walk in the door.

Part of it I like; part of it I despise. That's one reason I have to haunt the beach whenever I can, to retain my sanity. There seems to be so much money spent on trivia, and not enough gut-level talent. Ten goof-offs for one craftsman."

Janos giggled. "He's way-out! He drives us wild with the things he says."

Claudia knew she was in the presence of an original. And Belinda was obviously intrigued. For once she stared instead of being stared at.

"Well, you mustn't stay outside the fence," Claudia said. "Why don't you come over, maybe Sunday, and have dinner with us on the terrace? Just casually. We eat early, at six."

"Thank you, but I'll have to let you know," he said. "You'll forgive me, I have some business to attend to." He turned to Belinda. "I'm glad I met you at last. You'll have to be patient and really sit for me. I've done the wicked Lucretia—now I want the innocent one."

Belinda nodded.

He took Claudia's hand. "I saw the Augustus Johns portrait of you in London, and it was a primer for me. When I went back to the Sorbonne, I tried desperately to get those flesh tones and the transparency of your throat and the pulse in it behind that flower. I loved the haughty amusement in your smile."

"You have quite a memory," said Claudia.

"For beauty," he said. "Forgive me, I must go."

He left, and Janos stared after him and sighed.

"Nobody really knows him. He's thrown us all for a loop."

I just bet, thought Claudia.

"I'll be anxious to see what he does with Leslie Charles as Pope Alexander VI," she said.

"And Antonio Valli," said Janos. "He's such a handsome young man. It's too bad they have to stick that phony Borgia nose on him. But you know your husband, Mrs. Ziska, he's a stickler for authenticity."

Claudia felt a little peeved to be called Mrs. Ziska here in the studio where she had been such a star, but, of course this man was too young to remember—Well, they all were.

Later, as they walked over to the executive offices, Claudia looked at Belinda.

"Well, what did you think?"

"He certainly wasn't very anxious to talk to us," said Belinda, frowning. "Maybe he had a girl waiting for him."

"Maybe," said Claudia, noticing Belinda's disappointment. "Or maybe he's a serious artist who has his heart on his work, just like yours will be soon."

Claudia looked forward to getting Belinda into the excitement of the new production, and, if possible, into a friendship of some sort with this gifted young man.

When they entered Fergus's office, she saw that Max was at ease; he was going over some memos from the location department and pushing his hair back from his forehead in his characteristic way, which was indicative, Claudia knew, that he was visualizing facts as creative entities.

But his recent worried look seemed to have slipped onto Fergus's face. Fergus stood looking over the busy studio scene below, and as he turned to see her, he was scowling.

"Well," said Claudia, "I don't deserve that."

"Sorry," said Fergus. "My mind was elsewhere. How did you like the Kevin Frazier portrait?"

"I think he's terrific," said Claudia.

Fergus looked expectantly at Belinda.

"I hate it!" she said.

Even Fergus looked surprised. Max put down his papers.

"Why?" said Claudia.

"I don't want to be that person," said Belinda.

"Well—well," said Max, taken aback. "Perhaps that is only one side of Lucretia's character."

"The young man is going to paint the other side. He said so," said Claudia. "Look, dear, you can't be the innocent oracle all your life."

She saw the flash of resentment in Belinda's eyes, and she said, "You know, I think Belinda and I will run along and leave you two to your business."

As they left, she overheard Fergus saying, "This is as far as we can go. But we must have a written agreement from her. I'll have David send Sydney Keys over to Rome. The bitch."

Realizing it must be some dido of Jessica's, Claudia rushed Belinda away.

As the studio limousine drove them home, she looked at Belinda sulking in the back of the car. She knew that part of Belinda's rejection of the painting was because of the way Kevin had more or less dismissed them. The girl was not used to such treatment. As a matter of fact, he had been rather rude. At any rate, it was a good time to discuss the role. The Lucretia in Max's script was a very young woman who was the pawn of her family's lust for power.

"You know, Belinda, life is a series of decisions and rejections. I always had one image in mind when I decided I didn't want to play a role. I thought of my most hated rival playing it. And then I knew whether I wanted to do it. Often my ego told me I could do it better. What if they let little Barbara Pierce play Lucretia? How do you feel about that?"

"That upstart," said Belinda, bridling. "She's always trying to be friends with me in the hairdressing studio or on the set. She couldn't possibly play Lucretia. She has no classical training, like—like you gave me."

"Thanks," said Claudia, "but you've got a long way to go. Maybe you'd feel better if that artist Kevin—uh—what's his name—did paint you another way—"

"Kevin Frazier," said Belinda.

Ah, so the name had stuck with her. Well, that's one way to get them together, thought Claudia.

At four o'clock on Sunday, Kevin dropped by. He drove a secondhand Chevrolet station wagon. Effie was off; Max was in his studio. Belinda was flipping through magazines by the pool, dressed casually in pedal pushers cut off below the knee, hardly a glamorous costume, and a tucked-in blouse, wearing sunglasses, and her hair in pigtails, pretending she was not expecting a guest.

"You kids'll have to excuse me," said Claudia. "I'm chief cook and bottle washer when Effie's away, and taking care of my stepson, Alex. Kevin, this is Alex."

Kevin shook the baby's hand; they looked at each other gravely.

"There are too many good looking people to paint in this house," he said, impressed with the cherubic beauty of the little boy. "He is pure Botticelli." He turned to Belinda. "Like you."

And Barstow, thought Belinda. She wondered that anyone, especially an artist as perceptive as this young man with his piercing eyes on her, could look at the two of them and not notice. Anyway, they were supposed to be brother and sister. That might excuse the likeness.

She was relieved when Claudia hastily changed the subject. She must have been thinking the same thing.

"Maybe you and Belinda could run down to the pier market. We'll have a fish fry of some sort."

"Good," said Kevin. "Come along. If it's all right with you, I'll feed my dog, and you can see my pad. I'm certainly not going to paint you at the studio with everyone gawking."

As Claudia watched them leave, she realized that this was the first time Belinda had been on her own, aside from the elegancies of studio limousines with a chauffeur.

She felt a little concerned, as if she might have started something. What was plain and ordinary for any young girl could be a tension for Belinda, and anyway, she didn't know the young man at all. She smiled. He was only gorgeous, and gifted, what else could you want!

The two drove along Ocean Avenue, south toward the less pretentious part of the beach. Belinda, who had always thought of Santa Monica and Malibu as "the beach," was surprised as several oil wells and defunct canals marked the area so romantically started as a dream of Venice.

Now once-proud beach homes, rendezvous of California society and early film celebrities, had been turned into rooming houses. Oil rigs were few, their product diminishing, but they had stamped the community with the acrid smell and sound of commerce. Oily empty lots and stagnant canals still abounded. The thump, thump of a few active oil pumps perforated the sound of the surf as Kevin pulled his car into a garage off the ice plant bordered sandy roadway.

A sidewalk, used by bicyclists, wedged several blocks of houses in a communion of interests. The disoriented young forerunners of the hippies, winos, stray dogs, derelicts, and a few dedicated beach buffs walked, or rested, at random. Several waved at him and called out. He casually waved back.

Belinda, feeling more self-conscious than she ever had been, looked at Kevin. No one paid any attention to her in her sunglasses and pigtails. He was as nonchalant toward her as if she were just any girl. Was this where an artist wanted to live?

He opened a door at the end of the garage, and they entered a driftwood house. The ceiling slanted upward to an enormous north window. The other side of the house looked out beyond a patch of ice plant to a beach; it was a lonely, windswept vista. In a rush, the black object that threw himself at his master overwhelmed her. The black Italian whippet, Nero, was told to knock it off, and he did, throwing himself on a black leather chair, where he seemed to dissolve in darkness.

The studio was not like anything Belinda had experienced. There was a fieldstone fireplace. The only soft furniture was a large daybed, with a striped, fitted sheet pulled over it, several pillows, and a Mexican rug, barely hiding an electric blanket. An easel was set up, and a long paperhanger's table with folding legs held an arrangement of paints and brushes. Everything was in immaculate order. A coal scuttle held magazines, a reclining lounge chair sat beside a Parsons table with a reading lamp on it. A beige and gray Indian rug covered part of the brick floor; a plain round pine table had a hooded lamp with a Tiffany shade hung above it, flanked by four brown canvas-covered director's chairs. At one side of the large room was a small kitchenette, edged by a serving counter. On it were several large and intricate seashells, decanters, amber glasses, a wide cinnamon pottery dish holding apples and oranges, and a jar of pretzels. He spilled several on the counter and handed her one.

The high-ceilinged room was illuminated by his paintings. Vivid and experimental, they seemed to march like chapters of his life. Some seascapes, streets in foreign cities and villages, attractive boys and girls: various types in various places. Some sketches, caught on the run, some elaborate and painstaking cartoons of what obviously were studies for future portraits of wealthy, important personages. Kevin's brilliant view of the passing scene. She felt overwhelmed. He seemed to have been so much a part of things; she felt reduced to being less than a schoolgirl.

Belinda could smell the fresh oil paint and turpentine, and when Kevin flung open the upper half of the dutch door on the ocean side of the studio, the smell of salt air and crude oil also assailed her.

"This is it," said Kevin. "My retreat when all the captains and the kings depart after I've captured them on canvas."

He couldn't help but see the surprise on Belinda's face.

"I bought it for beans five years ago when I was a struggling artist just out of Otis Art Institute."

"It's—different," she said lamely.

"Want a beer?"

"Well—yes," said Belinda.

While he opened the refrigerator, she circled his easel to see what painting occupied the major focus of the room. The canvas had been sized, but there was nothing on it.

"That's going to be you," he said.

He tilted a tumbler, poured beer into it, and handed it to her, drinking his own out of a can.

"I never saw a place like this before," she said. "I posed for an artist in London. His place was very fancy. Of course, he was a photographer. Orville was his name."

"Orville," said Kevin. "My God, you're lucky. He's the maestro. Any portrait he did of you is priceless. I'd like to see them."

Belinda blinked, wondering what he'd think if he knew the old man had photographed her in the nude. For the first time she wondered where the pictures were. She'd like to show them to Kevin. Maybe it would make him see how sophisticated she really was.

"But this is where I work," he said, "not a photographer's atelier."

She felt put down, and she couldn't think of an answer.

After he finished his beer, he threw the cans in a trash can and put out some kibble for his dog.

"We'd better be going," he said. "The pier's probably crowded. I'll let you out at the fish market, drive up to the end, and pick you up on the way back. Okay?"

"Okay," she said.

He gave her a ten dollar bill.

She had never done an errand like this in her life. She asked the Japanese counterman what fish was good for barbecue, bought it, and stood clutching it like a treasure until he drove back and leaned over to open the door. Awkwardly, she handed him the change. He grinned at her, sensing her embarrassment.

At the house, Claudia had set up a buffet. There was a spinach noodle casserole, that Effie had prepared in advance, crusty dill rolls, avocado, orange, and onion salad, and a big bowl of fruit and a cheese board. Claudia broiled the halibut, and they ate with gusto. Later, they sat on the terrace. Max and Kevin talked about the Renaissance, its powerful contribution to the art and architecture of the world, the loss of Lorenzo il Magnifico contrasted to the evil ascendancy of the Borgias, the perfidy of the church. Remembering how she had boned up on ancient Greece, Belinda decided that she'd better get some books on Italian art.

She was half asleep when the evening finally broke up.
"I'll definitely paint you at my studio in Venice," he
said. "I can't cope with the panic around the Titan lot.
Okay?"

"Okay," said Belinda. She was suddenly shy; these were
grounds she didn't know.

Claudia felt the evening had been a flop. Even that
handsome young man, stunning in his navy turtleneck and
slim pants, hadn't seemed to have dented Belinda's facade.
She had been so aloof. Strange—Kevin was so attractive.

In bed, Belinda lay wide-eyed, reviewing in her mind
every object in the Venice studio. She thought of the big
bed and how it would be to lie in it in the dark, to have
Kevin make love to her, to see the firelight flickering on
the beams and on his naked body. She thought of how it
would be to be loved by him, to look up into his eyes and
pull his mouth to hers, her fingers in his black curls.

His studio was the most exciting room she'd ever seen
in her life because this handsome, mysterious man had
made it his domain. She didn't even think once of Niadas's
Villa Madonna della Rosa, the princely silver and blue
bed, or the silks and laces and opulence of the room where
she once, only once, had experienced what sex was all
about.

She thought only of Kevin, those wide shoulders, that
slim waist. His body, promising to be so strong and dominant in her imagination, inflamed her.

She would be posing for him in that studio, and somehow he would take her to his bed.

Meanwhile, she would have to pretend to be very unhappy about the cruel portrait of Lucretia at Titan. And
she must be very cautious so that Claudia would not get
the idea that she had a passion for this man. That would
ruin the whole thing.

Shrewdly she realized that Claudia and Max were
getting close to production and their own personal problems. They had forgotten she was an adult; they hadn't
even imagined that she was longing for a love affair.

Claudia was delighted that Belinda at last was taking an
interest in her role. Belinda toted art books around,
studied portraits, tried her hair various ways, suggested
wimples in some of the scenes, and enjoyed going to the

studio with Max, especially if she could say hello to Kevin, who was working on portraits to be used for the elaborate sets.

When she sat for Kevin, Titan sent a car for her, and she was delivered to his studio. The driver was ordered back at a designated hour. Sometimes for lunch they went to a nearby pub, where they had hamburgers, beer, and endless peanuts for a quick half hour between sittings. Kevin seemed to study her every move, as if she were a flower he was dissecting. She asked him if he wouldn't put his Italian whippet in her portrait, and she was disappointed when he told her he was using it in the portrait of Leslie Charles as Alexander VI.

She prattled of the Renaissance she was studying, and she was pleased when, after some of her enthusiastic outbursts, he would sometimes be amused.

She admired the painting he was doing of Leslie. It was a powerful portrait, in the style of Piero, giving the larcenous murdering pope grandeur and physical presence. Belinda remembered how Leslie had imitated her father in the first days of their filming in Rome, and she wondered if he would be able to sustain the power that Kevin had added to his effete face.

Kevin's preliminary sketches of Antonio Valli as Cesare Borgia were a different thing. He had one set of Valli with his own fine Roman nose and one set with the great, overpowering Borgia beak Max had insisted on.

Everyone at the studio was talking about Tony Valli. They called him the Golden Boy, for he was a blond with large brown eyes and a powerful physique. However, he was transformed into the evil Cesare the moment he stepped into the role. Belinda felt, albeit somewhat guiltily, that he was a finer actor than John Graves, whom she considered her ideal. But she did not feel intrigued by Valli. It was Kevin who had won her.

Kevin mentioned that he'd like to make a painting of Alex. She wondered what would happen if she told him that Alex was her child, not her brother. Would that make her seem more adult to him?

It was on her lips to blurt out, but she knew she would have to wait for the proper moment. She had never wanted to tell anyone before, but suddenly Alex seemed to be a secret she did not want to keep from this man.

She was glad to see the beauty that Kevin found in her portrait. It was, indeed, the young, unsullied Lucretia, the girl gazing into the world with a flower-wreathed innocence, eager to be alive. And, analyzing Max's script, Belinda now knew how she would play it: the dupe until the very end, when—embittered by her unnatural sexual affair with her father, after the murder of the one man she loved—she became at fifteen a woman who would betray the world as the world had betrayed her.

Claudia was helping Effie break in the new cook and the English nanny.

One day, as Belinda posed, she mentioned the changes going on at the house. "I guess Effie'll be with me at the studio," she said. "She's used to me, and she does things the way I like. But maybe I'll get someone else, and she can stay with Alex."

"What does *she* want to do?" asked Kevin, as he chose a finer brush and experimented with it on the pallet.

"Well, she'll do what we want her to do," said Belinda.

"Don't you ever ask her what she wants?"

"Why?" asked Belinda.

Kevin threw down his brush. "My God," he said. "Don't you know anything about her?"

"Well, yes," said Belinda. "She lives down near Central Avenue. She has a couple of grandchildren, two sons, and she goes everyplace we go. She was in Europe with us."

"She *doesn't* go everywhere you go," said Kevin angrily. "She can't. She has to drive twelve miles on her time off to get a sandwich at a counter, to get her hair done, or to try on a pair of shoes. If you stopped off in Dallas, there would be a sign at the toilet, White, and another, Black; she couldn't even piss with you. Don't you know that?"

Belinda looked at him, surprised at his disturbance.

"Well, I guess that's just the way it is. I never thought about it."

"Well, you'd better," said Kevin. "Did you hear what happened in Greensboro, North Carolina, a few months ago?"

"No," said Belinda, a little frightened by the anger that had suddenly crossed his face. She couldn't imagine what she had done.

"Four young men sat down and ordered coffee that never came. You know why? Because they were black. They started a storm of sit-ins all over the country. The whole nation joined in: sit-ins where blacks couldn't eat, sleep-ins in segregated hotels, read-ins when libraries forbade blacks to study, even swim-ins at white-oriented beaches. No violence, mind you. Dr. Martin Luther King only hopes for a recognition of human dignity. It's slowly happening. Nobody even knew how many places outlawed human beings because they were black. Now, because so many proved they cared, the barriers are beginning to fall. Don't you care about people like Effie? Or do you still think that in a way her love for you and your family makes her a nameless faceless slave?"

Belinda stared at him. She had never seen a man so angry. She looked down, humiliated.

"What's the matter with you?" he said. "Don't you live in the world? Don't you ever look at a newspaper, aside from the amusement section?"

He went to the sideboard, and for the first time since she had known him, he poured himself a stiff scotch and tossed it down.

"I've been waiting for some sign of imagination or originality to surface, so I could put it in my painting. But you parrot things out of books as if you were a pundit. You seem absolutely happy, like your little brother Alex, living under the protection of your oversolicitous reformed-alcoholic aunt, and your dear scholarly Max, who doesn't even know he has an asshole."

Belinda looked up at him, shocked.

"What's the matter with you?" he continued. "Don't you want to be alive? Don't you want to think? Will you always be a mental infant?"

She clasped her fingers and looked down. To her embarrassment, tears fell from her eyes onto her hands. She didn't know what to do.

"I'm no infant," she whispered.

Kevin set down his drink. "I guess I shouldn't have said anything. Titan's paying me a nice piece of change to paint your portrait, and I should let it end there. Only once in a while I see your eyes widen, and for a flash I think you are looking at the world. But I wonder. . . ."

He went to the counter, snapped a Kleenex out of a box, and handed it to her. She blew her nose.

A flash of lightning, followed by a furious roll of thunder, suddenly struck the sky. Rain began to burst against the sides of the wooden house and clatter on the glass of the skylight.

She started, and Kevin, looking up at the brief, violent flurry, set down his glass, seeming dejected.

"Forget it," he said. "It's too dark to paint anyway, even if it's only two o'clock. What time is the car coming for you?"

"We said four o'clock," she said. She was suddenly afraid he was dismissing her. Her heart beat faster.

"Sit down," he said, "and relax. I'll light the fire."

He twisted a piece of newspaper and lit it. The flame flickered against the gray driftwood walls, and the room seemed to dance; fire within, and storm without.

Belinda blotted her eyes. Kevin went to the refrigerator and took out a can of beer. He poured it into a glass and handed it to her.

"I shouldn't have sounded off," he said. "You're not programmed to think of anything but acting. And anyway, it's none of my goddamned affair. Maybe because I had to fight my way up, I have a different approach to what's good in life. I've been hungry and busted, and I've taken handouts with my paintings in a hocked trunk. I've had to be a street fighter. You never will."

He poured himself another scotch and drank it straight.

"You just don't like me at all," she said.

"Personally," he said, "my taste doesn't go to virgins. I prefer experienced women."

She put down her beer.

"I'm not a virgin."

He looked at her, genuinely surprised. It was the first time she'd seen a naked expression on his face.

"Believe me," she said.

"How did you ever get away from them?" he asked. "I thought they had you hog-tied."

"They were busy with their own affairs in Rome. It never entered their mind that I wanted a man." She looked sad.

Oh, God, he thought, I hope she's not going to tell me

all the sordid details and then pull that female thing of bursting into tears.

Instead, she looked at him and wiped the last tear from her face with the back of her hand.

Her heart was beating so fast and loud now that she wondered if he could hear it. This was it—this was the time. "And about Alex—," she said, "he's my child."

She turned to see the look, startled and frozen on his face.

"His father was Pericles Niadas," she said, almost enjoying the fact that for once he did not seem to be in control of the conversation.

"He died right after the night we—we made love," she said.

He was immobile, holding a can of beer in his hand.

"If you don't believe me," she said, "just look at the expression on my Aunt Claudia's face when you tell her I told you."

Relishing his astonishment, and in dramatic control of the scene, she stood up slowly, gliding.

She crossed the room and went to his bathroom next to the kitchen.

She disappeared a moment.

"I'd like to show you I'm a woman," she said, coming back into the room.

He turned and saw her standing by the fireplace. In the firelight her skin was like marble. She was naked.

And that's how I hoped it would be, only better, beyond my imagination. I didn't know it could happen so many times, Belinda thought as they lay gazing up into the skylight. Several gulls drifted by in their mad dance against the storm. The odor of paint and turpentine was the most exciting smell she'd ever known. His naked body had lain over her and it had been as she had hoped. He had loved her deeply and fully, and in his passion she had opened her eyes and seen him smiling in ecstasy, until his sensuous lips had closed again on hers so she could not see, but could only feel, and it was the only use of her senses she wanted. His body had a silken quality. And a lover . . . yes . . . yes . . . a lover who could plunge her into ecstasy and continue again and again was something she had never believed could exist.

She fell asleep in his arms for a delicious few moments, and then he kissed her awake.

"You'll have to get up," he said. "It's time for your keeper to arrive."

He watched her walk to the bathroom to put on her clothes. She was the most beautiful creature he had ever seen, even in his days in Paris, Rome, Tahiti, in all the places he had pursued beauty and beauty had pursued him. He knew he must paint her as she was, a gilded girl, her golden fleece of pubic hair, the high breasts and slender waist, long legs, the classically beautiful face. With a mystique and tenderness about her provocative mouth and the dream of fulfillment in her wide-spaced eyes, she was the embodiment of love, and he marveled at the transformation.

When she returned to him and sat at the side of the bed and once more put her fingers through his black curls, as she had dreamed of doing, she too looked at the transformation in his face, the glance of pride in his manliness, the first eye-to-eye encounter of joy and fulfillment she'd ever had after bedding with a man.

"I may not do a sit-in like you mentioned, but I'll make a sleep-in with you anytime," she whispered.

He smiled and held her closely a moment. She had been a revelation, and he was surprised. This had not been his intention.

He embraced her again, and then arose. He stepped into his jeans. She thought at the moment, he doesn't even wear undershorts, and look how wonderfully his clothes look on him.

Once he was up and into his clothes, he seemed to erase the intimacy they had.

He saw her politely into the waiting limousine. The studio driver greeted them smartly.

"Bad painting light," said Kevin in a matter-of-fact voice. "We'll try again tomorrow."

"We certainly will," said Belinda.

He saw her settle back and close her eyes as the car pulled away.

He went in and studied his painting. It wasn't soft enough, not tender enough for this beautiful girl. And, looking at the stiff costume he had painted, he mentally undressed it.

Max could not keep secrets from Claudia. Although he had managed an advance from Fergus to send to Jessica, and Sydney Keys had been sent off to Rome with proper documentation to be signed for her future investment in *Young Lucretia*, an assault had been made on Max's peace of mind, and during his sleeping hours he could not hide it.

Claudia sat wakefully beside him each time he cried out Jessica's name.

Finally, one bright morning, she turned to him. "Max, I'm going to sit here until you tell me what the trouble is with Jessica. I'm sick of hearing you scream her name in our bed."

There was no way not to tell her. He got out of bed, went to his study, and brought back the letter.

"You might as well read it," he said. "We're in deep, and there's nothing we can do. Fergus is taking care of the whole thing legally, but we'll have to pull in our horns for a while. What with taxes, cross-collateralization on the new picture, and the loan I had to get against my salary, all that money we thought we had is for the moment in limbo."

Claudia read the letter, biting her lip to conceal her anger.

"I know how it is, love," she said. "I've made and lost fortunes on the turn of fate more than once. It's incredible! That bitch! Well, we'll cut down; I'll drive you to the studio instead of getting a chauffeur. We'll do without extra help on days off. And the court gives Belinda a percentage of her money which doesn't have to be put aside for her until she's of age. Anyway, it's time for her

52

to realize that everything doesn't move along on a magic carpet. She can do her share."

Max waved away the trivia. "These things can be handled. I don't like to have you carry this problem."

"Don't worry," she said. "I'll just see that you're protected, and the rest will take care of itself."

But the rest did not take care of itself.

The first time Claudia realized it was when Belinda began to behave in a strange way.

"I'm taking Effie to have dinner at Scandia next Friday on her birthday," Belinda said.

"Whatever for?" said Claudia. "We can celebrate here."

"I'm making a point of it. And I want the best front table."

As Claudia went to the kitchen, she saw that Effie did not have her usual calm.

"I hear you're having a birthday bash at Scandia," said Claudia.

Effie shook her head. "Supposed to be complete with my Sam and Tom and my grandchildren. Good Lord, Miss Claudia, I don't want to make a Sunset Strip sit-in to prove some point that child's got in her head."

"Where did this come from? Not that I wouldn't like it if you care to go."

"I don't care to go," said Effie. "You know, I don't talk about it, but I don't especially feel I'm your 'token nigger' like my smart-aleck Tom says. He says I get in the front door on yours and Belinda's skirts. I just want to live out my life the way it is. It's been a good life. I don't live in the Deep South. I don't have to worry about getting a hotel room in New York or eating with you on the Super Chief. I earn my good pay; I'm good at my work; and I'm with Belinda, and Alex. But I'm afraid that Kevin fellow is stirring her up."

"What about your children?" said Claudia. "Aren't you concerned about their future?"

"Things are getting better," said Effie, "without B'linda getting us in the papers."

Claudia looked at Effie's handsome face and thought about her efficient ways. For the first time, Claudia became concerned about her private life. Like Jeffrey, and like Belinda, Claudia had simply accepted Effie's faithful service.

"And you know," said Effie, "now that you've brought it up, we don't need that Chinese cook. Let me run the house easy while you run Mr. Max and B'linda. She's a big girl now, and you can get her a fine girl to help her at the studio—someone who doesn't have to be here night and day. I know a girl, a cousin of mine, she's been a maid around town for twenty years. Her folks have moved east, and she wouldn't go. She'd be in heaven at a studio. Anyway, I think the baby needs me around."

Time was passing. Effie, without realizing it, had switched her allegiance from Belinda to Alex. Claudia was relieved. It would have been difficult to deal with a new nurse for Alex, manage the house, and be at the studio as well. This way, her ample salary as dialogue director would help run the expensive household, at least while Max pared off his surplus to Jessica and pawned his future, so to speak.

Belinda's friendship with Kevin was a comfort. They went to museums, galleries, sometimes to the Academy or to studio screenings of new films. Belinda was obviously intrigued with him, but as far as Claudia could see, he kept her at a respectable distance, almost as if he were an older man. His gifts were imaginative and proper: several of his smaller paintings, one a smiling face of Belinda; a chambered nautilus split in half, revealing its beautiful, sacred world; art books; an ivory figurine that was a small and perfect Venus, rising from the sea; a scrap of antique brocade so delicate that it was framed; a necklace of moonstones; and a sea-washed rock that had the form of a sleeping dog, which Belinda cherished on her dressing table. Things, Claudia mused, that she would never have cared for in her young life as a film star. But they were kid things, so to speak, and Belinda seemed in high spirits.

One evening, as the young couple came in late from an art exhibit, Claudia asked them how they liked the paintings.

"It was just wonderful," said Belinda, handing her the catalog. "We stayed late and had champagne with some of Kevin's friends."

Seeing the happiness in Belinda's face, Claudia was

relieved. If this was the way it was going to be, she could spend more time with Max and not feel guilty.

The next day, when she picked up the evening paper, Claudia saw a candid picture of Belinda and Kevin ducking out the back of the La Cienega Gallery. The gossip column read:

Belinda Barstow, Titan's star who is carrying the studio on her pretty shoulders, and Kevin Frazier, noted portrait artist, didn't seem as interested in art as they were in each other. They came into the gallery in a rush, snatched up a catalog, and left without bothering to view the brilliant paintings of Adam Guitry. The handsomest couple in town, maybe they'd just like to look at each other. Our private sleuth sea gull tells us there may be more than portrait painting going on in his studio along the Venice beach. . . .

Claudia set the paper down. Well, she had been responsible for getting them together, and now she would have to face the consequences. She'd better talk to Belinda. Be practical, get her over to Dr. Soames, have her checked out, and give her some birth control advice. After all, Belinda was an adult, or at least had stepped into the world of adults, even if she was not legally of age.

The complications of the situation hit Claudia. She had only thought of a passing romance. What would happen if it became serious?

The next morning, when Belinda came downstairs, she seemed like a child to Claudia, with her blonde hair tumbled around her shoulders. Yet, when she stretched and the voluptuous contours of her body were revealed in her silken robe, Claudia knew that this was a woman's body in the fullest sense.

She handed Belinda the paper. "I knew this would happen sometime," she said, "but I don't want you to lie to me. All that crap about staying late at the exhibit. You are having an affair, I suppose."

Belinda took the paper.

"Yes, I am," she said, smiling, "and it's wonderful. Hm, good picture. He's a marvelous man, I'm glad I love him. It's made up for a great deal of loneliness. And I guess I knew you'd find out and the cat would be out of the bag. Now I don't have to pretend anymore. I'm so tired of being cooped up like a child."

Claudia tried to control the churning inside of her. How different it was when it was Belinda. Her mind went back to the early days she'd had with Simon Moses, a married man who had so often left her bed to get back home so his wife would not be disturbed. Yet Simon had loved her; and he had died in her arms. She thought of the fact that now she herself slept with the man she loved, and she had accepted this time of complete happiness when there was a lonely young woman in the same house. Claudia disliked the situation, but she tried to convince herself that Belinda's being in love with a young man such as Kevin should be considered a blessing. He was a fine artist, he had style, and Belinda needed someone strong to balance her intrinsic Barstow willfulness.

"Well," she said, "we'd better get you to Dr. Soames and see that you are protected against pregnancy. We don't want that to happen again."

Belinda laughed.

"Oh, Aunt Claudia, Kevin has already taken me to a doctor. I told him about Alex, and he doesn't want *that* to happen again. It's all taken care of. I know the answers."

Claudia was startled.

My God! thought Claudia, she's already been in a gynecologist's office with this man! God knows who saw her go in.

And to think, to *think* she's told him about her baby . . . I must keep my distress from showing. This is the moment when I have to be casual. If this story gets around, she can kiss her career good-bye.

She swallowed, hiding the nervous dryness in her mouth, and forced herself to read a line as if she were in front of a camera. It was really a performance to hide her resentment of Kevin and his apparent take-over.

"He seems to have everything pretty well in hand. Was that wise, dear, to tell him?"

"As far as I'm concerned it was," said Belinda. "And I'm going to lead my life my way. And you'd better tell Max before he starts the Svengali bit again."

She arose.

"Oh, I forgot to tell you. I've taken my driver's test,

and I'm getting a car. I'm going on my own wheels, when and how I choose. And another thing, Kevin's tired of getting up in the middle of the night to deliver me to my own little bed. We think the pretense is silly. I may stay with him when we feel like it."

She left the room, and as she did, Claudia felt a welling of dislike for this man who was masterminding her Belinda. It was a terrible time, just at the start of production, for this emotional outburst to have to happen. She knew it would affect Max. And most of all, she felt like a fool. That's what you get for playing God, she thought bitterly. I all but pushed her into his arms, and now—now . . . !

She sat wondering what she could do, and slowly it came to her that she couldn't do anything. From her own secret rendezvous with Simon Moses through the years and her maneuvering confidantes, she knew now what she must expect. All the logistics of keeping the affair from the studio, being able to contact Belinda who was not home when she was supposed to be when there were set calls. She'd heard that Kevin had a rustic studio in Venice. She blamed herself for not having gone there to find out what was going on. She'd been so preoccupied with Max, and their problems.

And now, without a thought, Belinda seemed ready to move there, whether there was a closet for her things, decent living conditions, privacy, and any care for a girl who had never picked up her own clothes meant nothing. She suddenly realized how badly Belinda had been trained for a practical life. Under such conditions, this romance couldn't flourish forever. But what could an elder say or think when a passionate bed, with two beautiful young people in it, beckoned?

She wondered how she would face Kevin. The polite thing to do would be to make him welcome in the house; make him feel a member of the family. She smiled at the thought that she could probably work it out with Max, even if there was an uproar at first, but how was she going to face Effie?

Well, it would have to be a secret; a well-kept secret for the time being.

But this was not Belinda's idea. As the affair progressed, Effie was ordered to cook chickens and roasts and prepare food that was taken out of the house. Even Claudia was forced to remark to Effie, "She's beginning to use the place as a pit stop." For the first time, Effie tightened her lips and looked angry.

The new car appeared, as if Belinda now had her own corner on the magic carpet. It was a powder-blue fuel-injected Corvette, complete with folding top, and the new FM radio. Bill Chapman, the family accountant, called Claudia in a panic.

"For Christ's sake, what's going on at your house?" he said. "First of all you tell me to cut down, and then I get a bill for forty-five hundred dollars for a new car for Belinda. I didn't even know she drives."

"She does," said Claudia, "and I'm sure she has enough money to pay for it; most of her money is tied up in court until she comes of age, as you well know. But she must have some."

"Well," said Bill, "she's started on salary, and she gets 20 percent for living expenses, which, fortunately, because of some agreement with Max, her mother has just deeded to our care. But you know Belinda. If she gets shoes, there are a dozen pairs of various colors, and her dresses aren't exactly from Loehmann's."

"What do we do?" asked Claudia.

"Max or you, as her local guardians, can sign a contract for the car. She'll just have to go on a budget and pay for the car on the installment plan. We can afford to put down two thousand. Are you sure she's under your control? I'm hearing some funny rumors."

"Of course she's under our control," said Claudia too brusquely. "Give her a break; she's only a top movie star."

"I just wanted to remind you of one thing," said Bill. "We've had a problem with some of our other young film star clients. If she marries, even at the age of eighteen, her money comes into her own hands. She can move out on you, take her money, and the next thing you know, her husband could be setting up a production company, making new contracts with himself as producer, directing her every move, and telling her what to think and do. That is the number one hazard of the young girls in this town when a predatory male gets hold of them. What a jackpot she'd be!"

"Oh, my God," said Claudia, "I never thought of that!"

"Watch it," said Bill, "and tell her she's going to have to budget herself."

After he hung up, Claudia began to wonder what was in Belinda's mind. Her talk of freedom marches, students picketing in Washington, the new trend toward female liberation from the family bonds that had tied them to the hearth, and her latest, unexpected obsession, why couldn't they buy Pasternak's *Dr. Zhivago* so she could play Laura? On quizzing, it became evident she hadn't read it. Why did she press these ideas?

All of this had so far just been considered the chatter of a child interested in the world to Claudia and Max; but now Claudia began to trace down the source, and the more she thought about it, the more she became disturbed about Kevin's influence. These mouthings were not from Belinda's growing, seeking mind, they were the result of an indoctrination; she was parroting what someone else was teaching her.

It was a misty Santa Monica morning. Effie had let Belinda rest until the last moment, but it was the first day of the shooting, and by dawn's early light she had to be up and away. The new set maid, Polly, had been indoctrinated in the routine. With a pang, Effie realized that she would be losing her baby. No more busy, involved days of studio life and closeness.

She set up a pretty breakfast tray and quietly opened Belinda's bedroom door. She would open the drapes, turn on the radio softly and draw the bath. She tiptoed in, set the tray on the desk, and pulled the drapes.

Then she screamed.

Claudia came rushing into the room.

"Call the police!" cried Effie. "Call the police! She's gone! B'linda's gone!"

The bed was turned down and empty. It hadn't been slept in.

Max rushed for the phone.

Claudia stopped him. "No!" she said. "No! I think I know where she is."

Max and Effie both stared at her.

"Calm down!" she said. "Just give me a minute."

She rushed to her room and with a shaking hand got out her phone book. In a moment she dialed Kevin's studio. His sleepy voice answered.

"My God, Kevin," she said, "is Belinda with you?"

There was a pause.

"Yes," he said, "she's here."

"Thank God," said Claudia. "I mean, thank God she's all right. Can I talk to her?"

She turned and saw Effie's incredulous face and Max's bewildered one staring down at her.

"Hello," said Belinda's sleepy voice.

"Belinda! We've been so worried about you! Don't you know the picture starts today?"

"I'll be there," said Belinda. "I told you I was going to do it my way. Now maybe you'll know I mean it. Don't worry, Kevin cares as much as you do about my future."

Claudia wanted to comment about what she thought of Kevin's care, but she smothered her thoughts. "Your makeup call is at 6:30. It's 5:30 now."

There was a pause. Claudia was certain she heard Kevin's voice in the background.

Finally, Belinda answered, "They can wait. I'll be there when I feel like it. I just can't rush like this, and I won't. I'll have my calls later from now on. This hour is inhuman."

"Don't do this to Max," said Claudia.

"Don't do this to me," said Belinda, and she hung up.

Claudia sat shaking, holding the phone in her hand. She dialed back, thinking they might have been cut off, but there was no answer.

Claudia was in a fury. Max was still standing there with Effie.

"Well," she said, "now you know. Belinda spent the night with Kevin."

Effie put her hands to her face. When she took them away, there was sadness in her face. She remembered Jeffrey and his aberrations, and the night he had forced her into sex. She remembered the dreadful night she had found Belinda weeping in Rome, the very morning Pericles Niadas had died. That had been the start of sex with her beautiful Belinda, and now she knew, like the Barstows, this was an important thing in their lives, and her Belinda was no longer her sheltered baby.

"I'm going to go to his house and beat the hell out of him," said Max.

Claudia had an insane desire to laugh. Max, with his trembling hands, his wiry poet's body, beating a physical being like Kevin!

"No, Max," she said, "it would only disturb things more. There's nothing we can do but ride this thing through."

"But the picture—my picture!" said Max.

Claudia took his hand.

"Max," she said, "I don't usually tell you what to do, but listen to me. If you disturb her now, you've got a picture in bad trouble. Pretend nothing has happened. I'll cover for her. And you just go to the studio as if everything is normal, fuss around with your new camera crew, kill time with several complicated setups, and I'll appear with Belinda. And don't worry."

She turned to see that Effie stood, wide-eyed, looking stricken.

"And you," Claudia said to her, "you had a worse time with her father. As I remember, you cleaned up plenty after his drinking, and you survived it. This isn't a disease, Effie, it's young love, and it's an emotional power, the greatest explosion on earth, including the atomic bomb. So just go your way and take care of Alex. I'll handle the situation. I've been there myself."

Claudia sent Effie downstairs with Belinda's cold breakfast tray.

The sun was stifled by the morning fog. She called a studio car to pick up Max, kissed him, and after getting Kevin's address from the studio switchboard operator, got in her car and started down the coast toward Venice, the swirling mists slowing her journey.

She had thrown Belinda's most cherished leopard cape and fresh slacks and a sweater into the back seat, determined Belinda would make a star's appearance when she entered Titan's portals on the first day of shooting, even if it was only from the front gate to her dressing room. Jeffrey's old dressing room had been refurbished for his daughter, and there were even carefully selected and elegantly framed pictures from publicity along with theater collections and scrapbooks belonging to four generations of Barstows. Emotions were on the surface this day; it was too bad it had to begin in such a manner.

5

When Kevin Frazier found someone who suited his convenience, he was a lover and a companion; but at a certain point, his apparent innate self-sufficiency took over, and he became aloof.

When he was a boy of six, his drunken parents had been killed in a car crash, bringing a load of cheap white lightning from their still in the mountains near Leadville, Colorado. His Uncle Karl, who ran a hardware store, had severely disliked his sister and her husband, and reluctantly took him in. From the moment his body had blossomed into youthful handsomeness, Karl had turned his suspicions on the youth's beauty. Perhaps because in him there had been some secret yearning, himself being a Tony Lumpkin.

When Kevin was fourteen, his uncle Karl shot his hound dog before his eyes because it would not hunt.

"There's no place for an animal that doesn't do its work."

A dog was not to be petted or loved.

So the boy escaped to the world of make-believe. He was determined not to follow his classmates who would go to work when they graduated in the mining and smelting of molybdenum in nearby Climax. Outside his chores in the hardware store, he found his only retreat was the public library. He would devour every book he could get and not be a bigot like his uncle. Soon he had read everything in the children's section, and he asked for other books.

The fates had spun their mystic web when he stepped into the stark little library. The new librarian was a frail, displaced man, Philip Harvey, who had been shipped west by his family years ago after he spent his grandmother's hard-earned two-thousand-dollar inheritance on a trip to Italy.

Now, disinherited, his family long gone, he was a wandering wino, going from one small-town library job to another. He was thin, middle-aged, red-nosed, to the jeering kids a "swish," an old, white-haired, delicate-fingered wraith.

He was the town freak. When Kevin came into the library, lost in the misery of his dog lying in a pool of blood, Philip's pulse beat fast.

He saw in this youth the strange, misplaced beauty of a Donatello—remembering the idealized youth in his splendid *Saint George in the Bargello*, in Florence.

Philip, seeing Kevin's eagerness to learn, cautiously maneuvered an art book in his direction. In due time, the boy was his confidant. In his little shack on the outskirts of town where he tended a flower garden and lived in Renaissance Florence, he showed the young man a richness of life and beauty, glowing with unleashed enthusiasm and excitement, as he sipped on a jug of dago red. He told the boy it reminded him of Italy—but Kevin tasted it and said he liked Coke better; it was too sour.

Although he was madly in love, Philip never sexually approached the boy—his desires were too delicate. But several times, as he put his hand on Kevin's shoulder or touched his fingers while turning a page, he wondered if his reddened face and quick breathing betrayed the fact that in spite of himself he had reached a powerful, wrenching climax. He managed to escape the room under the pretense of preparing cocoa and graham crackers, and retired to the kitchen (he had no bathroom, only an outhouse) and cleaned himself quickly, flushing at the humiliation of his body betraying him, yet at the same time ecstatic.

Peering at his idol over his bifocals, he felt that life, even in this dreary mining town, had given him an unexpected bonus.

On Christmas, in a moment of inspiration, he sent to Denver for a sketch pad and some pastel crayons, mostly in sepia tones.

To his great delight, Kevin opened the package in front of the potbellied stove in his little house, looked at his rare da Vinci and Michelangelo prints, so dog-eared and cherished from his youthful flight to Italy, and began to copy them.

A month later, Uncle Karl found some of Kevin's sketches by the boy's bed. He picked them up angrily.

"That's against God, horses falling through the air, and it's pansy stuff for a kid to be home drawing when you could be earning your keep doing inventory at the store. Where did you get this junk?"

"Mr. Harvey over to the library gave them to me."

Karl looked at him wildly.

"You been hanging around with that queer? Well, we'll see about that!"

Philip Harvey was suddenly asked to leave town. But he never did. He was found dead in his cabin, an empty bottle of dago red and a box of pills on the floor by his body. Discreetly he had left no note to Kevin, and when the town took over the property, all the dog-eared prints in it were thrown in the stove by the cleanup woman who got it ready for the next librarian, an old maid.

In rebellion, missing his friend and his inflorescent life, Kevin had sketched and drawn during every moment he could spare, hiding his work under his mattress. He would read everything he could, listen to anyone who could teach; he wasn't going to be a hick like his uncle.

His Uncle Karl watched him suspiciously, and finally discovered his treasure trove.

"There'll be no more of this heathen behavior in my house," he said as he stuffed the papers one by one into the iron kitchen stove. His hands were trembling, but he was not a man of physical rage; he could shoot animals, but it was beyond his power to hit this wayward nephew; he could only destroy him with bigotry.

"You are a disgrace to your name. You better look around and get married, boy, or you'll have trouble in this town. You're a misfit."

Kevin didn't know what he meant.

He looked over the girls at the Saturday church sociable. They were either rawboned, mousy, or too plump, and he wasn't stirred by any of them. Even thinking of the beautiful, fashionable women in Philip's Italian reproductions made Kevin sick at the pit of his stomach at what Leadville had to offer. It was like the hot dishes on the sociable sideboard—a choice between meat loaf or hamburger. If this was being a misfit, he guessed he was one.

One Sunday he told his uncle to go on ahead; he'd be along to church after he cleaned up the breakfast dishes. When Karl had left, he took a bundle from under his bed. He had packed it in the middle of the night by kerosene lamp: one packet of crayons; old Philip's gift print of Donatello's *Saint George*, which he had saved; his one Sunday shirt; and his old lumber jacket. Aside from this, he had fifteen carefully hoarded dollars and a slab of ham he took from the larder.

With these, and his physique, and a natural curiosity about life, he left the town that had been his prison.

It did not take him long to use, and be used. He attracted men and women like flypaper. But through what he learned about the appetites of others, and himself, he managed to find his way to Los Angeles. It was a long journey in miles and much longer in awareness of what the world wanted of a young man; to give, and yet not give, to take, and get the hell out before there was trouble, or a frenetic grab for a permanent possession of what he had to give. But his objective was beyond the ways and means that were necessary. His path had a direction.

He discovered during this time that his greatest natural asset was his sexuality. Both men and women wanted him, and he soon learned that to be desired meant to be in control. And to be in control meant to have power. The fact that he was desired triggered his innate narcissism. He could accept being the love object, as well as the stud, if he felt his partner was enchanted with him.

In some of his first sketches, he caught the fleeting look of adoration on the face of his subjects. Even after he was the rising star at Otis Art Institute, on a scholarship given by an older woman who was in love with him, and had discovered him on a summer's day doing chalk sketches on the Venice sidewalks, a few people began clamoring for him to do their portraits. He caught them with the appearance of a joy of life they wished they had. He was a magician.

Men and women would come to his studio for a sitting, not realizing that his enchantment was as carefully worked out as a motion-picture script. He would set the stage with a scenario plotted on their personal desires. He pretended not to notice their admiration of his body, his classic face, and his simple well-fitted clothes. He would lead them into conversation, making them comfortable, then discover their preferences, and use them.

If his subjects did not want sex, he enjoined them with erotic poetry, beautiful music, fruit and wine; he found out their dreams and discussed the likelihood of fulfillment. Catching people in exoticism, he quickly sketched the moment of their excitement, and then skillfully continued to paint the person they would have liked to be.

His studio was not as primitive as it seemed. The lighting was artful, lights on dimmers were played by him secretly, as subtly as soft music; and stereo music carefully concealed turned on the moment he entered the room.

Wine, fresh fruits, fine cheeses, and the makings of gourmet dinners were in his refrigerator. His cooking utensils were of the finest French quality, and he was a gourmet cook. Everything he produced seemed casual, but was memorable; this he had learned from a grateful French nobleman.

His dishes, hand-thrown cinnamon pottery he had made himself, Spratling flat silverware from Taxco, amber glass goblets from colonial New England, and Venetian bronze oil lamps filled with pine-scented oil seemed primitive, but were the height of sophistication.

His library contained, among many fine art books, a folio of photographs of the great erotica in the Vatican; art too great to be destroyed, given to him most secretly by a panting man of papal title.

His usual pattern of selection of partners had been disturbed by Belinda. Her incredible beauty, and the first meeting of their bodies, when she had confessed being the mother of Alex, had surprised him. So had what was obviously her very gifted and pagan lovemaking. He knew that her postures, her desires, and her responses to sex were not learned from experience, but from instinct. And he was enchanted.

He thought about her when she was not with him, and he constantly sketched her in every way she had been revealed to him. Already a portfolio of her in the ecstatic postures of love were in a folder, and he filled canvases he had saved for other uses with an abandon that surprised him. Usually his schedule was completely planned.

In return, an inner warning seemed to trigger his actions. He could not allow himself to be dominated by this passion. He did not believe in the phrase "being in love." There was only one thing to do. She was born to be a great star. In spite of himself, he had been deeply moved by her in *The Oracle*, but he could not allow his life to get out of hand. He could only hand over his life to someone if his future was garnished with fame and fortune.

The natural step was to put her down, to make her realize that she was not a star to him, that she was only a young girl, dependent on his attention, interest, and talent. For this, she would have to follow the guidelines he set. He had seen too many men stare at her with hunger in their eyes, and he knew that any man who allowed himself to be enslaved by Belinda Barstow could not be important in his own right. But if he remained in control, new vistas opened up.

Kevin was proud of his talent; he knew his paintings gave life and depth and breadth to their subjects. He knew he had a fulfilling artistic life ahead of him. He felt he was the vessel of a talent beyond his learning. He would not abandon this force for any woman. He would use it. His strategy, in spite of his affection, his honest excitement about Belinda, and his unique position in being commissioned to paint her, was one of studied put-down.

And so love's dream had not been ideal for Belinda. Much as she loved the excitement of being with Kevin, she did not know him. And after pleasure, somehow, he seemed to have to give pain. He obsessed her waking thoughts—the only enigma in her life.

After the painting sessions were ended, as the sun went down, they often walked on the beach. Then they would come in, chilly and slightly cold. He would light the fire, the music would be switched on as they walked in the door; that always intrigued her. During these private hours he would take the phone off the hook so the world wouldn't interfere. He would pour wine, and they would listen to music. Sometimes it was Renaissance music and he would discuss it with her. Or it was modern—he could switch from Johnny Cash's "The Ways of a Woman in

Love" to Donizetti's *Lucretia Borgia* without losing his chain of thought.

To her delight, he would putter about the studio, putting his paints and brushes to rights, making a few sketch notes, and occasionally handing her an art book to look through. At times he would seem to forget she was there, and this, in the early days, was a pleasure to her. She could watch him moving without him seeming to know she was adoring everything he did, for she knew as the evening lengthened that they would make love and would be nestled together in his comfortable bed. At these times, even while she pretended to glance at pictures, she thought of what the touch of his broad shoulders and his silken skin would be, and how she would wait for the marvelous moment when they stopped playing with the tactile surfaces of each other's bodies, and the intense thrust of lovemaking, with its shattering explosion of fulfillment, would finally end in sleep in each other's arms.

He would prepare a simple meal, and after dinner she would do the dishes, something she had never done before. It was cozy and it was wonderful; that is, if it went well and she was cautious about what she said. She often paused on the brink of a gushing comment and analyzed it to see if it would suit his mood. Yet she never knew.

This past evening, after a walk, she had run happily toward the beckoning house, and once inside had commented on the sickle moon. The distant lights of Santa Monica, the Venice shoreline, and Palos Verdes beyond reminded her of the Bay of Naples, which she had seen by boat when she left Europe.

"If you thought it was so beautiful out there, why did you rush back when we could have walked farther?" he asked.

"Because," she said, "I wanted to settle down by the fire and talk to you."

He went to the door and listened to the sound of the surf.

"You know, Belinda," he said, "you remind me of a writer who lived down the pike. He used to take a walk on the beach so he could rush back to write about taking a walk on the beach. It'll probably be the same when you're doing a love scene; you'll leave my bed to rush to the studio to imitate it in your mind. Is the fulfillment of yourself as great as the fulfillment of your image of yourself?"

"I didn't mean that," said Belinda. She went over to him and put her hand on his shoulder. "Please, Kevin," she said, "I'm just enjoying the few hours we have together before I start the big grind. You know what I have to face. Even with Max, it isn't easy. I should be home studying right now."

Kevin swung around angrily. "I'll take you home if that's what you want."

She put her arms around him. "Oh, no! No! Please understand—"

He slowly pulled her arms away. "Don't feel guilty because of what you aren't doing. Are you with me, or somewhere else? You live in too many phony planes of existence. Sometimes I think your personality is created by that old bag Grace Boomer and nourished by queen columnists like Andrew Reed."

Her eyes filled with tears. "Don't be so mean. I love you."

He went to the fireplace, lit a cigarette, and sat on the sofa. She either had to follow or be left adrift. She followed.

"Love isn't the problem at the moment," he said. "You're here because I want you here. But let's not cloud the issue. You must realize the star system is only a specific institution of capitalism. A star's way of life is itself merchandise. Your personality is myth, and your reality is frozen capital."

"How can you say that! I work at my craft the same way you work at yours."

"Mine is real," he said. "Why do you think the trash cans in front of your house are raided by people wanting your used Kleenex? Why do you think kids come in and snatch the back clothesline free of your panties and nightclothes?"

"Effie should have put them in the dryer," said Belinda without thinking.

He put his hands to his head in despair. "I give up," he said. "I don't think we can make it together."

She stood there, frozen.

"Oh, don't *say* that," she said. "What do you want me to do?"

"Just be yourself. Adulation has given you too much self-importance. It's difficult to know you normally. Look what's happened to some of the greatest stars. Garbo is remote, not in this world. Marilyn Monroe is unable to accept happiness. You have to be a maverick and never stop moving, or you'll lose your identification."

Belinda was puzzled. She didn't understand his irritation.

"Well," she said, "you can't deny the talent of Max. He isn't a phony, and his writing ability is unquestioned. I'm very fortunate I have him in my corner, and I'm trying to learn."

For a moment her mind flashed back to that evening in London, when David Austin, who owned Titan studio, had faced her with the problems of stardom. He had tried to set her straight on what was ahead of her.

"You will assume power beyond your control. . . . If you knew what people would seek from you, you'd run."

She wished, strangely, as much as she loved Kevin, that bright, handsome, loner David Austin were here to tell her what was wrong, and why she was being attacked by the man she loved. She didn't understand the logistics of control, and she was adrift.

"Go right ahead," said Kevin. "Be the good little pupil. That's what Titan's banking their millions on. The good kid. And as for directors, don't chart your course on who you'll get during your career. You'd better know what and who you are. I've been around, kid, do you want the list? Your dear Max, the excited old man, image maker, Pygmalion, the best of the lot while he's on the beam. But the dream can sour, baby. Then there's *der professor*, usually a pipe sucker, with college and culture as his security blanket behind him. I painted one once and got a load of his id. He was a *spiegelschauspieler*, a looking-glass actor. He confessed that before he directed every day, he had a lone session with himself in the mirror to research the similarity of characters he observed. He stole from everyone who could help him, and that's what you'd get to inspire your dedicated performance—someone else's garbage."

He arose and mimicked, moving his hands, strutting.

"Then there's the out-and-out prick. The successful mediocrity who survives on put-downs and nightclub wit. He usually has the key to the front door of the board of directors room—the best houses, the raciest cars, and to the back door of any dame in town married or unmarried, he chooses. People are afraid it's unchic not to be involved with him. The cash register man, in unity with the New York money.

"And of course we have the young maniac, usually a one-time bloomer. He hits on the mod scene; startles the front office, who are afraid not to be with it, and the public who wants to know it all; and disappears after one stab, rich but artistically impotent because he told all he had to say in one film."

He shook his head. "You'll get 'em all, baby, and they'll make or break you, but they'll try to gobble you alive."

Tears were pouring down Belinda's face. She had no idea why she was suddenly being attacked as if the whole system was her fault.

He turned to her and took her face between his hands.

"You look so beautiful and washed clean when you cry," he said. "I either want to sketch you or screw you. I don't know which."

She put her arms around him, grateful that she had found him again. As she moved into his embrace, she felt the hardness of him; somehow she had excited him.

They fell into bed. They didn't remember to have dinner. Their lovemaking was fiercely passionate—more so than it had ever been! Exhausted, they slept soundly, and before she knew it the phone was ringing in the darkness, and it was Claudia's panicked voice, and the picture was about to begin.

It was not difficult for Claudia to find Kevin's studio. The blue Corvette was parked in the street, up against the sand and ice plants. Kevin's station wagon was in the garage.

Wouldn't you know it, she thought. *Her* car would be outside, with the top down, dripping with fog. But she smothered her anger. She had learned how to pussyfoot these last few years, and this was a time to do it.

She took Belinda's clothes with her and knocked on the door. After a moment, Kevin opened it. Belinda was sitting at the table, swathed in Kevin's robe, drinking a mug of coffee.

"I know you'll think I'm a fuddy-duddy," said Claudia,

trying to smile brightly, "and probably you're right. But Kevin, I have to have family priority at least today. Cameramen are probably waiting to photograph Belinda as she opens her father's dressing room. You see, they refurbished it just for her. Hollywood's proud of what tradition it can squeeze out. I know it's silly, but let's just get it set up. We can talk later about adjustments in our living pattern."

Although Kevin was ready to pounce, as he looked at the steely eyes of Claudia, which she could not quite conceal with her made-up smile, he knew he was facing a strong adversary.

"Come in. Would you like coffee?" he said matter-of-factly.

"It's going to be a little late as it is," she said, entering. "I know you care too much for Belinda to have her start this picture the wrong way."

Belinda stood up.

"Aunt Claudia, Kevin cares as much as you do about what happens to me. He just—" She waved her hands, trying to think of an alibi, and continued, "he just wants me to be grown up, that's all. To—to be adult."

"Well, then," said Claudia, her chin suddenly becoming firm, "the best way to start is to do the job professionally which you have accepted such good pay to do."

Kevin realized this was not the time to flaunt his sexual authority.

"You're right," he said. "I'm not used to being on an assembly line, with my work on call. But I guess you'd better go."

Belinda, abashed at his change of attitude, arose.

"Here, dear," said Claudia, "I brought your beige slacks and cashmere sweater. You can put on your leopard cape. We had planned on it, remember?"

Belinda took the slacks and sweater and disappeared into the bathroom.

There was an uncomfortable silence. Finally, Kevin spoke. "This wasn't intentional," he said. "It just happened."

Claudia turned to him. "Kevin, nothing in life is intentional. It just happens. But our family has gone through more crises than you could ever imagine, and we've gone on with our work. My brother, Belinda's father, was hauled out of a colored brothel in Kansas City to win one of the first Academy Awards. In accepting it, he gave a better performance than he did in the picture that got it for him. My long-time married lover was dragged off of me, dead, you certainly know that scandal, and I had to head for the hills. Well, I not only survived, I did my best work afterward. You know about Alex, but Belinda may not have told you that she gave birth to him in a cave on a Greek island and came back poised enough to face what Barstows are supposed to do. As far as I'm concerned, you may be a strong influence on her, I don't deny the great power of an emotional attachment. As a matter of fact, I'm for it. It's growth. That is, if it's good. And if it isn't good, I'll fight you tooth and nail. So just don't expect any sufferance on my part."

She was fuming. What had happened to her pussyfooting? She had blown the whole thing.

But to her surprise, Kevin was smiling.

"Bravo!" he said. "Hecuba aroused! I hope Belinda has your spirit. That's what I'm pulling for. All right, Mrs. Ziska, we're not shamming, are we?"

Claudia suddenly realized that she was facing a stronger force than she had believed. It frightened her, but she wouldn't let him see it.

She went to the bathroom door. "For God's sake, Belinda, get a move on!"

Belinda opened the door; she was radiantly beautiful, her hair pinned in a Psyche knot, her face scrubbed and glowing.

"Oh, damn youth!" said Claudia. "Just try to keep your hair that way. You couldn't pay Sidney Guilaroff enough to get anyone else looking that good."

Belinda smiled, relieved of tension.

Claudia threw the leopard cloak on her shoulders.

"Now you look like something. I'm driving you," she said. "We'll pick up your car later. It's sopping wet."

As they opened the door, Kevin looked at Belinda, and she reached up to peck his cheek.

"Well," was his parting remark, "who are you copying today? Liz Taylor, little leopard riding hood?"

Belinda was rushed out, Claudia's fingers pressing her arm firmly, before she could figure an answer.

As they drove along Olympic, Claudia tried to focus Belinda's mind away from Kevin.

"Now," she said, "I don't care what's churning around inside you. I've been there myself, as I keep reminding myself. We are going to have no open ticket to mediocrity in this family. You've got to pick yourself up. You have no right to damage your work because of a love affair, no matter how tumultuous it is. I just hope to God you don't do like I did and wait until it's too late to realize your potential. You'll find out that our family has a lot of talent and a desire to express it. Sometimes it's even a deterrent to the easy life.

"Max is waiting for you. So is a crew of about sixty, plus a nervous line of Hollywood and New York moguls. But they don't matter. Just you, in the end. Do what you're supposed to do, not that you'll ever be satisfied with it. Okay, lecture ended. I love you."

Belinda sat there sullenly. Where was their kinship? It took all of Claudia's concentration to contain her disturbance and plow through the slow traffic to get to the studio. She wondered how she was going to balance this change of power, Max . . . Belinda . . . Alex . . . and now, this Kevin.

Although Jeffrey's old-fashioned suite in Titan's star dressing-room area was her home base at the studio, Belinda also had a more modern facility, an air-conditioned trailer that would be moved to every sound stage or location as the picture progressed. In it was a small closet, a full-length mirror, several chairs, a sofa that doubled as a daybed for rest, a small portable bathroom washbasin, telephone, small refrigerator, and an elaborate lightbulb-framed dressing table with triptych mirrors. This little aerie was the proper place to study scenes, discuss script or wardrobe changes, repair makeup, or have production discussions of immediacy.

It was also a cocoon, where Belinda could retreat from the confusion of the set. Claudia realized that the closed door might mean she was on the phone to Kevin, if possible. But when scenes were shot, the phone was automatically switched off. Any electrical equipment could cause a disturbance on the sound track.

Claudia smiled when she remembered the story George Cukor had told about making a film with the magnificent Garbo. They could not understand what was buzzing on the sound track. One of the electricians suddenly realized that it was always when Miss Garbo was in her portable dressing room. The trouble was soon tracked down, she had switched on her vegetable juicer. The great star had laughed about it and followed orders to manufacture her health food snacks only between shooting scenes.

But this was a serious moment, thought Claudia. She would have to establish herself firmly to face Belinda immediately as dialogue director and coach, instead of aunt, or there would be trouble on the set.

For once she did not knock on the door. She entered. Fortunately, Belinda was not on the phone. She was lying on the sofa. Claudia realized, half-gratefully, that Kevin was too sophisticated to hang on the phone like a teenager; he had his work to do. In fact, he often, it was said, let his phone ring or unhooked it while he was painting. She had seen this irritate Belinda at home.

"I think," said Claudia, "we'd better get a little grasp on Lucretia before we get started today."

Aha, thought Claudia, looking at her, don't I ever know the picture. She's had a night of rampant sex, and now she's tired. What a rotten way to start a picture.

"*I* think," said Belinda, "I ought to know Lucretia pretty well. You've been drumming her character into me long enough."

"You may never know her character," said Claudia, "and you'll wake up to that, my girl, when you look at the rushes. Titan and Fergus won't cough up ten thousand dollars a day to do retakes just because you've been in bed with Kevin all night."

Surprised at her aunt, Belinda slowly sat up.

"Yes," said Claudia, "it's time for you to hear reality as long as you're living reality. Even as young as you are, the camera can tell. Why, Gordon Falconi can even tell you, through his camera eye, a day before you're going to get your period. As it is, we'll call in the makeup man and put a little white under your eyes. Don't ask me how I know, I've been there myself, and know all the reasons and all the tricks."

Belinda went to the mirror. She realized she didn't look as fresh as she should. "Call him," she said.

"Just a minute," said Claudia. "They're still lighting a new setup, we've got plenty of time. That's not why I'm here. Titan is paying me a good salary to be your coach. If I can't do it, I'm going where I'm wanted."

Belinda seemed startled. Then she started to smile.

My God, thought Claudia, she thinks she's in the driver's seat. "And don't think I can't," she said testily. "I've had an offer to coach Jennifer Joy, the new star at Paramount. Of course, they signed her up from the stage, and she's had plenty of experience. But they still need me, and they've offered double what I get here."

Belinda, trying to keep calm, said, "You wouldn't."

"Wouldn't I just," said Claudia.

Before Belinda could rush in with the abrasive remark that she wouldn't walk out on Max's problems, Claudia rushed the conversation.

"Let me ask you a question. What sort of person do you think Lucretia Borgia is at the beginning of this picture? That is, before life corrupted her?"

Belinda thought a moment. "I think she's tragic. As Max said, a pawn of fate."

"What is the most stirring way to express a young figure with a known tragic destiny?"

Belinda waited for the answer.

"With lightness," continued Claudia. "She must play with lightness. At this moment, if we get a wistful smile from this girl, not only entering an orgy at the Vatican, but realizing later what a life she was facing, then the audience's heart will go out to her. We must realize in the beginning that she is the victim—even with her beauty, her status, and her complete absence of moral responsibility. If her father and her brother are her seducers, and if they head the church and are the supreme authority and architects of life and death, then she is indeed adrift. You must think of Lucretia as a blossom, being forced to unfold under premature conditions."

"Like myself," said Belinda. "Like what happened to me in Rome."

She turned a bold eye on Claudia.

Claudia, although a little taken aback, was ready.

"That's a lot of crap," she said. "You were ready. You were panting after John Graves and couldn't get him, and I personally think you seduced Pericles Niadas. After all, he was your pigeon from the beginning."

Belinda blinked her eyes and said nothing, and in that moment Claudia knew it was true.

"Well," said Belinda, "I wasn't exactly a schoolgirl. You shoved me into a pretty big world."

"*I* did, my dear?" said Claudia. "All I did was to try to help you out—after the fact. But that's past history, and now I will not allow you to tarnish your family name. I admit we were all pretty freewheeling about our private lives, as you are starting to be, but by God, as my niece and your father's daughter and your grandmother's namesake, you will measure up when you do your work, or you won't know what wrath I can drop on your head. And you're not—by far—ready to be adrift in this competitive world. There aren't many stars anymore. It took expert handling to make you one, it wasn't just your own darling little personality, believe me."

She looked on the dressing table and saw the globule of transparent amber with the imprisoned paleolithic insects in it. It had been handed to Jeffrey when he was told by his father that he was worthy of being on his own as an actor—as his father had before him. And in his last note, Jeffrey had handed it in trust to his sister.

"Here," said Claudia, picking up the smooth globe. "Your father left this for me to give you when you won your spurs. Maybe I was wrong when I gave it to you at the premiere of *The Oracle*."

She held her palm open, the amber reflecting the dressing table lights.

Instinctively Belinda reached for it and set it back on the dressing table. Claudia realized that with all the emotional upheavals she had faced, she had brought the token amber with her this auspicious day.

"Okay, let's run lines," said Belinda, as if she were bestowing a favor.

As they opened their scripts, Claudia smothered her irritation. Here she was, working desperately to give Belinda training, knowing well how precarious her career was at the moment.

Once again, Max was starting an epic film at a time when Titan was balancing on a financial tightrope.

Even Fergus had come on the set to give Max his best wishes for a good beginning. If he knew what Claudia was facing with Belinda, Fergus's smile and those flowers in her dressing room wouldn't have been so generously given.

Claudia felt her back was against a wall.

Fergus! Why hadn't she thought of him before?

Max was in love with his script, Belinda was in love with love, and Claudia was terrified. But Fergus was the cool one.

Fergus. The original takeout kid. Since he was eighteen, he'd been snatching other people's coals out of the fire and getting insulted for it. Realizing that she needed him, his original role as everything from patsy to hatchet man suddenly seemed valuable to her. Good old Fergus, she thought, he's managed to be a pain in the ass for fifty years, but if all else fails . . .

She felt deceitful attempting to win Belinda with a fake affirmation of truce when she was secretly thinking of dethroning Kevin in any way possible. She also was going to win Fergus again for whatever need she had, and she was leading Max down a daisy path, pretending to be in control when she was scared, her inner self trembling over the authority that had been put upon her. She certainly was about to pay for her sins of having been such a carefree, thoughtless movie star in the days of her own youth. Now, with her own kin, the tables were turned.

Who was it who said, watch out what you ask for, you may get it? She had wanted to care for Belinda and the baby, she had wanted to be married to Max Ziska, and now all their burdens had somehow been transferred to her shoulders.

She thought of what the wonderful musician Satchmo had said: "Don't look behind you, something may be gaining on you . . ."

She didn't dare. She'd just figure it out bit by bit. The main effort at the moment would be to help Max get the required amount of footage in the can every day. What was it—ah, yes, at ninety feet a second, two or three minutes of usable film per diem. It seemed like little, but in the end it was a satisfactory output and, like a report card, gave the director a gold star for the day from the front office. But it had damned well better be good.

The main problem now was to enlist any aid she could find and try to get Belinda in line. This was the first time they had been strangers, and if it came to a real showdown, she'd call Fergus for help.

6

There was no gossip center in the world more incestuous than Titan studio. Having existed so much longer than the Johnny-come-lately celluloid factories, it had a web of internecine communication that could have been a pattern for the CIA.

Department heads usually heard the latest news from secretaries who lunched with other secretaries, who had dinner with other secretaries, who slept with members of various departments who heard from their secretaries— all within the great microcosm of studio life.

It also was no secret that Belinda called home to have Effie prepare hampers of food and ordered choice wines for Kevin's house. These items could not be delivered by messengers, for he worked at the studio on and off at odd hours. But it was known that her Corvette was on the ready, and well-equipped, for her to rush off to Venice as soon as she could get away from her work.

As the picture progressed, Claudia gave up trying to be her chauffeur and to hide the romance from prying eyes. Her only effort was to keep Belinda happy—and to keep as much of Belinda's private life from Max as possible.

Belinda fell into her role as Lucretia, Claudia suspected, not because of her constant drilling and effort, or Max's enthusiasm, or the familial affection of a well-geared motion-picture crew, but because she and Kevin apparently had discussed the importance of her stardom.

Belinda mentioned it several times in an idiom that seemed alien to Claudia. "The microcosm of the star system becomes a giant wave in the world," she said, "so it is an obligation, isn't it?"

Claudia wanted to tell her to stop mouthing nonsense she didn't understand, but she kept still. She wondered what the two had up their sleeves.

Max was engrossed in production problems and in developing a strong relationship with his large crew, his cast, and his cutters.

Claudia hoped that Leslie Charles would not get wind of where Belinda spent many of her nights, but from his lifted eyebrow when Belinda was on the phone or made sudden impolite exits at the end of the day, she knew he surmised plenty. He was gentleman enough not to say anything. After all, he had seen Belinda through her first puppy love mash on John Graves. Claudia breathed a sigh of relief when she realized that no one had been aware of Belinda's short and tragic romance with Pericles Niadas. But Leslie had been a good friend in Rome and in Greece and had helped Belinda over the difficult times of her first starring role.

As a matter of fact, Belinda was cozy with him. He was a father image; and that was the affectionate center of interest she could enjoy on the set. They had memories in common, and Leslie was shrewd enough to believe that he and his career might be around a great deal longer than this current hot affair with a young artist.

He had seen such passionate encounters blow hot and cold in a hundred pictures. Also, his lifelong friend, Claudia, who had really started him in the film business, was in the position of being almost "establishment" for the first time in her life, married to Max Ziska, not only one of the great talents of the industry, but with a predilection for writing the story of heroic types Leslie received such accolades for performing. It was a damned good living, being part of the Ziska stock company, so to speak.

He still quailed at the fact that he was no longer a leading man. His role as Hermocrates, the elder physician, in Belinda's first picture had closed the door on that; but he had won an Academy Award on it. He reluctantly decided to settle into middle age or old age, depending on the viewpoint, as suitable, as long as he played important character roles and had the money and social prestige to gather the beautiful and eager youths of Hollywood and

Beverly Hills around him. Aside from this, he had a high-walled, large Spanish house in Palm Springs, where, with the aid of various gay bars and dance clubs, he could gather the youth of southern California in a beautiful nut-brown nude panorama.

Claudia didn't care about Leslie's personal comments, if he did gossip, but she cared deeply about what he might say to his longtime lover and friend, Andrew Reed. Andrew had been foremost in promoting publicly his brannigan against the Barstows, and he had tried to blitz Belinda's career at the beginning in Rome because of a slight at the large party she was given.

A springtime romance was all right as far as the press went. In the old days the stars had their romances, but they were *affairs*, seemingly candlelight and roses, courting in the moonlight of a Jeanette MacDonald–Nelson Eddy dream. But now the more crude Anglo-Saxon words indicating more than a kiss which took the place of forbidden coitus were more likely to destroy the myth of a young star. Up to this point, as far as the public was concerned, Belinda was the fantasy of the cinema world; the hot-blooded virgin, whom every man who had bought a ticket thought of as the one he would most likely care to deflower.

Grace Boomer heard about Belinda's affair with Kevin and tucked it away with the other gossip and a bottle of bourbon in the bottom of her desk in her aerie atop the publicity department. Being an old trouper, and knowing that the forces were going to have to gather at the first bugle call, she kept her mouth shut, awaiting the time when Fergus would call her to his office and she would be asked how they'd plan to cut the Gordian knot.

On the set, Max was the last to hear gossip. Knowing Claudia was in his life, as his wife as well as dialogue director, no one would have dared approach him with anything that might supersede her authority. The whole hegemony of Hollywood tottered on an unwritten code which changed with the tides of fortune. Right now, Barstows were at spring tide. It was better to watch than discuss anything with the principals.

Max had hoped that Belinda would be intrigued with the Italian discovery, Antonio Valli. To his mind, Valli had more attraction than any man he'd met since John

Graves. The blond-haired, brown-eyed actor not only had the skills of a fine British and European training, he had the old-fashioned charm of a gentleman, and with it a mysterious withholding of himself. Max admired his ambition; he could be a star, flagrantly handsome, and as yet unplumbed as a personality. He played a brilliant, driving tennis game, and he was enthusiastically invited into the courts of Beverly Hills society. He had imported his classic Lancia, had a European household staff, and he had rented a house on Angelo Drive, not far from the Jules Steins. He presided at tennis lunches at his house on Sundays; in other words, he was doing everything properly, and he did not seem to be putting on airs about any of it.

He escorted the most fashionable women, few of them actresses, to various top parties, yet he was amiable enough about doing his publicity chores—lunching with press, distinguished visitors, department heads, or visiting brass from New York with a casual bonhomie.

"I wish," said Max to Claudia, "that Belinda would get out of Venice long enough to go play tennis once in a while on Tony's court. It would do her good to meet some of her peers."

"She's too busy to play tennis with Tony," said Claudia. "Wait a while. We'll give a few small dinners after you're well into the picture, and we'll get some people together she ought to know."

But meanwhile, Belinda looked at the handsome, broad-shouldered man who was to play her hated brother, Cesare, with the glazed calm eye of a woman in love elsewhere.

As for Tony, he was so involved with his first American role and his successful life in Beverly Hills that he did the proper things and went about his work with a vitality that delighted Max. Socially, he did everything a high-class star was supposed to do for his leading lady. He sent Belinda flowers on the opening day of the film and a rose each Monday thereafter. He invited her to lunch at the commissary where they were fodder for preplanned photographs; that is after he took off the false beak that Max made him wear, for he was properly vain about his own classic face.

The secretaries and women staff members creamed as he walked by, but Belinda was apparently untouched by his sex appeal. He tried to draw her into conversation; the best he could do was wrench a little enthusiasm about the Renaissance, and the portraits that Kevin was working on. Finally, he decided that, in spite of her dazzling beauty and talent, she was a somewhat dull young girl, and he gave up trying to impress her. Max and Claudia saw this and were distressed. Where was the fire and force, Claudia thought, that they had expected of Belinda?

Claudia began to be concerned about the film. Belinda, as Max and she planned, portrayed her role well in the first part of the script—the innocent being used; the pawn of a family of hates, fratricides, passions, and ambitions. Then Claudia began to realize the flaw in the story. There was no one for the young Lucretia to love, save the incestuous child she bore very young. There was no passionate interlude, as she had with John Graves in the first picture. She could not mention this to Max, for he was too involved. She realized that the whole crux of the drama lay in the hate-love relationship she had with the brother, Cesare, the man who was powerful enough in his diabolical cunning to be the pattern for Machiavelli's famous text for despots, *The Prince*.

But the production was rich, and everyone seemed satisfied when the rushes came in each day. The cast was splendid, and Titan rumors abounded, mostly promulgated by the publicity department, that the studio had another classic in the making.

It seemed absurd that the picture could not be made in Rome, but it was true, the goliath of the Mankiewicz-Tayor-Burton film, *Cleopatra*, had tied up practically every film and housing facility in Rome. To compete with this multi-million dollar blockbuster for space and equipment would have been impossible. Max, remembering the pollution and the pace of modern Rome, was finally satisfied with the constant pressure from Fergus to create the peace and beauty of the Renaissance in the bits and pieces he was shown in California.

As he had discussed the company's problem with the production designer, the suitable settings were found in various places: the Crocker mansion along the Seventeen-Mile Drive in Pebble Beach; Roman facades on several houses in Pasadena, terraced gardens in Montecito and Santa Barbara; a few venerable millionaire's vanities in

San Francisco; the great stone staircases and flowering gardens of Pacific Heights; among the quadrangles and in the chapel at Stanford University where Italian memories had been created with Senator Stanford's money.

Most of the architects of the new wealth of the West had their training in the Beaux Art school, which had focused on the classic and Renaissance buildings of the old world. Even sections of the University of California at Los Angeles, and the old campus on Vermont (now City College) were used, later to be skillfully edited, using establishing long shots that second units with doubles had made in Rome. The whole collage became a convincing Renaissance tapestry.

All the way from San Francisco to Exposition Park in Los Angeles, the company—with the public roped off, police protection, and jerry-built facilities—blossomed into action. The cavalcade was akin to a small self-contained army moving from fantasy to reality so quickly that costumed court members often walked out of a shot into an intersection where traffic halted as intrigued motorists stared in amazement at the splendor of the decadent court of Alexander VI.

There was the massive honeywagon, which was the portable dressing room and toilet facility on location. There were generators which made the night bright in country or city, under completely controlled conditions. Trucks carried makeup and wardrobe compartments for the extras and bit players. Aside from this were private trailers; one for Belinda, others for Leslie Charles, Antonio Valli, and such performers as the young Mexican actor, Ruben Padilla, who was playing the role of the sultan of Bajazet; the method actor from New York, Michael Sorel, who portrayed the ill-fated duke of Gandia; and Beatrice Condon, who portrayed Rosa Vanozza, the mistress of Alexander VI, and the mother of Lucretia and Cesare.

The camera truck and sound truck; the prop truck, Max's trailer, and the script girl's trailer—which was in essence the floating business office; and a crane, if necessary, were all in position, ready for instant action, for every moment meant money.

At mealtime, an enormous portable kitchen wagon opened up its chromed sides; steam tables and ovens poured forth the catered hot meals that were legally required for the entire crew and artists, no matter what the time or place. Of course, the stars, producer, and director always ate at a special place, with napkins and silver, above the salt, so to speak.

Location was a completely status-bound operation. Stars talked to stars, and the director. Featured players huddled together, usually in a long harangue about plays and past glories and disappointments.

Extras usually clowned and played cards and slept and were controlled by the bawling out of harassed assistant directors.

Crews, sound and cameramen, electricians, all performing their specific physical tasks, ignored the actors as much as possible until they focused in on them in work. They had complex jobs to glue this peripatetic world together.

During all this confusion, Belinda was moved with as much comfort as could be provided in such a caravan. Sometimes she drove in a limousine; stars always had chauffeurs, and elegance. The bit players were ensconced in "stretch-outs"—cars that were a cross between a long private car and a bus. Extras went by bus. Sometimes the company flew to locations, where a fleet of varied vehicles carried them to their destinations.

There was no time for anything but work.

Claudia was Belinda's tuning fork—keeping her voice placement, pitch, and pace in unity so the fragments of the film would fit together. Belinda and Leslie Charles began to move as a smooth team, understanding each other, becoming a creative unit. Max was pleased, Claudia delighted.

The press was kept away. Neighborhoods were jammed with onlookers. Eager youngsters and fanatic elders tried to get at Belinda with scraps of paper for her to sign. Cameras flashed and were barred as flashbulbs ruined scenes.

Finally, four studio guards and two policemen were posted to strong-arm people who tried to climb under ropes, peek through quickly erected canvas flats, or make their way into any park or garden where Belinda was working.

One man was thrown out of the corridor near her hotel room in Monterey. A chambermaid was found hiding in her closet waiting for an autograph.

Claudia stayed with her as much as she would allow.

During most of her spare moments, Belinda tied up the portable phone for a call to Kevin. Half the time she couldn't reach him.

"I'm sick of this!" she said to Claudia one night in her sitting room at the El Drisco, the old-fashioned little hotel on Pacific Heights. "Here I am, with the most beautiful view of the bay, my room full of flowers, and a whole evening with nothing to do. Why can't Kevin come up? We could go to Trader Vic's for dinner."

"Because you have to be up at five," said Claudia. "Honey, I'm sorry, but you'll be home soon. Just think— for once, the studio will look good to you."

Belinda sat down and creamed off her makeup. "I'm so tired," she said. "These people around all day. It smothers me."

"I'll have your dinner sent up if you'd like to be alone."

"I would," said Belinda testily, "since I can't do what I want."

Claudia wasn't surprised to hear that Belinda had tied up the phone an hour talking to Kevin. When she went to her own suite to join Max, she looked out to the street and could see the great lineup of Titan trucks and two night watchmen framed in a trailer window, playing cards. The whole studio flotilla seemed like a sleeping army, waiting to awake at dawn and start again.

They were all tired. They ran lines in moving cars, rehearsed with the wind flapping against the sides of the trailer, moved into hot sun, Belinda robed in velvet, brocade, and a towering headdress donned for a court ball. In reality she dressed at six in the morning, and the costume hung, a burden on her body, until the fading rays of the sun made shooting impossible and freed her.

Sometimes, fighting crowds and whistles and constant retakes, Belinda looked up at the sound boom twisting like an imprisoned serpent, and she felt as if she, too, were on a long leash, thrashing in every direction.

Finally, the company returned home. For a weekend, Claudia closed her eyes, and Belinda disappeared with Kevin.

On the first morning of studio work, Belinda called in. "Don't worry," she said, "I'll be on the set in time."

"I'm glad you called," said Claudia. "I'll tell Max not to worry."

"Kevin says the sets are marvelous. They asked him in to check the quality of the Pinturicchio murals. He says they're very well duplicated. He approves."

"Bully," said Claudia. "See you."

She hung up, biting her lip at her irritation. Was Kevin suddenly making himself the deus ex machina of Titan's production department? For some reason of his own, no doubt, he had decided to give his approval of the production, which meant Belinda would, too. Well, at least that would make it easier for Max.

The studio now was geared for the larger scenes.

The Borgia apartments in the Vatican had been copied. The low marble lintels, the gilded and vaulted Pinturicchio ceilings would be a background for the plotting and scheming of the ambitious and feral Borgias.

In contrast was the set for the dark room where Pope Alexander VI hides in deep despair when he discovers that Cesare has murdered his own brother. Here Belinda would have her most dramatic scenes, for in the story Lucretia remains closeted for three days with her father until she walks him out of the room of horrors into sanity.

Here, also, on the exterior lot of the studio, was the set, reconstructing the jubilee year of 1500, when Alexander watches his daughter ride by with her large court escort and her new husband, Don Alfonso, on her way to a ceremonial visit to the great basilicas.

Standing on the hillside with camera crews, staff, and five hundred extras, it was difficult to see the traffic flowing beyond on the freeway and know this whole scene would seem as rooted in stone and legend as the Castel Saint Angelo, where it had originally occurred.

The summer moved into the fall, and then, without warning, Claudia knew something was happening with Belinda, and she could not figure what it was.

For the first time, Belinda asked to have the few things from her mother's long-forgotten apartment taken out of storage. How long ago it seemed, just several years past, when as a schoolgirl she had balked at leaving South Palm Drive and her girlish memories. The crates were opened at her order in an empty back room of the servant's quarters over the garage, where Claudia had once housed a staff.

On a Saturday afternoon, while Kevin was busy paint-ing his portrait of Antonio Valli, Belinda tossed out great boxes of her childhood books and furnishings and toys which she had insisted on keeping; along with her mother's knickknacks they were sent to the Goodwill, and as the handsome picture of her father in top hat and tails, painted by Bellows, was opened, she exclaimed with delight.

"I'll keep that!" she said.

Claudia, pleased that she was interested in her back-ground, enthused about some of the small antiquities, Georgian silver and fruitwood end tables Jeffrey had picked up in London, an olive wood brazero with a copper tray from Spain, various mementos of other times and places. She was pleased that Belinda had them all set aside by the unpackers in one part of the room, but she was also puzzled.

When the men had left, and Belinda was finally en-grossed, sitting in a Savonarola chair, encircled by stacks of art and history books that Jeffrey had cherished, Claudia came to her and kissed her.

"I'm glad you're so interested in all the things your father loved. If he had only been here, you would have had such a wealth of enthusiasm to live with. He could have shared so much with you."

Belinda looked up, smiling. "Well, I'll have that any-way," she said. "You see, Kevin is going to give it to me. I'm getting all this stuff together for our house. We're getting married."

"You're—you're what?" said Claudia, her mouth turn-ing dry. "When did this—decision—come about?"

"Listen," said Belinda, "you didn't think we were going to hide out forever, did you? We've found a wonderful house in Laurel Canyon. Kevin signed the lease yesterday. It's rustic, but it has a studio and a wooded garden and lots of privacy."

"When did you plan on doing this?" asked Claudia.

"Next weekend," said Belinda. "I have four days off in the schedule." She flipped through an art book as if she had just made a random comment.

"It seems to me," said Claudia, trying to overcome a sudden dizziness, "that Kevin could have at least come to me before he made this decision."

Belinda waved the thought away. "Kevin's a very

private person," she said, as if it were a princely attribute. "We have to do our own thing, our own way. Of course, I'll be in control of my money when I marry. We have plans. Kevin will be a wonderful producer. He's already doing the production design sketches for our picture. We're going to do a modern story of a young woman picketing for civil rights in Washington, and what happens to her and her peers."

Claudia felt as if the world was tumbling around her; it wasn't possible that Belinda could look at her so sweetly and poison the air with such words.

"Don't look like that," said Belinda. "You should be very happy for me now that I've found the man I love. And it certainly will make things easier for you."

Claudia remembered Bill Chapman's warning about the hazards of a young star being taken over by a man who would ace himself into a fat life, using her name and fame. Well, it looked as if it had already happened. And there was no way to get to Belinda.

An intercom buzzed from the house. My God, thought Claudia, this old buzzer system still works from the days when I had a staff. If she was being buzzed by Effie, who was relishing the idea of their family togetherness, it must be important.

Seeing that Belinda was hardly aware of her departure, Claudia went to the house, her thoughts whirling. She was so angry she was glad to get away, whatever the phone call was.

How could Belinda be so callous about the rest of her life! What about Alex? Was she going to casually walk away from him? Claudia realized that the world thought Max was the baby's father and she the stepmother, so that was a social possibility. But what about Belinda's work, the picture, her life as a star?

A civil rights picture! On Belinda's money! Claudia's professional hackles rose; this was as much of a blow to her as the fact that Belinda was defecting from the personal part of her life.

She could just see Kevin with his fanciful production designs, preening, incapable of being a practical producer. The whole situation was repellent, and, above all, amateurish beyond belief. It had the makings of a disaster.

The minute Claudia picked up the phone and heard

Fergus's voice, she knew he was probably more aware of the situation than she was.

"I think you'd better get over here," he said. "You and I have to have a conference, pronto. I'm at the beach house. Just as well I talk to you away from the studio."

"I'll be right there," said Claudia. "Funny, I was just about to call you."

She unlocked the sacrosanct gates that were supposed to protect Belinda and had obviously not done the job. As she stopped a brief moment to kick off her slippers so she could walk faster in the sand, she realized with a wry smile that this was the very spot where she had looked at Kevin's sketches and started the whole bloody mess.

Fergus was looking out the window. He could see Claudia rushing down the beach. How many times in past years they had confronted each other here over various dramatic crises.

He thought of how surprisingly he had come upon the whole situation with Belinda and Kevin Frazier. It was unbelievable how strangely things came to light in this town.

For several years he had been sleeping with a woman who worked in the wardrobe department. Tall, slim, and chic, with a quiet manner, she labored diligently to educate her two boys.

A divorcée, Peggy Rush had been left on her own by an errant alcoholic and was shy of the casual sex life of the studio. Working as a wardrobe woman, she had little competition for her job. She was not ambitious, and she minded her manners, punching out the time clock, welcoming the long hours that gave her golden time, and knowing that if she could just hold out a few more years, her two sons would be on their own and she could make it for herself without such pressures.

She was one of the vast army in Hollywood of lone women homemakers, looking forward to the age of institutional and governmental pensions—her youth having fled without bounty. She accepted the fact that the prime time of her looks and life were passing, and she only resented the fact that there was not a man around to give her children some of the companionship that should have been theirs.

Fergus met her during several conferences with Janos, and he saw how neatly and efficiently she presented Janos's dramatic show. She was not on, and she didn't expect anything from anyone.

One night after a frustrating day, Fergus invited her to dinner when Janos had left the fitting room. Surprisingly, she told him she would have loved it, but she had a pot roast going in her slow cooker, and she had to get home to turn it off. Her kids were with their grandmother for their monthly weekend visit, and what was left would be their Sunday supper, but if he'd like to have potluck with her he was welcome.

Fergus bought a bottle of wine on the way to her house; she had her own Ford, but gave him the address.

When he got to her little bungalow in Palms, he saw that she was really a homebody. The house was neat and a cozier place than many houses he'd visited in Bel Air. She had dished out the pot roast, carrots, new potatoes and cabbage, and a savory mustard sauce. Somehow, in her apron, she reminded him of his first young days in Hollywood when he had rented a room over a cafeteria and had fallen in love with the owner, Kathleen, a sympathetic colleen. Peggy Rush was the homebody he had missed; her house a pale reflection of the good smells in his mother's boardinghouse kitchen in the Bronx. Now that these poor days were long past, he could relate to them with affection.

Over apple pie and coffee, he found himself chatting with her about simple things and enjoying it.

In time, he met her two boys, and it gave him pleasure to bring them tickets to athletic events and a color television set, perhaps to make up for the things he hadn't done for David in the busy years when David was small, perhaps to soothe the pang that had been so hard-hitting to his ego when he had discovered that David was not his own son.

Fergus's relationship with Peggy became one of many that remain hidden in the massive studio beehive of human lives. Once a month, when her children went to visit their grandmother in Sun City, he stayed with her, had pleasant sex with her, and left the next day, leaving a hundred-dollar bill on the breakfast table under the coffeepot.

It did not seem to humiliate her. It was money she could well use, and she was flattered by his company. He never was intimate with her when the children were around, and as time went on he learned a great deal from her about the underbelly of his own studio, things that the head of Titan would never have heard otherwise.

One day, Peggy, usually so discreet about her relationship with him, never coming to his office or calling him but waiting for him to summon her, had called, breaking all tradition.

"I think I'd better talk to you," she said. "Could you please come over to fitting room number 5? I have Belinda Barstow's court dress for you to see if anyone asks. You could say there's a problem in the selection of color."

He walked over to the wardrobe department, wondering if she were going to put pressure on him. If so, he'd have to drop her. That's the way it would have to be.

But when he walked into the dressing room and saw her welcoming smile, he knew it had nothing to do with any personal problem. She came close to him, holding the ruby velvet dress like a shield, to prove they had business together.

"I just thought you ought to know," she whispered. "My ex, who is dabbling in real estate at the moment, always calls me to brag about his success. Well, he has just rented the old Bessie Love log cabin up in Laurel Canyon to Belinda Barstow and Kevin Frazier. They paid a hot five hundred a month for the old place, and they say they're going to be married next weekend."

"My God," said Fergus, "are you sure your ex wasn't on the juice?"

"Of course he was on the juice," said Peggy. "He doesn't call me if he isn't. But it's real, Fergus, believe me. I know how he operates, and if he signed for a year with his commission, he wouldn't dare tell me if it wasn't true for fear I'd raise hell about getting money from him for the kids."

"Thanks, Peg," he said, unbending enough to kiss her on the lips. "I'll see you next weekend. You're a good kid. I'd better make some calls. You didn't tell anyone else?"

"No," she said. "I thought I'd better tell you first."

"Good girl," he said. "Let it end there."

"And now," said Claudia, "I'll tell you all I know of what's been happening. What do you think we can do, Fergus?"

He had refrained from drinking in front of her, respecting the fact that she was on the wagon; that's all he'd need, he thought, to see Claudia break her vow and hit the bottle again. But her austerity was frightening.

"You better leave it to me," he said. "I've handled some jim-dandies in my life, and I think with a little investigation I can handle this."

"I trust your power," she said, "but I don't know if I trust your methods. What do you have in mind?"

"You'll have to let me decide what to do," he said. "What I have in mind may not be very appealing to you; after all, Claudia, you've been pretty lax with Belinda."

She hung her head.

"I know," she said, "I just can't seem to help myself."

"Leave it to me," he said. "I have ways. And also, I can get a dossier on anybody you mention within forty-eight hours. And I can find out what makes 'em tick. From then on, it's just a matter of organizing."

"You'd better make it fast," she said. "The marriage, it seems, is next weekend."

Belinda was given an unexpected afternoon off on Wednesday. Close-ups were being made of Leslie Charles in the scene where he dies of poison. After all the ignominy of Alexander VI's reign of terror and murder, by happenstance he was poisoned by the potion he had intended for another man, put into his hands by a muddled servant.

The makeup, and the change from an arrogant, mighty pope to a man dying, in a sense by his own hand, involved an extremely complicated camera process, showing the incredible transformation of a man from a despot to a cringing animal, knowing that his life was coming to an end, and resenting every moment of the tortuous process.

Fergus had called Max.

"Max, do you think with the aid of your makeup man, the camera, and our new infrared technique you could do Rodrigo's transformation from life to death in one long shot? You know, with all the drama of a Jekyll and Hyde; it could be sensational."

"I'd planned on doing two shots of Belinda weeping and Leslie in death this afternoon," said Max. "But it's a good idea, since he has the makeup on now. Let me think about it."

In half an hour, Max called Fergus back. Fergus knew Max well enough to realize that his soaring imagination would shoot the scene before it happened. Fergus had challenged his creativity, and to Max this was catnip.

"We'll do it," he said. "I've talked to Joe on camera, and we're all excited about it."

"Of course," said Fergus. "And if it doesn't work, the other shots are great."

"That's not good enough," said Max. "We'll do it this afternoon."

So Belinda was freed.

Peggy, the wardrobe woman, came to Belinda's dressing room as she was removing her makeup.

"I hope you don't mind doing a little errand," Peggy asked.

"Me do an errand?" said Belinda, amused. "What's on your mind, Peg?"

"It's just that Janos decided that your portrait would look much richer with these ruby earrings and necklace."

She held them up. They were excellent copies of court jewels; set in traceries of gold, they were luminous.

"If you are going to see Kevin, would you take them to him? He needs them right away. Of course, if you can't, we'd send them over by messenger."

"Of course I'll take them," said Belinda, pleased. "We're going to have dinner, anyway."

It gave her an opportunity to see him earlier. She called, but as often happened, his line was busy. He must have taken it off the hook.

Four bottles of Lacrima Christi from the volcanic slopes of Vesuvius were empty on Kevin's sideboard.

"And the exciting thing, the triumphant domination of the homosexual and bisexual world, remains in art. What superbeings they were in those fabulous times. More liberated than we are today, living by our stupid conventions. What freedom, what glorious dominance of the human spirit above the restrictions of society!"

"Yes . . . yes . . . !"

"You can even see it in Botticelli's *Flora*; it seems the mocking face of a youth placed on the body of a slim, boyish woman."

There was a pause. The blond man received his alerting phone call. He checked his watch; it was time.

"And that is not all. Did you ever think of Michelangelo's *Pietà*? Come now, where are the soft lines? Instead, Christ's mother has the musculature of an athlete with woman's breasts glued like apples on a male rib cage."

Laughter.

"Ah, if you could see my villa in Fiesole. The tall cypress are the only sentinels. And, like Lorenzo il Magnifico's poem, the olive trees turn from dark green to silver as the wind blows."

"I'd like to see it."

"You shall. You belong in my galleria—the vines dripping with grapes, and you standing poised like a youth from our Golden Age."

The two came toward each other, each man admiring the other. The taller man was the aristocratic protagonist, the youth the classic male to be taken. The tall man set the two wine glasses down. In a moment their clothes were dropped, and they clasped hands, bodies taut, muscles rippling, as they fought, pressure against pressure, desire against desire, awaiting the moment when one would succumb. They approached the exciting moment when these erotic isometrics would turn to passionate subjection.

Antonio Valli, the blond-haired, olive-skinned man, took control. Perhaps at his will, Kevin's muscled arms trembled slightly, his feet moved for a firmer grip, and then he fell back, his eyes half closed with passion, toward the waiting bed.

When Belinda rushed into the room, she stopped short.

On the bed were two figures. One was on his back, his legs wrapped around the burly man on top. Kevin was playing the woman, and he seemed to be enjoying it immensely.

And then he looked aside and saw her standing there like Lot's wife, her face frozen in horror.

"My God!" gasped Kevin.

He pulled back, the two bodies separated in a violent spasm, and Antonio Valli rolled away.

Belinda was gone as quickly as she had come, dropping her handful of jewelry on the floor.

They could hear the screech of her car as she started off, the rip of metal as she crashed a fender against a fence post, then the sounds of the Corvette backing up and finally roaring away.

Kevin and Tony looked at each other a dazed moment. Tony sat down on the sofa, smiled a little smile, and said, *"Che será, será."*

Seeing Kevin trying to hide his disturbance by offering another glass of wine, Tony arose. "I'll see you again," he said. "It's better I go now."

After a moment, Kevin picked up the ruby jewels and held them like drops of blood in his palm.

Automatically he went to the portrait of Belinda as Lucretia and started to sketch in the jewels. But his eyes filled with tears and he had to put his brush down. For the first time he could remember, he was frightened, and he didn't know what he would do next.

Claudia was surprised when Belinda returned home in the middle of the afternoon. She heard the bedroom door slam, and, knowing how independent Belinda was these days, she smothered her annoyance, still wondering why Belinda wasn't with Kevin, as she had phoned she was delivering jewelry in Kevin's studio. Most likely she'd be staying there, she had surmised.

Then, as she went to knock at the door, she heard Belinda being ill in the bathroom. She rushed in and found the girl retching.

"Belinda, what's the matter?"

Belinda looked up, her pale face contorted.

"Just leave me alone!"

Claudia stood there, perplexed. Obviously it was emotional as well as physical. Tears were streaming down Belinda's face.

Atlas, the little Yorkshire, sensing drama, was jumping up at Belinda, trying to comfort her.

"Come on, Atlas," said Claudia, picking him up. "We'll just leave her alone." She left the bathroom, saying, "If you want to see me, I'll be here. Can't I help you, dear?"

"Oh, Claudia!" cried Belinda and rushed into her arms, clinging to her.

"There, there," said Claudia. "Maybe you'd better get to bed. You're shivering."

She settled Belinda in bed, and Atlas curled up in his usual place on her comforter at the foot of the bed.

Claudia sat in a nearby chair, discreetly silent.

"If you want to talk about it—"

"Never!" sobbed Belinda. "I don't want to talk about it. But I never want to see him again. Never! Never!"

And that's all she would say.

It took several days for Belinda to overcome her weeping and nausea. Dr. Saul was called in. He sedated her, gave her relief from the nausea, and suggested a bland diet and a possible session with a psychiatrist.

Claudia thought there had been a lovers' quarrel and that eventually phone calls and a distressed visit from Kevin would straighten it out, but there were none. Kevin had vanished. He was no longer to be seen on the beach, and he was not at the studio; she had inquired discreetly.

The smashed Corvette, now repaired, disturbed her deeply. There must have been a terrible scene. Belinda could have been killed.

Slowly Belinda came back to life. She studied the new scenes of the script with a ferocious look on her face.

Claudia finally talked to her one day, having urged her to go for a walk on the beach.

"I don't know what your trauma is," Claudia said, "but darling, I can see you're using it, and in this particular role, it will do you well. That old maestro Gielgud said that we as actors have an obscenity to draw on our own most intimate experiences of life and to use them publicly. Now's your chance."

She glanced at Belinda, pleased to see she was listening, not rejecting her.

"He also alerted me, long ago, and I should have listened, to take care that success does not vulgarize you for more success. I know you won't do that, because you're a—"

"Yes, yes," said Belinda, smiling for the first time in a long time. "You're going to say, 'because you're a Barstow.'"

"Right," said Claudia, pretending to dodge the cliché. "Everything you do is a preparation. Oh, I wish your father were here, he'd help you so much. He used to tell me, you can't see the whole scene, but try to look at it. Study your stand-in and the ensemble before you create your character. Don't just see yourself. Make servants out of placement, projection, facility, and variety, then forget them, and become the character you portray."

She let the words soak in. Belinda was silent, and Claudia had the feeling that infinity hung on her words. Claudia felt she had finally broken through the armor that had surrounded Belinda these last days. Whatever had happened must have been horrifying beyond what Belinda could express. Claudia was appalled at the angry expressions that sometimes flitted across Belinda's face when she didn't know she was being observed.

Longing to communicate, Claudia gushed out her feelings.

"Take this problem that is deep in you, Belinda, and use it; don't let it use you. Be a winner, not a loser."

"What's the difference in the long run?" asked Belinda, suddenly morose.

"Well, in a way," said Claudia, counting on her fingers, "having been both, I guess I'd say that a loser seeks, pursues, fears a loss of love, panics, wastes time with fantasy, and makes excuses for inadequacies. Also, a loser accepts crap and flees responsibilities for personal satisfaction.

"My God, that's a handful, isn't it? Forgive me, but I have to say this. Men like Kevin are poseurs. Sometimes an experience such as yours is like going to a movie—it's great while it goes on, but after it's over you see it had no reality."

Belinda ran on ahead. Claudia was afraid she'd ruined the moment by bringing up Kevin.

But then Belinda came running back.

"All right," she said. "You don't have to tell me what a loser is. I think *I* know that. But what's a winner?"

"A winner," said Claudia, eager to gain her ground, "is sought, is loved, loves, enjoys life, can accept loss, creates, faces truth without tragedy, accepts only true value, refuses nonsense, and cares for her own life and situation, whatever that may be. So go back to the studio a winner."

Belinda picked up a flat stone, skipped it across the water, and stood watching the tiny splashes it made before it sank. Claudia found her nails digging into her palms. It had been a nervous session. And she hated being a pundit. She had no right.

"I will, oh I will," said Belinda. "Lucretia Borgia is going to turn in her grave when she sees what I do to her!"

Her eyes glinted. For a startling moment Claudia felt she was looking at the vixen Kevin had painted in his first portrait, with the slitted eyes and darting lascivious tongue; embodiment of evil.

"Bully for you," said Claudia, trying to be light about it. "You know, we might as well face the fact that, as stars, none of us can be quite normal. All of our thoughts and actions are directed by the picture business; our relationships, our personalities, our time, our economy are all dedicated to the pursuit of fame and our particular situation in this possessive industry. And yours is in full flower right now."

Belinda returned to the studio. Grace Boomer called her absence "a courageous bout with the flu . . . returning to portray the most difficult scenes of her brilliant career." She was ready.

In the interim, a few things had happened.

Bill Chapman paid off two months' rent on the love nest in Laurel Canyon, and it was forgotten.

"Kevin Frazier," Grace Boomer also wrote, "the brilliant young artist who has finished his assignment of painting the Borgia family, has left California to tour Europe, becoming so intrigued with Renaissance art after working on the Max Ziska classic that he has taken a sabbatical to visit international art collections."

Antonio Valli, because of his brilliant portrayal of Cesare in *Young Lucretia*, was signed by Titan on a starring contract, most unusual these days. The studio had not yet decided whether he would follow his current assignment by playing Lorenzo il Magnifico, or whether the studio would attempt to obtain the rights to the life of Puccini so that he could play the great composer.

Peggy Rush also received a little bonus, a fine stereo set and a collection of records and tapes, which her sons enjoyed immensely, playing rock so loud she thought she'd go out of her head after a hard day's work.

Fergus Austin, reviewing the daily rushes, was often shocked at the change in Belinda. He couldn't believe there was such fire and fury in the girl who had played the gentle oracle. But knowing why, he hoped she would not ever blurt out the truth to Claudia, for if she ever knew what a setup it had been and how dearly the studio had paid Antonio Valli to destroy Belinda's romance, her fury would have made Lucretia Borgia look like a Brownie scout.

Antonio Valli himself wondered what was going to happen when he first met Belinda on the set. He was prepared for tears, hysterics, even personal assault.

Belinda managed to stay in the dressing room on the set until her first appearance. He was somewhat surprised to hear the sounds of Donizetti's *Lucretia Borgia* being played in her room. The tragic opera boded no good.

When she appeared, he was startled by her metamorphosis. She was regal and, at the same time, he felt, petulant. She avoided his eyes on the set, and when they confronted each other for a reading with Max while the final lighting was being set up, she first studied her stand-in, and then wandered about the set in her ruby velvet gown, touching the furniture, examining props, absorbing it all as if she were greeting friends. She then came back to her reclining board (her gown was too stiff to sit in) and, leaning back on it, did her lines letter-perfect, still avoiding his eyes.

No wonder, he thought. This was a hard situation for a young girl, and if Kevin hadn't been so eagerly seducible, he would have felt guilty. As it was, he decided, it was just as well that the girl had found out before she stepped into a hasty marriage with an unacceptable spouse. He had really done her a good favor, and one day she would realize it.

Once they were in place, Valli recognized that he was facing a money actress. She met him eye to eye, and, good actor that he was, he almost cringed at her contemptuous anger.

In her mind, Belinda accepted his sexual encounter with Kevin as the actual rape of herself. Now she faced him, as Cesare, the day after the orgy he had initiated in the Vatican. He had insisted on becoming her lover just when she was trying to break away from the unnatural relationship with her father, the pope. The scene was filled with hatred and tension, and Belinda used her sense memory to trigger anger that quivered on the verge of tears.

It worked. Max was overwhelmed. Belinda had finally come alive beyond his dreams.

At the end of the scene, Tony was sweating, and the gaffers, as they had when she was in her first hot clinch with John Graves in Rome, literally hung from the rafters, marveling at the incandescent image unexpectedly flung at them.

Afterwards, Tony in his dressing room wondered how

he had ever thought Belinda Barstow a dull young woman. He was more than a little nervous about the picture; he imagined nothing but overshoulder shots of his left ear and neck.

Throughout the remainder of the filming of the picture, she moved as a virago, a flame of anger and revenge. It was difficult for Max to give the scenes to Tony.

Leslie was astounded. "My God, Belinda," he said, "I never thought I'd live to see the change you've made from the docile Lucretia into this devilish creature. I must congratulate you, and Claudia, if she's partly responsible."

Hardly, thought Belinda; just look over your shoulder to Tony. But she said nothing.

Observing her, Leslie knew that her virginal days were long gone, and some inner fire was devouring a disturbed woman. Also, au courant as he was with the gay steam baths, social rooms, and dance halls of Sunset Strip, he had more than a suspicion that Tony Valli and Kevin had something to do with it.

One cool autumn day he got a call from Boysie Miller, longtime friend of Andrew Reed.

It had been several years since Leslie had heard from the newspaper man. Their affectionate relationship, begun years before when Leslie was a leading man playing opposite Claudia, had finally broken up in Rome.

Andrew had been exceedingly rude to Niadas at the party the Greek had given for Belinda. Niadas had just broken up with his wife, the film star Martha Ralston, who had run back to Hollywood, leaving their newborn child with Niadas.

Claudia had lambasted Reed for publicly asking Niadas a personal question about the breakup of his marriage which was embarrassing to answer at a social gathering, and Leslie had followed up by siding with the Barstows. He had been instrumental in having Andrew, his lover of many years, removed bodily from the party by Greek guards. Andrew had sneaked back the next morning to use the villa press facilities to report the news of Niadas's death to his newspaper.

In the ensuing excitement, with the possibility of the epic film being closed down, Leslie had not contacted Andrew again. The columnist had left for the States, vowing eternal revenge on the Barstow family and on Leslie Charles. His ego had been publicly damaged. He was a proud man, and from that time on he had pursued a vendetta against all Barstows, and his erstwhile lover, Leslie Charles.

Leslie, being a fair-minded man, considered that Andrew had gone beyond the realm of decency, and the rift had never been mended.

As time passed, Andrew had taken his young boyfriend, Boysie Miller, and trained him to work on his newspaper column. So when Leslie got a call from Boysie Miller, he was surprised.

"I just wanted you to know," said Boysie, "that Andrew is dead."

"What!" said Leslie, his heart turning for a moment with the thought of the good times they'd had years before, and a sudden wrenching that they had not had decent words together these last several years.

"Oh—I am sorry," said Leslie, shocked.

"Like hell you are," said Boysie. "Listen to me, Leslie. I want you to know that I am not only his heir, I am taking over the column. And I intend to follow *his* policy regarding the Barstows, Titan, and you."

"Isn't that a rather strong thing to say so soon after your friend has passed on?" said Leslie.

"Not at all," said Boysie. "I just wanted to remind you, after the shabby way you treated him in Rome, that I'm following orders that are very explicitly written in his will."

Leslie forgot about Belinda's romantic affairs and sank deeply into gloom as she continued to overshadow him during their scenes.

It was one thing to be on the outs with Andrew Reed, figuring that one day they'd meet over a cold martini and make up, and another to know that Andrew had carried his resentment and hatred into a pact that would continue in an ungoverned way at the hands of another person.

Leslie mentioned it to no one. He prayed secretly that Boysie would find someone who would make him forget that he had to revenge Andrew.

While the film was being cut and edited, Claudia tried to think of something for Belinda to do, aside from her usual publicity sittings and playtime with Alex, who was growing restless and more of a problem to handle. Soon he would be going to prenursery school. It seemed that just hanging around and being a baby these days was not enough.

And what would be enough for Belinda, to rescue her from the inverted sadness that was her state after the film was ended?

Claudia knew what a letdown and depression followed the change of habits and social patterns that the familial studio life brought.

What was happening to the world at the beginning of the sixties? Sometimes Claudia despaired of television, for it brought the troubles of the world into every living room.

The Cuban communistic crisis, and internal strife with political ideologies darkened many a life.

The H-bomb, and Oppenheimer's dislike of it, had put fear into the hearts of a people.

The young, some following the dream of their dead folk hero, James Dean, in *Rebel Without a Cause,* had gathered impetus, not only in the slums and among the dispossessed, but in middle-class families who were horrified at the new attitudes. Resentfulness and scorn became youth's banner. Juvenile hardcore robbers, rapists, and murderers began to flourish. Youth had joined the fatalistic rebellion which, in a previous time, had been saved for more adult criminals. Antihero was in.

The advent of rock and roll made a rich folk hero out of Dick Clark. His "American Bandstand," with its twenty million viewers, frustrated the elders with its noise and with the importance it gave to callow teen-agers.

Belinda had watched these rock and roll groups on television since she had come back from Europe. They were her peers, but their milieu was far removed from her isolated life.

Claudia, watching her, recognized her wistfulness.

"I suppose Titan could send you on your next tour to Philadelphia. Would you like to go to the TV studio there and watch them," she asked, "or doesn't it appeal to you?"

"I wouldn't know what to do," said Belinda. "It's not my scene, but you know, I bet Connie Francis and Bobby Darin and Fabian make more money than I do."

Claudia had no answer.

"Having fun, too," said Belinda.

"Listen," said Claudia, "I won't say I'm not prejudiced—
for I am. Thank God you're an actress. That's where you
belong. Believe me, it's a longer lived, more continuous
profession.

"For starters, in the new world there's payola, under-
the-table handouts, amateurs falling into sudden millions,
drugs, frantic fans snatching at your clothes. It's even worse
than the movie business.

"I don't even like you going on tour these days, but
when Elvis Presley makes his tour, it's complete hysteria
time. Whole police forces have to patrol the hotels where
he stays. Col. Parker, his manager, has to hire an elaborate
protective security force, and he can never be alone."

And this was only an indication of what was happening,
for the great American image was changing swiftly.

The Beat Generation, the new Bohemians, spurred by
the writing of Jack Kerouac, weary of the myth of American prosperity gained through a life of organized drudgery,
brought about a disregard of what every middle-class generation so far had considered the sterling aim of the land:
to be clean, keep good hours, and finally acquire a split-
level house and a permanent job with fringe benefits.

The decade of the fifties having ended, the old guard, Ike
and Dick, were on the way out, and, most importantly, fear
was in.

This was the world Belinda faced as an adult.

And then, there came a hope.

Like the rest of America, Belinda watched the Nixon-
Kennedy debates on the air. It was the first time that
television had become a major factor in the political history
of the United States.

Kennedy was a young face, a white hope, an image to
intrigue young and old. America had had Nixon, they had
heard him explain away the nonexistence of his wife's fur
coat, and such trivia, and seen him standing beside the
old warrior, Eisenhower, Nixon's vice-presidential smile
turned on like a twenty-five-watt bulb.

Here, in Kennedy, was a new man, who had stood behind no one. He was handsome, he was dynamic, and he
stood by himself. He was the longed-for magic after the
drastic changes of the fifties.

The first chance Claudia had to interest Belinda outside

her own orbit was the new era of commitment that was brought forth by the young presidential candidate who had the charm to bring the people of America to attention.

Claudia managed to get through to Kennedy one day in Palm Springs.

It was a bright desert morning, and as Belinda approached him, dressed in beige skirt and silk shirt, her blonde hair falling to her shoulders, it was obvious his eyes lit up at her beauty. She herself was the embodiment of a spring morning.

"Well, little movie star," he said, smiling, "are you going to dance with me at the White House?"

"I hope so!" she said, smiling at him.

"You'd better help me get the votes, then," he said. "We need all the help we can get." He grinned back.

She was taken by his charm.

"Well," she said, "maybe you're wasting your time." She gave him a dramatic pause.

He glanced at her quizzically.

"Because," Belinda continued, "I'm not old enough to vote."

This evoked laughter from him and the cohorts who always rallied around him.

The moment was photographed for posterity—an eager young girl and a smiling, admiring man.

The new dream, a promise to the youth of the country to create a better world, appealed to Belinda's dramatic mind.

Everyone was singing the words to "Camelot," hoping these words would presage a change. It would be the time of a blending of theater and the arts into the somber halls of politics and statesmanship; for once creative artists would be recognized and honored by the leaders of the country.

> Don't let it be forgot
> That once there was a spot,
> For one brief shining moment
> That was known as Camelot.

Belinda became involved in the campaign. She was ideal for photographs, she wore badges and buttons, and she did all she could to represent youth for Kennedy.

The president had not forgotten his promise. He telephoned her. She couldn't believe it, but there was his voice.

"This is Jack Kennedy," he said, "who hasn't forgotten you're a potential voter. Jackie and I want you and your aunt to be present at my inauguration."

So, on January 20, 1961, Belinda and Claudia sat in the cold rotunda of the White House, surrounded by top-hatted statesmen and furred ladies, and thrilled to the idealistic words: *"Let the word go forth from this time and place . . . that the torch has been passed to a new generation of Americans."*

That's me, thought Belinda. I'm the new generation.

Belinda realized she had never seen Alex's birth certificate. He would be the next generation. Where would it say he was born? Certainly not in a cave in Greece, you can bet . . .

There the new president stood, handsome and dedicated, and there was gorgeous Jackie, her hat way back on her head so you could see her stunning dark hairline and those wide eyes. She would have been a great actress. What a face!

"So let us begin anew . . . Together, let us explore the stars, conquer the deserts, eradicate disease, tap the ocean depths, and encourage the arts and commerce."

That's going to cost a lot of tax money, thought Claudia. Oh, the dreams of young rulers!

"All this will not be finished in the first one hundred days. . . ."

You bet, thought Claudia. Mankind hasn't managed it in thousands of years. Well, let us hope.

Back at the hotel, Belinda said to Claudia, "I never thought about it before, but what kind of birth certificate does Alex have? I hope he has American citizenship. My baby's an American!"

"I'm sure David Austin took care of it, but we'll look into it."

Claudia realized, feeling very happy, that this was the first time Belinda had expressed real maternal concern about Alex.

Belinda was invited to a dinner party at the White House. Janos designed her a dress, and she discreetly wore only her Barstow pearls, given her on her fifteenth birthday. Photographs of her were newspaper and magazine grist for months, and the crowning glory of the evening was when Kennedy himself danced her once around the floor.

His keen-eyed admiration for beauty was not lost, and again they were photographed together.

Aside from the personal thrill, the event made a difference in terms of Belinda's public image. She was accepted as the current sugarplum, pet of the elect, her picture on the cover of every magazine, and distinguished enough to be fodder for *Vogue, Harper's Bazaar, House Beautiful, Town and Country, Paris Match,* the *Tatler;* one magazine even had the audacity to caption a picture of her dancing with the new president with the remark, "Was Jackie Jealous?"

She stayed at the ball, being whirled around by all the eager-eyed diplomats until three in the morning, enjoying being a celebrity and meeting celebrities, and was escorted back to the Mayflower where Claudia was waiting. It had been a wonderful evening. She had danced with the president and it seemed a hundred others. Her feet hurt, and absolutely nobody had appealed to her personally except the president and Jackie. They had been darling. What a wonderful life they had! But you had to be born into it, she guessed. It all left her lonelier and more adrift. It was time to go home.

On the day of the "sneak" preview of *Young Lucretia,* Titan sent the usual staff to prepare the "fader" so that Max could control the sound effects. Tapes were rigged to record simultaneously with the sound track, so the moguls from New York and the staff could later coordinate audience reaction and discover weak parts of the film, which were usually revealed by coughing, minor rustling when there should have been spellbound quiet, and, of course, laughter or surprise at the wrong moments. Experts could almost tell by listening if anyone left the theater, they were so aware of the scrapings and movings of the elaborate programs that were handed out by pretty junior publicists at such events, indicating the cast and the glory of the product.

The city chosen was Pasadena; Fergus wisely felt that it would be proper to have an educated audience for such a classic film; and it would get better results from preview cards.

A booth was set up in the lobby for patrons to write out the cards, specifying their interest in the cast—a sort of report card grading of who they thought gave the best performance—and what they thought of the story. Fergus disliked this approach. It had been fine in the days when one film after another was a success. The cards sometimes helped to solve some puzzle that even conferences had not completely tackled.

But now that financiers were in charge of production instead of the old-time studio owners, Fergus was subjected to every whim of the East Coast boys. Hugh Fairfield had flown in, representing the banking interests. Gone was the old technique of warily tearing up bad preview cards and ditching them in the theater manager's wastebasket after a huddled conference. Fairfield stood by with his fat briefcase, and Fergus knew that the cards would all be studied in a group and then tabulated.

The back rows of the theater were roped off for cast, staff, and a few chosen Titan studio members. No press was allowed, and the phalanx of Titan advertising and press staff, after performing their chores and checking each exit to be sure that no newspaper spy was in the audience, settled down.

Max, with Fergus on one side, and his film editor, Jules Cadeaux, Jr., on the other, put nervous hands on the fader. Fergus trusted Jules, for he was the son of the man who, with his own father, had come out and started the Titan studio laboratories when their laboratory in Brooklyn had been demolished by the goons of the Trust. Young Jules had grown up in the world of film and cutting, and tonight he would be Max's most valuable asset.

An earnest man, taller, more slender, but an equally serious replica of his father, he held a unique position working with Max. Since Max was at once producer, writer, and director, the cutter and the cinematographer (a fancy name for cameraman) were the only other people who fleshed his dreams behind the camera.

The cameraman was now finished, unless added scenes were needed, so it was Jules who would have to control the pace of the film. If Max saw that the scenes were long, short, or ineffective, he and Jules could now edit before the answer print (the master print) was made.

Jules would build or cut the take, which was a series

of frames taken by a camera with one setup. He had assembled many of these in a mosaic to make an effective scene covering one dramatic situation, comparable to a chapter in a novel.

Sequences were the weaving of the scenes that made the dramatic entity of the film. Jules would get one light touch of Max's hand on his sleeve while the picture ran, and he would note the exact frame to be changed in tightening a scene or even going back to rearrange shots so the continuity might be more fluid.

Max could tell from a few coughs, a man walking out to go to the rest room, or a kid running up the aisle to buy popcorn, if he had missed a focus of interest.

Later, Max and the film editor would spend long hours tightening scenes, trying out variations that would make the picture more exciting. Sometimes a whole sequence would be put in another order to bring about a dramatic impact.

So it was, a preview was not a settling back to enjoy the product, but a nervous time to see if the millions invested looked like they'd pay off.

When the heroic, lightning-flashing, chained fist of Titan appeared on the screen, there was a ripple of interest. Cinemascope had finally been chosen by Titan, as against the clumsy Cinerama, or Vista Vision, or the new Todd-AO. And then when the wide screen revealed in its full glory Kevin Frazier's stunning portrait of Belinda as Lucretia—in her scarlet gown, ruby earrings, and the lascivious expression on her face—and dissolved to her own thick-lashed, wide blue eyes, the audience let out a murmur of delight. Antonio Valli was a newcomer, and Leslie Charles an old comer, so they had standard reaction to them.

As the titles came on, with the magnificence of Renaissance Italy, the audience waited to see, to be entertained, and to judge, having paid their fee of admission. This amateur jury was one of the most terrifying prospects a film maker had to face.

Claudia and Belinda sat together in the back row. As the camera zoomed in on Kevin's portrait, Belinda clutched her aunt's hand until she had to flex her fingers.

What was there to say? There was pain, and there would be more, Claudia knew, as the picture unrolled. For she knew that a large part of it would bring back some mysterious tearing memories to the girl who had broken off her love affair so abruptly that she could not talk about it. Claudia also noted how Belinda reacted to scenes with Antonio Valli. She really hated him; her acting had been on the level. Claudia saw her nervously brush her hair back and wince, while observing several passionate scenes.

It was one thing, Belinda thought, to playact with her enemy; it was another thing to see Tony with her in intimate scenes. She could only remember seeing him on that bed, embracing Kevin.

There was a gasp from the audience at the controversial scene where Cesare tied up the disemboweled bull, and as it was pinioned upside down, used its carcass as a bloodbath to relieve himself of his poisons. Of course, the scene had been manufactured with an artificial animal and blood, but several people left the theater, and the gasps from others made Claudia realize that as dramatically fanciful as it was, it would probably have to be cut.

By the end of the film, she knew there was trouble. The picture was too cruel for an American audience, and it lacked the pull, the love story needed to salvage it from its horror. The Machiavellian scenes of palace intrigue were beautifully played, but too complicated for the average viewer. She knew Max was in trouble before the final scene ended with Lucretia holding her son, the Infans Romanus, seed of incest and a family rife with fratricide and corruption, in her arms on a papal balcony facing the angry Roman crowd—her father, her brother, and her husband all dead, none of her own doing, and herself left to face the rest of her life.

There was an almost inaudible gasp of revulsion—and a pause; several studio hands attempted applause, but the audience did not join in.

A star of Belinda's magnitude had to get out of the theater quickly, unnoticed, or be mobbed, so Claudia and Belinda were discreetly rushed out of a side entrance and into a studio limousine in the alley.

Red Powell closed the car door swiftly from long practice before two shrewd teen-agers moved in on them. He recalled as he did it that he had done the same for Claudia. Now she looked more scared and nervous than she ever had before.

"You'd better go home," he said. "It's going to be a long session with Max and Fergus and the cutter; we just decided not to meet for supper as we'd planned. You know how it is. Would you like me to take you to dinner somewhere?"

Claudia, sensing doom, recognized his relief when she answered. "No, we'll run along. Thanks just the same. Tell Max I'll have something for him when he gets home."

She knew from experience he would return weary and white-faced. His mind would be so jumbled with the work that would have to be done and what was said that he would be a shell of a man, finished; unable to express himself, and unable to relate to her. At these times, perhaps because of the hunger he had suffered in concentration camps during the war, he would require sweets. She would feed him chocolate cake and milk, give him an antacid and a sleeping pill, and hope he'd be able to find a few hours of rest before he faced the next day and his grueling work at the studio cutting rooms.

"Well," said Belinda as they drove past the Pasadena bridge on the long trek home, "it was a bust, wasn't it?"

There was no use to deceive her. She was getting too wise to the world of film making.

"Not a bust," said Claudia. "Just strong medicine. It's a startling picture. Your performance was brilliant, but I'm not sure they're ready for their oracle to be an incestuous murderess."

"I felt resentment from the audience," said Belinda.

Claudia realized that Belinda had come of age. The girl who had been maneuvered by others had stepped out of her body, and the woman had stepped in.

"You know, Claudia—"

She didn't say Aunt Claudia . . .

"I played Lucretia the way she had to be played. She couldn't be any other way. She had to hate, just like I learned to hate." She stopped. She'd said too much. "But I want to say something. Please don't be hurt. Just for now, I think I'd better have someone else direct me."

"Belinda!" said Claudia. "What do you mean?"

"I don't mean to hurt Max or you. But I've got to be me. You've said I have to grow. I knew from the beginning that this script wasn't right. But how could I fight

Max? Now if I can get someone else, then I'll be able to fight."

"Actresses aren't supposed to be producers," said Claudia. "You'll be in trouble if you start thinking that way. We do what we're given to do. I think you'll get an accolade for what you did."

"Maybe," said Belinda. "And maybe I'm in trouble now. You know, the old order is changing. Stars are creating their own companies."

"And falling on their asses," said Claudia. "As an independent, your company would have to get your story okayed by a distributor and a bank before you start. If you defer your money so they agree to take the risk, you may end up with a handful of nothing. Even Gable and Lancaster didn't make it on *Run Silent, Run Deep*, and the great indestructible Duke Wayne stubbed his toe on *The Barbarian and the Geisha*. And if you get a percentage of the net, forget it, honey. The company'll gobble it up in hidden costs."

"I didn't necessarily mean being independent," said Belinda. "I just meant I think I'd like to do something different, even if it's a challenge, all by myself."

She looked at Claudia's face as a streetlamp flashed by. She was fatigued and pale, and as she leaned her head back against the cushion, Belinda realized that her aunt was beginning to age—and carrying a great burden. She had always accepted Claudia as vital and beautiful. She didn't want to desert a sinking ship; she just wanted to be herself, with no pressures from Max *or* (a light seemed to flash) a guy like Kevin. It was the beginning of her cure from her love affair.

"Oh, I'm sorry," she said. "I know this is no time to talk like this."

"Let's just see what we can do to make it easy for Max," said Claudia. "You know he has his pressures, you must understand, dear, that no man in Hollywood can be his own master."

"Of course," said Belinda. "I wouldn't hurt him. I love him."

They didn't say much the rest of the way home, and when they got there Belinda took Atlas out for a walk in the garden.

"Well," said a cheery voice, "how was it?"

Effie stood, smiling in the floodlights, the gold of her teeth gleaming.

"Ef, I don't think it went very well, so be prepared."

"Oh dear," said Effie. "I went through this once or twice with your daddy. It ain't good."

"It ain't good," said Belinda.

She heard Claudia fussing in the kitchen. It was her salvation to be waiting for Max. What would his salvation be?

Belinda went into the kitchen, pretending to open the refrigerator for milk. "Do you want me to sit up with you?" she said to Claudia.

Claudia poured herself a cup of coffee.

Although she was deeply disturbed, she felt Belinda reaching out. As much as she wanted to embrace the girl and feel comforted by her blood kin, she stopped herself. It was no time to reveal an emotional weakness, and she'd be damned if she'd burst into tears; somehow, that would be a betrayel of what Max had tried to do—an admission of failure. Best to deal in trivia. She swallowed her tears.

"No dear," she said, "but thanks. I know these conferences. He won't be home for hours. And I'll try to get him tucked in. He won't want to talk much."

As Belinda got into bed, she realized how different this was from her first picture. She had been just a child then, playing a role in a cinematic trance, being adored, with a powerful cast and great wealth sustaining her. Working in Hollywood was a different thing. She had managed to create a role under difficult circumstances, and she was afraid it hadn't worked. In her disturbed state, she had thought that her talent and her desire to use her emotions would pay off, as Claudia had suggested, and that she'd emerge a winner. At least that would have shown Kevin Frazier and Antonio Valli that she didn't really care. But apparently you couldn't just decide to be a winner.

8

Since Max had arranged to defer part of his salary for *Young Lucretia* in return for benefits, he believed himself in a fortunate economic situation. His reputation, which made him cinematically equivalent to a star, had garnered him a percentage of the gross, and he would be financially established for life if the picture was a success. At his age, and with his responsibility to Claudia, he hoped he would have no more financial worries.

But in the few months he had been focusing all his interest on his project, the economic rug had been pulled out from under him.

He realized that Fergus and Titan's staff of lawyers had stripped him; but he had asked for privileges and received them, and there was nothing he could do if he wanted his picture to be made. He could not blame Fergus, even though his old agent, Seymour Sewell, had screamed, but Sewell was a pale wraith compared to the powerful forces of the tough-scrapping Hollywood of the new decade.

Seymour retired to the deck of his decaying old yacht, the *Empress*, which had been moored so long in Newport Harbor that local yard hands celebrated her yearly dry-docking with laughter, wondering where the roots were that moored it to the bottom.

He was glad to have one client who still gave him an opportunity to get phone calls from Hollywood, from Titan legal counsels, and occasionally even from Max himself, who knew as much about business as the cat who kept the mice from crawling through the hawsers onto his yacht.

So Seymour, with a pittance settlement for himself, sold out his client to Titan and settled back to his yellowed memories and weekly *Variety*. Daily *Variety* depressed him too much.

With the money from *The Oracle* cross-collateralized, and therefore tied up, to get the new picture going; and with fifty thousand (on which he had to pay taxes, of course) shipped off to Jessica, Max was in trouble. In order to get advances for his personal household expenses, he had sacrificed the advantages of his deferment. His ownership in the picture had changed from the golden 2½ percent of the gross to 10 percent of Titan's share, after it reached twice the negative cost. (This would be a long wait, even if the movie was a smashing success.)

Taxes were high in the higher brackets, even if he declared joint income with Claudia. Belinda, of course, lived in the house expense free. There was never a thought of having her put money in the kitty and the amusing little bit he got off declaring Alex as his dependent was a private joke with the family. If his picture had been a success, the corporation would only have to pay around 50 percent tax, but any moneys he received personally were highly taxed. Out of the sums he earned during the past year, he faced the incredible situation of having only $15,000 in the bank, a business manager who received $100 a week, and a household that cost him over $2,000 a month. His film depended on several months of cutting due the company as part of his corporate interest.

He hoped his next production would be optioned by Titan as soon as the new film was out, but he dared not bring it up until the concern about *Young Lucretia* was settled. He hoped a few cutting sessions and several short new sequences would fix things up.

The reactions of the Pasadena preview were disastrous. The viewers had shied away from the intrigue and violence, and there had been a great hue and cry about the incest and the fratricide. Those who had enshrined Belinda as the beautiful young virgin in *The Oracle* reported in very strong terms that they were horrified that such a bright young star should have portrayed such a wanton character.

Too many viewers, including New York brass, had objected to the powerful scene of the butchering of the bull in Cesare's bedroom, where Cesare was cradled in living, pulsing blood to draw the poison from his body. Max fought a pitched battle; it was history, the story was classic, a check of the great author, Alexander Dumas's scholarly essay would prove the authenticity of the scene, the characters all got their just deserts, there was a moral in the story; after all, the script had been approved.

The scene had been done so graphically that it was unacceptable. And besides, even if they accepted it, the prints would be butchered by state censorship boards, and spottily banned all over the United States.

It was even suggested that the sweet portrait of Belinda as Lucretia be in the opening shot, and the evil one at the end, in opposition to Al Lewyn's film *Dorian Gray*, when the portrait turned beautiful as Dorian died, and his face became evil.

Max felt this change would destroy the dramatic impact at the beginning of the film. He wrote a new sequence, where Lucretia as a young girl is dispensing food and gifts to children in an orphanage. It turned his stomach to devitalize his product, but he tried.

The studio added another fifty thousand dollars for retakes. Then it was decided to have another love scene between Cesare and Lucretia, in which he showed his concern for her and she sympathized with his desire to be a commander of men (rather than a cardinal) like his brother, the Duke of Gandia. Pope Alexander VI, their father, revealed his dominance over Cesare's wishes.

It was one of the most difficult things Belinda ever had to face. She had to be loving and gentle to Tony Valli. Throughout the shooting he was overly kind to her. Her dressing room was stocked with his roses, and she could hardly bear to face his smiling courtesy.

As Max called "cut" on the last scene, and the cry "Save the lights!" rang out and the brilliant arcs were switched off, Tony turned to her and took her hand, which was heavy with the Borgia signet ring.

"I hope you will find it possible to forgive me," he said. "I am sorry you had to be hurt, but it was better for you to know now than later when it could have hurt you even more deeply. What happened between Kevin and me doesn't mean he didn't love you—"

She tried to pull her hand away, but he held her fingers in his strong grasp.

"Let go!" she said. "We're not acting now. Don't you touch me!"

"I want us to be friends—," he started to say.

She pulled her hand free and struck him on the cheek as hard as she could. The sharp amethyst ring cut his cheek, and a trickle of blood dropped on the white ermine edge of his cloak.

She saw Max's face transfixed as he rushed over from where he had been standing beside the camera. Leslie Charles, who had been watching the last shot, came running forward with a Kleenex.

"My God!" he said. "What happened?"

Belinda fled to her dressing room and slammed the door and locked it. She began to cry.

In a moment there was a pounding at the door. It was Claudia. "My God! What happened?" She echoed Leslie.

"I don't want to talk about it!" said Belinda. "Just let me out of here."

She began to weep again and became hysterical.

Claudia called the studio doctor who finally had to sedate her, and Claudia took her home in the studio limousine.

Once she was tucked into bed, Claudia closed the drapes and smoothed back her hair.

"Now," she said, "would it ease you to talk about it?"

Belinda's voice came out of the depths of her sedation.

"Tony seduced Kevin," she said, her voice so low that Claudia had to bend down to listen. "He—he—I walked in and saw them together, in our bed, *our* bed—where we made love together." She started to cry again.

Claudia patted her shoulder.

"Oh!" she said, remembering her talk with Fergus about breaking up the romance. He certainly had. "Well, I suppose the thing to say is that I'm glad you found out before you got married. But people hate to hear things like that. My God, Belinda, you had courage to go on with that picture. I'm not sure I could have done it. Go to sleep, honey, and just thank God you're with people who love you, in your own home."

If Belinda ever knew how Claudia had plotted, it would be the end of them. Despising Fergus, she wondered how he had worked it out; then she remembered Belinda calling that fateful day to say that the wardrobe woman had asked her to deliver jewelry to Kevin's house. Claudia knew then that Belinda's discovery was a setup. Wasn't it right after that that Titan had released those great blurbs about Antonio Valli's new contract? She'd wondered about it at the time, for he hadn't proven himself ready for stardom. She wanted to go to see Fergus and give him hell as soon as she saw the lights go on in his house down the beach, but she realized that she was as much of an accomplice as he was. Come the time, she'd go into it with him.

Fergus Austin, along with the other studio heads in Hollywood, faced a new era of dealing with independent producers who set up their own companies, and the vagaries of television series which could die aborning. The only autonomy he had left, after his years of power, was the right to edit pictures with his producers if they were in trouble. And it didn't take him many sessions in the projection rooms, with only Max and Jules Cadeaux, to realize that Titan's superproduction was in deep trouble.

Going to his office after one of these gloomy sessions, with Max's nervous energy reaching in every direction trying to improve his product, Fergus realized that Titan studio's future was in peril. *Young Lucretia* had been the great hope.

The actors' walkout the previous year had resulted in raising minimum pay of every strata of acting; writers' prices skyrocketed after their strike. Studios also had to put out vast sums to pension and health and welfare funds. Labor costs were way up, some over 50 percent. The new five-day working week had escalated overhead 15 percent. Taxes on property soared; and upkeep on the large lot and ranch seemed beyond control.

The large factory was busy on rental, but the overhead was prodigious and the interest alone on the loan of millions on current production was throwing Titan deeply into the red.

It was time to liquidate assets, and when that had to be done the studio lost its heart. The great cluster of real estate properties Fergus and Simon Moses had amassed year by year from a jerry-built little barn was in jeopardy.

Some of the studios had diversified; Disneyland, the

anthropomorphic plastic playground of the unreal, was one; record companies, broadcasting stations, music publishing, and electronics had made a new way of existence for many of the companies who had for years only concentrated on entertainment. They had all come a long way from their original intent.

But Titan had not diversified, and the only assets Fergus could name, aside from Titan's real estate holdings, were the distribution profits of 30 or more percent on their current films and the successful film laboratory, which the Cadeaux family had built up, and which at this moment was running full force. Long gone was the old grandfather who had gone back to the early days of Lumière in France. Fergus realized that within the cocoon of his studio were people who had been involved with almost the whole history of film making. If these talents were dissipated, many of them would never come back in focus again with the skills they had developed over fifty years. He knew that he and David would fight as long as they could to save the Titan water tower from toppling.

Now he was about to meet with David, who had just returned from Europe where he had sold Titan films to the foreign market, city by city, like the old States' Rights boys had done in the United States in the early days. He was following the pattern started by David Selznick in the mid-fifties. Owing the banks thirteen million dollars, the great film maker had sold such films as *The Garden of Allah*, *The Prisoner of Zenda*, and *Tom Sawyer* in Europe, and he had paid off his enormous debts.

Fergus had continued running the West Coast business, and David had been occupied trying to make Titan interests function internationally.

Now that the frozen funds in Europe were being released by governments, there was less money to be spent in foreign production. David was returning to see what could be done about the fluctuating fortunes of the home studio, and he was going to have to hand Fergus an extremely disturbing proposition.

Disliking the idea of facing Fergus over the studio desk, he'd arranged a breakfast at Fergus's house.

It was difficult for David to come to this house, where he had grown up. It brought back still painful memories of when he had returned from Stanford expecting to marry Jessica, his father's young secretary. He had gone to his father's office at the studio and discovered the two of them having sex in his father's private dressing room. The whole scene had been set up by Fergus to prove that this woman, his own mistress, was a worthless opportunist.

David had left this house that day and he had never returned.

Now, twenty years later, he had to return to the old house, where his father lived as a bachelor since his mother had been in a mental sanatorium these many years in Pasadena.

It was strange to David to be sitting on the rattan furniture on the sun porch he'd known as a child. He and Fergus faced each other at the glass-topped table, while a Filipino houseman served up melon, juice, coffee, corn muffins, a ham omelet, and a choice of bacon or sausage with the enthusiasm of a cook who was delighted to have an audience for his culinary efforts. The overlarge meal and his flourish of serving all bespoke of little entertainment in this house with its faded chintz.

David, with a pang for the life that was lost, recognized the same Marghab linen, Spode dishes, and Royal Danish flatware that he had known in his young years. Although he and Fergus had had a rift of many years, it had been mended by mutual need and respect.

Now, looking out at the strip of sand and a small fleet of sailboats on the sparkling sea, he thought of carefree days, sand baseball, swimming with so many stars, now gone, whom he had accepted as the most normal acquaintances.

Slim and elegant in his Savile Row suit, and tanned from the cruise he had just taken from Monte Carlo on a yacht while selling an Italian film distributor a Titan product, he looked less than his forty-one years. His face was a smooth, handsome mask.

Even Fergus could not figure what David was thinking. He knew David was a loner; and he knew that the women in his life came and went, or rather, were summoned and went, at his whim; and that he had never considered a permanent relationship.

"Fergus," David said, "we're in deep trouble. I was

able to raise around ten million on our product in Europe, but the studio is running at a deficit, and *Young Lucretia* is going to break our back."

Fergus interrupted. "From what I've heard, the critics are going to rave about Belinda's performance."

"That doesn't sell the picture," said David. "You know and I know that public opinion is going to be against it. Max had himself a fine intellectual trip. How do you think the public is going to react to Belinda playing the worst woman in history? And you have no backup of a love story. There's nobody to root for."

"I'm doing the best I can to fix it up," said Fergus. "We've shot new scenes. We've toned it down."

"You've degutted it," said David, taking out a cigarette.

Fergus could not help but admire David's economy of motion and his style. No wonder women were mad about him. He had a flair. Fergus hated to admit it, but he thought of how splendid Jeffrey Barstow had been in spite of his debauched habits. Although, it might have been better for David if he'd had a bit of Jeffrey's joie de vivre. He was too serious. It was difficult to deal with such a precise man, who seemed only to have business on his mind. Fergus caught himself short. Wasn't this what had always been said about him?

"You're not going to like it, but I've come to a decision," said David. "I know it's a great risk, but it's the only way. First let me give you a few statistics. There are now over fifty million TV sets in the United States, and over five hundred TV stations. The big theaters are gone, and our stages are mostly empty, save for fly-by-night TV rentals. What does that tell you?"

It was a rhetorical question.

"David Levy, who is the vice-president in charge of network programs and talent for NBC, has just sold Skouras at Twentieth Century Fox a bill of goods to put some of their features on the air. Skouras is announcing a *fifteen-million-dollar deal*. Fox needed cash and he decided that their backlog, sitting forgotten in vaults, was one of their biggest assets."

"Are you suggesting that we destroy our own business by selling out our product to television? Where would we go from there? I think it's death!"

"Just wait," said David, holding up his hand, "and listen to what I have to say. Fox is delivering thirty features with the network's right to repeat twenty. NBC can cancel out at sixteen if it doesn't work. They're just as nervous as the picture company. But Fox is getting $160,000 a running, with the option to run each feature twice at the same price. Then the films revert right back to their place on the shelves for future use, *and* income."

"We could dump some of our old stuff on them," said Fergus tentatively.

"Not so," said David. "The Fox films were all as recent as eight years. Levy looked at them, analyzing the product with the idea of how they would look three years from now in rerun. No dogs. Out of 102 he selected his 30. Fox sweetened the pot by throwing in several films that were recently made. They got such good pictures as *Kilimanjaro* with Peck and Susan Hayward, *How to Marry a Millionaire* with Monroe, *Desert Fox* with Mason, and *Sousa* with Clifton Webb. Not bad, what?"

"How is Fox going to handle the problem with the exhibitors?" asked Fergus. "They'll scream their heads off—it might empty their theaters."

"The hell with the exhibitors, they need our *new* product. They aren't interested in the pictures they've used up with us before. It's the studio that needs help, and our inventory would salvage us."

"You're asking me to cut our throat," said Fergus.

"You're bleeding already," said David. "This might just stitch it up."

"How are they going to present these shows?" said Fergus, still dubious.

"This is the amazing thing about it," said David. "It's going to be presented simply as 'Saturday Night at the Movies.' "

"*That*'ll help theaters," said Fergus sarcastically.

"Remember the bill of divorcement," said David, "when our whole theater chain was taken away from our parent company? And remember how the theater chains made it tough for us without block booking?" He turned and smiled. "Well, damn it, Fergus, here we are, right back with block booking again. We sell our product as a chunk to networks who now present the great films of Titan studio to an audience hundreds of times larger than our combined theater audience in our heyday. What a reassessment of our worth!"

Fergus pondered. This was bewildering. This new approach might be real competition to the theaters that were their market.

David pounded in his argument. "Our famous pictures appearing on TV with a lineup of great stars of another day will have an impact on our future product. We will be alive again. Titan, in the time of its glory! Think of the value of pictures with Claudia and Jeffrey Barstow—they'll be classics! Think of our roster of films of the old days, all of them showing again, and at no added cost to us."

"How do you know this is going to work out for NBC? Maybe it'll fall on its pratt."

"I'll give you a clue," said David. "The sales department at NBC has sold them all out before the series is starting. Saturday night is the best night for theater in America. And have they got a ploy! They are running the films uncut, not worrying about time. If they get through at 11:00 or 11:20, okay, *then* the news goes on. People see the finish of the film because they don't have to switch to another station right on the button of eleven to get the news. That makes NBC have higher ratings. And then—guess what a clever thing they've done?"

Fergus had never seen David so enthusiastic.

"Then they put on a second feature. On Saturday night, people are often in the mood to take off their shoes, snack a little, have a drink, and stay up late. They don't have to pay fancy prices, then get out of a theater into a parking lot and drive home. With prices and baby-sitters and creature comforts being what they are, this idea is a boon to the average family."

"Why is NBC paying so much for old movies?" said Fergus. "Why don't they just make more good one-hour original TV programs?"

"I'll tell you why," said David. "It takes at least a hundred thousand dollars to make a first-rate pilot. And you can be sure the star is not of the caliber of Gable or Cooper or Barstow; more often it's an unknown personality, not presold like a picture star, but someone who has to be built up to become known. Then they have to wait to see if the public buys the show. If the show doesn't go, you know damn well they're going to lose their shirts, for they can't amortize the sets and the initial costs. If we give them preadvertised pictures with star billing, the network is only paying what they would pay for a whirl on the roulette wheel of a new product. Think of it, Fergus, all your blood, sweat, and tears through the years of picture making can pay off all over again! It's a colossal annuity."

"What about blockbusters like *The Oracle*?" said Fergus. "What would we get for that?"

"Millions," said David. "We'd stockpile it. For warehousing it for two years, until it has the last run in theaters, we'd get an enormous advance against the TV showing, which would be most satisfactory right now to pay off the interest we owe on the millions borrowed on *Young Lucretia*."

Fergus arose and looked out at the beach.

"I never thought of TV as the proper place for movies," he said. "The screen is small, and most people have black-and-white sets."

"I have news for you," said David. "The very companies who are showing these films often have interests in the TV manufacturing business. By the 1970s, color sets and larger screens are going to be in almost every middle-class home."

Fergus turned his head, smiling wryly. "Talk about monopolies!" he said.

David knew he had won. Never mind; he had the control, and he had to face the disgruntled stockholders. He knew this made Fergus blanch. Even now, he was aware that this new scheme was not enough to stop the tide of rising costs. But it would be good for a first step.

Since the large studio was no longer being used in a total program of picture making, David knew that liquidation would be the only solution. The next step would be the ranch near Calabasas, now running amuck with cowboys and stagecoaches; it was far more valuable as a subdivision in the burgeoning California suburbia. Little towns were springing up all over the countryside; fake lath and plaster Spanish walls and safe dead-end streets planned for young married couples who wanted community swimming pools, golf courses, tennis courts, smaller school complexes, playgrounds, and cozy clusters of houses.

But it would be too much to drop any other plans on Fergus now. It was heady enough for an old-timer to face one new idea at a time. David had struggled enough with it in his own mind. The television sale was a comparatively easy out. David knew very well the story of how Fergus, who had worked for his grandfather, Simon Moses, had come out to California at eighteen and single-handedly produced Titan's first little film starring young Claudia Barstow.

David felt sorry for him; a bitter, tired man who had seen his power diminish and was facing the potential ruination of the only thing that glued his life together.

He didn't know how relieved Fergus was, for once, to have someone else make the decisions. "You'd better come to the factory," said Fergus, "and see what has happened to Max's picture. I think there are great things in it. But I don't know, David, I just don't know anymore."

In the last three years, David hadn't heard anything but determination in Fergus's scrapping Irish personality. Now he was a little surprised, and very touched, as Fergus put a hand on his shoulder as they started out the door. Somehow it made the familiar furnishings and tarnished memories less poignant.

Belinda awoke with a heavy head, and she began piecing together fragments of the day before. Then came the dreadful memory of her hand sweeping across Tony's face and the blood pouring from his cheek.

The whole company had witnessed it. It would be all over town, probably in the gossip columns. What could she ever say to explain it?

Somehow, like an alcoholic who has dim memories of misbehavior, she remembered having blurted the truth to Claudia.

She put her hands over her lips. Why had she done it? She had worked so hard to be a winner and behave impeccably in front of Tony. But it hadn't worked.

And twice she had rejected Max. Poor, dear Max, who was most likely in more trouble than she was. He was an old man, his career was at stake, and now it looked as if the picture was going to be a flop. It wasn't as important to her as it was to him. Besides, everyone said she was going to get good reviews. She was young, and there would be lots of people who would want her to work with them. Max's *Oracle* had done that for her.

She thought back on her brief romance with Kevin. She had managed to break away from the domination of a family who still considered her a child. Now that there was no longer a man in her life, she was back in the nursery. It wouldn't work. She couldn't stay.

It wasn't a matter of being in love. The hell with that. It was a matter of finding a man, of making a life as an adult. She thought maybe sex would be just as good, maybe even better, if you didn't care so much. If you cared, you could be hurt; if you just reveled in sex for itself, that might be more comfortable. She had heard enough around the studio to know that men and women had lots of affairs. It seemed to give them pleasure and laughter. They were always kidding about it, so it must be fun of a different kind, not the serious thing when you looked into each other's eyes and wanted to belong to someone forever.

She wondered if it would work for her. At any rate, she must find a man.

However, in her situation, everyone was spying on her all the time. Even her secret rendezvous with Kevin, as wonderful as they were, had been limiting. She would have liked to live with him, to have other people around to share their good times, and to do the things that some of her friends talked about—*acquaintances* was the better word, for she had somehow been rooked out of a circle of friends.

The solution would be to find a husband. Some wonderful sexy guy who would be crazy about her; she'd have a big house, and people would drop in, and it would be the life she'd never been allowed to have.

And marriage would give her control of her own money: 80 percent of her two starring salaries was now held by court order. There would be lots of it waiting for her, and then she could do what she wanted. She could go back to Greece and see Chloë, the Greek actress who had been so close to Niadas and could tell her a lot about the man who was the father of her child. And wonderful Ubaldo, the strange Italian prince who had sold his antique treasures to make her picture possible. They lived in Santorini now, married and happy, looking after their Institute for Hellenic Women. It would be good to go back, now that she was famous, and hold her head high in the place where she had hidden like a peasant girl when she was pregnant. In Rome wouldn't her mother, Jessica, have to kowtow to her now that she was on her own, and famous, famous, famous.

She'd like to go back to London where she had been restricted before, but to do all these things she'd have to have a husband.

Well, she'd look around, and, without the blinders of love, find a suitable husband; then her troubles would be over.

Claudia came into her room.

"Darling, I hate to do this to you, but the studio wants pictures of you in your wardrobe to be rushed off to *Paris Match*. They're going to do a big spread."

To Claudia's astonishment, Belinda jumped out of bed.

"I'll get ready."

"Do you feel all right?" asked Claudia. "That sedative gave you a nice long sleep."

"I feel fine," said Belinda.

It was time to get going into life, to look around.

She paused. "What am I going to say about hitting Tony?"

"I've been thinking about it," said Claudia. "You should have ripped out his jugular vein, the bastard. Just say you were clowning around and your ring hit him, and you're terribly embarrassed about the whole thing. After all, when people see something happen quickly, they don't know exactly what they've seen."

"I hope," said Belinda.

"Guess who's in town?" said Claudia. "David Austin is here, and we might run into him at the studio."

"Oh, I'd like that," said Belinda. "He's always been so specially wonderful to me. I'll wear pink."

Claudia, marveling at the elasticity of youth, looked at her and smiled. Thank God her spunk and spirit were back!

"You'd look great if you wore mud!" she said.

128

David was coming out of the projection room with Fergus when Belinda and Claudia saw him.

Belinda ran up behind David and flung her arms around him. "Surprise!" she cried.

He swung around and looked at her. She looked like a little girl in her pink silk slacks and blouse, her hair tied back in a ponytail. He threw his arms around her.

"Hi, movie star!" he said. "That was quite a wrestling hold! I'm glad you haven't lost the common touch."

"Never with you!" she said.

Fergus watched them. What a pair of handsome humans they were. People on the studio street wanted to look at them. Strange, he thought, that they couldn't see the resemblance. It was painful for him to look at them, and it brought back long-hidden resentments he had tried to contain throughout the years.

As Belinda took David's hand and looked up at him, she remembered the warm, embracing concern that had helped her so much on the island of Santorini when he had brought treats and magazines for her and Claudia and Effie, and, at the end, a layette for her baby. He understood her; he knew her secrets, and there was no sham between them.

This is it, she thought. This is what I want. This is the man I want to marry.

9

Claudia was perplexed when Belinda announced that they should have more of a social life at the beach house. She suggested they have a brunch for David, and why not have Fergus, too; they weren't very neighborly to him. After all, Belinda pointed out, the Austins had been more than just studio heads, they had helped her and Claudia when the baby was born. Fergus had even taken Alex to Switzerland when it was decided to let the world believe that Jessica was the mother. Belinda and Claudia, in spite of their personal problems, had to do a last publicity stint in Rome and sail home in splendor on the *Christoforo Colombo* before they faced the hurly-burly of Titan publicity in New York.

As for David, Belinda remembered him on the pilot boat, meeting the ship in New York Harbor. She had left American shores a little girl in a blue coat with brass buttons and her hair in a ponytail.

She had returned in a Paris suit and a smooth coif, and she had faced the curiosity of a whole nation. She had become the newest sex symbol, and David had bridged the gap for her with his protective presence.

For Belinda's Sunday brunch, David postponed a golf game and Fergus canceled a meeting; they all sat under an umbrella table by the side of the pool.

Effie laid out a grand spread, and in no time they were involved in studio talk. It was decided to stay away from discussions about *Young Lucretia* until the final cut.

Belinda did everything she could to charm David. She talked knowledgeably about Renaissance Italy; she had boned up on movies for television, having heard rumors of what was going on.

These five all had so much to say it was impossible for anyone to dominate the conversation.

David told them about the change in the film world. He turned to Claudia and Max. "There are no more Niadas's left to hand out fortunes on a golden platter."

He glanced at Belinda.

"It's all right," said Belinda. "That's ancient history."

At that moment Effie brought out Alex.

He was a golden child. His hair curled in ringlets, and his skin had the pale biscuit tan of a California child carefully exposed to the sun.

His chin showed a small dimple that would be a cleft, and his widely spaced blue eyes looked into what was his— a happy world.

The small hands in their infant grasp already revealed long tapered fingers.

Both David and Fergus were emotionally shaken. David, because he knew Alex was his nephew, and Fergus, because it gave him a pang to see how much the boy resembled David at that age. Both of them had to smother their feelings.

Alex was picked up by Claudia and fussed over. He greeted David and Fergus abstractedly and was soon deposited, wearing his swimming belt, in the pool, where he paddled and played with a toy sailboat. They all watched him, Atlas barking and yapping at his small charge.

"Well," said Belinda, "at least we can talk about him among ourselves. But not in front of him for long, as Claudia's been warning us. He's awfully bright."

Her sudden smile at the child touched David. Her life with her child had to be so private.

"He's a knockout," said David. "When does he start school?"

"Prenursery school next autumn," said Claudia. "There's a great school here in Pacific Palisades. Even the furnishings, doorknobs, and toilets are infant size so the children will feel secure."

"I wonder," said Max, "if that's such a good idea. I seem to notice that the children who come to play with him with their nannies and cars are smothered with a sense of security; a feeling that life is tailor-made for them. What happens when they discover that in the big world they may not always sit on toilets that fit their little behinds?"

"I remember on my last birthday with my father how he and Aunt Claudia and I ran away from the same old clowns and caterers and fancy doings and fled to the beach near here to get away." Belinda laughed. "And how pissed off mother was. It was great!"

They all laughed.

David and Fergus and Max, Claudia, and even Belinda realized how free they now were from Jessica, as if she were the Wicked Witch of the West and had dissolved. It was a moment to be shared. She had become a ridiculous figure. The shackles of the past, on this pleasant morning by the sea, had freed them all from Jessica in various ways.

"Well," said Max, "if any of us call on her, we'll at least know that her villa has the best plumbing and roof in Rome. I ought to know, I paid for it."

With all of them in good spirits, the meal broke up.

David bent down to shake Alex's little hand in the pool.

"I'll walk back to the house with you," said Belinda to David.

They opened the beach gate, ignoring a cluster of young people nearby. Apparently, someone had managed to peer through the greenery and see the party dining outdoors. Tourists with cameras and autograph books at the ready—all were waiting for any contact with her. They began to rush toward her.

"Oh damn," said Belinda. "I forgot. It's the middle of the day. I can't go out, they'll mob me."

As the crowd came running, Belinda slammed the gate shut and bolted it, and she and David retreated quickly into the garden.

"Sorry," said David. "I forgot too. Fergus and I can walk home along the sidewalk."

Belinda escorted them through the house, and David leaned forward and kissed her cheek.

"I know it isn't easy. I warned you in London."

She smiled up at him. Fergus stood behind him, watching them.

"How long are you going to stay?" she asked.

"A few weeks this time," he said. "Fergus and I have enormous tasks ahead of us. And I want to see the final print of *Young Lucretia* before we plan our advertising campaign."

"Good," said Belinda. "Maybe you'll take me out to dinner some night, and we can have these Sundays together. It would mean so much . . ."

David was aware that she was a prisoner in this beach house. Her face held an echo of his own loneliness. He knew she had had an abortive love affair, but he didn't know how deeply it had cut or why it had broken up. But somehow, the panicked, lost look in her face concerned him. It seemed akin to the blow he had had in his youth; it didn't show, but the scars had influenced the rest of his life.

"I'll call you," he said.

He and Fergus walked along the sidewalk, past the flat facades of the big houses that lined the Pacific Coast Highway. The roaring traffic passed by; there was little indication of the fine rooms and gardens in the walled fronts along the area that had been called the Gold Coast in its heydey. Only the rich, nowadays, most of them merchants, were the ones who could afford to live in this oceanfront area.

"Watch it," said Fergus. "She's got a crush on you. This kid is hankering for a love affair. She had a bad experience."

"Don't be silly," said David, waving it away. "What happened to that romance?"

"He was a switch-hitter," said Fergus, "and she caught him at it."

"My God!" said David.

He wanted to choke. No wonder. It was like his own experience, finding someone you loved *in flagrante delicto*. He suddenly had a distaste for Fergus, for it brought it all back as he remembered what he had done to him.

At Fergus's house, he said, "I have to run. I have an appointment. I'll see you tomorrow at the office."

As he got in the car, he wondered how Fergus knew all the details. He might talk to Claudia someday and see if she knew what really happened.

Too bad, he thought, as he drove through the Olympic tunnel, leaving the beach, that Belinda had managed to be involved with a man who was part of the new androgynous society.

He thought about Alex, a dividend of fame.

In due time, say five years from now, Alex should have been conceived and born in a stable home atmosphere.

Stability! he thought. What chance did Belinda have of finding such a thing? Fergus was right. She was longing for a relationship. And this was a perilous time for her.

In spite of his business problems, he should do something for her. Perhaps just by taking her away from the pressures of Max's gloom and Claudia's obvious role as duenna he might somehow help this natural sister of his by getting her around to meet people.

Claudia sat near Belinda's dressing table as Belinda finished the last touches of her makeup. David was waiting to take her to dinner.

"We're going to the Bistro," said Belinda, showing Claudia her jade green silk dress. Her hair touched her shoulders like trimmed cascades of corn silk. She wore her strand of pearls and small pearl-drop earrings.

"You know," she said, "it's time for me to get some decent jewelry. What do you think of aquamarines? Someone said they'd go well with my eyes."

"Who said that?" asked Claudia, delighted that Belinda was excited about going out. David's company had been good for her.

"Leslie Charles," said Belinda.

"Well, he has good taste. Let's see how the exchequer can handle it. The next picture, maybe."

"Maybe," said Belinda, slathering violet cologne on her hands and wrists and splashing her neck and throat. "How do I look?"

"Disgustingly gorgeous," said Claudia, smiling.

Belinda came to her. "Oh, Claudia, he really likes Alex, doesn't he? I always had a crush on him. Don't you think he'd make a wonderful father for Alex?"

Claudia's lips were still in a smile, but they felt frozen.

"Well?" said Belinda.

Claudia jumped up. "Look at your dress!" she said. "You've splashed that cologne all over the collar. You'll have to change!"

Belinda looked in the mirror.

"Oh, well, I've got the same dress in lilac. What do you think?"

"I think lilac will be fine."

"I mean about David," said Belinda. She opened the closet door and started moving hangers.

"I—I hadn't thought about it," said Claudia. "He—he's twice your age. And he's a bachelor, dear. I told you a long time ago, he's not the marrying kind."

"I could change that," said Belinda. "I know I could. From the first time I saw him, there was something, the way he moves his hand, even the look of the back of his neck when you see him leave a room. I feel—so close to him."

"Stop it!" said Claudia sharply.

Belinda looked at her, surprised. "What's the matter? What did I do?"

Claudia unzipped the back of Belinda's dress to avoid facing her.

"It's just that I—I don't want to see you lose your head again. And he's not suitable."

"You mean you don't want me to get involved," said Belinda, her face clouding. "You'll just never let me grow up. You want to tuck me in like Alex every night."

Claudia picked up Belinda's purse. It was blue. She took a silver one out of the cupboard.

"Not really," she said, "I just want you to take your time and not give yourself any more heartbreaks. Here, change this, along with your dress. I'll see you downstairs."

Belinda watched Claudia's retreating figure. What was the matter? Claudia loved David, too. What was so upsetting? Was she supposed to remain in limbo forever in this prison? She would have loved to tell David she would give anything to get away, but if he was the man for her, it would be very wrong to let him think that was the reason she wanted him.

They had dined several times, and once gone to Santa Anita racetrack with some of his friends, and he had looked at her with affection, sometimes taking her hand when they walked through a crowd or putting his hand gently on her shoulder as they waited for a car to be driven up to the crowded entry at Scandia or Trader Vic's. Once, when they had been leaving Chasen's and the cloakroom girl was busy, he had taken her wrap and fastened the top button, looking at her fondly.

She had loved his suave manner and had felt very grown up. Actors, directors, and executives had greeted them both with warm smiles, and she had even liked it when one of his friends had called him a cradle snatcher and they had both laughed. Her social circle had enlarged. She was invited to various houses in Bel Air and Beverly Hills, and, through David, she was learning to be part of the town.

Claudia had seemed to relish this attention for Belinda, but all of a sudden she had turned cold. Was it possible she was jealous of Belinda's social success? Maybe Max had smothered her too much. Maybe she wanted to get around more herself.

Belinda felt warm, loved, and she wanted to include the whole family. Soon Alex could join up as her little brother and meet some of David's friends' children.

She was glad David hadn't married. The columnists gossiped that Belinda Barstow, the brilliant young Titan star, was the first girl David had taken to several parties in a row. That was something for this freewheeling studio head who usually was jetting in and out of the country, dating briefly here and there, or, as was rumored, often went underground in his amours. Many disappointed and beautiful women had been known to admit that he was hard to catch. And here was the new young superstar, with him constantly.

Belinda enjoyed it all; he was the most eligible and handsome bachelor in town.

Now she decided she liked the lilac dress. She changed her shoes to silver, repacked her purse, tried a pink lipstick, and recombed her hair. It was going to be a wonderful evening. She must look perfect.

Claudia found David on the terrace.

"I can't waste any time, David," she said, "and I have to tell you, but it must be fast."

"What's wrong?" said David.

"It's Belinda," she spoke quickly, in a low voice. "The crazy kid. She's got a big crush on you. She thinks your interest in her is—is very personal. She's got you in mind as a possible father for Alex. She—she asked me what I thought."

"My God!" said David.

He sat down dejectedly, took out his cigarette case, and lit up, so disturbed that he didn't offer her a cigarette.

"I'll take one, please," said Claudia.

He apologized and saw her hand shake as she took it.

"What did you say to her?" he asked.

"I just jumbled it, I was so disturbed. I told her I thought you were too old, twice her age, and that you were a confirmed bachelor. What else could I say?"

"Nothing," said David.

He shook his head. "I like being with her, taking her around. It gives me a feeling of belonging to someone." He lit her cigarette. "Should we tell her?" he asked.

She put her hand out. "No! She's had enough trauma about relationships already. If she knew Jeffrey was your father, her relationship with Fergus would also be blitzed. And she's so inexperienced. She told Kevin all about Alex. I couldn't trust her with any secrets."

"I guess I'd better stop seeing her."

"I don't know what to say," said Claudia. "She's loved being with you. I don't want her hurt again. Maybe you'll have to romance someone else publicly and get your name in the paper."

David shrugged. "It's not my style."

Belinda opened the terrace doors.

"What are you doing out here?" she asked. The ends of their cigarettes burned in the dark.

"Making love, of course," said Claudia lightly.

Belinda pirouetted. "How do I look?" she said as they walked into the house.

"Terrific," said David, "and much too young for me."

Belinda made a face. "I should have put my hair up," she said. "I just knew it."

"Look, young fry," said David. "It wouldn't make any difference. Let's get going."

As they left, Claudia went upstairs to Max, who was switching out the lights in his study.

"Let's have an early dinner and go to a movie," she said. "I'm getting claustrophobia."

"Of course," said Max. "Any movie. I'd like to see some

137

strangers jumping around in front of me. Have the young ones gone?"

"They've gone," said Claudia, sighing.

Max took her hand as they walked down the stairs.

"They're a good-looking pair."

"Yes," said Claudia, "but don't say that."

"I thought of that," said Max. "Too bad."

As Effie served dinner, Max began discussing the last session of looping that was forthcoming.

"Maybe," he said, "we'll do our dubbing session in the afternoon, and, if you feel like it, we might have Leslie and Tony Valli over for dinner afterwards. They've gone through some big changes valiantly."

"We'll have Leslie," said Claudia, "but I don't think we'll have Tony."

"Why not?"

"Well, Belinda just doesn't like him."

"Thought he'd be a good tennis partner for her. What's she got against him?"

"Who can say? Just personality problems," said Claudia. "We've got two choices for a movie, *Judgment at Nuremberg*, or *West Side Story*."

"*Nuremberg*'s out," said Max, waving his hand. "I couldn't possibly live through that again. It's *West Side Story*. I want to see how Robbins tackled that rumble in ballet."

Later that evening, as they pulled into the garage, David's car drew alongside. Claudia could see that Belinda was in a depressed mood, and David seemed flustered.

"Hi," said David. "I'm bringing Belinda home early. I have to get some papers together tonight and catch an early plane for New York in the morning."

He came into the house with them.

"A drink?" said Max.

"Wouldn't mind," said David. "I'd like to have a couple of minutes with you before I go."

He turned to Claudia and Belinda, who stood by expectantly.

"You'll have to excuse us," he said. "I'd like to talk over some last-minute business with Max."

He took Belinda's hand and kissed her cheek.

"When I come back, we'll do it again. You'll excuse us?"

"Come on upstairs, honey," Claudia said, "and we'll catch the ten o'clock news."

Pretending she didn't see the hurt in Belinda's eyes, Claudia switched on the television in her bedroom.

Belinda stood there a moment as it flickered on. "I guess I'll hit the sack," she said.

"Did you have a good evening?" asked Claudia.

"I had a rotten evening," said Belinda and left without an explanation.

Poor David, thought Claudia, it's just as tough on him as it is on her. Wonder what happened . . .

Belinda sat at her dressing table, looked at her face, and flushed. She was glad Claudia didn't know what had happened.

Belinda had never acted that way before, and the very thought of it was humiliating.

As they had come down the beach road on the way home, she had told David she wanted to park by the state beach and walk in the sand.

"Come on," he said. "Another time, if you don't mind."

"I do mind," she said.

So he had pulled the car over to the side of the road. As soon as he parked, she put her arms around him, and before he realized what she was after she had put her hands to his face, pressed her mouth against his lips, and put her tongue into his mouth.

Surprised, he had pulled back. "Wait a minute!" he said.

She pressed against him, arching her breasts against his shoulder.

"Don't you know I want you?" she whispered. "You don't have to be afraid, David. I know how to take care of myself."

She had unbuttoned her dress. One of her white breasts was naked.

"Don't you want to make love to me?" she said, moving her face toward his lips, her eyes closed. But when she opened them, he was leaving the car. As she moved back in surprise, he opened the door on her side.

"Button your dress and get out."

He pulled her roughly out of the car and walked her

down the cement steps to the beach. Then he took her by both elbows and shook her.

"Don't you ever try a cheap trick like that again!"

"Don't you like me?" she asked, buttoning her dress as he released her arms.

"Not that way," he said, "and not with you acting like any cheap broad in a parked car at the state beach." He pulled her along, walking with her, their shoes crunching in the fine sand. "This is just as stupid as the time you pulled it on me at the Dorchester, tearing your dress open at the age of fourteen to show your half-assed idea of being a movie star. I said then, and I say again, that is not maturity, Belinda."

She had to move quickly to keep up with him.

He stopped and looked at her.

"I don't want to be a moralist. I know you get lectured too much and you've been put in the miserable situation of being a sex symbol too young—all the things I warned you about. As I told you in London, a corporation is a calculating machine, based only on financial morality. That's the part of the scenario that found you valuable. That's why you're a star—a very rare commodity in this day and age."

He held up his hand.

"Yes, I know you're thinking it's my company, and it's my profit, and my organization that set you up, just like my grandfather set up Claudia to be a star when Titan began. But goddamn it, this is different. It was a rough-and-tumble world then, and your Aunt Claudia had to crawl up the ladder, rung by rung. She was one of the pioneers. She helped create film acting technique. And she worked hard."

"I work hard, too," said Belinda. "I haven't let you down."

"You've had a hell of a lot of help. You started at the top with Max Ziska. We won't go into the Niadas situation now, but you had the wealth of a Midas at your command. The jury's still out on *Young Lucretia*, but your performance is our hope. But I'm not talking about that. I'm talking about you, Belinda. What's going to happen to your talent? You have a great heritage. Your mirror tells you that you are beautiful. Claudia is the best coach in the world, and you have her, and that's only the beginning. But what's happening to the young woman who has just had an abortive affair with a man who wasn't right, and then several months later tries to make out with an old friend in a car on the state beach?"

She hung her head.

"Come on," said David. "You aren't in love with me. You know it, and I know it."

She didn't answer.

"Are you opting for sex to prove you're a woman? Let's be honest about it, Belinda. You know what it's all about. Do you think if you start now and go down the line of all the eager bedmates it will make you glamorous and wanted? You can have sex in a car, on yachts or private planes, or in châteaus in France or palaces in India. Eventually, it all amounts to the same thing." He suddenly looked sad. "Even for a man."

"What?" she asked.

"Lonely. Goddamn lonely. There's nothing lonelier than waking up next to a body after having sex when there is no love."

As suddenly as he had wanted to talk, he was finished.

"I'll take you home," he said.

When he opened the door to the car, he bent over and kissed her cheek.

"Now, don't take it badly, Belinda. We once said we'd keep our relationship impersonal so we wouldn't have the luxury of hostility, didn't we?"

"Yes," said Belinda. "I remember. You said, 'or the blinders of affection.' I can't do that because I like you too much." She smiled at him. It was a relief to have some memory of the past to obliterate the embarrassment of what had just happened.

"That goes for me, too," he said. "Now we'll forget this whole incident. Okay?"

"Okay," she said.

They had pulled up in front of the house just as Claudia and Max were returning home. Max was full of enthusiasm about *West Side Story*. Natalie Wood was a bright young star; Rita Moreno and George Chakiris had put a new dimension into musicals, their choreography and their acting blending so splendidly together.

He mimicked Chakiris, doing a few dance steps.

Belinda smiled to see him suddenly becoming a young Puerto Rican in a rumble.

"You can be anything!" she laughed.

He turned and grimaced. It was the old Max, excited by creativity, lambent. Claudia laughed.

"I wish I had wings!" he said.

"You have!" said Belinda.

Then they had gone into the house, the magic of the moment of fun gone for Belinda as she realized she had probably spoiled everything with David.

As he left the house, David was saddened. He had seen *Young Lucretia*, and he knew the picture was in trouble.

For once, even as a studio owner, David resented the breakdown of the motion-picture production code of censorship. Since the dissolution of the theater system, which had rejected pictures with questionable scenes, and the advent of television, which was a parade of violence, the film industry had broken away from the once-needed seal of approval.

The mother studios no longer sustained their own product, and if the drug scene, prostitution, rape, sexual perversion, seduction, depravity, erotic language, adultery, nymphomania, satyriasis, and sadism were exposed verbally or physically on film, the audience was likely to fill seats and wait on line around the block, eager to be exposed to hitherto hidden delights.

Now David—and Titan—had to face such competition or not get bookings.

He had just heard the results of Red Powell's last conference with the publicity department. The advertising campaign had been steamed, brewed, and distilled by the heads of the advertising and promotion departments who were seeking a solid platform from which to launch a difficult picture.

A million-dollar campaign would almost sneak in on kitten feet.

What happened later—when airplanes flying banners, blimps flashing lighted signs, the news crawl on Times Square, newspaper, magazines, and TV channels flashed the startling message: "DON'T SEE BELINDA BARSTOW

IN YOUNG LUCRETIA—IF . . ."—remained to be seen.

In another day, the studio could have stopped the madness of *Young Lucretia*, but since a seal of approval was not necessary, and since Max had wanted to be daring in terms of historical truth, Fergus had given in.

David felt that he himself was part of the perfidy. Perhaps he, too, had wanted to compete with the art of the foreign films that had been daring in their portrayal of the seamier side of life.

Max had convinced them that the study of lust and incest of another age was a moral revelation. And so the film, unthinkable ten years ago, was taken as a daring gesture on Titan's slate. It had been framed so carefully around the beauty and innocence of Belinda that it had passed even the critical New York boards. They had all felt that with Max's genius, they were coming into an exciting art form.

Now David was faced with the problem of protecting the release of a picture he disliked.

The campaign would have to be based on Belinda's metamorphosis.

Already Red Powell had brought him the program.

IF YOU CANNOT TAKE THE NAKED TRUTH IN HISTORY . . . OR YOU'RE EASILY HORRIFIED . . . *IF* YOU DO NOT WANT TO KNOW WHAT HAPPENED TO A YOUNG VIRGIN IN THE HIDDEN ORGIES IN THE VATICAN OF THE BORGIAS . . . DON'T SEE BELINDA BARSTOW IN *YOUNG LUCRETIA*.

This would be provocative, would strike at the very flaw in the production in such a way that it would counteract any criticism that would fall on their heads.

Belinda would be forced into a sexual image much more difficult for her to bear than the unripe sex object in *The Oracle*. Men would not only want her, they would seek depravity in her beauty as a special dividend of the macho they all hoped lay within themselves.

Sensationalism was the word, and Belinda was the victim.

It was the only way out for Titan. David battled his

143

thoughts about the three people he had just left—that oddly matched triumvirate who, in spite of himself, had become so important to him—two of them strangely related to him by blood.

Claudia had tied her future to Max, who, in this new era when a director was only bankable if his last picture was a smash, could easily become unemployable. Cold, calculating box office figures, instead of the human equation of another day, were the only judges of future employment. There had been a time when a studio head like Simon Moses could keep a director working endlessly if he believed in him. No longer so. Even David was not in a position to count on his future talent without the bank account of a current smash.

As for Belinda, David was disgusted with the scene he had just been put through, and he was disappointed in her; he wondered if she had any of the wealth of spirit that had seemed to shine through in her first film. Or was she just the product of Max's brilliant imagination?

Her scenes in the new picture had been astonishingly feral. He had been excited about her acting and startled by her fierce dominance in her scenes as the vituperative Lucretia. But the young woman he had just encountered on the beach was neither attractive nor, in any sense, maturing.

Disliking himself for the thought, he was glad he would be away for a few months. He wanted no part of this personal responsibility.

He had to be a realist. At the moment, Belinda was the lifeblood of Titan studio. She had been forced into stardom, and she must continue; millions were at stake. Her corporate worth could not be ignored. And it was too late for her to sink into oblivion and retreat to the girlish life that had been hers a few years ago. It was necessary for her to move on, to achieve maturity in her life as well as her career.

He thought of the girls and women who had been abandoned after a quick flash of career; he knew only too well how many had found surcease from the disappointments of a blighted career in too much sex, in narcotics, in drink, and how many ended on the frightened, lonely path to suicide.

He felt he must somehow see that she moved on from

her ambiguous situation. Perhaps he might send her flowers to let her know he valued her, after the dressing down he'd given her. But he rejected the idea: It was a cop-out to soothe his own embarrassment. This sort of blind apology was exactly the behavior he would have resented from another man with her.

The intelligent thing to do was to see the advertising and publicity department heads and have a realistic conference with Red Powell. Belinda must be backed up by a publicity campaign based on her skillful performance. She must be given kudos as a serious actress. No more the beautiful novice, she must be recognized, given dignity so that she would be beyond the sort of behavior that he had just experienced.

He knew this would plunge her into maturity in the eyes of the film business, but there was no other way out. She would never be able to live the life of a normal young woman; she would never have substantial men in her life unless she had a substantial position of her own. Again, another burden would be placed on her shoulders; "measure up" were hard words to give a girl not yet twenty.

In his mind he rearranged his schedule. He would stay over a day for conferences with advertising and promotion heads, and a different approach to the publicity campaign of *Young Lucretia* would emerge.

As a result of this decision, he unwittingly changed the lives of the three people he had just left.

Sweet charity, thy name is publicity, Belinda learned.

Red Powell, being an old hand, realized that since the film business had scattered its gold dust all over the world, the glittering Hollywood premiere of other days was finished. As head of the publicity department, he had to make immediate connection.

The next step, therefore, was to wheedle a prestigious local charity group into giving a gala premiere for *Young Lucretia.*

Red Powell had survived decades of studio turmoil by his splendid instincts in snatching victory from defeat. And now he knew he would have to enlist the help of the very force that usually despised the film industry. It was all done with an inner knowledge of larceny.

From Grace Boomer, the senior publicist, also a war-scarred member of the staff, down to young Laura West, the new breed junior publicist, with the masque of a Kabuki dancer, and a perpetually gloved left hand, they all awaited Red's final word. What they would think, and how they would make it come off would all spin from his carefully chosen words.

"Our plan will give the film a glossy introduction— before the Legion of Decency, the church groups, and the Bible Belt give us the double whammy."

Red relished the puzzled glance on the purse-mouthed face of old Gracie Boomer.

He would lay out just enough of his scenario to put them on their toes. He'd get more out of them that way. And they'd better dance, or they wouldn't be getting that weekly paycheck.

"There is no problem with the upper crust," he grimaced, "if you know the ropes." And he did.

The first step was for a prestige film to be offered to a charity organization for a premiere. This meant studio cooperation, which was eagerly given. The second step was to contact Flora Stone Random. She was the woman most capable of larceny in Los Angeles.

Flora Stone Random was in her mid-seventies. She dressed in the style of the turn of the century, and lived like a grande dame on a pittance and her wits.

Her mansion was atop a small rise above the encroachments of business buildings, facing the new freeways of Los Angeles.

She still maintained vast lawns with sculptured shrubs, iron stags, and lacy gazebos. The old coach house and its two acres had been sold for a restaurant, which would have piqued her neighbors, but they were long gone, and rezoning had destroyed the neighborhood.

She kept a slew-footed staff of elderly retainers and an unpaid spinster slave secretary, Miss Monk, who disliked her intensely but was afraid to leave as she had no place to go. She was allowed to live in the old gardener's hut, and this had sealed her doom twenty-five years ago.

Mrs. Stone Random (as she insisted on being called) still had a butler's pantry crammed with china and crystal from many an overbuying European jaunt. Her husband, an insurance broker, had allowed her to spend anything she wanted to get her off his back. But the wealth had ended with his death and the stock market crash.

She had discovered a racket, which she organized with skill. Although she agreed, like all of Los Angeles society, that film people were anathema to the sacrosanct Los Angeles Country Club, Hancock Park, and June Street citizens, she also knew that, even if the men were not too interested in film folk (aside from private liaisons with up-and-coming starlets), their wives and daughters would still come running to a premiere of a prestige picture, especially if the audience was laced with celebrities and they could attend a dinner in a ballroom and stare at their favorite stars.

Mrs. Stone Random also knew that if a studio had a preview for charity, the organization that was being honored would come in full force; society would join up (it was deductible at $150 a ticket); and the company would do anything in its power to urge the press to attend.

There were many advantages in searching out charities in need of an event. Although she was known as one of the major hostesses of the town, she had never paid for a party in her life.

Her cateress, eager to be mentioned in the papers, gave her a good price for the large dinners in Flora's home when committees met to glue the event of the season together. She put a bill in to the charity doubling what she put out, after she received compliments on her generosity.

For Titan's premiere, for the party at the Crystal Room of the Beverly Hills Hotel, she got an old friend to underwrite the liquor bill. Her favorite wine dealer always gave her a large kickback and provided her with liquor for her home, which of course she added to her chit for a PR payback for entertaining in her gracious home.

The same went for the florist, the orchestra, and the party planners who worked out the motifs of tablecloths, chairs, and the setting for the band.

She suggested a fleet of limousines to take the Golden Circle ticket holders (at $250 apiece) to the gala at the hotel. Her favorite service sent her a pleasant check.

As she was the "finder" of the Titan film, she accepted a legitimate salary as public relations counselor for the Project Babies charity event. It was worth it; her secretary wrote good press releases—she could copy the style of any columnist in town.

Titan also presented her with a handsome check for "out-of-pocket expenses," to insure the fact that Titan studio, as well as high society, got in all press releases.

It was fortuitous for the charity, of course, to sponsor the film. Out of the $150 to $250 a ticket, they garnered 50 percent.

By the time the premiere of *Young Lucretia* was ended, she figured on a personal profit of over six thousand dollars.

In the interim, aside from major Los Angeles social leaders, she corralled a Nobel Peace Prize scientist, a Pulitzer Prize winner, an authority on Renaissance history who was flown in from the British Museum, two senators, several duchesses who would fly anywhere to meet film stars and get a free ride, and all the society press from Orange County to San Francisco. Many of her subscribers would never have attended a premiere if it hadn't been for the fact that a large amount of money would go to Project Babies to help orphaned children, many of whom were a result of the United States' commitment in Vietnam.

Everyone was getting nervous about the accelerating military involvement in Vietnam, and people wanted to take a stand.

Mrs. Stone Random got some pitiful pictures of ragged little toddlers in Vietnam, had her secretary contact the proper people to agree it would be marvelous to be able to have a lovely evening, see a great picture, meet some enchanting picture people, and at the same time help stamp out communism.

As soon as Red Powell met her, he saw that she would be delighted to have Belinda meet society. Mrs. Stone Random was a natural pusher. About twenty years before, she had bought fifty of Jeffrey Barstow's discarded neckties at Goodwill and sold them for five hundred dollars' profit at a charity event. This gave her a warm feeling toward the Barstows. The first meeting was at a tea in her mansion, and Claudia was invited to accompany her niece. Many of the committeewomen were the right age to have been Claudia's fans.

Claudia, following the memory of girlhood days in London, remembered her actress mother taking off her plumes and rouge on the rare occasions when she had been invited to high tea.

Claudia wore a black frock, pearls, and a small hat that had been sitting in a hatbox for ten years. She allowed the ladies to chat, joined in, and then managed to shock them a little with the latest gossip, most of it invented. They found her slightly racy, but elegant.

Belinda wore a pearl-grey wool dress, a matching coat with a mink collar, and Claudia's coral necklace and earrings that had belonged to her grandmother. They hadn't been worth pawning, Claudia thought gratefully, and now it had a value that this type of society would recognize from jaunts to the coral shops of Italy. Belinda played it in a reserved manner; that was the advantage of beauty— nothing else was needed.

"Now," said Claudia, "thank God these occasions are

rare, but it'll fatten your pocketbook if all these people shake your hand and each one tells their ten best friends. You've no idea how they will talk it up. There's nothing like a charity premiere to make people feel noble."

Both of them ran the social gamut. Belinda, engulfed in Mrs. Stone Random's wave of scarves and lilac sachet, saw her hostess as a smart character actress who was playing her role well, if a bit overdone.

"My dear," the hostess said, "Miss Barstow—or I should say Mrs. Ziska—would you honor us by sitting at the other end of the table and pouring the coffee while I greet my guests? Mrs. Fraser, our president, will do the tea at the other end."

"I'd be charmed," said Claudia. "My, what a lovely Georgian tea set."

"Of course," smiled Mrs. Stone Random, "you, with your British background, would recognize its value."

Wouldn't I ever, thought Claudia, having pawned the same in my day. I wonder if she knows the genius of the hour, my husband Max, is a Jew. I wonder if she knows that I was more than slightly scandalous around town about the same time she was buying out Europe . . . Oh, well, what difference does it make?

So she poured coffee. The two maids, busy passing cucumber and walnut and cream cheese sandwiches, were surprised at the long lineup for coffee. Everyone wanted to talk to the lovely movie star, Claudia Barstow, and they all gushed with remembrances of having stood in line to see her pictures. Some of them even admitted that their mothers had been her great fans. Claudia, looking at women at least ten years her senior who talked as if they had been carried to the matinee, smiled; she'd been through this before, and so had most of her peers.

Belinda was surrounded by a group of enthusiastic women; they'd adored her in *The Oracle*; such a high-principled picture. Mrs. Stone Random introduced her to everyone. "My dear, aren't you lovely!" she said, holding Belinda's hand in her jeweled claw. "I must find you a suitable husband. I'm sure you haven't met the proper people in your métier."

Belinda looked at her, surprised.

"I—I know some very nice people," she said.

"Oh, of course, but I mean someone, well, a fine lawyer, or banker, or even a doctor—from a good family, of course," she ended, putting down the medical profession a notch.

Claudia and Belinda had already been alerted by Grace Boomer that the Chinese Theater, chosen for the gala, had 1492 seats, and that the charity would be fortunate if they managed to sell 700. The house would have to be papered. Of course, Titan and the press would take up a great deal, but everything that could be done to make it look like a sellout would be important. You could only paper a house so much without it showing.

During a rare moment, Belinda managed to speak to Claudia. "I feel like a salesman," she whispered.

"You are, dear," said Claudia, talking through her teeth. "Let's lam out of here as soon as we can. But remember, the most important showing of *Young Lucretia* depends on this group, so multiply it by the first week's gross, take another walnut sandwich, and grit your teeth on it."

They laughed.

"My," said Mrs. Stone Random, sailing up to them like a frigate with all sails furled, "you two are chums, aren't you?"

Suddenly a photographer appeared. "Don't move, ladies," he said.

Their hostess lifted her scarves higher over her chins, and they posed. Women they had just met were pushed into the picture, in pecking order. Some of them were attractive, and Claudia would have liked to talk to them, but their hostess ordered them about like a marine sergeant; it was impossible.

When the photo session was finished, Claudia said, "I must get my wrap; we do have to get back to the beach. It's been so nice of you to include me with Belinda."

Mrs. Stone Random was enchanted. "This must be the first of many meetings," she said. "I know we're going to be friends. But don't rush. My nephew, I feel, is coming in early to meet you; you don't think he'd miss the chance to shake hands with Belinda Barstow."

She rushed off.

"Oh, God," said Claudia. "I'll go get our wraps way down yonder in that guest room."

Several more women were bearing down on them.

"Do that," said Belinda. "She's already planning on finding me a husband."

"That'll be the day," said Claudia as she fled.

As if on cue a young man approached her. Her first impression was of grey.

He wore a pearl-gray suit, a slightly darker necktie, and as he came closer, she saw that he was suntanned and his eyes were gray. He was tall, slender, broad shouldered, and his light brown hair shone as he passed under the chandelier.

Cutting across a group of women poised with teacups, he rushed up to her and took her hand.

Surprised, she allowed it.

"Now," he said. "You're coming with me to the solarium, right now. Don't you dare refuse!"

He smiled and, taken aback, she let him move her along the hall to a solarium that was jammed full of ferns, gardenia plants, and wicker furniture. Several women stared at their precipitous retreat from the drawing room.

"What is this?" Belinda asked.

"This is a necessity," he said. "If my aunt got hold of me we'd be stuck forever in a forest of women, teacups, and chat, and I had to see you by myself."

He drew her to a bench. He looked at her as if he could devour her, but this had happened to her often, and it didn't bother her.

"So you must be the nephew," she said.

"Oh, let me introduce myself," he said. "I'm Scott Stone. My father was Aunt Flora's brother. Does this make our introduction proper?"

"I—don't know," said Belinda. "Anyway, my name is Belinda Barstow. Hello."

She put her hand out. He took it and laughed.

"As if every man in America doesn't know. I ripped out of my law office early. If I hadn't met you, I think I would have picketed Project Babies. Listen, Belinda Barstow, I saw *The Oracle* twelve times, and aside from you, I don't know who the hell was in it. Except that John Graves, who had love scenes with you. I hate him."

She smiled. He was attractive. His high cheekbones and slightly jutting chin showed a promise of strength; and he certainly was determined.

"He's a good actor," she said. "You know those scenes aren't real. They're directed."

Oh, what a lie, she thought. How much I wanted those love scenes to be real. But she realized as she said it that John Graves had been away from her thoughts for a long time. It was pleasant to have an attractive man so intrigued with her.

"Well," he said, "let's get down to basics. They'll be looking for us any minute, you can be sure. What are you doing tonight, and the next night, and the next?"

She could see Claudia in the hall, with their two coats over her arm.

"I'm going home with my aunt."

"I'll drive you."

"I have my own car."

"I'll follow you," he said.

"Oh, I couldn't. Not tonight."

It was too sudden.

"Then I'll sit in front of your house and battle anyone who comes to pick you up."

"You're crazy," she said, laughing. "I haven't a date, but—"

He looked so pleased that she bit her lip.

"I mean, maybe tomorrow—"

"It's a date," he said.

Claudia came up to them. "I was looking all over for you—"

"I'm Scott Stone," he interrupted, "and I have to introduce myself. I'm Flora's nephew, and I have to get a word in—my God, here she comes."

They were shaking hands as Flora bore down on them.

"Well, I see you two have met. Scott, you are incorrigible, dragging Belinda away. The photographer is looking all over for you."

As she spoke, the photographer found them. "May I have a picture of you two, right in front of those gardenias?"

Scott smiled, picked a gardenia, and handed it to Belinda. "We're going to look like a garden wedding, posed in this bower."

"Oh, Scott!" said Mrs. Stone Random. "You are outrageous!"

Indeed, the picture did look like a garden wedding in the newspapers. Scott was holding Belinda's hand and looking down at her. She held the white gardenia. His aunt on one side was beaming, and Claudia on the other was regal. Inside, of course, she was wondering what this pushy young man thought he was doing.

Several days later, as Belinda dressed for an evening with Scott, Claudia chatted in her usual catbird seat on a blue slipper chair.

"Not that I want you to be conniving," said Claudia, "but this mad passion Scott has for you is taking the place of a hot romance with your leading man, which usually gets you publicity while you're making a picture. At this time, it will do our premiere nothing but good."

"He's really very nice," said Belinda.

"Well," said Claudia, "frankly I never had the experience of a 'very nice' man being a hot romance. My Lord, three nights in a row. Are you by any chance taking it seriously? Have you—uh—kissed him yet?"

"Heavens, no," said Belinda. "I think he's too scared of me."

"Maybe you'll meet someone you like among his group. That's always a possibility.'"

Belinda laughed. "Hardly. The Los Angeles Country Club was once reputed to have an average membership age of eighty. But that's a lie. It's sixty-five."

"Well, anyway," said Claudia, pleased to see Belinda laughing, "it's fun to be romanced by a handsome man. And maybe you'll get him away from Aunt Flora's apron strings after this charity gig is finished."

"He promised," said Belinda, "and for a change I'm enjoying the attention."

She clasped a silver chain over her gray satin dress, put on silver drop earrings, then took them off, and added a Greek coin medallion to the chain instead.

"I'm glad," said Claudia, "that you have the knack of underplaying your clothes. That's perfect. When are you going to break out the fabulous gold and pearl octopus that Niadas gave you? It's in the vault; too valuable to leave around the house."

"I was thinking of wearing it at the premiere again," said Belinda. "What do you think?"

"I think it will knock them for a loop. You know, your good luck token."

"Good luck . . . ," said Belinda, remembering the villa in Rome, when Niadas had lifted the golden treasure from her neck and they had made love, she for the first time in her life, and he for the last, a few hours before his heart stopped.

"I wonder," she said, "what would have happened if he had lived; mostly what it would have meant to Alex?"

"I do, too," said Claudia. "And thinking of that, you know, if you do fall in love and want to be with someone, we'd always take care of him. You deserve a little freedom. By the way, dear, you know from your experience with Kevin it's better you don't tell anyone about Alex. It's a dreadful sin of omission, but it's necessary in your young life."

"Yes, I thought of that," said Belinda.

She was suddenly dejected. Oh, if she hadn't seen Kevin in bed with that dreadful Tony Valli, he might have been the one celebrating all the excitement of the premiere with her. She longed for him, his body, their walks and talks together, and the delicious Bohemian life and freedom they had shared.

But no use to think of the past.

"I'll be downstairs with Max," said Claudia. "I have a hunch this young man will be right on time."

Downstairs, Claudia opened the newspaper. "Look at Belinda spread all over the Sunday society section. And your name's splashed all over the article."

Max looked at it. "Good," he said. "Nice-looking man. What is he? What does he do? Is he decent?"

"Too decent!" said Claudia. "He's supposed to be a big catch. Of course, we're more into casting directories than Blue Books in this house, but I borrowed a Southwest Blue Book from Mildred, next door. He's a graduate of Harvard Law School, and he belongs to the Bel Air Bay Club, the California Club, and the Los Angeles Country Club. He's in a Westwood law firm—Something, Something, Something, and Something." She made a face. "That doesn't sound like the right style for Belinda, do you think?"

Max shook his head. "What do I know about young American men? He seems mad about her."

"Is he ever!" said Claudia. "Anyway, it's better than shacking up in that artist's pad in Venice."

"I think he was probably more fun," said Max.

"Up to a point," said Claudia, thinking of his betrayal of Belinda. "Anyway, it's good publicity for the picture. Of course, he insists on taking her to the gala opening. And the romance is selling tickets."

Prince Charming arrived for Belinda in his steel-gray Porsche. He greeted Claudia and Max affably, a small corsage of gardenias in a plastic box in his hand.

Belinda came down the stairs. No matter how simply she dressed, her fluid body denied the propriety of her dress. No wonder, thought Claudia, that he was bonkers about her. He stared at her with such awe that any conversation at this moment was impossible.

"My favorite color!" he said, admiring her dress as if she had invented gray.

Claudia had been told by Belinda that he was a "gray" man. How premeditated it all was.

Claudia was struck with the fact that this whole situation was ridiculous. Belinda going to a dinner at the Los Angeles Country Club, given by Mrs. Stone Random. The officers of the Project Babies charity would be the other guests. Well, it was a business situation. Belinda was being a clever little bitch. But this was a man, not a boy, and she was going to have to cope with him somehow, so to speak, after the fair was over.

"Have a good evening," Claudia said, feeling like a cross between a hypocrite and a housemother.

After the two of them left, she turned to Max. "I'm glad I'm not that young again. What she has to go through reaching maturity. Well, this one at least is good for our picture."

Max wasn't too involved with the publicity on the picture. These things never mattered to him. Now that the film was out of his hands, his mind was on the next one.

He had chosen another classic theme, and Belinda was right for it. It was the story of the beautiful Egyptian queen, Nefertiti, the Asian princess from Mitannie, who had enchanted the mighty Akhnaton, who had become the first monotheist in history. The great royal court had moved from Thebes, abandoning and defacing the shrines of many gods, and created the new city of Akhetaton. It had become the splendid center of worship for the sun-god, Aton. And lasting longer than the great capital, now the rubble of a modern village, Tel-El-Amarna, was a new, liberated, more natural attitude toward art which had advanced the skills of the great artists and craftsmen of the Eighteenth Dynasty.

The rivalry of the priests, the dethroning of many gods, and the worship of the sun-god had intrigued Max. The acromegalic figure of the great Pharaoh innovator, and the driving beauty of his consort, had excited Max when he had thought of the theme. Never—before he saw Belinda's maturing beauty—had he known a woman beautiful enough to portray the frail and divine creature, the legendary Nefertiti. As a young man, he had haunted the Berlin museum, looking at the beautiful limestone bust of her: the swanlike neck, the royal headdress, and the almond eyes that looked out from centuries past with a serenity and, he felt, a singleness of purpose that made her one of the fascinating creatures of all time.

He wondered what stresses had made a woman, at this time in history, cling to the god Aton, battling political, religious, and personal forces, after her husband had compromised to serve other gods.

But there was no certainty of his dreams being fleshed until Titan gave him the go-ahead. It was a difficult project, for there was no chance of a motion-picture company with a Jewish director shooting it in Nasser's Egypt. Again, a film would have to be fashioned of plaster and gilt, and it would be incredibly costly.

Also, Max feared the studio would question a film in which Belinda would have to age. But thinking of how *Giant* had only advanced the acting career of young Elizabeth Taylor as she aged through several decades, he felt it would be a worthy challenge for Belinda, and he was already tracing steps through ancient Egypt. On his desk sat a copy of Nefertiti's bust from the Agyptisches Museum in East Berlin. It, like himself, had survived the perils of the war. To him, it was a symbol of eternal beauty, both physical and spiritual.

As always, he was pleased by this new story, casting aside like a lizard skin his complete absorption in his previous epic.

Claudia was delighted to see him cast off the horrors of

the Borgias, and she prayed that he'd be working again soon.

It seemed to Belinda that the premiere would never happen. It would be two more months until the combined forces of Titan, Mrs. Flora Stone Random, Los Angeles society, celebrities, and merchants would merge to achieve one homogeneous mass of goodwill toward men.

Scott was called out of town on a court hearing, but he bombarded her with gardenias, phone calls, and his distress at their being apart. The coming gala seemed to be the main event in his life.

She was in demand for fashion layouts, it seemed, in every magazine in the world. She posed on chilly mornings in bathing suits, sat through heat waves in fur coats, and was either elegant, aloof, or smiling as various photographers and fashion editors demanded. It was wearying, but all part of the big chess game Titan was playing.

She was finally called to the studio for a sitting with Leslie Charles. Elegant furnishings from the film were placed in a setting that evoked the Renaissance. Kevin's portraits of herself and Leslie were hung against rich velvet damask, and the two of them were to pose in costume with the paintings.

For a moment, the shock of seeing the portraits overwhelmed her. Here she was, contained in pigments and oil, as still and yet as alive as she could be. The warmth of her love affair showed in her eyes. The ruby earrings and necklace she had brought Kevin at that dreadful moment when she saw him in bed with Tony had been added with consummate skill. The idea that Kevin was able to finish his work with such precision, after what he had done to her, ravaged the calm surface she had achieved so painfully.

"Well, my dear," said Leslie, "here we go again. I wonder if you and I are doomed to stalk through history together. I do hope the next film will be more cheerful than this."

"So do I," said Belinda, grateful for his presence. "Oh, Leslie, let's do a comedy for a change!"

"And for a few laughs," said Leslie.

He was thinking of other times, and of the death of his lifelong friend, Andrew Reed. Dear acerbic Andrew, his first and most real love, the man who had taught him the most. Andrew's death had saddened his work on the picture. He remembered the remote melancholy he had seen in Belinda at the end of the film, and her hot scene with Antonio Valli. And he thought he knew why. What a bad start this youngster had. He remembered her desperate crush on John Graves during *The Oracle*. He had witnessed moods in her he could not fathom, not knowing their origin, but it made him realize that she had somehow missed the natural joys of her age.

"I must tell you," he said, "now that the film is ended, I think you were splendid, and you have *my* vote when the time comes. Now let's cheer up and look properly mysterious and wicked."

She smiled at him, and they posed hand in hand.

"It isn't every day," he whispered, "that a father gets to have incest with a beautiful chick like you. Since I have neither had a child, nor performed incest, it's another unique trip in my colorful career."

They both laughed.

He put her in a good mood. George Ritt, who had taken Belinda's first Titan pictures at the studio bash introducing her to the press, was delighted. "You look splendid!" he said, grinning. "Who would think that the little kid I photographed a couple of years ago would become Lucretia Borgia so fast."

It was a pleasant sitting for Belinda, as long as she didn't look behind her at the portrait.

In spite of herself, she had a longing to go to the studio in Venice and be with Kevin as she had so often, fall into his arms, and get lost in music, talk, and books, and, most of all, in love, fulfilling and wonderful in its ups and downs, challenges, quarrels, and emotional conciliations. It had been a time of magic. Why couldn't it have stayed that way!

Leslie took her hand. "Endings are always sad, Belinda. But the wonderful thing is, there are always beginnings."

He stopped suddenly, his mouth slightly open. He put his hand over it.

"I must be getting old—sentimental. My dear, we can't afford that, can we? Well, it's been charming."

His dresser and Belinda's maid, Polly, met them at the doors of their adjacent bungalow dressing rooms.

"Mr. Fergus Austin wants to see you, Miss B'linda," Polly said.

"Well, when you finish, maybe we can have a 'cuppa' in the commissary," said Leslie. "It'll take me a little while to peel off old Alexander VI's face and nose. That's where you're lucky. All *you* need is a little cream."

Belinda got out of her heavy court clothes, unfastened the piled-up curls, and cleaned off her makeup. In a blue silk blouse and jeans, she looked far from a film star. What a relief; Fergus could take her the way she was. She was going to have to dress up tonight. Scott was back in town and taking her to dinner at the Bel Air Bay Club. At least it wouldn't be formal. Two of his friends, the Howards, were planning to take them sailing over the weekend; he found great pleasure in giving her new experiences. She only wished she could be thrilled about the plans he made with such enthusiasm.

Belinda could see by Fergus's jammed-up ashtray that he was chain-smoking. Although he had been kind to her in Europe in her time of trouble, she did not relate to him as she did to David. But he was a part of her adult life, and she attempted to ignore his cold blue eyes and abrupt mannerisms and gave him a peck on the cheek. He managed a smile. Anyway, it was good to be called in alone and for once not feel that Claudia was looking over her shoulder trying to direct her conversation.

As soon as she settled in a chair, he walked around the front of his desk and perched on it—his idea of an intimate gesture.

At first glance at her, Fergus was taken aback. Claudia had always entered his office in a chic suit, hat with veil, wafting her little cloud of French perfume. But it was a different time now, and this would be a touchy meeting. He plunged in without ado.

"We're going to need your help on this picture, Belinda. We don't have as much working for us as we did with *The Oracle*. I have hopes you'll be nominated for an Academy Award for your performance, and we're slanting our promotion on this."

She waited for what was coming. What else did he want her to do? What was his gimmick?

"Right after your opening, we're going to swing you around the country; there will be premieres in key cities as the picture opens, and you'll have to represent not only your picture but the company. We need you. The tour will include TV interviews, talk shows, game shows in New York for national coverage. It'll be lunches and banquets and flights from one place to another. I'm not conning you. It's going to be tough.

"At least six cities will have charity benefits. Not as important as the one here, but of great value to our box office. And you'll be the main attraction. Now, we'd like to have another cast member go with you, and that's why I wanted to talk to you. Would you like it to be Leslie Charles, or Tony Valli?"

He looked down, not meeting her eye, knowing the answer.

"Leslie, of course," she said quickly, trying not to reveal her emotion at the sound of Valli's name.

Fergus lit a cigarette. This had been a poser, bringing it up casually, knowing what he knew.

"Good," he said. "Of course, you'll be on an extra month's salary."

"Naturally," said Belinda, having been clued in by Claudia on what to ask for on a PR junket. "And a decent expense account. Limousines, of course; and a specially designed wardrobe—which I'll keep," she added.

"Naturally," said Fergus, thinking that she was every inch a Barstow. "A number one star treatment—that's what you are, Belinda. I'll have Janos make you whatever you want. Now we feel that Grace Boomer would be best to handle your PR since she's done it so well before."

"Okay," said Belinda, "as long as she stays out of my hair when I don't need her."

Fergus remembered the trouble Claudia caused Grace as a young press agent on her first jaunt. He knew that poor old tired Gracie would dislike this junket as much as Belinda. But who else could he trust to watch a Barstow?

He smiled at her. "We count on you."

She stood up. The session seemed to be at an end. The bargain had been struck.

"Well, I'll be glad to get the salary," she said, "and I'm also glad you didn't include Claudia."

Fergus lifted his eyebrows.

She waved his unspoken question away. "No trouble at home," she said. "It's just that I want to be me. I'll do my own interviews without someone making waves in my direction. I'm glad you didn't suggest her coming along. I want to be on my own. Oh, I'll need Polly to take care of my clothes."

"Of course," said Fergus. "You couldn't be expected to have a new maid in every town. She's used to your things."

Belinda wondered why he was being so affable.

"And one more thing," he said. "We're going to ship Kevin Frazier's portraits along with you. They'll be featured in two museum openings and at several social events. They are brilliant portraits. They have a unique value in promotion, and they'll be a great focus in artistic circles for high-class publicity."

Startled at the idea of posing with a smiling face with this tragic memorabilia, she wondered which of the two portraits would express what she was—the youthful victim of high ambitions and lust, or the young woman who had realized the depths of her degradation and joined the dance of power and death.

They'd undoubtedly be displayed side by side, with herself in the middle like a goody to be consumed by the public—the cream in the Nabisco wafer.

And she supposed the exhibit would include the portrait of Antonio Valli. That would be another cross to bear.

She glanced down, choked by the idea of traveling all over the United States bearing the phantom of her love like the albatross in the *Ancient Mariner*. But what could she do? There was no way she could complain.

Fergus took her hand. "I think you might give Leslie a call and tell him you want him to go on tour with you."

"I'd already planned to have a cup of coffee with him in the commissary. I'll run along, then."

She wanted to get out of the office fast. She'd be damned if she'd cry.

Fergus saw her to the door. From his eagle's nest, he watched her as she slowly walked down the street to meet Leslie. Her whole posture revealed sadness. He felt a pang of guilt at the fact that he had set up her distress, and he compensated for it by thinking she was saved from a worse situation. If that Kevin was a goddamn fag, it was just as well she found out about it before it ruined her life. Then he remembered how he had done the same thing to David and Jessica. Well, he'd saved David from making the dreadful mistake of marrying that bitch,

Fergus's own mistress. He'd often had to make decisions that seemed dreadful for those involved at the time, but the means justified the ends: Titan studio had gone on in spite of niggling human interference.

As he watched, he saw Belinda turn away from the commissary and start running toward the dressing room area. As she put her hands to her eyes, he could see that she must be wiping away tears. He wondered what she was going to do and if it would interfere with his plans.

Leslie's door was ajar. He saw her wiping her eyes with one hand as she fumbled for the doorknob. She paused, her head bent.

"Belinda," he said, coming toward her, "what's happened?"

Instinctively, she clutched his arms, holding on tightly.

"You'd better come in, my dear," he said. "Let's not make a spectacle."

The presence of several cowboys rushing to their afternoon libation in their dressing rooms alerted him. He recognized them as prominent TV personalities; of course, he wouldn't talk to them, and the fear that they might be privy to any emotional disturbance of legitimate actors made him move quickly.

He drew her into his room. The wardrobe man had already left.

"Now," he said, "what's the trouble?"

She took a Kleenex from his dressing table, wiped her eyes, and blew her nose.

"Would a drink help?" he asked.

"I'll take a Coke," she said.

He opened his refrigerator, handed her one, and poured himself a vodka. Then he settled back, and she smothered a sob.

"If it would help," he said, "you know I'd be glad to be your confidant. You have to be careful, dear, so it might as well be an old friend if you wish to unload your problems."

She composed herself. "Fergus Austin wants you to go on tour with me all over the United States."

"Well," he said, raising his eyebrows, "that's hardly something to weep about! At least I hope not!"

"Oh," she said, managing a smile, "I didn't mean that. Will you go? On salary, of course."

"Yes," he said. He wondered briefly why Antonio Valli wasn't going, but he had an inkling. After all, he had witnessed the time Belinda scratched Valli's face, he knew that Kevin had disappeared, and he had heard a few things around the pool at Fantasy Palms, a gay motel in Palm Springs. "You know we'll make the best of a grueling assignment. We did it in Rome. Remember when I taught you what kind of wine to drink with what kind of food?"

She smiled and sipped her Coke.

"Instead of that rotgut you're swilling now, why don't I give you a small glass of an excellent California Chablis?"

"Why don't you?" said Belinda.

He poured her a glass and sat back, waiting.

She looked up at him, her blue eyes wide above the rim of her glass. He was touched by her beauty; she looked like a little girl, except that a mask of sadness added a quality to her face that made her very much a woman.

"Oh, Leslie," she said, "I have to appear with those portraits—even the one of that louse, Tony Valli."

"I see," said Leslie. He suddenly did.

"Well, Belinda," he said, "if you are willing to listen, I am willing to talk to you. It's going to be rough, but I wouldn't say anything if I didn't think I could help you. Can you take it?"

She glanced at him and nodded.

"I don't know exactly what happened," he said, "and I don't want to hear the lurid details. But I do know that Kevin got his walking papers. And that when I thought about that haymaker you landed on Tony's cheek the last day of shooting, I put the whole monkey puzzle together."

Belinda nodded. "You seem to know all about it."

"There is no secret in the gay world of Hollywood," said Leslie. "And I'm sure I hit the nail on the head. Did you hold the lantern, or did you walk in on them?"

"I—I walked in on them." She set down her wine, and her face contorted with anguish.

"Oh, dear!" he said. He went to her and gently patted her shoulder. "Now, lay off the waterworks," said Leslie. "I'm going to tell you a few facts that may make it easier for you. First of all, you should feel sorry for Kevin."

Belinda was so surprised her tears stopped. She sipped her wine. "Sorry!" she said. "After what he did to me!"

"He also did it to himself," said Leslie. "Don't you understand, dear, he couldn't help himself. He wanted to love you; for a while he tried, but his nature asserted itself. It would have happened eventually, maybe after you'd made a real pattern of your life with him, perhaps had a child. Then it could have been worse."

"That's what Claudia told me," said Belinda.

"She knows, then?"

Belinda nodded.

"Well, that's good. She's matured quite a bit from the madcap who started me on my career. Now listen to an old hand, and remember what I say because I may never have the guts to go into it again." He saw that he had captured her attention, and he plunged on, disturbed within himself, but needing to tell her. "You no doubt know my predilections. Well, when I was young, of course, I had an occasional affair with a woman. Sometimes, I'm embarrassed to say, for ambitious reasons."

"With Claudia, I heard," said Belinda.

"My God," said Leslie. "There really are no secrets in this business, are there? This venerable studio complex never forgets anything." He waved it aside. "I don't want to digress. Fortunately, at this time in my life, my sexual starch is in darling boys. It's very convenient. They are replaceable objects. You know, one of the great benefits of the gay world is its accessibility. It's all at hand. Even if one does decide to live with some man one cares for, one day he will probably bring home another boy who is in favor and stays, and then the threesome usually doesn't work out. But there's always a lineup of handsome lads waiting. Broken relationships can happen in heterosexual life, too. True love is so rare, Belinda, its magic cannot be bought or sought. It just happens."

"I thought I had it," said Belinda, her eyes brimming again.

"Impossible with Kevin," he said. "It's too bad you have to be involved with the growing androgynous society of our times. What I am trying to tell you is that homosexuality and heterosexuality are two conditions which can both be understood. They are the result of basic sexual drives that come easily to an individual human's need. If you want a certain thing, no lecture or punishment in the world is going to keep you from seeking your desire.

"But bisexuality is a different thing. The bisexual who seesaws from one sex to the other, to me, is the tragic figure. He may think that freedom and abandon are the badge of liberation. I have heard some of them smirkingly say they are try-sexual—they'll try anything. But whatever he chooses, he eventually seeks the other, and someone is punished. Usually, in the end, himself. Sometimes he has sex with a woman to prove he is a man—macho, the stud, the master. Then again, he can love or be dominated by a male and punish the male with the idea that he really likes to make it with women. Sometimes this is done as a bribe to get more out of a male partner, for usually the woman doesn't know about him. But wherever he is, he is not complete. His sex is his proving ground. And sometimes his performance is just egotistic masturbation. It might as well be a warm melon. He's doing it to get something or prove something."

"It sounds horrible!" Belinda put her glass down. "I think Kevin really loved me. Was I wrong?"

"He really wanted to love you," said Leslie. "He told everyone how much he did. He wanted to make a life with you."

"You—you said sometimes such a man does make a relationship for—for career. We had planned to go into pictures when we could, together."

"That could be the legitimate dream of two creative people who love each other. But that's another story. I'm just trying to make you realize the tragic nature of the bisexual. He's two different elements, not whole in either one. When I was a young man, I attended an event at a local college in Pasadena. One of the sponsors of the college had given a hundred-thousand-dollar pipe organ, which was being dedicated in a new auditorium. But the donor, in spite of all the caps and gowns and fanfare, was not there. You know why?"

She looked at him, intrigued. He had deliberately diverted her from her own problems.

"Because," he said, "he and about a dozen other fathers of the city were in jail. They were caught with their pants down in a house of male prostitution, with young boys.

There were educators, doctors, lawyers in that group. Three of them resigned from important positions in the community. There was one suicide. Now mind you, dear girl, they were all married men with children and grandchildren. Many of them thought they loved their wives. But most of them really hated women."

He made a face.

"It was a cute undercover joke among those who were not affected. But it was also a great tragedy. Families were broken up, lives ruined because the uncheckable passionate desires of men were involved. Now in these more liberal days, many of those men might not have been married. I feel sorry for the closet queens. It's an iceberg, Belinda, much more homosexuality below the surface than above the calm waters of society. These men might have found happiness with their own sex. As it was, they were really what I consider perverts—deviating from their true natures by trying to be normal husbands."

"Can anybody make a life with a man who loves her, yet has that—that problem?"

Leslie looked at her. "It isn't just a problem, it's a schism. I believe our Puritan background has forced many homosexuals to feel they have to prove they can relate sexually to a woman. In the end, they prefer men, if that's their bent. The other is society's phony moral proving ground. A very mature woman might be able to face it, but I'm afraid she'd be hurt eventually because a man who truly enjoys sex with a man will go back to it. Of course, if she had some hang-ups of her own, she might forgive, and love him without too much anguish. But that would be very rare. As rare as monogamy, which is rarest of all. You know, a so-called normal man could mow you down, too, if he sought a relationship elsewhere and you were left holding the bag. Would it have made much difference if you had found Kevin in bed with a woman?"

"I think," said Belinda, "he could have explained that, and we might have patched it up. I don't know. Do you think we ever could?"

Leslie shook his head. "You don't seem to be hearing me. I don't think the impact of what I just said has really hit you. You're still young enough to think that love is magic. The truth is, love is ephemeral; never expect it to be a constant state. Now, just to give you the other side of the homosexual story, I fell deeply in love with a beautiful young man I met—a long time ago." He gestured. "Tall, slim, wavy black hair and blue eyes; his name was Bill.

"I took him into my life, my home, and my bed. Oh, he was not only handsome, but grateful, a rare combination. I taught him what socks to wear, what forks to use, what wines to order. I showed him the wonders of Europe, got him Roman suits and London shoes. I really educated him in literature and art. I was a successful actor, and he was glamorized by me. He allowed me the use of his body, and I mistook for love his gratitude for the world I was showing him.

"Well, my dear, several years later he met a young girl, fell legitimately in love with her, and finally told me he could no longer live with me. Then I realized that even though he was considered—because of our relationship— a practicing homosexual, he really wasn't at all. He was just the passive victim of my passion. I had the grace to let him go without a scene.

"He is now happily married. You may be surprised, but I occasionally visit him and his family in Southampton, and I am the godfather to one of his children."

Belinda looked at him, startled. "Does—she know?"

"His wife?" Leslie shook his head. "No, my dear, I don't think it ever entered her mind. I was just an old and valued friend. Bill and I talked about it and decided that there was no reason to disturb her. And right now, in fact, he bores me. He's a successful real estate broker."

Leslie gulped a good swallow of his drink and looked up, an almost crooked smile on his face.

"Of course, he never really enjoyed me. If he had, it would have been different."

With a pang, Belinda remembered the look of passionate pleasure she had seen on Kevin's face the fraction of a moment before he had seen her staring at him and his lover in bed.

"But think about your situation. Pity Kevin's loss. He's probably wandering around Europe somewhere, trying to solace himself with museums and galleries, no doubt without any comfortable personal relationship. Bless the experience of your love affair for what it gave you; it seems to have been wonderful, or you wouldn't hurt right now.

Go into it, analyze it—aside from the last scene. I've been to his studio, I've posed for him. I like him. He's an original. I know the whole scene. Delightful Bohemia."

Seeing a flicker of her lids, he held up his hand quickly.

"Oh, no," he said, "no whoopsie-boo between us. Thanks for the compliment. You must understand, homosexuality doesn't necessarily mean constant promiscuity. As a matter of fact, he bored me, talking endlessly about your beauty and your bright mind and the great times he'd had with you, talking and looking at books, and your enchantment."

"He said that?" said Belinda.

He saw the hopefulness in her eyes.

"Belinda," he said sharply, "forgive me, but he was trying to convince himself. Also, take a look at the rest of his life. What would the quality of your life be? And speaking of that, don't neglect your talent. You'll discover it's your best friend. You had some pretty fantastic beginnings in Rome. By the way, I understand that social fellow, Scott Stone, is mad about you."

"He is," said Belinda, "but I just—just don't feel anything for him. He's been out of town on business, and I don't miss him a bit; just the getting around is attractive."

"Have you tried very hard to be—ah, personal with him?"

"Well, no. He treats me like a china doll."

"That can be corrected," said Leslie. "It's up to you, dear girl." He arose imperiously.

She embraced him. "You've helped," she said. "Thank you."

"Well," said Leslie, "I hope I haven't confused you, talking about sex and love. I'm certain, since even great philosophers never quite worked it out, it's beyond me. These are only my findings; others may feel differently. The only thing I've convinced myself of is that love is rarely permanent, and if we just accepted it for the moment and relished it as it is, we'd be much better off."

"You mean we should just take it day by day?"

"I guess we'd have to have constant amnesia for that to work," said Leslie.

He looked at his watch. "I must run. I have an engagement. I mustn't keep him waiting. He's too good-looking and too young to take the risk." For a moment he looked sad.

"I'm getting old. Even though I have a gymnast come to my house every morning to keep me fit, how can I compete with all those gorgeous physiques in my society? It takes fame and money to make up for not being young. And even then I have to turn a blind eye and a deaf ear to what goes on behind my back."

He turned to the mirror and patted the perfection of his carefully groomed hair.

"You look great," said Belinda, feeling sorry for him. She kissed him on the cheek. As she left, she had the fleeting notion that Leslie was like an old sugar daddy who was going to take out a young chorus girl. Well, she thought, maybe it's the same, only it's a chorus boy.

Even though she was trying desperately to be sophisticated about the Pandora's box he had opened, her car almost steered itself with her thoughts.

She drove toward the beach, abandoned Wilshire Boulevard, and turned south on Lincoln; past the marshland to the tacky part of Venice, where the old houses and the oil pumps were interspersed.

Leslie had told her so many things her head was whirling. But her feelings about Kevin were revived. He had really loved her, no matter what his other problems were.

She came to Kevin's house, and her heart beat as she parked the car. Stepping out, she saw where her car had smashed against the fence post.

What would happen if she opened the door and saw him standing there at his easel?

A plastic tricycle lay on its side in the center of the open garage, and she saw a string of laundry where his small garden had held several chairs. As she entered, her heart beating, a woman came out of the house, followed by a snotty-nosed little boy who rushed to his bicycle and got on it, looking at Belinda as if he thought she might steal it. The woman pulled the dry laundry off the line and stared at her.

"Yeah?" she said. "I suppose you lookin' for Kevin Frazier? He isn't here anymore. We're renters."

"No," said Belinda hastily. "I must have the wrong address."

Belinda walked down the street to an empty lot. She waded through wild oat weeds to the sandy beach. The tide was low, the wavelets made a soft sound as they sucked sand into their rills. Ripples of foam looked like soapsuds. A few strands of seaweed and some globs of oil littered the edges of the surf. Several gulls swooped and soared. Sandpipers on their thin legs skittered along pecking at their unseen dinners in a veil of tide—reflecting themselves, letting out their thin, sad cry.

She walked along the shore and looked back at the house. Where she and Kevin used to come back to the welcoming glow of the fire, there was no light.

The dwelling that had once been a repository of so much love was a shabby old driftwood shack with a raised peak where a skylight had been added.

She slowly walked back across the sand, halted once by the limp carcass of a dead pelican, its broken neck somehow twisted into the noose of an oily piece of rope. She wondered if it had died that way, or whether the two things had drifted in a strange juxtaposition of fate to lie at her feet on the desolate shore.

She got into the car. The street was full of the stink of creosote and oil, the flowers were flattened, and the sky was dull. Cats and stray dogs and shabby people inhabited the dirty streets.

She drove back to the beach house where the entrance was neater and cleaner than she had remembered.

"How did it go?" asked Claudia.

"Fine," said Belinda. "Guess what? I'm going on tour with old Grace Boomer and Leslie Charles."

"Well," said Claudia, smiling, "at least you'll be safe."

"I'll be safe," said Belinda.

How sad it is to be safe, she thought as she went upstairs.

11

The *Sprite* cut through the foaming crests of the waves, which made a hissing sound. Belinda sat at the bow looking up at the billowing sail and half-closed her eyes, seeing rainbows of fine spray against the sun.

In the distance, the clusters of buildings along the shore, and the brown hills beyond, with occasional clumps of greenery, and the bright blue afternoon sky were a clean, pure panorama, without the close-up of clutter that coursed so busily over the many streets and highways. How the sea and the coast disassociated itself from the land, on a boat, Belinda thought. Her cheeks were hot, and the cool, stinging spray felt good against her skin.

Scott moved up from the cockpit and joined her, balancing a paper plate of sandwiches.

"I'll bring you a drink next trip," he said.

"Never mind," she said, smiling up at him. "This is tonic enough!" Tanned, handsome in his white ducks and crew neck sweater, he belonged on this beautiful Rhodes sloop. They'd gone out of San Pedro Harbor in the morning on a broad reach, headed toward Catalina. They had leaned toward Newport, picking up mileage. The sloop, canvas billowing, bucking a hard sea, sometimes careened, her lee rail underwater.

At first, Belinda had been astonished that the tilt was so severe, bracing herself and digging her heels against supports. Penny and Harry Howard, who owned the *Sprite*, watched her to see if she was going to go below seasick and sack out like most landlubbers. But she asked if she could do anything and struggled below, braced her knees against the sink and the small refrigerator, and managed to hand them chilled cans of beer on deck.

"Excuse me," she said, holding a railing, "if I'm clumsy. I didn't know boats leaned like this. My last boating experience was on Niadas's three-hundred-foot yacht in the Aegean."

Penny Howard sought to look into her eyes through her fluff of billowing blonde hair, wondering if she were trying to one-up them. She decided Belinda was guileless; much younger and more forthright than she had expected a movie star would be.

Belinda laughed. "But the *Circe* was like a hotel. I used to long to get into one of the Greek fishing boats where people were having fun."

"Good lord," said Penny, "tell us about the *Circe*. I've read about it, but I never thought I'd know anyone who actually lived on it."

Belinda saw that Harry, too, was intrigued with her story; suddenly, for the first time, she saw interest on their faces.

"Sometime, but not now. I don't want to miss anything," she said. "Can I go up front?"

"Forward," corrected Scott, smiling and taking her hand. "I have a lot to learn," she said.

The Howards had signaled approval of her to each other. She had dressed properly, wore no makeup; she fitted in.

Belinda thought about her father's yacht, the *Zahma*. Somewhere among her books was his log. She had looked at it often, longing for him. Now, for a moment, Jeffrey Barstow was with her as the waves turned transparent through the sun. But her solitude was not for long.

Now that the trip was ending, Scott moved closer to her and put his arm around her shoulder.

"I'm so proud of you! You're a good sailor. I've tried to be very circumspect," he said, "but I just can't be much longer. I think I love you more now, sitting with your hair blowing in the wind, than I even have holding you in my arms when we dance."

Belinda looked up at him, wondering how such a sophisticated man could be so defenseless. Before she could say anything, he moved close to her and kissed her.

She couldn't help but compare. It was not an earthy, promising kiss like Kevin's; there was no fire in it. He pressed his lips against hers; there was no force in him to part her lips; to find the woman, search her mouth. It was a tender, surface kiss.

She considered parting her lips slightly to see if he would pursue with his tongue, but as Harry turned the boat against the wind, in the snap of canvas and the jolt of hard sea against the hull, the moment was lost, and they scrambled back to the cockpit.

Once there, as they sat, backed by canvas pillows, the Howards started planning the evening.

"We'll have drinks aboard at the dock and then dine at the club. I'm starving, are you?" she said to Belinda.

"Famished," she said. She put her hands to her face. "But I'm afraid I got sunburned. My face is hot."

"I hope you're all right," said Scott.

"Oh, I'm fine," she said. "It's just that I have a sitting tomorrow. You know, getting ready for the premiere. My dress for the fashion sections of the local papers, and all that."

"Oh, it must be fun!" said Penny.

"It's not," said Belinda. "It's all hard work. Getting the act together, as they say."

"Why don't you go below? There's some lotion in the cabinet in the head," said Penny.

After she left, they turned to Scott.

"Well," said Penny, "she's a great gal. Too bad she's a film star."

She said it kindly, as a woman who was pitying the flaw in a pet.

"Well, she may not always be," said Scott. "I think I'm going to marry that girl."

"Scott!" said Penny. "Have you asked her?"

"Not yet," he said.

"Isn't she a bit pampered? How are you going to measure up to Niadas's three-hundred-foot yacht?" said Harry.

Scott waved it away. "You heard what she said. She's not a bit pretentious."

"Does Auntie Flora know?" said Penny.

"For God's sake, skip it," said Scott. "I was premature."

"Well, darling," said Penny, "I'd like to be there when you tell *her*! Once a film star, always a film star."

Belinda, in the small cabin below, heard them. There was no motor, no sound but the soft sea. She stood staring into the mirror in the head, putting lotion on her reddened face, stunned, automatically shaking the bottle over and over while she gathered her thoughts. She quietly closed the door to the head and sat for a moment on the toilet seat, bracing herself against the odd angle of the boat. These people had liked her, she had done her best to fit in, and yet the innate snobbery in their voices cut her. Even Scott, dismissing her career by saying she might not always be a film star, as if she might possibly recover from a disease. How dare he make such an ultimatum on so little authority! What did they know about her, or what she could do? Or what she had to be.

For the first time, she came face-to-face with herself as an actress. It had never entered her mind that anyone would criticize what she was doing. She had thought it set her apart. Nobody was going to stop her from doing what she was supposed to do. Nobody was going to tell her what her future was going to be. She came from a line of distinguished performers, that was where she belonged, and anything else that entered her life was going to be secondary. No more men to put her off her path. Thank God Kevin's affair hadn't ruined her performance as Lucretia. Instead, she had used the turmoil. It had helped her. And if this socialite thought she was going to dance to his tune, he was wrong. If there was to be any dancing, if it suited her, he would do it.

It was a good thing her face was flaming from the sun; it saved her from flushing when she came back on deck.

After they docked and sat in the evening on deck, drinking martinis, friends from other boats dropped by.

She noted that the men eyed her furtively, looking for that publicized sex symbol in her, and disappointed that red-faced, dressed in her white slacks and sweater and her blue pea jacket, there seemed to be no evidence of her publicized charms. The women, she noted, were a little more inclined to pretend she wasn't a celebrity, but just one of them. Not knowing exactly how to treat a celebrity, they addressed their conversation elsewhere. Several she had met with Mrs. Stone Random, and they all made a fuss over Scott, telling him how handsome he was and asking where he had been lately, they hadn't seen him. She was aware of the fact that he was the catch of the lot.

They talked endlessly about yachting. Someone had done the *funniest* thing in the Ensenada race. They'd dropped a cherry bomb in the toilet at Hussong's bar, and flushed it, and the explosive had gone off in the pipes, blowing up the floor and scattering sewage all over the commodore and the committee at the bar.

This was greeted with roars of laughter, as the apogee of wit.

Someone else had been locked up in the local hoosegow, and it had taken large bribes to get him out, and then he had gone back to his yacht, fallen overboard, and had to be fished out, saying he wanted to go back to jail, it was safer. Someone else had picked up two hookers and brought them to his yacht, telling his wife they were the chief of police's daughters.

Out of context, it was deeply depressing to Belinda. Her face hurt more and more. Scott, watching her between his jaunts as bartender, came to her.

"Your face is bothering you, isn't it?" he said.

"It is, Scott," she said. "I hate to do this, but I'm shivering. I think I'd better get home. Do you mind?"

"You poor darling!" he whispered. "Of course I'll take you home."

He made his apologies. Everyone could see Belinda's face, and they said how sorry they'd be not to have dinner with her. It was as if they'd lost a Brownie point with other fellow members; they'd had a captive actress for the day.

As Belinda and Scott walked along the dock, there was a sudden silence on the boat. Belinda knew that as soon as she was out of earshot, they'd start gossiping. *What* was Mrs. Stone Random going to say when Scott told her he was going to marry an actress? No doubt they just hoped he'd wait until the charity was over; it might interfere with their benefit.

Scott bundled her in his jacket in the car, and his concern made her ashamed of herself for not appreciating him. He hadn't done anything except be, at least for her, a very dull man.

But she was too involved in her own misery to do anything but put her head on his shoulder and close her eyes.

Claudia met them in the hall.

"I'm sorry," said Scott, "but apparently Belinda got a fierce sunburn. The reflections on the water can creep up on you."

Claudia touched her face. "Oh my! I'd better put her to bed and call Dr. Saul."

"I'll stand by," said Scott, "and rush right to the drugstore if you need a prescription filled. It'll be faster that way."

"That would be nice," said Claudia.

She put Belinda to bed and put cold packs on her face. Scott rushed out for Benadryl, an antihistamine, sedatives to soothe the pain, and a steroid cream that was ordered to take away the redness.

Scott was desperate. "I feel terrible," he said. "It was all my fault. I should have taken care of her. That beautiful skin!"

"Don't worry," said Claudia. "Now you run along. She'll fall asleep soon. It's not your fault. She'll be fine. Call me tomorrow."

After he left, Claudia went upstairs, wondering what was going to happen with this young man. Belinda's face would certainly be well in a few days, but this man's emotions were a deeper problem. Belinda's impact on men was something that was going to have to be faced. There was nothing anyone could do about it.

She went into Belinda's room. Effie had just put icecold cloths on her face, and the pain pills were beginning to take effect.

"Is there anything you want?" said Claudia.

"No," said Belinda drowsily. "Effie gave me some broth by straw. Oh, Claudia, I overheard these friends of Scott's on the yacht. They were alerting him. They seem to think that being a movie star is being a freak."

"They're absolutely right," said Claudia. "We *are* freaks, darling. Nothing else seems important but being an actress when you are one."

"Don't make me laugh," said Belinda. "It hurts. And Scott said that maybe I wouldn't always be one—that he might marry me. How do you like that!"

"The nerve!" said Claudia. "He'd have about as much chance as a butterfly in a car wash!"

It seemed incredible to Claudia that a man who was practicing law could find so much time to call. He was finally told that Belinda was resting and the phone was out-of-bounds.

"Tell him I'll see him at the premiere," said Belinda.

The plans were organized by Mrs. Stone Random like a field general. Scott would pick up Belinda in a Rolls Royce limousine. They would join her at her mansion, where they would all have a little snack (which, by itself, would have paid the plane fare to and from the United States for two Vietnamese children) with the Project Babies president and her husband; the lieutenant governor of California; Leslie Charles; and dignitaries from Europe who had come to add éclat to the affair. They would all convoy to the theater where, in truth, the red carpet would be rolled out, with television cameras and radio microphones, master of ceremonies, interviewers, press, and a covey of photographers awaiting their every word and gesture.

After seven days in bed with cold packs, peeling skin, and medication, Belinda had rallied; her complexion, if anything, more pink, shining, and beautiful. In the interim, Scott had sent her so many dozens of gardenias that their sweet scent sickened her, and as they arrived they were put all over the house save in her bedroom.

"I never want to see another gardenia as long as I live!" said Belinda. "They give me migraines!"

He had sent her books, champagne, even a little pillow from Grande Maison Blanc on which was embroidered Browning's words, "One born to love you, sweet!"

Belinda had been gowned in a draped dress of scarlet silk jersey. The studio had decided it was time for her to look provocative. The classic, pure beauty of *The Oracle* was finished; as a mature actress, she was to be exciting.

Her hair was sleek and smooth, with a chignon at the nape of her neck, revealing the sculptured beauty of her forehead and cheekbones. Janos, delighted with the gown and a matching pleated cape that fell open and flared when she walked, like open poppy petals, suggested that she wear the ruby necklace and earrings that were in the Borgia portrait. But when they were presented to her, even Janos, who was used to scenes with spoiled female stars, was startled.

She picked them out of the satin-lined box and dashed them to the floor.

"I never want to see them again!" she said in a voice so quiet that it belied her actions. "Get them out of here! I hate them!"

Peggy, the wardrobe woman, knew why Belinda hated them, but Janos couldn't understand.

"She's going to be worse than any of them if she goes on this way!" he said later in the fitting room. "I don't understand. I did my best. Well, I give up. The little bitch can do her own thing with jewelry. I wash my hands!"

It seemed strange, for Belinda had never expressed anger or temper before.

On the evening of the premiere, she wore Niadas's ancient Mycenaean gold and pearl octopus with the uncut emerald eyes. It hung on its slender chain, dazzling and priceless against her bare shoulders, clinging to the curve of her breasts. It was her only ornament.

For the first time, her face was heavily made up.

Max, looking at her as she left with Scott, shook his head.

"I don't like to see that beautiful face masked like that," he said.

Claudia consoled him. "You can't hide her beauty. It's that damned sunburn," she said. "We had to cover it. The makeup does make her look older and more sophisticated, but that's what all young girls want to be."

"We're losing her, aren't we?" said Max. "Claudia, we can't fight anymore, we'll just have to let her go."

"It's inevitable," said Claudia. "We can't keep her wrapped in cotton wool, dear. We took her girlhood when she stepped into fame so quickly. Now we can't rob her of her young womanhood because we want to protect her. God knows it will be hard enough for her as it is; that *damned* pedestal. It puts her on constant display, privately and publicly. There's no way out."

Max took her hand as the doorbell rang and Effie went to answer it.

"Is it my fault?" he said.

"No, Max. Jessica pushed her too early. But it would have happened eventually. Well, maybe she'll get lucky when she's an old bag like me and find someone like you."

He kissed her.

Fergus was picking them up for Mrs. Stone Random's party. They would have to go through all the motions of being part of the glitter, but the evening would belong to Belinda, and that was the way it should be. Of course, Max would get his acclaim. Tony Valli was on location in

Australia; Titan had lent him out to Twentieth Century Fox. Leslie Charles would add style, escorting their hostess. He had been a sophisticated film figure for so long he had become a status symbol, forgiven, even by society, for being an actor.

When Belinda entered the Chinese Theater with Scott, even she was amazed at the ovation. Scott, seeing that his aunt and Leslie Charles were properly moving with them, was abashed by the bright lights. In the acid glare, he blinked. But Belinda, incandescent and illuminated, moved along the red pathway of the carpet. She seemed to flow, and then she paused, smiling slightly, looking up at Scott. She was magnificent, exotic from her scarlet slippers and clinging gown, to her cape falling away from her arms, revealing the ancient pearl and emerald jeweled octopus. There was a gasp at her beauty. And when Scott took her arm, there were cheers and whistles from the bleachers, a roar of doubled excitement and delight.

Scott was startled, but Fergus, following along, realized what was happening. The two of them made such an incredibly handsome picture that the audience had invented their own version of a famous scarlet and slightly scandalous Cinderella and a tall, classy, elegantly groomed American prince, and had elected them their favorites. The pair fulfilled the current fantasy of a romantic-hungry public.

Even Flora Stone Random didn't realize what was happening. She took it all as a signal of the success of her charity bash.

They made their comments on the dais, the master of ceremonies greeting them effusively. Belinda didn't even remember what she said. She moved on, and they started to interview Max.

The foyer of the theater had been transformed into one of the elegant Borgia suites. The Pinturicchio paintings had been erected on a false ceiling, and against a brocade wall, bright lights shone on the gallery of Kevin's paintings. They had been hung dramatically—her twin portraits, the innocent and the wicked, side by side. Red Powell came forward and shook her hand and greeted Scott.

"This is your night," he said. "I never saw a star get such an ovation. You look terrific!" He turned to Scott. "You lucky man!"

Scott smiled and held her arm.

"Now," said Red, "would you pose between your two pictures, Belinda?—Oh, look, what a break!"

He gestured, and Belinda followed his glance. There was Kevin Frazier. He was not wearing a dinner jacket, but a dark suit and a cashmere turtleneck. He was looking at his paintings.

Her heart beat fast. Why did she have to see Kevin under these conditions, with this crowd around her? Why couldn't they have been alone?

Scott was looking at her, as he had been all evening, enchanted with her. She wondered if he could see her pain, or if the flush of her hurt was showing on her face.

It really made no difference. He was suddenly boring to her. She couldn't think of anything to say. She stood spellbound.

"Well!" said Red, "this is a surprise, Kevin. I didn't know you were back. How fortuitous! We must get your picture with Belinda and the paintings."

Kevin turned and looked at Belinda. He had been drawn to the theater. He had no wish to be noticed, but he had been away for a long time, and he wanted to see his portraits, framed and dramatically lighted and presented as had been planned. They were his masterpieces—the final product of his life and skill, and he knew it.

Red took him by the arm. He stared at Belinda a cool moment and then pulled away from Red's grasp.

"No—," said Kevin, "I think not."

He moved away. Belinda, shocked, watched him, his dark tousled hair, the face she had memorized. How could he walk away like this? He joined another man, and they drifted into the pushing mass of people who were being held back by several studio guards.

She was frozen. The moment to contact him was gone. The evening was spoiled.

Red smiled. "Shy, I guess. You know how artists are."

"That man certainly is rude," said Scott. "Who is he?"

"He's the man who painted these portraits," said Red hastily. "Eccentric."

Red wondered if Scott Stone had heard the gossip about Kevin and Belinda. Probably not; it wasn't in the *Wall Street Journal*. Anyway, it had been a mistake, an impulsive gesture on his part. Fortunately, the bank of cameramen were focusing on the next celebrities who had come into the foyer.

"You'd better get to your seats before they let in the cattle," Red told them.

Belinda and Scott followed the elect who were segregated behind gold-tasseled ropes in the choice seats.

For the first time at a premiere, Claudia was not next to Belinda. On one side of her was Scott, on the other Leslie Charles.

The picture began with great applause and fanfare. The audience had paid, and it was going to enjoy the evening. As the film progressed, Belinda could tell, as in the preview, that the Borgia court scenes, heavy with intrigue, were too long. But as her character grew in the scenes she dominated, the large programs stopped rustling and people moved out of their lethargy to watch her. In the one scene where she castigated her brother Cesare and threw poisoned wine in his face, there was applause. The crowd gasped at the slaughter of the bull in Cesare's bedroom, and several people left the theater.

Several seats away, during Belinda's dramatic scene with Leslie, as he wept over his murdered son, she saw that Claudia was leaning forward slightly. Claudia raised her hand in a salute. Leslie patted her arm fondly. It was their moment in the film.

Belinda felt in her purse for the talisman, the chunk of amber her father had given her aunt to keep for her. As a matter of fact, Claudia had given it to her, almost in this same row of seats, when *The Oracle* had finished its first showing. Belinda clutched it and felt it grow warm in her hand, but in her heart was no feeling of exaltation as she had known before.

She felt she had sold herself short in doing the role as she had. A girlish bitterness because of an unfortunate love affair had triggered her performance. She had not faced the reality of acting, the inner stimulation and spirit, supported by her craft, that would have made her rise above herself if she had listened to the role and known the woman. Talent was a platform from which one was carried beyond one's own self. She had not been the vessel of talent in this picture. Her performance was spotty, and she would have given anything to do the first scenes over, where she had drifted soporifically in the grasp of an off-scene love affair which at that moment was possessing her strength and drive.

She was in a turmoil. How brutal Kevin had been just now in the lobby. She could have been a stranger. He hadn't even had the grace to speak to her. Her insides twisted with the thought that he would see all the scenes she had done so bitterly and violently with Tony Valli, and he would know why.

She wondered about the man he was with, and she was washed in a wave of misery. This was no evening of triumph for her.

During the scene where she embraced the child of her dreadful incest, Scott took her hand.

"You're a magnificent actress," he whispered.

She looked up at his eyes, glowing in the reflection of the screen, and the moment seemed symbolic. He loved her, and he protected her as no man ever had. She thought of her decision, after the first knife thrust of her broken affair with Kevin, that she wouldn't fall in love again. It hurt too much. She would find a man who would care for her, she would get married and be free, have friends around her, take sex on its own terms, enjoy it all, do her work, and have a good life.

She took his hand and put it against her cheek.

"You're pretty wonderful yourself, Scott."

His doom was sealed. His heart was so full that he couldn't focus on the screen. He simply sat there waiting for it all to be finished, so he could somehow see her alone, take her in his arms, and ask her to marry him. It seemed incredible after all his courting and her shyness that at this moment of her triumph on the screen, she had revealed her love to him.

The evening seemed endless. He had looked forward to it, but now, with the hopes that caused his pulse to beat faster, he suffered. He went through the endless Crystal Room banquet and then the drop-off at his aunt's mansion, having to stop for another drink and excited chat, as much about how much money the charity made as about the film. He jettisoned the car and chauffeur, and having left his Porsche at his aunt's house, he drove Belinda to the beach.

"I'm so tired," she said. "Isn't it a long evening when they crowd you in? Did you mind that fanfare so terribly?"

"I wouldn't mind anything if you were with me," he said.

They went into the house; Claudia and Max had already retired.

"Let's go out by the pool," she said. "It's quiet out there, and we can walk on the sand. I'll kick my shoes off."

It was brilliant moonlight. He opened the gate and they walked out by the sea. As he looked at her in the darkness, her slender throat seemed to rise out of the duskiness of her gown and cape like a flower stem—her face the blossom, the tendrils of her blonde hair escaping like petals and curling at her temples.

As she looked at the water, she thought of Kevin's house and the dead pelican. She mustn't, she mustn't! It was poison to her soul.

She looked at Scott and as they stopped she saw the adoration on his face. She put her arms up and wrapped them over his shoulders.

"Hold me," she said.

He bent to kiss her, and her lips parted slightly. This time he kissed her as a man should, for he felt that now she wanted him.

She hoped he would stimulate excitement in her, but it was not there. At least, she thought, not yet . . .

He reluctantly pulled away. "We're going to get married," he said. "There's no other way I want to spend my life but loving you."

She looked up at him. She knew every girl in Los Angeles society would give anything to have him.

"Yes, Scott," she whispered.

After they walked back to the house, she held his hand.

"It isn't going to be easy," she said. "You know, I have to go on with my work. I have obligations. Can you take them? I hope so, for it is the only way I could say yes."

For a second he was taken aback. But looking at her, he was ashamed of himself. He could not be selfish. Things would work out. Most of all, he wanted her.

"Whatever you say," he said.

He looked down at the beauty of her breasts.

She smiled at his glance. "You'd better go," she whispered. "We're not married yet."

He left her reluctantly, but in his heart he was thrilled at her modesty, her decorum. It was going to be so fantastic to take that beautiful body in his arms, to strip her of her shyness, to love her and give her everything she should have, including passionate devotion.

On the way out, he almost stumbled over a little plastic wagon that had been left by the side of an umbrella stand near the door.

My God, he thought as he found his way to his car in a daze, she even has a little brother, and a mother I haven't seen. I'll have to know them and, for her, I'll have to love them all.

On the way home, fighting euphoria, his mind whirled. He'd have to tell Aunt Flora immediately. His father was dead, and his mother lived in an apartment on Wilshire Boulevard. They hadn't been so well-off during the last years. He'd had to struggle to get his law degree at Harvard, and he had been a peon in Mulveny's law offices in Los Angeles. Sometimes the young hopefuls worked so far into the night that they had to sack out in a small dormitory hidden behind the library in the offices.

Only recently had he been more than a junior partner in his law office in Westwood. But things were moving. He had ideas that would have upset Aunt Flora, but it was not her life, it was his. And what he aimed to do would fall in very well with Belinda's career, since she chose to continue it. Well, give her time and love and a family, and she would certainly change her point of view.

Feeling too excited to sleep, he went to his apartment at Century City and looked out toward the ocean. He could barely see the rim of the sea; but he looked at it, smiling. That's where his love was sleeping.

```
★★★★★★★★★★★★★★★★★★
★                    ★
★        12          ★
★                    ★
★★★★★★★★★★★★★★★★★★
```

Flora Stone Random sat in her queen size bed playing
queen. Her girlish ruffled canopied bed was in contrast to
her florid face and the wisps of gray-blonde hair that hung
to her shoulders. They did not have to be very long, for
she had practically no neck.

Two apricot poodles sat on her feet, and her satin comforter was littered with phone books, newspaper clippings,
and the latest issue of *American Astrology*.

On her bed tray was a Haviland china breakfast set and
a rose in a Waterford bud vase. The side slots of the tray
were crammed with mail: announcements, advertisements,
and invitations, which had all been gashed open by her
busy silver letter opener. She did not allow her secretary,
Miss Monk, the intimacy of looking at the dividends of
her life until she herself had assayed their worth and separated the pay dirt from the dross.

This morning Flora was utterly ecstatic, holding her
scepter, the earphone of her silver-mounted telephone, and
reaching out to bestow favors on her subjects. She was
gloating over the returns of the previous evening. A dozen
sycophants had called saying she had never looked lovelier,
the party was superb, the food divine, and the take a great
success. There was little criticism of the film—this was
not the time—for the charity was the main event.

She had already relayed the good news that the $28,000
required by the theater to break even was more than paid,
and the overall profits were accelerating.

Half the people she spoke to commented on the fact that
Belinda Barstow and Scott Stone were the best-looking
couple they'd ever seen.

Her gushing answer to this was always a decibel louder than her previous conversation.

"Of course," she said, "Scott is so darling. He always does his best to help me with my charities. All the girls are mad for him. I don't blame that young Barstow girl. I imagine in her métier she hasn't met anyone with his style. But wait until you see what's coming up! Senator Schmidt's daughter is coming in from Washington next month for my Books for Our Boys Abroad luncheon. She's adorable—black curly hair, blue eyes, a great horsewoman, a real blue-ribbon winner, my dear. Pure aristocrat. She and Scott are going to look divine together, and they'll help our benefit no end!"

She had just hung up when her secretary buzzed. She picked up the phone, raptly smiling as if it were a TV camera.

"Mr. Stone is here to see you," said Miss Monk's eager voice. She always perked up around Scott.

"Well, isn't he the early bird? Of course, have him come up." She dropped her smile; Miss Monk didn't deserve it.

She picked up the hand mirror that was tucked under her lace pillow, fluffed her hair, took a lipstick from the side table and inexpertly overrouged her mouth, sprayed a little lily of the valley on the bedside lamp bulb, and told the doggies to be good and not bark, their Uncle Scott was coming in.

Scott entered, circumnavigating delft dog dishes, scattered newspapers, and some pink satin mules on the floor for show (two lambskin moccasins were half-hidden under the lace dust ruffle).

Flora looked at him. "Well, aren't you the happy one? You were an absolute darling last night, helping me out with Belinda Barstow. Dear, what brings you here so early?"

"I wanted to talk to you," he said.

"Well, Scott," she said archly, "aren't you going to tell me how successful the party was last night?"

"It was great."

"Did you have a good time?"

"That's what I wanted to talk to you about, Aunt Flora. Your party has changed my life."

"Well, that's nice. How, dear?"

"Aunt Flora, I'm going to marry Belinda."

Her knees jerked, the two dogs were kicked aside, the wicker bed tray rose up, and the empty teapot fell sideways, splitting the thin teacup neatly in half.

"You what!" she said, her face a mask of horror.

Scott set the tray on a table and continued. "Don't look so startled," he said. "You certainly must have thought that one day I'd fall in love and get married."

She leaned back on her pillows, staring at him. Her hand reached for the cloisonné phial of smelling salts that she always kept on hand.

"I just can't believe you!" she said, inhaling deeply. "You must be mad!"

He suddenly realized he was facing a hostile.

"But Aunt Flora, you must understand. I know you aren't wild about theater people, but Belinda's different. She's a very sweet and gifted girl. And her Aunt Claudia is a darling. You've been proud to have her help you in the charity."

"Proud!" said Flora. "You must be out of your mind. Claudia had a very chancy reputation around here as a young woman. I have heard she was the mistress of that man who owned Titan studio. *And* she got around on the side, mind you, a great deal."

Scott flushed. "She's a married woman now, and devoted to her family. It's all right for you to use them," he said, "then discard them like a squeezed lemon."

"I gave her the dignity of helping me with a worthy cause. And by the way, that is a *dreadful* film. I'd never have taken it if I'd known there was so much depravity in it. How could you think of marrying a girl who portrayed a character like Lucretia Borgia?"

"She's an actress," said Scott. "She can't play little Mary Sunshine all the time."

Flora resorted to her last stand: tears.

"To think," she said pitifully, "that you would do this to me. After all the trouble I went through to make you the social catch of the town, in spite of the fact you don't have a fortune behind you. You will be *drummed* out of the Los Angeles Country Club. They won't allow an actress to belong. Well, my dear, even my friend Hector Dunne was turned down for membership because he worked as an assistant manager at the Biltmore Theater twenty years ago. And when the club has its dinners, what will you do about her stepfather? He's a Jew. Have you thought of that!"

He stared at her, shocked. "You're just like most of the old guard in this town. When you need theater people to perform or give you a little publicity, you use them. Then, heave-ho. Well, let me tell you, this time you're going to be stuck with it because she's going to be in the family."

She wiped her eyes and blew her nose. "I'm only trying to help you, Scott. You must not be blinded by this—this foolish infatuation. You must think of her heritage, my dear. Her father was a dreadful drunk. And a man-about-town in the worst way. She comes from a long line of *thespians*." She spit out the word as if it were the pox.

"You were reared to be a gentleman. You went to Harvard, you belonged to the best clubs. You've only known the best. Where is your gratitude? You don't know how often I have scraped to make you a prince—A prince!"

"Now wait a minute," said Scott. "My father wasn't quite destitute. He managed to get me through Harvard, and now I earn my own way."

"I'm not talking about money, I'm talking about prestige. I cannot allow you to mix our blood with that of wandering minstrels."

Scott started to light a cigarette and then he crushed it out on the bed tray.

Flora threw back her bedcovers; she wore a peignoir over her nightgown, and as she moved, the sheets tangled with her heavy legs, and her fleshy oyster-white feet were revealed. She slipped into the high-heeled mules, walked unsteadily to the window, and gestured.

"Look at that garden," she said, wiping her eyes and snuffling. "I designed it with the dream that one day you, my heir, the child I never had, would bring your bride and our friends to stand among its graceful poplars."

"Bullshit," said Scott.

She turned and looked at him, her mouth agape. "How dare you use that word!"

"I'll use any word I want," he said, "and there are plenty to express how I feel about the way you are behaving."

She lifted her hands in despair.

"Already your association with her and her way of life is making you vulgar. I have no words for how I feel, but she'll never enter *my* doors again."

"I have words for how *I* feel," said Scott. "Don't you be so uppity about Belinda. You could drive an angel to hell with your way of life. It's completely larcenous."

She looked at him, her face mottled, and she swayed as if she were going to faint.

"Don't be so shocked," he said. "You were hell on wheels to your poor husband. You were psychologically behind that smoking pistol that ended his life."

She sank into a chair, her hand at her heart, or at least at her breast, which without her corsets was just above her navel.

"I know the poor bastard blew his brains out in the wine cellar because he was broke. Broke, with $5,000 worth of fancy French wine behind him; too bad the bullet also smashed several precious bottles. Broke, with $350,000 worth of Wedgewood, Royal Berlin, Dalton china, Georgian silver, Aubusson rugs, and uncomfortable Louis Quatorze furniture in a jumble all around him."

He walked in front of her. "Don't give me the waterworks; it's too late. You lost him, old girl, to hang onto your friggin' vitrines jam-packed with crap. Everything in them is tainted with his heart's blood."

"I only tried to make a fitting life for our dynasty," she sobbed.

"Dynasty!" he snorted. "Since when are we aristocrats! My great-grandfather was a grocer in Peoria, and he moved west because he got caught selling flour full of weevils. And even he would be dismayed at what you are doing."

"What do you mean!" she said. "I contribute my *life* to charities."

"More bull," he said. "Look, I know what your trust fund is, and I know what your living expenses are. It's very devious. You are a crook. Every time you give a charity, you're on the take. You're milking money out of the mouths of babes, so you can be the hostess with the mostest. You should be in jail!"

She collapsed, sobbing. She was deflated, smaller than she was a moment ago when she had stalked across the room. Gone were the sweeping gestures. She looked up at him, her eyes wide under her thin hair, her hands clasped.

"Don't try to pull that scene on me," he said. "It won't work. For the first time, I'm rising up on my hunkers. In my business, I have had to use social connections. I know it, and all the guys who slaved with me to get their law degrees know it. All of us who worked earned our tickets to wear Brooks Brothers' suits and Charvet ties and be polite—if that's what we need to get where we're going. We worked eighteen hours a day until our eyes dropped out. We won the prestige of being associated with the *Law Review*. We danced with plain girls and opened the doors for old clients who bored us to death with their niggling made and remade wills, their sour breath, their tediousness. After all this, if we made it, we earned ten thousand a year as a junior partner, paying our back debts and putting up a front so we could get into more debt. So don't one-up me with your morality—you with your illicit income."

"I only want the best for you," she whispered.

"You wouldn't recognize the best if it bit you," he said, "because your values are so lousy. You've done your best to reduce Belinda Barstow to a beggar in rags."

She hobbled back to the bed and pulled back the covers to protect her.

"I never should have seen you today," she said. "I should have known Uranus is squaring Saturn."

He looked at her as she plumped up the pillows. It came to him that she had always lived in a world of illusion, bounded by the pedigreed poodles, the Chantilly lace pillows, the silver phone, and her dreams of elegance. He doubted she saw herself in the mirror. Instead, a little Dresden shepherdess smiled at her as she fixed her hair and relished her social dreams. In a moment, secure in her own nest, she corked her phial of ammoniated smelling salts. As if preparing a momentous statement, she put her hand out and smiled at him.

"You don't know much about this girl," she said. "At least wait a little while. After all, you are used to the establishment, and you may miss it more than you think."

"I love her and I'm marrying her," he said. "And there's no use talking to you. You just won't listen. What do you think I'm doing, stepping into a goldfish bowl?"

He walked out angrily, slamming the door.

At the beach, Claudia was facing a similar scene. Belinda was sitting up in her bed, Effie's breakfast setup on a wicker tray in front of her.

"I'm sorry," she said. "I know it distresses you, but Claudia, it's my life, and I'm going to marry him."

Claudia sat in a slipper chair and looked at the transparency of her own hands to keep from looking up. She didn't want Belinda to see the pain in her eyes.

"Couldn't I just ask you to wait a little while? You're young, you know, and so many fascinating men will cross your path. I like him, dear, but he just doesn't seem to be the one who has excited you. There's no reason to rush—is there?"

Belinda waved her hand, then sipped her orange juice. "If you mean what I think you mean, heavens, no! I haven't had anything to do with him."

"Well," said Claudia, "this may seem strange coming from your elder, but don't you think it might be a good idea to find out how you feel about him in bed before you plunge into marriage?"

"I can't this time," she said. "It's a different thing with him. He's crazy about me; I think he'd consider it wrong."

"Well, what are you going to do? Are you going to tell him about your past experience. What about Alex? And Kevin?"

"I've been thinking about it," said Belinda. "You told me you'd take Alex. I could always take him in as my little brother later. But what am I going to do about not being a virgin? I know he thinks I'm—pure."

Belinda looked down. Claudia pitied her. She was so naïve, in spite of her experience.

"You think it would be better if he thinks he's uh—deflowering you on your wedding night, is that it?"

"That's it," said Belinda. "Look, Claudia, I don't expect bells to ring anymore, but I want to be free, to have a home of my own, have friends, do my work, and have a handsome man crazy about me. Is that bad?"

"That isn't bad at all," said Claudia. "Half the girls in the world would think you're the luckiest. But it doesn't always work that way. And also, you must be prepared to land in a nest of WASPS, because that's his background."

"I'll be busy," said Belinda. "I won't have to play that

game too much. But about the other, what do I do? Go have an operation?"

"You mean about virginity?" said Claudia.

She nodded.

"Heavens no!" said Claudia. "If you insist on going through with this, you need ingenuity, and a little courage."

"How would that work?"

"Well, first of all, get a douche bag and some alum. Give yourself an alum douche just before you get in bed. Believe me, that has been done before. Some men prefer that little thing tight anyway. I understand when the deposed King Carol of Romania, and his mistress, Madame Lupescu, had to abdicate, they found a sack of alum under her bed in the palace."

Belinda made a face. "That makes everything awfully clinical."

"Well, dear girl, that's what it is. And that's not all."

"What else?"

"You know the old Arabian legends about the bridegroom hanging out the sheepskin after the first night so the whole village would know by the bloodstain that he had deflowered his wife. In some societies, if this did not happen, the bride could be sent in disgrace back to her family."

"You mean I have to bleed, too?" said Belinda.

"Absolutely, if you're going through with this farce. You'll have to hide something, like a little penknife, nearby, and have the courage to cut yourself so that you will bleed. Are you up to that?"

"It's no worse than having a baby in a Greek cave."

"Right," said Claudia.

She went to the bed, bent over, and kissed Belinda on the forehead.

"I like Scott," she said. "I know Scott will be honorable with you. I hope you will be honorable with him, although I deplore you taking this step."

"Why?" said Belinda. "I think I'm lucky."

"I think you don't love him," said Claudia.

She left the room, hoping the details she'd given Belinda on instant virginity would make her change her mind. It was sad to think that Belinda, so young, was already learning that her way of life was not a gift—it was a negotiation.

```
*********************
*                   *
*        13         *
*                   *
*********************
```

Belinda and Scott's romance caused much more turbulence in various circles than either of them realized.

Belinda was torn with the thoughts of stepping into a living relationship with Scott, but she had no choice. It was her only way out of a situation where she had no control of her actions, no choices in what she was going to do for herself.

She remembered her decision to marry an attractive man who would adore her. From then on, she would do what she wanted. Forget being in love.

When Scott had come into her life, he seemed to have been prefabricated for the plan she had in mind. And he was much more attractive and important than she had dreamed for someone who would be the deliberate solution to her problem.

Before meeting Scott, she had considered getting in touch with Si Merkle, the slick young agent who could have taken care of her career; he would have been her slave. She had even considered patching up the feud with Vernon Miles, the brilliant writer who had picketed her dressing room. His play had opened in New York, and it was a smash hit. She knew that with a few words and a dinner she could have won him. Perhaps he could be the Arthur Miller in her life. Look how Miller had advanced Marilyn Monroe's background when they were together; and he certainly could take a more modern approach to her career needs than Max, with his overwhelming historical dramas. She even considered Homer Case, the attractive choreographer who wrote sensitive poetry to her and had a beautiful physique. He had the potential of being a dancing star on his own, with a little help and promotion.

Even Hugh Fairfield, the New York banker, had come to mind. Elegant and attentive, he was in his late thirties, a bachelor, and his Wall Street connections might help her establish her own corporation.

Any of them would have been satisfactory for her deliberate plan to be an independent woman.

The only way to beat the time machine was to marry immediately, so that she could gain access to her own funds and set up her life on her own terms.

But Scott had surpassed all of her previous considerations. He was not only attractive, but he could give her even more importance than she had expected, and he would not have to be carried along on her power. The two of them, in appearance alone, would hit not only picture publicity, but the slick magazines; wherever they went, they would be a photographic event.

She put their pictures upstairs in her room; she took his numerous phone calls and tried desperately to find the deep instinctive sexual stirrings she had known before. She wanted to have a feeling of excitement when she talked to him, she wanted to long for his body when she heard his voice, she wanted to dream of rushing into his bed.

When it did not happen, she hoped that their day-to-day life would eventually make it come true. She had heard a marriage could grow into a love affair.

But she had no idea of the larger problems that the change in her life was bringing about.

It began at home with Claudia and Max. It filtered into the life of Mrs. Flora Stone Random, and a social feud with Henrietta Stone, Scott's mother; it went into the studio with Fergus, and to David Austin flying back from Europe; it flowed into the whole publicity campaign of Titan's picture. It eventually would spread into the coffers of Titan Corporation, which was gasping for life.

While Belinda was thinking of what flat silver and dishes she would start with, and Scott was dreaming of the time he would get Belinda away from her career and into his bed, the distress of many people was hidden from them.

"Can't you do anything with her?" Fergus paced in his office, a cigarette almost burning his fingers.

"Watch out, Fergie," said Claudia, "you're going to burn your bloodless index finger."

He looked down hastily and snuffed out the cigarette. Too nervous to even give her an amused grimace, he went to the window overlooking the studio. It was late afternoon. Claudia wondered how many times he had computed in his mind how many people under salary were losing him how much money by leaving a few moments early instead of being where they should be.

"At this time in her life, and with our picture promotion so important, why does she have to get married? It disturbs her image tremendously."

"It disturbed her image when you sicced that Italian sexpot on Kevin."

"We won't go into that," said Fergus. "Otherwise, she'd be shacked up with that bisexual in Laurel Canyon right now."

"Well," said Claudia, "you've got a point. That would be worse, wouldn't it? This Scott is a very attractive, nice young man."

"Who doesn't know," said Fergus, "that she has a child, and that she's always had hot pants for someone else. My God, aside from deploring the situation, I pity him."

"So do I," said Claudia, "and I pity her, too."

"Why is she doing it?" said Fergus. "I don't see any signs of mad passion. I've seen them enough to recognize that it's all on his side."

"She's doing it," said Claudia, "partly because of the breakup of her first love affair. You ought to know enough about women, Fergus, to realize that she has to prove that someone wants her madly. And also, and very importantly, she wants to belong to the grown-up world. She wants to lead what she thinks will be her own life; she wants to get away from me and Max. I might as well admit it. We're momma and poppa figures who tuck her in, structure her days, and tell her what her future is going to be. It's a strange quirk of fate, Fergus, that of all people, I should be her duenna, but it's true. When I think of how *I* was swinging at her age, and how free I was, I marvel that she's stuck with it as long as she has, considering."

"We've made her the last of the stars," said Fergus.

"She kept Titan from going under for several years," said Claudia, "so don't complain to me, old buddy."

Claudia got up and looked out the window with him. "My God," she said, "why don't you pull the curtains? Look at that motley group of TV people out there. Titan has no class anymore, has it?"

"It's nothing but a rental facility. And it'll have even less class," said Fergus, "when they turn the whole lot into a business complex. Maybe even one of those plastic interchangeable-unit shopping centers that are going to spring up all over southern California: cocktail lounges, coffee shops, banks, travel bureaus, department stores, beauty parlors, savings and loans, escalators, underground parking. It makes me sick."

He looked down at her. Petite, slender, and still lovely, he always saw her as the young actress he'd brought out west on the train, with her whimsical smile and her joyous, troublemaking, piquant self.

"Me, too," she said. He put his arm around her shoulders.

"Ah yes," she said, sighing. "I can see it now. Where we had country streets, boulevards of every land, even our back lot lake and trees, and flowering gardens. So it's good-bye to our fantasyland. Maybe we've lived past our time, Fergus."

"I have to tell you something," he said. "Belinda's not the real reason I asked to see you."

There was an uncomfortable silence.

"It's about Max," she said. "You're not optioning his new property."

He took his arm away. "You know me too well."

She sat on the sofa, curling her feet under her as she had so many times over the years when something important was to be discussed. But this time she was not the star in the Chanel suit, wafting perfume and dramatically waving a gold cigarette holder. Fergus saw her concern.

She put her hands to her cheeks. In her mind the threat had hung like the sword of Damocles. Now it was final.

Oh God, how would Max take this! She felt the terrible wrench of reality . . .

"I'm sorry," he said. "I had to tell you first. I know what it will do to him."

"I'm not surprised," said Claudia. "Obviously Titan can't

go ahead with another blockbuster historical film until this one makes back its colossal expenses."

"You took my words," said Fergus, lighting another cigarette. "We tried, Claudia. But the bankers said that the Eighteenth Dynasty Egypt was out. Even with Queen Nefertiti, it wouldn't be good box office today. That society is too far from our own roots. It's like a trip to a museum; it might draw some people, but not the big theater audience. It's going to be hard enough to get them to step into the court of the Borgias."

"I see," said Claudia.

As she spoke, her thoughts were on the fact that she would not have a salary, that no one knew what Belinda would do next. As for Max . . . he had been bled anemic by Jessica's demands; he had hoped for a large down payment for his script and a future that would involve production plans for his next picture. Film makers of his stature in the last several years could count on a large expenditure and benefits while a production was in preparation. Now there would be a void. It seemed as if her whole world was being pulled from her.

"Perhaps he has something in his trunk, of a lighter vein, which we could have him develop. That's all I can offer, Claudia. David is coming in from London. Now we've got a new pain in the ass. The discovery of the transistor radio has brought about a wave of rock and roll madness. Every kid can carry his music in his pocket. Kids are doing their own thing. You can forget the Saturday matinees. The rock singers are the new cult figures. Look at Elvis. And David tells me this trend is exploding in Europe. We are even thinking of going into the record business. Can you believe this, Claudia? Giving up pictures to record that racket!"

"I can believe it," said Claudia. "I get it at home all the time. The garden used to be peaceful, but now Belinda's out there with her head against her set, competing, I might add, with a dozen others on the beach right outside our windows. But that doesn't solve my problem."

"Or mine," said Fergus. "Claudia, I don't know what to say. I suppose you've thought of the possibility that, at least for the time being, you're on your own again."

She looked at him sharply, suddenly angered that after all these years Fergus could sit in the office that had once belonged to Simon Moses and tell her she was on her own.

Her memory went back to the time (could it have been 1931!) when Simon died in her arms at the ranch. She had not even been allowed to attend his funeral, and she had come to the studio the same day to remove her things, thinking she would never be back again. And then, by a turn of fate, almost thirty years later, her own niece, Belinda, had zoomed into stardom and Claudia had returned in dignity to the Titan payroll. Now Fergus was telling her that the door was closing again. Well, what did she expect—coaching was only a picture-long job.

Then her anger dissolved.

"Claudia, I've loved you for years. I've been happy for you because of the life you've made with Max, even though at times I've resented the bastard and wished it were myself alongside you in my older years."

"Thanks for the compliment," she said, smiling. "You and I would never have been very peaceful together, I'm afraid."

"Well, anyway," said Fergus, "I'm not exactly what you would call a bargain. Sometimes when I go to Las Cruces to see Esther, I wonder that I just don't say, 'move over, kid,' and stay there with all the nuts myself. It's very hard to see your work and power dissolving in front of you. My only job is to carry the messages of other people. I have no choice. If I'm not a studio man, I'm nothing. If Max is not a director, at least he's still a writer."

"Of course," she said, "and brilliant."

She thought of the things Fergus didn't know. That Max had gone deeply into debt with his publisher, getting an advance to keep up their expenses—property, state, and federal taxes, insurance, all the things that didn't show in an economy.

She knew it would take him at least a year to deliver another book, six months more for editing, rewrite, final galleys, and, after the publication date, another six months to get royalties if the book made more than the advance. It would be a long, dry spell, and Max would be nervous without the backup of the studio behind him.

"Claudia, you know this business as well as I do. Even I, after clinging tooth and fang to stay within these walls, may be blitzed at any time. And I know, and you know, that we end up on our own, no matter how many Simons and Davids and Maxes and Belindas cross our paths. I'll repeat what I said to you way back when. You have too much talent to get lost. There's only one Claudia."

She was close to tears. She uncurled her feet and stood up, almost limping.

"Oh, damn," she said.

He took her hand, and she clung to him for a moment. He put his arms out to steady her.

"Wouldn't you know," she said, "at a dramatic moment like this my damned foot would go to sleep."

It made him laugh. "Well, sit down while it wakes up. We have to face logistics. I'll call on Max, tell him that at this time we can't afford a blockbuster, and ask what he has in his trunk. I'll compliment his talent and try my best to make him feel valuable. Of course, the Nefertiti script will be his, but I doubt if any studio will go for it. It's too big."

"I know," said Claudia, sitting down again. "And now, what about Belinda? You know Titan has an option on two more pictures for her. That's the contract that Jessica arranged when she was in control."

"It's a puzzle," said Fergus. "If Belinda marries, you know, all guardianship controls would be gone."

"That's true," said Claudia. "So what happens?"

"David's coming in to talk the whole thing over with me. We have to find her a property. The consensus in New York is that her next picture ought to be light. Do you think she can handle comedy?"

"She can handle most anything," said Claudia. "You know, while you were preparing for the picture, I had her working. We went through everything from Shakespeare to Tennessee Williams. Don't worry about her."

"I guess I shouldn't," he said. "She usually lands on her feet, and covered with roses. Anyway, for the time being, she owes us about a month of her time, so Cupid will have to wait. I'm sending her on tour; she'll have a heavy schedule of personal appearances—TV, radio, and newspaper interviews; and magazine sittings in various cities. I'm sending Gracie Boomer along with her. The old war-horse seems to know how to feed material to the press so they think they've invented it when they write it."

"Do you think Grace can handle it?" said Claudia.

"After all, she's not as young as she was when she kept me out of Dutch on the road."

"She can handle it," said Fergus. "And Leslie Charles will be there, too, to escort Belinda. It won't be too bad for Belinda, she's on salary and she's getting a wardrobe that will be some trousseau. Press representatives and sales people will meet them at every airport. They'll have protection from the public, guards, limousines, the best suites, and Polly is going along to take care of her clothes and packing."

"I wish it were Effie instead," said Claudia, "but you can't tear her away from Alex."

"Which reminds me," said Fergus, "what is going to happen to that child in this new marriage? Is Belinda going to tell Scott?"

"We decided not," said Claudia. "What can it do but mess up everything? Max and I will keep the baby. He's a joy to us, brings laughter and life into our house, and Effie takes care of everything. Do you think we're wrong?"

"How can I?" said Fergus. "Imagine what would happen if news got out of Belinda having that baby. I think you're doing the right thing."

" 'Oh what a tangled web we weave,/When first we practice to deceive,' " quoted Claudia. "Max is stuck with the fable that the baby is his, and Jessica's got us forever by the kishkes."

"Does she know Belinda's getting married?"

"No way," said Claudia. "Let it be a fait accompli before she finds out or she'll show up in lace and orchids to sit in numero uno seat, left-hand front pew, as the bride's mother."

Fergus shook his head. The picture was too vivid, even in his mind. He hated his ex-mistress.

"I think I should tell you," he said, "if anything, God forbid, should happen to me, Jessica signed a waiver with Titan—for the payment of certain funds—that if she ever mentioned the true story of Belinda's child or denied the parentage herself, all the money she received from Titan by her own pressures, as well as what she received from Max, would be payable on demand."

"Great," said Claudia. "That'll shut her up." She stood up. "My foot's ready to leave. When will you see Max?"

"Let me get the final word from David. Then I'll see

him. But I had to let you know first so you can brace yourself. Make it easy."

Easy . . . she thought. Nobody but myself knows the groove Max has worn in the carpet, walking in his study night after night, day after day, worrying and fretting about his work and his life.

But she smiled at Fergus.

"Thank you," she said. "Get it over with as soon as you can."

"You know, Claudia, it may be just a few months lay-off, and you'll be working again on Belinda's next picture."

"We'll hope," said Claudia, and she gave him a ceremonial peck on the cheek.

As she went to the parking lot and started her car, she thought about changes. She couldn't trail along with Belinda forever. Fergus had given her advance warning, time to find herself. She'd have to figure another way to keep on making money. After all, she was in good health, and she carried the Barstow name.

She was tired of dissembling, tired of the unspoken silences that hid so much deceit. She was tired of putting up a front for the role Belinda was playing with Scott.

Claudia was getting suspicious of Flora Stone Random's lack of communication. Something was wrong. Even Scott seemed to be avoiding the issue.

She had met Scott's mother, Henrietta Stone, who seemed to have a minor position in the social hegemony. Perhaps it would be wise to invite Mrs. Stone to tea and see what was happening.

There were so many things to do. It was time to get more clothes for Alex. He was growing out of everything. He was a walking menace, snatching everything off coffee tables, having to be watched around the pool. Her life was a web of responsibilities, and her sword and buckler was Effie. Her main problem, the man she loved. What would happen to Max?

She wished she could just go to bed, pull up the covers, and be alone without a thought in the world. But it was impossible. Love and care for those she loved had come to her life late, but in full measure.

She'd get on home, check on Max, and run her ship on a tight course as best she could.

To her surprise, there had been a phone call from Henrietta Stone. Her instincts were right; it was time to meet with Scott's mother. And she must not allow her concern about Max's problems and her own to interfere with this important time in Belinda's life, a time of change, of what should be celebration. Belinda had had such a cruel share of personal life in the middle of her overwhelming stardom.

Claudia wasted no time in calling Henrietta back and arranging tea the following day.

All she had to do was to inform Effie, and out came the pastry board, the silver polish, the best tea cloth and napkins for pressing. Effie planned an elegant little tea.

"You must have been English in one of your past incarnations," said Claudia. "You have this thing going in the most Mayfair tradition."

"Wish I could serve her a dinner," said Effie, grinning.

"That comes later," said Claudia. "Right now, let's just act like we do this every day."

"Wish we did," said Effie. "Maybe after Mr. Max relaxes a little, we can do it more often. 'Specially when winter comes on and there's fog or rain outside and we have a fire. That makes it cozy."

As Claudia smelled the fresh apricots cooking for the tiny tarts, she too wished that their life gave them more opportunities to sit by a shining tea service and relish the quiet moments. She loved Max, and she was proud of Belinda, whom she cherished as her own, but she realized that they were not a family that had many casual hours; they always seemed to be in a crisis. And this one, she feared, was going to be as bad as any, especially with economy looming up in such a fast, shocking way.

Compared to Flora Stone Random, Henrietta Stone was a weakling. She lived in the Maria Christina apartments on Wilshire, her large old-fashioned rooms furnished with remnants of antique furniture from the square mansion on Irving Boulevard where she had lived with her lawyer husband, Clarence. He had long since perished of a heart condition induced by too much bourbon, too little exercise, and too much fright at competing with the legal eagles of his time.

Just when Scott was in law school and his father could have enjoyed the prestige, Clarence Stone had died, and

Flora, his sister, had swooped in like a chicken hawk, taken Scott over, and also taken all the bows.

At the same time, Flora had relieved Henrietta of rooms of furnishings and a butler's pantry of silver and china, for Flora had space in her mansion, she said, to keep the precious things in the family.

Henrietta's life had been bordered generally between Bullock's Wilshire and Perino's restaurant, with occasional sorties into the ladies' dining room at the Jonathan Club where women were taken by their own elevator to a seragliolike area, the rest of the club being restricted to males. Occasionally, she went out-of-bounds to the Jonathan Beach Club where she wore silk dresses and flower-laden straw hats, and dined behind closed windows, avoiding the sea breeze.

She had done her obligatory social chores for the Junior League, Mills Alumnae, her cultural oasis—the Euterpe Opera Club, and occasional service at the Assistance League Thrift Shop.

When her husband died, her membership at the Jonathan Club and such benefits ended.

Her main dream was to have oodles of grandchildren and get the girls into the Ticktockers, to be recognized as part of the honored order of well-sung grandmothers. In her dreams, she had blanked out Scott's wife-to-be. It would all be a love affair between her and the grandchildren to make up for her smothered resentment over the fact that her pushing sister-in-law Flora had literally taken her son and goods away from her.

Now, in her fantasy future, with little ones who needed her love and attention, she would find her proper place. For years she had accepted secondary roles in Flora's grand social scene. Flora had the clout, and Henrietta was a widow without prestige. She became a victim of Flora Stone Random's driving ambition, and she was sick of it. Come the time, *she* would be the grandmother, and she would avoid the pitfalls for her grandchildren; Scott h·ʹ literally been snatched away and made a princeling. Now Henrietta would have her revenge.

None of Henrietta's friends would have believed how much she disliked her sister-in-law. She had always presented a smiling face, posed two or three from the center, poured tea in an emergency, sold tickets, run errands, and accepted small bounty while she faced defeat, seeing her son seduced with gifts and glamor. But a grandmother was a grandmother, a mother of the groom always wore lace and orchids, nobody could take that away, and even in the social columns her bloodline would give her first billing after the bride and groom.

As soon as she heard about Belinda and Scott, she exalted that Flora hadn't chosen the bride. There were rumors of discord. What did she care? A bride was a bride. Scott wanted to get married, and they'd certainly have pretty children. Henrietta braced herself for the first good fight of her life. She'd be on his side—anything to be against Flora Stone Random.

She knew that Flora was a snob and had put her nose high in the air against Claudia. Ah, there was her ally—that darling, attractive woman. She had admired Claudia as a movie star when she had been a very young girl, so Henrietta was delighted to come to the beach house on the exclusive Gold Coast. After all, even Flora hadn't been there yet. She was greeted effusively by Claudia, who wore a stunning green tea gown.

Max was in his study. Claudia had alerted him that this was going to be a woman-talk hour, her heart sinking at the sight of him deeply involved in polishing his Egyptian script. Her guilt at not telling him that it would be jettisoned was somewhat alleviated by the role she would play as Belinda's surrogate mother while arranging the wedding plans.

Belinda was at the studio fitting her wardrobe for her forthcoming trip, so Claudia had the house to herself, and she was glad to get away from her current problems, even if it involved talking to a bird-brained woman such as Henrietta. The silver and tea cloth were all set up elegantly by Effie, like a Freddie Lonsdale parlor comedy.

Henrietta admired the melon pattern set.

"It's only silver plate," said Claudia, "not half as lovely as that Georgian tea set your sister-in-law had."

"Oh," said Henrietta, "I'm glad you liked it. It's sort of on loan-out. It's mine."

"It is!" said Claudia, surprised, handing out Effie's little tarts, which made Henrietta's eyes light up as she quickly ate one.

"How does it happen that Flora has it?"

Henrietta looked at her conspiratorially. "How does it happen that she has practically everything of mine? Including furniture, French vitrines, Crown Derby china, Beleek tea sets. A Venetian bed. An Italian dining set. Most of the furniture is just shoved away in the attic, except for a few showpieces in her drawing room." Henrietta's eyes brimmed with tears.

"Why, I think that's terrible. Oh, I'm sorry, I didn't mean to bring up anything unpleasant," said Claudia. "Excuse me."

To Claudia's surprise, Henrietta set down her cup; and her tears made a river down her powdered cheek.

"I was a defenseless widow," she said. "Much younger, and not as ambitious as she was. You'll forgive me, Mrs. Ziska—"

"Claudia," said Claudia, patting her hand.

"Well, anyway, she was getting ready to give her big parties for charity—and money—and she latched on to everything! Oh, dear, you'll have to excuse me."

She reached into her bag, pulled out a lace-edged handkerchief, wiped her eyes and blew her nose.

"I—I just feel so terrible. I wanted to have these lovely things to give to Scott and his beautiful bride for a wedding gift. You wouldn't believe it—Claudia—thank you—but she even took my son from me. And I hate to tell you this, but she's just furious about him marrying Belinda."

"She is!" said Claudia, shocked and angry. "I think he's a very fortunate young man, and I'm proud to have him in the family."

Henrietta felt a surge of power rising in her. This would be her revenge. "You know," she said, "I'm so glad we talked. I feel that through this marriage I'll get my boy back. He won't be a social pawn of that terrible woman."

"You poor thing," said Claudia. "Here, have some more tarts."

While Henrietta ate several, Claudia had a vision of what one-upmanship it would be to go against Flora Stone Random. How dare she object to Belinda!

"Is there any way you can prove that these—uh—items are yours?"

Henrietta thought a moment, and the light dawned.

"I never thought of it, but we did have a complete inventory made for insurance purposes just before my Clarence died. Yes, I have proof."

"Well," said Claudia, "how very fortunate that you brought this up. You know, if I were in your position, with a wonderful son like Scott and a future daughter-in-law as famous as Belinda, I'd just get a van and get your things out of the grip of that woman at once, with legal advice of course, and I'd store them until the proper moment came for your very own family to enjoy them."

Henrietta's eyes lit up.

"Well, I think it's wonderful for you to think of that. You know, my little apartment wasn't big enough to take them. I wish I had more of a place to entertain for the children. But I'm just as glad that Flora isn't doing it and taking all the bows."

Claudia put her hands over Henrietta's. "We'll do very well here," she said. "We'll have a garden wedding. Thank heavens it will be a lovely time of the year. Don't you worry, Henrietta. The bride's family should do it anyway."

"And a tent," said Henrietta, "and a little orchestra with just piano during the breaks, and of course gardenias all over the place." She smiled fondly and patted Claudia's hand. "You must remember, they were Scott's courting flowers."

Remember, thought Claudia. They inundated the place; Belinda couldn't stand them. But she smiled.

Henrietta gushed on. "Lovely little topiary trees of gardenias, and screens of them over your pittosporum hedges. I can just see it. Oh, we'll show her! And I'd love to help you with the proper lists. I know you'll want celebrities. But of course we'll have a hard time weeding out all the people we've always known, and just having, well, perhaps a hundred of them."

Claudia managed to pour the second cup of tea without spilling it. She set it down and looked up bravely.

"Well, fifty-fifty," said Henrietta, waving her hand in a generous gesture. "A hundred of yours, a hundred of mine. Right?"

Claudia did not even have to nod. Approval was accepted. Her heart sank. Where was all this money going to come from?

"Oh, it'll be such fun!" said Henrietta.

Claudia realized that she had stepped into a feud, and Henrietta, with a gleam in her eye, would have her revenge. Well, Belinda would get enough beautiful furniture to set her up splendidly. She realized that the Stone family had bought in a much simpler market, and today's prices would have made it impossible for even a well-off young couple to duplicate the treasures of yesterday.

They sealed a pact with mutual excitement about the wedding, which, they figured, considering Belinda's commitments, should be in several months, giving them time to make all their plans.

"Believe me," said Henrietta, "I'm going to get a moving van right in and take every single item out of that woman's house!"

"Bravo," said Claudia. "That'll be a fabulous wedding gift. We'll get our act together, and the wedding will be something the whole town will remember. Don't you worry!"

Henrietta left, her euphoria flowing like a chiffon scarf. Now she would make up for all her past humiliation.

Claudia walked out by the pool. It was a beautiful day. A little fleet of snowbirds, sails atilt, was skittering along the bright sea.

Effie and Alex were strolling up above in the Palisades' palm-fringed park.

She looked over the sixty feet of her garden. She'd have to have Abbey Rents construct a dance floor and tent over the pool. That would be the only way to stretch the space. The band could play at the far end of the veranda. Tables could be set around the edges of the pool; there would be room for two hundred people. Caterers could bring in most of the food, and a bar could be set up at the inner court entrance. The gardenias and potted ferns would make the garden seem like an exotic jungle.

She stopped short. Good God!

Playing the grand lady has really done me in! That silly ding-a-ling, Henrietta Stone, has managed to rescue her ego through this wedding. And I'm supposed to pull it off! How . . . How . . .

If she pawned all her jewelry, the most she could get was about three thousand. She'd been through that enough times to know.

There was no way Max could be asked to help. He was deeply into his own world.

She walked out the gate and over to her neighbor Mildred Hammond's house.

One of the derelicts of the film business, Mildred was married to Terry Hammond, a retired ace cameraman. Mildred had been a starlet and never advanced beyond that calling; fate and overweight caught up with her. In a few scrambling years before she gave up her fight against talent and chocolate creams, she had ventured into the Cape summer playhouses. Now a fervent reader of *Variety*, the *Reporter*, the *New York Times* drama section, and the strawhat reviews, she welcomed Claudia's visits like plasma, and she was always a refuge in a storm for Claudia. Now Claudia needed to get away, even if just to listen to another voice outside the house. No matter how much she loved her husband and her niece, they were both involved with their own needs. And what she had just agreed to do overwhelmed her.

It was as if fate had led her to this moment. Mildred was waving the theatrical section of the *New York Times* in her hand.

"Oh, scandal! Scandal!" she cried. "Remember old Stuart Plimpton who used to direct at Titan?"

"My God, yes; he was my first director," said Claudia. "What are you so excited about? Did he die?"

"No!" said Mildred, "he directed me in my last job in summer stock at the Elderberry Playhouse at the Cape. The old boy is still at it, and he was going to do *The Madwoman of Chaillot*, and *The Glass Menagerie* later. Well, he was using Rebecca Keely. She just got busted for drunk driving, hit and run, and he's in a terrible flap. He's signed Bruce Dennis to play the Ragpicker, and he's stuck with the contract. They're supposed to start in two weeks. *Glass Menagerie* to follow. Each playing two weeks. Oh, boy, I can just see it now, that whole village in an uproar. They live all year on summer theater. That cottage craft junk in all the windows, and those pies and scones and doodads that people make all their money off of. It's a disaster!"

"What will he do?" said Claudia. "He was a nice Joe, even if untalented."

"I just feel like calling the poor thing up. He was always so nice to me."

"Do you know how to reach him?"

"Of course," said Mildred. "He's lived in his own wing at the Elderberry Inn for thirty years. He owns it. He's the lifeblood of the town. Practically runs Elderberry."

"Call him," said Claudia. "I'll come with you."

Mildred rushed into the house. As she dialed the number, she turned to Claudia. "I'll put you on the phone. Boy, will he be pleased to talk to you!"

"I hope," said Claudia, wondering if he remembered how she had refused to have him direct her and had chosen a fancy Englishman because talkies were coming in.

But after Mildred reached him and gave him her sympathies, Claudia took the phone.

"Hi, Stu," she said. "Too bad you got mixed up with that rumpot. How much were you paying her?"

He groaned. "I've got a nine thousand weekly nut to crack," he cried, "and I've got contractual obligations, and, between us, I own the inn and the tea shop next door to the playhouse. I've a ton of perishable food ordered, and I've hired ten extra college kids. Idiot that I was, I was to pay twenty-five hundred a week, plus a 25 percent guarantee over the nut. She could have made maybe a thousand more. Plus her own suite and transportation. And a two-week run on each with a hiatus in between, so she could do a TV show. Oh, God, Claudia, I'm ruined."

"Not necessarily," said Claudia. "That is, if you think the Barstow name on the marquee would make it. I'll get Fergus to give us a little plug through Titan's PR, and I can get there in—uh—a week. . . . Hello—are you there?"

There was a gasp on the other end of the line.

"Your name make it! You'd—you'd do it?" he cried. "My God, Claudia, you'd *do* it! Are you up on the play? It'll take one week's rehearsal around the clock!"

"I'm up on both of them, and I'll study in the interim," she said. "Now, Mildred will get on the other phone and be witness to the terms."

She frantically signaled Mildred to run upstairs to the bedroom phone. She ran up, three at a time.

"I'm on," she screamed, "with pad and pencil."

"My God!" said Stuart, "Claudia, you've saved my life!"

"The terms," said Claudia, "are three thousand a week, plus 30 percent over the nut."

"You're killing me!" said Stuart.

"Stu, you talk too much. I know what you have to lose. Forget it, then," said Claudia.

"Wait," said Stuart. "Could you stay on?"

"I doubt it," said Claudia.

"You're picking on an old man," he said. "Well what about it?"

"We'll talk terms for that when I get there," said Claudia.

"You're killing me, but anyway, I'll meet you with a limousine," he shouted. "You'll have the bridal suite, and I'll bring you yellow roses. I'll hire an extra press agent. Oh, Claudia, God bless you and forgive you all the shitty things you did to me so long ago."

"See you, sucker," said Claudia. "And you'd better arrange an extra room for Belinda in case she can work it out with her PR tour to be there part of the time while I play."

"Oh, my God!" gasped Stuart. "What a season! For all I care, Rebecca Keely can rot in jail!"

Mildred was ecstatic. "You're getting right back into show business where you belong!" she said. "Oh, how I envy you!"

"Envy me!" said Claudia. "Don't you know what a grind it's going to be? Imagine being directed by Stuart Plimpton again. Josh Logan, he ain't."

"Well, it's better than watching sea gulls," said Mildred, sighing. "I wish I could go, but my old man won't let me out of his sight. Nobody can prepare his ulcer diet like me, he says."

"Mildred, those star package shows. Don't I know. I've been warned; amateurs all around you except for several beached old pros who come on too, too strong. The grind of rehearsals—competing with the belches after those shore dinners and the three-martini snorers. Shouting through hail and rain on a tin roof. Working out the lighting plans because some freebie kid doesn't know pink from yellow. Endless country club luncheons just to boost the ticket sale; dead chicken in a cardboard patty shell and peas, peas, peas.

"I'll have to study both plays at once. I'll be lucky if I don't play the Madwoman of Chaillot with a Tennessee Williams southern accent!

"Well, I'll concentrate on the Countess—and hope *The Glass Menagerie* works out during rehearsal time.

"Doing two shows in a rush just because that old boozer Keely messed up the season! I must be out of my mind! It's too much!"

Mildred was reflective. "You're right," she said. "I guess I forgot. Well, why do you do it? Get out of it. I'll watch the sea gulls with you."

"I'll tell you why I'm doing it," said Claudia. "Because I seem to be launching a very fancy wedding here in a couple of months. And I have to do it right. I can't just sit on the front porch and rock."

What have I done? thought Claudia on her way home. I'm walking out on Max, on Belinda, on Alex, and I'm putting the whole load on Effie's shoulders.

Well, at least Fergus will understand, and he'll be a backup in case of any disaster.

I'll work until the last minute and get back in time to get Belinda's wedding together. Who knows? Summer theater pays big; it might lead to enough work to bail us out until Max finds what he has to do. I've got to be careful, though, not to let Max know how desperate we are, not to let Belinda know we're busted, and not to let Henrietta Stone ever know that we don't have plenty of loot. She'd fall apart. And not to let that ego trip, Flora Stone Random, realize what a pinch we're in. That's all we'd need to blitz Belinda's wedding.

Thinking of the web of deceit she would have to spin, she went into the house. She would tell Max that she had a great chance to do summer stock, she'd been longing to do something for herself, and she'd always wanted to play *The Madwoman of Chaillot*.

She thought nostalgically about Laurette Taylor and how thrilling she had been in *Glass Menagerie*. It was a challenge! And this was a good time, while Belinda was away, and Max was so busy with his work.

Her most painful thought was the realization that soon Fergus would have to tell Max about the picture being dropped.

But Max had been through plenty in his life, he was a survivor, and perhaps it would be a relief for him not to have to see her concern. It would give him time to look over his other properties and adjust his thinking. Knowing Max's brilliant mind and his unflagging talent, she felt he would involve himself completely in seeking another property.

Belinda would soon be on the road, and Effie, as always, would run the house, take care of Alex; she'd been doing it since Belinda was her special charge as a baby, and it was her chief joy in life.

Claudia didn't have to worry about the creature comforts of the family she loved. And it wouldn't be bad to be on the stage again.

Already she was beginning to think about her characterization. The Madwoman of Chaillot was a renegade, an individualist who had thumbed her nose at what the world expected. As a matter of fact, she reflected the insanity of Claudia's own life. The play showed the pitched battle between the givers and the takers. The Madwoman was a true eccentric, a life lover.

It would be exciting to create a role for herself after all these years, to have the excitement of sustaining a characterization for two hours with vitality, pace, timing, voice projection, and *no* retakes.

Even with all the irritations of summer stock, working with young people wasn't bad. If they had any sense she could teach them. If not, she'd just overwhelm them.

She knew she'd only have one week of rehearsal business and blocking. Well, she could do it! She'd know the script cold before she left.

For several years she had been at the disposal of Max and of Belinda. Now she was on her own, and what she did would bring joy and comfort to her family.

With these thoughts, Claudia stepped into a world of planning, of luggage, of clothes, of cosmetics, of her play to study. She ordered her tickets from the local travel agency and realized that, for the first time in a long time, she was Claudia Barstow, her own woman, and her mind was in Elderberry on the Cape, instead of on the ocean front in Santa Monica or at Titan studio in Hollywood.

It was as exciting and engrossing as the time long ago when she had done her independent film in London, launching John Graves, a cockney boy, into stardom. How life reflects itself.

But this time she was not only doing it for herself, but for her husband and her niece. It was a good feeling.

14

As the large Bekins truck pulled out of the driveway, its bounty all documented by a ten-year-old insurance policy, Flora Stone Random looked at her living room. The large vitrine that had held a treasury of gimcracks was gone. The carpeting where it had been was mashed flat, the varied coloring of the thick fabric revealing a loss more overwhelming to her than the memory of a lost dear one. In the center hall, an Aubusson rug had decamped, leaving pegged oak floor that did not match the well-worn surrounding territory. Rude men had carried an attic full of furniture down the double staircase.

The pantry also was emptied; some of the hinged doors still stood open, with the incredibly soiled look of raped shelves that had once held silver and china to please the appetites of the local Four Hundred.

Flora wept, alone. Miss Monk, her secretary, after finishing the duplicate check-out sheets, had retreated to her gardener's cottage where, over a bottle of sherry, she was gloating over the takeover of her employer's lifted largesse.

The staff, two flatfoot floogies, after helping to assort and pack, were gone, claiming exhaustion, eager to get away from Mrs. Random's fury at the unexpected hegira of the possessions they had cared for and had constantly been warned were valuable beyond belief. The fact that they belonged to the milquetoast Henrietta Stone was as surprising as the fact that Mrs. Random was unable to do a thing but stand by and watch the exodus.

Flora wept because she felt she did not deserve what had happened. Prince Charming had left with that damnable glass slipper—and the furniture to boot.

She had only meant good, and Scott had the nerve to

invade the musty dwelling of her inner soul. Or at least that milksop Henrietta had done it, and it must have been with the aid of his devilish legal training. Flora would never forgive them. So this was what happened when you were kind to relatives!

When her special white hope, Scott, destined to carry on her family name (much better, she thought, than her husband's), deserted her, it was too, too unfair.

She went back to the irritating memory of her husband, Hector Winfred Random. Poor, dear man, it was all his fault; such a coward that he blew his brains out over a few paltry overdrawn bank accounts. And just before the Candlelight Ball!

What was left of him was taken to Forest Lawn to be repaired, waxed, and dressed with his Stanford Phi Beta Kappa key becomingly draped on his Savile Row threads—for a last exhibit of her worth.

Like many women of her background, Flora had spent her obligatory first year of wedded bliss sleeping with Hector in her ruffled silk lace bedroom, and after the first year, armed with loving comments about his snoring and his darling but disturbing thrashing about, she moved him to a newly built screened sleeping porch where he could look out on his garden and leave her alone to her mail and her long phone calls.

She was relieved to be rid of his body, of his man smells, and of his puffy pink face.

Every evening, she carefully stirred a small innocuous sleeping potion into his Ovaltine.

He adored her concern, called her his dear buddy. In spite of sedation, he occasionally roused himself to make quick missionary-position love, and he went to sleep marveling that such a faithful woman was his.

Flora's friend, the douche bag, hanging under a fluffy towel, was put to immediate use. There was no room for a child in Flora's busy social life.

It had been a joy to her that her brother's child was so handsome. He would be her heir, her child to guide, the lovely little one to be photographed standing by her side in velvet, not unlike the *Blue Boy* at the Huntington Museum in Pasadena. She herself, a lovely Romney, standing in the background.

But after Mr. Random's patched-up face had been

relegated to the earth in one of Forest Lawn's prettiest hillocks, with Gabriel blowing an ever-silent "watch out!" Flora had to take stock of herself.

The pretty little Dresden shepherdess would have to work it out alone. The shepherd's crook with its pink bowknot would have to turn into a bludgeon, until her nephew Scott's croquet mallet would become Excalibur.

And now, after the years of waiting, instead of finding a princess, he had selected an orange girl from the Globe Theater. It would never do.

But sometimes the darkest moments came before the dawn. Out of the drawers of one of the Venetian cabinets, she had pulled some old magazines and stacked them on the floor. She sat down, exhausted, and wiped the tear from her eye with the sleeve of her gown. She didn't even know where the Kleenex in its golden container had gone in the holocaust.

She picked up a copy of *Town and Country* that must have been two years old. She opened it idly, and there before her eyes was a layout of expatriate Americans who had found a life in Italy.

"The Principessa Bonavente, in the gardens of her beautiful Villa Jessica outside Tivoli. This lovely American, the former Jessica Barstow, widow of Jeffrey Barstow of stage and screen, is an important member of Roman society with her husband Principe Carlo Bonavente. She is the mother of the American film star, Belinda Barstow, but she has chosen to eschew her connections with the film industry and join the ranks of high Roman society."

Flora stared at the layout. Well, how strange, how very strange. This woman was never mentioned by Belinda. That upstart Claudia Barstow had undoubtedly taken over. Wouldn't you know she'd want the child to be an actress!

She took a look at Jessica's picture, her high-fashion figure framed by the ordered cypress walks of her garden, a marble fountain and steps in the background. What an aristocratic face, what an elegant woman, thought Flora. And a title, too, a *principessa*!

Forgetting her sadness, she went up to her boudoir. Sitting down at her desk, she pushed papers and bills aside and unearthed her best stationery. After a moment's pause, she took her plumed pen, discarded it because it scratched, got out a ball-point, and wrote.

Dear Principessa Bonavente,

I was enchanted to see your lovely face peeping at me from between the covers of *Town and Country*.

Unfortunately, we have not yet met, although my nephew, Scott Stone, is betrothed to your beautiful daughter.

I would be delighted to have you as my houseguest when you come to Los Angeles for the wedding. My maid will take care of your clothes, and my limousine and chauffeur will be at your disposal.

I do hope your charming husband will be able to accompany you. You must let me know the date of your arrival, so I can plan a proper reception. My friends are eager to know you.

I hope you will not consider me presumptuous, but I feel we shall be friends, and am eager to meet you.

Most sincerely,
Flora Stone Random

There, she thought, as she lit a candle and dropped sealing wax on the envelope, using a coat of arms she had purchased a few years before. Now, we'll see what happens! As soon as I hear from her, I'll inform the society editors. If Scott and Henrietta think they can cut me off—they'll see!

As for the drawing room, great Italian pots of ferns, flanked by Regency chairs juggled from the music room, would hide the blank spots where Henrietta had tried to cannibalize her social life. Hah!

Had she known what a Pandora's box she had opened, she would have been even more eager than she was now, as she licked the overseas airmail stamps, pounded them on furiously, and went to the postbox herself to see that her chit went winging.

Scott Stone was enjoying the most exciting time of his life. Aside from being madly in love for the first time, he found himself the focus of more interest than he had ever expected.

He had no idea of the inner currents and emotions his betrothal to Belinda was causing. He knew his mother was happy and promising gifts he was certain she could not give—but this was not unique with her. He knew he had put down his aunt beyond belief, and, resenting her, he decided to let her cool off and miss him. In time she would join up, and Belinda would never know there had been a rift. It would be terrible for her to discover that anyone could reject her.

But Scott had been morally seduced more than he knew by his Aunt Flora, and by the privileges he had received, no matter how much he had revolted.

While he was still at Harvard Law school, she had given him Ivy League argyles, regimental club symbols, summer-weight jackets with gold buttons, navy blazers, two dinner jackets, six pairs of Bass Weejuns, two dozen alligator shirts, four cummerbunds, Hermes handkerchief sets, madras and paisley sport shirts, Shetland sweaters, cashmere turtlenecks, silk pajamas and monogrammed robes, gold cuff links, Lynx golf clubs, Wilson tennis rackets galore, and memberships in the proper clubs. Later, when he returned to Los Angeles, there were dinners in the best cafés (paid for by social climbers) and knowledge in wines (which he selected elegantly without checking price lists). He accepted the best tables in restaurants, the best seats in theaters and concerts. He had never waited in line for anything in his life.

These were only small indications of where his life would lead. He believed in the quiet, orderly sweat of the club handball court, his opponents always men of substance. He accepted as natural the right people on the tennis courts and fairways at the right time. He had been sent to Harvard instead of the law school at the University of Southern California. He lunched with his jacket on, even at home. He wore silk pajamas and robe in his own room and going from his bed to the bathroom. He believed that a bride should have the best silver and china, and he expected his whole living pattern to be completely adjusted to suit the importance of his marriage. It was time.

He intended that his children should go to private schools, and then, of course, to college. He would give his wife every privilege. In time, there would be trips to Europe, a summer house in Newport, if possible a small but comfortable boat at the dock, or, if not that sort of life, at least a place in the winter at Lake Tahoe or even Aspen where the skiing was worthwhile and pleasant important companions would augment the family scene.

He realized he was stretching a point to make such plans, but these were the grand values that had been handed him, so insidiously that he believed they were the proper pattern of the good life. He looked on them as the natural advancement of work, and the social adornment that valued marriage should have.

It never entered his mind to think of the talents involved in the Barstow way of life, for he felt that what he had to offer Belinda was a world she would love; he desperately wanted the best for her, and, to him, this was the best.

He forgot the embarrassments of his extreme youth because of the largess his aunt had handed him—with definitive penalties attached. After his father died and his mother moved to an apartment, any luxury, any benefice was from Flora. Everything she had given him she remembered with an elephantine memory. Where was the cashmere, where was the Shetland sweater? Where the cuff links? Did he like his golf clubs?

He vaguely remembered one incident in a summer hiatus when he had been ordered to wear a certain Scotch sweater. One of his schoolmates had offered to buy it, and Scott had needed the money to take out the local prom queen. But one of his pals had a similar sweater given by an equally doting grandmother. They had sold one sweater, pooled the money, and pooled the other sweater, to wear when asked by their inquisitive elders. The sweater had become the joke of the summer.

He had often been forced to escort Flora's socially prominent misfits, when he would have preferred to be elsewhere, but these inconveniences were all forgotten in the euphoria of the one wonderful thing she had done for him—the meeting of Belinda.

He remembered the scene in Flora's bedroom with embarrassment; he had been hasty in the vulgar words he had used and the anger he had revealed. Of course she was shocked. He had always been her takeout, her comfortable boy, her social rock. But he felt her dismay would change to pleasure when she saw how wonderfully Belinda would fit into his life. She was not only a beautiful girl, people were drawn to her like a magnet.

His first reasoning had been that Belinda would not be in the picture business for long. But one of his own peers dispelled this idea and even planted another in his head.

"You've struck it rich," said Harry Howard when Scott announced his intention to marry Belinda. "Have you ever thought of the corporate value of that gorgeous corporis?" He grinned.

At first Scott had resented the crack, but he quickly got used to it, and he even began to enjoy the innuendo from acquaintances as well as friends that he must be hiding something special, and what did he have that they didn't know about.

Open discussion of sex had filtered into the fifties, and now the sixties were unleashing current myths. Behavior and secrets of the great lovers were analyzed in print, on the air, and over cocktails. Even Scott's friends were beginning to categorize him in terms of the great studs who had become the folk heroes. He was, through his affiliation with Belinda Barstow, a candidate to step right up with Errol Flynn, Ali Khan, Alfonso Portago, and even triple-threat man, Porfirio Rubirosa.

It was generally accepted that he and Belinda were having a torrid affair. If they only knew how sweet, how modest she was, he thought, they wouldn't believe it. He couldn't explain it if he wished, but it was his secret delight to know what a wonderful girl she was.

It made it possible for him to sublimate his sexual desires. Sometimes, tossing and thrashing in his bed, he was forced, before he could sleep, to relieve himself of his sexual tensions, but he did so with such a fantasy of Belinda that it was as though he were preparing for the time that she would be in his bed, and her tender flesh and his meshed together.

He had had plenty of eager girls who knew what they were doing. He had never deflowered a virgin, and he was secure in the knowledge that he was considered a good lover, had a good physique, would one day find a partner for life, and that would be that.

But his passion for Belinda was something he had not expected, and it was disturbing, a flood of excitement that possessed his thoughts and actions more than anything in his life.

The fact that he had to struggle to make it all work out

properly had complicated his life more than he would have thought possible. It took all his control and his training to decide not to rush pell-mell into an elopement.

Many times in the night he decided he could no longer go on with the waiting, that they'd just dash away. But when he got to the office in the morning and considered what he needed to do, he realized that there were several important steps to be arranged before he could even ask her to set the date.

It never entered his mind that she was reticent about entering into a physical relationship with him.

First, he would have to find a suitable house; no doubt they'd have to start with a rental. With Belinda there could be no makeshift. Everything would have to be perfectly arranged, even before the honeymoon. He must win his Aunt Flora after their unfortunate confrontation. She had attics full of furniture, and he had heard some of it had been salvaged and packed away when his father died and he and his mother were forced to move out of the old Irving Boulevard house. He had been a youngster then, and secretly delighted to get out of living with his stolid mother. Now he thought of the family things that should be his.

His next step was to get a raise from the senior member of his law firm. He was surprised at how it came about.

Old Frederick Cotter, his father's classmate and partner, who had been his sponsor, offered him a six o'clock scotch behind closed doors.

The elder of the company was both privately derided and forgiven by the younger men, who had accepted his verbiage and drinking, and yet learned from him. Once handsome, now possessor of a thatch of white hair and thick, ruddy, alcoholic nose, he still was a vital force, probing and seeking dominance in the world around him. He had had the courage to sweep his whole firm from the venerable Spring Street building to the new field of Westwood. Now another move was in the wind.

His first words as Scott entered his office were, "Scott, I envy you."

In his dentured smile was the spice of remembered times, for in his day he had been a connoisseur of women as well as wine.

His greatest pride, including many civic awards, was a

carefully polished replated cup that he had won in the twenties doing the Charleston at a Cocoanut Grove te' dansante with Joan Crawford.

A bachelor, younger and younger girls decorated his arm as he moved around town. It was as if looking at their young faces and holding their slim bodies made him reflect youth into himself through them.

"And I congratulate you. Lovely girl . . . Lovely. Now, I want to talk business with you. You know I have always deplored the old-fashioned techniques of some of our hidebound profession who remained mentally and physically in the inner city. It took some courage to move out here to Westwood, but I have my ear to the ground, Scott. We haven't ended yet. We'll be moving to new offices in the Avenue of the Stars in Century City. It's a new world, and many picture people are taking on lawyers because the agents don't have the clout they used to have."

Scott sipped his drink. The old duffer was selling him a bill of goods.

"You know, since the picture business has splintered, the major studio has no part in protecting individuals. Producers and directors and actors need the constant aid of legal personnel every time they set up a new deal. It is a very complicated business; each motion picture set up independently is a world all its own, and it is time for us to step into this fascinating area."

Scott still didn't say anything. This was going to be a soliloquy.

"The stakes are very high," continued Cotter, "and objective advice is a valued commodity. You're a valuable man, Scott. You have already progressed from associate to junior partner. You have youth, the finest training, charm, social position, and you're marrying the most beautiful, sought-after girl in the film business. I would say the only great star left in this time of change."

"Thank you," said Scott. "I know that. I want to do everything I can to live up to what she is."

"That's a boy!" said Cotter, pouring himself another drink. He waved the decanter in Scott's direction, but Scott shook his head. He was going to pick up Belinda, and he didn't want to have too much to drink before they had their wine together. She had said she had some important news for him, and he wondered what it was. There was so much to say. And he hadn't even picked out her engagement ring. He had to talk to her about what she wanted. She had said a freshwater pearl, and he didn't think it was important enough. He got his mind back to the situation at hand.

"You will be in a position to meet the top people of the film world. It is really an open sesame."

Scott resented the implication, but he said nothing. One didn't interrupt a man like Cotter when a raise was in the air.

"I am leading around to what must be most obvious to you," said the old man. "I may be stepping down soon, but I want to set up the most modern, prestigious office I can for my boys. And you are one of the best. Scott, I want you to be the head of the packaging department. That's where the money lies—getting producer, script, director, and star into a unit that is satisfactory to the finance— and there's plenty of that with the proper elements. I want you to gather the valuable independent forces that are capable of making pictures throughout the world. The stakes are getting higher. A blockbuster picture is the way the great talent is going."

Scott set down his drink. The old man went on, his hands arcing in enthusiasm as he spoke. "Independent companies are the bloodstream of this fragmented industry, and every star has to have shrewd advice behind him, or her, and every director, producer, and actor in the flowing industry is going to need crack legal advisers. I want you to head this department." He paused dramatically, as was his wont in court and in private chambers. Scott knew that what the boys called "the zinger" was going to follow.

"With it would be a participation in profits; with a raise and proper diligence on your part, it should be above twenty thousand dollars a year more than you make now. I will cut you in on a share, to be determined when we make a package deal and get our percentage of the investor's money. Also a bonus with every new client you bring into Cotter, Sullivan, and Gregg. Incidentally, as a senior partner, eventually the company might be Cotter, Sullivan, Gregg, and Stone. Now, how's all this for a wedding gift?"

The old man beamed and came around from behind his desk to shake hands with Scott.

Scott was astounded. The concept of his future income, and the personal maneuvering that would go with it, made his mind whirl.

At the same time, the idea of so much wealth was overwhelming. It would solve many problems that had been keeping him awake nights.

He put his hand out and shook, wondering if he had sealed a bargain. This was startling. He didn't like fastening it all on his relationship with Belinda, but the necessity of his future and the sudden flash into what it could mean hit him with an impact.

No longer would he have the sort of life he had been leading with his aunt as his social mentor. No longer could he get along on the comfortable money he had been accepting with his work and his moderate inheritance from his father. He had seen some of his friends go into talent agencies and others into personal management. It was surprising how quickly the inductive leap made him realize what might be in the future. Somehow, the idea excited him. He would get over the sudden wrench in his gut as he adjusted his thinking. Belinda, for example, did need management. As if answering his thought, Cotter went on. Scott realized how shrewd the old boy was, and how Cotter had been a jump ahead of him as he had gone his blind way, slowly setting his own pace in standard legal practice.

"I took the liberty of investigating the situation," Cotter said, "and I discovered that Belinda is most naïve, as are her aunt and stepfather, about the progression of her career. She has a contract with an old agent which can be abrogated very easily once she is an emancipated woman. Of course, that she will be legally, even if she isn't of age, when she marries you. Her funds, of course, will revert to her, and most of all, negotiations for any future films she wants to do will be in her own hands. She will no longer be under the guidance of any guardian; she will be her own woman."

"I hadn't thought about that," said Scott.

Cotter pinioned him with his next words.

"How fortunate for her that she will have the know-how at hand," he said. "Scott, do you realize the position she is in? She was indeed used by her mother, Jessica Barstow, and, unwittingly, by Max Ziska. She was signed by a studio without any participation, only straight salary. She should have her own production company and be sharing the profits. Fergus Austin and David Austin have been very fortunate in the millions they've made off her."

"They took a risk," said Scott. "After all, she was an unknown quantity when they started her. Just a child."

"That may be," said Cotter, "but she proved her value. If she hadn't been magnificent, all the publicity in the world couldn't have made her a star. But now she's a multimillion-dollar property, and she may be in the wrong hands. Max Ziska, from what I've heard, was not really with it in his selection of that Borgia story. Am I wrong?"

"There has been some discussion at the studio," said Scott. "I've heard about it. They haven't approved his newest script. And it seems she alone is hauling them out of the soup by her performance."

"I'm not surprised," said Cotter. "Perhaps you can have a talk with her."

Scott stood up, disturbed.

Cotter noted his expression. "Look," he said, "this new assignment doesn't necessarily have to have anything to do with your fiancée. But you must agree, it is a field that has more and more promise now that the studios no longer own their top talent. You don't have to rush. I'm not going to hand this on a silver platter to anyone else—that is, unless you refuse. So go out with your lady love and have a fine dinner and think it over. By the way, you'll have a large expense account—so order the finest wine—it's on the company."

He sipped his drink. "You must understand one thing, my boy. I am proud to have you in the firm, and if you choose to stay on in your current situation, I will still be delighted to have you.

"I don't like to presume too much on the fact that I am the executor of your father's estate, but I know your trust situation. Upon your mother's death, which we both hope will be a long way off, you will receive the trust, without tax, but, as you know, it won't make you a rich man."

Scott nodded. It had always embarrassed him, fed by comments from his aunt, that his father had not been able to give him more.

"But I must tell you," continued Cotter, "that you are young and have great opportunities ahead of you; you shouldn't worry. On the basis of my trust in you, the firm would be willing to advance you ten thousand dollars."

Scott's face reflected the disturbance that this gift might represent. "I couldn't accept it," he said.

Cotter quickly waved away any suspicious thought. "Nonsense. You're stepping into immediate expenses with this marriage," said Cotter. "You'll damn well earn it burning the midnight oil learning all the ins and outs of being a nursemaid to gifted people. It won't be easy. They'll call you from the jungles when they have a fight with their leading ladies. They'll wake you up from New York when they don't get their money on time or the star in Paris is threatening suicide. You'll wet-nurse talent with headaches; don't I ever know."

"You make it sound very chancy."

"So is any law," said Cotter. "Well, you sleep on it. I have no respect for a man who makes an immediate decision. And by the way, you are going to be very surprised at the incredible tour de force your mother has pulled off for you. I didn't know she had the guts to go up against Flora. She had to come to me for legal advice." He put his hand over his mouth. "I've talked too much. That third drink always does it."

Scott was puzzled. "You're not going to tell me," he said, "now that you've got me intrigued?"

"Let her," he said. "She's a good mother. Don't underestimate her just because she's old-fashioned."

He beamed, as if he had put himself in a different category. "Well, good luck, my boy, and may this talk disturb your sleep. Those tossing abouts are the times we really decide where we're going. Oh, and one last thought. The fringe benefits—travel, large expense accounts for entertaining current and future clients, a company car—are very convenient in your current circumstance. I don't see how you could really cut it otherwise."

He shook Scott's hand warmly and fell back into his elegant leather swivel chair.

Scott was glad there was a chauffeur awaiting the old boy, for he wouldn't have been safe on the street.

As he left the building, Scott realized that if he didn't follow this new opportunity, Cotter would give the assignment to someone else, and he would be backwashed into the regular office routine and would lose his clout as the promising white-haired boy. And of course, his raise.

On the way to the beach, he thought of corporations, ownerships, the potential of expense accounts and travel for himself and Belinda on corporate largesse; he thought of the life he would lead with an open sesame to a world of growing importance for the independent operator, if he was the right one and was clever.

There were three things in the world that had to be accepted as earthmovers. Expertise, energy, and money. Without these, there was nothing in the modern world of business. And a lawyer with know-how would be able to get them together.

It did not end there. Personal management could be involved. Participation in profits. One great picture in the hands of the right person could mean financial security for life. Imagine having a piece of *Lawrence of Arabia* or such recent blockbusters as *The Apartment* or *Ben Hur*. What a variety of choices! Frederick Cotter had opened his mind, and he felt foolish that he had not recognized the possibilities himself. He had been too much in love.

Scott hadn't the slightest idea of what kind of life he was going to face with Belinda, or of the chess game taking place with her as the pawn. Had he known, he wouldn't have so blithely planned a happy evening. He also knew he couldn't help himself. He'd have to tell her he was going to become a senior partner in the firm.

Claudia began to live the character of the Madwoman of Chaillot. In spite of the fact that the Countess held up her skirt with a clothespin; wore button shoes and a hat that imitated her dream of Marie Antoinette; added beads, a lorgnette, and a full capelet dripping with sequins that were dangling on threads; and carried a dinner bell in her bosom, to Claudia she was magical.

As Claudia grew to know her character, her subtle European humor, she found her warm, womanly, straight-backed in her determination to save Paris from the monsters who would destroy the city's beauty for the riches of oil. She was wise and strong in her insanities, and there was dignity and aristocracy in her straight carriage and straight thinking.

Belinda came into Claudia's room as she was practicing.

"Whatever are you doing?" said Belinda as she watched her aunt's regal posturing.

"I'm finding the Countess," said Claudia. "A week after I arrive, there will be a final dress rehearsal. It isn't like a Broadway play, slowly progressing to concept and maturity." She swung her chair around and faced Belinda. "You know, I'm glad to be getting back to live audiences and the day-by-day challenge. I feel free again. That's why I have to get into the skin of the Countess before I work with the cast. It isn't the actor who makes the style of comedy, it's the writer; so I have to face my own reality before I see the tapestry of Giraudoux's splendid play. I hope you experience this someday."

"So do I," said Belinda. She sat down and sighed. "I hate to face this chopped-up personal appearance tour. I envy you."

"I'm glad to hear you say that," said Claudia. "And one day you'll do it. All actresses worth their salt occasionally take a flier into theater. Film is wonderful, but it's only part of it. That live audience watching you . . ."

"The thought of it scares me," said Belinda.

"It scares *me*," said Claudia, "and it scared your father, no matter how many audiences he faced. Did I ever read to you what George Bernard Shaw said about the theater?"

Belinda shook her head.

"Well," said Claudia, "I have it at hand. I sometimes read it when I feel life getting humdrum."

She arose and took the book out of a rack by her bedside, opened it, and read, " 'The theater is as important as the church was in the middle ages. It is a protector of the conscience, an elucidator of truth, an army against despair and dullness, and a temple of the ascent of man.

" 'Whether you have made a shout or a whisper in the time of life, the faceless multitude which once had a grasp on life and missed it, and seeks self-involvement in your image—if you really touch them, then you are the idol.' "

She lowered the book and looked at her niece.

"You did it in *The Oracle* without knowing it."

"Why didn't you ever read this to me before?"

"It's strong medicine," said Claudia. "Let me go on with it. 'When you lose your grasp in this mass hypnotism called fame, then it can never be really recalled—even in the frenetic eyes of your aging acolytes.' "

"I don't believe that," said Belinda.

Claudia looked at her, surprised, and then smiled.

"I can't tell you how glad I am to hear you say that. That part to me is an apostasy of the human spirit. I've had a renaissance when life seemed worst. We can't always win. Be prepared for failure, Belinda, but don't ever let it overwhelm you. Even when life seems worst, it is as if you are finding another path. And often it's a better one. It isn't easy for me to do this play, but I must."

"Why?" said Belinda.

Claudia was tempted to tell her it was for the money, but she realized that was no longer the reason. She really was into it, and she longed to be on her way. She was a little ashamed, but suddenly both Max and Belinda had been relegated to their own places, and she was moving into her own orbit.

She looked at Belinda wistfully. "You can't help yourself sometimes; you never stop learning. That's the pain and the joy of maturity. I'm an actress, and now that you and Max don't need me, and someone else does, I'm turned on again. I was hoping you might have a day or two in New York where you could find time to come to Elderberry and see me."

"I want to," said Belinda. She stood up, stretching. "Oh, Claudia. I hate this whole thing. Two months ahead of me as Titan's puppet. Seeing myself either scowling or wide-eyed innocence on billboards wherever I go—as the two Lucretias. Everything connected with it was like a bad dream."

"Don't say that," said Claudia. "Your performance was outstanding. You learned a lot. Most of all, control of your characterization under difficult conditions. I respect you for it."

Belinda came to her and embraced her. "Enough of that. We haven't set the wedding date yet. And Mrs. Stone is pushing it. I can't understand Mrs. Random's absence, can you?"

"Yes," said Claudia. "She's not on center stage, and she's piqued. Can't you wait until I get back before we make definite plans?"

"That's just what I wanted to talk to you about," said

Belinda. "Scott's pushing me, you know. He's got the loan of a friend's beautiful lodge on the north shore of Arrowhead Lake—pine trees, private cove, motorboat, and all that for our honeymoon. I'll enjoy the peace and quiet after what's ahead of me, but I don't know what to say. If I tell him your summer theater is holding us up, he'll resent you. I don't want that."

"Well," said Claudia, "just tell him you have an obligation to the studio, and you can't set the date until you get back from your tour. You'll miss him terribly, but he must understand how fatigued you are after the long grind of the picture. Play hearts-and-flowers, dear; he loves you, and he'll give in."

Belinda sat silently.

Claudia swallowed. "Do you want to break it off?"

"I can't," she said. "And he really is a darling. But I have to settle a couple of things in my mind."

"Everybody gets buck fever before a wedding," said Claudia.

"A couple of—I guess you'd call them hang-ups. And one of them is David. I have to see him. He's going to be in town tomorrow."

"Who told you that?" said Claudia, surprised. Her heart sank. It would mean the final showdown. Max would be learning that his option was not going to be picked up.

"Don't you know I call Fergus's office every day to see where he is?" said Belinda, smiling. She went to the window and sighed. "I know he's too old for me, and I know, as you say, he's a confirmed bachelor, but oh, Claudia, I wish David was the man I was marrying."

Claudia picked up a perfume bottle as she sat down again at her dressing table. She could see Belinda in the mirror, her head bent, her whole pose one of dejection.

"He's not for you," said Claudia.

Belinda turned. "Don't get me wrong," she said. "I'm not in love with him—I just love him. I feel so—so complete around him. Isn't that awful to say when I'm expecting to marry another man? But it's true."

"Maybe we'd better ask him to dinner," said Claudia.

"No," said Belinda. "I want to see him alone. As a matter of fact, I didn't tell you, but I called him in London. It's arranged."

Claudia's first thought was that there would be an expensive telephone bill. Then she realized there was more than that in the air.

"How about Scott?" she said. "Isn't this a little strange?"

"I told him it was a business meeting."

"Well," said Claudia, "keep it that way in your mind. I told you, it's no go." She set the perfume bottle down sharply.

Belinda looked at her quizzically. "I don't understand you," she said. "You're always so sharp with me when we discuss David."

"I'm sorry," said Claudia. "I have a lot of things on my mind."

They heard the faint sound of chimes from the outer gate.

"There's Scott," said Belinda. "We're going to Jack's at the Beach. I hope we have a quiet booth. I'm going to have to tell him we can't set the date yet."

"Be gentle with him," Claudia said. "I've never seen a man more in love."

After Belinda left, Claudia struck the proud, spine-erect attitude of the Countess and looked at herself in the triptych mirror. Then she slumped and grimaced at her reflection.

It was a tired face, she thought, having none of the true aristocracy and purposefulness of the crazed woman she was going to portray.

What a fake you are, she told herself, giving fine advice to Belinda. You haven't really done any of the things you talk about in such lofty terms. You blew it when you had the chance to be a real actress. You were an important movie star just because you were there early and were photogenic. You never lived up to the advice you're handing out like an apostle of the theater. What Shaw said is true; once you lose your grasp in this mass hypnotism, it never can be recalled . . .

"I told you that was the way it would have to be," said Belinda. "You know I have to go on with my work; you agreed the night you asked me to marry you."

The waiter set the lobster plates in front of them. Scott, masking his slight hurt at her defensive attitude, waited until the man was out of hearing, and then he took Belinda's hand.

"I'm not complaining, sweetheart," he said. "I know you have to go on tour. There's nothing we can do about that. But, as you said, your Aunt Claudia deciding to do two plays in summer stock is going to hold us up a month beyond the time I'd planned."

"Well, she decided it wouldn't be worth it if she didn't do two plays. She'll finish with *Glass Menagerie*. I used to rehearse that play with her when she coached me. She made me study a dozen plays! But she told me I had to be Laura because the lost, fragile little crippled girl was everything I wasn't. You should have heard Claudia read. She gave me such gooseflesh when she was Amanda that I could hardly remember my own lines. She'll be wonderful!"

Scott suddenly realized that her enthusiasm about acting recalled a world he could not enter. He felt a little resentful, but awed.

In a second she came back to their problems of the moment, but he wondered if he'd ever win the respect and admiration he saw on her face as she talked about Claudia's talent.

"Anyway," she continued, "I'll be worn out from hopping around from city to city. And the way your mother and Claudia are planning, I think it's wonderful that they can put it all together a month after Claudia returns."

"Did your aunt have to do summer stock at such an important time?"

"You never know what our family will do," said Belinda. "Besides, an opportunity like this doesn't often come along."

She looked up at him, smiling. It wasn't his fault that she was edgy. Sometimes his very presence made her feel guilty. She took his hand. "You might as well get used to Barstows," she said, "since you were foolish enough to get mixed up with us."

Warmed by her smile, he felt better.

"Not foolish—lucky. I was going to tell you something later, but I'll tell you now. Belinda, it's going to be a big surprise, and you'll see how our lives will mesh together in more ways than one."

She had started to cut her lobster, but she put down her knife and fork, seeing the excitement in his eyes.

"I've had a great opportunity offered me. Fred Cotter just told me I'll be a senior partner in the firm. I'm opening up a department that will include coordination of film industry talents and finance. And we're going to live very well. A big raise, travel, and I'll be able to give you the things you deserve. It has worried me more than you know," he smiled, "asking a film star to live on my junior partner's salary."

Belinda looked at him, surprised. "I never even thought of that," she said. "What is mine is yours, wherever we are. Polly could come by in the day to take care of things. We can always get away at the beach and weekend with Claudia and Max—"

She almost said "and Alex," but she didn't risk it.

She saw by his expression that the idea of weekending with her family didn't intrigue him.

"Well," she amended, "I mean, Claudia said my room would always be my own. It doesn't mean we have to use it."

"Look," he said, "leave it to me. There will be so many things for us to do. Sailing, golf at Del Monte Lodge, deep-sea fishing in La Paz, occasional trips to Europe on my business. Give us a chance to make our own pattern."

Her heart sank at the idea of Catalina on the *Sprite* with the Howards; golf, a game she didn't know, in cold, foggy Monterey (the alternative being sitting on some club veranda with the wives); fishing at La Paz (she could already feel the early-morning competitive dedication); and trips to Europe on his business, *his* business . . .

But then her mind dutifully traced back to his excitement. Of course—the other side of the coin; she'd handle the rest when the time came. A raise, benefits, involvement in the entertainment business. That was the trigger.

"Why Scott," she said, "all those, what Claudia calls corporate fringe benefits, are wonderful, but they don't really matter. You're going to be involved in the entertainment world. *My* world. How marvelous!"

"Yes," he said, "can you believe it, I'll be able to help you."

Seeing the interest and pleasure in her face, he parroted what he had learned from Frederick Cotter. He might as well plunge. After all, in spite of the wrench at his ethical gut, it was time to find her reaction.

"It's a new world, darling. Many picture people are taking on legal advisers because the agents and studios don't have the power they used to have. It wasn't their intention to use you, for you were a minor when your career began; but you are a multimillion-dollar property now, my little superstar. You should have your own corporation, share in the profits of your pictures, as well as having an immense salary with nontaxable expense accounts. You know, you are the keystone to an independent company. On your name alone you can bring a company into production. You're in the driver's seat."

Belinda realized that Scott's attitude was completely altered. What had happened to the man who had said that if she married him she might not always be a film star?

Once again, she thought, once again, I'm being used. This man who loves me has changed because it means advancement for him.

But her chagrin was followed by a sense of sudden relief. Wasn't that what she wanted? Hadn't she deliberately planned this marriage so she could be free to do what she wanted? And if he went along with it, she wouldn't have any problem. She could have her career, be her own person, and he would be involved with the business end, making it easy for her, putting all the details together so she wouldn't be bothered.

"Why Scott, that's just wonderful. You'll take care of things for me. Can I choose my own stories and director, and can I have artistic control?"

Scott was amused. "How did you learn so much about the business? You'll have to teach *me!*"

She was touched by his eagerness. What a strong ally she had in him.

"I've heard nothing but this sort of thing at home for several years," she said. "Claudia is into it all, hoping that Max will have a better deal next time around. You know, he's not very practical. Neither am I. But now that I'm going to be able to make my own choices, you'll protect me."

"Darling," he said, "you know you've already got me, and as far as I can see, you can have anything else your heart desires. We'll find you the best properties; we can go to New York and see the plays, contact publishing houses for the cream of the new novels that might suit you, or comb the European market. You'll have the sort of creative freedom you deserve. And you know I'll protect your interests."

"I know," she said. "I'm dizzy thinking of the possibilities. I'm sure you can work out my contractual obligations with Titan. At least, I'm not exclusively tied up. I know you'll think I may be ungrateful, but Scott, I don't want to do another heavy historical drama with Max. How can I get out of it?"

Scott took a deep breath and sipped his wine. He was surprised by the conversation. It had been so easy to have Belinda accept him as the controller of her career. At the same time he was taken aback at her immediate concern about artistic control, that bugaboo he had heard about from his confreres. Little words alone had wrecked many a career. Actors were noted for not being as shrewd as the old moguls about what proper elements went together to make a commercial success. They were inclined to see the script in terms of themselves rather than the whole, and favorites instead of talent were often hired, and many a production floundered.

Also, her quick decision made him realize that behind that placidly beautiful face she knew what she wanted.

This practical conversation, the first they'd had, was far removed from the sweet talk of courtship, but, since what they both accepted as moments of truth were laid on a platter along with their lobster, he might as well plunge further.

"I must tell you," he said, "that through the legal grapevine I have learned Titan has refused Max's Egyptian script. As much as they would like you to be the beautiful Nefertiti, they feel that the story is not a commercial item, and Titan is in trouble. They have to recoup on *Young Lucretia* before they can get into another superproduction."

He saw a look of relief cross her face.

"Oh," she said, "how awful for Max! At the same time, what a relief for me!" She put her hand out quickly. "Don't misunderstand me," she said. "Of course I love him dearly, and he has been wonderful to me. But I'm tired of being a puppet. Without meaning to be, he was my Svengali. I want to be my own person. I want to do a light comedy, and I want to work away from the domination of Max and even of Claudia, as much as I love her."

"I'm glad to hear you say that," said Scott. "Oh, Belinda, we're going to start together in a new and exciting world. I needn't tell you how grateful I am that I can protect you as well as love you."

He was so moved that he only toyed with his dinner. He sipped his wine, often stopping to look at the clear cameo of her flawless profile. Undoubtedly, he thought, she was the most beautiful young woman in the world. It was difficult to avoid being annoyed at the other diners who stared at her, and even the maître d' was too obsequious. Wine they didn't want was sent courtesy of the house. Two notes were delivered to the table. Belinda looked in the direction of the waiter who brought them and nodded politely at two tables.

"Sorry," she said between her teeth, leaning toward Scott. "One of them was the art director on the Borgia picture, and another is a newspaper columnist who was at the big bash Niadas gave for me in Rome. I always get this sort of thing. You'll have to get used to it."

While they were having coffee, the maître d' came up to them.

"Forgive my interruption," he said, "but when you're ready, I think you'd better leave by the kitchen. There are about twenty fans perching at the entrance with cameras and autograph books, and that newspaperman went to the phone and called a photographer to rush over and have his picture taken with you two for his Sunday supplement. I respect the privacy of our customers and I thought you'd like to know."

"That's very thoughtful," said Scott. "I'll take the check now, and we'll slip out."

Belinda set down the lemon peel she was about to drop in her demitasse.

"I didn't really want it anyway," she said, pushing the little cup aside and making a face.

"Oh Scott," she said, "it's a goldfish bowl. I'm so sorry. I'm afraid that's another thing you'll have to get used to."

They escaped through the kitchen, stared at by two fry cooks, a waiter balancing a full tray, a checking girl who unabashedly grabbed a slip of paper and got an autograph before they could pass her stand, and the maître d' who accepted a crumpled ten-dollar tip from Scott.

In the pier parking lot, they managed to drive off with a sigh of relief as they saw the cluster of fans at the entrance doors.

"Well!" said Scott, "I guess we outwitted them."

"It doesn't always work," said Belinda.

He looked at her, concerned, and put his hand on hers as they swung up onto Ocean Avenue.

"What are you going to do on tour?" he said. "Who's going to look after you? These mobs could be dangerous."

"Titan protects me," she said. "Grace Boomer arranges everything. But it's no fun. I'll be so glad when it's over."

The evening was ended as far as any romantic notions were concerned. Scott felt as if he could hear the jingle of thirty pieces of silver in his pocket. He had delivered Belinda to Cotter, Sullivan, and Gregg to guarantee his future.

Belinda felt she had used his devotion to protect herself, and to get away from the binding, smothering ties of family. They were both eager to get away from each other and to explore in their minds the plans the evening brought forth.

As they kissed rather casually and said good night, both of them defined the problem concerning themselves in a different way, but the enigma was the same—where does progress end and exploitation begin?

It was not until Belinda was alone in her room that the impact of the evening hit her.

What a change this marriage would make! Scott was not just a playboy—she was not just entering a new social life. He would be the builder of her business future as well as her husband.

A partner, someone to protect her, to give her freedom to do what she wanted with her life.

She fell asleep feeling comfortable.

The storm that Claudia feared, like many anticipated problems, came to naught. After it was all over, she decided that the unexpected and the insignificant was sometimes the trigger leading to a holocaust, and great fears could dissolve like the hot morning's Santa Monica mist.

Friday, two days before she was to leave for Elderberry, David came into town. He would only be in for the weekend, he had to fly back to Europe; already Titan was beginning to listen to the British music scene, and he was busy signing artists and arranging proper recording facilities. There was a suitable sound stage in Soho, where some of the best film scores had been recorded, and it would be possible for the parent company to record and test their first platters before the artists were considered important enough to tour the United States.

David made a quick phone call to Claudia in the morning, explaining the necessity of the new diversion in corporate interests.

"I don't like to go into it too deeply," he said, "but we both have always had a potent interest in the company, and you must know how difficult it is to diversify while trying to keep Titan functioning in Hollywood."

"I know," said Claudia. "We're not as lucky as Fox and Metro, finding oil in our backyard."

"Well," said David, "we still have the back lot and the ranch in the valley."

"Please save my little casita by the lake," said Claudia, "for my old age—which, I may add, is upon me."

"Never that," said David. "By the way, how is the little one doing? Is she happy?"

"She's not a little one anymore," said Claudia. "I hope this man will be strong enough to help guide her through the shoals. Anyway, she still has a fixation on you. Are you going to see her?"

"Perhaps it would be wiser if I didn't."

"I was going to suggest it," said Claudia, "except that I'm tired of being God. Besides, it doesn't always work."

"Right," said David. "I'll send her some flowers and tell her I'll see her next trip, which will be soon. You know I'm seeing Max today. Fergus told me he's already alerted you."

"Be kind," said Claudia.

She was grateful that David didn't know what a bind they were in economically. It would have been too humiliating for both herself and Max. It was incredible, even if true, that two talented people, after years of work, could have their backs against the wall, but with the fluctuating Hollywood economy and the escalating expenses and taxes, such a situation was not unique.

"Of course," said David. "Trust me, Claudia. When Max leaves, he'll think everything is great. He has too much talent to be stifled. And let's hope we can continue with him in the future."

"Thank you," said Claudia.

"I hear you're doing summer stock," he said. "I told Red Powell to give you a little boost in the trades and the New York papers. It doesn't hurt. How did you decide to do that?"

"You know, an old war-horse," said Claudia. "There didn't seem much for me to do at the moment, and the hambone in me said it's time to hear the audience again, mano a mano. I think I'm just crazy enough to play the Countess in the *Madwoman of Chaillot*. Don't you?"

He laughed.

"You sound great," she said. "Are you happy? Is life being good to you?"

"Who's happy?" he said. "Yes, I like the challenge of trying to glue everything together in this changing entertainment world, and by God, do I have it! I think you have plenty of challenge ahead of you too, Claudia. You don't fool me. It must be a wrench to see Belinda off on her own. How is she going to fit into the establishment? This seems a strange way for her affections to go."

"Well," said Claudia, "they're very attractive together. He's a nice man. I hope it works."

"Not only attractive," said David. "They're probably the most handsome couple in the world. The coverage they'll get on their photogenic qualities alone is incredible."

"Doesn't always work," said Claudia. "Remember Zelda and Scott?"

"Well, I hope there's no bottle involved here."

"None," said Claudia. "You'd better be here for the wedding. I'll give you advance notice."

"Of course," said David. "This is as close as I'll ever come to seeing a wedding of a member of my family."

"Too bad you couldn't give the bride away. I suppose Max will do the honors."

She wondered if she had been tactless. Did it grieve him to know that Belinda was his sister and he couldn't claim her?

For a fleeting moment she thought of what a trauma it would have been for Fergus to see David give Belinda away. It was a Greek drama, this whole relationship of the two families.

"We're sending a car for Max," David continued. "We're having lunch and a meeting. Fergus and I decided it would be the best way. Making a call at your house might seem too much of a kiss-off. We'll discuss plans for the future if and when the time comes that a property is suitable. I hope I get a chance to at least say hello, but I doubt it. Tell Belinda I send her best regards and all that sort of thing."

As Claudia folded some summer cottons into her suitcases so she would be free to spend the next day with Max in case he was in a turmoil, she tried to put away her guilt. She could not mother the world—or perhaps the word should be *smother*. They were beloved to her, Max and Belinda, and they both had their own lives to lead. So be it.

As the afternoon hours lengthened, she worried, like many a Hollywood woman when an important meeting for her man was scheduled at a studio. She knew every move that would be made, and she knew that the system itself was intrinsically cruel.

Max would be driven to the studio by a company limousine, with gatemen and varied personnel greeting him effusively; Max Ziska, the great talent, who had finished one big blockbuster and might be doing another that would help keep them all working.

David and Fergus Austin would meet him in the executive dining room, where anything personal would be smothered by the presence of top brass. There weren't as many important faces these days around the long table. Directors of one or two movies, a few television executives, and heads of departments who were allowed to rub elbows with the elect in the private room, the last stand of privilege in a fading society. A long row of special condiments, Kosher dill pickles, cole slaw, sauerkraut, imported mustards, Swedish rye crisps and Armenian slabs of bread in baskets showed the dispensations to the elect. A special waiter served them, and those who wanted to could order steaks or diet food not on the menu in the commissary beyond.

Max would order his usual pastrami sandwich with coleslaw. She wondered if he'd have indigestion during the meeting. Somehow it seemed cruel that he would be fed, so to speak, then taken to the slaughter. But if the meeting had been held earlier, David and Fergus could hardly have had lunch with him. His food might have turned to gall.

After the lunch (where Max would be greeted effusively, for many of the diners did not often have the opportunity to meet with such a legendary director), they would go to Fergus's office, where he would be told that his services were no longer needed. Even though it was said politely and with great respect for premium product, he would leave the studio a has-been.

It would take no time for the rumors to filter throughout the studio. Whether it was a report from the legal department rejecting his submission on the new script, whether it was a chance remark from a secretary to another secretary, the word would soon be out that Max Ziska no longer had a contractual obligation to Titan studio.

He would be unemployed, his failures and the expenses and extravagances of the last two epic pictures noted, and, after a few tart remarks in trade papers, his possibility of employment in other studios would diminish to a vanishing point.

Claudia had been through it herself, she had seen it happen with her brother Jeffrey, and she knew that these would be terribly difficult days for Max.

She thought seriously of canceling her summer stock

commitment. What did it matter if one old actress didn't appear?

It was only three o'clock when she heard the door close in the inner court. She rushed downstairs, her heart beating, to greet Max, trying not to look too apprehensive or to let him know in any way that she had been alerted about what was to happen.

Much to her surprise, he greeted her with a smile.

"Well," she said brightly, "how did it go? Did you have a nice lunch?"

"The usual pastrami," he said. "Saw a lot of the old team."

"I mean," said Claudia, "what did David have to say? And Fergus, of course."

"Not much," said Max. "Let's go out by the pool and have a breath of fresh air."

As she opened the glass doors, she glanced back. He seemed in good spirits.

They sat on a hammock.

"Well," he said cheerfully, "I am relieved. We're not going to do the Egyptian story."

"Relieved?" she said.

"Yes," he answered. "Somehow, like many a Jew, I've lost my taste for Egypt. Am I foolish?"

She took his hand. It was not shaking. He really seemed relieved.

"Not at all," she said. "I thought of it, too. What do you want to do?"

"I want to take out all my old manuscripts and find something lighter. David suggested it."

"Well," she said, "you've worked hard, dear. If that's what you want, do it."

It hadn't even entered his mind that there would be no income. He had been too busy creatively for such thoughts to seep into his brain.

"I think you should slow down, anyway. You'll be busy reading while Belinda and I are away, and you'll have the house and your thoughts to yourself."

He looked at her, his eyes warm, his clasp endearing.

"I'll miss you deeply," he said, "but it will be a good time to look into myself while you're doing the same. Perhaps I could fly east and see you."

"Perhaps," she said. "But do what you must do while I find my audience again. I love you, and waiting to come home to you will be one of the exciting things in my life. It all works well, doesn't it?"

He smiled, rather absently, she thought.

"It does," he said. "I have an idea; and it might just work out. Not an expensive picture while we see what *Young Lucretia* does."

Thank God we have Effie, thought Claudia, to take care of Max. And Alex, of course.

Hand in hand they walked up the stairs. He was eager to get to his study. A man like Max had creative juices that flowed no matter what the circumstances. Claudia almost laughed at herself. What did disruption of a property mean to him? Or the temporary absence of a person? He had already left her. Max had written in prison camps and hospitals, he had come through better than many of his peers, civilians who had remained in the United States at their chosen work and fallen by the wayside.

As she packed the last of her things and prepared to spend the evening with him, she thought of what she could do after she finished with Belinda's wedding. She would have just enough money to get through it all, and then she would remortgage the beach house. Prices were escalating, and she could take the chance on refinancing. The worst that could happen would be that she could rent it for a high price during the summer season, and she and Max and Effie and the baby could go somewhere inexpensive, maybe a cottage in Palm Springs, even a hotel in Mexico, and sit it out, if nothing came up.

Life was changing. Belinda would be gone, and there was no other way but to go along with it.

There could be more summer stock. There might even be a play. And Max would eventually come up with something. Talent like his could not be stopped permanently. She had always landed on her feet, and she would do it again. Max had made her life these last few years, and she could do the same for him.

What the hell have I been worrying about? she said to herself as she heard the familiar sounds of his files being opened and shut. Already he was on his own trip. No matter how many miles away she was planning to go, he was already ahead of her.

I'm just right to play the Madwoman, she thought. It's easy to compare her with the insanities of my own life . . . Here I am, a woman born before the century began, going through all this upheaval to pay for caterers, rented plates, silver, chairs, tables, mixed help, and all those bloody gardenias, for a wedding that isn't even based on love—at least on Belinda's part. Oh, Jeffrey, I wish you were here to guide your daughter a little better than I have. But I'll do the best I can.

Stuart Plimpton met Claudia at the airport in a limousine. She was a little shocked, but secretly amused by his appearance. He was neat and dapper, but he seemed to have shrunk. His liver-mottled skin clung to his skull tightly, and the effect was accentuated by the fact that he dyed his hair and moustache, which was pasted to him like shining jet black satin, to match what he remembered as his image of his youth.

He was alert and dynamic, darting, she thought, like a salamander in the shoals of his domain. The star players were the comfortable rocks upon which he basked. The stream flowing, sometimes tumbling him about, held the irritations of economy, apprentices, and local upheavals, depending on the floodtimes of the year.

As they drove through the country, he regaled her with his problems. The town of Elderberry, with its fake-fronted stores, trying to copy Stockbridge, put up an equally fake front of joviality while he slaved to make the merchants rich in the summer theater season. Then, when the season was ended, they lapsed into sullen criticism of the whole system. The gays imported their friends. Limp wrists were prevalent, and he had to protect the handsome young apprentices from stage-door Johnnies.

On the other hand, rich middle-aged nymphomaniac women came prowling after the visiting stars and character actors, and he had to protect their privacy as well. Occasionally, there was a coronary problem in the audience; many older people, sweating it out in the heat, couldn't take it.

Seeing Claudia's dismay, he felt he had said too much. He put one withered hand on hers and changed his story.

"You'll love the season," he said. "I have dear Bruce Dennis to play the Ragpicker, and you know he's a real pro. And I'm lucky that one of our local matrons is Helen French, she'll play the Madwoman of Passy that Estelle Winwood played on Broadway; and I got old Ginger Woods to play the Madwoman of St. Sulpice, which Nydia Westman did. I had to promise her enough actors to get up a bridge game or she wouldn't come. I tell you, it's going to be great."

Claudia shook her head. "All those beauties now playing these roles? I remember when Cecil Beaton and Orville were pleading to photograph them!"

"Ah yes," said Stuart. "Time passes, doesn't it? But people still have dreams of the past. They see things as they were. And so many are your fans. That's one thing that will make this play so exciting."

Realizing that he had hardly complimented her, as his habit seemed to be to have his thoughts tumble out before his wisdom dictated them, he turned, his mouth open. Claudia could see, as his heavy-lidded lizard eyes blinked, that he was about to pay her a fatuous compliment of the "but not you" school.

"Don't say it, Stu," she said. "We've known each other too long to crap around. I'll elevate the conversation by quoting something Dudley Fitts wrote after Plato, called 'Dedication to a Mirror.' I found it and remembered it myself after I took a look into a mirror one hot Roman morning:

> I Lais whose laughter was scornful in Hellas,
> Whose doorways were thronged daily
>   with young lovers,
> I dedicate my mirror to Aphrodite:
> For I will not see myself as I am now,
> And I cannot see myself as once I was.

"You see, I'm too happy with Max and pleased with Belinda's career to have to lean on what I looked like forty-odd years ago. As a matter of fact, I think it helped do me in."

"Lucky you," said Stuart, "and lucky me. You've no idea what trouble I've had with some of these old belles who still think they can play ingenues. They need a special makeup man to tape their chins to the back of their necks and special wigs to cover the wrinkles that get dragged up into their foreheads. One of our erstwhile stars had whole foam rubber bodies, like leotards, made with high tits and youthful thighs. After one wore out, she threw it away, and one of our local gayboys got it out of the trash can and wore it down the main street after a drunken party that night, screaming loudly that he had the body of Lola LaMonte. It was a terrible scandal!"

"No fooling," said Claudia. "Lola has a rubber body, after all the trouble she got into with the real one?"

"She wore it in all her last movies!" gossiped Stuart. "You can't believe her spindle shanks and knock-knees."

"Well," said Claudia, "beauty is one thing in life we don't have to worry about; time takes care of it. Now, how are we going to take care of ourselves? When do we start rehearsal?"

"Not until tomorrow," said Stuart. "But don't count on any spare time after that. That's why I always have my new people come in on Sunday. This current play's been on the boards a week, so it's not such a problem next week. The house is dark on Monday, so we can have our first reading and blocking on the stage. Your show, being a week later, we'll rehearse daytimes. You'll learn how it all functions. It's mighty hasty."

"You don't fool around, do you?" She smiled.

"I live and breathe it," he said. "You'll get a couple of hours to settle in and wander into town and take a look around."

Her suite at the Elderberry Inn was better than she had expected. The sitting room and bedroom were furnished in colonial style, the four-poster bed had a canopied ruffle, the flowered chintz on a sofa and chairs was old enough to be mellow, and it was all comfortable to live with.

Rag rugs, polished floors, floral paintings on the walls, and brass fenders at the hearth were cozy.

As Stuart had promised, there was a great bouquet of yellow roses with an affectionate greeting:

> Time and tide have brought us
> together, bless them both.
> Gratefully,
> Your first director,
> *Stuart*

Well, not quite the first, thought Claudia. Fergus was first in those infant days, if you could call it directing. She smiled.

Two bay windows looked out over a green meadow and a nearby lake fringed with trees and flowering dogwood. The sweet scent of cut grass drifted in, and the tang of salt air from the nearby seashore.

Before sunset, she wandered into the village. It was a festive street; people were wandering into the stores, and entering the tea shop and the restaurants.

The lobby of the theater was festooned with posters and pictures of the current attraction, *The Corn Is Green*, starring Connie Blake, a character actress she'd known in Hollywood.

She looked at the glossy eight-by-tens.

I could be playing that, she thought. I'd be better than Connie. *She* couldn't sustain a belch through a Boston baked bean dinner.

And then she smiled, ashamed of herself for wanting to devour every play. She had enough on her hands! It was good though. She had a feeling of belonging. No wonder the old pros liked summer theater. There were no Broadway critics pouring venom on them, and they were accepted affectionately.

There was an easel up announcing coming attractions:

The distinguished star
CLAUDIA BARSTOW
in
THE MADWOMAN OF CHAILLOT
★★★★★★★★★★★★★★★★★★★★★★★★★★★

Following Attraction
Broadway Tony Award Winner
ARTHUR DeWITT
in
LOOK HOMEWARD ANGEL

My God, she thought, an assembly line. Stu Plimpton really doesn't fool around.

She stopped in the drugstore to buy a tube of toothpaste. The druggist, Mr. Whitcomb, a tall white-haired man, introduced himself, greeted her warmly, gave her a card with his private phone number in case she wanted anything when his store wasn't open, and gave her a bottle of mosquito repellent in case the maid forgot to close the screens.

Entering the tea shop, she was waited on by a pretty blonde girl who sat her at a little table by the window.

"You can look out here and watch the action, such as it is, Miss Barstow."

Barstow, thought Claudia. Isn't it great, for once, not to be Mrs. Ziska . . .

She was served proper hot tea in a flowered porcelain pot, tiny scones with sweet butter, and bitter English marmalade.

The waitress smiled. "I'll be seeing you," she said, her scrubbed cheeks pink in the late-afternoon sunlight that filtered in. "You see, I'm playing Irma in your play."

Claudia looked at her, a little surprised.

"Well," she said, "as the description says, you certainly have the face and figure of an angel. But how do you do that and this, too?"

"Oh, this is my last day. I picked up a little money while we were waiting for you. I'm getting my master's degree at Bennington next year. I want to be an actress, of course, but teaching always keeps the wolf from the door. I love it here." Her eyes shone.

Claudia realized how times had changed. This kid, wanting to be an actress, but getting a master's degree so she could teach.

"Good for you," she smiled. "It comes in handy. I've been doing a little dialogue directing myself for my niece."

"Oh, don't I know!" said the girl. "Maybe you could get me an autographed picture of her." She flushed. "And I mean you, too, of course. My name is Joan McGowan."

Claudia extended her hand. "What a nice way to meet you. Well, I see you've already done your homework on being a waitress in the play."

When she finished her tea, she asked for the check.

"There isn't any check for you, Miss Barstow," said Joan. "This is on the house. It's your first day, and we're honored you came here. And the management said if you like this table, it's always yours."

Claudia felt as if she were a star again, cared for, sought after for herself alone.

Joan called over the hostess, a heavyset woman who wore a regal coronet of auburn curls on her round head. "Oh, Miss Barstow, we're honored to have you. Anytime you want a pot of tea or a sandwich when the inn dining room isn't open, we'll be glad to send it over. You're next door, you know."

Feeling she had already made a friend, Claudia thanked her warmly. Then she wondered what she should do about a tip. After all, the girl was going to be in the play with her. It would be demeaning. Maybe a gift would be more suitable.

She had a phial of lily of the valley cologne in her purse, and she turned to the girl as she held open the door.

"Here, Joan," she said, "I think you'll like this; it's my own favorite."

"Oh, Miss Barstow!" the girl gasped.

"Claudia," she said.

In the lobby she took her key from the affable young desk clerk and went to her room.

Once inside, she plumped down on her bed, comfortable with goose down shams and pillows, and looked out at the pastoral scene. It's too good to be true, she thought. Not that I'm a pessimist, but I wonder if this euphoria can keep up. I know rehearsals will be rough. I'm ready for that, and I can stick it. I will, and I won't complain, and I'll be kind to dear old Stuart . . .

She picked up the phone and called home.

Max was fine. He was busy. Mildred had invited him to Sunday dinner and of course wanted to hear all the news. Fergus was sending a car for him the next day for an interview with *Cosmopolitan* about *Young Lucretia* to be held in the studio dining room. Belinda was packed, ready to go on tour. She and Scott were going to dinner with his mother; Max had been invited, but he didn't feel like leaving the house. He seemed comfortable and happy, and his work was going well.

She assured him that everything was fine.

She hung up missing him, but her new world had taken over. If there was any gimmick in the near future, she thought, she couldn't see it.

The next day the reading was good. Of course, Joan McGowan was her slave. Claudia had an instinctive feeling that they'd soon be running lines together. Stuart was all right at blocking scenes; he had earned his ticket in these years where he reigned supreme in his summer kingdom, but, as far as Claudia could see, the nuances of characterization would have to come from heaven.

The young man who played Pierre, the would-be suicide who falls in love with the waitress, Irma, was a handsome, shy young man. Claudia wasn't surprised to learn he was getting his degree in engineering. This was another of the new breed. But when he stepped into his role, he lost his own identity and played to the hilt. Claudia also felt, with a shudder of instinct, that he and Joan McGowan would undoubtedly fall into one of those passionate summer stock love affairs as their roles overwhelmed them. They were such babies!

Bruce Dennis, who played the Ragpicker, was the type of character actor who could play any role, any age. He had worked here at the Cape for years. Summer stock was comfortable for him, and it supported him all year if there were slim pickings in TV and on Broadway.

"It's good to be flexible," he said, grinning.

There is another type, thought Claudia. I have really been on the cinematic shelf too long, where everyone is cast as himself or herself or they are out of the race.

The only problem she had was trying to avoid the smothering possessiveness of Helen French and Ginger Woods, who were anxious to chat with her, find out what was going on in Hollywood, and tell her all the news and gossip of New York.

But sometimes the three, so beautiful and acclaimed in their heyday, put their heads together and chatted like mad, revealing secrets of old times, old lovers, old bosses, directors, and actors, unlocking a treasury of memories as fragrant to them as lavender and rose petals long forgotten in a closed chest.

It was not only amusing, but a pleasant catharsis for Claudia. Stuart was shrewd enough to get a photographer to record their reunion and euphoria, hands flying in dramatic gestures, heads thrown back in laughter, and eyes widened at sudden revelations that wove them together in a hitherto unknown pattern of relationships.

When she could find a moment, she also studied *The Glass Menagerie*, aching at the tragic pride of Amanda as she reached vainly from her southern belle illusions to try to make her own youthful glory come to life for her fragile, fearful daughter, Laura.

Amanda was a far cry from the bold, zany organizer, the Countess.

Stuart had told her that, of all the apprentices, Joan McGowen was the best; she had done some stage bits on Broadway and several television spots.

But *The Glass Menagerie* was not Claudia's immediate concern. The Countess was more than enough of a challenge for the moment. A week of study, and the following week of rehearsal would suffice to change her image. Thank God she was a quick study.

She recalled that in her days in England this had saved her, after many a debauch and aborted love affair. And the same was true for Jeffrey. He could rise out of the fumes of a bottle and play Hamlet when he could hardly find his way back to the dressing room afterwards.

In the days that followed, the play took form. Claudia felt she was working well, surrounded by pros.

Stuart as director was letter-perfect in knowing the play. His manuscript seemed to have cuneiform writing on every page, and he carried a sheaf of notes in his shirt pocket, shuffling them like cards in a game of solitaire. But his enthusiasm won her when his talent bogged down.

She and the main cast understood their roles and their characterizations. Some sought Claudia privately to work on fine points, and they all felt that the play was a joint venture; that as a family they should share.

One evening she called Belinda in Detroit. Belinda seemed tired and irritated.

"Listen," said Claudia, "don't pull any sad songs on me. You should be working as hard as I am."

"I'm doing three stage appearances and four interviews today," said Belinda. "I'd rather be doing just one play like you. Why didn't you tell me Gracie Boomer was such a rumpot?"

"Are you having trouble with her?" said Claudia. "They shouldn't have sent the old bag with you."

"I'm so tired," said Belinda, "and Gracie isn't helping."

"Well, I hate to have you ring the bell on her after all these years, but if you have a real crisis, you'd better call Fergus, and Red Powell will replace her."

"Why couldn't they send somebody like that new girl, Laura West?"

"She's kind of green," said Claudia, "but you could always ask. After all, Gracie was green when she started me, but she did okay. I wish you could see the play."

"I'll see if it's possible. The way they have me routed, looks like I'm due for the South next week. Texas and New Orleans. That ought to be fun, if anything can be on this route. Maybe I could make it when the tour winds up. Anyway, the reviews are good; that is, for me."

"Good," said Claudia. "How about Scott?"

"He calls night and day. I've missed a lot of his calls. He suggested coming to New Orleans, but I blitzed it. Too busy."

"You're right," said Claudia. "Love and PR tours don't mix. I've talked to Max every night. I even dissuaded him from coming."

There was a slight pause.

"How is Alex?" said Belinda. "Oh, Claudia, what am I going to do about him when I get married? I didn't know how much I'd miss him on this trip."

Claudia's heart leaped. She had waited a long time to hear Belinda talk like this. Thank God she wasn't the frozen mother, denying the child privately, as she had been forced to do in society.

"Don't worry, honey," Claudia said, "we'll work it out. As his mean stepmother, I can always pretend to foist him off on you and Scott."

"I love you," said Belinda.

"I love you, too, darling," said Claudia. "Now be patient. You're going to have a glorious wedding. You'll be able to go on with your life in a better way. Things are looking fine. You have a wonderful man madly in love with you. I'm surrounded with talented people who like me, and Max is very happily hacking away on a new project which he thinks will be good for you. So don't let a little fatigue get you down. If we all did, there wouldn't be any careers."

"I'll try," said Belinda.

Claudia was pleased. It was true Belinda had her problems. She hoped Belinda wasn't making too many waves being a star. Three shows! Four interviews! And New Orleans could be hot and jammed up and a strong piece of meat for a young girl alone. In a sense, she hoped that Laura West would not be a replacement if Gracie defected. What did they know about that strange young woman who always wore a cotton glove on her left hand and had such a pale face, her brows and the etched line of her black hair sometimes making her face look like a mask?

If there was time, she'd call Fergus before any change was made. She'd like to know a little about the girl.

But she didn't have time, for the power and grasp of the play occupied her.

The opening night was a new experience.

The village was filled with elegant visitors, the parking lot glistening with Rolls Royces, Cadillacs, Mercedes, rented limousines, and the well-kept station wagons of affluent country people.

Members of the New York press were disgorged from a special shuttle run by Stuart Plimpton. A dinner was held for dignitaries, preceded by a cocktail party.

Claudia would meet them all after the show at a party in the main sitting room of the hotel. A few VIPs would be received previously in the Green Room, which had been set up comfortably with cold drinks and coffee.

When she first stepped on the stage and was greeted by a wave of applause, her heart leaped. Of course, her appearance alone was enough to be titillating. She rustled with her taffeta petticoats and skirt, her grand plumed hat, her ancient buttoned shoes, and her dangling beads. She had sharpened her features with heavy makeup, frizzed her hair in a pompadour above her large eyes. When she removed the dinner bell from her bosom and rang it, the acclaim was so great that she had to wait and do it again.

In her first long speech—"To be alive is to be fortunate, Roderick. Of course, in the morning when you first awake, it does not seem so very gay. When you take your hair out of the drawer, and your teeth out of the glass, you are apt to feel a little out of place in the world. Especially if you've just been dreaming that you're a little girl on a pony looking for strawberries in the woods."—the audience held its breath, enchanted by the words, the magic of her lovely face, and the mellow Barstow voice.

At the end of the speech the audience applauded.

So the play went. When the valiant old woman fought the wicked of the world and gathered her tattered remnants of society about her to do in the evil forces in her basement oubliette, there was an emotional response from the audience that hit Claudia in the stomach. It was as if they were all loving her en masse, and it was almost too much to bear. She carried the cast along with her, and at the end, when she told the lovers to never let a single instant wedge itself between them, the audience's emotions could be heard.

In the Countess's fantasy, her eccentricity bordering on insanity, her words rang out at the end: "Nothing is ever so wrong in this world that a sensible woman can't set it right in the course of an afternoon. Only next time, don't wait until things begin to look black. The minute you notice anything, tell me at once."

It was the triumph of mad reasoning against the insane power of bureaucracy.

Claudia, her face illuminated, arose, a symbol of right against wrong, carrying her tattered dignity and essential aristocracy like a banner in a high wind.

For a flashing moment her mind skipped out of character. That's me, she thought. This is how I am and have been. If this doesn't come off, I've failed.

There were a few seconds of silence. Her heart seemed to pulse into her neck. Please God, she prayed, don't let me stand here like a fool in front of all these people. Did I mean it too much and overplay?

Applause suddenly thundered in the auditorium, and she took a deep, sighing breath.

Curtain call after curtain call followed, the cheers and applause and stamping of feet moving like a summer storm.

After it was ended, she stood there, sweat pouring down her face, as one after another of the cast embraced her. She turned to Bruce Dennis, trying to play it lightly.

"No wonder you love summer stock," she said. "Is it always like this?"

"My lord, no!" he said, staring at her. "I've never seen anything like this in my life!"

Stuart Plimpton was ecstatic. In one classic performance, Claudia Barstow had elevated him to becoming a director of importance. The whole company had come into acclaim as the crowning glory of summer theater. The pictures of Claudia, Helen French, and Ginger Woods were on the front page of the Sunday theater section of the *New York Times*, and they were sent by wire service all over the country. It was not a lampoon, a cruel light shone on fading beauties, it was triumph of remembered loveliness, character, and vivacity over the years. People who had known the three as young beauties, sought after by the swains and artists and photographers of their day, took courage.

A hairdresser's chain created a frizzed hairstyle called the Countess Claudia pompadour. It ran in full-page ads in the New York papers. She was a Toulouse-Lautrec poster come alive.

Elderberry became the place to be; there were Standing Room Only signs in the theater lobby, and even motels in neighboring villages were filled up. Stuart begged Claudia and got permission to put on a Wednesday as well as Saturday matinee. The theater was usually dark on Sundays after a play closed, but he convinced her and the cast, with the promise of a heavy bonus, to put on a Sunday matinee and evening performance at the end of the run.

She agreed and also settled on added fees for future rehearsal time above the basic Actors' Equity minimum, as well as the extra week hiatus that had been planned for her predecessor. Of course she would keep her suite.

She decided to coach Joan McGowan privately in the role of Laura, for both she and Stuart felt the girl had won her spurs and could play the sensitive young cripple. Michael Ross, who had played the role of Pierre so successfully that one of the reviewers had called him a young Paul Newman, and a reviewer of another generation had referred to him as the Jimmy Stewart type (My God, thought Claudia, how could anyone ever merge those two!), was to play the Gentleman Caller. Joan was ecstatic.

It seemed the summer held a cornucopia of rewards for the young and old.

The very skies seemed to celebrate with them, the days were golden, sometimes a quick gentle shower refreshed the air.

Claudia, after her morning calls and riffling through a new excitement in her life, theater fan mail, would walk along the country roads, savoring the fragrances of the countryside and of her success, blending together in a feeling of physical well-being.

Max was working well; he even thought his new idea would be optioned once he got it down on paper. Alex had taken his first baby steps into nursery school, cared for by Effie, who wouldn't take a day off while Claudia was gone. She said she couldn't stand being parted from Alex.

Belinda called from time to time, always from a different city. Gracie Boomer had twice gotten up too late to take her to TV interviews. She and her maid Polly had worked it out by themselves with the limousine drivers. Belinda was going to have to ring the bell on Gracie. Claudia told her to let Red Powell handle it.

"Call and raise hell. You're a star, not a starlet. He's handled worse before, believe me!"

Belinda wouldn't be able to make it to see the play, but after New Orleans she'd come up; even if they were only rehearsing the next one, she'd get a chance to visit and to sack out for a couple of days before she went home and faced the plans for the wedding.

Claudia pushed all personal responsibilities into the back of her head. It took all her time and effort to do what she was doing. The adulation of the public, the reviews, the affection of the cast, and her teacher relationship with Joan made her life very full. Yet, in spite of all the benefits, she was weary. Bone weary.

17

As Laura West threw some clothes into her Vuitton fort-niter, she wondered how anyone with the name Barstow could possibly be lucky for her. For she had grown up with a hatred of the name.

She had been born in the sere, hot town of Barstow in the Mohave Desert in California, and her foremost ambition in life was to get out of it.

The town had been named after one of the founders of the Santa Fe Railroad, and as far as she could find out, there was no possible relationship with the acting Barstow family. But the name still made her nostrils quiver.

Her father had wandered into the dusty town in the late thirties and met her mother, a cocktail waitress at the Lucky Deuce Café and Cocktail Lounge.

They had married and merged their miserable lives in a sweatbox near the railroad tracks. A brother had been born first and then Laura. She grew up with the hubbub of a fighting brother, drinking parents, and a struggle for identity in a lonely world.

She was reared on canned beans and corned beef that she opened herself and ate out of tins, hot dogs and bulk store cookies, and if she was lucky and had been given a few coins, ice cream and candy bars from vending machines.

Once in a while some drunk ordered a T-bone steak and forgot it. Her mother brought it home, threw it into a pot with an onion and some potatoes, and left it on the back of the stove until it was used up.

Her mother told her to stay the hell away from her café—she didn't want any knock-kneed kid interfering with her customers.

259

During the day, her father either walked the rails or rode a handcar, covering about ten miles a day, examining the Santa Fe tracks that led toward Needles from the junction where the Union Pacific branched off to Las Vegas. It was a lonely job, and the few brains he had were fried in the desert heat under his straw hat. She remembered him as a man whose neck was red brown and wrinkled, his teeth yellow, and his smell that of rotgut whiskey, which he sipped from time to time in the hundred-plus temperatures to bear the wretched tedium of his work. He usually came home drunk just before her mother went off to the Lucky Deuce, and she often came home in the morning, after he had stumbled to work.

When Laura was fourteen her father raped her while her mother was at work. Her older brother Pete watched, and when the old man was asleep, he tried it himself.

Her struggle did no good, for she was pummeled by both of them into submission. But she was not surprised, for some of her girl friends at school had told her of their own experiences with relatives. Incest was not unusual among this society—the dregs, the jumping-off spot of the railroad world, aptly situated near Death Valley. Her friends talked about birth control, for pregnancy was the communal fear, and a trip to a quack doctor with five dollars worth of stolen money bought her the protection of the pill.

Until she was sixteen, she bore the humiliation of her father's and brother's advances. Just lie there, she thought, don't fight; get 'em on and off and over with.

At sixteen, her mother got her a job in a hash house. She used the birth certificate of an older cousin, and at least the job kept her away from the house until her father had drunk himself to sleep, and her brother, a cocky stud, was out prowling the town. He told her anybody was better than she was; she might as well be dead.

At seventeen, with her false papers, she worked the Lucky Deuce bar alongside her mother. She graduated from high school with a passionate interest in movies. Her two escapes were the movie theater and the library, and between the two she managed to develop an ambition and an education way beyond that of her family.

Because she had been so cruelly introduced to sex, she rejected the invitations of the boys in her class, quite certain that their lives would end up like that of her father and brother.

Since she had been a little girl, she had seen and heard of the behavior of some of the men who had worked in the Marine Corps' supply depot and the Fort Irwin desert training center. She wanted none of this.

But one day, by accident, while she was looking for a Kleenex in her mother's purse in the employees' rest room at the Lucky Deuce, she came upon two things: a small wad of bills snapped together with an elastic band, and a savings account book; she opened it, and to her surprise saw deposits, most of them less than ten dollars, that totaled almost two thousand dollars.

Her mother came in, saw her, and smacked her halfway across the room.

"You keep your goddamn hands off that!" she said. "When it hits five thousand, you won't see me around this dump anymore. And I earned it all the hard way—on my back—so your old man couldn't grab it out of my paycheck."

Laura began to think about getting all that money for doing what she had been forced to do for nothing. What difference did it make if you didn't enjoy it? You could tick off the strokes and think about what you'd get.

Some of the older sisters of the girls she knew in high school had drifted off to Las Vegas and Reno. Several had become dealers, and some had gone into prostitution in the rich late fifties. One or two had even made connections way beyond their dreams and had married.

None of that marriage crap, thought Laura. One guy having a contract to bang you free whenever he wanted. Never!

For a while she worked out of the Lucky Deuce; having no connections, she went on her own, a loner. It was a snap. There were a dozen motels where transients stayed briefly, some on the road commercially, some on their way to Las Vegas. As time went on, there were the men who were planning the Goldstone Tracking Station operated by the Jet Propulsion Laboratory at Cal Tech.

As she brought them their short orders in the bar, she could make contact. It was up to her to use her looks and her body to provoke them for a later assignation. It was easy, for the lower strata of Barstow held little to entertain transients, save a few stolen moments in a motel room or trailer.

It took her a short time to realize that she couldn't lie there like a piece of wood. She learned what the expression meant to turn a trick. She groomed herself, did her nails, selected perfumes that weren't from Woolworths, copied hairstyles out of fashion magazines, girdled her belts tightly so her hips would swing, copied little things from Marilyn Monroe, Sophia Loren, even the innocent Belinda Barstow, three years her junior, in *The Oracle.* Everything Laura learned was one more chance to get more money.

She was afraid to put her money in the bank because someone would find out that she was a minor and tell her family. As time passed, she turned her bills into fifties and hundreds and sewed them into the corner of her shabby mattress. She was sure nobody would ever look at anything in her room.

She carefully counted her legitimate paycheck in front of her father and brother, and allowed them to know that she hid it in a shoe box in the closet, accepting that a certain amount would be pilfered before she screamed and threatened to tell her mother what they were doing with her when she wasn't home.

She wasn't going to head out of town until she knew exactly where she was going. She wouldn't end up like some kids in a sweltering motor van traveling from spot to spot, avoiding the law, taking on cheap Johns. She was going to enter Las Vegas with a wardrobe, a hairstyle from the pages of *Vogue,* a gold necklace that could be recognized as Tiffany's, and classy luggage. She was going to land in a top spot, or none at all.

Class, that was it. When you got your stake, you could get out of the gutter and lead the life you wanted, have a steady income, property, a good car; you could travel and wear fine clothes, and most of all you would have doors of your own you could lock against the world. The fastest way to get all this was to be a first-class hooker, not a second-rate street hustler.

She read the Bullock's Wilshire and Magnin ads in the *Los Angeles Times* occasionally left in the bar by customers. She shopped for several expensive outfits with money orders, and hid the things in the back of her closet.

One day when she came home, she found her dearly bought wardrobe missing, and when she rushed to check her hidden bankroll, the mattress was ripped, the money gone.

She never saw her mother again.

She moved out of the house, for there was no use to even try staying there with her father and brother.

With the last dollars in her purse, she rented a dilapidated trailer and a campsite on the outskirts of town. She fixed it up as best she could, put in an electric fan and heavy drapes, and played loud music when she needed privacy.

She opened her ears to the talk of others of her kind in pickup bars. The trailer became her laboratory: she learned the ways of the freaks and kinkys, how to cope with them, how to pleasure them, and how to get the most money out of their need to have their hidden fantasies realized.

She soon was recognized and referred to as the weird scene queen.

She learned the when and how of payoff to local law—sometimes in trade, sometimes in money.

She took on customers until she had enough money to get outfitted again. Then she took the next Greyhound to Vegas, where she checked her luggage in a locker at the station. In her white silk dress and coat and her Tiffany gold necklace, she thought she looked like a well-off tourist.

She headed for the Desert Inn and wandered around. The cheap trade, mostly old women, were at the slot machines. Forget that. Then she watched the blackjack tables. This was a chance to sit knee to knee in one spot. There were a lot of men alone, some playing for high stakes. She left the tables and sat demurely in the bar at a table near the blackjack section, looking at her Patek Phillipe watch as if waiting for someone.

Finally she took a plunge, played blackjack for four hours, and lost two hundred dollars, pretending to be casual. Nobody gave her the eye.

This is for the birds, she thought. It would take a lot of tricks to make up for this.

She went back to the bar, and she wasn't there more

than ten minutes before a young man from San Bernardino, who had come to town on a motorcycle, struck up an acquaintance with her. He had been watching her, he said, and he thought he knew what she wanted; he was the one to give it to her. He unpeeled a big wad of bills from his pocket and bought them both drinks.

He took her to his room, upstairs. He was a leather man, and he beat her up. Frightened, with a black eye, a welt across her cheek, and lashings on her back, she locked herself in the bathroom until she heard him slam the door.

When she came out, he had gone. There was a hundred-dollar bill on the bed.

At a drugstore, she bought some covermark and a large pair of sunglasses. She sat in the hotel lobby facing the reservation desk to spot the men who were checking in, and she found a place next to them at the tables. She picked up two men; all she got was twenty from one, and the other got so drunk he couldn't perform; he passed out in his room; and she took the top off his bankroll.

That night, as she entered the casino, a tall, curly-haired security guard met her.

"I've been watching you," he said. He told her his name was Pete Yorke. He looked like a movie star; as a matter of fact, she had heard that some leading men had started here.

"You better watch out," Pete said. "Vegas is tough. You can't be an independent bar or street hustler here. And you sure are square. I spotted you hours ago. You don't know your way around, kid. The law of the jungle in this casino is that you don't pick up a high roller. While you're earning your hundred bucks upstairs, the casino could lose ten gees because he isn't at the tables. Of course, if he wants a girl, it can be arranged. But you've gotta have connections. Are you sure this is what you want to do?"

"I'm sure," she said, staring at him.

"Well, you'd be better off at one of the ranches out of town. You need protection. You won't get picked up by the management, and you can make plenty. And on a schedule you don't have to run yourself."

"What's your gimmick?"

"I want you for free once in a while," he said. "I like your looks. You're not all trimmed up like a firehorse. You've got class."

"How do I get in touch?" she asked.

"I'll take you when my shift is ended in two hours," he said. "Just stick around and play the slot machines and don't pick up nobody else."

She started to move away.

"I could remove you from the premises right now!" Pete said.

There wasn't a way out.

"Could you help me pick up my luggage at the bus station?" she said.

She realized she hadn't changed her clothes in twenty-four hours.

"Sure," he said. "Remember, I'm keeping a bead on you."

She knew what would happen. He picked her up, and on the way he drove her to the motel where he lived. He threw her on the mattress and pulled at her dress. She helped him so he wouldn't tear it. There was nothing under it. His eyes popped. He stopped quickly.

"Baby, you're built for it! I'm not taking no chances," he said. "This is a down payment."

When he had finished, after a running dialogue about how good he was, he affably told her she could shower and freshen up. He had his reputation with Gertrude and Chuck to think about. They owned the place, and he didn't want to take a bum to El Coyote Ranch.

"I'm no bum," she said, "and listen, mister, I always get paid."

She put her hand out and he laughed. He reached in his pocket and gave her a silver dollar.

She looked at it scornfully and put it in her purse.

"Don't worry," he said, "I'll send you a lot of Johns."

As they drove out of town, she glanced at him. He was handsome and arrogant and had a pleased look on his face as he told her how great it would be to work at El Coyote. The bastard was undoubtedly getting a payoff for delivering her. She had nothing but contempt for his good looks and his shoddy charm. Cheapskate. She kept the silver dollar as a token of what could happen to any woman dumb enough to get mixed up with a good-looking guy with no financial background. You could believe he'd show up for the freebies.

Out in the desert they approached El Coyote. It looked like a standard high-class dude ranch, rimmed with sand and mesquite, with a large social building in front and scattered adobe bungalows done southwestern style at the rear of the property, except for the fact that it was surrounded by a high iron fence and gates that opened or closed by electronic control at a gatehouse with two men on guard at the entrance.

Pete ushered her to an office at the left.

Although she could hear music and voices in the distance, the office was as austere as any businessman's domain.

Pete introduced her to the Hunters. Obviously they had a deal going. They shook hands with him and he left.

Gertrude was an older woman whose painted face was a map of her past life. Her glasses, hung around her neck on a silver chain, were decorated with turquoise beads. Like many of her kind, she had run to fat, and in her middle years she could afford to be good-natured because she was in control. With a smile she could kick a girl out into the desert. It had just happened; that's why there was an opening.

Chuck, her husband, was younger, thin, and, Laura figured, undersexed. His pleasure was taking care of the books of the ranch. That he did at night.

They took a look at her and approved.

"What's your speciality?" asked Gertrude as if she were hiring a cook.

"Money," said Laura.

"How about the s. and m. and the tv scenes? Problems?" asked Chuck.

"I take on problems," said Laura. "I dig all the freaks, the slave and master, and the tv's. I can dress a transvestite faster than I dress myself."

"Okay. Fifteen minutes for the regular Johns, but of course if you take on kinky dudes the price soars by time and the nature of the trick. You've got the best spot. You're insured for any physical mishap, and you've got buzzers all over in case of panic."

Chuck smiled like a kindly host.

"We protect our girls. Some have been here ten years. That shows you."

The terms were set of what services she would perform and what she would get. She would split fifty-fifty with the Hunters. She would work a sixteen-hour shift for sixteen days. After each shift she could leave the ranch for an hour to have a drink in a nearby bar or do what she chose, but no visits to town.

No money would pass through her hands—the front office handled these details.

"You're right for the Dragon Lady," said Chuck. "Now all you gotta do is darken your hair a little more, keep your face white, and concentrate on the makeup around your eyes. Look bold. We'll give you the slaves. Wear leather, boots—we've got some slick wardrobe for you."

When she realized that all the girls were cast according to type and the client's tastes, the irony of the situation hit her. She had tried so hard to be elegant, to be chic, and now she was cast like a Gorgeous George wrestler, to be the heavy. What the hell, the money was beyond her dreams.

Later she learned their checking system was almost computer organized. A patrol ticked out time with a stopwatch, and if a customer couldn't make it within a certain time, he was bounced out or he paid extra. Tough.

She also found out that her predecessor as the Dragon Lady had left with two broken arms. She'd have to be on constant alert.

She realized later that she had been let in because they needed her type. Most of the girls were pretty; all had stacked bodies, but many wore wigs and tottered on high heels; some wore evening gowns, some bikinis, others, the petite ones, dressed in ruffled underwear and wore ribbons for the men who wanted little girls. Some sat in the large social room with their Johns where there was music, drinking, laughing, and conversation.

The farthest bungalow, with a path hidden by fences and desert foliage in the highly fenced compound, was to be her domain. The walls were thick adobe, the windows shuttered, and the doors double-locked.

There was a bar setup and comfortable furniture. It was obviously the elite suite. Thick rugs covered the floor with animal skins interspersed, and there was a fireplace of baronial proportions.

She was shown a light panel; strobe lights could be flashed on and off, as well as blue or red lights, as the whim chose.

There was a projector and a library of blue films; choose your desire and watch it to stimulate your action.

A sophisticated sound system played everything from Wagner to recordings of animal calls, moans of ecstasy, human cries, and shrieks.

The bedroom had a low bed, suspended on chains hung from the ceiling, which was mirrored, along with one wall. In the closet she found an assortment of ropes, shackles, whips, dildoes, and fine chains with Spanish leather handles. Also a wardrobe of silken finery in large sizes for the tv—transvestite trade. She realized that she had taken on a big job.

But she figured she could handle it. Most of the poor bastards who came for help with their hidden desires would rather be punished than punish.

And most importantly, in both rooms, and in the elaborate bathroom with an oversized tub, sauna, and shower, she found push buttons that would alert help immediately, including two strong-arm men with the proper tools to unhinge a locked door in a flash and get her out.

A dormitory at the back of the property contained a sitting room and small rooms where the girls could sleep between shifts. They often were given sleeping pills to help them let down. Many of them instead chose liquor or narcotics.

Anything they did privately was condoned as long as it didn't show during working hours. It was standard to take Nembutal to sleep, Valium to calm down in case of jittery nerves, and uppers to get moving after a bad night. And in the final moments before the "paradise stroke," she sometimes popped ampules of amatol nitrate to turn on the customers.

Liquor was used by many of them, but too many girls were fired for being awkwardly alcoholic or breathing boozy breath on their customers, no matter what the state of their trick's breath was, from garlic to brandy fumes, the most sweat-stinking alcohol of them all. Often they playfully got the VIP boys into a large shower "to turn them on"—but in reality to clean them up.

The girls were addicted to a variety of narcotics: some dropped acid, tripped on speed, or took amphetamines, barbiturates, goofballs, secobarbital, amobarbital, and rutalin, an antidepressant.

One of the girls, a silent and sullen young mulatto, always started her holiday with two balloons of heroin.

Another got PCP, angel dust, the animal tranquilizer, from a veterinarian. One day she got up and couldn't come down. When she lashed out at two girls who were peacefully sharing the *Christian Science Monitor*, she was wrestled out by two guards and never seen at El Coyote again.

There were as many types of escape as there were girls. Lolita, a Mexican girl, freaked out on psylocybin, synthesized from mushrooms used in Mazatec Indian ceremonials. She had exploding visions which she attempted to share in unintelligible gibberish. The girls tried to hush her so she wouldn't get sacked.

One of the tragedies of the house was a young Swedish girl, Elsa, who was addicted to cocaine. Her habit cost her half the money she made. Her pimp was also her narcotic procurer, and he kept her satisfied to secure his income. She often slumped from fatigue and went into a corner where she took out an inhaler filled with white powder and sniffed coke to get back into action. In her spare hours, she used a delicate golden spoon, given her on Christmas by her lover, to sniff up the powder. One day she didn't wake up. She was carried away quickly by night to another county, and her body was dumped in a lonely canyon.

They were narrow footpaths, these escapes. Laura, for the first time in her life, associated closely with others of her ancient trade, and saw the pitfalls of their lives exposed daily. It made her retreat more and more into a state of mind that warned her that while she was young, and still—as many said—beautiful, she had better figure how to get the hell out. Although she enjoyed marijuana as an occasional relaxation (she never cared for alcohol), she feared that she too, in time, could become addicted to the five-fingered leaf and find herself, like the others, bargaining with her hard-earned money for the finest Acapulco gold. And later, as often happened, escalating for more kicks to more potent drugs. It was a rotten way to lose money earned on her back.

The first week, Laura was broken in carefully. She handled thirty-six men on the first shift, each for about fifteen minutes. Then she started with the exceptional trade—masochists, the poor slobs who carried a bundle of guilt and wanted to be whipped, scolded, mistreated. A few men shoved her around, but they were warned to keep hands off on anything that hurts too much or shows. The first week she tucked away fifteen hundred dollars.

Of course there were expenses and the cleanup maids to pay. Laura was fussy; everything must be immaculate. There were always salesmen around on off-hours to sell the best in cosmetics, wigs, clothes, furs for vacation times, stocks and bonds, holiday travel packages, new gleaming automobiles, expensive jewelry, clothes that could be bought by mail order from the Paris couture, even real estate.

It was natural for these women to buy status symbols. They must own what they considered only the best to comfort them in their free time.

Laura met hookers as a group, saw the vapid blankness in most of their faces. They were merely fornicating machines. She despised them and decided that she would use her time to discover how she could belong to another way of life.

Meanwhile, she would buy what was needed to create the image she was building for herself. Everything would be the best. These girls didn't understand class at all.

In her first months, she bought a Jaguar, and then later a Paris wardrobe and a fine string of matched oriental pearls and earrings. Then she decided that she wanted a Rolls Royce. Too many of the girls had Jaguars.

In her second year, she selected a Phantom Three classic Rolls in mint condition. She didn't want anything she owned to look too new. A classic Rolls was the thing. It was fortunate, she thought, that as the Dragon Lady she used a masklike makeup, long lashes, heavily darkened eyelids, eyebrows that were penciled to turn up in a diabolical manner, and lips drawn into a dark red curve. This was as concealing to her natural looks as clown makeup, and she felt that no man whom she would meet in real life would recognize her.

As time passed, she became more and more sickened by the confinement, the forced association with a group of women she considered subnormal. The lesbians (of which there were many) had unsuccessfully made passes at her. In group sex, she performed with both men and women for the pleasure of the customers. It didn't make any difference. It was all the same, a job. She had never had an orgasm (although she was adept at faking it) and she hoped she never would. She was disgusted with some of the girls who had pimps and turned everything they made over to them. If that's what love was, she wanted no part of it.

She read in her spare hours, studied French, and picked up Spanish; her image, she thought, would be to be a rancher's daughter from Nevada, newly widowed. That would explain the license on her car. A California license on her Rolls would cause questions about where she came from, where she had gone to school, and whom she knew.

After sixteen days on duty, the girls had half a month off. Most of them headed for San Francisco or Los Angeles where many of them owned houses or apartments, and some had families. They were proud of their kids and their old men, or brothers and sisters being put through private school or college by them, and had their family pictures propped up in their private sleeping quarters. Most of them led a square life on the outside; some belonged to country clubs where the members would have been astonished if they knew which men on their board had recommended these women for membership.

Searching for a place to spend her holiday time, she came upon the Bel Air Hotel in the elegant suburb of Los Angeles. Its entrance bridge was over a pond, where swans floated among the water lillies. The well-appointed bungalow suites, the Garden Room, dining room, the casual life around the swimming pool, where she sunned in a modest one-piece black bathing suit, was all part of her incognito life. She wore sunglasses, pulled her hair back, wore no makeup, and rarely spoke to anyone save a few conservative regulars at the hotel.

Her doors were never open to anyone socially, and she led an austere life, with constant room service, fine low-key music, and armfuls of carefully selected magazines and books. She was an enigma to the management, but her behavior was so correct that she was honored as a lady. An inference was made that she was a widow, and overcoming a great depression.

It was there she met the man who was to change her life.

He was in his late seventies, his forehead and bald pate speckled with liver spots, but he had the entourage and demeanor of a man who had much money and power at his command. He came to the Coast on business regularly.

His name, she heard, was Abe Moses. He was the brother of Simon Moses, founder of Titan studios, and as the head of a New York–centered chain of theaters, he controlled the fate of many Titan productions. He was always surrounded by a group of young girls, some of them starlets, obviously for show. Business was first with him. He usually had a phone to his ear; otherwise his prime interest seemed to be an endless game of gin rummy with other executives, while he sat in the sun and burned his skin to a deeper leather.

It was good to be sunk in anonymity, Laura found. Her nose poked into a magazine, she enjoyed eavesdropping on conversations around her. And as she listened to Abe Moses talking, she learned a great deal.

One of Titan's great problems, it seemed, was *Young Lucretia*. She heard the gossip that Belinda Barstow was the only hope for the picture. She also heard rumors about Belinda's affair with a young guy, an artist, who it seemed was a switch-hitter.

"That Barstow kid's such a baby; she'll get hassled, you can bet."

"She has been already," said Hugh Fairfield, the young banker who had come out with Abe.

They looked at him expectantly.

"I've taken her out, but lately she's only had eyes for this Kevin Frazier. He had a big idea of getting into a company with her until it hit the fan."

"You're just pissed off because you couldn't get her," said Abe, shaking his head. "I've been through 'em all at Titan. Claudia, her drunken brother, and six others who were a constant pain in the ass. But this kid, even at her age, is controlling millions. She's catnip for bankers. She's the only woman superstar around, and she's so square you wouldn't believe it. And one of the tragic consequences of this business is the reputation of a star and what one misstep could do for our economy. We had it with her aunt, Claudia, when my brother died in her arms: we had to pull out her latest movie from the Bible Belt circuit."

He mentioned his brother's death as if it were another business statistic.

"The publicity department is more concerned than even the front office. They know what can happen with this little hot pants. Thank God I'm out of that rat's nest." Abe shook his head.

"Isn't it strange," said Fairfield, "that a young woman can have such power? And doesn't seem to know it."

His comment seemed to trigger Abe Moses into anger. "Women!" he almost screamed. "Women's power has deballed us *all* in America!"

He went on with his diatribe as they sat by the side of the pool, almost out of control with anger. It was the first time Laura had noted any emotion in him, aside from noisy social anger at losses in gin rummy.

His irritation, his quick movements, and his argumentative high made her suspicious. He was on something.

She had learned so much as a hooker that she knew hang-ups. No needle; pot wouldn't do it.

As he sniffled slightly, she suspected the old boy got his energy and fake vitality from cocaine. That was becoming the in thing in upper circles.

After this explosion, she thought about him. And about Belinda. That kid needed someone around who knew what was going on. It was true what the banker Fairfield had said, she controlled millions and didn't know what power she had. She must be an easy mark.

Laura heard with surprise that Belinda still lived with her aunt and stepfather and a baby brother. She decided to listen more closely to Abe Moses and learn about this rich, screwed-up Hollywood scene.

She noted his disinterest, almost aversion, to married women, especially the wives of some of the successful men who gathered around him. One of his little entourage married a popular young screenwriter, and the next day Laura overheard his comments on the subject. He disparaged the girl, and strangely enough his pity was for the poor sucker who had married her. She was a ballbuster; she'd lead her husband a chase, he said. Too bad, the guy was a good writer. She'd take every cent he made; she'd picked him for his success. He was disgusted with the women of America who were inheriting some poor bastard's money. In his own family, he cried, power and inheritance had given women money they didn't deserve.

All his life he'd worked and hadn't nearly the clout that some man's relative or wife had gotten without any effort of her own.

Sure he'd never married. And you could bet he never would!

When Laura returned to El Coyote, a convention of theater owners came to Las Vegas. Although their headquarters were at the Sands, they took over El Coyote for one weekend.

The girls were told that everyone would be called Joe, and that any resemblance to celebrities was coincidental.

Laura wondered who would be given her VIP suite, and which aberration would be handed her as if her John had invented it himself. She would have to pretend to be startled, intrigued, and perform whatever he wanted with him, for him, with the dramatic implication that this was a first and a unique turn-on for herself.

She was surprised when her trick turned out to be Abe Moses. My God, that old mummy couldn't do anything. It had to be freaky! He had obviously been drinking, and she noticed with interest that he was quite different from the businesslike mask she had seen around the Bel Air Hotel swimming pool. He was scowling, and he seemed to be intent on some inner plague.

He had been on a big trip before he got to her suite, and she saw the room was prestocked with what he had ordered. She had no fear of his recognizing her. She wore a leather bikini, patent leather boots with high heels, and her face was masked in exotic makeup.

He asked for a double Pernod on the rocks and a cocaine spoon; he'd left his at the hotel. No expense spared on this one. Good God, she thought, this is really going to be weird. She poured his drink and for herself masked ice water with enough of a float of Pernod to make it look cloudy.

After he tossed down the second drink, she asked him what music he liked. He asked for Brahm's Lullaby.

Well, she thought, this joker really is on a trip.

He asked for a third double Pernod, drank it off, and settled back.

She wondered when he was going to start to tell her the

story of his life and how terrible it had all been, or when he was going to ask to be hurt or to hurt. At the rate he was drinking, she could anticipate either his flaking out, or some miserable, long funky session.

Fortunately, Brahms's Lullaby had been preordered. After all, he would have her for twenty-four hours. Maybe the lullaby would put him to sleep and she'd have it easy.

But as she turned, her drink in one hand, she was taken off guard. He leaped at her and threw her on the thick rug. As her glass went flying, she thought, so this little old man is going to play the phony rape scene. She wondered how soon he would rip off her leather bikini.

The first thing she saw was the flash of gold. He had a pocket knife in his hand, and she saw the blade flash as he pinned down her left hand. She was too late. His blade sliced into her ring finger. Feeling no pain at first, she saw the finger lying there, severed from her hand, blood gushing and staining the thick rug.

"Aha!" he cried out crazily, "now you'll never get a wedding ring from me—or any poor sucker!"

He picked up the finger and put it in his pocket.

She wondered if he were going to try to kill her. She stumbled up, the pain now throbbing into her hand as the blood pulsed out. She was faint, but, knowing she could bleed to death if she didn't get help, she managed to get to a buzzer and ring for help.

Abe Moses curled up into his fantasy, whatever it was, and by the time the guards rescued her and took her to the infirmary, leaving a trail of blood behind her, he had been strong-armed to the main building.

She was stitched, bandaged, and sedated, and she came to the next day.

Chuck was bent over her, Gertrude standing in the background.

"You sure got yourself a gilt-edged bond, kid," he said, "and as long as you have to get your finger cut off, you chose the right dude to do it. Know who he is?"

"I know," said Laura. "I sure do."

"You could get a half million at least," said Chuck cheerfully. "Of course our contract calls for half of it."

"I'm not getting a settlement of that kind," she said. "I'll take care of it myself."

"We'll do it," said Chuck strongly. "It's better that way. We're smart in these things. Honey, let us take care of you."

And yourself, thought Laura.

"I'll let you know what I decide," she said.

Chuck and Gertrude looked at each other. Obviously they didn't like it.

"Now you just rest up," said Gertrude. "We're going to knock you out, honey, for a day or so. Don't worry."

"No way," said Laura. "Where is the guy?"

"He's back at the Sands Hotel sleeping it off. When his friends got him out he was too stoned to make sense."

It took Laura about three hours to get her things together, she was so weak. Some of the sympathetic girls helped her pack her few possessions into the trunk of her Rolls. That was it. Good-bye to this scene.

"Honey," said Lolita as she put Laura's books in a carton, "they tried to get me to do the Dragon Lady bit —but after what happened to you and the last three I'd rather be a street hooker in Tampico. I ain't goin' to end up in some shallow grave out there in the desert. Not for all the money in it."

Laura shuddered. All the money—she'd put away twenty-odd thousand, and she would be maimed, a freak for life. That wasn't enough money. She had to do something, and fast.

She took a pain-killer and managed to sneak out in the darkness. It could have been the time for her break. The guards on the new shift signaled her as she waved and drove away.

She managed to wheel the car across the interminable desert road, and eventually she faced the late-night strip traffic into town, wondering if she'd blank out. She'd lost a lot of blood.

At the Sands, with a scarf covering her bandaged hand, she gave the desk clerk a fifty-dollar bill and sent a message to Abe Moses that she had to see him personally. She had come for her ring finger. If he didn't see her alone, at once, she would call for outside help.

Abe Moses was scared. All his adult life he had buried his hostilities. He had fantasized doing this to a woman for years, his fantasy growing as his power and ability

276

dwindled. And now, under the influence of drugs, he had been able to express his hatred. He knew he was in for it.

She sat looking at him, her face pale, her bandaged hand held up. She wore no makeup, and he recognized her as the young woman at the Bel Air pool.

"My God!" he said. "I know you!"

"You sure do, Mr. Moses," she said.

"What do you want?" he said, his face gray under his yellowish tan.

"I want a job at Titan," she said. "Of course, I don't want to be an actress, and I couldn't—with this." She waved her hand. "But I want to meet people, know them, be part of a business. I guess the publicity department would be the way. You see, I thought about it a lot. It sure was a stroke of fortune that brought you my way."

He looked at her bandaged hand, startled at what she considered good fortune.

"That's all you want?"

"All I want," she said. "Except I want a room here to sleep in for a day or so, and a nurse to take care of me."

She started to stand up, but she felt giddy, a wave of pain swept over her, and she had to sit down.

"You've got guts," he said. "Sure, I'll set you up here. Of course, you will sign a paper absolving me from any other payment."

"Yes," she said, "providing you guarantee that this job will last at least a year. And I want an apartment, not too splashy, in Beverly Hills. I don't want to be conspicuous. I want to be straight."

He stared at her, relief plainly showing on his face.

"Done," he said. "I have the right connections. I'll get in touch with Fergus Austin and Red Powell."

"What will you tell them?" she asked.

"I'll tell them you're my girl," he said. "That'll shock 'em. I never had one I set up."

He was concerned, for she hadn't signed any papers, but he'd have her sign the proper documents before the deal was set. There wouldn't be any trouble getting Red to put her in the publicity department. Red owed him from a few plush times Abe had provided in New York when Titan had cut down on large expense accounts. The Titan publicity department was a little heavy on the older staff, anyway. Nobody ever need know where she came from or what she did.

Secretly, even in his disturbed condition, he was delighted with the idea of putting a tough hooker into the sanctum sanctorum of Titan publicity.

He knew a few reformed girls of such persuasion. They were usually glad to get out of their profession, and they did a good and thorough job when they got into the straight world.

He put Laura in a suite in the hotel, got her a nurse, and settled back, for the first time in his life grateful to a woman—one who could have ruined him.

Once established at Titan, there was nothing too much Laura could do to learn her way around. Red Powell was obviously in on a long-term ticket, past the age of retirement, but kept on, as were others of the nucleus of Titan old-timers. In a studio, it seemed, special skills and experience kept men working longer than would be allowed in another type of business.

Red had a well-earned reputation for being a fair man; the secrets he kept were tucked away forever. He would never reveal what he knew about the private lives of stars, directors, and tycoons, but it would have been worth a fortune on the book market.

Even though he was very busy, Laura was summoned to see him the day she came to work.

He sat her down and looked at her keenly.

She was slender, yet full-breasted, her dark hair smooth against her white skin, and her brown eyes met his gaze unflinchingly across the desk.

She was neither coy nor nervous, and, as she looked at him, he had the feeling that maybe he was the one being appraised.

"Let's get to the point, Laura," he said. "I don't usually let people in to work in my busy department because someone asks me to. As far as I'm concerned, the gentleman who asked, although he has lots of power and is a big stockholder, means nothing to me. If you get out of line or swing your weight in the wrong way, you're out, even if we have to keep you on payroll to fulfill the deal. Okay?"

"Okay," she said.

"Good," he said. "Now, I will start you as a junior publicist. If you're any good, you'll get moved up. I could use new blood. Some of my stable is getting a little long in the tooth."

He looked at her gloved hand.

"There is one thing," he continued. "I know everyone will be asking about your hand. Leprosy?" he grinned.

She allowed herself the privilege of wanting to like him. He seemed like a good Joe.

"Not quite," she said. "I have a finger missing. An accident. I don't like to talk about it. People don't like to see a maimed hand."

"Harold Lloyd had one," said Red. "He managed to disguise it with gestures and a glove, and he delivered some of the best comedy in pictures. I guess you can work it out."

"Of course I will," she said. "Thanks, I didn't know that about Harold Lloyd."

"This is not a luxury job. You'll have to do your own typing."

"Can do," she said.

"You'll attend all meetings, punch the time clock—figuratively, that is. Each day you have to do three items in triplicate aside from your other work. Our legmen will get in touch with the columnists; that's not your bag at first. You will be assigned to production sets and some players, and you will get to know your people, but you must not abuse the privilege. Many of them will be very much in the public eye."

"Of course," she said, thinking of some of the important men she had serviced at El Coyote.

"I'll start you out studying the requirements for our idea campaigns."

He opened a folder and handed her a blue mimeographed page.

"This is your primer. Study it. Get to know the Titan lot. Keep inconspicuous. Think of what the public will like to read without fabricating too much crap or being scandalous. Look for the unique. Protect us if you see something that shouldn't be known. Sometimes the stuff our department keeps out of the papers is more important than what we put in."

He picked up his phone. The interview was obviously ended.

She returned to her little cubicle and looked over the blue sheet: "In making up campaigns for forthcoming pictures, please list ideas in the following order, and under designated numbers so there is no misunderstanding concerning specific purpose for which ideas are intended."

There were seventeen points, from cast and credits, synopsis of picture plot, art layouts, magazine features, to the suggested finality of local planting with the press.

The little blue page became her primer. She also studied all the trade papers, columns, and fan magazines. Soon she could copy the style of the various columnists so the legmen could plant her material easily.

She wandered around the departments, seeing how furniture was assembled, how sets were fashioned, how wardrobe came to life in the lofts, how scripts were written and finally mimeographed in sequences. She even investigated the TV departments, watching their assembly line techniques. She studied how the transportation and business end of the great studio functioned to make everything run smoothly and come together in time; which was money.

Old shoes like Gracie Boomer, whom she recognized as a boozer, told her how glamorous it had all been in the old days when labor was cheap and dozens of pictures were made at the same time.

Laura finally won her spurs and was assigned with Grace as her senior to handle the production of *Young Lucretia*. She saw Belinda Barstow at work and carefully stayed out of sight as much as she could. She'd rather have a little more power in publicity before she approached her.

Laura analyzed Belinda's beauty, recognizing the inborn spark of talent as she watched her do some of her scenes.

She spotted Claudia Barstow as coach on the sidelines and saw her dedication. It looked like a smothering relationship, for Laura had no idea of what had gone on before in their lives.

Max Ziska was undoubtedly a wonderful old man, a fine director, and he had the mien and the outlook of a poet. Laura had never seen a person like him before, for he was not a brothel man; he lived in some other world.

Her early days on the lot, she saw Kevin and Belinda together, and she knew instantly that he was a double gaiter. His stance, his tight trousers, and his underdone elegance cried out the narcissist. At the moment he was absorbed in Belinda, but Laura wondered.

Whitey, the old guard at the back lot gate, let her meander there, glad to see some action—the place was almost forgotten. One day she wandered, enjoying the lake and imitation jungle, remembering how real it had looked to her as a kid. She smiled to herself. This was a make-believe world in every sense, but it was the first real world she had ever seen.

Instead of always lunching in the commissary, she decided to pick up a sandwich and a malt and spend some of her lunch hours sitting under a fake banyan, scribbling notes for her first picture campaign, just enjoying being by herself.

One sunny noon, as she sat looking at the riverbank, a man came along the path and stood gazing over the water.

He wore a suit she recognized as being English, and she spotted the elegance of handmade shoes. He was unusually correctly dressed for a man on the back lot.

He took out a cigarette, tapped it, and then, obviously thinking the grass could be tinder, put it back.

He turned and saw her just as she was biting into her ham sandwich.

"Hello," he said. "I thought I was alone."

He did not smile or put out a hand. He stood there for a moment and then, with an economy of movement, sat on a log and looked out toward the distant greenery.

"Hi," she said. "You've found my secret place."

"It's been here a long time," he said. "And it's going to have to go. Along with the back lot . . ."

"Too bad," she said. "I guess a lot of us had our dreams built around it."

He nodded, and a faint smile touched his lips.

"Believe me," he said.

He sat in silence a moment and then stood up.

"Back to the treadmill," he said.

He glanced at her. She picked up her malted milk and stirred it with her straw.

"I'd offer you some refreshment," she said, "but I only have one straw."

"Thanks," he said. "If I'd known, I'd have brought one."

He signaled a quick good-bye and left along the footpath into the jungle. She admired the back of his head, the casual way he moved. She wondered who he could be. Certainly not an actor, and too elegant to be the run of Hollywood top brass. But obviously he belonged here. She had never met anyone the least like this man. He had not questioned her, he had not been disinterested, nor interested for that matter. He had been obviously himself, and that was a cool, somewhat introverted self. Yet she felt he was very much in charge of this domain.

After he left, Whitey, the old cop who had been put out to pasture as back lot watchman, came by.

"Just checking you don't light up a cigarette," he said.

"Yes," she said. "I don't smoke."

"You have to watch out for that David Austin. He forgets. Known him since he was a kid. Caught him swimming bare-assed in this pond when he was a toddler."

Laura's eyes widened. So that was David Austin. The grandson of the founder, Simon Moses. The man who owned the studio: heir and chief stockholder. No wonder he had style. She should have recognized him from the pictures she had seen in the slick magazines. He was always hobnobbing with the great in Europe.

She finished her malt, put the plastic cup and straw in her brown bag, and walked back into the bustle of Hollywood.

David Austin . . .

The rest of the day he kept entering her mind. She had never thought of a man this much before. He was a person. And she couldn't figure him. Usually she had them all pegged in a category, and she thought she was pretty sharp in looking beneath the surface.

Laura grew to know the department routine, and she learned faster and was more interested than any of the newcomers. She was stepped up in salary, no longer a junior publicist.

She had worked hard, minded her manners, had a keen grasp on the machinery that made publicity, and had been screened carefully. She had gone out with a few men but was not promiscuous. As a matter of fact, men only dated her once or twice. The rumor got out that she was an ice maiden.

Abe Moses occasionally took her to dine at Scandia, the Bistro, or Chasens, when he was in town, but Red noticed that they were not into any noticeable sex scene. After all, thought Red, Abe Moses was probably too old to be involved sexually. He must have seen what a bright kid she was and wanted to give her a break.

Red had heard the carefully initiated rumor that she was widowed, her husband an aviator who had died in a crash.

That was the vantage point that made Red give her a break. She never complained, she went about her business with singular dedication, unusual in his department, for most of the younger people looked on the publicity department as a stepladder to another connection. The situation blinded him to the fact that he really didn't know a thing about her. All he knew was she wore very expensive clothes and jewelry and drove a well-kept Rolls. Obviously she didn't need her salary. So what difference did that make? The poor kid was trying to make a new life for herself, and no doubt was plagued with old memories. She deserved a break.

Belinda was fatigued and nervous. Dallas was suffering a hot spell, and she was facing a continuous round of press interviews and personal appearances.

It wasn't that people weren't nice. They were too nice. They overwhelmed her with flattery, admiration. Cameras flashed for press interviews, and crowds of citizens stood outside of any building where the word had spread that she was inside.

Two bodyguards had to be hired to hold back the people who rushed at her for souvenirs, ready to snatch bits and scraps of anything that belonged to her. Since her confrontation at the beach in Santa Monica, she had a fear of scissors, which could be whipped out of purses or pockets to snip a lock of her hair or a button from her clothes. Life could be a nightmare of unprotected, unscheduled confrontations during a tour. The public became a beast trying to devour part of her magic.

Leslie Charles supported her during interviews, a comfortable presence to share limousines and planes, although his nightly wanderings and late dates often left her ending the evening with strangers, or, worse, with Gracie Boomer.

But Leslie was no longer a stellar attraction, and he did little to garner publicity for the picture. Titan had arranged for her to have a personable local escort so it would not seem that the current sex symbol was escorted by an elderly man. It was obvious that no one cared about an old character actor outside of the sophisticated circles where he was remembered as a bon vivant or forerunner of the gay chic.

Belinda had not realized how much his image was waning. It had been difficult to get him on prime-time programs, and as a once-stellar attraction he was disgusted at the caliber of some of the shows on which he did appear. He was old hat, and being a sensitive man, he realized it.

After several of Leslie's panic calls to the studio about the caliber of his publicity, Fergus had carefully called around town. Fortunately Paramount was doing a large-budget historical picture, one of the flashy extravaganzas spawned by the success of Michael Todd's *Around the World in Eighty Days*, with the producers seeking drawing power in cameo star roles to make up for the lack of power in the leading roles. It took little persuasion for Fergus to ace Leslie in to portray General de Gaulle. The producers agreed it would work out beautifully, especially with Titan handing over half his salary under the table.

Before he left, Leslie had a late breakfast with Belinda in her sitting room.

"Well, dear," he said, "the old war-horse has been kept from being sent out to pasture. I hope you don't mind my defection. After all, it is pleasant to be wanted."

"I wish I could get out of the rest of this tour myself. But thanks for being so dear to me. Leslie, I know we'll work together again."

He put his hand on hers. She could see that he was controlling tears.

"You know, Belinda, in our day, mine and your father's and your aunt's, we belonged to a studio family. We had continuous protection, great care from a large publicity department that had handled us for years and always kept us glamorous before the public. The same contract players knew us and worked with us; the same staff, crews, directors, and producers protected us. Sometimes we fought, scrapped, loved, broke up, and got together afterwards. It was a life and it had continuity."

He paused, as if the clock had stopped. Belinda glanced at him; he was remembering, and she had a rush of emotion herself, for this was a tie-in with her roots, and she suddenly saw it as part of the history of a dynasty, so to speak, of privileged people, and, so far, she was one of them.

He went on. "Continuity—," he echoed, "isn't that funny! That's what they called screen treatments in the early days. Continuities. For years I was a prince. Well, my dear, one day you'll think of what I said to you at the start of your career. You're fortunate. Someday, only someday when it isn't there, you'll remember."

They faced each other for a moment until Belinda broke the silence.

"I haven't mentioned it," she said, "but thanks for the conversation we had about—about Kevin."

As she mentioned Kevin's name, she knew she wasn't over him yet.

"I hope it helped," said Leslie. "Believe me, Belinda, forget it. You have that divine Scott Stone waiting for you."

It was time for him to go.

As he turned to blow her a kiss, she remembered how he had left the last scene of *The Oracle*, realizing that his glory was past, that he had been demoted from star to character actor. She had seen the look of a man who had long been champion and knew his time was ending.

Now that Belinda was more or less on her own, she discovered that being on the road was not as easy as it had been when she traveled for *The Oracle*.

Gracie was a walking disaster. She still preplanned with the ingrown formula of experience, but she was often unable to follow through. At interviews, her speech was often slurred as she dipped her nose into her third drink, and, instead of being protected, Belinda had to cover for her. Other times, she sent a local PR substitute, saying she had to make phone calls and set up appointments in the next town.

Belinda spotted her several times in hotel bars, chatting with newspaper cronies, as she passed through on her way to the elevator.

When Belinda made a public appearance, she looked fresh, beautiful, and effortlessly put together, but the disorder in her room was the price her permissive life had exacted. She had never had to take care of her possessions; she had always walked away from such realities.

As the tour progressed, Polly was less and less help. She was easygoing and cheerful, but she certainly wasn't any Effie. A handsome young woman, she was sought eagerly by the black society of the towns they visited, her place assured as the maid and traveling companion of Belinda Barstow.

She did take care of Belinda's clothes and managed to get her wardrobe on and off trains and airplanes, or into limousines with the proper change of hats, jewelry, and makeup for her interviews.

Belinda began to realize how much planning had gone into Claudia's and Effie's seemingly effortless organization of her life.

One afternoon when Belinda returned to her hotel room, Polly disappeared, saying she had to press her gown for the premiere that evening, and Grace vanished with the tale that she had to make phone calls to the press. Both were to meet her at six in her suite.

Belinda had been up since dawn, starting with a morning TV show, sharing the spotlight with a local swing band and a religious cult leader.

Belinda knew that Polly and Gracie were both sacking out. She ordered the phone switched off, and, fatigued to the point of tears and facing the dreary, lonely impersonality of her Louis Quatorze suite, she pulled off her dress, ran her fingers through her heat-dampened hair, and looked at herself in the mirror without assaying the beauty that had put her on a pedestal. Having been born to it, she accepted it and often tried to forget about it. Born beauty did not have to be achieved. After all, she wasn't looking in a mirror when people looked at her. Through the eyes in her head, she looked at other people and tried to forget the bias her own person triggered in them.

She wished she looked like just anyone; the pretty girl who waited on her in the coffee shop this morning, or the tall, slender blonde on the TV show who was too involved in getting her show on the air to be overwhelmed by a picture personality.

It would be good to finish this tour, get home, have Claudia back from summer theater, and just sleep.

She threw herself on the bed and drifted off, wondering how she would feel when she saw Scott again. She remembered how elated she was at the thought that he would take care of her; it would be a partnership. Wouldn't it be wonderful if she could cure herself of her heartache over

Kevin and fall in love with Scott? Wouldn't it be even more wonderful if David Austin were here to be with her and to comfort her?

She tried to think of the other men in her life. She'd had such a crush on John Graves when they played opposite each other in *The Oracle*. She'd been so mad about him, but of course it had never come to anything; she'd been so young. She wondered how he was doing in his new company, filming now, she had heard, in Spain. Maybe she could work with him again. She thought fleetingly of Niadas, who like a conquering Caesar had come into her life one night and fathered her child.

They were all different, these men she had known, and all the result of her work, and this enshrinement when Titan had literally taken her out of bobby socks and made her a star. Well, Kevin was the only one with whom she'd really lived, slept, awakened in his arms, and pretended to keep house; the only one who had given her excitement and adventure. And that had ended in shocking heartbreak.

It was time, she decided, for her to take off her spiritual bobby socks and get on with life. It was time for her to forget Claudia and Effie and face problems on her own.

She drifted off to sleep. How wonderful it was to close her eyes and slowly sink into various levels and finally turn everything off for several hours.

She was awakened by her phone ringing furiously.

She picked up the phone, wondering for a moment where she was; what time, what city, for hotel rooms had been so alike these last hectic weeks.

It was the manager at the front desk.

"Miss Barstow," said a harassed voice.

"I thought I ordered my phone off," she said sleepily.

"We're sorry to disturb you; this is Mr. Simpson, the manager. But it's an emergency. Your representative Miss Boomer in Room 301 is in trouble, and we had to call an ambulance. I think you better come down."

"What's wrong?" said Belinda. "What's wrong! Is she ill?"

"We think she has delirium tremens," said Mr. Simpson, as if she had the flu.

"Has *what*?" said Belinda.

"Dt's," said Simpson. "Hallucinations from drinking. We've faced these problems before."

"I'll be right there," said Belinda.

She pulled on her dress and rushed to the elevator. The starter stared at her, and one of the passengers asked for her autograph.

She dashed out on the third floor. A group of hotel employees stood in the hall. Before she arrived at the door, she heard a keening wail inside the room.

Mr. Simpson met her. "I'm sorry," he said, "but maybe you can do something. She knows you."

Belinda went into the room. Gracie was huddled in a corner, clawing at her arms, staring, her eyes glazed.

Belinda was shocked. Grace looked so tiny and ancient curled up against the wall.

"Get those ants off of me!" she cried.

Belinda bent down. "Gracie!" she said. "There aren't any ants! It's your imagination."

Gracie swung out, and Belinda backed away from her.

"The hell it is!" she said. "Get them off me!" She began to scream, clawing her arms until streaks of blood flowed.

Mr. Simpson lifted Belinda up.

"You can't help," he said. "I'll get her out of here. You'd better reach the proper people in Hollywood."

"Of course," said Belinda. "What time is it?"

"It's 6:30," he said.

"Oh, God," said Belinda. "The mayor's picking me up at 7:00 for the premiere!"

Two men with a stretcher stood at the door. They pulled aside as she passed, then they struggled with Gracie, and put a straitjacket on her as she flailed and screamed.

"I'd better call my maid," said Belinda.

"She's right down the hall," said Simpson.

They walked to the door and knocked. There was no answer.

Belinda banged on the door.

"Polly!" she cried. "Polly, let me in!"

In a moment the door was unlocked. Polly was in a wrapper, and she looked ill.

"Get up!" said Belinda. "Get up and get to my room right now."

"Miss B'linda," said Polly, tears pouring down her cheeks, "I can't. I just can't."

"Why not?" said Belinda.

"I'm sick."

"What's the matter?"

She started to cry. Belinda walked into the untidy room and took the girl by the elbows.

"Pull yourself together. What's the matter?"

The girl retreated to the bathroom. She could hear her being ill.

Belinda went to the door. "I'll get a doctor."

"No," said Polly. "It won't do no good. I think I'm pregnant."

"Go back to bed," sighed Belinda.

She saw her lilac evening dress thrown over a chair. She snatched it up and left, slamming the door.

Simpson stood, concerned, in the hall. "What can I do?"

"Get me a maid to press my dress. I'll call Titan."

As Simpson watched her rushing to the elevator, he was a little startled. With the panic in 301 and the scene he had heard with the maid, the only thing this little movie star seemed to be interested in was her evening gown. Show people!

Belinda got through to Hollywood. David Austin, as she feared, was on an airplane and couldn't be reached. Fergus was at a meeting in New York. In a panic, she finally reached Red Powell. He had already been called by the hospital.

"I was trying to reach you," he said. "My God, I'm sorry for what you've been through. I'll arrive tomorrow with a replacement, or I'll stay on. What do you want to do?"

"I've already talked to Claudia about Gracie's drinking a few days ago," she said, "and we discussed that girl Laura West. She was around the set on the picture. I think I'd like someone young, not some old fuddy-duddy."

Thanks, said Red to himself. But he was relieved. He had too much to do to chaperone one teen-age film star.

"I'll talk to David when he gets in," he said. "I've already put a call in to Abe Moses. It's his theater chain you're opening. He'll get in touch with the manager and see that you get the A1 treatment tonight, and he'll get you on the plane tomorrow morning. Take it easy and try to enjoy yourself. I'm sorry about Gracie. We'll take care of her."

Take it easy! She thought of trying to pack the shambles

of her wardrobe and getting on a plane. It was too much!

Her first instinct was to call Claudia, but then she thought it would be better to wait until they could have a long conversation and she could describe how the opening and the evening went.

She dashed into the shower, brushed her hair, which she was wearing in a long straight bob. She had barely put on her dress and stepped into her slippers when the phone rang. The brass was on the way up. Champagne and caviar had been ordered. Gracie had made all the arrangements before she stubbed her toe on the bottle. "You don't meet the mayor and his entourage in a hotel lobby," she had said.

The waiter, who was arranging the hors d'oeuvres in the sitting room, answered the door. The room was filled with flowers, the candlabra on the tables were lighted, and soft music came out of concealed speakers.

She snapped on the amethyst necklace and earrings the studio had provided, took one last look, and decided she had done pretty well. She made an entrance into the salon, the full sleeves of her light silk dress floating behind her. The gown would look spectacular, Janos had told her, as she came down the curving steps of the new theater. He had keyed the gowns to match the decor of the theater in which she was to appear.

The mayor and his wife, six local dignitaries, and the local glamor bachelor, a cattle baron in his mid-thirties, stared at her, tongue-tied.

She was used to it; it happened all the time. Then conversation and the run of the evening always leveled it off. After a while, she knew, they would bring out their bag of tricks to prove their worth so she would remember them.

"My," said the wife of one of the bankers who had been invited as a favor by the new theater chain, "you movie stars really live it up. It must be fun!"

Belinda could only give her a faint smile. There was always one in every gathering.

"Sometimes we work," she said, "but it's such fun being in—in—" her mind almost went blank, but she caught herself, "in Dallas," she said quickly.

She gratefully took a glass of champagne from the tray.

Her escort, Harry Gilman, was a counterpart to other young or middle-aged men who had shared the arms of theater seats, limousines, and receptions with her. This one was robust, slightly red-faced, terribly impressed, and he tried to overcome it by telling her how great his ranch was.

He paused occasionally to shake his head, grin, and say, "Nobody will believe me! Nobody will believe that li'l ole Harry Gilman took out Belinda Barstow! We'll have to have some pictures to prove it!"

Then he would signal the nearest photographer, put his burly arm around her shoulder, grin like a chessy cat while the picture was being flashed, and squeeze her shoulder in an outburst of affectionate excitement as he let her go.

The theater manager and the PR man, seeing her dilemma, moved her from person to person to meet local celebrities.

Then she sat through the picture for the hundredth time.

"Gorgeous!" Harry Gilman kept saying. "You're just gorgeous."

She realized that he had little interest in the context of the picture, except when Cesare Borgia soaked his poisoned body in the carcass of the bleeding bull. Then Harry shook his head in amazement.

"Well, my Lord, who ever thought of such a thing!" he said. "If I ever get snakebit at the ranch, I'll remember that." Then he let out a chuckle and squeezed her hand.

Dallas was a typical premiere situation in a rich city; where an important charity was involved, it was difficult to know how the public was going to react in later runs. New, expensive gowns, many of them ordered months before from New York, Paris, and Rome; jewels that had been taken out of vaults and delivered by armored cars to mansions for the evening, were all part of the excitement. As far as sophisticated Dallas was concerned, it was a glamorous evening, and they were quite satisfied with the picture. It was rather shocking; Belinda had debuted as a very worldly actress; and they were all in on it; topic for many phone calls.

Belinda sat at an orchid-festooned table while an imported New York band played, alternated by a fine Mexican string trio flown in from Mexico City.

Belinda suffered through several dances and then sat at an endless banquet of chilled shrimp, mushroom soup, roast duckling flanked with rice and peas, Belgian endive salad, and of course the standard banquet show-off, flaming crepes suzette. Each course had a different wine, and Belinda noticed with some concern that her dinner partner was imbibing it freely. It loosened him enough to lean toward her and make several personal remarks.

"I didn't know 'til I saw this movie you were such a sophisticated little lady. Nobody knows what lies behind that beautiful, cool exterior, huh?"

Later, he put his hand on her forearm. "Why don't we get rid of these people and hit a couple of night spots— or whatever?" He gave her a nudge.

She had the sickening feeling that he was confusing Lucretia with herself. Was this to be her fate from now on? Was she worthy prey now, instead of the untouchable young goddess she had been in *The Oracle*?

"Look, Harry," she finally said, "you are a very nice man, and thank you for being my escort. But I am tired, and I have to get some rest. This is not all fun and frolic for me, even though it may look like it. I have a heavy day tomorrow."

"Oh, come on, be a sport," he said. "You must be lonesome, all by your little self on this trip. If you want, you can get into something more comfortable and we'll make a different kind of plan."

She looked at him, startled. How could it be possible that a wealthy rancher, a graduate of Cornell as he had told her he was, would pull a line at which a chorus girl would laugh.

"Also," she said, "I am engaged, and I'm going to be married when I get back home."

This startled him. "Some big actor, I suppose."

"No," she said. "He's a lawyer, and a very successful one, and one of the handsomest men in Los Angeles." She arose and turned to the mayor who was seated on her right. "You'll have to excuse me."

The mayor arose, helping her to escape.

Back in her room, Belinda called Claudia, waking her.

"I'm sorry," she said, "but I had to tell you. Well, it hit the fan. Gracie's gone. She has the dt's. Oh, Claudia, it was awful! She was all curled up in a corner, moaning and screaming; she thought she had ants all over her."

"Tough titty," said Claudia. "After pulling that on you,

just wait till I get my hands on her. Better yet, I'll send her an ant farm."

"And that's not all," said Belinda. "When I tried to get Polly, she was throwing up. It seems she has twenty-four-hour morning sickness. She's pregnant."

"My God! You poor kid. How did you ever make out?"

"I got through an interminable evening by myself. Oh, how I miss you."

"I'm proud of you. I wish I were there," said Claudia, "but the Madwoman finally did its run. They're playing *Look Homeward Angel* now and I'm starting rehearsal on *Glass Menagerie*. I've got two weeks. Joan McGowan is going to be good as Laura, but she needs as much help from me as I need help from me. I'm beat to the socks, too, honey. Did the public go for the movie?"

"At two hundred dollars a plate they ate it up along with an endless banquet—can you believe it?—*after* the showing."

"They do everything big in Texas," said Claudia.

"Including coming on strong," said Belinda. "My red-faced escort wanted to take me home. Anyway, Red Powell's flying in, I hope, with Laura West, after he talks to David. Oh, Claudia, I can't wait to get home."

"Well," said Claudia, "you're learning the cardinal rule of a personal appearance tour. The unexpected is to be expected."

After she hung up, Claudia thought about Laura West. She wished she had called Fergus to find out more about her. She remembered the strange paleness of her face, her phlegmatic, unsmiling attitude, and the mystery of the gloved left hand that had caused comment on the set. Nobody knew her very well, and even at meals she had never taken that glove off.

The fact that Red Powell was considering bringing her was certainly proof that he thought she was right to get Belinda through the last few days of the tour. And since Polly had decamped, it would do well for Belinda to have a young woman with her.

But most of all, thought Claudia, as she turned off the light and looked out on the dark landscape, silver-tipped by the moonlight, she was proud of Belinda. She was growing.

She had handled a bad situation without hysterics. Fortunately, she only had a short time left on the tour. Perhaps she could come to Elderberry and enjoy this blessed peace for a few days and see another life and a different part of the country.

She mused, actresswise, putting her thoughts and words into Tennessee Williams's southern accent. She was going to need lots of sleep and rest to be able to play the mother of a young girl. Everyone told her she looked wonderful, and she should, for success and life in the country had given her a bloom. She only wished Max could be with her to enjoy it. But he was doing well, cosy in his nest by the ocean shore, cared for by Effie, and writing madly.

David was sorry to have missed Belinda's call, but he thought no more about it, since she often telephoned him to share some experience or thought.

He had been wary of being too close to her since she had tried to make love to him, although her engagement to Scott had alleviated his fears.

Reports of her tour had been satisfactory. Of course, he knew that the hypo of her appearances would not prove the box office potential of *Young Lucretia*.

He called her hotel in Dallas, but she had ordered the phone switched off for the night.

Wearily, he prepared for bed. Beverly Hills could be a quiet place at night, and after the hurly-burly of listening to talent in supper clubs, and quick survey of theater, in London pressed by agents and business problems, the quiet gardens and peace of his rambling Mediterranean house on Lexington suited him.

It had belonged to Rebecca and Simon Moses, and he had inherited it as a young man and kept it even when he went to war. Later, he settled into it like an old shoe. From time to time the studio decorators had given it a modern slick-up, his secretaries kept it staffed with a cook, houseboy, and gardener, and celebrities and business people of the current moment were entertained when necessary, when he was on the Coast.

The next morning Red came to David's office and alerted him about the panic.

"Belinda handled it very well," said Red. "And she was

protected by the theater management from harassment last night at the premiere. The kid's so green she didn't know we had to hire six nice stalwart cops in dinner dress to take care of the mob that wanted to touch."

David shook his head. "What a nightmare. I wish I could go with you, but I've got the City Planning Commission on my neck about the plans for subdivision of the back lot, and I'm meeting Sidney Keys again in London in two days; we're laying out almost a million on our new recording facilities and studio space. Do you think she'll be all right until you get there?"

"Yes," said Red. "I have my friend Jill Jackson who writes a column for the *New Orleans Times Picayune* standing by, and she'll take over and get Belinda settled in the Royal Orleans Hotel. She's set up for an early interview and lunch, and by the time we get there Jill will hand her over to us for the most elegant press dinner money can buy at the Commander's Palace in the Garden District."

"Who is we?" asked David.

Red grimaced. "Belinda didn't mean it, but when I suggested I finish the tour, she said she didn't want an old fogey, but would rather have someone around her own age, more or less, and she asked for Laura West. You know, that new girl who wears the white glove. She's the best new member of my staff."

"Oh, yes," said David. "I know her. Met her on the back lot. Interesting person."

"Good," said Red. "I didn't want to do anything about it until I talked to you. What do you think?"

"Go ahead. I tried to reach Belinda, but she'd already flown out to New Orleans alone. Get there as soon as you can, and if everything's going well, get back fast. I need you. It looks as if we're going into real estate. Sharpen your pencil—you'll be glamorizing new urban development."

"That's a switch!" said Red. "I'm getting a little old to have to face a complete new set of editors. Well, at least there will be no personality problems of actors to cope with."

"Right," said David, smiling. "No one but local politicians."

Red groaned.

"Anyway," said David, "I'd like to talk to Laura West."

Laura came into his office and sat on the chair facing David. There was no posing in her manner, no social amenities, none of the feminine ploys women often attempted to use when they saw him alone.

Her hair was smoothed into a short cut, she wore a gray silk dress with white piqué collar and cuffs, and he noted that a broad gold circlet at her neck and wrist were those he had recognized on some of the status seekers recently in London.

She was an enigma. He studied her carefully, but, if she noticed, she made no sign.

"Well," he said, "we meet again. I guess you know why. We have an emergency. As you may have heard, I am very fond of Belinda Barstow. I saw her through some hard times when she began at fifteen. Stardom hit her too soon. She has adulation, which is like a pox to someone so beautiful and so young. Fortunately, along with it, she has unquenchable talent."

"I know," said Laura. "She was my ideal when I saw her in *The Oracle*."

"You're not alone," said David.

He offered her a cigarette. She shook her head.

"Good for you." He lit his own. "A placebo. Red told me he informed you that Gracie Boomer has to be replaced at once. I'd go with you, but I have an important meeting. We have decided it would be good for Belinda to have someone younger, who understands her, to be with her for the few days of the tour in New Orleans. So you're to take over."

He saw the flicker of her eye and was satisfied that she did not smile or look flattered or coy. That would have spoiled it for him.

He went on. "We'll send you out immediately. How soon can you be ready?"

"Just give me time to pack," she said.

"Good," he said. "Now if there is any problem, here are my private numbers wherever I am—which will probably be London, New York, or here."

He went to the window and looked out toward the green fringe of the distant back lot.

"Belinda used the European number when she was in a

jam. I hope you won't have to use it in New Orleans. After all, the tour ends in several days. But here they all are."

He handed her a slip of paper.

"If you're a good kid and take good care of her, I'll give you a picnic lunch in our jungle when you get back." He smiled. "I'll even bring two straws . . . We won't have our secret place very long. It's all going into real estate."

He shook his head. "Glamor is leaving, dreams are being dispelled. But after all, new dreams take their place, new illusions are manufactured. Don't you think?"

"I wonder if they can take the place of the old ones," she said.

He put his hand out. "Good luck," he said, "and don't be afraid to call me if necessary. I know you can handle it. Red Powell is your big booster."

She shook his hand and left the office.

On her way out of the administration building, she thought about his elegance and his manners. He was a gentleman, but under it she sensed a wistfulness. What was he? Cool, obviously cerebral, but he certainly wasn't gay, and he was a man without being macho.

And so Laura faced the first job she had handled outside the studio. She felt Belinda would be no problem. The big thing would be the public, the image she would have to help manufacture. The way she would manage the moment in an unexpected crisis. For she had heard enough long tales of the perils of a tour to know that Red Powell had indeed, as David Austin said, had great faith in her, even as a greenhorn in this business.

So now, as she threw her clothes into her luggage, she thought quickly of the rough road that had led her to being, of all things, chaperone to a young movie star, and she wondered what Red Powell, and most of all David Austin, would have thought if they knew she had come out of the worst brothel that existed in the Las Vegas desert to take care of Titan's young superstar.

For the first time in her life she was disturbed. This wasn't a set-up trick with a captive audience, so to speak. It was a challenge, a trust, and it would take careful handling.

She felt she had stepped so far from her early days as a crumby little waitress in Barstow and the painted Dragon

Lady at El Coyote that even if she met anyone from her past, no one would recognize her.

She almost came close to prayer, but she thought it was a cop-out to ask heaven to please protect her, so she gave up the idea and busied herself throwing her clothes in her suitcase.

It had been an overwhelming experience for Belinda to get all her wardrobe together. She had the help of a nervous Irish chambermaid who had never seen more than six pieces of luggage with anyone in residence in the Dallas hotel. A movie star with four wardrobe trunks and ten pieces of small assorted luggage had overcome her.

In the end, Belinda had jammed everything as well as she could into the complicated containers. She barely made it to the airport with the aid of the hotel manager and a local theater representative. She felt that the management was relieved to get rid of her and all the trouble her group had caused.

It was a short flight to New Orleans, but the confusion of her departure and what she would face when she arrived would make it a long day.

Jill Jackson, a kind and efficient young woman, met her at the airport in New Orleans.

As she feared, someone had alerted the press, and a mob stood at the terminal, pushing and shoving to get near her as she deplaned. Security guards had been called to hold back the throng, and her limousine was allowed to meet her behind closed gates at the edge of the airfield. She was whisked away, barely escaping a few wily autograph seekers and camera fiends who knew the ropes. A few people banged at the closed windows before the car gained momentum, and several snapped pictures through the window.

Belinda leaned back and closed her eyes.

"You'll have to get used to this city," said her companion. "New Orleans is a combination of the courtly and the mad."

On the way to the hotel, Jill pointed out the wonders of the city, but Belinda was too tired to enjoy it.

In her rooms, the air heavy with fragrance and the clutter of bouquets, she sat down to study her itinerary. There would be three days of heavy publicity and meetings to get the city ready for the opening of the Royal Lafayette Theater, the most elegant and baroque of the new jewellike motion-picture theaters that were beginning to take the place of the large picture palaces.

Jill ushered her through a breakfast interview at Brennans and a lunch at the Court of the Two Sisters, where the elite of the city and the press met her. Cameras flashed, hands grasped hers, and beaming faces moved into proximity to be recorded as the elect.

Fatigued, she returned to the hotel. Red Powell and Laura West were waiting, and she saw Red's briefcase literally perched on his foot and knew he was ready for flight. Laura sat back, after greeting her, and waited for her boss to make his say before she took over.

"We're all behind you, Belinda," said Red. "Laura knows exactly how to handle things for you, and you can relax." He gestured at the elegant sitting room. "With Laura in one bedroom, you in the other, and a hotel maid to take care of your things, you should have a great time. The city is wild about you."

Belinda felt she should smile, but she was fed up. She didn't want the city to be wild about her.

"Can't I just take it easy tonight?" she said. "I'm so tired."

Red was all sympathy. "Oh, I wish you could. But a dinner has been set up at the Commander's Palace and half the New York brass are here for the Royal Lafayette opening. There's no way out of it. Laura will take care of everything, now don't you worry."

Before she realized it, he was on his way.

Laura turned to her. "Now," she said, "first of all, you can sleep. I'll wake you up at six o'clock. A hairdresser will be here, and we can work out your little makeup together. I'll get your clothes unpacked and assorted. We'll ship back all the stuff you've used. It should have been done before." She checked a list. "It says here the green lamé cocktail dress. Your jewelry is in a box to go with it, and shoes and purse. We think violets would be pretty on your purse—you know—the unknown admirer bit for the press." She smiled.

"Oh, it's great to have someone take care of things," said Belinda.

"I'll unpack while you're resting, and I'll run your bath," said Laura, "and have some pine bath foam in it to make you feel fresh. And if you're still weary, don't be concerned, I'll give you a pickup."

Belinda went into her room. Laura came in, closed the drapes, carried some of the flowers out of the room, and folded back the coverlet to plump up the pillow.

For the first time Belinda really looked at her.

Laura was a girl not too far from herself in age; stylish and efficient, she was organizing without making a fuss about it.

It was time to turn these petty annoyances over to someone else.

"With you around, maybe I can make it," said Belinda as her head hit the pillow.

As Laura got things in order, she saw the inner workings of this young girl's life. She was a patsy, a pigeon, waiting to be ripped off by anyone who managed to get a foot in the door. Impractical, naïve, she needed a keeper. Like most talented people, she only reacted fully when she was performing.

Laura answered messages in the sitting room. Three aristocratic men, laying out their lineage and their right to meet Belinda. Offers of limousines, drivers, escorts, small gifts, perfumes, boxes of pralines, a brown velvet café au lait doll dressed in all the finery of the famous courtesan beauties of the Quadroon Ball. There were the usual hostesses offering the mostest, and a constant parade of flowers—from handpicked bouquets to great swags of orchids and gardenias.

There were two calls from Scott. Laura introduced herself on the phone and explained that Belinda was very tired and was resting. Scott suggested that he come on, but Laura explained the impossibility.

"Mr. Stone, she's terribly tired. If you came, it would just be one more responsibility. It would be a kindness to wait until she returns. She just can't wait to get home. She's told me."

"Did she get my flowers?" he asked.

Laura looked at the flowers on every conceivable surface.

"Of course," she lied, "and she has them right by her bed."

He hung up, somewhat mollified.

When it was time to wake Belinda, Laura pushed the curtains open. The late-afternoon shadows made a filigree of tree branches. Looking out on the square, she saw the mellow glow of antique facades. It all looked so charming, so peaceful. She thought of Bourbon Street and the Quadroon Ball, and the varied, sometimes rabid night life hidden behind these seemingly peaceful historic walls. And she should know. Even she had learned a few startling tales from some of the prostitutes who'd had a stretch here. But, of course, that could happen anywhere.

Belinda awoke and got into the foamy tub. Laura let in the hairdresser, an effete young man who was "thrilled to the core" to be doing Belinda.

"Now cool it, Jack," she warned him. "She's tired of being gushed at; she doesn't want to be told how divine she is and how you love her acting. Just do your thing. If you mind your manners you'll be asked back, and, above all, don't ask for any autographs for yourself or for any buddies."

She saw by the look on his face that she had guessed his plan. But he wanted to come back, so he would behave.

She went into the bathroom. Belinda, her head back on the edge of the tub, had fallen asleep again.

"Hey," said Laura, "you've got to get cracking and get your hair done."

Belinda looked up at her. "I just can't make it."

"Well, I'll give you a break."

Laura went to her purse and took out a little phial. She got a glass of water and handed her a capsule.

"What is it? Vitamins?"

Laura smiled. "Not quite. It's an amphetamine. It'll pick you up, and you'll feel great."

By the time they were ready to go to the dinner, Belinda was euphoric. The pill had reduced her tensions and given her a feeling of well-being. Well, it was necessary.

The next three days were a whirl. Brief impressions, the Quarter, Fat City, a parade of parties in the historic resi-

dence section, Faubourg Marigny, Pete Fountain's clari-
net, Al Hirt's horn, Alvin Alcorn's great Dixieland sound,
restaurants, elegance, polished woods, lush gardens, pools
stocked with turtles and fish at the Commander's Palace,
Galatoires, fabulous foods and drinks, each host trying
to outdo the other, turtle soup, seafood gumbo, oysters,
soft-shell crabs stuffed with crab meat, trout, soufflés,
crepes, Sazeracs, wines, champagnes, and above all, the
mixture of frantic jazz and forced hilarity.

Belinda was courtèd, romanced, admired, photographed, getting Titan more space than it had since its
golden days.

Each night she was tranquilized. When she reached a
high of nervousness because of too much pressure, Laura
handed her a Valium. So in the morning, she had to be
fortified with another amphetamine. It was the only way
Laura could get her through the ordeal. She would have
been a basket case, she thought, without it. She had lost
weight during the tour, and only the splendor of her
clothes and studio jewels, the beauty of her abundant hair,
and faint rouge on her cheeks kept her weariness from
being noticed.

The Royal Lafayette premiere was dazzling. Belinda
wore a cloth-of-gold gown and wrap and the Niadas
octopus.

"Now," said Laura, "Mrs. LeSeur, who handled this
charity premiere, has invited us to a party at her mansion.
Of course we have to go."

There, Vernon Hodine, a rotund man with a neat Van-
dyke beard and an elegant manner, greeted them. He was
one of the white musicians who lately was joining with
black talent to become a successful songwriting team. In
his early forties, a serious tunesmith, like others of his kind
he had been spawned at Julliard. Outgoing and well-off, he
held a social position in the city.

"Let's split out to my apartment and have some coffee,
and get away from this dullsville stuff," he said. "This
scene is folding anyway." He turned to Laura. "She must
be sick of having all these dowagers tell her how great the
picture was. I don't think they dug it at all."

"Could be," said Laura.

"My place is in the French Quarter on Decatur," he

said. "We can have coffee and beignets and just put our feet up and relax."

"Are you sure?" said Laura. "No swinging with this kid."

Hodine looked at her. "You're a kid yourself," he said. "Now you know better than to think I'd risk a scandal. It's tough enough in my situation, hobnobbing with my black friends to get good music. I'm heading for another gold platter before I finish this gig. I'll meet you outside, a cream-colored Fleetwood," he said. "Let's not make a spectacle of splitting out together. Of course, my invitation's kosher. If you don't like it, you can leave. I'm right on a courtyard."

Laura glanced over at Belinda. She was surrounded by five men, and one of them was pressing her. Laura recognized him. He had been a customer at El Coyote, and she knew what he liked. The nerve of him.

"Why not? It's time to get out of here," she said, relieved again that her makeup as the Dragon Lady made her unrecognizable in society.

They paid their respects to the hostess and left.

"Those are the perils of fame," Hodine said in the car, "I have to do some of these numbers to keep up with society because I live here. We've paid our ticket, so let's just relax. I'll give you the best café au lait you've ever had." He looked at Belinda sympathetically. "I'd love to take you to a little all-night restaurant almost next door. Everyone from stevedores to society would recognize you. So I'll just pick up a box of fresh beignets. They'll make you want to stay in New Orleans."

His apartment was in an old mansion. Large, high-ceilinged rooms, a combination of French and modern furniture, shining brass, polished wood, and potted ferns, and a low, glowing coal fire, made it cozy and elegant. At the side was a private courtyard. A collection of Dixieland records and photos of famous musicians decorated the walls of his study.

Hodine put on some records and went to the kitchen to prepare the refreshments.

Belinda settled into a plush red velvet sofa and kicked off her shoes. Soon she had a cup of coffee in her hand. She ignored the powdered sugar that fell off the puffy beignets on her gold dress, the little triangular pastries were so delicious.

"This is the first time I've relaxed since I hit this crazy town," she said.

There was a loud rapping of the brass door knocker.

Hodine went to the hall door.

Laura and Belinda heard voices, one moaning and another raised in excitement.

"No, Bert, you can't come in now. You just can't!" said Hodine.

Laura arose, suspecting trouble.

"Go away, Bert," Hodine said. "You can't bring him in. Why do you have to do this to me! Take him away."

"The hell I can't! This is an emergency, Hode. The kid's in bad trouble. He'd get busted if they found him, and he's a two-time loser. We need him."

They heard the door close, and Hodine came in ahead of two figures. A tall, well-dressed black man was holding up a slender white youth. As they entered the room, the young man slumped to the floor.

"What is this?" said Laura, suddenly alert.

"He's on a trip," said the black man. "I don't know what to do. I can't just let him lay, can I? He's my drummer."

Laura looked at the man on the floor. "What is this all about?" she asked Hodine.

"Oh, my God, I don't know what to do. This is Bert Galen, my partner. He's always dragging some musician in for help. They're always on a trip. And I'm supposed to be Big Daddy and get 'em back on the track. This guy's Little Jimmy. He's been recording with us."

Laura looked at the frail boy. "He's deep," she said. "I don't like his looks. What's he on?"

"These dumb kids," said Bert, "they get keyed up on bennies to play for ten hours, they take God knows how many barbs to cool it, then some pal comes along and they stumble down Bourbon Street and tie one on. We gotta get your doctor!"

Laura had seen the synergistic function of drugs and liquor multiplying the effects of each. This kid was close to respiratory arrest.

"I told you to stop bringing your basket cases here. I'm not Big Daddy." Hodine was nervous. He picked up a phone book and scowled at Bert. "This is it. Never again."

"Okay, okay! But he's just a kid. What could I do?" said Bert, looking apprehensively at the boy who was lapsing into unconsciousness.

There was a knock on the door. "We know Belinda Barstow's here!" said a loud voice. "We want to see her. Let us in!"

"We'd better clear out of here," said Laura.

Belinda stared at the young man on the floor. "Look at him. Look!" she pointed.

His face was turning cyanotic. He convulsed, his hands clenching, his teeth grinding. He began to breathe heavily, his thin face contorting.

"Hey buddy, wake up. Wake up!"

Bert bent down and shook him. As he did, the young man gave a gasp and seemed to slide deeper into the floor. His quick breathing stopped.

Laura stared at him a moment. "He's dead," she said.

There was more banging at the door. "You'd damn well better give us an autograph!" The man sounded intoxicated. "We could break the door down, you know. Don't give us any bullshit. We saw that gold dress flash in here. We know who you are. We saw you on TV."

Laura took Belinda by the hand. "Come with me," she said, leading Belinda into the bedroom off the hall. "Get out of your clothes."

Frightened, Belinda did as she was told. Laura quickly put on the gold dress and handed Belinda her own white crepe gown.

"Get into it fast."

"What are you doing?" said Belinda.

"Trust me," said Laura.

She called out to Hodine. "Have you got a large scarf?"

He found her a cashmere evening muffler, and she quickly pinned Belinda's hair up and wrapped the scarf around her head, making a turban. They went back to the living room.

"Now," she said, "let me go to the door in this dress. I'll tell 'em they made a mistake. Bert, you get the hell out through the back door. We don't want a black man in this mess. That could bring on a real brannigan. Then Hode, you and Belinda take this kid and walk out into your car with his arms around you, holding him. Belinda'll have to do it with you. It's the only way we can get her out of here and get this dead kid out without the cops finding him. He's drunk. You're getting your boyfriend to your car."

Bert was shaking with fear. He knew what a tough spot he was in, and he fled out the back door.

Something heavy was being banged against the front door. In a moment it was pushed in.

"Duck your head, Belinda, so they won't see your face."

Laura rushed to the hall. As the door slammed open, she faced two burly stevedores.

"Well, men," she said, "you sure broke up a dull party. Come on in. But as you can plainly see, I ain't a Belinda Barstow."

They looked at her, surprised.

"You'll do," one of them grinned. "Baby, you're built."

She moved toward the first one. "Okay with me," she said, "but let's keep it low. This kid in the next room just had her boyfriend pass out. She's scared. What a damper these kids are! Now just let me get 'em out, and I'll take care of you, both of you. How does that grab you?"

They stared at her.

"For free," she said. "I'm turned on. Okay, you squares, get the kid out," she gestured to Hodine, "and no more junior trade. They can't handle it. I'm giving these big handsome guys a party."

Hodine and Belinda managed to get the young musician propped up. Belinda ducked her head, with the boy's arm around her shoulders. She clung to the dead fingers, horrified. Hodine supported the weight of the body, and the men pulled back to let them by.

Hodine's Cadillac was parked in front. He slid the body into it and helped Belinda into the seat next to the boy. She was gasping with terror.

"Now," he said, "no hysterics. There's no other way but this."

She slid into the seat. The boy's head fell against her shoulder. A patrolman was strolling toward them.

"Oh, God!" said Hodine looking down Decatur Street. "A cop. He knows me. He always says hello. Duck down, like you're looking in your purse or something. He mustn't see your face."

"Evening, Mr. Hodine," he said, saluting.

"Evening," said Hodine pleasantly as he pulled the car swiftly away from the curb.

The darkness seemed smothering to Belinda. They traveled upriver, soon the city was left behind. Shacks and plantations interspersed the swampy land, desolate trees thick with choking moss, blackness beyond black. It was a hell ride. Hodine was silent; she could see by the dashboard light that his face was pale and he was sweating. He kept mopping his brow with his handkerchief. She was afraid to look at the body that leaned against her as they took the bends along the lonely road.

Finally, they come to a secluded stretch down the batture; the levee rose, the Mississippi beyond it, the smell of roots and mud thickening the heat.

Hodine parked the car alongside the left lip of the road, getting off the main highway as much as he dared without miring in the sandy mud, and he doused the lights.

"Now," he said, "I'm going to get rid of him. If you see a car coming, call me. I don't want anyone to see you alone in this car. Okay?"

She nodded; it was impossible for her to speak.

This was the moment of truth, Hodine realized, as he lifted the inert body out of the car. Panting with the exertion, he set the body on the ground, and dragged him, pulling his arms, up the side of the levee.

He disappeared over the lip. Panicked, Belinda, sitting in the smothering darkness, saw a truck chugging along the highway. She figured it must be a mile away. She had to alert him.

She slipped out of the open door and ran to the top of the levee. Hodine was struggling against the mud, dragging the body by the back of the coat collar.

"There's a truck coming!" she said.

"You'll have to help me," he said, breathless. "Here, hurry, take an arm."

In terror, Belinda grasped a sleeve, and the two of them dragged the body to the edge of the river. Hodine waded into the shallows and pushed the body until the water took its weight and it began to drift.

For a brief moment, Belinda saw the boy's blue white face against the darkness, then it seemed to turn green as he sank into the water.

"Get back to the car," said Hodine, "or we've had it."

They rushed to the car, slid into the seat quickly, and Hodine turned music on the radio. In a few moments the blinding headlights of the truck struck them.

Hodine took Belinda in his arms and pressed his lips against hers, pretending they were lovers in the night. The truck slowed, and, as they clung together in frozen fear, honked a cheerful salute to l'amour and passed on.

Hodine released her and let out a gasp.

"Thank God they didn't stop to investigate," he said. "Not only would they have wondered about my muddy feet and legs, but this place isn't exactly safe for a beautiful young girl."

The road back seemed endless. Belinda was shaking. The horror of the evening was beginning to take hold of her.

"I think I'm going to be sick," she whispered.

"Be sick," said Hodine. "Lean over, if you must, and be sick. Get it out of your system, Belinda. Things like this happen. It had nothing to do with you or me. You can just thank your lucky stars that you had a woman like Laura to be your takeout. I never would have worked it out on the spur of the moment like that."

He slowed the car. "I think I'm going to be sick myself."

He parked, got out, and then came back wiping his mouth. She saw how terrified he was.

"I'm sorry," he said. "Just remember, in case anything goes wrong, you never saw my apartment."

Belinda was sunk in despair.

"But we'll have to go back to it now. You must change into your dress before you return to the hotel. I hope Laura's okay. We'll go in the back door cautiously."

The coast was clear. No one was on the street. It was almost dawn. They walked past the shrubbery in the patio, and Hodine unlocked the back door. The place was quiet.

He walked into the living room. Laura was sitting on the sofa, nude. The gold dress was on the floor.

"Well," she said, "come in. The party's just over."

There was an empty bottle of cognac on the table.

"Didn't even dirty your glasses," she said. "They drank right out of the bottle. But after that, well, you can imagine . . . Then they lammed out. A little scared, I guess. I told them some big-city officials were supposed to come over and join the fun."

"Belinda," she said, "as your press representative, I think we'd better try to put your dress on you, and I'll take mine back if you don't mind."

She looked at the splattered mud on the hem.

"I'll just have to give it a quick rinse-out and hope nobody's in the lobby at this hour to see how untidy I am."

The exchange was made in the bedroom. Hodine shook his head as Laura came back into the room.

"I've never known a woman like you in my life."

"Well," said Laura, "we'd better call a cab and wait for it as if we came out of that apartment foyer across the street . . . Just in case."

"Right," said Hodine. "Just in case . . ."

He turned to Belinda. "Now," he said, "I think it's all right. If you read the New Orleans papers, you'll know that people like this kid are washed up quite often in the river under the same sad circumstances. If I were you I'd get out of this town fast—I am. I've had it."

They reached their rooms at the hotel without incident. Once inside, Belinda was shaken with sobs; finally Laura grasped her by the shoulders.

"Now look," she said, "there's nothing we can do. It wasn't our fault. Because you are what you are, you can't be a private person. That's why it got so complicated. Otherwise we could have sat by, called the police, and had the whole thing cleared up. Obviously the poor kid was just one other on a bum trip in any city. I think Hodine is clean. He's just a patsy for the floaters who run for help."

Belinda didn't seem to listen. "I'm going to call Claudia," she said. "I've got to tell her."

Laura went to her makeup kit and took out two pills. When she returned, she felt Belinda was close to hysterics.

"Now," she said, "you'd better take these. They'll knock you out for a few hours."

Belinda looked at them in a panic.

"No!" she said. "After what I've seen tonight, no pills!"

Laura shrugged. "There's a lot of difference between taking two of these, and the amount that guy took before he doused about six drinks. Some of 'em get up to a dozen pills or so a day before they conk out. You must know the other stars, Marilyn Monroe and Judy Garland, take 'em like popcorn. That's what pressures of a career can do when you're not able to face it."

Belinda buried her face in the pillow. She wanted to get away, but she realized that there was no place for her to go. She didn't want to return to the beach house alone. It wasn't home without Claudia.

Laura sat in a chair.

"I can't help you, really, Belinda. I've done all I could."

Belinda raised her head and looked at her. For the first time it crossed her mind that Laura had taken on those two men to get her out of the dilemma. Laura, reading her, waved it away.

"Forget it," she said. "There's one thing you'll understand someday. I'm not ready to lay it on you now, but not everyone has been as protected as you. Tonight's nothing, forgotten. I had to fight the hard way to get out of the situation I was born in."

"So did I," said Belinda. "Maybe sometime I'll tell you!"

Laura was surprised. Something in her voice told her that Belinda had more spine than she thought.

"I have to call David Austin and ask him what to do," said Laura. "So why don't you call your aunt and get it off your chest?"

"I want to talk to him, too," said Belinda.

"Later," said Laura. "Call your aunt."

Belinda woke Claudia in Elderberry. She was in a sound sleep. Finally, she answered the insistent ringing of the phone; the call had been put through as an emergency by the night clerk.

Belinda attempted to steady herself. She dug her nails into her palms; perhaps if she gave herself physical pain she could obliterate the horror of the night.

As she told Claudia what had happened, her emotions seemed to crawl up into her throat and she had to stop occasionally, her voice choked with sobs.

"My God!" said Claudia, "this could wreck your career. Why weren't you better protected?"

"It was just one of those things," said Belinda. "As Laura said, it wasn't our fault. Not even Vernon Hodine's. He's a nice, fussy little man, and he's scared to death, too."

"I should think so," said Claudia. "Now, exactly who might have seen you?"

"Well, the parking attendant at the party saw us leave together, and then, after—after, at Hodine's apartment, the two stevedores, but I don't think they saw my face. A patrolman passed us on the street, but I ducked. And then there was the truck driver on the road—where we—where we got rid of the body. But he didn't see my face. Just the back of my head."

"Good God!" gasped Claudia. "I think you better get right out of there. Come to Elderberry. I'll get a room next to mine, and you can just get over it here with me."

There was silence. Belinda was crying.

"Are you all right, honeybun?" said Claudia.

"Yes," cried Belinda. "But it was so horrible. He was just a young kid!"

"Now listen to me," said Claudia. "You've got to keep your chin up. There's nothing you can do but sit it out. You mustn't let anyone see you're upset. Have Laura get you on the first possible plane. I'll be waiting. Look, I think it's going to be all right. That Laura is some girl to take you out of it. That was quick thinking. Where is she?"

"She's in her room calling David."

"Well, you go right in and tell him you're coming to Elderberry with me. Get his permission. Tell Laura to say you have the flu and cancel your other appointments. I'll be waiting, dear, now don't you worry."

Belinda rushed to Laura's room.

She could see by the look on Laura's face that she was listening to David, and was engrossed. Belinda signaled to interrupt, she wanted to speak to him.

"Here's Belinda," said Laura. "She wants to talk to you, then I'll get on the line again."

"Oh, David, it's so terrible!" said Belinda. "Where are you?"

"I'm in London. But I'll get to you as soon as I can. Now play it cool. Laura's told me everything. I understand you were the victim of an uncontrolled situation. We'll discuss it when I see you. So now just close up shop."

"That's what Claudia said," said Belinda. "She suggested I say I have the flu and go to her in Elderberry. Oh, David, I need you. When are you coming?"

"Elderberry sounds like a good idea. Get out of town as fast as you can. I'll see you in several days. Put Laura on."

As Belinda left the room, she turned to see Laura's face. She was still engrossed and smiling faintly.

"Thank you," she said. "I did the best I could in an emergency."

Belinda found herself being jealous of Laura. Anyway, she'd see David in Elderberry soon, he had promised.

She returned to her bed. What if Scott heard about this? There were so many things Scott didn't know about her, the things that had happened, Niadas, Kevin, and now this horror. If he knew, she was certain he would stop loving her. The thought of his not loving her hadn't entered her mind before.

She began to think about him, his handsomeness, his concern, the fact that he was going to protect her with his love; the way he planned to organize her working life so it would run smoothly for her. What a comfort it would be to be protected by someone who really belonged to her.

She had accepted courtship and adoration from him as easily as she had accepted stardom from Titan. But now that she was facing a hazard in her career and realizing for the first time what she had been hiding in her life, she evaluated some of the things she had accepted as her right.

Never before had she had such a heaviness in her heart. When she had been pregnant and kept it to herself, she had been nervous and frightened but had never understood responsibility. In a sense, she had thought it happened "at" her. She carried no personal burden. It had been put on the shoulders of other people, who hid her dilemma and erased her concern with love and understanding.

But this situation wasn't something that could be hidden until a pregnancy was ended. Clauda had shaken her when she had said "this could ruin your career."

Surprisingly to herself, facing the possibility of loss, Scott began to take on a different value. He was her stalwart, her Galahad, and she had accepted his relationship thoughtlessly.

Kevin wouldn't have helped her at all, she realized. He was an eccentric, in his own world a superstar—he wasn't in anyone's orbit—he didn't revolve around another body, they revolved about him. He could go on painting pictures, enchanting the sitters, enjoying his carefree sexual life, and it wouldn't have made any difference to him at all. Any more than when she had told him Alex was her child. He hadn't sympathized or been shocked, it had only turned him on, stimulating him sexually.

This thought was the beginning of her cure from the bond of love and passion she had for a man who had given her a glimpse of sensuality and free-living Bohemianism, which at the time was needed in her sterile life.

She was alerted suddenly to her sin of omission. Scott didn't know her at all. He was in love with her beauty and the inborn attraction she had in spite of herself, which made men desire her.

In Scott's case, he had fallen in love with her, not as a mere sex object, but as the person with whom he desired to spend his life.

But he did not know her, he did not realize that she was devious enough to step into marriage without letting him know that Alex was her son; that she had borne a child and kept it from him.

The realization added to the heaviness of her situation. She was deeply disturbed; peril on all sides seemed to be engulfing her.

Her mind flashed to the dreadful memory of dragging the dead boy to the river and watching his body and white face as he sank into the water.

Laura came in. "It's all set," she said. "We'll get an early plane out. A car will meet us at the airport. We're shipping most everything out but your necessities and several things you can wear in the country. I'll get your things packed. You can just jump into your slacks and silk shirt in the morning. I'll lay them out. Tie a babushka over your hair and wear dark glasses. We're to say you have the flu, and we'll be in the country before anyone knows you're not asleep here in your rooms. A car will be waiting to get us out quietly and quickly."

Belinda looked at her. "You look tired. You won't get any sleep."

"I'm used to crazy hours," said Laura. "Before we leave, I'm to call Hodine from a pay phone and have him get to another one and talk to me. From now on, we have to be very cautious. So far we've lucked out."

20

Claudia awoke at dawn. It was no use trying to sleep. She relived the moment when Simon Moses had died in her arms at the little casita at the Titan ranch in California. How long ago it had been. And how vivid it still was. Her screams of terror, Jeffrey coming to her aid, Fergus and all the uproar, and her exile from Hollywood because she had been proven in the most public way to be the mistress of the man who owned her studio.

Now Belinda faced the same sort of scandal, an encounter with a young musician, dead from an overdose in the French Quarter of New Orleans. A famous composer's apartment. No one would ever believe Belinda wasn't involved in the drug scene. It could shatter her life.

It sounded so terrible, Claudia thought. Worse than it was, as far as her involvement would suggest. Belinda had a talent for having her life seem like a soap opera!

And, as a secondary thought, her forthcoming marriage to Scott. Scott, who seemed like a staunch pillar, a man to guide Belinda through the shoals of her career at a most crucial time in the history of this splintered entertainment industry.

As she poured bath salts into her tub, Claudia was ashamed of herself for thinking of Scott in such a mercenary way. He was a nice man and would undoubtedly be much more interesting once he stopped being moon-eyed every time he looked at Belinda.

What really disturbed her was the fact that Belinda had not yet grappled with life as an adult. She had been cared for and used by others. Was she capable, after what she'd had from life and fame, of thinking in a way of growth?

Would there ever be anything spiritual in her life to give her sustenance when all the success had passed her by, if that had to be? Would she grow into a beautiful woman in her old years, a Lynne Fontanne, an Ethel Barrymore, a Gladys Cooper, a Cathleen Nesbitt?

Claudia smiled at herself. Here she was, wishing her niece all the joys of splendidly educated women who had grown in the theater, all disciplined, who had also managed to live their lives fully.

What had she herself done? Not much, really. She was playing this summer with a last gasp of her misused talents, a feeble reach for the stars before it was too late. What right had she to tell Belinda what to do?

She laid out her terry bathrobe and lifted one foot over the edge of the claw-foot tub, indulging herself in a favorite Barstow trait, remembering a fragment of quotation and fitting it like the missing piece of a jigsaw puzzle into the current problem, fashioning it all together. It was Browning: "A minute's success pays the failure of years."

Well, she had grasped it, this moment, and she would attempt to help Belinda. Help her here in the country, away from the trappings of success and stardom.

As she absently stepped into the tub, she slipped.

The next thing she knew, she was lying on the bathroom floor. Startled, she raised herself up on her elbow. She'd given her head a sharp bang on the lip of the tub, and for a moment she had blacked out.

God, God, what if she'd broken an arm, or leg, or that old person's curse, a hip? She cautiously moved her arms and legs. She seemed to be sound, although her head ached from the crack she'd given it.

She pulled herself up, shaking from the shock, but she seemed to be all right.

That's all I need, she thought as she gratefully stepped back into the tub.

Later she ordered an early newspaper. She had had an interview with the *New York Times*. Strange how bulky the paper seemed when one was looking for an item of personal importance.

She turned on the lights and scanned the papers, squinting as she looked for page numbers. Why was it so difficult to find something? She put on her bifocals. They must be dirty. She polished them and peered again.

Something strange was happening. A gray veil seemed to be moving up from the lower lid of her right eye. As she glanced at the paper, blotches of black seemed to be swimming on her eyeball, and the printing was crinkly, as if the words had been waved, she thought, like a special effect man does with a shimmer on the screen.

She set the paper down, blinked, and went to the mirror. There didn't seem to be anything in her eye, but the veil crept farther up into her sight. Perhaps she was getting a cataract. But did that happen so fast? She waited until the hour was decent. She looked out the window. Her left eye was all right, but the other one was acting most peculiarly.

She called Stuart Plimpton.

"I'm sorry to get you up early, Stu," she said, "but I seem to be having some sort of a problem in my eye, and I'd better get it checked before the rehearsal. I know it's nothing."

"Of course," said Stu, "I'll take you right over to Dr. Parker in the village. Don't be scared because she's a pretty blonde. She's the best ophthalmologist around."

"I'll walk over," said Claudia.

"No such," said Stu. "I'll drive you. I can't take a chance with my star!"

And your meal ticket, thought Claudia.

"Oh, and by the way, get me a room, next to mine if possible. Belinda is coming to join me for a few days. She's worn out from her tour."

"Belinda coming!" said Stu. "*Now* you tell me! My God, that's going to be a news item. Famous niece visits famous aunt. What a break!"

"Knock it off for now," said Claudia. "She's tired."

When he came to get her he was so excited about Belinda's arrival that Claudia's eye examination was almost routine.

"You'll probably have to wear dark glasses for a couple of days," he said. "Well, I can work on the scene with Laura and the Gentleman Caller, and you just take it easy and get Belinda settled."

"You'd better be alerted," said Claudia. "She's liable to be pestered to death. We may have to get a little security for her. You've no idea!"

"Anything you say," said Stuart, looking at his watch nervously.

"You run along," said Claudia. "It's silly to stay. It's only a few blocks; I'll walk home afterwards."

Young Dr. Parker was pretty and affable. Claudia was given medication so her eyeball could be probed. The doctor examined her, her brow furrowed with concern. Finally she moved up the slit lamp on its swinging arm. It reminded Claudia of a studio crane. She took the indirect ophthalmoscope off her head and switched on the room light.

"Miss Barstow," she said, "I'm sorry to tell you this, but you have a retinal detachment."

"My goodness," said Claudia, "what is that?"

"It's a tear, a rip in your eye," she said. "Have you recently had a fall or a blow?"

"Yes," said Claudia, "I fell and hit my head on the tub early this morning. Is it serious? No wonder I don't feel so well. I guess I'll have to go back to the hotel and take it easy for a couple of hours."

"No," said Dr. Parker, "you're not going back to the hotel. You'll have to go to the hospital right away. I'll see what surgeons I can reach at the hospital in Hyannisport."

"Wait a minute," said Claudia, holding up her hand. "This is a little sudden, doctor. My niece will arrive in several hours. I'm rehearsing a play. It'll just have to wait."

"You can't wait," she said. "You are in danger of losing the sight in one eye."

Claudia stared at her, in shock. "Are you sure?" she said.

"Of course at Hyannisport I'll turn you over to a specialist who only deals in detached retinas, but you have no choice. You wouldn't want to face the possibility of complete blindness in one eye, would you?"

Claudia was irritated that the young woman was so abrupt. But she saw the compassion in her face and knew that she was being efficient.

"Well," she said, "I—I just don't know what to say!"

"I'm sorry," said the doctor. "Would there be anyone I should reach?"

"Well, I guess Stuart Plimpton could get me to Hyannisport. Is it a good hospital?"

The doctor grinned. "What do you think? The Kennedy family's residence! Of course. The best. You can rest in my reception room while I call and see if I can get Dr. Nolan off the golf course."

Claudia sat waiting, her mind whirling. So sudden! So very sudden.

The doctor came back. "Did you have breakfast?" she asked.

Claudia shook her head.

"That's a break," she said. "You can have the proper tests done immediately and Dr. Nolan can operate as soon as possible."

"Wait a minute!" said Claudia.

"Miss Barstow," she said, "I can't take any further responsibility. This is such a delicate operation that only a specialist can do it. He will give you a better examination than I can in my office, and you must rely on his judgment. Believe me, you will be glad. It's a matter of the whole of life ahead of you, not just what is happening to you this week. I wish I could say it isn't necessary. But you may be very fortunate and have good vision later."

Plimpton was stunned, but he drove her to Hyannisport, hoping against hope that it was a mistake.

But it was not.

Before Belinda arrived, Claudia had been wheeled into the operating room.

When they got to the Elderberry Inn, Belinda and Laura were surprised that there wasn't a welcoming committee. There was a message at the desk. They were to get in touch with Stuart Plimpton at once. He rushed to their suite. "This is a terrible way to greet you," he said. "Your Aunt Claudia is in the Hyannisport hospital. She fell and has had to have an eye operation. A detached retina they call it."

"What!" said Belinda, paling. "Why didn't we know before?"

"It was an emergency," said Plimpton. He pulled at his moustache.

"She's going to be literally sandbagged to keep from moving for a week, and then she has to be in bed for three weeks; maybe here. She can't move too much. My God, I'm in a mess!"

"Well, what about *her*?" said Laura.

"Of course!" said Plimpton apologetically, "my first concern!"

Belinda seemed to crumple. She sat on the edge of the chair, her face a mask of fear.

"I want to see her," said Belinda.

"Nobody can see her until tomorrow," said Plimpton. "I guess you'll have to take over. She told me she had insurance. You can look through her papers, and you'll have to take her nightgowns and robe and toothbrush and all that stuff over to her. They didn't even let her come back to her room after her examination."

After he left, Belinda walked into the sitting room. She saw *The Glass Menagerie* open on the desk, Claudia's careful marginal notes, and her notebook, which Belinda knew was a progression of the study of the play—an analysis of the lines. She saw a half-finished memo to Joan McGowan about the character of Laura. And, with a pang, Belinda realized the work and time Claudia must have spent so she herself could portray the roles for which she had received such kudos.

There were the fond family pictures in silver frames: herself with Jeffrey, herself and Claudia at the villa in Rome, even a picture of herself and David—and, of course, one with Max. She must get in touch with Max. Suddenly she was in charge of things she had never thought of before.

She picked up Claudia's bifocals and saw the newspaper folded on a chair near the window. In it was a glowing interview of the emergence of Claudia Barstow as an important figure in American theater—and the value of summer stock as a showcase for talent of all ages. She looked out over the peaceful landscape and wondered how many times Claudia had looked at it with an eye that now could not see.

Belinda had the sinking feeling of loss, of the absence of Claudia's ever-present vitality, which she had always taken for granted. The room had the sight and scent of Claudia, more poignantly for Belinda because Claudia wasn't there.

There was a knock at the door. It was Plimpton again, more nervous and bouncy than ever.

"I forgot to tell you," he said. "I hope you haven't called Max Ziska."

"No," said Belinda, "I was just going to do it."

"Well, Claudia called me just before they wheeled her in. She was half punchy from sedation, sort of talking Swahili, if you know what I mean, but she said not to call Max, to wait until the ordeal was over and she could contact him by phone herself. She didn't want him to come on. 'He's not a hospital person,' she said, 'and if I talk to him myself later, I can keep him away.'"

"Don't you think I should call anyway?" said Belinda.

"Listen," said Plimpton, "if Claudia said you shouldn't, you shouldn't—Oh, God, what's ahead of me? I have to try to get a replacement for her in *Glass Menagerie*. I suppose it will have to be one of the gals who played in *Chaillot*. Local talent, so to speak. I probably won't sell a ticket since *her* name's been splashed all over the countryside. I don't know what I'll do without Claudia."

"Neither do I," said Belinda.

In spite of her operation, Claudia's vitality was at a high. Even though she had to lie supine, her commitment to what the summer had brought her was foremost in her mind.

The doctor had put his foot down on Max coming east.

"You're having too much stimulation as it is. As long as your niece is here with you, that is enough. Your husband will be doing you a service to stay away. I'll talk to him and explain. Too much strain could tear your eyeball, and that would be real trouble."

"I suppose you're right," she said. "I'm trying to do the right thing. This has caused so much trouble already."

She was thinking not only of Max and the house, but of Stuart Plimpton and the blaze of glory her performance would have been to end his season.

The doctor gave orders that Max was not to call, the hours might be difficult, but wait until she would call when it was convenient for her schedule and well-being.

Max was mollified by her calls, selected carefully by her when the rates were lowest. She thought ironically of all the profligacies of her youth, and the care she was taking now to save pennies on the phone calls to Max, the man she loved.

She thanked God that he would not be coming to be with her at the added expense that such a trip would cause. It would serve no one, and she knew his nervous nature would put him into an unhappy situation when he could not be with her, or be surrounded by the comforts of his study and his incessant work.

Claudia was lying in the hospital bed a week later, her eye still bandaged. Pillows had been placed on each side of her head to keep her still. Her conversation was on the voluble fringe of Valium. Belinda sat in the standard visitor's chair, her back to the light, the position she had taken for hours each day.

She observed the finely etched planes of Claudia's face. Her Barstow profile held a handsomeness that time and sickness had not obliterated.

"Well," said Claudia, "this is just great. Me on my back, unable to move, just when I'm supposed to make the summer theater bloom again for poor old Plimpton."

"I hope my call from New Orleans had nothing to do with your eye," said Belinda.

"Of course not, silly; when an old woman slips and falls, it's only her own fault. As for your dilemma, darling, as I keep saying, it wasn't your fault."

"I guess so," said Belinda, "but I always seem to be getting into a mess, mixed up with the wrong people."

"Don't tell me," said Claudia. "That's life. We can't evaluate people from the start, you know. I never told you the garish details of my own life. Oh, the chances I took. Did you ever hear of a famous gangster named Mike Cuneo?"

"No," said Belinda. "Don't tell me you got together with a gangster!"

"Yes," said Claudia. "He was a handsome young squirt in the Bronx when Fergus and I made our first picture. I think he even bankrolled Fergus with a crap game. He drifted off to Chicago and made it big. Years later he was my lover for a while. Gave me a diamond bracelet that was fancy enough to sell and get me to Europe when things turned sour in Hollywood. If the public had known about him, I would have been finished. But life is funny. You know what happened?"

"What?" said Belinda, intrigued.

"Well, he got by with it. Now he's establishment. Went into the California wine business early. I even saw a picture of his elegant children and grandchildren in *Town and*

Country, living like barons in the family vineyard in
Sonoma. The youngsters, all college graduates, are so-
called dynasty wine family; he's the paterfamilias instead
of the capo regi, and he looks like aristocracy in his old
age. His wine company is always giving parties for VIPs
in underground caves that are decorated like medieval
keeps. We should go sometime and get a couple of laughs."

Belinda moved closer and took her aunt's hand. Claudia
was gesturing to make up for the fact she wasn't supposed
to move her head.

"Take it easy," said Belinda. "You're moving around a
little too much. Oh, Claudia, I haven't had much time to
think during these busy four years. But since you've been
sick, I've thought so much. I know I am young, and
started out young, but I botched it with Kevin. What a
mess that was. And now Scott—I don't know how to handle
this. He's so vulnerable. Oh, if he only knew. About me.
And Alex. What can I do?"

"I don't know, said Claudia. "I've been thinking about
it myself. I told you not to tell him. I had no right. It's up
to you to decide. There are pros and cons both ways. You're
fortunate in the fact that Max and your mother are supposed to be his parents. Alex can stay with us, dear."

"I don't want you to think about it now," said Belinda.
"Let me do that—for a change."

Claudia pressed her hand.

"I'll come back early tomorrow," said Belinda, "and get
your things together for the drive back to the inn. The doctor says you can go in a car, and Plimpton's sending the
famous limousine. I'm saying good-bye to Laura tonight.
She's called back to the studio tomorrow."

"Give her my love and thanks."

There was a silence. Belinda picked up her purse.

"It seems dreadful I can't do that play," said Claudia.
"If it had only been a leg, I could have winged it somehow."

A nurse entered with a tray and a little fluted cup holding
a pill.

"Time for your medication, Miss Barstow."

Claudia lifted her head slightly.

"Now, now," said the nurse. "These downers seem to
be uppers with you. You're supposed to rest."

"I know she is," said Belinda. "I'm leaving soon so she'll sleep."

As the nurse left Claudia said, "Sit down a little longer, honey. You know I'm talking so much because I'm a little afraid; afraid of just being a statistic. I guess you get that way on the shady side of sixty-five."

Belinda sat back. Let Claudia talk. At this time it was all she had.

"Maybe I could start coaching Joan McGowan when I get back to the hotel."

"That's a good idea," said Belinda. "She came by the other evening and said hello. She was very upset about you and can't wait to see you. She had her boyfriend, Michael Ross, along. He's nice, but he didn't say much. Just listened and looked. But she's pretty."

"And talented," said Claudia. "I suppose that old bag Helen French will play my role. She's not bad, but they'll have to watch her phony southern accent."

Belinda smiled. "You've really loved this summer. It's wonderful what happened to you."

"Yes," said Claudia. "If you know what you want, you can do anything."

For a few moments, Belinda thought she was asleep. She could tiptoe out and leave her. But as she half rose, Claudia put her hand out; she felt she was soaring high on the sedative, and her words were spoken overcarefully.

"I'm glad for success," she said, "but I'm sad about the money cutting off."

Her voice became more vague.

"The money?" Belinda said.

"For your wedding," said Claudia. "That's why I came. For your wedding. Scott's mother has grand ideas. And we have to get even with that old bitch Flora Random Stone."

Belinda leaned forward.

Claudia continued drowsily. "She didn't want him to marry you. She thinks we're—mountebanks. Max is canceled at the studio. Jessica shook him down. He paid her off to keep from having you go to Rome to live with her. We've run out—run out—And we're going to have the fine wedding you deserve. The finest—" Her voice dwindled, and she whispered, "the finest."

"Oh, Claudia, that isn't necessary. We can elope."

"No way," said Claudia. "Not possible. Oh, it's so hard to be alone. All the years until I met Max. I want the best for you. It's all arranged. You're starting this marriage right. It's what I want the most. It makes up for so many things . . . so many."

Belinda saw her bandaged face light up with deep affection.

She watched Claudia drift off to sleep and sat a moment, shocked, putting the pieces together. Looking at her aunt's pale, quiet face, tears came to her; tears of gratitude for the love and spirit of this courageous woman.

She left the hospital. So that's what this unexpected summer had been all about. This was why Claudia had uprooted herself from Max and Alex and her happy life. So she could give Belinda a wedding.

On reflection, Belinda realized that things had been slim lately. Effie was taking care of the baby and the house, Claudia did the work on Effie's days off and drove Max to the studio. There were no frills. No new clothes, no new cars. Belinda was the one who had been blind. She had no control of her money; only an allowance for her personal wishes. In the excitement of the picture and her romance with Scott, she hadn't noticed anything.

She was learning a lot and it was coming at her fast.

Of course, when she married she would get her money. But now—now.

She had spoken to Scott on the phone many times. He was involved in a lengthy legal case, shuttling between San Francisco and Los Angeles. He hadn't been able to come east, and she told him it was just as well; things were tenuous with Claudia. There were long visits to the hospital, then she'd be settling her in at Elderberry and getting her home as soon as possible. He had told her of his longing for her over the phone, and as she heard each word, she felt guilty.

She'd make it up to him; she'd be a good wife; and she'd let him know how grateful she was for his plans and dreams. He'd never know she wasn't passionately in love with him.

Laura was all packed. She'd be leaving early in the morning, before Claudia came back from the hospital.

Red Powell had ordered her home. He intimated he had heard from David that Laura had rescued Belinda from some complex situation in New Orleans. David had been very sketchy. He was anxious to hear all the details. That'll be the day, thought Laura.

Now she was to work on the residue of the campaign, get all the material together, caption photographs of local celebrities, and get them off to the proper regional periodicals and national magazines for future consumption. The big Titan publicity machine was working to hypo box office on *Young Lucretia* during its first run. Everything to create long runs must be done, and Laura had suddenly become a key woman in the publicity department.

Most important was the clipping she had received in the morning mail. She had kept in touch with Hodine through prearranged pay-phone calls, and now an envelope addressed to her had relieved the tension. It would be a great farewell gift to Belinda.

Hidden in the back pages of the *New Orleans Times Picayune* was an insignificant item. The body of a young man had been washed up below Canal Street. He was identified as Jimmy Booth, an itinerant musician who had been seen recently around New Orleans. There were no signs of violence, and, according to the coroner's report, he had died from an overdose of barbiturates and alcohol. There was a local drive on to halt the pushers of illicit drugs.

Just another kid, thought Laura. Who would miss him? Who would care? The only people really interested were the few whose lives could have been ruined if their brief encounter with his last few moments had been known. And several pushers who would have to watch their contacts if the fuzz was on their particular trail, thought Laura.

It was the same old story. She remembered the Swedish girl at El Coyote, and the pimp who had vanished after he'd made his killing (and that was what it was) when she died.

Anything had been fair game in the illicit world in which she had lived; it was dog-eat-dog, and anyone who asked for it deserved it. After all, no one shoved dope at anyone unless they accepted it.

When Laura moved into Belinda's life, she had controlled her by a judicious use of pills. In no time, she knew the girl could have been dependent on her, as she eased the strains of her career. She knew from the studio gossip which quacks and which "friends" had helped Judy Garland and Marilyn Monroe. They had done it several generations before with Wally Reid, Mabel Normand, and Barbara La Marr, she had heard. She had even met a wide-eyed little redhead in the publicity department at one studio (trusted girl friend of a spaced-out star) who was really a pusher. And, Laura thought, she had actually been leading up to the same situation—control of a star, moving into a more lucrative position where the most important people, unwittingly, would depend on her influence, not knowing how it had come about.

When she had been a waitress and part-time hustler in the desert town of Barstow, she had both resented and envied the innocence of Belinda in *The Oracle*. Why did one young girl have it so good, adored and pampered, when life had given another such a rotten deal? Laura had been avenging her past through this girl who now could have been her patsy.

Lately she had seen that life on the pedestal was not as much fun as she thought. And she had found Belinda to be a better companion than she had expected. She had thought Belinda would demand instant service and want such eccentricities as one star who, while on the road, made her press representative get out her antique Revere silver bowl and fill it with fresh-roasted peanuts before she would deign to answer the phone or grant interviews.

But Belinda was nothing of the sort. She seemed either unaware or uncaring about her sexuality—which made men of all ages enchanted with her. As a matter of fact, Laura decided, she was an innocent, and probably had been used by everyone, just as Laura had planned to use her.

But it was not going to work out that way. Watching her overcome the problems of New Orleans, refusing tranquilizers when most would have eagerly taken them, and having seen her devotion to her aunt and heard some of the sane phone calls she made to Max and Effie about the house, she decided that although she was awfully square, she was okay.

Laura found herself pouring all the uppers and downers down the toilet.

No . . . No, she convinced herself, I'm not doing this for any phony morality. I'm making it on my own steam; they aren't necessary, and I don't want any leftover crutch from the lousy past.

Laura prepared to meet Belinda—they might go for a walk along the elm-lined lane and she could show Belinda the good news in the New Orleans paper she had just received—when the phone rang. There was a Mr. Austin in the lobby.

David! David had arrived!

She rushed to the lobby.

"Oh, Mr. Austin," she said, "how wonderful you got here!"

She had wanted to greet him warmly. But he was so elegant, and his gaze so straightforward, that she stopped short.

He stepped up to her and took her hand.

"It's good to see you," he said. "Where can we talk? I just came from New Orleans."

She looked up at him, startled. "Upstairs in Claudia's sitting room," she said. "Belinda ought to be back from the hospital at Hyannisport any moment. Claudia gets back tomorrow. I'm leaving."

"You've just about handled everything in that sentence," he said. "You'd make a good journalist."

Upstairs, he set down his bag and walked to the window. There was a moment of silence.

Her heart skipped a beat. What did he know about her? Had he discovered something? This could be a showdown. What would she do if Titan released her?

"Laura," he said, "I saw Hodine."

Oh, God, she thought, Hodine must have told him how I serviced those two stevedores . . .

"Oh?" she said.

"I guess you know that everything's all right. The young man is gone and buried. Another incident in the night life of any big city, and many a small musician."

Why doesn't he get to the point? she wondered. Let's not play cat and mouse.

He turned his back to her, smoothing his hair with his long fingers. While expecting him to ring the bell on her future, she was impressed by his manner, his forthright dismissal of the usual social amenities.

"I'm so glad," she said. "It was a rotten deal for Belinda. Anyway, she's out of danger, I guess."

"She's out of danger, thanks to you," said David. "Hodine is your greatest admirer."

"I see," said Laura.

For a moment panic seized her, but looking at his warm, open smile she realized that Hodine hadn't mentioned the stevedores.

She wondered momentarily if David would try to pay her off to keep her mouth shut about Belinda's escapade. If he tried, she'd spit in his eye. Maybe that was why he was being so strange. He didn't know how to go about it.

"You needn't worry about me," she said.

"I don't," he answered. "You seem to be able to take care of yourself."

That was a rotten way to put it, she thought.

"Of course," he continued. "I am grateful that you got Belinda and Titan out of the mess. Thank you, Laura. I'll stay over to see Belinda, and then I'll return with you tomorrow. I guess Red told you how necessary it is for you to carry on with the campaign. Good that Belinda isn't here. We can talk."

She sat down. A feeling of relief such as she had never known before flooded her. She could face this man eye to eye.

"Maybe I'd better tell you more about myself before we go back," she said.

"Maybe not," he said. "I don't much care for confessions."

He took a cigarette from his case and lit it. He reached to offer her one, then put it back.

"I owe you a picnic on the back lot," he said, glancing at his watch. "What were your plans this afternoon?"

"I was going to take a last walk along the lane, into the woods," she said. "I never saw country as beautiful as this before. It's so clean and fresh, the ponds and the ferns, and the wood violets in the hidden places; and the rhododendron—"

"Let's go," he said.

They walked along a lane of English elm which gave way in the countryside to oak and maple. They cut past a pond, thick with birch and willow, and along a rocky path, the sloping land beyond dappled with pink bursts of rhododendron.

Neither spoke for a while.

He stopped and took a deep breath.

"It's a rotten rat race between Los Angeles, New York, and London. The whole world is changing."

He looked at the slanting rays of the sun filtering down through the lacy leaves of a gigantic oak.

"It doesn't seem to matter much here, does it?"

They sat on a fallen log, ankle-deep in fern.

"How is Belinda?" he asked. "How is she taking what happened in New Orleans?"

"Well, since you asked, she must be disturbed. I've learned to know that she isn't your standard run of actress. She has less ego than many of the so-called starlets at Titan. She hasn't mentioned the last part of that evening to me—how they got rid of the body, and how she felt about it. But it must be disturbing her deeply."

"It was dreadful," said David. "Hodine gave me a long description."

"She talks about you with such affection. She's been wondering when you would arrive. Maybe she'll tell you."

"Could be," he said. "We've been very close. I've seen her through troubled times before."

He could tell by the open interest in Laura's face that she had not been Belinda's confidante, and he was relieved.

"When she comes back," said David, "leave me alone with her. I want to tell her about finding the boy's body. In a sense, it closes the door on the incident. Perhaps she'll open up to me, and I'll help her get the horror out of her mind."

"Good," said Laura. "She's got a long haul ahead of her with her aunt. Do you want me to stay on with her?"

"Certainly not," said David. "Belinda and Claudia are very close. It's time for her to grow up. Besides, Red needs you."

As they walked back, David seemed lost in thought. Laura wondered whether he was concerned about Belinda because she was Titan's prime asset or whether there was a stronger bond between them.

She also wondered why she had suggested returning to the inn. Never in her life had she had such an idyllic time

331

as this escape from the world in this glade. It had been a few moments of enchantment.

But she didn't believe in enchantment, she reasoned with herself as they walked along the narrow footpath. Occasionally she looked back at David, pointing out some beauty of nature as they moved toward the scattered houses of the village.

Would it be peaceful to live here, or would the intrusion of the world prove that it was an illusion? After all, she had always felt she didn't belong. She wondered if she ever would find a home. She also alerted herself: never fall prey to sentiment. There is no possible way you can love anyone. If he knew . . . if he knew, it would only end in heartbreak.

When they reached the inn, Belinda was there in the lobby. She had just come in and was standing at the desk expectantly.

"I'll split out," Laura said. "I want to pick up some maple syrup and some gifts at the country store. I'll return for early dinner. Okay?"

"Thank you, Laura," he said. He wanted to take her hand, but the gloved hand was the one closest to him. He had been particularly aware of it as they had walked through the woods, for as she pushed branches and ferns aside, that hand had been held rigidly to her body.

Laura noticed the swift flicker of his eyelid as his gaze turned from her glove. He had almost taken her hand. She had seen that look on others before.

Well old girl, she thought, let that be a lesson to you. You're thinking about this man. What if he knew his monstrous old great-uncle had chopped off your finger in a brothel. Snap out of it, kid. Violets and ferns and a fallen log don't make romance. Nothing does for you.

In the lobby, Belinda rushed to David and put her arms around him.

"Oh, David, I knew you'd come, I've been waiting for you!"

He saw she was close to tears.

"Well," he said, "if we're going to have waterworks, let's have them upstairs in privacy."

"I'll run along," said Laura. "Shopping for the gang in publicity and all that stuff. See you later."

As she left, she noticed that neither Belinda nor David seemed to have heard her as he took Belinda's arm and they started up the wide old-fashioned staircase.

When they had closed the door, Belinda turned to him. Her eyes filled with tears.

"I'm sorry," she said. "I just can't help myself. I know you must think I'm a crybaby."

"I saw you in a Greek cave, holding your newborn infant in your arms and proudly saying, 'I told you, it's a boy.' Now after that, Belinda, how can you call yourself a crybaby?"

She attempted to compose herself.

"Sit down," he said. "I have news for you. They found the body of the boy in the river. There is no investigation. He was just one of many who drift off in life. He's at peace in a way, Belinda. His chapter is finished. Look at this little scrap of paper, the worth of his poor life. 'That was the third body in three months which had been picked up under similar conditions,' " he read. "And the circumstance of his death could have ruined your career."

She arose, her face distorted. He gave her his handkerchief. She pulled at it, twisting it.

"It was so awful!" she said. "I'll never forget dragging him over that muddy levee and seeing him sink in the river. It was as if I murdered him!"

She began to sob.

He put his arms around her. "Now, now," he said. "It's over. You helped Hodine get rid of a bundle of trouble and tragedy. I talked to him. He has respect for how you helped pull it off."

She clung to him, relishing the scent of his woolen jacket, the comfort of his presence.

"Oh, David," she said, "don't let me go. Don't ever let me go! I need you. I've loved you since the first day in London when you told me not to be a movie star. You're the only one in the world who understands me, even though you know all about me. It doesn't matter to you, does it?"

"Of course it doesn't," he said, smoothing her hair. "You know, as the saying goes, the crimes are of the times. You were rushed into an untenable situation. It's an unfortunate payment for fame. So how can you be blamed?"

"Then why can't you be with me? Why can't you love

me? I wouldn't have to make any pretense with you. I'd be good for you. I truly love you. You've never given me a chance to show it."

David broke away from her. "This is not right, Belinda," he said. "You're planning to marry Scott Stone. You'll be sorry you were so foolish as to say this."

"I know," she said, "but I can't help it."

He saw the distress on her face.

"Oh, David, Scott doesn't really know me. You do, and yet you understand. I feel closer to you than I do to him. I can't help it, but I do."

"It's impossible," he said.

She saw the same closed-in stubbornness on his face that Claudia had revealed every time David had been mentioned.

He went to the little table where Claudia had set up her treasured photographs in their ornate silver frames.

There was Jeffrey in his younger years, his handsome and famed profile, his casual elegance caught by the lens of Orville so long ago. And there also was a picture of himself with Belinda and Claudia at the villa in Rome. By chance, his face was in identical profile, as he had glanced down, smiling at Belinda.

"All right, Belinda," he said. "I guess it's time to level with you. I didn't want to, but I will."

He picked up the two photographs.

She stood, surprised at the way he had broken away from her and the anguish that was in his face.

"You see," he said, "sometimes pictures tell all. And you will see what I mean. Of course I love you. I should. I'm your brother."

Early dinner in the dining room was quiet. Belinda, seeing David across the table, was still shaken. At first shock she had felt a loss, and then she considered the incredible possibilities that lay in having him as her kin, her half brother, looking so much like Jeffrey. Memories of her adoring father, who had died when she was a small girl, rekindled a flame in her. Here was someone to cling to, someone who belonged to her, another Barstow.

Laura could see that something had happened between them. Belinda's sudden glances, David's attention to her and concern with small details—what she ordered, how she would take care of Claudia—were fraught with interest and underlying affection that seemed a departure from his usual cool manner.

Once or twice Laura thought she saw a faint tear in Belinda's eye, which she was working manfully to conceal. Laura briefly thought it might be a lover's quarrel, then decided against it. For there was no sign of withdrawing, or approaching, which any lovers would have at a point of crisis. Instead it was almost a balance of mutual tenderness.

After dinner, the summer evening still glowing with the gathered light of the day, David took over on his own.

"Why don't we go for a walk while Laura's packing."

I get the message, thought Laura. She agreed, that would be fine. They would have to leave so early in the morning that Belinda would hardly see them to say good-bye.

The fragrances of the day were distilling in the gloaming. David took her along the same lane where he had walked earlier with Laura.

The first star was beginning to gain ascendancy in the pale sky.

"This reminds me of the first time I met our father," he said. "Of course I had no clue of our relationship, for Fergus always thought *he* was my father . . . Poor Fergus." He smiled. "I guess he just got shortchanged. No wonder he's such a sour old bastard. Well, let's not dwell on that. Anyway, I was swimming in the ocean in Santa Monica. Jeffrey had been visiting Claudia. I tossed a piece of seaweed in the air over my head, and I heard someone near me in the water, laughing at my abandon. I told him I liked to swim until the first star came out and the sky turned purple. He was so alive, so alert to the sea and the moment. I remember what he said: 'Ah, yes, the lengthening shadows wait the first pale stars of twilight.' "

"That sounds like him," said Belinda. "I remember how he used to love to quote poetry. And he used to hold me close and smell my cheeks and say it was honeysuckle time. Funny how I remember moments with him so clearly."

"Yes," said David, "he was old, and I'd say gone into alcoholism, but it didn't seem to matter, he had such joie de vivre. I was so fascinated by him that when we got back to the shore I walked backward so I wouldn't miss a glance of his face or a word of his splendid voice. After that, he always sent me wonderful books on Christmas and my birthday. I think he left me a heritage, a treasure trove of literature I never would have known if he hadn't shared his innermost passion for beauty with me."

Belinda, warm with shared memories, took his hand. "I'd like to see them if you still have them."

"So you shall," said David.

"Tell me," said Belinda, "how is it that no one realizes he was your father? You look so much alike, now that I know, it amazes me. Does anyone know?"

"Strange," he said, "people rarely see what's right in front of them. But Claudia did. She put the pieces of the puzzle together on the yacht in Greece when we were shooting your picture. I didn't even know it myself then. You know how I discovered it?"

Belinda glanced at him quizzically.

"Fergus got angry at all Barstows. How he must have hated Jeffrey when Jessica, that sainted mother of yours, told him he wasn't my father, to get even with him. But I won't go into that. Strange, the two mothers that brought us into the world. My mother, insane and gentle. Jessica, sane and cruel." He frowned. "I've often thought about it, Belinda, but I'd never tell you the whole story of Jessica and what she did to me. I don't even want to think about her."

"I hate her, too," said Belinda.

He glanced at her sharply and waved the comment away.

"But to get back to the story, when you got pregnant and we had to protect you, Fergus blew up and told me I was siding with Barstows because I was one of them. He had no idea how his bitterness released me from a miserable young manhood. I never knew why he hated me, but now I was able to understand it. And, strangely, we became friends."

"That's why you were so close and wonderful to me in Greece; you knew."

"Partly," said David. "I think it did me good to know I had you for my sister. I was a loner, and now I felt I belonged to someone. Even if you didn't know."

Belinda struck her palm against her forehead. "Now I know why you were so shocked when I tried to make love to you on the beach at Santa Monica. Oh, my God!"

He smiled and strode on ahead. She had to walk faster to keep up with him.

"I almost told you then," he said, "but it was not the time. I've been watching you. You've matured a great deal in these last few weeks. And I admire the way you're taking over Claudia's problems."

"She never told me," said Belinda. "How could she not tell me!"

"It was something that had to be resolved between us," he said.

They approached the meadow. It was getting dark. He stopped for a moment, and Belinda inhaled the fragrances of the flowers and the tender green ferns, which were sending out a signal of summer in the warm stillness.

He thought of the moments he had spent here with Laura. This place seemed to be a confessional.

"You know," he said, "I never said this to anyone before. I love you deeply."

"I love you, too," said Belinda, "but I'm simply trying to adjust."

"The wonderful thing about us," he said, "is, now that we know, we will have each other as long as we live. Lovers and husbands can get lost in the course of tide and time, but brother and sister are bonded together by nature."

He bent forward and kissed her cheek.

"It's a helluva wonderful secret, isn't it?"

She smiled, and he turned to go back, leading the way. For a moment he reflected that when he had come back on this path with Laura, he had courteously allowed her to lead, and to look back and point out the beauties of their few moments.

But this was different. He was the elder, and he protected her.

Belinda followed. Her emotions were close to the surface. In a way she felt a comfort and a security she'd never felt. But in another way, which she felt she would learn to live with, she was bereft. Her Galahad would never be a suitor, as she had dreamed. Instead, he was kin.

He reaffirmed it when he said good night to her.

"I won't see you in the morning. We'll leave too early. Keep in touch with me about Claudia; if you need anything, call me. And, of course, what we discussed is to be our secret."

"Of course," she said.

"And," he said, kissing her cheek, "you know now that you are not alone. As long as I'm around, you have someone."

Her eyes filled with tears.

"So do you," she whispered.

In the suite, Laura was ready. She seemed in good humor. After all, thought Belinda a little jealously, she was going away with him, back to Titan, she'd be right in the middle of things.

"Did you have a nice visit?" asked Laura.

"The best," said Belinda.

She went to her room. Let Laura wonder. Anyway, what could she say?

"Laura, thank you for what you did in New Orleans. I— I haven't been able to talk about it, but now that they found the boy, I feel in a way he's put to rest."

Laura nodded. "I'm glad you can think of it that way. And if you don't mind, I think we'd better keep it to ourselves. I wouldn't even tell your fiancé. He might wonder what you were doing in some musician's digs. I never should have let you go there."

"It's taken me a while," said Belinda, "but I'm catching on. I guess I just can't be a private citizen. Anything I do can be magnified, and I'm suspect."

"True," said Laura. "But let's forget it. It's past."

"Do you think you can forget the past? Can you hide something awful that happened to you?"

Laura glanced at her. Could she possibly have been told anything about *her* past? Seeing the guileless look on Belinda's face, Laura decided that she was trying to relieve herself of some past burden.

"What happened in the past can't be helped," said Laura. "If we dwelled on past mistakes we'd never be able to go on." She smiled faintly.

Belinda noticed that Laura was changing, the white Kabuki mask that had been the face she previously presented seemed to be softening. There was more joy in her, and her smiles were becoming a natural part of her personality.

"At least I hope the past can be ignored," Laura said.

"So do I," said Belinda.

When she retired, she turned the light out and looked out at the landscape, so peaceful, so gentle in the summer night, it hardly seemed possible that a turbulent world existed.

She thought about David, and she felt an aching, yet a deep pride that he was her brother. And she was glad that Claudia knew. They were a family group, a strange family group, but nonetheless related.

She pondered on the conversation she had with Laura about keeping a secret. Of course she had only referred to the night in New Orleans.

Then she thought about Alex. Laura said past mistakes should be forgotten; the past should be buried.

It would be wrong to ever let Scott know about Alex. There was nothing she could do about it. After all, his father had died. His death was an accident of nature. No less terrible than the death of that young boy.

Ah, there was another reason that proved to her that a secret should be kept. Look at David. All these years he had been thought to be Fergus Austin's son. What a well-kept secret his natural father being Jeffrey Barstow had been! She related the plight of David's birth to the plight of herself and Alex. If David's birth could be kept secret, why not Alex's?

The guilt that had been building in her was relieved. She had been thinking that she would have to go home and face the truth about Alex with Scott. Now she put it out of her mind.

It was late before she fell asleep. She'd be busy arranging to get Claudia home. She'd already enlisted one of Claudia's fans, who was a practical nurse, to take care of her. Everyone at the inn adored Claudia, and the glamor and success she had brought to the summer theater showed in their personal care. Flowers had already begun to arrive, many of them home-picked and fragrant, much nicer, Belinda thought, than the usual city offerings from fat purses and prestigious florists.

Some people sent plates of home-baked cookies, jellies, and cakes. Belinda was beginning to see the roots of a personal country life. It was good. She liked it. And it also made her realize how different these personal kindnesses were from some of the glossy success-oriented behavior of a film studio where everyone was as close to the top and success as they could get, and made every overdone effort to stay there.

The phone woke her in the morning. Stuart Plimpton was on his way up to take her to pick up Claudia.

She hastily washed and dressed in her slacks and shirt and met him at the door, still brushing her hair.

"I have a driver," he said. "Let's run. Can you skip breakfast?"

"It really doesn't matter," she said. "I slept late. Let's go."

He was so lost in thought that he only managed to grumble absentmindedly that she looked better than anybody who took two hours to make up.

On the way to Hyannisport he put his head back and closed his eyes wearily.

"I have to tell you," he said, "because we will have to face Claudia, and it isn't going to be easy."

He paused, deep in reflection.

"What is it?"

"I'm going to have to close the play. We aren't going to do *Glass Menagerie* without Claudia."

"Oh, Claudia will feel awful. Isn't Helen French any good?"

"She's adequate," said Plimpton. "But after a talent like Claudia, and that old Barstow name on the marquee, nobody would be right. People are just canceling out. The magic is gone."

"Oh, that's terrible!" said Belinda.

"Yup," said Plimpton, "it is."

He was so sunk in misery that he didn't even attempt to be the vital personality he usually presented to the world.

"I guess it puts you in a bad spot," she said.

"Well, I did lay out a bundle on publicity and promotion. After all, you don't find a break like that very often in a lifetime. At least I can remember how wonderful it was!" He patted her hand. "Wish you could have seen her. She was splendid."

"I wish there was something I could do," she said. "This is going to hurt Claudia, and she shouldn't be hurt. But I guess there isn't anything, is there?"

He smiled and flipped his hand trying to be light about it.

"Well, there really isn't," he said, tugging at his moustache. "Unless of course you got out the magic wand and played Laura. Another Barstow on the marquee. Sounds like that corny line from an old movie. 'Mr. Shubert is in the audience, Miss Haver, so kick high!' "

She laughed. Then she turned and looked at hm. They stared at each other; the thought had struck, like sudden lightning in a summer storm.

"I'll do it!" said Belinda. "I'll do it! I can play Laura."

"Oh, now, come on!" said Plimpton. "The sex image of the picture business playing a plain, crippled little girl who can't cope with life—an escapist, a misfit, a loser. But thanks."

Belinda stuck her chin out. "So you think I can't act. That I'm just a personality product. Well, let me tell you something. I have the best teacher in the world. Would you believe Claudia had me learn the whole play with her, scene by scene, just to prove to me that I could do something outside this so-called star buildup. She said that first and foremost Barstows were actors. My ancestors belonged to itinerant stock companies; they played everything. And she didn't want me to be typecast. So there!"

He stared at her. "You'd do it?"

"Yes," she said, "of course I'd do it. Do you realize what it would mean to Claudia? She can coach me from her bed, if she has to. You know her."

Plimpton was still in a state of shock. "Titan wouldn't let you," he said. "It's a wild notion!"

"Titan *will* let me; just leave it to me. I'll call David Austin as soon as his plane gets in. You can leave the name Barstow on your marquee," she grinned. "Think of the money you'd save!"

"It's impossible!" said Plimpton. His mind was racing. Already messages were being sent out in his imagination; theater and film society would be rocked, the publicity would be overwhelming, he could prolong the run as long as she would do it. But of course, it was impossible.

"Impossible," he said again, "but thank you for getting me all excited when I needed it. You're a trouper!"

"You'll have to tell Claudia yourself that you're closing the show, and that you wouldn't let me do it!"

"Won't let you do it!" gasped Plimpton. He sank back and put his hands to his forehead, overcome.

His mind darted feverishly as they drove on. Even if Belinda couldn't sell herself as the crippled, shy Laura, if she could run through her lines, she'd create an excitement such as Elderberry had never known. And it would get him off the hook. It would make him.

He had a crazy, quick flash. One of the fantasies that a man could have who saw life in terms of his own world, for after all, he owned Elderberry and had created the season that made this dream possible.

He saw the press gathered about him in a knot.

"Tell us, Mr. Plimpton, how did you ever get Belinda Barstow to play at Elderberry?"

He would glance down at them modestly and then say, "She talked me into it."

The audacity of that quote alone would get him in every publication from *Variety* to the *Reader's Digest* . . . Helen French would be okay as the mother, nobody would really care. They'd just like to see Belinda Barstow in the flesh. Why, even a Broadway producer couldn't have afforded to have her.

"I couldn't afford you!" he echoed his thoughts.

She patted his hand. "You can give me what Claudia would have had in salary and I'd ask you to put us both up, of course, and you'd have to pay for her practical nursing because I'd be too busy to be with her. She'll have to stay in bed most of the time, you know."

"I know," he said. "Don't think I didn't talk to the doctor." He put his hands over his eyes. "My God! What about poor Joan McGowan? She's been working so hard. And her boyfriend, Michael, is playing the Gentleman Caller. That kid'll shoot herself."

"Well," said Belinda, "it's too bad, but if you have to close down the show, she wouldn't be in it anyway, would she?"

"You've got a point," said Plimpton.

"How will we tell Claudia?"

"Don't say a word! Let's just get her settled at the inn, and then you can bring it up as a natural progression of things."

"Which it is," said Belinda. "Mum's the word."

In her mind, she was already playing Laura. Plimpton didn't believe her. Well, she'd show him she could do it. Thank God she had the family total recall. Memorizing lines had always been easy for her.

She leaned forward, hunching her shoulders slightly, and pulled a wisp of her hair over one cheek. She waited a moment for the feeling of Laura to filter through. Her cheeks seemed to become thinner, and the fullness of her lips was drawn back as she pressed them tightly, self-consciously over her teeth. She glanced up, her chin still low, as if the very act of speaking was an apology. And in a faint voice from the nervous, restricting chamber of her throat, a barely heard whisper of her fear escaped, it seemed unwillingly. She glanced sideways at Plimpton as if seeking pardon for her presence, lifted her hands tenderly as if she were proffering a jewel to him, and spoke Laura's lines, the tiny imaginary glass unicorn held in her cupped hands like a king's treasure.

Her voice, as thin as spun glass, reached him: " 'I don't do anything—much. Please don't think I sit around doing nothing! My glass collection takes up a good deal of time. Glass is something you have to take good care of.' "

Belinda paused to take a breath, and then moved on to the next speech.

" 'Little articles of it, they're ornaments mostly. Most of them are little animals made of glass. . . .' "

Belinda gestured delicately, bringing the invisible collection of glass creatures into life. As she continued evoking the fragments of Laura's wistful being, nurtured with illusion, doused by an overbearing belle of a mother, Plimpton stared, astounded.

She stopped, put her shoulders back, and resumed her own stance.

"My God!" whispered Plimpton.

Belinda waved his awe away.

"Of course," she said briskly, "Laura doesn't have the long speeches. I can't read her very well alone. She's a reactor. But she certainly takes over the stage, don't you think?"

Plimpton swallowed. For once, he couldn't speak.

Claudia left the hospital in a blaze of dramatic glory. She wore a black patch to protect her eye against the glare of the bright summer morning. It made her look dashing and mysterious.

There was the usual flurry of good-byes to the people who had entered her life so importantly and briefly: interns, nurses, and orderlies who asked for autographs; the special one who wheeled her to the waiting car. A young anesthetist who wished her good luck, and also wished he had the opportunity to be on the stage and hoped someday he could look her up and get his foot in the door; the doctor who would visit her at Elderberry and had been promised tickets for his whole family the first time she'd step on the stage when this was all in the past.

Exit the courageous grande dame.

Plimpton fluttered about, concerned and helpful, gathering the necessary insurance forms for her to sign so she wouldn't be fatigued. He walked in a daze, trying not to let his euphoria show, at the same time convincing himself that the wunderkind would not defect. He would have to be most cautious not to reveal his ecstasy when the news was broken to Claudia about Miss Superstar taking her place. Claudia Barstow might be news, but Belinda Barstow was an avalanche.

Belinda gathered her aunt's little treasures: cologne, sachet, feather powder puff, bath powder, new pills in little hospital vials, robes, gowns, laundry, facial unguents, get well cards, telegrams, potted plants, and fresh flowers in fancy containers all to be saved.

Of course, several people, mostly youngsters, had rushed up to Belinda for her autograph, and a few people from other floors rushing up back stairways had been sent packing by the officious head nurse who had the privilege of wheeling Claudia to the parking lot.

This was Claudia's moment. She certainly was the star, and, for once, Belinda felt like a supporting player.

She noticed with affection Claudia's pale, thin face, the black eye patch and white powdered chin and neck. She still had the scent of glamor. Even with her hair on end, for the doctor would not allow her to brush or comb it, but only smooth it until the tortured eye was more solidly in her head, she was splendid.

Lavender and Chanel Number 5 followed her triumphant procession. A wisp of marabou was at her neck, and she had the mien of a Bernhardt. Fate might have rung the bell on a much younger woman, but Claudia had the air of standing in the wings, perhaps slightly unsteadily, yet ready to step up to the footlights and play L'Aiglon.

She had the vanity to pull a little mirror from the silk clutch bag on her lap and dab a bit of crimson rouge on her lips before she faced her public, the hospital staff at the third-floor reception desk.

And she didn't disappoint Belinda. As they stood waiting for the interminably slow elevator, Claudia lifted one thin arm dramatically. She gestured back to the doorway of her room and then to the cluster of nurses who awaited a chance to see her famous face.

She spoke:

> " 'The play is done, the curtain drops
> Slow falling to the prompter's bell;
> A moment yet, the actor stops,
> And looks around to say farewell.
> It is an irksome word and task:
> And when he's laughed and said his say,
> He shows as he removes the mask
> A face that's anything but gay.' "

This is pretty corny, thought Belinda, smiling to herself.

The elevator appeared at that moment, the doors opened, Claudia was wheeled in, and she turned to face the surprised group, staring in arrested motion. The sliding door, as majestic as a theater curtain, folded her from sight. As the elevator slowly moved downward, she turned to Belinda.

"Well, damn, William Makepeace Thackeray certainly gave me a good curtain, didn't he?"

Belinda laughed.

"You'll always have one," she said. "Where did you ever pick up all those quotes?"

"It runs in the family. You should have heard your father. I guess it's our protection against the banal. 'Good-bye, thank you . . . you were so kind . . . We must meet again . . . ask me if you want tickets . . . Oh really, your child should be on stage, how interesting.' My God, Belinda, what a multitude of clichés are avoided by one good joust into the crevices of some poet's mind."

"I'll remember that," said Belinda.

Once they got in the car, Claudia, moving slowly and majestically, settled into a mound of pillows at the back of her head, and Belinda sat next to her, straddling pots of ferns and baskets of flowers. Plimpton tucked his pleasure into an apparent study of the landscape.

"You should be here in the fall," he babbled. "The dazzling rich shades of the trees—crimson, orange and red, even golden yellow. The fragrance of balsam, spruce, and pine, and ash whose leaves turn plum colored, and of course the great elms, viburnum, the scarlet hawthorn bush—"

"For the love of God," said Claudia, "shut up, will you, Stuart? It hurts my eyes to have to listen to all those colors. Why are you babbling so? It's not like you."

"Because I'm so happy," he blurted, a broad smile revealing his perfect porcelain teeth. He tugged at his moustache. "Claudia, Belinda's going to play Laura and we're going on with the show! With your coaching, of course."

Claudia opened her mouth. She turned to Belinda. "Is this true?"

"Don't turn your head so fast," said Belinda. "Put your head back on the pillow."

Belinda turned to Plimpton. "You said not to say anything!"

"I couldn't help myself," he said. "Claudia—we almost closed down. Belinda will save us. Is it okay with you?"

Claudia put her head back on the pillow.

Finally she spoke.

"Look, they gave me a sedative before we left. I'm still not quite with it. This is startling, to say the least. How can you?"

"I can," said Belinda. "You know I'm off salary with Titan. And you also know David will let me do anything I want to. We had a long talk about—about many things."

Claudia glanced at her. Ah, David had told her! The whole world was whirling too fast. She wasn't really up to it. It had only been a week since her eye had literally been out of her head, patched, stitched, and stuck back in. It ached in spite of pain-killers.

"Let's not talk anymore," said Belinda. "Close your eyes."

Claudia drifted off, putting herself into the hands of her niece. It was the first time it had happened to them, and they both felt good about it.

```
********************
*                  *
*        22        *
*                  *
********************
```

Claudia was forced to lie still, and sedated, in her hotel suite for two weeks.

In the evenings she was allowed to lie on a chaise in the sitting room, and she and Belinda dined at a card table, served from the dining room.

Molly Johnston, a retired nurse around Claudia's age, a petite red-haired Scottish woman who adored film stars as nuns adored saints, was there during the day, cosseting her, sponging her, giving her cologne rubdowns, reading to her, answering phones, sorting callers, and tending all the flowers and gifts that poured in. Her most difficult chore was to restrain Claudia; she sedated her by doctor's orders on the clock.

The little woman was in seventh heaven. She was promoted to instant prestige in Elderberry, and she handled the situation with dignity.

Claudia, grateful for the attention, wished Molly could stay with her always. It was wonderful to be cared for.

Belinda was busy with rehearsals in the daytime, and in the evenings, after dinner, Claudia went over scenes with her; they dissected each line of the play.

"There are two schools of thought on acting," said Claudia. "There are the actors who study their roles and analyze them line by line. Students like your father, of course, and Spencer Tracy, Humphrey Bogart, Katharine Hepburn, Helen Hayes, Paul Muni, and George Arliss, mostly from the theater, always followed the tradition of deep study. Then there are the others, spawned by the film business. Strangely, most of them have splendid memories, and they learned their roles in great chunks, like Gable, Cooper, Jean Harlow, Joan Crawford, and, sometimes I hate to admit, in my early days, even myself. This school relied on their star personalities to carry them through their characterizations. I hope you will belong to the former group. I've always been a little nervous about your memory and your built-in star quality. It makes it so easy. But remember, those gifts are only a stepping-stone, not nearly enough for a superb performance."

"I know," said Belinda. "I've heard how Marilyn Monroe is suffering, trying to get away from her sex image. How hard she works with the Actor's Lab!"

"Your biggest problem," said Claudia, "will be to overcome your screen image in playing the mousy little Laura. You have to face the fact that on account of your over-publicized image, the public may not accept you in a character role."

Belinda was annoyed. As she worked with Plimpton, with Helen French, who was obviously nervous at stepping into Claudia's shoes after all the fanfare of *The Madwoman of Chaillot,* and with Michael Ross, who was also in that play, she felt that she had her hands full just trying to coordinate. She didn't want to seem to dominate the company because of her film success and her fan following.

As Plimpton had anticipated, the press hounds had come rushing in, triggered by the startling news that Belinda Barstow was going to appear on stage locally. Plimpton had to hire a man to guard the door at rehearsals and station another at the desk to check pushy visitors and keep camera freaks away from Belinda.

Gifts and flowers began to fill the suite to the point of confusion. These, too, had to be assorted, and Molly sent the overflow to a rest home and orphanage nearby.

Requests for press tickets inundated the box office. So many wanted to see the opening that season-ticket holders would have been pushed out of the theater, so it was decided to have a press preview before the opening. Claudia was disturbed about that, too, for she knew how rough the press could be. She was wise enough to realize that part of her success had been the forgiveness of the press for her failures of many years. But a renaissance was completely different from the acceptance of a glamorous young star who had just been on a nationwide tour playing one of the most lascivious young women in history.

"What am I supposed to do?" said Belinda crossly.

"Put on a body pad and erase my face? I hope my acting will overcome this problem. I'm trying hard."

She saw that she was agitating her aunt. It would never do. Claudia had to have serenity. The doctor had warned her, disturbance and sudden movement could end in partial blindness.

"I'm sorry," Belinda said. "I'm just on edge. I couldn't help hearing that Joan McGowan is so upset about me getting her role that she's leaving Elderberry. And I have to tell you something—Settle back," she said, fluffing up the pillows. "That's right, lean back, close your eyes. I just like to keep you up on what's going on."

Claudia did as she was told, eager to hear what went on in the outside world.

"Well, Michael Ross, you know, who was kind of stuck on Joan when you did your play, is giving me all sorts of goo-goo eyes. I really have to be careful to stay away from him during breaks. I feel badly about it."

Claudia reached for her hand. "Oh, my dear, don't I know! How many fine actresses have been hurt when the role goes to another person. And I hate to say it, but one day you might have to eat crow yourself. I'll never forget when I wanted to play Catherine the Great and Martha Ralston got the role."

"Oh, that one," said Belinda. "I always wondered about her. And about the little girl she had by Niadas."

Belinda paused. She hadn't thought about it much, but this child, less than a year older than Alex, was his half sister and the heir to the Niadas billions. Belinda remembered that Martha Ralston had been the Titan sex symbol in the war years and afterward, until she had married the Greek tycoon.

Obviously, Claudia's memory was focused on the mother, not the child. "Martha could never act. She's rich, and of course the child is an heiress. But that stupid girl got the role *I* should have played. And of course she blew it! Anyway, don't worry about Michael Ross. I've been through so many of these crushes. It goes on like mad during a production. There is always an empathy with the drama of the roles. It's part of the fantasy you're creating. He'll get over it if you don't encourage him. And if he really cares for Joan, they'll get back together again after you're out of their lives. Maybe she might come to see me. It might make it easier for her."

Belinda shook her head as Claudia opened her un-bandaged eye.

"No way!" she said. "She's too unhappy. You're not going to be exposed to someone's misery. I'll see her and tell her how much you admire her. Would that help?"

Claudia looked at Belinda with admiration. She was maturing. Imagine the courage of a girl who was taking over a role to consider facing the young hopeful who had literally had it and lost it!

"If you think it's all right," she said. "But that certainly takes guts. How's Helen French doing in *my* role?"

"Oh, she's hacking it," said Belinda. "I think she's a little touchy about the situation, too. But she's solid, and of course old Plimpton is trying very hard to make her feel relaxed about it."

"Now, I think you're beginning to realize that there is more to a production than just acting," said Claudia. "Raveling out the backstage personality problems from the onstage performing problems is sometimes incredibly fatiguing. Remember, as I've said to you before, success is not always a popularity contest. Even if you have to seem cool, play it that way, and don't be a Humpty-Dumpty who can be knocked on and off the wall by the way the current emotional breeze is blowing. Onstage you have to maintain a long level of concentration; it's so different from the chopped-up segments of a film."

"Yes," said Belinda. "I'm learning that. You know the play cold. Could we run through the scene where Amanda tells Laura that she's found out she hasn't been going to business school? I think Helen's playing it too scolding, instead of feeling that life has given her such a cruel cut to have a crippled daughter like Laura. And I have to listen to such long speeches, to react all curled up inside myself. Poor Laura. She listens and gets crushed so much more than she is able to express herself. Help me to learn to react."

Claudia's face softened with pleasure. Belinda was on the right track . . .

They played the scene. Claudia was delighted to be in-volved. It gave her something to think about. Unfortunately, the doctor had already told her she could not take the excitement of the opening night. Perhaps she could attend the final performances, if she could restrain herself from being emotional, for tears would do her damage.

As soon as the play closed, they would fly home. She would face a time of increasing activity, but she couldn't drive for several months, and exercise would be curtailed.

She would press Scott's mother, Henrietta, into doing her errands. She smiled wryly. That lady had little to do. The wedding would be the most exciting thing that had ever happened to her. She blessed the fact that Flora Stone Random and her social pretensions were out of the picture. And Max would be working at the house, that would be another blessing.

In due time, Belinda invited Joan McGowan and Michael Ross to have Sunday lunch with her at the inn dining room. She larded the meal with compliments to Joan and made several remarks about Scott and her coming marriage. She finally saw Joan's clouded face begin to break into smiles.

"And I have a surprise for you," Belinda said, once she realized the tension had been lessened. "Claudia can see you both for a moment. You know, of course, that emotions have to be smothered. She looks rather thin and pale, but don't be alarmed, she's going to be fine." She smiled at Joan. "She has something special to say to you."

It was a touchy moment. Claudia had wrapped her hair in a chiffon scarf and was sitting on her chaise as grandly as Colette, wearing a royal blue dressing robe and using a cane for a hook, which eased books and papers and pens to her side without too long a reach to her side table.

She allowed Joan to bend down to kiss her.

"I just had to see you, Joan," she said. "You know how sorry I am not to have played this role with you, but I have good news. Providing you're available next summer, I'm going to do the play with you. Would you?"

"Would I!" said Joan, wide-eyed. "Oh, Miss Barstow!"

"It's Claudia to you," she said. "I hope you will enjoy telling people that Belinda was your successor, but only fate got her into your shoes."

They all enjoyed a laugh.

Michael stood by shyly, enjoying the excitement in Joan's face.

He's going to be okay, thought Belinda. She suddenly felt lonely, seeing their love. Well, she thought, I've got Scott.

Joan brought forth the little empty phial of perfume Claudia had given her the day they met.

"I'll keep it as a talisman in my purse forever!" she said.

The fences were mended. The two of them left happily with a future and a promise sealing their high spirits.

After they were gone, Belinda turned to her aunt. "Well," she said, "you didn't have to put me down quite so much. Only fate put me in her shoes! That's the limit!"

She flounced into her bedroom.

Claudia smiled. She thought Belinda had been too good to be true. This wasn't all quite as easy for her as being the pet of a hundred people at a studio. She was performing on a bare stage with a small cast of actors who were not exactly the elite and working with a director who had been a movie dropout for a quarter of a century.

There was no comfortable dressing room. Thank God they could do her stage makeup right in her room.

But Belinda would have to stand on her own feet. It was a good experience for her.

It was impossible for Scott to come to the opening. His office had him working night and day. Belinda was relieved, for his arrival at this time would have been an added pressure. And fortunately for Claudia's economy, Max caught a summer cold and was afraid to come east because he might pass it on to her.

They both hoped David might be with them. But he called Claudia from London. He was setting up a new sound-recording studio for Titan in Soho, off Charing Cross Road. The sophisticated equipment was costing over half a million dollars. There were bugs to be worked out; he was determined that the new sound studios would be better than the current IBC in Portland Place, the Olympic Studios in Baker Street, and CTS in Westbourne Grove.

The thought of London brought back tender memories to Claudia; she suddenly had a longing to be there again.

"Oh, David," she said, "I wish we could be there with you. Now that we—well—"

"We all know," he finished.

She swallowed, trying not to be emotional. "How I'd love to show you our family haunts, Drury Lane, and Jeffrey's hangouts . . ."

There was a moment of silence. She wondered if she'd gone too far.

"We'll do it sometime. You and Belinda and I will catch up to our past."

"It seems strange, all this sound stage excitement," she said. "Why is it so important?"

"Because rock and roll music is becoming so important," he said. "It's changing the face of entertainment. Tell Belinda I'm not going to add to the collection of flowers and gimcracks that must be cluttering up your lives. I'm bringing her a present from London."

"She'll be excited," said Claudia. "She's working her little tail off."

"How is she?"

"Good," said Claudia, "really good, David. You won't be sorry you gave her permission to do it. I'm only worried about one thing. She's so damned beautiful that you just can't help feeling that she'd be anything but the most sought-after girl in town."

"Don't worry," said David, "she'll make it." He sounded fatigued.

"Are you all right?" she asked.

"I'm very tired," he said. "I've been having meetings all day and half the night."

Something in his voice made her suspect he wasn't happy.

After he hung up, Claudia cradled the phone in her hand. Her brother Jeffrey had left her the legacy of two pretty unusual human beings.

So the two Barstow women faced their problems by themselves.

"These days strangely remind me of the villa in Rome," said Claudia. "We had to work it out there doing our studying in that amphitheater where you learned your skills in that beautiful Roman hillside. And now here we are in a hotel room on the Cape going through the same thing. It all seems a far cry from the finished product, Belinda, but we have to be flexible."

Belinda was withdrawn these days, less flamboyant than

usual. She was trying to fit into the carapace of the pallid girl she was going to play.

"Yes," said Belinda almost wistfully. "I guess no matter who we have in our life, we still are on our own when it comes to performance."

"I'm glad you've learned that," said Claudia. "I have a good marriage, but it hasn't helped me much lately, has it? I had to cut the mustard myself. You're marrying a fine man. It seems he is doing his thing right now, without you, too. There will undoubtedly be times when you'll desperately want to be with the man you love, but if you really care about who you are and what you do with yourself, those other elements in your life will have to be washed clean for the moment. I hope you're very happy with your new life, Belinda, but I do hope your happiness won't cloud what you are supposed to do with your talent."

I wonder, thought Belinda. I wonder what it will be like to be happy. I just want to sink into my life with Scott, that's all I can think of now . . .

Looking forward to returning home, and beginning to dream more and more romantically about her marriage and Scott, gave her the strength to face both her work and the responsibilities of looking after Claudia's emotional health. They became close in work and affection, in spite of the pressures of the play and the gathering excitement of the first night; it was a happy time in their relationship.

The company was enchanted with Belinda. Plimpton virtually threw a red carpet down wherever she walked. Photographers and a TV camera came to interview her the day before the play opened. The fact that Claudia could not meet the press made it seem all the more dramatic.

The whole village of Elderberry became Belinda's showcase. Her picture adorned every store window. A bunting hung over the entrance to the theater lobby: WELCOME BELINDA BARSTOW. Cars were lined up double in front of the inn. People drove in from the countryside and stood in line to get tickets for whatever performance was not sold out.

The restaurants stocked up with food, the hotel moved in extra folding chairs and tables to take care of the large pretheater dinner trade, and the shops all arranged to remain open longer.

All available rooms were filled for fifty miles around. It made Claudia's previous success seem minuscule. It was a personal experience, being adored by a community to which she'd brought prosperity.

In the center of it all, Claudia managed to help Belinda maintain her calm; she was satisfied that the core of Belinda's life was her work. She was a trouper. With her, the play was the thing. She related well to her fellow actors; she had managed to tiptoe cautiously with Plimpton, so he would not be disturbed by the fact that Claudia was coaching her.

The rest, she thought, was up to Plimpton, the cast, and the presentation of Belinda in her first stage role. She knew the critics would be a cool audience, and she was sorry she couldn't attend the post-theater champagne party that Plimpton had arranged in the dining room of the inn. He was obviously getting rich on the summer. What had started as a disaster with Claudia's eye problem had turned into the jackpot for him.

The set had been beautifully constructed by a designer brought from New York. The wardrobe was carefully selected to the last character analysis. The complicated lighting—focusing on the selected dramatic moments of the actors—concentrated on an illuminated lighting of Belinda as Laura, revealing her slightest reaction even to long pauses between her speeches. She was the visual center of the play at all times; a moth illuminated by candlelight. Belinda wore her hair combed back from her pale forehead, tied with a ribbon and falling in a cascade between her shoulders.

Looking at Belinda's heart-shaped face, the thick-fringed eyes, large and luminous, Claudia was touched by the transparency of her beauty. That wistful face would hold the audience's attention even during the long pauses when Laura had to listen to the weak brother and the dominant Amanda, her mother.

The only thing that disturbed Claudia was Belinda's beauty. A shiver came over her; a premonition that it might be wrong to cast her in the frail person of Laura, who had never attracted a single suitor in her unhappy life.

But Belinda worked on her characterization and tried hard to disguise the magnificence of her body. She had chosen tacky clothes, tied them in a low, long sash at the waist, and worn her sleeves at wrist length, hiding the grace of her arms and shoulders. In every way, Belinda had attempted to make her body into that of a lame girl.

The day of the opening, Elderberry seemed to gather a strange life, different from any it had known. The streets were festive. The hotel lobby was alive with visitors, the local gentry coming in early to shop and dine and celebrate the excitement brought about by a genuine celebrity in their midst.

Claudia, in her suite overlooking the open country, saw a stream of cars pouring down the distant highway and heard the roar of hot rods and the explosion of motorcycles. She wondered about it.

Early in the evening, Plimpton made a ceremonial visit to her. He brought a magnum of champagne.

She was sitting up, dressed in a lilac silk slack suit, the sitting room laden with flowers, the sideboard full of snacks and a liquor setup to receive a few visitors afterwards.

Plimpton rushed in and kissed her on the cheek.

"What a day!" he said. "What an evening. Claudia, I want to thank you—Yes, I know what you've been doing. I know the coaching was beyond me. And don't think I resented it; I'm deeply grateful. She is splendid, this girl. I only wish I could have fulfilled the dream of the two of you on the boards."

For the first time he noted that the patch was off her eye. Devoid of eye makeup, she still looked good.

"My God!" he cried. "Your eye! It looks great. Nobody would know anything had happened!"

"Save me," she said. "One eye is out of focus. But give it a chance. I guess I'll be able to witness at least the last performance."

"Well," he said proudly, "you'll be thrilled at what I did for Belinda. Of course, a hundred of the press is here, and they're devastated not to see you. But the audience can't all be critics—so I pulled a coup."

"What did you do?" said Claudia, "get the local bank presidents and founding members of your theater?"

"Better," said Plimpton, beaming. "They come in tomorrow. A group from New York called me, begging for a block of two hundred tickets for the press preview.

They're the New York branch of the Belinda Barstow Fan Club.

"I thought it would be a wonderful idea to have a bunch of young kids in the middle of that staid press to adore her and cheer her on; the press will be overwhelmed."

"What was your connection?" asked Claudia.

"Well," he said, "the New York Belinda Barstow Fan Club. Of course, you know them."

"No," said Claudia. "Actually I never heard of them. Who are they?"

"Well, they're very well established. Their head is prominent. His name is Boysie Miller. He's the man who has taken over the column that Andrew Reed left to him. You know, a very bright young man with great newspaper connections."

Claudia put her hand to her heart.

There was no use to tell Plimpton about Andrew Reed. Flung out of the party of the year in Rome for his misbehavior in handling scandalous items, the incident had broken up his relationship with Leslie Charles, who was the love of his life. Reed had been a bitter enemy of the Barstow family ever since Fergus had stopped him from coming to Titan studio after he had reported serious private items about the family. And Boysie, his young lover and the inheritor of his column, had undoubtedly been left a message in his will to keep up the vendetta.

"My God!" she said. "How many came in?"

Plimpton was exuberant. "Several hundred. Youth! Youth!" he said. "The one thing we need to get out of the slough of our aging theater group. They've been pouring in in hot rods, motorcycles, stretch-outs, buses, all of them eager to be part of Belinda's success."

Claudia stared at him. Maybe she was wrong. Maybe this was the new wave needed to push a career. There was no use to alert Stuart now. It was too late. Maybe this was just the new way.

"Well, Stuart," she said, "you certainly have tried your best."

"For you, Claudia, anything," he said. "We'll pop up right after the show and break open that bottle before Belinda has to run the gamut of the party downstairs. Go easy on the Valium so you can have at least one little sip."

"Stu," she said, "I haven't had a drink in years. But I'll pop the cork for *you*."

He kissed her hand and left. He had his speech ready for the curtain calls, for the celebration, and for the launching of the brilliant career of Belinda Barstow as the young stage star she would be, as well as a fascinating film star. What a career these two worlds could give her! It was his fate to be involved with her beginning, as he had been with Claudia's.

Claudia sat listening to the increasing sounds of roaring engines and motorcycles as the evening lengthened. It could be youth celebrating its own way, not the sports cars and limousines of her time. After all, Belinda was beautiful and famous.

She could not see the theater lobby, but she heard the many whispers of footsteps in the village street, and she knew when they had stopped that the theater was full, the doors closed, and the fate of Belinda as a stage actress in limbo for several hours in the confines of the theater.

She thought of all the training that had made it possible for this girl to step into the breach, and she prayed that it had been sufficient to put Belinda in the position of doing honor to herself; that was really what mattered.

Generations of her family had stepped on the stage to fame, to fortune, and to a long life of dedication to the theater. She thought wryly that she and Jeffrey had blown it in the quick magic of Hollywood at one time or another, even though they had both risen like the Phoenix out of their ashes. And now Belinda, of an illustrious stage family, was to tread the boards in this village playhouse.

Claudia knew and loved Hollywood, and Belinda was the second generation in this new film industry. But all the same she came from a long line of stage actors. This was the original calling of the family, the platform of talent upon which this young girl could always stand, no matter what happened to the splintered world of cinema.

She waited in the quiet room. How dreadful that fate had played her such a trick—she couldn't watch her own niece make her debut on the stage.

The audience settled down. The press had arrived in all manner of vehicle. But in the middle of the theater, a solid pack of young men had filled up the seats, most of them in leather jackets and sweaters, an unusual first-night aspect.

In the beginning they had seemed to listen attentively to the long speech of Laura's brother Tom, explaining the intent of Tennessee Williams in presenting the play.

When Belinda appeared, the roar of applause was immense. The cheering and whistling of the young men was deafening. At first, Plimpton hoped it was an indication of the admiration the audience had for Belinda.

But the ovation became a horror. It turned into a stomping of feet and rhythmic clapping of hands, which eventually halted. It became obvious that it was not the intention of this claque to stop the play. It was allowed to go on long enough to keep the curtain from being rung down. But when Belinda appeared in her lavender kimono in the second scene and her lameness was mentioned, a voice rang out: "Take it off! Take it off, let's see what's underneath!"

Belinda stumbled on with her lines.

"We don't care, babe!" "You'll be okay horizontal or any way, with *that* bod!"

Whenever a point of Laura's unattractiveness was brought up, a voice or two from the audience denied the lines with a vulgarism. The cast was devastated, but they carried on courageously.

In the sixth scene, when Amanda tries to stuff the powder puffs into Laura's bosom and says, "to be painfully honest, your chest is flat," the young members of the audience broke into a roar that could be heard a block away.

The play had been sabotaged.

The performance was destroyed. As soon as the play ended, the parade of young hoodlums vanished, the hot rods and bikes moving off as noisily as they had come.

There was no violence, no destruction of property, no need to call for police aid, only the assassination of a stage career.

The opinion voiced, as people walked up the aisles, was that Belinda Barstow was too beautiful and too sexy, and that in her recent film about the Borgias she had been exposed too lasciviously, to play a role of the dramatic significance of Laura in a classic such as *The Glass*

Menagerie. She obviously belonged in Hollywood and should stay there.

A few reporters, mostly women, shook their heads and said it was a rotten deal that the younger generation had been so rude; but they agreed that Belinda Barstow belonged in front of the camera, not behind the footlights.

Plimpton rushed to Belinda's side.

She stood, stunned, the short bow she took still in her mind, the catcalls and innuendos ringing in her ears.

"It was a setup," said Plimpton. "Believe me, honey, it was a setup! It had nothing to do with your performance."

His face crumpled. It was a personal disaster.

"Come on," he said. "We'll sneak out a side door and get into Claudia's suite through the fire escape."

Plimpton took passkeys out of his pocket, and they circumnavigated the crowd. He took her hand, and she walked behind him, blinded by tears.

When they reached Claudia's suite, they both could see that Claudia had heard enough to know what had happened. She was on her chaise, her fists clenched.

"She was heckled," said Plimpton. "Someone has it in for her. It wasn't her fault. It wasn't!"

Belinda fell on her knees and put her head in her aunt's lap.

"Claudia, it was horrible!" she said. "Horrible! Worse than anything; worse, even, than what happened in New Orleans."

"What was that?" said Plimpton. "This sort of demonstration? You should have told me."

"No," said Claudia. "What happened in New Orleans was not death to the living."

Plimpton was curious, but so disturbed that he passed it off.

Belinda settled back on her knees on the floor. She was wracked with sobs, her stage makeup streaking down her cheeks, her hair unloosened as the ribbon slid down her shining curls.

Claudia handed her a Kleenex. "Pull yourself together, honeybun," she said. "It's not your fault. I think it's a vendetta from that lousy old queen, Andrew Reed. Remember how we put him down in Rome? We broke him up with Leslie Charles, and he vowed revenge. Unfortunately, there's no way you can get even with a dead man."

She arose from her chaise and walked over to Plimpton.

"I'm sorry," she said. "I'm sorry."

Belinda, wiping her eyes, went to Claudia.

"You'd better take it easy," she said. "Now Claudia, sit down, don't get upset."

She turned to Plimpton. It was plain to see the anguish in his face. His whole dream had fallen apart in the last two hours.

Belinda walked to the window. She swallowed the tears still in her throat. The last of the noisy crew had left; there were few cars on the distant highway. The guests must have flocked to the party downstairs. It was certain there was plenty to talk about—and to write about.

Ironically, they could hear the festive sounds of the small orchestra Plimpton had provided for the gala occasion.

Both of them stared at her, not knowing what to say.

"Well," Belinda said, managing a smile, "what do we do next?"

They were too surprised to answer for a moment.

"What do you think we should do?" asked Claudia.

"You really believe it was a vendetta?" asked Plimpton.

"I do," said Claudia. "It goes back a long way. Earlier, when you mentioned the name of Boysie Miller, I was scared."

She looked at Belinda. "You see, it had nothing to do with your performance."

Plimpton arose. "I guess I better go downstairs and face them."

Belinda still wore the frilly old-fashioned dress selected in the play as a mother's desire for her daughter to be a southern belle.

"I'll wash my face and go with you," said Belinda.

She went to the bathroom.

Claudia and Plimpton stared at each other.

"What do you think?" said Claudia. "Dare she?"

"You can just bet," said Plimpton, "that it'll be all over the papers. But it'll fill my theater—Oh, God, Claudia, is it too cruel to let her?"

"It's up to her," said Claudia.

Belinda came out of the bathroom. She had skewered

her hair up, and it fell in a crown of curls on the nape of her neck. Her face was scrubbed clean. She had tied the sash of the dress, and in spite of her efforts, which Claudia recognized, not to look like a sexy actress, her beauty had never shone so bright. There was something about Belinda's face, when the tears were freshly gone, that brought about a luminescence. It was too bad it had to be that way at such a price, she thought.

"Screw the doctor," said Claudia. "I'm going with you."

The press reacted exactly as Claudia feared they would. Belinda was a private heroine and a public disaster. She and Belinda were both lauded for their courage in facing the crowd. The press, of course, was unable to review the play. They deplored the behavior of young America. What had happened to manners? Plimpton was pilloried for dreaming of putting America's sex symbol into *The Glass Menagerie*, and all joined in the decision that Belinda Barstow was too sexy and too beautiful to attempt to play a role such as Laura.

Belinda seemed to make light of the disaster at the theater as she met one person after another. She dared not show her distress in front of Claudia, for Claudia had taken enough of an emotional and physical risk in going downstairs to shake hands with dozens of the press. With a smile she listened to all the remarks about how stunning Belinda was. That was an old song, and they were both tired of the refrain.

From experience, Claudia knew such surface cop-outs were a poor takeout when a performance had bombed.

Glancing at her niece occasionally, she had seen, as she well knew, that there was nothing Belinda could do about it. She not only was endowed with a classic face and figure, she had something which often not even great beauties could achieve. She had a sexual magnetism she did not even understand herself, which made men gather around her, fascinated.

Belinda's pillow was wet with tears. She felt she had let the Barstow name down. She had been so certain of herself as she had stepped into the role of Laura.

Only a few days before, when the play had been taken away from Joan McGowan, Claudia had warned her that she might have to eat crow herself someday. And now, how unexpectedly it had happened.

It would have been better for everyone if Joan McGowan had played her role, she thought.

The next day, although she refused phone calls and would avoid the newspapers or more interviews, she went on again. The theater was jam-packed, and the requests for seats had increased so that the box office phone was switched off.

The play had to be attended by the town and country elite who had come from miles around. The reception was enthusiastic and warm. But Belinda realized that she would never be accepted in the role. She had been tagged a novelty, something to stare at and talk about. Beauty and sex appeal were sometimes a deterrent to a legitimate performance. Titan's publicity department and the power of the press had seen to that.

As far as asking the press to come back and see her again under different conditions, that was impossible.

She gathered several fine reviews from small-town newspapers—editors and columnists who had not been invited to the important initial showing. But it was too late. The deed was done.

Fergus Austin was disturbed.

He was on the brink of taking a step which was beyond the forgiveness of all the people he had cared for in his life.

Absolving himself from blame for the thing he was about to do, he convinced himself that everyone in his life had been a disaster for him, no matter how much he cared, giving him no comfort or security. Since, he thought wryly, he had suffered from emotional constipation, anything he did was understandable.

Even though he had covered for Simon Moses by bringing his mistress, Claudia, out west as a young woman, and he had literally founded the studio while Simon remained in the East with his family, and he had protected her in her romance, what did it get him? Only long years of sweat while others got the gravy. He had never been owner of the studio, only a hireling.

When he married Simon Moses's daughter, Esther, not only because he cared for her, but because it would accelerate his career, that hadn't worked. She became mentally ill and had to be removed from the active world, thus canceling out his social life at home and minimizing him in the eyes of the town.

On top of this, the foolish young woman had gotten herself pregnant by Jeffrey Barstow, and years later, when he discovered that David wasn't his son, there was another private humiliation to face. Jessica, his mistress, had betrayed him with David, and, adding insult to injury, had married the aging Jeffrey Barstow. So he had a double hatred of Jeffrey, whom he was forced to star at Titan.

To top it all, Jeffrey and Jessica had spawned Belinda,

who now was the prime asset of the studio. Again, he had been forced to raise a Barstow to stardom, and just when it looked as if the young woman was going to be the stellar attraction of Titan studio, she was going to marry a shrewd young lawyer who would manage her professional career and undoubtedly set her up as an independent star.

He convinced himself, to cover the pangs of guilt, that even if Belinda were eager to step into a Titan production when she returned to Hollywood, it wouldn't have done any good. The gaps in the organization were beginning to show. Since Max's talent had gone off beam—for they had depended on the success of the big blockbusters—they had been caught short. There was no script waiting for her, no usual preproduction planning that would have kept her going, as it was in the old days when a star hopped from one film to another.

By the time a property was selected, a stepsheet worked out, the wrinkles ironed, a first-rate script written and rewritten, a cast assembled, with massive starting-date problems, sets and wardrobe designed and built, it would take months, perhaps a year or more, to go into production. With overhead going on all the time.

He remembered how long Titan had waited between *The Oracle* and Belinda's new picture. It had seemed proper at the time because the windfall of their shining star, Belinda, and their genius Max's efforts had brought in the money, and it had seemed provident to plan another superproduction.

He should have known that a hiatus was murder to the future, but Belinda, and Claudia as her guardian, had accepted the waiting period, using it for Belinda's training and the building of her adult image, while Max was on salary and half the studio was getting the production of the Borgia film ready, after *The Oracle* was finished.

It had been a lush time, but now Fergus knew that he had been lax. Belinda's first picture had given him false security. *Young Lucretia* was going well in key cities because of the Belinda cult, but it was bombing in the Bible Belt. And his biggest blow, which even David didn't know yet, was that because of censorable scenes there had been no television sale. He had counted on it to recoup.

In the old days, Belinda would have been just one more on the roster. But those times were gone. He had tried to lower costs by cutting the payroll where it hurt the most. Stars, contract players, and directors had been dropped when their options came up. Now, it was a matter of making a deal for each needed stellar personality. Like many another studio executive in Hollywood, he woke up sweating when he thought about Elizabeth Taylor making way over a million-dollar salary, spread over a period of years, with the money tied up legally, plus 10 percent of the gross over seven million on *Cleopatra*.

This hit a hard blow to every stellar ego in town, and they reacted by asking for every advantageous frill they or their agents could dream up, including massive untaxed expense accounts.

And when it came to the old-timers who were still hot box office grossers, he thought of the wry comment about Doris Day, when some wag had said that they were running out of plots for forty-year-old virgins.

Of course, the sale of pictures to television was always a help in considering financial advantages, but he felt very nervous about movies when it took television for a bailout. Somehow, it was the chance you took feeding the monster who might devour the hand that fed it.

He was not happy about David spending most of his time in diversified interests—the sound stages for the new music scene in England, the television and radio stations in various suburban communities which were opening up to the tube. They all seemed to Fergus to be lurking enemies of Titan, the studio he loved, for in the months and years he had spent in it were contained the most real life he had ever had.

What disturbed Fergus most was the thought that in a year the back lot would not exist. Encroaching upon his kingdom would be the new real estate development which was necessary to keep them going.

The studio was like an old man with an insurance policy that made him more valuable dead than alive.

He picked up the real estate section of the *Los Angeles Times*. Here it was; it existed in print. Not just a dream to chase away in the morning after a bad night: "TITAN LOT 2 DESIGNATED FOR HOME DEVELOPMENT"

Abetted by David's endless hours of effort, the final support of several councilmen, and the unraveling of much red tape, the City Planning Commission had finally recommended that a new, specially planned development of high-rise housing, with proper use of combination land for uses except industrial, be built where dreams had once become real.

The new district zoning gave the developers of the 140-acre site the right to lay out the area without the rigid limitations of conventional houses and duplex residences.

The sprawling area around the studio perimeter had mushroomed through the years with modest homes, pleasant tree-lined streets, and a middle-class golf course. Now this area would be forced into a rigid complex of housing, and shopping center. Naturally a certain amount would be apportioned to small parks and trees, but the steel, concrete, and high-rise buildings would change the whole complexion of this area of Hollywood.

Fergus, looking out his window, past the main business body and sound stage of the studio which would remain, realized that even his mighty water tower, the proud focus of the studio and the community for almost fifty years, would be dwarfed by urban development.

He thought of all the sets that had been laboriously constructed, from the make-believe African river and swamp to frontier stockades, foreign streets, a railroad station, castles, mansions, villages, and the well-known New York avenues and western streets. They were all jam-packed side by side in a lunatic juxtaposition, but the magic of the camera had made them seem as far apart as if they were in their original geographical setting.

Each one had a memory to Fergus, of the original cost, the film that had introduced it, and the actors that had trod and postured on it. To him, they were pages in the photo album of his life.

All of them had paid big dividends for the company throughout the years, having been amortized a hundred times.

Even the maverick TV companies that rented his facilities would be forced to go elsewhere for their sets. He would have to work hard to keep them used in production in the next year, before massive machinery would plow them under.

He recognized that contained in them were the craftsmanship of another time, when manpower was not so high. They could never be duplicated again.

Labor costs had zoomed so that, even though he had a much smaller staff, his production costs were up at least 30 percent because of inflation. Now it took a larger group of men with higher salaries to stand behind a camera before the unions would allow the first foot of film to roll.

Trying to jockey the collapsing studio economy was an impossibility. He was too old and too tired to fight, and his back was against the wall. There had been several malfeasance threats by the usual small stockholders, and soon he would have to face it with David.

Then came a bolt of lightning, unsuspectedly throwing him into confusion. And this was to change his whole life.

In the postwar years, the high-breasted, yellow-haired Martha Ralston had been the sex symbol of Titan studio. Later, she had married Pericles Niadas and had left him after their child was born. But before the divorce had been completely settled, Niadas had died.

Martha's lawyers, in for immense fees, established that she was returning to the States for medical care resulting from the primitive conditions she had to face when her child was born in Greece.

Martha had walked out with a settlement of fifty million dollars, perhaps, Greeks claimed, in return for her child to remain in Greece.

The American press said it was the greatest sum that had ever been paid for nuisance value. One jokester figured she received roughly a million dollars each time she went to bed with Niadas.

For a while she drifted. She bought a mansion in Bel Air, a town house in Paris, a house in London, a yacht and apartment in Monte Carlo, and a villa in Majorca, and she held court for young lovers and down-and-out aristocrats. She provided food, room, and entertainment, and while seeing that her bed was not empty, she had several unpleasant bouts with not only shakedown artists, but venereal diseases. Her doctor had warned her that she had to be more cautious about whom she let into her boudoir.

Finally, after a session with an eager Near East admirer, she fled to the familiarity of Hollywood. She had discovered, in spite of her lush body, that he preferred the type of sex he could have had just as easily with young men.

In Hollywood she was known, and she could deal with

the sort of people she had grown up with. She would be a star again.

It didn't take her long to realize that it was not as easy to be a star as it was when she left Hollywood five years before. The whole picture had changed.

Studios were not signing stars, especially one who in a sense was over the hill in her mid-thirties, and had literally been dumped by her husband, with a film half finished.

The motion-picture business, hearing of the scandal in Hollywood, was irritated that one man was in the position to throw out fifteen million on a production. It was an uneasy sign of what could happen even if you were Midas.

So Martha had sat in her mansion, served by a staff of fifteen servants, with a party list she could command by the phone calls of two secretaries.

She made great entrances down a baronial staircase to meet people she hardly knew. New faces came once, twice, thrice if they had nothing else to do, and were eventually jettisoned because they got too pushy, or were simply boring to her.

Those who were important took a look at the fine paintings, dined on the best chefs could offer, and, having had the trip, often did not return.

She soon realized the one prime rule of Hollywood: if you aren't in action, you aren't alive.

She was the loneliest woman in town.

One day she picked up the phone and called Fergus Austin.

He had avoided her parties, for he was not a party man.

But as far as he was concerned, when an ex-Titan star asked him to dine with her alone, he was curious. First of all, he was intrigued. Of course Martha Ralston did not know about Belinda having a child by her former husband. He wondered what she would have to say about Niadas, or if she would bring up the little girl, whom it seemed she had jettisoned so easily, reared in Santorini.

So he came.

Even he was impressed with the trappings of wealth that surrounded her. It made even Atwater Kent's hilltop aerie in Bel Air fade far away in memory.

Curving driveways, marble loggias, rich antiquities, fine paintings were as beautiful as the fabled splendors of

Niadas's villa outside Rome where headquarters had been kept for Belinda when *The Oracle* was made.

When he entered the drawing room, it seemed to him it took several minutes to walk across the priceless Persian rugs. Although the fire was lit, and the lights and candles were all aglow, there was no one in the room. The butler showed him through a spacious corridor, past an enormous study, and then to a smaller sitting room.

Martha was curled up on a cut-velvet wing chair, looking at the seven o'clock news on an immense television screen. A fire glowed in the hearth, the paneled walls were hung with paintings—Marie Laurencin, Fragonard, a Renoir and a Utrillo. She wore a pale green smocked velvet gown, festooned with pearls.

She looked at him, setting her cigarette down on a jade tray, and jumped up eagerly. She seemed delighted to see him. This startled him, for he was not used to it.

"Oh, Fergus!" she said. "How wonderful of you to come!"

He ordered scotch, she took a glass of white wine, and a butler set down a crystal iced bowl of Iranian caviar with Dutch pickled pearl onions, grated egg, lemon, toast, and two crystal and silver knives for spreading.

"My God," he said, "this caviar's big enough to string!" She smiled.

"It's flown in to me every week from Iran. The Shah's private stock. Let me know if you like it, I'll send you some when you give a party."

"I don't give parties," he said.

"I don't much anymore, myself," she said.

She looked sad.

He waited.

"Well, Fergus, there's no use to be polite and wade through dinner waiting to see what I have up my sleeve. So here it is."

She sipped her wine. He hoped to God she wasn't going to ask for a contract at Titan. And then he realized she didn't need it. She had that fifty million to sustain her.

"I've learned a lot the hard way the last five years," she said. "Fergus, I've looked into your current situation at Titan. Your wings are clipped. A creative producer like you can't run a studio that's collapsing. And you have no authority. Your ego must be hurting. You can't even make a deal anymore."

Fergus put his drink down and stood up. "I didn't come here to be insulted. If you'll forgive me—"

"Now wait a minute," said Martha. "Please hear me out. For God's sake, sit down."

A little surprised because no one ever talked to him that way, he sat.

She pushed a button and the butler came in, freshened his drink, and vanished.

"It isn't your fault," she said. "Things change. You know and I know that the independent film maker is the one who takes the risks now instead of the mother studio. And also gets the gravy. And every butcher and baker and candlestick maker in the country that has money wants to back movies. True?"

"They usually haven't enough money," said Fergus. "We've been leaning on Wall Street."

He stared at her. Her jaw was firmer than he could have believed. Where was the simpering girl who had been his bane as much as she had once turned on every American male and then finally Niadas?

She seemed to read his mind.

"Yes," she said. "When I finally got that great hunk of money, I said to myself, Martha, it's time to stop the act. You don't have to talk baby talk and flatter and cajole and play the dummy. You don't have to lie under a man to get your way. With this money you can walk over him with your spike heels if you like it."

She picked up another cigarette and allowed him to light it.

"I had a real party for a while. Rollses and Alfas, Isotta Fraschinis, Humbers, and Ferraris cluttered my driveways all over the world. Even the rich can be freeloaders—because they have nothing else to do! I tried them all out for size."

She waved her hand in his direction. "Don't get me wrong; it's not that I don't enjoy sex, but I'll tell you something I never told anyone before. I had the money to find out what every woman secretly wants to know. That is, what the man who is balling her does when he's not with her. Every time I had a lover, I had him tailed night and day; just hoping that once, one who made such protestations of affection for me in bed would carry it through away from me. Well, I have news. There never was one who played it straight. They went from me to brothels, to other rich women, to girls, to boys, and one, even with my maid on the way out of my house."

She sighed.

"It was harder to replace the maid, but of course I had to. I couldn't stand her sly eyes looking at me as she selected the clothes I'd wear with him.

"Of course I was lucky. If I got into a jam I could ring the bell on them, or move to another place and get rid of them. But all in all, it wasn't any fun."

Fergus said nothing. She was on her own wavelength, and he had undoubtedly been invited to listen. While she talked, he studied her. She still looked beautiful. She should, he thought, she had everything going for her that money could bring her. Somehow it seemed depressing, and as he saw this woman sitting in this enormous house in a small room with the television still flickering, the sound turned down, he understood her loneliness.

"You've changed," he said. "I wouldn't believe it."

"Yes," she said. "It started with voice lessons, tutors. That wasn't it. Body shaping, high couture—" She waved. "For the birds. I got a brainstorm. I decided I would study money management."

She stood up.

He saw a fortune in diamonds and emeralds slide in the bracelets on her arm; great chunks flash on her fingers.

"Do you know," she said, "I not only gained back the great slice I had to pay my lawyers to get that bloody Niadas estate settled, I made a profit."

So, thought Fergus, she was a stone maiden. There was no thought of any relationship she'd had with Niadas. And the child was obviously a by-product she'd dropped on the way.

"And now," she said, "living here without anything to do, without being related to this industry, is driving me up the wall. I have tax problems, Fergus. I could use a loss."

He was beginning to see the light.

"I know your wings have been clipped," she said. "Well, so have mine. You need money to fly. I need a career again. So let's merge."

"Meaning?" he said, knowing what was coming.

"Meaning," she said, "what about you breaking the umbilical cord? Become an independent producer. You and I. Who needs Titan? Ralston Productions, headed by Fergus Austin, ought to be a pretty good combination. If we find a property we like, nobody can outbid us. Who's afraid of a loss? Not Martha Ralston. If we need a leading man, we can buy him. Most everybody likes money. That is, almost everybody. Except me. Now that I've got it, I'll trade it to be in the saddle again. Who cares? I couldn't possibly spend it all."

She looked dejected and, Fergus decided, mighty hard.

The butler bowed at the doorway.

"Well," she said, "dinner is ready. If you don't mind, I can't face that big formal dining room. We'll dine in the morning room."

An exquisitely appointed table was set for two in front of a fire, which was encased in a porphyry mantel. The room was done in white wicker and pale green chintz, with a wall of orchids at one side, falling in clusters of white. A modest Modigliani, two of Diego Rivera's most charming Indians with bunches of lilies in their brown hands, and a Rosa Covarrubias painting of lacily garbed Oaxaca brown girls, waiting to be asked to dance, were the decorations.

Again, Fergus saw a television set tucked in a corner opposite Martha's chair.

His mind was spinning so he could hardly down the meal. Later, back in the little sitting room, he settled his nose in the mammoth Corvoissier snifter while she outlined plans.

She had been preparing a long time. She had control of two novels that had not yet been published, one of them a future Literary Guild choice; she had obtained a European play, and one to open on Broadway. He was amazed at their acquisition, they were such important properties, and appalled at the high sum she had paid. Obviously, nobody could outbid her.

She had analyzed the financial necessities of every male star in the business who had been let out of the studios in the current upheaval. Fergus was astounded at some of their plights. They had been living way above their means in a time of depression.

"Tonight I'll only focus in on what I want to do," she

said. "I have a business staff of sixteen who will do any research you need before we set up offices. Preproduction expenses don't bother me, they're a write-off. Name your salary. We'll talk ownership. All the production details are up to you. I won't interfere. That'll all be in writing."

Fergus glanced at her sharply. "You're asking me to step down from a situation I've been deeply involved in since 1913. Do you realize that?"

"It's ending, Fergus," she said. "I have a list of Titan's assets and debits. And I know how deeply David Austin is dipping into his personal fortune to keep things floating."

He said nothing. What was there to say?

"Also," she continued, "I know what your paper loss has been on Titan stock. You should have diversified a little on your own."

"I don't have sixteen advisers behind me," he said acidly.

She sighed.

"Forget bank accounts," she said. "Just think of getting the best everything."

He had noticed that she was sparing on the carbohydrates, and her sipping of wines during dinner had been minimal. When the champagne had been served with the lemon soufflé, she picked up a contraption the likes of which he had never seen. Through the years he had observed many sophisticates take a little many-pronged silver or gold spray and swizzle the bubbles out of their champagne. But Martha had hit the jackpot with hers. Every tiny little branch was tipped with a diamond. It flashed like a miniature mobile.

Odd, he thought, what she has gone through for this Moët et Chandon, and then she twirls out the bubbles.

"Aren't we going into business, if we do, for money?" he said. "That is usually the reason behind an independent company."

"Not in our case," she said. "What you want is power. Money doesn't get that by itself. Look at Louis B. Mayer. When he was shorn of his studio, he slowly died of a broken heart. Even with his magnificent stables, a lovely young wife, and all the money a man could want. He wanted power. So do you."

"And you?" he said.

"I want to be in pictures again. I want to be a mature

star. I want everyone to—to really want me again. How about it?"

Her lip quivered. She had laid it on the line. She wasn't quite as stony as she seemed, he decided. She had sold the memory of a marriage and abandoned a child for money, and she had come up empty.

"I'll have to assess it," he said.

"One more thing," she said. "As you know, that little Barstow bitch was a pain in the ass to me. Perry Niadas was creaming over her rushes all the time I was pregnant in Greece. He hadn't even met her. But all of a sudden, I was the has-been and she the divine creature."

She wrinkled her nose in annoyance. "And you remember when I did one of my first pictures with Jeffrey Barstow? *Tiger of the South.* He breathed his boozy breath on me in all those scenes where I was supposed to be his loving daughter. And remember how we had to prop him up and do his scenes a dozen times? I'll never forget the last day when we had the usual set party. He came up to me and said, 'You'll never learn to act, Martha, but you certainly have a nice ass.' And then he pinched me on it and left the set without a backward look."

Fergus couldn't help but laugh.

"Well, damm it, it wasn't funny then," said Martha testily. "I don't much cotton to Barstow's, so if any of their names should come up, forget it. I know you've been close to Claudia in your day. But what have they ever done for you?"

Indeed, what had they ever done for him? David, the unmentioned Barstow, the hurt of his life—so what if David had kept him on when he had control of the studio. By God, he'd made the studio. Even Claudia had withdrawn from his emotional life now that she was happily married to Max Ziska. Their relationship was long gone.

What this Martha Ralston would do if she knew the true story of Niadas and the baby, Alex! She was bitter enough without it. Belinda had dethroned her personally and professionally.

David would be outraged at his decamping with, of all people, Martha Ralston. And there again, the Barstow name hit him. What a convoluted situation. Everyone would say he was leaving a sinking ship.

As he said good-bye to her, she put her hand out like a man and shook his.

"I think you'll be a good partner, Fergus," she said. "I'll start you out with a good stock setup and sweeten it with a six-figure salary that can be published as the highest for an independent head of a company in Hollywood. It will jack up your prestige and give our company clout. No doubt everyone will think I'm a patsy, but you and I will know differently, won't we? I need your know-how. You need my bankroll. May I say, two things that are essential, but hard to come by without proper planning. Right?"

He nodded. She certainly had planned. And he was intrigued. He'd never seen such a character turnabout in his life.

As she let go his hand, he thought that perhaps she'd be a good partner. He didn't like her, and that was a smart way to begin a business deal. Both partners would be cautious.

24

Belinda returned to Hollywood with even more newspaper coverage than when she left to go on tour. The press had made so much of the fact that her sex appeal destroyed her stage performance that Titan had picked it up and used the insinuation of her sensuousness in additional advertising copy; periodicals screamed it—along with reproductions of Kevin Frazier's paintings.

"The woman who could not escape from the passion men had for her." "No matter how she tried to forget her beautiful face and voluptuous body, she could not escape from what she was."

The copy was used to hypo *Young Lucretia*, but the personal inference was obvious.

Lines of young people eager to see the vaunted charms of the star whose beauty had caused such a riot in summer theater, and who had been called lascivious by the press, became members of the new Belinda cult.

Youth was beginning its open revolt against the establishment, and Belinda's portrayal of Lucretia, added to the comments about her sexuality, were wrongly interpreted. She was held up as a renegade, an actress who refused to play goody-two-shoes and was not ashamed to flaunt her body.

Out of the sittings she had made, the most revealing poses and the most passionate clips were discussed and exposed by press and magazines.

She became a symbol of revolt, the throwing aside of the Puritan morality that had long made sex a shameful secret. She was unwittingly the trigger of the young to bring sexuality out of the closet and rejoice in it.

For privacy, her meeting with Scott at Los Angeles

International Airport was set up ahead of time. Claudia suggested that she and Belinda fly to San Francisco and take a commuter plane to Los Angeles, arriving unexpectedly midafternoon, stepping off a shuttle instead of an important transcontinental flight, and they managed to get off the commuter unnoticed.

Molly had suggested it was time for her vacation, and had paid her own way to be able to be a houseguest and spend a few weeks taking care of Claudia.

Thinking of the empty suite over the garage, Claudia had gladly accepted and therefore had the luxury of an unpaid companion who was having the time of her life.

Thank God, thought Belinda, I'll be able to be with Scott and not feel guilty about Claudia. So the three of them deplaned and Belinda rushed off the escalator into the arms of Scott.

She had forgotten how handsome he was, tall and tanned. As he embraced her, the familiar scent of wool and aftershave seemed wonderful as she fell into his arms. And his look of joy overwhelmed her. She had held back from loving him, but now she felt that the experiences of the last few weeks had changed her attitude.

As they waited for the luggage, clinging to each other, a man with a camera slung over his shoulder recognized her. He was not the usual fan who rushed up, asked for pretty poses, or alerted the bystanders. He pulled out his camera quickly, shot several pictures as they kissed, and rushed to his film laboratory. In two hours he sold the negative to Globe Films, who in turn syndicated it. The next day the papers revealed a passionate meeting, which was front-page news. "The sex symbol of the world," wrote one imaginative reporter, "was marrying the handsomest man in the world."

Flora Stone Random looked at the news picture in distress. She decided it was time to call her nephew and break the silence. She called him at his office.

"Well," she said, "I told you that you'd be living in a goldfish bowl."

"Aunt Flora," he said, "there's no use talking to you. You just won't hear anything I could say about Belinda. I love her, and I've made my choice. So that's it."

She spoke again, her voice quivering. "Scottie, please don't hang up. You know all I want is your happiness."

With this last sentence she twanged the lute that elders have pulled since Noah talked his children into stepping aboard the Ark.

He felt sorry for her. She was alone, missing out on his happiness. She'd been good to him all his young life, and he had really been cruel to the poor old woman.

"What is it?" he said.

"Give me the decency to let me just give one party for you. You know, all the friends we've had through the years. After all, it's been very hard for me these last few weeks." She began to choke up.

"Now, Aunt Flora," he said, "cut it out. I'm very busy."

"Well, I can never reach you at home."

She blew her nose.

"Right," he said. "I'm seldom in."

"Just a nice reception at my house. After all, I am family."

"We are trying to avoid everything that's a mob scene," said Scott. "Belinda gets so much of that. Believe me, our wedding is going to be as simple as we can make it. Penny Howard is standing up with Belinda and Harry with me. And, of course, it's at Claudia and Max's beach house."

"Well, it's your life," she said, thinking of the fanfare she could have had. At least she could use the social clout with her reception.

"All right," he said. "I'll have my mother and Claudia get in touch with you."

"Oh, I'm glad," she said, suddenly recovered from the vapors. "You know, dear, it wouldn't look right for your own aunt not to give you a proper send-off."

"Thank you," he said. "Call mother. I must ring off now."

He had a moment's discomfort. For the hundredth time, he wished he and Belinda could just elope. But it wouldn't be fair to her. Anyway, what could Flora do wrong? A big fancy mob scene, a lot of social people she could impress.

Just what she liked. He and his friends would protect Belinda. And he didn't want an open family rift about his marriage.

Belinda deserved a little pleasure after the restrictions she had been forced to lead in her work and the adulation of her public life.

So he gave it little thought save to call Claudia and alert her.

Claudia was secretly pleased, for it seemed that Flora Stone Random had lost the game and was going to get in line and not ignore Belinda socially.

Scott had hardly hung up when Flora took to her bed, wicker writing tray on her lap, her hand on the silver phone, her world surrounded by social registers, society columns, and party lists. She paused for a moment, took a deep breath, and thought perhaps the past months' depression would go away.

It had not been a vintage year for her. Aside from the criticism she had received for having that scandalous film *Young Lucretia* for her Project Babies charity, and then having Scott actually decamp with that young actress, she had been beset with escalating expenses and a general gloom about what was happening to her world.

It was all turning topsy-turvy, she thought. There didn't seem to be any security anymore. After the Bay of Pigs everyone was nervous about Cuba; some Russian cosmonaut had orbited up there in a six-ton satellite. That meant the United States would pour millions into their space program, and that would raise taxes. She could hardly cope with property taxes as it was.

Goya's portrait of the Duke of Wellington had been stolen from the National Gallery in London. It just showed that nothing was safe. She had immediately hired a night patrol service, which was very costly.

And that was not all to be concerned about. Those young men in green berets shouldn't have been in Vietnam training those natives in guerrilla warfare; freedom riders were causing no end of havoc in the South. *They* should have stayed home where they belonged.

What was coming of the world? Everything was out of control. To top it all, imagine a picture in the papers of Scott kissing in public!

Her fists clenched.

Although there were a hundred people she wanted to call immediately, being an expert at social promotion, she knew that there would have to be an extraordinary event to make the party come off; a surprise that would cause tongues to wag, where she could experience the excitement and triumph.

Of course, everyone who could read would be terribly intrigued to see Scott and Belinda actually together; she had to admit that they certainly were a picture, whatever they did. But that was not the end-all. People expected that.

Of course, the party would cost an arm and a leg, but she'd wangle it.

She knew her house would look lovely; she would have white flowers—everything white and gold. She could commandeer dozens of candelabra from her caterers; half of her solarium ferns and orchids could be scattered all over the house on rented pedestals, all festooned with tulle and wedding bells.

The empty solarium could be filled with round café tables and rented gold chairs (courtesy of her caterer; she'd done plenty for him!). And gardenias, gardenias on tables, in topiary trees—again she'd get a handout. These were all essential! An orchestra would play there in front of a screen of fern and white gardenias. But that was still not enough.

So, after pausing in deep thought, the inspiration came to her. Would this ever be the *pièce de résistance!* It was not only a coup, but since Scott insisted he would marry this girl, it would give the bride cachet.

So she cleared her throat, got long distance, and called Rome.

Wedding plans moved on apace at the beach house. Claudia was amused that two of the most excited people she could have invented were at hand managing the complicated arrangements. Henrietta Stone, her thumb literally in Emily Post's etiquette book all the time, worked with Molly, who had a fine, Spencerian hand and was at her happiest addressing envelopes, sending notes, marveling at the names of the invited, answering phones, and keeping a journal and a scrapbook of all the activities.

"I never saw such a pair of eager beavers in my life!" said Claudia, watching their excitement and delegation of what would have been chores to her. They merely smiled at her absentmindedly and went about their business, their heads together.

Belinda faced the problems of every celebrity who is a

target for publicity. Unsolicited gifts came pouring in, and offers from many famous houses—Dior, Balenciaga, Galanos, and Scasi, all vying to be the one dressing the bride of the year. But Claudia warned her what would happen if she accepted a free wedding gown.

"They'd expect you to buy a trousseau at their house to go along with it. Like everyone, they think that a film star can throw away tens of thousands of dollars on a wedding."

They both smiled, for Belinda knew how Claudia had scraped the barrel to give the wedding.

"Why don't you get Penny Howard to help you? She knows more about this sort of thing than I would."

"Great!" said Belinda, for she'd never shopped in stores as most people did.

She managed to wangle five thousand dollars from Bill Chapman, the family accountant.

"I'm overstepping legal bounds to give this to you now," he said, "but you'll be getting about two hundred thousand of your own money the day you marry."

It had never entered her mind there would be so much, for it had been put in trust.

She called Penny Howard to help her out.

"I could just charge everything, and pay for it after I get the money," she said gleefully. "I guess the sky's the limit."

Much to her surprise, Penny held her back. Disguised in a black wig and sunglasses so she wouldn't be mobbed, they cut a wide swath through fashionable stores.

"Listen, Belinda," Penny said, "my husband's a lawyer, too, but we don't live in the stratosphere you're used to, with a corporation tending your needs. For Scottie's sake, as well as your own, you've got to learn to think on a different plane. You don't want to overstep his standards of living; he's a man, and a proud one. Let's stay within bounds on your trousseau and what you want to buy for the house. And remember, you're not moving into a mansion."

"Of course," said Belinda gratefully. "I hadn't thought that way."

Anything was fine; she agreed to everything these days. She and Scott had searched the town for a house.

Like all young people in love, on the brink of marriage,

who had not yet been in bed together, each house was a promise of the life they would lead. Bedrooms were a passionate promise, living rooms and studies, playrooms, kitchens and breakfast rooms held a structure for the life they would share; practicality, at the moment, was blinded by emotional surges.

When it came to looking at bedrooms, both of them thought of making love, of how it would be at night and how wonderful it would be to wake up in each other's arms in the morning. The most exciting part of the dream of love was the stimulation of unfulfilled desires—moving toward an ultimate ecstasy that each anticipated.

Make your dreams come true. Find a house—move in it. That's it. After one of these house-searching sessions, Scott put his arms around her in the car and kissed her, even though they were parked on a city street.

"It's taking all my discipline to wait," he said. "I could have taken you right there on the floor, if that damned real estate woman hadn't been watching."

Belinda felt her excitement rising hotly. She longed for him to love her.

"Two weeks and four days," she whispered.

They turned to the roadway and the bright California sun, and went on, awaiting the time they would fall into each other's arms and their desires would be fulfilled—endlessly.

They considered old June Street houses, the heart of the Los Angeles social establishment, but they were too formal, Belinda decided. Then they looked in the Los Feliz district at neo-Spanish mansions of the twenties and thirties with their countless cut-up rooms, arched bay windows, and steep-sloping hillside lawns, but these did not seem comfortable to Belinda.

Finally, they selected a large, comfortable Mediterranean-style one-story house on Beverly Drive above Sunset. It had a large living room and what was called a library-playroom overlooking a garden with a pool and terrace for outdoor dining and barbecue, several sycamore trees, and a pleasant flower garden.

There was a dining room, a breakfast room, a comfortable kitchen, pantry and maid's room and, along a gallery hallway, a small study and three bedrooms. They decided that one could be redone as a dressing room with closets built in for Belinda's voluminous wardrobe, most of it gifts from Titan left over from her tour. She certainly had enough evening gowns for some time to come, Scott said.

The house was slightly run-down, which made the rent cheaper, for it was part of an estate. But Scott ordered it painted and refurbished with a two-year lease.

"With all the furniture mother's given us and the wedding gifts pouring in, the house will look great. We'll have the floors polished and just use scatter rugs."

"We'll have a fire going every night, and bright paintings flickering on the wall!" Belinda said.

Scott laughed. "And you flickering in my arms!"

They were ecstatic. They ran through the empty rooms, their feet clattering, their excited comments echoing in the empty rooms, furnishing them, planning.

"And we'll get the best cook and housekeeper," said Belinda, "no matter what she costs!"

Scott tried to hide his disturbance. Of course they'd have to have a housekeeper, but he was stretching his current economy to the limits. They would need sofas, chairs, refrigerator, freezer, and a new stove, the purchase of which enchanted Belinda; two ovens and a warmer would be fun, she said. She selected a gleaming one that cost five hundred dollars.

Scott was grateful for Penny Howard's practicality. Apparently, the Barstow family rarely thought of such things; Claudia's house had grown on her over the years.

One evening at the Howards, Penny had sat down with pad and pencil and informed Scott and Belinda what was necessary in the sort of a domicile he was going to have to set up.

"Well, Scottie," she said affectionately while Belinda was called to the phone, "we're about eight years ahead of you on this deal. I think you're a lucky guy, but you've got a girl who's going to have to learn a lot about running a house, and at the same time you're going to be her business partner, so you mustn't lean on her too hard. You will have to get a pretty smart housekeeper, even if you do pay through the nose. After all, you got yourself a working girl."

She turned to Harry. "Now, Harry, you may not like me

bringing this up, but we have to help him. Scott, have you made any arrangement with Belinda about splitting household expenses?"

Scott was annoyed. He got up and poured himself another drink.

"Of course not," he said. "What kind of a guy do you think I am?"

"A smart one," said Harry. "Come on, old pal, be real. You're marrying a movie star. I don't mind saying that Penny had an inheritance when we started out. You don't think we could have done it all on my salary, do you? What's the difference? It's the American way."

He looked at Penny affectionately. "Marry a rich girl if you can, for starters," he said. "It helps. Then later on, you make it up."

"And he does," said Penny. "Don't be stuffy, Scott."

"But she earned hers," said Scott. "It's different."

"I earned mine," said Penny, "being very courteous for years to a mean old grandfather."

They laughed.

Belinda came into the room.

"Guess what!" she said, smiling. "David Austin just called me from London. Titan's having Janos make my wedding gown. Isn't that great!"

"He certainly takes good care of you! All that Crown Derby table setting from London he sent you."

"He's like family," said Belinda, smiling to herself.

She came to Scott and embraced him. "Now," she said, looking up at him, "we'll have that extra thousand to get that down sofa I loved so at Sloane's. Please let me!"

He shrugged. "If you insist."

Penny and Howard smiled at each other.

"Great!" said Penny. "Just be sure Janos doesn't think it's for a movie and make a thirty-foot train to drag through those steps to the poolside."

She turned to Scott. "You see," she said, "she's turned practical. Every time you sit on the sofa you can remember that you're really sitting on a wedding gown."

They laughed. It was going well, and they all were happy together.

Fred Cotter had promised them the use of his lodge at Arrowhead Lake. It was nestled in several acres among the pines, with fences and steps leading down to the lakeside. This time of year it was too cold for swimming, and the boats had been put up for the season, but it was a comfortable chalet, with a master bedroom with a fireplace overlooking the terraces and gleaming lake below, the cozy living room done in red, and toile quilted sofas and chairs. Scott had visited there many weekends in summers.

"You'll love it," he said to Belinda. "The black velvet nights and the stars are unbelievable, and the wind in the pines. Oh, Belinda, it's as close to serenity as anything could be, and to imagine being there with you is heavenly. We won't have to see anyone or talk to anyone for a week!"

"We'll take up hampers of food and wine. I'll have Effie pack it all," she said. "Oh, Scott, what a wonderful honeymoon!"

Effie had been put out that caterers were going to handle the large wedding luncheon. The young couple were marrying in the morning and getting away early in the afternoon to be at the lodge by nightfall. But Effie was appeased that she could plan hampers and portable ice chests of food, some precooked, in casseroles ready to be heated, all the delights she could think of that Belinda could share with her husband for a week. She stewed and roasted and baked and froze with joy in her heart. A car would be hired to take her up the day before, get the house settled, put the food away, and leave directions for each meal in an envelope on a table in front of the hearth in the commodious kitchen. Then she would rush back to the joy of seeing her darling married.

Effie had never had the opportunity to be so romantic. It made up for the fact that her own children and even her grandchildren were breaking away from the old traditions. She knew less about what they were doing and who their friends were than she ever would have believed. So she appeased herself and reveled in memories of her honeybun's childhood, as she packed Belinda's trousseau in tissues, set up the wedding presents for display in the downstairs study, and prepared the simple clothes Belinda was taking on her honeymoon: jeans, slacks and woolen shirts; a down jacket, walking shoes and boots, and a leather coat, a wonderful contrast to the soft negligees, lounging gowns, and pajama suits she would wear in the evenings.

Effie watched the weather reports. She had two wishes: a fair wedding by the sea, and a snowed-in honeymoon at Arrowhead Lake.

The new house stood in readiness. Penny promised to have all the wedding presents installed, cupboards arranged, and everything ready for them when they returned. She and Belinda had made charts of where the furniture should be placed.

"That's my big wedding present for you," said Penny, "and I was a fool to offer it, but you'll be all set."

25

David returned from London, bringing with him a star sapphire and diamond bracelet for Belinda. Under the umbrella of a gift from Titan, the great jewel from Asprey could be given to her properly. It amused him that the studio, as a surrogate father image, could take the place of his real blood relationship without criticism. He had noted a fleeting expression on Scott's face on occasion as he and Belinda had been together. David realized he would have to tread on light feet with this adoring young man watching her every move.

Having been exposed to the didoes of the reigning spectacular personalities in the performing arts, he noted that there was always a loved one and one in love in a relationship. He immediately recognized the seeking, passionate desire in Scott. He would be the one on the alert, the one who could be hurt, the disturbed one, the ever seeking. David instinctively felt he would be obsessed by jealousy, and he also suspected that Scott might never be fulfilled in his love for Belinda. He would always want more, no matter how passionate their encounters might be. He would want full possession of her in mind and body, and David wondered if he would ever get it.

Again, it was a modern manifestation of goddess worship, but since the idol Scott had chosen was flesh and blood, he could never enjoy the peaceful adulation of a man kneeling at a shrine in front of a stone image. He pitied Scott, for he knew how untried and how juvenile Belinda still was underneath the mask of her beauty and fame. She had never assessed normal values; the very framework of her life had kept her from it.

He knew, without being told, that Scott had done the

pursuing, and that Belinda had only fallen into his arms at last because she had no other place to go, and he was a suitable image for her needs.

Remembering the night she had tried to make love to him before she knew they were brother and sister, he realized that Belinda was seeking a relationship. It was not Scott who had overwhelmed her. She was in love with love, not with the person.

But as far as he could see, Scott was a good man, and, if he were strong enough, might make it go. He only wished for Belinda's sake that she could have been more ecstatic, a little less sure of herself and the love and life she was offered. It was strange that she was stepping into the establishment of old Los Angeles. He wondered how it would work.

What would her life be? Would Scott mastermind her in finding a successful career for herself (and himself)? Would he be one of those manager husbands who were the anathema of Hollywood, often with their complicated maneuverings and corporate desires leading a hard-earned fortune down a daisy path to destruction?

He knew several movie stars who could not retire and hacked on as character actors because of ill-fated adventures—films that did not come off, tax-dodging deals, ranching, get-rich-quick schemes in hotels and resorts, and foreign exchange blitzes—masterminded by spouses-cum-producer-managers. He remembered hearing about one old-time male star, a friend of his grandfather, Simon Moses, who had papered his walls with hundreds of thousands of German marks and then shot himself, spattering the wallpaper with his blood.

But this was all a depressing reverie on the eve of a young woman's wedding. Perhaps this was the beginning of a great life for Belinda—a growth of herself that could lead her to a purpose that transcended daily living, that's what a good career could bring under the most fulfilling conditions.

If he could give her any gift, this would be his wish for her. He cared more deeply than he would have admitted to himself previously about what happened to Belinda and how her life would be fashioned. No doubt Claudia was going through the same emotional turmoil, as well as thinking about Alex. He realized again that Belinda had been surrounded by a fake life, protected by a corporation, for a time by an ambitious feral mother and a fearful aunt, removed from the problems and ethics of most young people.

Remembering London, he castigated himself. He had warned her to step away from the entrapment of fame. But he had not been strong enough. He had only commented.

He wondered, had he known at the time that they were both sired by Jeffrey, whether he would have behaved differently. It was only in a later encounter that he discovered why he had been so attracted to her and why he had cared so much about what happened to her. Had he been stirred subconsciously, was there some genetic gemmule that had cried out to him?

He scoffed at himself. What right had he, who had never had a relationship of any consequence with anyone, to enjoy the idea of a weird pangenesis bringing them together.

He drove through the Titan gate, waving at the same hoary old gateman who had greeted him obsequiously a thousand times. The phony, the fake, all engendered by a cardboard kingdom that was about to collapse.

A twenty-thousand-dollar bracelet was in his breast pocket to prove to Belinda that he cared and that she was valuable. It was another prop. At most, something she could sell if she came upon bad times. What the hell was a star sapphire, even if it was called Queen of India? Another status symbol.

Was *she* valuable? Or was she just a beautiful puppet made dear partly by pity and partly by guilt? The little girl who bore her baby bravely in a cave in Greece didn't have any way out. The little girl who was an heiress to fame and fortune, yet who had been so distressed that Laura had to take over when she faced the raw reality of helping an anonymous dead musician into the swirling waters of the Mississippi on a dark night. To save her reputation. Or was it Titan's moneybags?

He began to think about Laura. Who was she, that mysterious woman who had sat next to him on the plane coming back from Elderberry? Most women who had saved a studio from a horrendous scandal would have thrown their weight about a bit. But she had not tried to make character. She had been a pleasant companion, as evasive as he was. What had she really done to get Belinda out of the mess in Hodine's apartment? She had been less than explicit. She had just not cared to talk about it.

He smiled at the thought that he'd like to have a ham sandwich and a malted milk with her and sit on a fake grass bank stinking of paint and creosote, muddied water being pumped by explicit instruction of the health department, pretending the two of them that they were living in the dream factory of their youth.

The lot looked seedy. What was the use of refurbishing anything that had a time clock ticking away at its gut? As he got out of his car and started across the parking lot, he saw Laura parking her car down the way where chief staff of the publicity department was allowed to park. He had been thinking of her so deeply that it did not surprise him to see her materialize.

He saw the flash of keys as she locked her car.

"Protecting your property, I see," he said.

She looked up at him, smiling. She wore a navy jumper, white sleeves and collar ballooning out of it, a gold chain and bracelet matching. She always had cachet, he thought. Her dark hair swept away from her forehead, and he noticed that her smooth skin was without makeup, save for scarlet lips and a way she had of painting a fine line on her eyelid above her long lashes, which were without mascara.

"No," she said, "not protecting my goods, but yours."

"Oh?" he said, curious.

"Well, in a way. Red asked me to handle the press releases on Belinda's wedding. Anything, I guess, to get people in to see her picture. I have a list a yard long of all the gifts. It's incredible. Enough semiprecious cigarette boxes and doodads to fill an antique store. Paintings, lace tablecloths, a few pieces of antique furniture. I guess that's how everyone thinks a movie star should live." She looked at him and smiled.

He noticed her white teeth. They were small, not the usual regular square Hollywood teeth that were patterns like a piano keyboard.

"Not one electric percolator, or iron. You know what I'm going to give her for a wedding present?"

She dropped her keys in her purse and squared her hands.

"A toaster." She shook her head. "Oh, the fun she's missing as a bride, exchanging three toasters for one electric roasting oven." She smiled.

"I suppose," said David, "you got all those things when you were married."

Laura looked at him, her face suddenly cool, her look withdrawn.

"I was never married," she said.

Well, his mind clicked, that destroys the rumor that she's a rich widow . . .

She ran her gloved hand lightly over the rear fender of her Rolls as she moved on. He had the fleeting feeling that she had earned the money for this car herself, and he wondered how.

"I didn't mean to be personal. By the way, when are we going to have our picnic?" He looked at his watch. It was ten o'clock. "How about in two hours? I have to see Fergus, but it won't be long. You pick up the food. Two ham sandwiches. I'll bring the drinks. Two malts."

She looked surprised. "I can do better than that," she said, smiling.

"No," he said, "it's got to be traditional. See you by the African riverbank."

He was gone as quickly as he had been by her side. He didn't look back. She stood there, wondering if she had really heard right. Well, the worst thing that could happen was that she would sit on the side of the African swamp river with two ham sandwiches and a copy of *Variety*.

Fergus was smoking and pacing the floor in his office. David had always insisted that he keep Simon's office, for he was there in residence all the time. David was the traveler. His office, which looked out on the alley, had once belonged to Fergus.

"Sit down," said Fergus, crushing out a cigarette in an ashtray that was already heaped high.

"Sit down yourself, Fergus," said David. "You look like you're about ready to blow up."

"I don't know how to tell you this," said Fergus. "David, I know everything's going to hell on a slow barge, but it's going. And I know that I'm the last man you'd let go."

David sat down. "That's not exactly the situation," he said. "You're not only a large stockholder, you created this studio. Don't think I don't know it. What are you trying to do, fire yourself?"

"Yes," said Fergus.

David leaned forward. "What's wrong?" He noticed that Fergus's hand was shaking.

"What keeps us going?" said Fergus. "Aside from your diversifications, it's our laboratory, which is the best color process in town, and everybody's getting on to that; and our distribution of independent films. If I could bring an important independent company into the studio, unlimited funds, and Titan could distribute the films I make, it would be a great asset."

"Of course," said David. "But how could you do that and manage the company?"

"Wouldn't it be better for me to step down from running the studio and come in as an independent producer?"

David walked to the window.

"Fergus Austin's beehive," he said, looking out. "And you'd walk away from it? What are you getting at?"

"I'm bringing you a company." He looked down, almost afraid to look at David's face.

"With Niadas's money, in a way. It's a coproduction company. I might as well get it over with. Martha Ralston Presents—"

There was silence.

"My God!" said David.

"Sky's the limit with funds," said Fergus. He made his pitch, fast and clear. "With the exception of Goldwyn and Disney, who could rock their own boat economically, there hasn't been a producer who could buy anything he wanted. As you know, Goldwyn's been known to toss out a hundred thousand dollars on a sequence and do a new one." He gave David the semblance of a grin. "That, of course, horrifies me. I think my only battle as a so-called creative producer would be to accept the creative use of money and forget the budget."

David's mind whirled. This defection was an apostasy he had never expected.

"Why Titan?" he said. "You could work anywhere."

"Because," said Fergus, "not only do I know it well, but

we'll need your laboratory facilities. After all, I built them up from the time those two itinerant Frenchmen walked in on me at the old barn and hid upstairs developing film and keeping from getting knocked in the head by the Trust with our illicit film."

David nodded.

"And we need Titan's distribution."

David was disturbed that Fergus had said "we" and "you" so glibly. For it did not mean Titan. It meant something quite different. He felt the rug he had always trod so casually was being yanked from under his feet.

"Independent production," he said. "The giant swap. Facilities for talent. You'd better have the talent."

"You don't even have to approve star and script," said Fergus, waving the comment aside, "for you're not in the position of raising the money."

"The hell we don't have approval," said David angrily, snapping open his cigarette case. "We're not going to let you use Titantone, or our lenses and laboratory and distribution and advertising, unless we know exactly what the product is going to be. Listen, Fergus, don't try to bullshit *me*. You know damned well that even Selznick paid MGM a million dollars and gave them his colossal 30 percent of distribution because, as well as needing Clark Gable for *Gone with the Wind*, he also needed major distribution."

"Okay," said Fergus. "Okay, don't get hot! We'll haggle out our problems. Credits and all those ridiculous things that no one reads, but which we all live by."

"Of course, 'Titan Studio Presents' will have to go first, even before your star," said David. "But all these matters can fortunately be settled legally."

He took a deep breath.

For several hours they traded back and forth, discussing the changes. As the conference lengthened, he saw that Fergus was weary. The previous planning he had gone through—with concentration on each detail, since he had accepted the amazing reality of an endless bankroll and what it could mean—had drained him.

Yet David was piqued. Fergus was leaving the sinking ship. He looked at him, the man he had so long thought was his father. His face had the dry, greenish hue of a man who was getting old and who was more at home with scotch than with a balanced diet. David saw the frost in Fergus's red hair, and the tremor of his nicotine-stained fingers, and he pitied him.

"I can't imagine the studio without you running it," he said, softening. "I guess this will chain me down quite a bit."

"Well, it's time for you to stop galavanting," said Fergus. "It's your studio." He sat down, dejected. "Will you forgive me?"

To David's surprise, Fergus's eyes were bright with moisture.

David went over to him and put his hand on his shoulder. "It's okay, dad."

For a moment, both forgot that Fergus, knowing David was not his son, had said, "Goddamn it, you're a man, don't call me that . . ."

Was it just a few years ago?

"There's one thing—," said Fergus, recovering. "She hates Barstows."

"Tough," said David, his jaw set. "After all, you're only one independent unit. She can't have any say in my studio policy."

"Of course," said Fergus. "But I had to tell you."

David was used to quick decisions. He had always been a peripatetic executive, and now his mind was clicking.

He began to pace, himself.

"This will take massive legal separations, this corporate divorce," he said. "I'm so used to you being the old dray horse that we can't just sever this quickly. You'll have to double for a while as consultant while we gear up differently."

"All right," said Fergus. "We'll work it out. But Martha insists on going into immediate production. She's a hard-case. She wants all sorts of gimmicks—like her picture announcing the company in posters all over our choice street-side billboards. Believe it or not, she has already asked for Kevin Frazier to paint her portrait. Better, she said, even than he did Belinda. She wants all-out publicity, and she wants Belinda's dressing room suite because it's the best on the lot."

"She can have it," said David. "Only I have news for you. As much as she wants to be, it won't make her Belinda Barstow."

Fergus looked at him. "How did you know?"

"Because Belinda, as we know only too well, at the age of fifteen unseated her personally and professionally. She'll never get over it." David looked at his watch. "My God! It's twenty after one! I have to dash. Excuse me. I'll meet with you later."

Fergus had never seen David move so quickly. As a matter of fact, he had always resented the casual way David had moved through life. He wondered what was triggering him.

David rushed to the commissary, astonished the counter service waitress, who generally saw him only on his way to the executive dining room, by asking for two malted milks, slapping down a bill, and rushing away without change.

When he got outside, he hailed one of the trolley carts that drove personnel around the maze of streets.

"Get me to the African river on the back lot, fast as possible," he said.

The trolleyman, watching David juggle his two cartons of malt, straws, and a packet of paper napkins snatched hastily from the counter, pushed his electric go-cart as fast as possible, left the main studio gates, and entered the portals of the back lot, where old Whitey stood on guard.

Whitey smiled and would have passed a word, but David said, "Step on it."

He left the cart at the path that led to the jungle. As far as he could see, there was no one there.

He wandered through the fake trees, scraping his head once on a papier-mâché boa constrictor. Laura was obviously not there.

As soon as he knew it was so, he went to the large trash bin nearby. On top of the heap he saw a *Hollywood Reporter* and a *Variety*, both stamped *Laura West, % Publicity Dept., Titan Studio*. And there was a ham sandwich, still in its paper wrapper.

He tossed in the two malted milk cartons and walked back across the Paris streets, over an English country bridge, and into the traffic and the business compound of his studio.

He called publicity.

She wasn't there.

The next day he discovered that she'd gone on location to Durango, Colorado.

"She's an odd one," said Red. "Asked to be on loan-out to the *Johnny Grizzly* series. It's just as well. If their Nielsen rating goes down the drain, we lose our stage rental."

"When will she be back?" David asked, adding hastily, "She's handling Belinda's wedding."

"Oh, in about a week," said Red. "She's got it all lined up, don't worry about her."

Surprised at himself, that evening he called the location, but she was unavailable.

The next few days he was closeted with Fergus's problems.

The general consensus was that the company announcement would read: *"Titan release of the Martha Ralston Production Presented by Fergus Austin."*

Everything but the kitchen stove, thought Red Powell as he prepared the announcement. He held out his notes to his secretary. "Another defection from the ranks," he said. "We might as well Xerox these items. You see more and more of 'em in the papers every day. I can't believe this one!"

If Fergus left Titan, things were worse than even Red thought they were.

"It'll go like this," he dictated. "Headline: 'FERGUS AUSTIN LEAVES TITAN STUDIO' then, 'Fergus Austin, longtime Titan executive, citing the tremendous pressures an administrative program requires, has announced to his son, David Austin, that he is resigning as senior vice-president in charge of production.

" 'Austin will head the banner of a new company starring top film star Martha Ralston, which will headquarter at Titan. Miss Ralston is returning to the screen by popular demand.' "

Red made a wry face, but continued doggedly, " 'Austin's resignation becomes effective in three months; however, he will remain in an advisory capacity for one year and will maintain his association with the studio as an independent producer of the Ralston unit.'

"Blah, blah, blah, etcetera," said Red. "Look up his

bio. Not quite an epitaph, I hope. But maybe this article ought to be labeled, *For Whom the Bell Tolls*."

He stopped short. "For us, or for Fergus. Who knows?"

He dismissed the secretary and poured himself a double drink; scotch for himself and milk for his ulcer.

****
26
****

Claudia was nervous. She had longed to talk to Belinda privately the week before the wedding. The problem of Alex hung heavy on her mind. How did Belinda feel about separating from her child? How was she going to handle it? Did she have plans? Or hadn't the idea entered her mind that someday she would have to face the problem. Claudia sometimes lay awake at night wondering if she had been right to allow Belinda to keep silent about the child with Scott.

But, as she watched them together when Scott picked Belinda up in the evenings and she saw the happiness reflected in both their faces, she tried to blot the disturbance from her mind. They seemed so in love. Belinda was getting her share of the life she should have had. It would not have been possible, Claudia was certain, if Scott knew about Alex. And yet, if he was not strong enough to know and to weather the truth, then he was not the right man for Belinda. It was a puzzle.

Claudia decided to bring it up on the evening of Mrs. Stone Random's big party.

"I hate to go through with this," said Belinda. "It's like being on display again, like that wretched PR tour."

She was dressed in one of Janos's gowns she hadn't worn as the tour had ended early. The pale blue chiffon gown was dramatically edged with starched Alençon lace. The girdled waist and the lace-cuffed collar and sleeves lined in pale pink were a perfect adornment for her blonde coloring.

"You look like a cream puff," said Claudia. "You know there are often things you have to go through for someone you love. I know Scott's not so mad about the old girl, but she's trying to give you both a big send-off."

"And herself," said Belinda.

"Well, you'll meet all his friends. And *you* got him. I bet there'll be plenty of jealous women there."

Belinda smiled. "I guess so. Oh, Claudia, I can't wait for this all to be over, so I can get away with him."

"I'm glad to hear you say that," said Claudia. "Have you had a chance to talk to him, I mean really, to tell him what you want out of life and find out what he wants?"

Belinda looked at her, surprised. "That'll come later, I'm sure," she said. "Right now I guess we just want each other."

"I mean," said Claudia, "about, well, what happened to you in your life—"

Effie buzzed. "Mr. Scott's waiting," she said.

"Oh," said Belinda, "here we go. Are you ready!"

Max came into Claudia's room carrying his tie.

"Sorry," he said sheepishly, "but I need help. My hand shakes."

"You look elegant, darling," said Claudia. "No one would know you're in a state."

"I hate these things," he said. "I'm a fish out of water."

She took his tie and turned him toward her mirror as she reached around and tied it.

"Don't be nervous," she said. "It's going to be such a mob scene that we can get by with being just dress extras. Anyway, lots of our friends will be there. We even got Fergus into a black tie, and David promised he'd be there to run interference for our team."

Belinda had gone to her room to pick up her wrap and her purse. They heard her rush down the stairs, and they heard Scott exclaim as he stood in the hallway staring up at her as she descended the stairs.

"How can anybody so beautiful belong to me!" Scott said.

"Does she?" asked Max, listening.

"She thinks she wants to," said Claudia. "Just pray for them."

Max knew what she meant.

Claudia was wondering if there was actually any substance to Belinda, if she had any desires beyond the momentary excitement of being a bride. Alex and her creative career seemed to be in limbo.

Scott had hired a limousine. Aunt Flora's seemed to be busy; no doubt, thought Claudia, picking up swells.

The mansion grounds were alight. Flora had had an electrician light the curved driveways with special illumination, trees festooned with gardenias were spotlighted. Cars were lined up, and red-coated attendants rushed up and down the hillside, parking cars and taking others out of the way for the crowd of elegantly dressed people who were entering.

As they got out at the porte cochere, the sounds of a band and the buzz of people could be heard.

"My lord," said Claudia, "it looks worse than a movie premiere. I'm surprised there aren't arc lights."

"I'm sorry," said Scott. "I told her to keep it simple, but you know her. We'll make the proper motions and cut it as soon as possible."

Claudia saw how tense he was. "Now, Scott," she said, "we've been through worse than this in our day, so don't be nervous. This is for you. She's giving you what she would like the most, so don't fret."

Belinda pressed her hand. "Thanks," she said.

She got out of the car and took Scott's hand, looking up at him and smiling. "Here we go, honey."

A phalanx of photographers caught them as they walked in.

Scott moved on angrily, trying to block them.

"No!" said Belinda, her eyes briefly blinded by the flash. "You can't do anything about it, Scott. At least they're not inside."

But as they entered the main hallway, she saw she was wrong. Flora Stone Random had a society photographer in black tie taking pictures of everyone who entered.

It took Belinda and Claudia a moment to get the lights out of their eyes.

Mrs. Stone Random stood in front of a canopy of gardenias. She was swathed in yards of pale pink chiffon edged with marabou, alight with pearls, and wafting a cloud of Shalimar. Beside her stood Scott's mother, Henrietta, dressed in pearl-gray lace, and beaming, for she was in ascendancy.

Flora stepped forward slightly. "There you are, my dears," she said. "Have I ever a surprise for you!"

She gestured next to Henrietta.

Belinda blinked. It could not be!

There stood her mother, Jessica, and Prince Carlo, known to his friends as Bobo.

"Darling!" said Jessica.

She stepped forward and kissed Belinda on the cheek. Claudia stood frozen. "My God!" she said under her breath to Max, "I don't believe it. The Wicked Witch of the West has come back to life."

She moved forward. Belinda still stood in shock.

"Well, Jessica," said Claudia, "imagine you coming back to Hollywood. I guess Belinda has been taken by surprise, to say the least. So I guess I'll just introduce you to Scott myself, Scott, this is Belinda's mother."

Scott, astonished, put his hand out and took hers.

He saw a slim, elegant woman, gowned in shimmering Nile green satin, wearing white kid gloves up to her elbows, her head coiffed to the point of being plain, but the high cheekbones and her wide, green-flecked eyes giving her style. She wasn't what he could ever have imagined Belinda's mother to be; he felt her coolness as he took her hand. He felt she was appraising him, and her admiration turned on too soon. Before she could say anything, Flora broke in.

"The Principessa Bonavente," she said, beaming and rolling out the liquid name. "And this, of course is the *principe*."

The *principe* put forth his hand and bowed stiffly.

"A pleasure," he said, "and congratulations."

Somehow Max had escaped the receiving line and had found David standing by a cluster of potted palms, watching.

"What is this?" Max said angrily.

David drew him aside.

"Don't worry, Max," he said. "Whatever she's up to, I'm standing by. Just to see to it that we keep her away from any lengthy chat with Belinda and Scott." His lips were compressed in anger.

As they waited, Belinda received another cold peck on the cheek and regained her poise long enough to say, "What a surprise!"

David cut in, taking Jessica by the arm. "You must come with me, Jessica," he said. "I want to tell you something."

"Oh," said Flora, "do you know each other?"

"Intimately," said David.

They all moved on as other guests entered.

David walked Jessica into the solarium. A dance floor had been set down and a few people were dancing.

"Shall we dance?" he said.

He took her by the waist and moved her into a waltz. She looked at him, astonished.

"If you open your bloody mouth to disturb Belinda with anything unpleasant, I'll take legal action on the letter you wrote to Max," he said.

She turned pale. "You—you read it?"

"Yes," he said. "Fergus and I both had to read it for contractual reasons. It goes under the title of blackmail, madame—or should I say *principessa*."

Her mouth drooped. She stopped dancing.

"I—I think I'm going to faint," she said.

"You've never fainted in your life, and you won't now. I'm going to keep right on dancing with you."

"You're a bastard," she said, and then she gasped at what she had said.

"Right," said David. "I understand you discussed that matter with Fergus. You know, Jessica, for a smart woman, you talk and write too much."

Seeing that Bobo was moving in to protect his property, David veered in that direction, relieved when he was tapped on the shoulder and could relinquish Jessica. Bobo gave David a charming smile.

"A pleasure," he said, and danced off with his wife. He was a good dancer. He damned well had to be, thought David.

A little later David saw him lumbering Flora around the floor, to her delight, while cameras flashed, and he heard him say, "A pleasure."

David turned to Max. "He seems to have a rather limited vocabulary."

As far as a big social jam-up went, the evening was a success. Los Angeles society had a chance to stare at Hollywood society, with a real imported *principe* and *principessa* thrown in. Belinda and Scott managed to join their own friends, and Penny and Harry stayed close by. Claudia, begging fatigue, sat out the excitement with Max in an alcove of fernery.

"We can't let that bitch out of our sight," said Claudia. "Has she spoken to you?"

"No need," said Max. "She squeezed all the money out of me she's ever going to get, and she knows it. Therefore I don't exist."

Scott said to Belinda, "I have to dance once with your mother."

Fergus joined up with David. He had come in late to make a token appearance, and he came alone, not having the courage to invite Martha Ralston, even though she'd hinted that she'd like to see the Barstow tribe in action for once.

"My God!" Fergus said to David, staring at Jessica, "I don't believe it. I've had a couple of stiff ones. I hope it's just the dt's."

"Sorry," said David. "It's real."

"She's got her nerve," said Fergus. "How did this happen?"

"That barracuda, Mrs. Stone Random, thought it would be a coup."

"I don't like Jessica dancing with Scott," said Fergus. "Maybe I ought to break it up and have a word with her."

"I've already had a word with her, but you could break it up. Go dance with the *principessa*." David grinned.

"Me!" said Fergus, aghast, pulling at his bow tie. "What do I talk to her about? How's the plumbing in the villa Max paid for?"

"I can't do it twice," said David, grinning. "People will talk. Go on."

Fergus frowned, but as he turned away, he saw the panicked expression on Belinda's face as she watched Scott and her mother.

"Okay," he said.

He tapped Scott on the shoulder. "May I cut in?" he said. "Hello, Jessica."

Scott was surprised. "Do you two know each other?"

"Through the years," said Fergus acidly, taking her in his arms.

"My, it has been a long time—"

Jessica received the second shock of the evening as they danced off. As graceful as she was, she stepped on his foot.

"Sorry," she said.

"No more than I. When are you leaving?" asked Fergus.

"After—after the wedding," said Jessica.

"Oh, that's a pity," said Fergus. "Why don't you leave before?"

"You son of a bitch," whispered Jessica.

At this moment her husband cut in.

"A pleasure," he said.

Fergus walked back to David. Jessica was staring at him over Bobo's shoulder.

"You know," said David, "she was so cocky when the evening began. I don't think she's having a very good time."

David went over to Belinda. "Dance with me," he said. He swung her around the floor.

"Don't worry, honey," he said. "I think we've taken care of it. You know, I still haven't given you my special present. It's blue—for you to wear when you step up to the altar. And we'll say it was a gift from Titan. Okay?"

"Okay," said Belinda. "I'm glad you're going to be at my wedding. David, I'm happy. Really."

Scott cut in.

"You're a lucky man," said David to him, smiling.

Scott looked down at her. It was difficult dancing with her. The house photographer's camera flashed so often he could hardly see.

"We have about as little privacy as if we were doing a scene together," said Belinda. "Let's get out soon."

"I could almost be jealous of that David Austin," said Scott. "He's very handsome, and he's very fond of you."

"He's like a brother," said Belinda.

Claudia met them as they stepped off the dance floor. "Couldn't we split out of here before they bring in the flaming pheasants?"

"Yes," said Belinda. "I have so much to do. Just think, Scott. It's day after tomorrow. Are you getting cold feet?"

"Opposite," said Scott, smiling. "I'm getting hot all over."

They sought out Flora. Guests were beginning to leave.

"We have to run," said Scott. "So many things to do. Thank you, Aunt Flora. It was a winger."

Flora beamed. "I knew you'd be surprised to see your mother, Belinda. Is she going to take your little brother back to Rome with her?"

Belinda gasped.

"No," said Claudia quickly. "Perhaps you've forgotten. It was a little awkward, you know, because Max was married to her. And I am Alex's stepmother. We're keeping him."

"Oh, dear," said Flora, her mouth pursing into an *O*. "I *had* forgotten. You must forgive me." She turned to Max. "I hope it wasn't too awkward for you, Mr. Ziska."

"Far from it," said Max. "I had forgotten it myself."

They paid their respects and left. When they got into the limousine, they rocked with laughter.

"Well," said Scott, "you certainly gave it to her."

"I like this boy," said Claudia. "I think he's on our side. By the way, where was Jessica when we left?"

"I saw her for a moment," said Belinda. "She had to go upstairs. She had a terrible migraine."

They all leaned back, glad to be finished with the fanfare that apparently had to go on before two young people in love could get together.

Even the press, alert for the unusual, could only call Belinda Barstow's wedding flawless.

The whole event had been a happy amalgam of Claudia's determination that it would not be too spectacular and Henrietta Stone's desire that it be properly social. Above all, it was a setting for two who, by the sound of a soft sea on a sunlit noon, reflected in their personal beauty all the dreams anyone could have had about a perfect couple.

Belinda was gowned in a white lace and chiffon sheath, embroidered in seed pearls. A flowing cape fell from her shoulders. She wore a coronet of white lace and pearls. A tulle veil covered her face as she walked into the garden bower with Max. At the end of the ceremony, when she reached up to Scott and he raised the veil from her face, everyone gasped at her beauty, her thick-lashed blue eyes alight with happiness as she lifted her face to be kissed.

She carried a small bouquet of stephanotis and gardenias, as Scott had desired. Her wrist flashed with the splendid bracelet David had given her the night before. It was her "something blue," and her "something borrowed" was the strand of pearls Claudia had lent her; she had been given them when she married Max.

Penny, as matron of honor and only attendant, wore a gray satin frock, and her sentimentality at Belinda's beauty and Scott's handsomeness made her almost burst into tears. She didn't even dare look at her husband Harry, who was standing up with Scott, for she knew, as she had said to Harry the night before, that he was the one who was the sentimental slob.

Henrietta and Mrs. Stone Random stood together, Scott's mother for once in the ace position.

It had finally been decided that, since Max gave the bride away, it would be possible for Jessica to stand with Claudia. Bobo Bonavente was wedged between them, the ham in the sandwich, for he dabbed at his eyes with a yard-wide linen monogrammed and crested handkerchief, and in spite of the fact that the ceremony was Episcopalian, occasionally crossed himself surreptitiously, until he was nudged by Jessica.

She wore a Nile green lace gown and a many-layered tulle hat, which brought out the green in her eyes and the henna in her hair. Behind her stood David and Fergus, which made her feel slightly nervous.

The press was stationed discreetly at the rear of the garden, and only George Ritt, who had shot Belinda's first pictures at the Titan studio commissary, was allowed to photograph the event.

Outside the gates in front of the house on the Pacific Coast Highway, a cordon of policemen flagged traffic and handled the crowd that stood by to catch any glimpse of the principals. On the ocean side, more policemen had roped off the public beach, despite a few protesters. The garden hedges had been doubly screened so no one could look in. Claudia also knew that four off-duty policemen from the Santa Monica Police Department, dressed in civilian clothes, were watching for any possible interference.

One room downstairs had been made into a cloakroom with racks brought in. The police had alerted Claudia about a "fish-pole burglar," known to pry windows open at such functions and fish fur coats right out into his possession. So a maid was stationed in the cloakroom to protect the thousands of dollars of fancy furs that had been worn by the elite, since this was a winter wedding.

Caterers functioned in the back quarters, electric roasters and ovens had been plugged in, aside from the usual facilities of the house, to carry the overload. A massive bar, draped in white damask and swags of gardenias, had been set up at one side of the dining room. Six waiters served champagne for the toasts.

Gilt café chairs and little tables bursting with tiny gardenia trees awaited the guests. A dais for the wedding party was in front of a screen of gardenias.

Once the marriage ceremony was performed, the elegant meal laid waste, and the innumerable toasts drunk,

Belinda and Scott were stationed at the five-tiered wedding cake, flashbulbs popping, and the pace began to let down.

David found a moment to greet Belinda. "This is not the time to say all I have on my mind," he said. "You know I wish you happiness. And I know you'll do everything, Belinda, to make this marriage work. Forget the past. Forget everything. Start anew."

She looked at him, a line of concern between her brows.

"I'm so happy, David," she said. "I hope that whatever happened in my life before will never be a cloud. Do you think I should have told him?"

"I've thought about it," he said. "I don't quite know."

Penny interrupted their conversation. "You'd better get into your traveling suit," she said. "Time's awastin', and you don't want to be on that mountain road too long after dark."

Belinda kissed David. "Thank you for everything. Including the beautiful bracelet."

He kissed her wrist.

As they went up the stairs, Penny turned to her.

A cluster of young women stood below, and Penny handed her the bridal bouquet.

"You're supposed to throw it now," she said.

At the back of the room, Belinda saw Laura West. She'd been masterminding the press and had hardly joined in the festivities. To Laura, it was a job; she had barely come back from location for the event.

Belinda deliberately threw it in her direction. It arced over the heads of everyone and literally hit Laura on the head. She lifted her hand to protect herself and caught it.

Laura looked at Belinda in surprise, held the bouquet aloft like a torch, and waved at her, smiling.

"Who's that?" said Penny. "Isn't that the girl who handles your publicity?"

"She's the girl who saved my career," said Belinda.

They rushed for the privacy of her room.

David pushed his way through the celebrants and found Laura, holding Belinda's bouquet. There were no friends or staff around, and a glance or two at the social personages surrounding her had told her plainer than words that their thought was, who is this person who caught the bridal bouquet, and why did she have to be the one?

If they only knew what I really was they'd peel away from me like I had the pox, she thought.

When David took her arm, she was relieved at the same time she was flustered. The white-gloved hand was awkwardly holding the flowers while her ungloved hand held a guest list for the *Los Angeles Times* society editor who was also vainly trying to push her way toward Laura.

"Come on," said David, "let's get away from the crush. I want to talk to you and apologize. I tried to reach you on location. Were you avoiding me?"

As he took her arm and moved toward the terrace, she looked up at him; no smile, no disturbance on her tanned face. She was wearing a beige dress, with touches of gold at her ears and throat. She looked trim, and all of one piece compared to the furbelows and frills of some of the other people who stood gaping, exchanging cliché small talk about how beautiful the bride, how handsome the groom, depending on what side they were on.

"No apology," she said. "I got your messages, so I know you tried. You get an A for effort."

David wasn't used to being thrown off-balance, but she disturbed him. He hadn't tried hard enough to reach her for missing such a personal date. He, too, was flustered.

"Not good enough," he apologized.

They stood on the deserted terrace while the caterers cleared away the debris. The afternoon sun shone on a crashing surf, and the gulls whirled, crying out a storm warning.

"Listen, Mr. Austin," said Laura, "I'm not naïve enough to think the head of the studio is going to meet a member of the publicity department on the back lot for a picnic in the middle of a business day."

"It was the hour when Fergus announced that Martha Ralston and he were stepping into a corporate marriage," said David.

"I figured that later," said Laura. "News seeps around a studio like poison gas."

"That's a hard way to put it," said David.

"It's a hard world," said Laura. "I thought feature pictures on the lot were a vast gamble, but you should see what happens on location for a television show. The production manager has to be a Simon Legree. The stunt men and featured players get drunk every night out of sheer distress. The leading star personalities bear down on their lines, thinking of their residuals and ownership, and are sour and sober. The pace is killing, and joy or despair reigns on the wings of the Nielsen rating. It's hell. And you know if old Johnny Grizzly falls on his face with the public, twenty eager beavers are standing on the sidelines pushing a replacement show. And Titan's lost the race in the rental space."

"Do you want to quit the series and come back? We're doing a drawing-room comedy, believe it or not. Jennifer Joy has come on loan-out from Paramount with her independent unit. How about it?"

"I'll stick it," said Laura. "It's the new world, and I'd better get with it."

She looked at him, smiling at last. "That is," she said, waving the press list, "as soon as I get rid of this cupcake assignment."

She put the bouquet to her nose and sniffed the sweet stephanotis. Then she stopped suddenly and pulled it away.

"And," she continued, "also unload this bouquet, which some young girl is going to grab."

She set the bouquet down on an empty table.

David noticed that one of the fingers on her gloved hand, her ring finger, in fact, seemed to be stuffed with cotton. It was limp and bent back as she put down the flowers.

He had never realized what was the secret of her ever-gloved hand; it must be an amputation.

He found himself wondering if she was rejecting the bouquet because she'd never wear a wedding ring. Whatever trauma brought this about must be the reason this woman is so aloof. Perhaps she drives herself in her work because she's rejecting a personal relationship.

But then he thought, so am I; no one can see the wounds we carry inside. How can I know what makes this attractive woman almost glow and then turn off the flame? Look at me, skating along in life, avoiding everything except Belinda, who was thrust at me as my blood kin . . .

Already Laura was turning away.

"Wait," he said.

He pulled a blossom from the bouquet, looked for a place to put it, and saw her tapestry purse hanging on a slender chain from her arm. He unsnapped the purse, tucked in the sprig of stephanotis, blossom out, and snapped it securely in place.

"You have to have some remembrance," he said.

Then, motioning toward the house, he said, "She looks happy. What do you think?"

"Since you asked," said Laura, "I think she's got a long way to go."

"Don't we all," said David. "Will you have dinner with me?"

"Again," said Laura, "you picked the wrong day. I have to rush the photos of this gig to the society editors. It seems Titan has stepped up a social notch with this wedding."

She looked toward the house. Sure enough, a woman was waving at her.

"There's four columns and a picture in the *Times* waving at me. Thank you, Mr. Austin."

"For God's sake," said David, annoyed. "*David.* After all, I'm not that old."

She smiled at him, and again he noticed her teeth, not squared off and photogenic, but small, matching her oval face and slim trimness.

As she walked away, he was thoughtful. Why was it that a woman like this intrigued him. He could have almost any beauty in town at the crook of a finger. But she was the one he thought about.

Claudia, dressed in coral crepe, looking beautiful but fatigued, went into the downstairs library where the wedding gifts were all set out. Max joined her.

"Well, Max," she said, "it's a good start. We did our best."

He kissed her.

"It seems strange to me," he said. "The whole pattern is odd. Does it have to be like this?"

"I know what you mean," she said.

They were startled to find Jessica carefully examining the lavish array of presents.

At that moment, Alex toddled in, followed by Effie, regal in a blue satin dress.

"Come on, honey," said Effie to Alex. "Back to the nursery."

The little boy looked like a Gainsborough child in his red velvet suit and ruffled shirt.

Already he was beginning to resemble his grandfather in the way he lifted his brows when he smiled.

Claudia smoothed his curls back from his forehead, and as always her heart turned as she saw the promise of elegance and humor in his face.

Oh, Jeffrey, she thought, I wish you could be here on this day . . .

Jessica turned and stared at the little boy.

"Oh!" she said, "couldn't I just pick him up for a moment?"

She moved toward him, but Alex immediately stepped behind Effie's skirts.

"He's very shy with strangers," said Claudia acidly.

Jessica lifted her chin. "Hardly a stranger," she said. "After all, I am his grandmother."

Max stepped forward. But there was no stopping her.

Music in the garden, and the conversational hubbub of the guests in the living room seemed to enclose them in a circle of privacy.

Jessica turned to Claudia with a saccharine smile. "Tell me, Claudia," she raised her voice slightly, "what are you planning to do with Alex? Is he going to live with the bride and groom, or doesn't that nice young man know that Belinda is his mother?"

There was a movement behind them. They turned.

Scott was standing there.

For an eternity he stood, and the color drained from his face.

Claudia put her hand out to hold him, to do anything, to try to explain. But he slowly pulled away. Harry was standing on the steps that led upstairs.

"Come on, Scott," he said, "Belinda's dressing. You better get into your traveling duds. It's getting late and you'll hit the afternoon traffic going up the hill from San Bernardino."

Claudia wondered if Scott would bolt.

Instead, he walked up the stairs.

"Well, you've done it," said Claudia, looking at Jessica in anger. "You've really done it."

"I'm sorry," said Jessica, her lips pressed together. "But

really, I think *you've* done it. You didn't have the courage to tell him the truth, did you?"

There was nothing Claudia could say.

Bobo came into the room. He broke it up by taking Claudia's hand.

"A pleasure," he said, kissing it.

Max interrupted, a look of fierce anger on his face.

"Get those two clowns out of here," he said, "or I'll personally kill them both."

Jessica, looking at his glowering face, retreated.

The last they saw of them, Jessica had gathered her eleven-foot ermine stole and the two headed for the door and their waiting limousine.

Claudia was sick at heart as Belinda came down the stairs. She wore a pale blue traveling suit, and Penny followed, carrying her white fur coat. The rest of the luggage had been previously stowed in Scott's car.

Claudia rushed toward her.

"Belinda—oh, Belinda!" she cried out.

But she was literally pushed aside by Flora and Henrietta.

"Oh, be good to my son!" said Henrietta, embracing her first, which was a feat, for Flora outweighed her. It didn't last long, for Flora elbowed in.

"You were a beautiful bride!" she gushed, looking out of the side of her eye to see if the photographer was catching her best side.

Claudia managed to get to her niece. "Oh, Belinda," she said, "Belinda, I must talk to you—"

"Thank you, Claudia," said Belinda, her face shining. "It was a wonderful wedding. I can't thank you enough. I know what you did—"

"Belinda—" wailed Claudia.

"I'll call you from the lake," said Belinda happily.

Scott came down the stairs; little tulle packages of rice were torn open; and the contents were thrown.

The front gates were opened, and the crowd was held back by the policemen. Belinda threw a kiss to Claudia and was washed away by the tide of celebrants.

The last thing Claudia saw was Scott's strained white face as he opened the door on his side of the car. Before he got in, he looked across the crowd and glanced at her for a brief moment.

She had never seen such a tragic expression on anyone's face in her whole life.

They drove off, amidst cheers and the flashing of many cameras, and two police cars escorted them out of the jammed highway onto the road that would eventually lead to their honeymoon at Arrowhead.

It took over two hours on the road, passing through the downtown traffic of Los Angeles; the smog-ridden inner city with its dark commercial veil of mourning, the onward-battling traffic adjacent to the Rose Bowl and Pasadena, the Valley towns, El Monte, Pomona, Ontario, bypassing San Bernardino on curving Route 18, heading uphill beyond the old Arrowhead Springs Hotel. Then up toward the Rim of the World drive, where the flatlands—now sprinkled with glittering lights—lay below in a vast tapestry, pine and greenery taking over the chocolate-colored earth and scrub of the lower land.

To Scott, it was a drive through purgatory. He knew that hell instead of heaven awaited him, and he didn't know what to do about it.

He was stunned, speechless, and the girl . . . no, the woman, his wife beside him . . . at first had clung to his arm.

To her surprise, he pulled away. Choking back his emotion, avoiding her eyes.

"This traffic is very hard to drive in," he said. "Please."

He could feel her hurt. Then he could not resist glancing at her. She had taken off the small hat she had worn, a little off-face confection, he thought bitterly, suitable for photographic reasons, for God knows there had been plenty of that. Her hair had been unfastened and fell about her shoulders. The large blue eyes, framed in dark lashes, glanced at him. Her pale face and the brow he loved so well, the classic serenity of eyebrow, disturbed at his coolness. He seethed at the seeming innocence of her glance.

"What's the matter, Scott?" she said. "Have I said anything to make you unhappy?"

"It's what you didn't say," he said, his lips thin with anger.

"What was it, darling?" she said. "I'm sorry—"

"Skip it," he said. "I can't go into it now, or I'll wreck the car."

She looked at him, startled. What was this man she had just married? Was he going to be so difficult, so strange?

The drive seemed endless. She watched the stream of Los Angeles traffic, tried to observe the countryside, and then put her head back and closed her eyes. She was fatigued from all the fanfare, and now she was alarmed. This man was a stranger, lost in his own thoughts, alien to her.

A rest stop along the road near a stand of pines was rimmed with a low stone wall, against a drop of several hundred feet.

Evening had settled into the warmth of the day. It was chill, and no one else was parking. Below, San Bernardino stretched out its crazy quilt of lights, and beyond, up the road toward Crestline, along the curving mountain road, the mountains, now purple, were awaiting the black of night.

Scott brought the Porsche to a halt, and to her surprise he got out, ignoring her. He stood staring over the canyon, one foot on the low wall. Belinda sat in the car, forgotten. Then she saw that he was bending his head, his hands to his face.

She got out of the car and came up to him. He did not look up. She sat on the stone wall.

"Scott—"

He turned away. "I feel like driving this car right over the edge," he said. "Why didn't you tell me? How could you do this!"

For a second she looked puzzled; then she realized what it was. Somehow he had learned about Alex. That had to be it.

She felt her cheeks flaming, then the blood seemed to drain away, leaving her limp and icy cold. She thought she would be ill. Her hands trembled. She couldn't bear to see the anguish in his face.

"Oh—," she said, "oh, Scott. I didn't know how. I was going to tell you when we were alone and had time—"

He broke in.

"How convenient," he said. "After you had shared my bed? What else were you going to explain, I wonder—"

She flinched from his anger. And also from the fact that following Claudia's advice she had brought the alum for a tightening douche and planned to seem virginal on her wedding night. Guilt had never fallen on her before, but now there was no alibi, no Claudia, Effie, or David to be her takeout, no privilege of being looked after by others because she was such a valuable commodity.

What could she do? What could she say?

"If you only knew how it happened," she said. "It was only once—I must explain—"

He took his foot off the low wall.

"I don't want to hear the lurid details. Especially on our wedding night."

She hung her head.

"It's my fault. I should have told you."

"Not only yours," he said angrily. "What sort of woman is your Aunt Claudia? She also led me into this trap. It was time for you to have a substantial background. Maybe what I heard and ignored about that Bohemian artist you were mixed up with at the studio is also in the script. I didn't believe it."

Now there was nothing she could say.

"Believe me," she said, "I love you, Scott. I love you, and only you."

He looked at her angrily. "I love you, too, Belinda, God help me."

It had become darker. Several cars passed on the highway. It was getting colder, and clouds were lowering on the mountains above. She pulled the lapels of her jacket close, but the chill was from within.

She turned and ran past the Porsche onto the road. There was nothing she could do, no way out; she would flee from Scott and his anger, hide from everything. She didn't care if she died, but she had to get away.

She stumbled along the road, and a truck chugging up the grade honked at her. Her slipper caught in a thin frozen snowdrift and came off. She hobbled on without it.

Scott, startled, watched her run. She was like a detached little doll in her pale blue suit and white fur jacket, fleeing along the darkening road. Another car came by at a faster clip and honked, swerving to avoid her. The car stopped a moment, then raced on. Thank God, thought Scott, it didn't stop! Belinda Barstow, the face that everyone knew, running along a mountain road on her wedding day.

He rushed after her and caught her as another car whizzed past, barely missing her.

Taking her in his arms, he held her head against his chest and drew her to the side of the road. She was sobbing with great gasps, and he had to hold her, as painful as it was to him, to keep her from falling into a heap.

He finally got her back to the car, settled her in, and locked the doors, starting the engine.

"Look," he said, "there's nothing we can do about it now. I'll get us to our destination. You mustn't do anything foolish."

Her breath still came in racking gasps.

"Stop it," he said. "It won't do any good."

His eyes filled with tears. A cry of despair made him keep from sobbing himself. He couldn't allow it. If she had to be a child, he had to be a man.

He took out his handkerchief, wiped his eyes, blew his nose, and, after swallowing, turned to her.

"I'm trying to keep together myself," he said. "You'll have to help me. When we get to the lodge, I'll try to put the pieces together. So just sit back and stop it."

Belinda fished in her purse and took out her handkerchief, dabbing at her eyes and wiping off the mascara. At another time she would have fished for a lipstick, but she realized that this was no good. In a sense she was naked, her face, her soul, everything that she was, more than she had ever been in her life, even when she had suffered in that Greek cave giving birth to Alex. For this was her future, and it was ruined. With a heavy heart, she realized that she loved Scott, and that was ruined, too.

As they went higher above the snowline, clouds began to press down on them, and finally a swirl of large snowflakes began to fall. The road was slushy, and driving was doubly difficult.

The drive seemed endless as they moved above five thousand feet into thicker pine forests and snow. They passed the faint lights of the village and moved around the edge of the lake and followed the road over the dam to the north shore.

Cottages, Swiss-style chalets, and larger estates encircled

with walls and gates revealed the privacy and seclusion of the area, which had managed to keep a shuttered aristocracy away from the summer water-skiing and winter snow-skiing jumble of the village environs.

Scott pulled into a private road, the end of it surrounded by a high stone wall. Iron gates were opened by a caretaker who came from his lighted gatehouse to welcome them, carrying a flashlight in the storm. The man rushed up to the car to greet them.

"Welcome, Mr. and Mrs. Stone," he said. "Everything's waiting for you, the fire lit, food in the oven, and champagne on ice. Effie called to say you was on your way. Good thing you got here. We might be snowed in! Happiness!"

He gave him a broad smile. Scott had known him since he was a young boy.

"Thanks, Henry," he said, managing a smile. "We'll be just fine. You'll protect our privacy, I know. I'll handle the luggage myself."

He drove on quickly, and Henry wondered why Scott hadn't introduced him to his famous wife. She was a pretty thing, as well as he could see, although her head was turned away. After all, they wanted to be alone, and fast, he thought, grinning to himself.

Scott had promised Belinda that he'd carry her over the threshold—but it was forgotten.

He helped her out over the slippery crust, noticing that she only had on one shoe. He had been so distressed he hadn't noticed before. She limped in and kicked off the other slipper.

Then he returned to carry in the two night cases. Effie had unpacked everything else and settled the house for them the day before. Henry had set it all up. Music was playing softly. A fire was roaring, giving its flickering fragrance to the beamed room. Champagne in a cooler, two glasses, and a spread of caviar were on a sideboard, and from the kitchen came the fragrance of Effie's bubbling casserole.

A small linen-covered table and two chairs had been set by the fireside.

Belinda took off her coat and stood, looking miserably at the promise of the room and the setting.

Scott disappeared and came back from the bedroom.

"Your things are in there," he said.

She saw him turn into another bedroom with his own suitcase.

She stood by the fire, trying to warm her shaking hands. In a few moments he returned. He had taken off his suit and was wearing slacks and a dark red turtleneck sweater. She looked at his blonde handsomeness, and her heart turned.

"You'd better change," he said. "I'll pour you a drink to warm you up, the hell with the champagne."

She went to the bedroom. Effie had outdone herself. Her clothes, fragrant from sachet, were hung in the dressing room closet and her personal things were laid out on the dressing table. Even, she noticed, the little lump of amber that had always followed her everywhere. The talisman that had belonged to her father, which Claudia had given her the night of her first premiere as a gesture of the fact that she had grown up and earned it.

She had proudly showed it to Scott. Now the amber, with its imprisoned little insect, seemed to mock her— proof of the fact that she was not grown-up at all. As a matter of fact, she felt like a little girl, and if she had the chance she would have fled to her father or Claudia, had either of them been able to be there, and escaped from the pressures of being adult and facing a problem all on her own.

But there was nothing she could do. This snowstorm and the sudden guilt placed so heavily on her had made her a prisoner, a prisoner in the very place set up to be the treasured nest of what should have been the happiest hours of her adult life.

She sat down and clutched the little talisman, hoping to gain strength from it, to face whatever she would do about Scott.

She glanced up at her white face in the mirror and shuddered. What a sight! She mustn't run scared; it wouldn't work. She went to the closet door. Near at hand was the wedding nightgown, especially made by Juel Park, the white lace and frothiness a web of enchantment. Even Penny had said that in this case expense was no object. Penny had been delighted when Belinda confessed they had not yet been to bed together.

What a wonderful and romantic way to start a honeymoon! Penny had blushed and admitted that she wished she had started that way, but after all, she and Harry had gone to college together and fallen madly in love. "And you know how that is," she had said apologetically. But of course Belinda hadn't, and undoubtedly Penny too thought she was a virgin. That's why she had delighted so in the pure white, madly exciting lace wedding nightgown. But now . . . now . . .

Looking through the array of negligees, evening pajamas, and lounging robes, she pushed them aside.

Effie had packed slacks and warm sweaters, a down-filled quilted jacket to wear in case it snowed, boots, and little fur-lined moccasins to wear around the fire after an afternoon walk.

She put on slacks, pulled a soft blue sweater over her head, stepped into the white moccasins beaded in blue, and brushed her hair back after washing her face. If that's the way it should be, that's what she would have to do. No makeup. No cajoling.

When she entered the living room, Scott was sitting on a chair near the fire, a glass of scotch in his hand. Beside him was another, which he handed her.

"Drink it neat," he said, "to warm up."

He glanced at her, the beauty of her face, washed with tears and emotion. He disliked himself for the yearning he still felt for her. He tried to put the thought away.

She sipped the scotch and choked a little, but ignored it as soon as she could and courageously took another sip. Outside, the storm seemed to blanket the house. Now snow was falling heavily.

"Are you hungry?" she finally said.

He shook his head.

"I'll turn off the oven." She went to the kitchen, took the casserole out of the oven, and set it aside. No use to ruin Effie's offering.

On the sideboard she saw salad dressing and serving things set out. In the refrigerator was a salad, ready to be unveiled from its plastic wrap, and Effie's small heart-shaped cake with LOVE spelled on it.

She put her head against the refrigerator door and wept. After a moment, she recovered and went back to the fireside, where she sat on a chaise and picked up her drink.

Scott was staring into the fire.

"You'd better drink some milk and eat a piece of

bread or something so you won't be sick tomorrow," he said.

He went to the hall and opened a closet. He took out a storm coat and some boots, sat at a bench and put them on.

"Where are you going?" she asked.

"To clear my head," he said. "You might as well go to bed. I'll see you in the morning."

As he walked out, a flurry of snow blew in the doorway before he slammed it shut. Belinda rushed to the window. She could see his form in the swirling storm as he walked toward the gate.

The minutes seemed like hours. She thought of calling Claudia. But it was no use, she thought, she'd only disturb her. There was nothing she could do. Maybe he'd come back and at least say good night.

She finally went to her room, hoping that he'd be all right in the storm. Of course he knew his way around here, he had spoken of it so many times, enjoying it in winter and summer.

She sipped another drink, hoping she'd forget the quivering that was attacking her, inside as well as outside. But it did no good. Following Scott's advice, she drank a glass of milk, nibbled on a cracker, and went to her room.

The bedroom fire had turned to embers, lighting the yellow and white room with shadows. Effie had arranged flowers on the bedside tables; it had all been prepared with love—for love.

She finally took a hot bath to get the chill and fear out of her, but that didn't work.

Automatically she put on the cobweb wedding nightgown, chiffon and lace all fitted to her body with such care, looking at herself in the mirror, mocking her image. Hello, bride . . .

She went to bed, leaving a crack of the door open hopefully. She turned out the lights and snuggled under the comforter, but of course she couldn't sleep.

It must have been an hour later that he came in.

She heard the click of a decanter top as he poured himself another drink. She heard the clomp as he kicked off his shoes. She waited, it seemed an eternity. She heard him pour another drink. And another. The music was still playing. Of all things, the "Liebestod"—the Love Death.

She couldn't bear it. She had to see him.

She got out of bed and walked into the hall.

He was deep in thought. He had moved close to the fire and pulled off his sweater; his shoulders and chest were gilded by the firelight.

She came to him and stood before him.

"Scott," she said. "Oh, Scott, please—"

He stared at her, seeing her body through the chiffon and lace gown, the glow of firelight on her, from the top of her head to her feet.

"Scott," she said, "I love you. I'm your wife."

He arose. "Yes," he said, "you are indeed. I guess I paid for the license, didn't I?"

"Of course," she said, startled as he moved toward her.

He reached up, she thought for a moment, to be tender. But he clutched at her nightgown and ripped it off her shoulders.

She stood still, her breasts exposed, as he tore it again and pulled it off her body. It fell at her feet.

"Lie down," he said, "lie down on the floor."

He pushed her off-balance and she fell.

He quickly undid his belt and slipped out of his trousers.

Before she realized it, he was naked, and he had thrust her on the floor under him. He caressed her breasts savagely and bent for a moment to bite the nipples.

She cried out. "You're hurting me!"

"That's nothing," he said.

Without tenderness he forced his mouth on hers, drove his tongue into her. He kissed her fiercely, bruising her lips, not giving her enough breath to cry out. She tried to push him away.

This excited him to a passion. He halted for a moment, looked into her face, and moved his hand down her body.

"Now," he said, "is that what you like? Tell me what you like from your men."

She stared up at him miserably and put her arms around his neck.

"No," she said, "you don't understand. I love you, Scott, I want you to be gentle with me."

She pulled his head down and tried to kiss him. He turned his head away.

"You're not a woman to be gentle with," he said.

In a violent thrust he entered her, and his anger and his passion beat fiercely against her. She struggled to get away from him, scratching him and beating him with her fists. This was not love, it was rape.

She cried out, "No! Please, don't do this to me!"

But it was to no avail. The crescendo of his movement was hurtful, and his anger made his urge slow to come to fulfillment. Try as she could, she could not get away from him. She was pinioned. And in a moment that made her ashamed of herself, lying like a whore on the hearth in the arms of her husband, she felt an intense excitement come over her and found herself responding to him, moving with his movement, being carried in a tide she could not help, going with him on the wave of passion. She found her lips clinging to his, her hands caressing him as he held her, and in a mutual, fulfilling explosion, totally unexpected, they fell, panting and sweating in front of the fire, released from the passion that had fallen upon them.

He rolled away from her and was silent a moment.

She arose, ashamed that she had responded, picking up the shreds of her gown to hold in front of her.

His arm thrown over his eyes, he turned toward her.

"Well," he said, "you're everything they said about you on the billboards."

"That's not true!" she said. "That's just publicity. It isn't true!"

"But it is," he said. "In spite of myself, you made an animal out of me."

She turned on him. "You did pretty well yourself!"

The "Liebestod," the Love Death, was still playing. She bit her lip in anguish.

She went to her room and slammed the door, snapping the lock so he would hear it.

In the bathroom she cleaned herself from him, furious and crying. He had managed to make a whore out of her because that's what he thought she was.

She put on another nightgown and went to bed.

It was impossible to sleep, and she waited through the long winter night for dawn. It was a steel-cold morning when she got out of bed and looked out the window. It was still storming, and she couldn't even see the lake a few terraces below.

She dressed in slacks and a warm sweater and unlocked her door. There had been no need to bolt it. He hadn't come near it.

The curtains in the living room were drawn and the fire was embers. Scott, dressed in his turtleneck sweater and slacks, was on the chaise, his eyes red, his hair disheveled. He undoubtedly was hung over.

Without a word she went into the kitchen and brewed coffee and poured orange juice.

She brought it to him and put it down.

"Here you are," she said. "You need it. I'm going for a walk."

She put on her storm boots and hooded coat and headed for the door. A drift of snow had filled the entry, but she climbed over it and started out. She had to get away from the house, from Scott, from herself.

She had no idea it would be so difficult to walk. Each deep footstep was a struggle. She moved on as well as she could, heading toward the front gate. The snow whipped against her face and stung her eyes, but she went on until the hateful lodge was out of sight.

She finally realized that a farther walk was impossible, and when she turned back there was a blur where the house should have been. She looked for a light, but remembered that Scott had closed the shades.

The country was deathly still, with only the abrasive rasp of snow and wind against pines. Perhaps she'd never find her way back. Perhaps she'd freeze. She didn't care.

She stumbled on and tripped once, picking herself up. She began to cry. What a terrible way to die! She thought of Claudia, of David and Max, and most of all of Alex. She had taken him so lightly. He was hers.

She saw the shadow as he came for her. "Scott!" she said. "Oh, Scott!"

He picked up her and carried her through the drifts to the house.

"It's a blizzard, you idiot," he said.

He carried her into the house, peeled off her coat and boots, and rubbed her hands and feet.

"You're just a stupid kid," he said, "wrapped up in a fancy package."

He poured her a cognac and got her into one of his woolen robes.

While she thawed out before the fire, he scrambled some eggs, made toast and coffee, and they both sat at the neglected dinner table having their first meal.

He leaned back and looked at her. She felt that all the love she had expected from him had evaporated; he was appraising her.

"Now," he said, "the phone line is out. Looks like we're snowed in. So we can't tell the world that we're quitting."

She looked at him, startled.

"That is," he said, "if we are. I've been doing some heavy thinking. You don't need to be scared, Belinda. There's not going to be a repetition of last night."

Belinda blinked, wondering if he could know that it hadn't been so unfortunate for her. But, of course, she couldn't tell him.

"I'm a proud man, in case you don't know it. I've thought it over, and I realize that I courted you without question. It was my fault for being so stupid. *The Oracle* was in my mind and I ignored *Lucretia Borgia*."

Belinda felt anger rising in her.

"How dare you come to such a conclusion! I'm neither one. I'm me! What are you, some sort of great casting director? You're just as dumb as any movie fan—living in your fantasy. I didn't expect this of you. Look, Scott, you did court me. And it took me a long time to fall in love with you. I didn't know you were thinking of some celluloid image when *you* fell in love with me. Talk about being stupid!"

He looked at her, surprised. In his mind she had always been the gentle, affable beauty, for that was the role she had played during their courtship.

"I am stupid," he said angrily, "for expecting a bride and discovering I married a woman with a child. That really takes the cake."

"Well," she said hotly, "don't preach to me. You certainly weren't a thoughtful lover last night. Talk about rape! Let me tell you something. The man who gave me Alex was a remarkable man. He was gentle and loving and made me feel like a goddess. And then he died the next day. If he hadn't, I'd probably still be with him. His name was Pericles Niadas."

He stared at her, startled.

"So," she continued, seeing her edge, "don't think it

was any fly-by-night experience. He made me feel like a young Cleopatra to his Julius Caesar. I was very young and I wanted to be important. And I'm not ashamed, I'm proud. I wish the world knew he was Alex's father. But it would have wrecked my career."

Seeing her advantage, Belinda did the unusual. She picked up the plates to carry them to the kitchen. And then she paused.

"And another thing, Scott, I imagine from last night that you're a man of experience. Let's turn the tables. How many women have you slept with? How many women could you have made pregnant? For all you know, you could be a father, too. But that doesn't count, does it? It's the woman, the poor dumb female who gets pregnant and takes the rap in society. True?"

She walked out past the pantry and turned. "I wonder how a man would feel if he thought he might need an abortion whenever he had sex?"

She walked into the kitchen and put the plates in the sink. For the moment she had stopped quivering inside. Her anger had taken away her terrible fear. She had stood up to him. Of course, it wouldn't work as far as they were concerned, but she had done it. At least she wasn't craven.

The next few days were a truce rather than a siege, although unhappiness and loss of what had seemed to be a lighthearted love hung over the lodge.

The blanket of snow thickened. A snowplow opened up the roads for necessary traffic. Since the telephone lines were out, Henry managed to get a message sent down to San Bernardino with a road repair crew, so Claudia was alerted that the bride and groom were well and in no peril.

There was no physical contact between Belinda and her husband. Scott did not accept her as his wife. It was obvious that the shadow of her past hung over him, and he was ashamed of himself for the fierce attack he had made on her body. But he was a practical man, and he spoke to Belinda in terms of his life and his work, not as a lover or husband.

"We'll have to set ground rules for the time being," he said. "Because of you, I have completely changed my work. I have been put into a prestigious situation in my law firm, and I'm now in control of the corporate entertainment field of our office. I have already set up two independent films and a television series, and as you know we have established the Belinda Corporation to further your career. All this has taken not only time, but expertise, and, aside from this, I have gone heavily into debt to set up our style of living. I couldn't very well back out, as much as I'd like to."

"I didn't ask you to do this," said Belinda. "You chose it."

He looked at her angrily, all the gloss of being in love seemingly removed.

"How does one compete with a trousseau and wedding like yours, thousand-dollar down sofas, Coleport and Waterford crystal, Porthault linens, and twenty-thousand-dollar star sapphire and diamond bracelets from the head of the studio?"

Again, she felt his suspicion about David. Well, that was one secret she would never reveal. In his proper Los Angeles upbringing there was no room to admit a bastard brother as well as a bastard child. It tickled her. Knowing what David was and had been to her made it easier to bear the thought of Alex. He'd be lucky to be as fine as his secret uncle.

"Don't get any wild ideas about David," she said. "There are lots of people in my life who have been friends with me. And who believed in me, and my talent."

She put her hands on her hips angrily. "Which, by the way, you have ignored. Doesn't it hit you slightly between flashes of distrust and jealousy that at the age of eighteen I have enough talent to allow you to form a corporation— of which you are partner, and manager?"

He paced to and fro, running his fingers through his hair.

"I know, I know!" he said. "Don't think I haven't stayed awake thinking about it these last nights. It's all a Gordian knot, this circumstance, and my basic desire is to get out my sword and hack it all to pieces."

"Do it!" she said angrily. "Just do it, Scott Stone. I can do without you."

She started to cry.

He wanted to take her in his arms, but he couldn't. He wouldn't be a pawn to this spoiled girl who hadn't cared or believed in him enough to tell him the truth about herself. He had been taken, and it wouldn't happen again.

"No you won't do without me," he said. "Neither you nor I are going to be humiliated by the fact that we're not working out our marriage as film fans planned. I do respect your talent. And I think you are going to have a great career. You've just begun. Your potential is enormous. And, if I say it myself, you need my help. You've been spoiled and overprotected. God knows you need a strong person beside you in a business way. I know I have had a new facet of law open up for me because of you, but I intend to use it well. I will work as your partner and adviser, and I'll do everything I can to make your career flourish."

She blinked her tears away. Why show weakness? She stuck out her chin. "So what am I supposed to do? Play the loving wife?"

"You're damned right," he said. "You're a good actress. Look what a fine snow job you pulled on me, the sweet virgin I had to marry to get." He looked at her angrily.

"Let's not play that song anymore," said Belinda. "You were the one who treated me like porcelain. So what do you expect for all of this?"

"I expect to settle you into a firm career, to get you started on your way solidly. I expect you not to embarrass me with any flirtation or affair that will besmirch our reputation, and I expect for the time being we will pursue what appears to be a good marriage. And if at any time you, or I, find someone else of legitimate significance, we will disolve our bonds and each go our own way. But for now, no one, and I mean no one, for business reasons as well as our personal dignity, is to know that we are not living as husband and wife."

And that was the plan.

At night, doors were closed, with two proud people tossing and finally falling asleep, fatigued with the pressures of their emotions and the turmoil of their lives.

Belinda arose late one night. Scott had had too much to drink, as had been his pattern these days, and gone to his room. She could see the light under his door. He was studying the innumerable papers he had brought with him in his briefcase.

The fire was banked into high white and red embers. She took the torn wedding nightgown, the precious lace and chiffon confection that had been the awe even of an exclusive shop used to such luxuries, and tossed it on the coals, watching it shrivel and curl as the lace went up in pinpoints of little flame.

So that's it, she thought. Good-bye dream of a wedding night, farewell settling comfortably into a marriage that was going to solve everything. Why does my particular booby trap have to be romance? Why is it everything turns out so badly for me? Will I ever be happy in love?

Later in her room, as she tried to read a book, the words blurred. She was in love and it was very uncomfortable and had no future.

Soon the week would be ended and she and Scott would return to the rapacious gaze of people who would conjecture about how their honeymoon had been, how many times they made love, and what heaven it must have been for two such glamorous people to have spent their first week together, most likely in bed making love most of the time, in the mountains in a paradise all their own.

She could imagine the fan magazines gushing over how she ran her house, how they entertained, speculating on their private moments. She couldn't imagine Scott standing still for all this balderdash, but he'd have to face it. And above all, she'd have to present a smiling face, turned up to his at everything from tennis matches to restaurants, anywhere they would have to be to belong to the pattern of Hollywood.

She had been indoctrinated in the motion-picture business long enough to realize this was necessary. It could not be ignored. The public demanded their idols to keep in touch with them. And if they didn't they fell from their economic pedestals.

Without the buffer of love, this would be an endless battle with Scott. But the charade would have to go on.

When she awoke, the sun was shining. She jumped up to look out on a wonderland. Icicles hung from the eaves. A pristine blanket of snow lay over the mountain, down to the sparkling lake. To her enchantment, she saw rabbit footprints, the only mark on the crystalline crust.

She got into her clothes, her parka and boots, and rushed out on the terrace. The sharp, clean air cut into her lungs as she ran across the steep drift and suddenly sank into the powdery heap waist-deep.

She pulled herself out, half laughing, and retreated to

the shelter of the eaves, where the snow had not drifted. Wouldn't it be fun to build a snowman! Wouldn't Alex have chortled to see it!

Then she paused, the winter sun beating its thin but welcome warmth on her face. She missed Alex. For the first time she realized that she hadn't thought of what it would be like to be away from him. In her excitement about her marriage she had not considered her child. Plans for him had all been left in limbo, with Claudia as the takeout.

Well, Scott was laying down *his* rules, and she would abide by them. On the other hand, she would have some rules of her own.

And her work.

She moved around the protected eaves of the house to the front, where the snowplow had engraved a path. She moved slowly along the crunchy road toward the gatehouse, listening to the soft song of the pines, looking up into the pure dome of blue sky.

She breathed deeply, her lungs almost hurting, but she felt full of life, full of joy. What had happened to the frightened girl who had allowed her husband to throw her on the floor and treat her like a cheap whore? How could that have come about? Never again would a man use her so.

She would have a good career. She wouldn't take mediocrity. She wouldn't do a picture just to make money for a corporation. She wouldn't listen to anyone who was singing a siren song to entice her.

Not Claudia, or Max, or David, or Fergus, or even Scott, now that he was so determined to do well with the corporation. The first thing she would do would be to fall in love with a script. Then, after that, be meticulous about cast. No favors, no favorites, no idols of the moment to be used as a gimmick. She would be her own person, an actress, a growing talent, and she would work and study so that any personal unhappiness would be forgotten, for the first thing in life should and would be her work. Turning from it for frills or privilege hadn't worked.

And then there was Alex. There was no reason in the world he couldn't be with her a large part of the time. Of course he could stay with Claudia and Max when she worked, if necessary. But there would be a permanent room in her house for her "little brother," and if Scott didn't like it, he could go live in some club.

Refreshed in spirit, she entered the house. Scott was in the kitchen fixing breakfast. He looked at her and for once a smile broke across his face.

"Well," he said, "you look chipper. Guess what? French toast."

For a moment Belinda felt that if their retreat lasted one more day and night, they might get together.

"Thanks," she said. "I'll set the table."

When they settled down over their grapefruit, she looked up at him.

"I've been thinking of what I want," she said. "Since you suggested ground rules, Scott, these are mine. First of all, I don't care what is offered, I want story and cast approval on all our deals. I won't accept anything I don't like, even if we have to cut down."

He smiled again. "We haven't even started," he said, "so let's not worry about cutting down."

"And that's not all," she said. "I want our guest room to be a nursery. I want Alex to live with us most of the time."

The joy came away from his face. She could see the muscles tense in his jaw.

He picked up his spoon and then put it down.

"I suppose you had this planned all along," he said.

She looked at him wide-eyed.

"No such thing. I was very selfish. When we started I thought only of us. But I've come to my senses, Scott. Alex is mine, and he's not going to be shuffled off. And since I no longer have your love to consider, that's the way it will be."

He dug his spoon into his grapefruit.

"I know how wrong it was," she continued, "not to have told you about Alex. My only excuse is that I was afraid to lose you. You would have run from me, as you are now—or you would have understood and opened your heart to me. But I was stupid enough to think only of loving you, and not considering Alex. Well, I'm not apologizing, I'm only saying that the baby is going to stay with us, and Effie is going to run our house so she can be with him."

"What is she, your slave?" he said. "Does she do everything you tell her to do?"

"Almost," said Belinda, "because she loves me and she loves Alex."

He shrugged, as if anything that was said meant little to him.

"And I need all the love I can get right now," she said.

She dropped her spoon and ran from the table.

In her bedroom, for the first time since the ill-fated confrontation had occurred, she succumbed completely to tears. She threw herself on her bed and allowed herself the release until her head ached and she forced herself to stop. Scott had paid her no heed.

She bathed her face and went into the living room. He was gone. She looked out the window and saw his footsteps. He had wandered out to the road that led to the lake beyond.

She went to the kitchen, began cleaning up and packing away the carrying containers and dishes Effie had sent up for the holiday. It was the first time she had confronted being domestic, and she tried to be meticulous. It had been so promising when she and Effie had discussed the menus. Now, with a heavy heart, she decided that she wouldn't in any way reveal to Effie—or even to Henry the caretaker—the truth, as she threw away so many dishes which had been ignored. Smoked pheasant, a roast, stew, and pastries, all left over. She set them out in the snow; anyway, the hungry coyotes she had heard howling in the night would have a royal feast.

After that she went into the bedroom, folded her clothes, most of them not used, and again packed meticulously for the first time. There was no hurry; the day, like others, would drag along.

In a sense, she thought, she was folding away a dream. Well, she intended to make the best of everything.

She was moving into a new, beautifully furnished house. She had wanted to get away from the confining life as a young girl with Claudia and Max. Now she had her wish. She would pretend the house was hers alone, for now she was liberated.

Perhaps the best thing that had happened to her was being on her own at Arrowhead. Otherwise, she would have switched her dependence from Claudia to Scott and never have realized that she would have been in bondage to another person, unable to make her own decisions.

When she got over the hurt of Scott, she might even think of him as being a houseguest. Effie would be there to take care of her and Alex, and if anyone didn't like it, to hell with 'em. Effie had taken care of her since she was born, and she knew she loved it. And instinctively she knew that, no matter how surprised they were, both Claudia and Effie would be proud that she was bringing the child into her life.

Already the thought formed in the back of her mind that someday she would tell the world that Alex was her own. He had a right to know who he was.

She heard Henry's Jeep start down by the gates, and she rushed to the window. Scott was getting into it, and they were off on some errand.

Late that day the car returned, and she saw the two of them fitting the Porsche with snow chains. Scott, too, was making plans to get away from the lodge and back to reality. He, too, thought Belinda, must feel that his booby trap had been romance.

It struck her that the two of them were chained together as solidly as Henry was clamping snow chains around the Porsche's tires.

She didn't want to talk to Scott tonight; she wanted only to live with her own thoughts, to try to plan for the future and not stare at the dead present.

She heated the last of the soup, ate a bowl of it quickly in the kitchen, and left the pot on the stove with a note: "I'm packing. Will see you in the morning. Let's leave early, I want to see Claudia."

From her room, she listened for the glass top of the decanter to clink its announcement as he poured drinks for himself, but instead, she heard him go to the kitchen and stay there a while. Finally, he turned off the music on the hi-fi and went to his room.

Well, she thought, he's back to earth again, too. His mind is clicking away just like mine. The honeymoon is over.

★★★★★★★★★★★★★★★★★★★

29

★★★★★★★★★★★★★★★★★★★

Belinda's first meeting with Claudia had been her challenge. If she did not keep her pledge with Scott, she knew her whole house of cards would tumble. She realized that Claudia's face alone would reveal the betrayal of her promise.

If she told Claudia the truth, that her marriage was a sham, the information would reveal itself in the way Claudia looked at Scott. The same would go for everyone she knew.

Claudia would be the test.

Play it cool, she kept saying to herself, digging her nails into her palms, preparing for the first meeting.

They reached the beach house, as had been arranged, in time for lunch.

"Let's get it over with," said Scott testily as they entered the garden.

Belinda rushed upstairs to greet Claudia alone in her bedroom.

"Well," said Claudia, embracing her, "how was Arrowhead?"

"Oh," said Belinda, holding Claudia close so she could not see her eyes, "sorry I couldn't reach you by phone—the storm, you know—but it was glorious. Claudia, I never saw snow like that before, the purity of it, icicles on the eaves, tall pines covered like a Christmas picture, with drifts that fell in soft thumps in the night."

This kid's certainly talking about the weather a lot, thought Claudia. But Belinda presented a smiling face.

"It was wonderful. And wait until you see the house."

"I've seen it," said Claudia. "Didn't you recognize a few of my touches? Did you like the Bellows portrait of your

437

father over the fireplace in the library? His elegance ought to overwhelm even Flora Stone Random! And all the pictures of the Barstow clan I put up in the library, and the log of your father's boat, and his scrapbooks and books, and all the good junk I had in storage. A lot of silverfish lost their homes!"

"Oh, dear, I'm sorry, I didn't see it," said Belinda. "After all, we've only been home hours. Would you believe I haven't been near it!"

Good, thought Claudia, what bride is going to rush right to the library?

"That Penny is a darling," Claudia said. "You can thank her for blending Scott's mother's stuff stylishly together with the wedding gifts and all the things I sent over."

"I hope you didn't strip yourself of too much," said Belinda, glancing at Claudia's bedroom. Many of the gewgaws were gone. Looking out the window, she was relieved to see Scott and Max chatting amicably in the garden.

"How is Max?" asked Belinda. "How is the work going?"

"I honestly think he's on the track again," said Claudia. "And this is no wife's alibi. He has a good, very modern story, which would be fine for you, come the day, but he's meticulous, you know that, and he can't be rushed." She looked out at the two men.

"Max has aged," she said. "You know, his handwriting is getting more difficult to read, and it takes a typist with a European background to get used to his script. But the old head's right where it ought to be, and between that old German secretary, Miss Trondl, and myself, we can work it out." She turned to Belinda, her eyes alight with affection. "The fire burns bright," she said. "What else matters!"

"Let's join them," said Belinda.

They went downstairs. Scott was attempting manfully to play his role.

Fortunately, Max was on high, and he embraced Belinda with fervor. Effie had stayed over to greet the bride and groom, and she came down the stairs with Alex.

Alex rushed to his mother, embracing her knees.

It was a delicate moment. Belinda bent, kissed him and picked him up, and they hugged each other.

What Scott did next turned her heart and made her grateful to him with a pain that cut at her like a knife.

"Claudia—and Max," said Scott, "Belinda and I want Alex to come live with us."

Max looked surprised, and Claudia stared at Effie.

Effie's eyes widened, and her mouth opened in surprise.

"With you, of course, Effie," said Scott.

Effie's handsome face broke into a smile.

"Praise God," she whispered.

Belinda turned to Claudia. "What is this going to do to you?" she said, her eyes brimming.

Claudia took her hand and Scott's.

"Well," she said, "this is all very startling. But what can I say?"

"Listen," said Belinda, attempting to recover, "we hope you won't mind taking him on lend-lease from time to time." She looked at Effie. "Is it okay with you?"

"Okay with me?" said Effie. "What do you think?" Tears began to roll down her cheeks. She pulled a Kleenex out of her uniform pocket. "I've never been so happy in my life!"

They all laughed.

At lunch Alex sat at the table in his high chair. Now that his status was changed, Claudia and Max and Belinda all looked at him as if they hadn't seen him before.

Once or twice, Belinda, out of the side of her eye, saw Scott staring at the boy. Her food suddenly turned to cotton in her mouth, and she apologized; she was too excited to eat.

After lunch she went up to the nursery with Effie to decide what was to remain in the nursery and what could be moved to the new house. Both rooms would be intact so he could move wherever he wanted.

Later, they sat before the winter fire. The sky was pewter, and gulls circled and swooped and cried, expecting another storm.

Molly had returned to Elderberry. The beach weather was not good for her arthritis, Claudia explained.

"What are you going to do? Who will you get to keep house for you?" asked Belinda. She stayed close to Scott, not wanting another session with Claudia to explain how she and Scott had faced the truth about Alex.

"Well," said Claudia, "Max and I have been thinking about it. Of course, having Alex here made it difficult, but now that he's going with you, we feel we might not stay here. The house is too big for us. Taxes have gone up, all those grand aluminum window frames crack the panes in the salt air, and central heating in a house with unused rooms and pool upkeep for a pool that isn't used is silly. We might lease the place—we could get a bundle—and we were thinking of renting a little cottage in Palm Springs while Max does his polishing. Of course, we'd have a room for Alex wherever we went, and it might also be a pied-à-terre for you and Scott. What do you think?"

Claudia was smiling her brave smile. Belinda saw through it. Everyone was playing polite games. There wasn't any money. Claudia had scraped the barrel for the wedding. There was nothing coming in. Looking at the guileless face of Max, Belinda knew that he accepted Claudia's strength and most likely had no clue of the thin ice on which they were skating.

Perhaps, thought Belinda, some of the treasures missing in the house were not in her new library. They might have been discreetly sold.

She looked around for the first time as an adult instead of as the young girl of the house, seeing things she had taken for granted.

She kept her silence. What could she do? She couldn't change the whole life-style of a valiant woman who had her own man to look after. Belinda realized that her marriage had changed the life of everyone in the house. The responsibilities and the whirling pace of events overwhelmed her.

She went over to the window and looked out at the wide-flung beach, where she could not walk because she was a star. The place where Kevin had sat sketching in the sand. The garden that had been Alex's territory since he had been brought home as an infant. Here was Claudia's house, such a bower a week ago, where she had left so exuberantly as a bride. And here, a week later, disaster had struck. Here a family was planning to leave, and the lives were all tumbled askew.

"What have I done!" she cried out. "It's all breaking up!"

In a moment, Scott was at her side. "You haven't done anything, Belinda," he said. "Life changes."

"Yes," said Claudia, "you mustn't feel upset. This will

be a welcome vacation. We're not selling the place, dear, we're just renting it. When Max is ready to go into production again, and that could be easily in a year, we'll probably come back here again. But for now, I'd really welcome a simpler way of life."

It seemed reasonable.

As they left, Belinda tried to be practical. She took her aunt aside in the library.

"Are you really all right?" said Claudia.

"I'm fine," said Belinda. "Look, that's not the problem right now. First of all, give me a month or so to get settled, then you can announce that you and Max want a warmer climate. Say that the sea air is not good for Max's arthritis, and get yourself settled. But Claudia, you don't have to go. Anything I have is yours. How much do you need to stay here?"

"Don't be silly," said Claudia. "I don't want to stay here. That time has passed. But thank you."

"What will you do when I go back into production? I couldn't work without you."

"Yes, you can," said Claudia. "But come the time, I'll come up and be with you. You can't get rid of me."

She turned back to her favorite subject. "You know, Max has really got a great story. It's going to surprise everyone. Even you."

What would Claudia and Max do without each other? thought Belinda. It had taken a turn of life and fortune for them to come together in their older age. She wondered if there ever would be a mellowing that would make it possible for her and Scott to come together.

On the way to the house, Scott was silent. She didn't dare speak to him.

They entered the house. Her first thought was to rush to the guest room and see how it would work out for a nursery. But she couldn't, it would irritate Scott.

He had taken to his study. A daybed made it his bedroom. His dressing room and bath fortunately connected with it.

He saw her looking into his study as they went along the galleria toward the suite that was to have been theirs.

"Well," he said, "I guess we'll have to work out some plot with Effie. How about I snore, so have to sleep alone?"

Belinda flushed. "Whatever you think," she said.

"Well," he said, "the first hurdle is over. I'll be back in the office tomorrow, and you can make plans. Go ahead with whatever you choose to do. Good night."

He went off to his room, and Belinda retired to the spacious and pretty bedroom. It was furnished with all the comfort that care and money could buy. Thick white rugs, a sprigged chintz, two comfortable armchairs, a delicate fruitwood desk, a table and two chairs in a bay window overlooking the garden, suitable for meals à deux for two people in love. Venetian mirrors, courtesy of Mrs. Stone, delicate English flower paintings in velvet-rimmed frames, and an elegant Venetian bed with a painted head-board.

The dressing room was a vision of muted blues and whites with occasional sprigs of violet. Mirrors and innumerable drawers, all lined with scented quilted padding.

A bathroom dressed in finest velour towels, initials intertwined.

Belinda looked at it all, then unpacked her luggage in the dressing room. She pulled out the necessities. Tomorrow, when Scott went off to the office and her Mexican cleaning woman came in, she would have time to pick up the threads and get the house alive. Undoubtedly, Penny and Howard would come over and another charade would be performed.

She glanced around the warm, lovingly put together room, which so far had no loving in it.

A hell of a prison, she thought.

Now let's see, which side will I take? Well, I guess the one near the phone would be the wisest. I can switch it off if I want. Or the one nearest the dressing room. I won't have so far to go when I undress.

She abandoned the phone side. After all, to whom would she want to talk, and who would call her? It was a private, unlisted phone, the number not yet given to those who would share her new life. Maybe Scott's friends and business connections, and he had the duplicate of the phone by the daybed in his study.

The thought struck her that for the first time since she was a film star no production or specific role was in her future. She was truly adrift.

Already she felt the emptiness of the house. Her direction would have to be in work. She'd get her house in order, move Effie and Alex in as soon as Claudia and Max moved to Palm Springs so the house would have some life, and then most of her time would be spent searching for new properties.

There was no reason her company couldn't work on the Titan lot. It would make her feel at home. She would ask for Laura West to be her personal publicity woman, Claudia would be her coach, and that part of her life would be taken care of. She thought of her comfortable dressing room and remembered the days she had spent in it, the excitement of her career—phones ringing, interviews, fittings, staff, everyone fussing over her. A built-in social life.

In a week or so she would have lunch with David. Strange, she thought, in the last several months she hadn't thought much about the studio; all the excitement of a new life had occupied her.

But now it had become very important to her—a nest, a focal point filling her life.

One of the first things she'd do would be to have Scott alert the literary agents. Scripts would be pouring in, and her career would continue. As a matter of fact, it had to. She needed lots of money to do what she wanted.

Perhaps in the early summer she could go to Greece and take Alex to visit his godmother, Chloë, and Ubaldo, both of them so involved with the early part of her life and her first picture.

She wondered if Chloë would see Alex's resemblance to Niadas; these were threads of a life she would make all by herself.

As the weeks passed, she realized that life was not so easy. One fantasy could not take the place of the other. Reality and emotions somehow seemed to be partners, they could not be denied. She couldn't wait for the scenario to write itself. She must start moving on her own.

David was in Europe. Fergus was involved in a new company, Belinda heard, with Martha Ralston, that monster of a mother, she thought, who had given up her child in exchange for some of Niadas's money.

One day, Belinda drove by the studio. The prominent corner billboards were crying out that Martha Ralston was going to be a Titan star again.

SHE COMES . . . SHE CONQUERS . . . was emblazoned in gold beneath a stunning portrait of Martha looking much more beautiful and exciting than the original person. Belinda almost drove her car into the curb as she saw the portrait. No one could possibly have done that portrait but Kevin.

Martha was portrayed with thick blonde curls resting on her milky shoulders, her bold eyes wide, black-penciled eyebrows lifted in surprise, her glossy mouth half opened in the old-fashioned tradition, and her slim neck rising from a strand of expensive pearls. Belinda recognized the Kevin touch; he had made her seem like a woman of great price, haughty yet provocative, lush and intriguing. Kevin had used his magic; he had caught what the woman wanted to be; he had entrapped the dream.

For a moment, the blood came rushing to her cheeks, and she wondered if Kevin and Martha had been together in bed. But as she saw the portrait she knew it couldn't be. There was no love, no eye-to-eye contact. The portrait was compelling, dramatic, but not personal, not fulfilled.

As she drove through the studio gates, she was greeted with the admiring salute of the policeman on duty.

"Congratulations, Miss Barstow," he said, "or should I say Mrs. Stone."

She smiled automatically, and then realized that the rest of the visit was going to be like this. She couldn't help it, she'd have to smile it off.

Fergus had new offices in the independent producer's rental wing. So she went to the publicity department.

Red Powell's secretary greeted her warmly, and after felicitations and admiration of her ring—which had been made up of an assortment of rose-cut Stone diamonds—she was ushered into Red's slightly shabby office.

"Well," he said, kissing her cheek, "Mrs. Stone, this is a treat. What brings you here?"

"Well," said Belinda, "I just thought I'd see how the—the old gang was getting along, and what's new."

"What's new!" said Red, clasping his brow. "The usual. Lots of television."

"What about movies?" she asked.

"Now," said Red, "don't give me any of your gallows humor. Just get your company going, honey, and give us some real class. Where are you opening your offices? Here I hope."

"I wish I knew," she said. "Scott won't let us get into that until we find a property. It's no use facing overhead, he says. Oh, Red, why can't it be like the old days?"

"I wish I knew," he said. "When Madame Ralston gets off her keister, maybe there'll be a little action. They have offices on offices. They've Charles Eamed him up to the elbow, and there's so many plastic legs on the furniture that six people have sprained ankles from running into them. The rumor is that Fergus dropped a script on the rug and it's so thick that they haven't found the script yet. And her dressing room. Oh—my God . . ."

He stopped and stared at her.

She looked at him quizzically. "What is it?" she said.

"Nothing," he answered. "Anyway, she's bought three Broadway plays. I wouldn't be surprised if they move into production within three months. Fergus is closeted with a playwright from New York and a top scriptwriter moved down from Santa Barbara for the chore, both of them holed up in bungalows at the Beverly Hills Hotel at four hundred bucks a day. Each of them has nothing but contempt for the other, and I hear Fergus is wearing a referee's uniform to work. Don't get near him, even if you can. He's in a foul mood."

Belinda realized this was no place for a visit. The phone kept ringing, and Red answered it, with studio problems at hand, while she looked around. There were pictures of herself, Claudia, and Jeffrey among a batch of other personalities. She noted that Martha had been strategically put in a prominent place. It made her feel as if she had been demoted. A situation she had never considered.

"Pardon me," he said, as he hung up. "This is a busy time."

"Where's Laura West?" she said. "I thought I'd like to say hello."

"Fat chance," said Red. "Martha has her working. Right now they're in Palm Springs doing a layout of her Dior clothes and her Cartier jewels; would you believe a photographer, a maid, a makeup woman, a hairdresser, a wardrobe woman, a private dick to protect the half million worth of ice, and Laura masterminding three limousines and a suite of bungalows at the Desert Inn. Sounds like old times, only it ain't our money—or profit, if any. It's hers." He shook his head. "Never heard of a star paying her own way like this."

Belinda was doubly shocked. She seemed to be having all the props pulled out from under her.

The thought flashed in her mind, the unspoken, disturbing trick of fate—all this Niadas money. While she had his son and was realizing she had to make her own way.

"And also," said Red, "she was so impressed with the portraits your friend Kevin did that she's got him shackled to his drawing board here doing six portraits of her."

Belinda wondered if her disturbance showed. Kevin here, on the lot!

"Well," she said, "guess I'll run along. Given Laura my best and tell her to call me."

She scribbled her phone number on his note pad.

"This is unlisted, Red. Keep in touch."

"I guess you're pretty busy with your new life, but, anyway, wish you were back."

So do I . . . she started to say, but she realized it wouldn't be a good idea. She gave him a peck on the cheek.

"Red," she said, "would it be too much to ask if I might see my two pictures. Could you have them run for me?"

"Of course," he said. "Any time." He looked at her, a little surprised.

"Don't get me wrong," she said. "I'm not being a ham, I just want to see where I'm going as an actress, for the next time out."

He grinned. "Well," he said, patting her shoulder. "You sure are a branch off the old tree."

For a moment he looked at her almost sentimentally, which was rare for him.

"Right now, if you want."

"I want," she said, smiling. "Time's a wastin'. Since Scott's in San Francisco on business, I have time."

Red went back to the phone. After a moment he turned to her. "In luck," he said. "Projection room one in fifteen minutes."

As she walked down the halls, all emblazoned with polychrome one-sheets of various pictures, she hoped she wouldn't have to see anyone else. Everything in her life had changed, even on the lot she knew so well.

But the worst was yet to come.

She decided to visit her old dressing room. At least
it was a place where she and her father had been at home.
It was part of her, and she would have it again. She
walked along the lane of carefully trimmed pittosporum
hedges.

As she approached the environs, she heard the sound of
hammering and an electric buzz saw.

At first it was difficult for her to relate. Then she realized
that the little patio that separated her dressing room and
that of Leslie Charles was gone. The whole front had been
torn out of her rooms, and a new facade with mullion
windows, and a French provincial roof added. The gardeners were already planting primrose and pansies in window boxes, and a neat little sign hung on the wall, done
in delicate gold script, *MARTHA RALSTON*, and underneath it in even more delicate letters, *Ralston Productions*.

The doors were open, and Belinda could see carpenters
fitting drawers in French provincial furnishings.

A large sun-room with high skylights connected the
spacious sitting room with the patio, and it seemed to be a
complete gutting and enlarging of her dressing room. The
addition of rooms, one of them apparently an elegant
chandelier- and mirror-decorated dining room and private
kitchen, was where once had been Leslie Charles's cherished
suite.

Shocked, she stood there a moment feeling violated
by this gigantic commercial enterprise, which seemed now
to have erased everything she had thought was her natural
right.

One of the craftsmen recognized her and waved. She'd
have to move fast. She waved back quickly and rushed
down the path to the protective stages and projection
rooms.

Projection room one was on the main studio street near
the commissary and production departments. She ran into
the foyer. The projectionist looked through the small
aperture and waved at her, signifying he was ready.

She moved into the comfort of the last row where even
the projectionist couldn't see her. She had often sat in
this seat looking at her rushes on the Borgia film. But to
be alone was a blessing, for once. The gush of tears that
came now was not to be seen by anyone.

She hoped that as the picture unreeled she would be able to control herself. She must forget all the trivia of her life, try to discover who she was and how she could find herself in her work.

As *The Oracle* played, she remembered how Max had taught her, how innocent she was at fourteen. How really dumb, she thought, she had been to allow him to control her completely in the role. But of course she needed it then, for she had only been a vessel.

When the love scenes with John Graves unrolled, she tried to recall what a terrific crush she had on him. He had not yet been a superstar, this picture had done it for him, but she tried to feel what she had felt when he kissed her. That had been the first sexual stirring she had and, of course, it had never been fulfilled, although she had tried everything she could to get him to make love to her. She even remembered stepping naked into the shower with him at the villa in Rome, and his rejection of her. She smiled. How funny to see it all in her mind now, as the pictures of them flashed in these memorable scenes that had also helped to make her a star. It was wonderful to know that such passion could be remembered without pain.

She'd like to work with John Graves again. Of course, he was a renegade; after being a superstar for three years, he had announced that he would do things his own way, if necessary, with his own money. She liked him and remembered how Claudia, who had discovered him as a cockney kid in prewar London, had said that in spirit he was more like Jeffrey than anyone she had ever met.

As the picture went on, Belinda remembered her pregnancy, the death of Niadas, and the shock of her predicament. Since she was playing a mystical young seeress, the oracle of Delphi, it had fitted the role.

What a life the picture had revealed, the plot within the plot as she watched it. She sensed Claudia behind the camera being her coach. She almost felt Max's presence as she saw the various scenes unfold. Well, she had overcome these difficult times, and now she was her own person.

While the projectionist set up *Young Lucretia*, she looked back on this springtime of her life as if she had never seen the picture before.

She tried to analyze herself through the picture. It was good because she had much help: Max's euphoric magic,

Claudia's expertise and love. But that was just fortunate, not her doing, and she had to move beyond it.

Seeing herself as Lucretia Borgia was not going to be pleasant; she'd seen it too many times. But here, by herself, without the mosaic of rushes and the disturbing acclaim of previews, premieres, and charity galas, was a different thing. She must analyze herself.

In the beginning of the picture, the overlay behind credits of her two portraits by Kevin disturbed her. This was quite a different thing from her long past feelings about John Graves and Niadas. This was still emotional, and she wondered what would happen if she saw him again. Would she be in a turmoil? Would his sexuality disturb her? If she loved Scott, as hopeless as it was, perhaps that would have turned off the passion that she had felt for this strange, incomprehensible man.

Thinking of Kevin, it entered her mind that as a superstar, her image had created desire in many people. That was one of the reasons for her success; why Scott had been so enamored of her. In a way, Kevin was a man who had such inherent attraction for herself—and others, as she had grown to realize. Strange, Miss Public Superstar meets Mr. Private Superstar and finds her nemesis! Her great sexual attraction for Kevin was perhaps a retribution for what she had done to thousands, flaunting her body and face—a magnet to inflame the imaginations of many.

There was no question about that; a superstar was more than a great actress. He or she was an explosive force of sexual attraction. It was a starglow which had nothing to do with acting; a circumstance that could not be denied. You had it or you didn't. Many fine actresses did everything in their power to be superstars, but it didn't work. It couldn't be manufactured at will.

Thinking of Kevin, she realized that there must be many men and women in private lives, aside from being in the performing arts, who had this innate charisma. They could not help it, and, depending on their characters, it was either used happily or caused misery and unearned privilege.

She was fearful that her father had been damaged by this so-called gift of the gods. Claudia had it, and had only in her very mature years overcome it. Love had done it.

Unwittingly, it had come to Belinda. It was a force she

could not ignore. But she vowed to herself that she would try in every way to be a true actress and not allow it to overtake her performance or career.

As the film ran, she studied herself. In this picture she was on her own a great deal more than she had been before. Of course, the glow of her love affair with Kevin was revealed in the young Lucretia, she thought. She'd heard studio gossip about how some female stars always needed a passionate love affair during the making of a film. Sometimes it was the leading man, the director, or the cameraman. She hoped she'd never have to be the sort of actress who was a parasite, having to feed on a body other than her own to perform a role.

As the film moved into the half-innocent, half-diabolical side of Lucretia, the love-hatred with her brother and father, and the mad protection of her illegitimate child, the Infans Romanus, born of an orgy in the Vatican, Belinda felt that she had earned her spurs as an actress. The picture may have been raw meat for some of the viewers, but she was moved by the performance, and a feeling of satisfaction which she felt was deserved welled up inside her.

A strip of light hit across the darkness of the room as the door to the corridor was opened and quickly shut, but she was so engrossed in the scene, and so used to doors being opened and closed during runnings, that she paid little heed.

But suddenly in the dark, two arms were thrown around her from the back and, before she could move, a man was kissing her.

In a panic, she pushed away. The projectionist, she realized, couldn't see her. As the man moved in front and pinioned her, she was defenseless.

Finally, she turned her head away, but the man grasped her hair and pulled her head back. She cried out with pain. By the flickering light, terrified, she looked up to see it was Kevin.

She gasped, and then he kissed her again. For a moment she felt his pressure against her, the hardness of him against her body, the breath that she knew so well mingling with hers.

"Kevin!" she gasped, "are you out of your mind?"

He looked at her, smiling, and slowly released her, but

he put his hand on her breast, caressing it softly in contrast to his obvious passion.

"Out of my mind for you," he said.

He put his arms around her, and as she breathed the familiar closeness of his warmth in her own loneliness, and her mind recalled what he had done, she felt more alone than she had been when she had tossed in the dark, yearning for him and disliking her desire.

"Oh, Belinda," he whispered, and it, too, was a cry in the darkness of his own loneliness.

He reached forward to the panelboard and turned the sound fader down. Belinda sat, shocked. How many times she had thought of him. And now he was here, and his pervasive way, the very movement of his wide shoulders and slim waist as he turned, the glisten of his dark curls and his shining eyes, made more dramatic by the flickering of varying lights as the screen changed scenes, were startling.

"How could you do such a stupid thing," he said, "as marrying that guy? Don't you know we belong together? We fit together."

"How can you say that," she said, "after what I saw with that—that despicable Tony Valli?"

"That had nothing to do with us," said Kevin blithely. "Don't call me homosexual, bisexual, or heterosexual—why categorize? I'm just a man who likes sex. Why put a label on me? I'm sorry you walked in on us, but if you didn't know, it wouldn't have made any difference between us. Don't be simple, Belinda. It's what we are to each other that matters. Believe me, I didn't expect that to happen with him. Now I realize; with lots of wine and Tony's complicated phone calls to the studio, it was a setup to break us up."

"That's ridiculous," said Belinda.

"Don't you believe it," said Kevin. "You don't know the studio underground like I do. Listen to this. Your dear friend and protector, Fergus Austin, has been shacking up with a gal from wardrobe, Peggy Rush. He's stupid enough to park his Mercedes, with the license plate showing, in her carport. A lot of studio people live near her in Palms.

"Also, right after the rumor went out that we were getting married, it turns out that Peggy's ex-husband handled the lease on that house I found for us in Laurel Canyon, and of course, called Peggy to brag.

"So Fergus got a panic call. A boy I know in the wardrobe department saw Fergus rush to see her in the fitting room. So what happened? Tony Valli got a new starring contract without any film to show for it. Peggy gave you that jewelry to bring to me, and Valli shows up with some high-class Italian wine and his famous sexuality. Phone calls arrive, which now I realize meant you were on your way to find us in action."

He looked at her and sighed.

"He did very well. Mission accomplished. He got out right after you left."

Belinda looked at him aghast. She remembered the sudden change in filming Leslie Charles's death scene instead of her scene with Tony. How neatly Peggy Rush had put those jewels into her hands, to get to Kevin! It all fitted. However, her focal point was anger at Kevin.

"It may have been a setup," said Belinda, "but you didn't have to do it."

"I know," said Kevin, "and I regretted it more than you would believe. No one but you ever moved me to tears. To lose you was terrible. I think if you and I had made a life all this would have gone from me. But don't believe it's so rare. Don't you know that bisexuality, or homosexuality, is like an iceberg in our society. There's more beneath the surface than anyone would imagine. You wouldn't believe how many thousands are involved."

"I don't want to imagine it," she said.

"Oh, Belinda, help me. It was easy for me to take the path at hand. Maybe I lived like most people would like to live, day by day, moment by moment. The gay world is easy. No responsibility. And lots of sexual excitement. But I love you. That's the difference. The kind of love we had doesn't have to be fulfilled all the time. It just has to be felt even for a moment to be immortal. What we were is on that screen. You were aflame, beautiful. So different from that placid girl who was the oracle. Whatever we felt will express itself in my work as long as I live. I need you. Help me. I think we can make it together."

He put his arms around her and his lips met hers. For a moment she accepted his mouth and his tongue, and then she pushed away.

Help me . . . he had said. No one had ever asked her that, they had only helped themselves.

"What do you want?" she asked. "I'm married. You know that."

"What does it matter?" he said. "I know why you married. You don't love this Scott Stone. He'll never give you the romance and life I could if you'll give me the chance."

For a moment the memory of their passionate love, the studio, the fire, the wine, and the sharing they had stirred her. But then she remembered the criticism, the constant petty put-down that an egotistical man dared give who lived on any crest of passion he could summon, his body and personality a target for anyone he chose.

"What makes you think I don't love Scott?" she said, moving his hand away as he tried to seek her breast through the opening of her dress.

"I looked out my window in the production department," he said, "and I saw your face. Belinda, I'm an artist. I study emotion. I know sadness and despair when I see it. Then I discovered that you were running your pictures alone. Any young bride would be seeing it with her husband. If I were your man, I'd have you on the floor right now, the hell with the picture. It's you who excites me."

On the floor . . . on the floor . . . Belinda's mind flashed to the memory of Scott throwing her on the floor on their ill-fated wedding night. Suddenly, Kevin's whole ploy seemed another senseless pattern, a man driving his symbol of supremacy into a woman, the woman supine and defenseless, feeding his vanity, and sex used as a weapon instead of a fulfillment.

She pushed him away and stood up.

"Kevin," she said, "I feel sorry for you. You're a yo-yo. You'll never be satisfied. You're not real. You're a trip and, for me, the trip is over."

She moved away from him quickly and walked out of the projection room.

The projectionist in his booth was surprised when she opened the door.

"Thanks," she said, "I've seen enough."

30

David Austin wearily stepped off the 707 at Idlewild Airport, disliking the task ahead of him.

He had just finished his meetings with Sidney Keys at the Dorchester in London, preparing him to take over his international interests, for he knew there was a long haul ahead of him at Titan, when a call had come through from New York. His great-uncle Abe Moses was dead, and since David was trustee of his estate he had to be in New York at once.

He had dealt with Abe Moses all through the divorcement of Titan from the theater chain, and he had always found the old man secretive, self-seeking, and, most of all, outside the usual pattern of business associates.

He had deplored Abe's constantly changing companionship with young women, figuring the old man obviously ran on an economic basis alone in his dealings with young flesh.

Now he would be forced to find out about the core of Abe's life, and he would be saddled with the responsibilities of a life he didn't know. It would have been more comfortable if there had been a widow or children and grandchildren to comfort and look after, at least in a financial way, but that had never been.

When he reached New York, Hugh Fairfield, vice-president with Abe's theater chains, met him. Fairfield looked pale and weary.

"Glad you could get here," he said, looking deeply disturbed. "The services are tomorrow."

"Yes," said David. "Poor old Abe, I guess he missed the boat."

Fairfield gave him a strange glance.

"What is it?" said David.

"I guess you better come with me to his apartment at the Dakota."

David walked into the familiar lobby. So many theater people he had known through the years lived in these spacious, sought-after apartments. Abe's apartment had been lived in so long that, in spite of moneyed elegance and a collection of valuable paintings carefully bought for him, it had a shabby look.

Abe always kept his rooms in a bachelor's organization of locks and keys, letters and paraphernalia neatly filed. Yet what a strange existence it seemed. The bar had always been better stocked than the kitchen. His manservant and housemaid came in by the day, but the collection of records and music system suggested, along with rows of bar glasses, a nocturnal private life that had little to do with his driving business life or any ordinary homelife.

Fairfield unlocked the apartment door and closed it. David noted the elaborate inner locks, chain, latches, and bolts.

"You're going to be shocked," Fairfield said, switching on the lights, "so be prepared."

He opened a drawer in a table at the side of the king-size bed. Out of it he drew a little tray. On it was a mirror, a tiny golden razor blade, a small golden double spoon, measured to fit each nostril, and a phial of fine white powder. Alongside were two balloons of heroin, several marijuana cigarettes, and a spidery gold roach holder shaped like a pitchfork.

"Varied tastes," Fairfield said succinctly.

David looked at the collection. The mirror had dozens of small scratches. He picked up the razor blade. It had an inset edge.

"Diamond edges," said Fairfield. "The finest of the fine cutter for cocaine. But this is just the beginning."

He took him to the closet. Silk robes, smoking jackets, short Chinese coats and silk pajamas were carefully hung. Fairfield pushed them aside. Behind them was a panel.

"It took McBane, our lawyer, about fifteen hours and a slight heart attack to discover where this key belonged," he said quietly. "But it was necessary to show it and some papers to you before they are disposed of."

He turned a key in the lock. A panel opened with a

light flashing on it. Hanging in rows were various chains, whips, manacles, and a pair of gold handcuffs. Set in the middle of the display was a shelf. And fitted in it, in a jar of alcohol, was a woman's finger.

"And here," said Fairfield, closing the door, the sight an abomination, "is more to be considered before the estate is closed down. God knows what would have happened if any of this got in the papers."

He went to a desk, unlocked a secret compartment, and pulled out a folder.

"These," he said "are all payoffs for little tricks he did with different girls. Several hospital bills. But the weirdest of all is here."

He took out a paper.

"It's a release from a girl who worked the El Coyote Ranch outside Las Vegas. She let him off without a cent, with a signed paper that he'd get her a job at Titan studio. In return for what he did to that finger."

David took the paper. It seemed to burn his hand as he stared at it.

Fairfield's voice broke through the shield of shock that engulfed him. "Who is it?" he asked. "You must know."

"Skip it," said David.

He folded the paper and put it in his pocket.

Fairfield didn't question his terseness. What a startling revelation. He, himself, was horrified. Thank God David Austin was in command. It helped to take the pressure off.

As Fairfield took him through the rest of the apartment, David hardly saw anything. Sickened, he kept thinking of Laura, of her aloofness, of the withdrawal that came over her. And now he knew. He thought of her fine, delicate body, her honest gaze, her neat appearance, and all that he had admired in her, seemingly of one piece, one driving, ambitious, meticulous person.

As he went through the papers and he and Fairfield reviewed and removed the proof of his great-uncle's wretched life, David was struck with a depression he had hardly ever known, even in the vortex of his own loneliness.

The ramifications of the human condition, the drive that sometimes swept people away from their potential path of sanity and growth, overwhelmed him.

In a few hours, Abe Moses, who had started life as an impoverished son of an illiterate immigrant, and who had ridden on the success of his brother and that first nickelodeon, the Little Diamond, to a fortune, was buried in pomp and circumstance.

Wealth cleansed him of his perversity. His obituary read like a great American success story: his directorships, his charities, the nature of his will—leaving money to a home for unwed mothers, his collection of fine art to a museum, hundreds of thousands to Jewish, Catholic, and Protestant homes for wayward boys. Generous, varied in thought, embracing a world of less-fortunate beings . . . How good, how generous, how perceptive Abraham Moses was of the unfortunates of the world, said the press.

David was revolted. The old bastard was making a name for himself in death to atone for the evil he had done all his life; he was copping out.

It damned well was not atonement; it was the last status symbol.

With Abe finally laid to rest, and his personal objects up for sale (with the exclusion of those private hobbies that had been conveniently jettisoned), the fortune would be immense. David washed his hands of the experience.

Even Fergus, with all his petty intrigues and his battle for power to keep the studio functioning, didn't have a clue of the depths of Abe's depravity. It had certainly been one of the best-kept secrets David had ever known. Yet it had pervaded the inner reaches of his own life, for he had cared for this woman, Laura. He had wanted to know her, to be with her. He had thought of her as a potential part of his life.

Why did I allow only two women to stir me? Jessica, Fergus's mistress, and Laura, obviously a sadist's hired playmate. Was it because I didn't know them, because they had a facade, a fascination that didn't reveal what they really were? Do I unconsciously seek disaster, punishment, because I have so much wealth I did not earn?

Why did my poor crazed mother allow herself to get involved with Jeffrey Barstow, and to have me as the result of that passion? She could never have been a wanton woman. That drive must have been strong to cause her to risk her whole life for a few moments of love.

Why did poor little Belinda allow herself to be involved with an aged and dying Greek tycoon, and to have a child just when her career was beginning?

He thought of all the plane trips and hotel rooms and meetings and casual relationships he had endured during his life after he discovered the basis of Fergus's hatred for him.

He tried to relate his own loneliness to that of Abe. Abe had been overshadowed by his brother Simon; he was a secondary figure, riding on the skirts of a brother's success and wealth.

Simon had been handsome, Simon had owned the vast Titan studio, complex, and theater chain. Simon had his prime star, Claudia, beautiful and vivacious, as a mistress, and Rebecca, his wife, a steadfast and loving woman.

Abe must have been twisted and torn by living in the shadow of an unlettered man, when he himself had become a lawyer and still remained in the background. Jealousy must have twisted at his gut, and he had escaped in fantasy, a hatred of women and society, revolt against the establishment that had made him rich.

But Laura, Laura, what was she? What did she want? Was her life an escape, or just a living out of reality over which she had no control. How young she must have been when she stepped over the line into prostitution.

Men like Abe, glutted with money and power, could buy her. Her clothes, her car, he thought bitterly, were proof of her past life. But she had asked to be released—she could have shaken Abe down for a fortune. Yet, she had not. He knew as well as anyone how diligently she worked at her job.

Had all these people been victimized by the false importance that the motion-picture business had given them?

Abe, by being able to buy any perversion he wished. David himself, pursued—to the point of rejecting everyone —because he was heir apparent to a vast picture empire. Belinda, by being a superstar almost before she was out of bobby socks. Esther, a simple, pretty young woman who might have been a happy housewife, put into the position of being the golden heiress of a cinema empire, and thought of, even by a prince of beauty and talent such as Jeffrey was in his heyday, as an intriguing focal point for his famous sexuality.

They had all been blown up into symbols of greater attraction and mystique than they really deserved because they were connected with the greatest publicized mover of emotions the world had ever known, outside of religion —the many-templed kingdom of motion pictures.

He thought of his mother at Las Cruces Sanatorium. He wished he could look beyond that lineless, beautiful face and probe her mind to discover the secret of the lost love she lived with and to know what sustained her mindless happiness.

He wished he could know what sort of person Laura really was. If she was living a life of atonement, closed in, unable to face a personal life, or if she was just an immoral wanderer looking for a cover.

He would like to know whether Belinda was happy in her marriage, or if she had chosen her own symbol of security and prestige to help her get away from the sex-goddess image that had been thrust on her.

Fergus came to New York for the funeral, being one of the pallbearers. It was a ceremonial event, replete with dark suits, studied long faces, and lack of emotion.

Everyone already was asking themselves who was going to be the new chairman of the board? Certainly one of the pallbearers. How solid was the theater chain since its divorcement from Titan studio? Was real estate going to be the greatest asset of the giant company?

Abe Moses would be put to rest next to his brother in a cemetery in Hollywood, scattered with graves of stars, directors, and producers, alongside a street that once had been a lane of pepper trees and barn studios where the Moses brothers had their beginnings. No one really cared where Abe Moses's brittle bones were laid to rest. The main question was, who was going to get whose job in the imminent corporate shuffle?

Fergus flew back to California with David, who could not refrain from studying the man he had thought so long was his father.

As usual, Fergus chain-smoked. David wondered how he could drink his double scotches and not have an ulcer attack, he was so nervous. But he laid it to his Irish ancestry. He'd always heard that Fergus's father was a barfly, and he knew his grandmother Mary Francis had carried the whole boardinghouse, where they had lived in the Bronx, on her shoulders. How often David had listened to the endless story about the prowess and success of Fergus against great odds—the eternal justification of a life, and the desire for approbation, of a man who had carved his own way.

True, Fergus was a scrapper and a fighter, and he was helping Titan immensely by bringing the Ralston fortune into the production schedule.

"You don't know," said Fergus, looking down at the Kansas plains far below, "what whoredom is until you work for Martha Ralston. She gets harebrained ideas any time of the day or night and calls me. Her preproduction extravagances are insane. The fact sheet on our first production would cause a congressional investigation if she didn't have the purse strings herself. She's given away points and half a million for the best seller, *Blitz*. And shelved the other I was sweating out. There's no board to take a vote on her expenditures. And she's so goddamn lonesome that I have found myself, imagine, me, putting on my black tie and escorting her to ceremonial dinners, listening to all that bullshit about how wonderful it is for films to have her back."

David couldn't help smiling. "I hear she jettisoned Belinda's dressing room," he said. "How could you let her do that?"

"Well, the kid wasn't working. Have you heard rumors that Scott's found a property!"

David nodded. He certainly had. He'd been the mastermind behind the scenes.

"Yes," said David, "and that's going to be interesting. He bought *The Promise*, Vernon Miles's screenplay. Remember how mad that guy was for Belinda and how he picketed her dressing room saying she was unfair to young writers? But it's a great role for Belinda. It's the story of a child whose mother was the sweetheart of a GI during World War II. The girl is brought in as the heiress to the man's fortune, the GI having become a man of importance. The girl has to earn her father's love against great odds. It's a tender story. She'll be great as a little cockney girl who steps into wealth and social position. Different for her. I think she can handle it very well."

David did not mention the fact that he was one of the prime investors. Under the umbrella of a varied-interest investing corporation, he had put up a million dollars. He had convinced himself that he was not doing it because he wanted Belinda's career and life to flourish, but because he believed it was a good investment. Of course, Scott did not know it. He and the young man had literally circled each other like fighting cocks, appraising and conjecturing. He knew Scott was jealous of him, undoubtedly noticing the affection he and Belinda had for each other. And of course Scott could not quite fathom it. And David's instincts realized the coldness of Scott. He was sparring with something—not David's idea of a contented husband.

When David arrived at the studio the next day, he could see how much it cried for attention. Fergus was immersed in the private vagaries of Martha Ralston. It was obvious that she didn't care whether her picture made money or not, she simply wanted to be the darling of the world again, the tootsie pie of fate, with important men panting after her. Fame was her narcotic, and she craved it with an insatiable appetite and a pocketbook to match.

Fergus confided to David that he was a lucky s.o.b. to have been needed enough to ask for and to get a percentage of the gross of the picture that was about to go into production. A percentage of the net, with her expenses, wasn't worth a farthing.

Sets had to be refurbished for Belinda's picture, *The Promise*. The London street was put in order. It was on the back lot, adjacent to the African river where David had planned to have a rendezvous with Laura. He bypassed the little jungle footpath, not wanting to see it. As he visited the set, seeing it given the character of the old part of postwar London that he remembered so well, he admired the expertise of the men who made the whole thing seem so authentic, down to the last barrow, daffodil stand, and stall of the vendor of jellied eels.

Leslie Charles was cast as the father of the man who was Belinda's father in the picture. Arthur Adams, a handsome, fortyish man who had the good fortune to resemble Cary Grant and was a new television star, of all things, won the plum role.

Strange, thought David, how time moves. A short time ago Leslie would have played the father. Now he was identified with a grandfather. He had just come back from a sortie in Switzerland with a new face-lift. His face had been ironed out so much that in spite of looking younger he looked more stupid. But he still rolled on as a substantial Academy Award winner.

While the preproduction was being arranged, the family unit that had circled around Claudia was changing. She had found a pleasant house with a pool, wide verandas, flowering hedges of white oleander, and rooms that would be comfortable for herself and Max, and for Belinda and Scott and Alex and Effie when they came to visit.

"It's white wickerish and green, on one of the prettiest streets in Palm Springs, called Buena Vista—" she said to Belinda, pausing as she helped pack some of Alex's clothes at the beach house.

Already the nursery looked vandalized.

"These new renters have two children," Claudia continued. "New-rich oil people from Texas. I guess they'll enjoy it when they aren't counting their money. And the kids will like the beach."

She took several pictures off the wall.

"We'll all be back one day," she said cheerfully. "Max is packing all the material he needs, and we've kept a room over the garage for files and my personal treasures. It'll be just great."

Smiling a very crooked smile, she glanced at Belinda, and her eyes brimmed with tears. She sat down, pushing the pile of Alex's clothes aside.

"Oh, shit, Belinda, why do we pretend!" She put her hands to her face. "You know why we're going. Everything changes. Max is taking forever doodling on the script, and you're starting off, really by yourself, and I know what a long haul that is. Why isn't Scott with you more during these family changes? Does he really have to be at the office and in meetings so much?" She took a Kleenex and wiped her eyes. "Sorry," she said. "I guess I'm just tired."

She looked up, managing a smile, and then saw that Belinda's hands were clenched, her eyes filled with tears.

"Oh," said Claudia, "I'm sorry. I didn't mean to do this to you, darling. I'm glad you're taking Alex with you, as much as I'll miss him. But we'll see each other often."

Atlas, the little Yorkshire, sensing distress, pawed at

Claudia's foot. These days he was just a feathery little postscript, following Alex, Claudia, or Effie, whatever the focus of his immediate attention was at the moment.

Belinda came to Claudia, knelt on the floor, and put her head in Claudia's lap. As she sobbed, Claudia stroked her hair and reached for a tissue.

"There, there," she said, "get it off your chest. What's wrong?"

Belinda lifted her head, no longer a young girl going through her first adult passions. She was a woman. She took the Kleenex, wiped her eyes, blew her nose, and pulled her damp hair away from her cheeks.

"I wasn't going to tell you," she said, "but I have to. Scott and I aren't lovers. We're not even friends. We're living a lie. It's all a phony setup until we get my career going."

"Oh, God," said Claudia. "I was afraid of it when I saw you together. There wasn't that—" She waved her hands expressively, not finding the words. "Not that—that living thing that is between two people who share the same bed."

Belinda told her about the wedding night.

Claudia stood up angrily. "I could wring his stupid neck," she said. "Doesn't he have any humanity? Couldn't he know it wasn't exactly your fault? You were a victim, darling, and you mustn't let him victimize you again."

"I won't," said Belinda. "I made up my mind there in the mountains that I wasn't going to let anyone do that to me again."

"Good luck," said Claudia, making a face, "until you fall in love again. Then you'll be thrilled to be a patsy."

"That's the trouble," said Belinda. "I am in love with Scott, and I'm going to make him love me again."

"He doesn't deserve it," said Claudia. "Maybe you just think so because he rejected you."

"Oh no," said Belinda. "Would you believe it, I just had a big session with Kevin? I could have had him and all the sex I wanted under my own terms. And guess what—" She laughed. "I turned him down to go back to my empty bed."

She picked up Alex's clothes and put them in a box. "Anyway, I have Alex, and I know where I'm going in my work. I guess we're born alone and we die alone, and what we do with ourselves—all by ourselves—in between is what matters."

"Bravo," said Claudia. "Please excuse my silly tears. You don't deserve them."

They embraced each other.

Belinda wondered how Claudia would face Scott next time she saw him.

And Claudia thought, someday, somehow, I'm going to talk to that egotistical young man about what a woman is all about. I hope he will be able to understand.

Belinda would never have dreamed that her favorite room in the house would be the library. The bedroom had been accepted as a place of defeat, the tempting never-never land that was not entered by the conquering soldier.

Friends visited, wined, dined, made small chat, and admired the elegant wedding gifts. Effie ran the house, turned out splendid meals, and her cousin Louise, a cateress, came in to add elegance to evenings. It was all well ordered and too easy.

There were parties at clubs and private homes, and both Belinda and Scott were so lionized by friends that they did not need to pretend a togetherness.

She adjusted to the routine of having Alex with her. He was busy with Effie and seemingly countless appointments, prenursery school, and visits to play with other children.

But she found that the ultimate facing of herself occurred in the library when Scott was at the office and time belonged to her.

First there was the scrapbook Jeffrey had kept of her first six years. There were the little celebrations and galas, all remembered by him. She discovered that he was much more sentimental than the world had ever realized. And he had kept a meticulous record of her birth and early years. In the pages were imprisoned the dreams and beauties of her young life and her father's joy in celebrating her. The sudden disruption of the story was as poignant as the telling of it. She knew she had not been cherished and loved by her mother; and sketchy memories kept by Effie and a few snaps of her on the beach and at children's parties were all that remained of her young childhood. She had forgotten most, but flashes of memory both warmed her and brought her close to tears.

There was a large gap between those childhood days and the sudden emergence of the chrysalis as a film personality.

Looking at the motion-picture production scrapbook Claudia had kept for *The Oracle*, Belinda saw how naïve that young person had been, a little girl in makeup playing a charade.

One day, Belinda realized that she had always wanted to prove herself instead of simply being herself. It was time to stop seeing only her own image, time to relate to the world around her.

She began to analyze the behavior of people around her, and patterns came into view.

She foresaw the time that even beloved Effie would have to be stopped from cosseting Alex. He was not being allowed to do as much as he should on his own. His small willfulness amused her. As she walked with him in the park near the Beverly Hills Hotel sometimes she felt that he wanted to wander on his own, to examine the ant, study the plant, or just observe the other children at play. His little half smile and his quizzical brow were already indications of his own special personality; he was becoming a little boy.

Belinda felt inadequate. She would have to look at the world herself so she could share it with him. And thinking of what her father had done for her, she expanded her life and his, showed him the wonders of a shell, let him listen to the sea with it cupped to his ear. As she had played with the little piece of amber with the tiny isoptera imprisoned in it, he, too, took the little globule and began to study the small world. She remembered how much she had cherished the earning of it, being on her own, and she thought that someday she would hand it on to him and tell him how his great grandfather had done so to Jeffrey.

For the first time she realized that here was another generation, that one day she would be the elder, and he would come to her with his problems, and, please God, she would be wise enough to help him as Claudia had helped her.

Claudia was ensconced in Palm Springs, settling the

house, looking after Max, and adjusting to being away from Belinda and Alex.

She was cheerful on the phone. As soon as the picture was lined up, she'd come into town. She had a nice Mexican woman housekeeper who could cook well enough to look after Max when the time came to do her dialogue work. Belinda wasn't to worry.

There was joy in Claudia's voice when she heard about the little sorties Belinda and Alex had had together in the big world. And she delicately refrained from asking about Scott.

As time went on, Belinda realized that Scott was testing her. Every man she had ever mentioned, or who had ever been linked with her in fan magazines or gossip was brought into her orbit, as if Scott were trying to see where her weakness lay, and if any of these men were involved with her.

Si Merkle, the young man who had worked his way up to be one of the top men in the Star Lists Agency, was signed by Scott to be in charge of production of the Belinda Corporation. She saw him in many of the business conferences that were held outside Scott's law offices. He was in and out of the house by invitation, using Scott's study, working on the complicated maze of bank loans, budgets, potential exploitation, releasing deals, contracts, studio space, and assemblage of cast and crew.

It astounded Belinda to discover that the daily production requirements, once under way, would include over sixty people on the set, all at high salaries.

Merkle was a good man, she was glad he was with them, but she saw the shadow of a frown on Scott's face as she enthused with him over production planning.

This was just the beginning. Homer Case, the choreographer who had once written poetry to her, was brought in by Scott as the right man to do her dance sequence in the script for the coming-out party her father gives her in New York.

Hugh Fairfield, who had taken her out several times, was invited to the house when he came west to settle Abe Moses's estate. She heard Scott ask Fairfield if he'd like to join the company, since there were such great changes in the theater corporation in New York. Several times when Scott was busy he asked Fairfield to take her to the theater or a private showing at the Academy. Hugh was a nice man and a solid, boring companion.

Her suspicions were almost completely verified when Scott suggested that Kevin Frazier do portraits of her both as the little cockney waif and the successful New York debutante.

"Why not?" she said. "He's the best. . . . But of course maybe he's too busy with Martha Ralston."

She walked away, pretending a chore in the kitchen, leaving him staring at her.

Oh, she thought, if that big dumb guy only knew the scene we had in that projection room, I wonder what he would think . . .

Poor Kevin, she found herself thinking, he's always trying to prove himself the great renegade lover because he's scared. He knows he can't sustain love.

Then she smiled to herself. Well, she was over Kevin. Completely.

But when Scott suggested using Tony Valli in the new picture, she was ready to turn on him in rage—until the thought struck her that, if she were explosive, he might think that there had been a lovers' quarrel.

"Forget him," she said casually. "I just don't care for his acting."

It annoyed her to have to consider her reactions before she uttered a word, or to feel she was being tested when it came to any random discussion.

Then he mentioned John Graves. My, he really has gone back into ancient history, she thought angrily. But she put on a pleasant face.

"I think John Graves is the best actor I've ever known," she said, "but he's a big star and we really couldn't afford him now. Someday it would be great to work with him again. Let's look for a proper vehicle."

She watched Scott when he wasn't noticing. This bit of conversation disturbed him, and it amused her. Let him wriggle about on the horns of his own dilemma. It served him right!

Scott sealed her annoyance by suggesting that Tex Arthur, the cowboy who had once had such a crush on her, be called back from Italy to play the unsuccessful Texas suitor in the picture.

"After all," said Scott, "he has a great following in Europe. He's a big drawing card there and would be an interesting counterpoint to our American actors known so well here."

"As you wish," said Belinda, thinking that he must have dug into some silly fan magazines to bring up the false ghost of that relationship. All poor Tex had ever done was to be exiled by the studio for being fresh with her. Trick of fate; it had made his career.

She decided to test her theory. There was a new young man at the studio who had been brought in from Broadway. As the shooting date neared and she came to the studio to have some fittings with Janos, she noticed him. He had red hair, blazing blue eyes, a slightly uptilted nose, and an Irish grin, and he was undoubtedly going to be a comer. She watched him from several tables away in the commissary at lunch and heard him talking enthusiastically and loudly to an interviewer about the current Broadway season.

Then she dropped by Red Powell's rumor factory.

"I just noticed that new import from Broadway, Barry Norton," she said sweetly. "I think that guy has a real career coming up. I'll buy his lunch any day. It's good to hear someone talk about theater instead of TV ratings. You can say I said so, if it'll help him."

"Good," said Red. "He's up for a part with Martha Ralston."

"Well," said Belinda, "I'll get him in my picture first if I can."

She walked away, knowing that Red would get a good item out of it. Already he was relishing building a feud between two stars—that kind of excitement hadn't gone on since the days of Gloria Swanson and Pola Negri.

Sure enough, several days later in Hank Grant's column, the item ran: *"What two stars at Titan studio are having a secret feud about who gets Barry Norton for their upcoming film? It seems the redheaded male bombshell from New York has won the attention of two of the most important ladies in Hollywood."*

The next day at breakfast, Scott brought it up.

"You know," he said, "maybe that Barry Norton would be good for the young socialite who tries to run away with you in our picture . . . play him like one of the Philadelphia Kellys, a real Irish charmer."

Belinda looked at him and said nothing.

"Well," he said, "what do you think?"

"I'll tell you what I think, Scott," she said angrily as she deliberately poured his coffee cup too full, so he would have to lift it with a steady hand to keep from spilling it.

"I think you should stop trying to entrap me. I set up this red herring with Barry Norton to see if my suspicions were true. You're trying to throw in my way every man you think I might be interested in, to see if I live up to the reputation you've made up in your head about me. I'm alerting you right now. It won't work. When I love, I love. When I don't, nothing could get me into an affair. I will never get into someone's bed to get even with you. So lay off, and concentrate on making a good picture. As a matter of fact, I think Barry Norton is a loudmouth. Who needs him! Let Martha Ralston take that trip."

She left the table and went up to Alex's nursery.

"Come on, old boy," she said, "you and Effie and I are going to Uncle Bernie's toy store. Christmas is a-comin'."

She heard Scott's car as he raced out of the driveway. He was upset, and he deserved to be.

After the jaunt with Alex she went into the library, closed the doors, and looked up at the portrait of her father. He seemed to be glancing sidelong at her, with the wit and joy of his eyes teasing her.

"All right," she said, "I'm not as clever as you were, daddy, but give me time."

She wondered if Alex would ever look so sophisticated. And she thought of David. If he had more humor, more joy of life, he'd look a great deal more like this man.

She took out her script and studied it, remembering apocryphal tales of how Jeffrey Barstow had dissected scripts and made them come to life.

Thinking of all the things Claudia had told her, Belinda prepared for the first scene. She had grown her hair for the role. It had been decided that she would play the London waif with long, unkempt hair. When she became the petted New York heiress, her hair would be trimmed in a fashionable style.

She was glad Claudia was coming in to help her with

the cockney dialect. It would be fun. She could imagine the two of them—working on the exact opposite of the diction she had learned so painstakingly in Rome. Claudia had said, "All you California kids talk like Irishmen, now let's get some Bond Street in your voice."

Now Claudia would teach her the sound of the people of London who were reared within the sound of Bow Bells, those wonderful costers she had heard about, the pearly kings and queens who came in their pearl buttons, sewed by the hundreds on antique garments, nodding their white ostrich-plumed bonnets, to have tea with the Mayor of London once a year from the Church of Saint Martin In the Field—filling Trafalgar Square with their gaudy, proud procession at their October festival. This splendid raggle-taggle parade, with herself as a sort of latter-day Eliza Doolittle, would be the most spectacular scene in the movie.

She found herself feeling very much kin to her Barstow ancestors of the British stage; she was enjoying the creation of a role, hoping to find the fey enchantment of the character; discovering the worth of Vernon Miles's comedy. Comedy was the great humanizer, she realized, the peccadilloes of human beings laid bare. The wellspring of laughter was characterization in counterpoint to another person's view.

She felt an empathy with the character of Hester Watts. She thrilled bringing the imaginative projection of her own consciousness into the ramifications of another being. She wanted to be Hester, the little waif who was so satisfied with her own little bits-and-pieces shop in Petticoat Lane that she resented being asked to go to New York. Belinda could imagine Hester with her street life, happy and carefree, belonging to a society of feckless charms.

Before Belinda knew it, the short November day had turned to evening. Effie lit the fire and, after a few moments, returned with a tray. She shook her head, smiling. "You're just like your daddy," she said. "You've got that same absentminded happy look on your face. Where *are* you, honey?"

"I'm in Petticoat Lane in London," said Belinda.

"That's nice," she said and left without another word. Alex was already asleep, and she didn't bother to tell

Belinda that Scott had phoned and said he wouldn't be home for dinner. That seemed usual in their house.

Several hours later, Belinda closed her script and went to her room. Soaking in a hot tub, she wondered what her own life would have been like had she been born near the sound of Bow Bells. London came alive to her as she peopled Hester's life with imaginary friends.

Unthinking, she latched her door and went to bed. She was weary, yet happily so, and she slept soundly.

In the middle of the night, she heard a pounding on the door.

She sat up sleepily. "What is it?"

"It's Scott," he said. "I want to talk to you."

She shook her head, awakening. She could tell by the overprecise diction that Scott had been drinking. He got very Harvard instead of California when he had been imbibing.

"Not now, it's late."

"But I want to talk to you."

"It'll wait till tomorrow," she said. "I'm half asleep. Good night."

She knew he was standing there deciding what to do. If he broke open the door and came into her room, if he took her again, another scene of rapine, she couldn't bear it. She would have to leave this house. She could not go on with this dreadful situation.

She drew in her breath, frightened.

She heard his hand as he ran it along the panel of the door. Oh, God, please don't let him try it again.

Then she heard a sigh.

"Belinda," he whispered, "I love you."

The agony and the loneliness in his voice seemed to seep into the room. Suddenly she wanted him to come in. She wanted to take him in her arms and tell him that it wasn't too late.

She heard him walk away, and she waited for the sound of the running water as he prepared for bed. For a moment, she considered going to him.

No, she couldn't go to him like this. He had been drinking heavily; she couldn't take him in her arms under these conditions. He would have to take a stand. He would have to communicate with her first, or she would still see that searching in his eyes, that unspoken question about what her life had been before she met him. If he wanted her now he would have to be a man, not a suspicious, frightened boy looking for his manhood in the arms of what he thought was the world's most enticing sex object.

She realized that they both had been wrong. If it ever could be possible for them to mend the breach, he must learn to think of her as his woman, not as a film star. And she must learn to know him as her man, not as the most handsome, eligible bachelor in Los Angeles. Both of them had married symbols instead of people.

She looked out her window. The lights cast by his bedside lamp on the garden shrubs suddenly went out, and she knew he had gone to bed.

She sat up, annoyed at the fact that because of his drinking he would probably fall right off to sleep. Now that he had disturbed her, she was wide-awake.

Damn it, she thought, why did he have to say he loved me? I want him, and I know that his silly pride is keeping him from me. What can I do?

She knew he was making every effort to get her career started again. Only last month he had suggested that she defer her salary to take the risk for large ownership in their first picture. Her salary, if she were on loan-out to another company, would have been $750,000—a sum that seemed incredible to her.

"We go for broke," he had said. "No salary. But you take 10 percent of the gross of every facet."

"What does that mean?" she asked.

"That means," he said, "theatrical rights, television, American and European rights, the whole spectrum."

"Oh," she said, "Scott—are you sure?"

"Belinda, you are a star. And you are going to trust me. I'll do the right thing about your talent."

He had turned away. And then he had amended his statement.

"At least," he had said.

She finally fell asleep, longing for him. When she awoke, he was gone.

She looked forward to a busy day at the studio. By her side was her invisible sister, a little cockney girl named Hester Watts who was getting ready to step into her shoes.

472

Palm Springs was at its best in December, so it was a good place for Belinda to celebrate her birthday. She wanted to avoid any festivity Scott would have to give her, the false gaiety in her own house when she knew it was no home in reality.

It was decided that Belinda and Scott, Alex, Effie, and the dog, Atlas, would spend the weekend visiting Claudia and Max.

Belinda suggested that she and Scott stay at the Racquet Club, leaving Claudia and Max the chance to be with the baby and enjoy themselves without a mob scene on their hands.

Claudia knew the real reason; there was no possibility of the two sharing a room. Of course, Scott didn't know that Claudia understood the truth.

And so, after a festive evening, Effie having cooked Belinda's favorite "little girl" meal—avocado and grape-fruit salad, roast chicken, whipped mashed potatoes, and an eggplant and mushroom casserole, topped by a double fudge birthday cake, they all sat in the garden by the pool.

"It was an orgy!" said Belinda, "but I loved it. My last bash before the picture."

While Effie busied herself putting Alex to bed, they turned out the lights and gazed at the black velvet skies and the glittering desert stars.

After a while, Max went back to his work, saying that nights like this always turned on his imagination, and he had to jot down a few lines before they got lost in the stars. He kissed Claudia and Belinda, shook hands warmly with Scott, and retired. Thank God Claudia didn't tell him about Scott and me, thought Belinda.

Effie called Belinda. Alex wanted to kiss her good-night. He had been practicing a week to wish her a happy birth-day. He'd done it three times already, and he wanted one more chance before his day was ended.

Claudia sat relishing the stillness, finding the crisp air pleasant after the sunstruck day.

She glanced over at Scott. It was not difficult for her to realize that he had lowered a veil with her. Obviously he did not like her. And she knew why. He blamed her for allowing Belinda to marry him without telling him about Alex.

She tried to bridge the gap.

"Scott, Belinda has a wonderful grasp on the character of Hester. I think it will be a great role for her. I also think it was very courageous of you to take the risk on her salary, and to defer her interest. I'm glad you trust her talent."

"Yes," he said, "my partners think it's a brash move in our corporate beginning. But I think it's a good idea."

His voice was cool. He stopped to light a cigarette and glanced up at her.

"It may be difficult for Belinda to realize that we're not making a superproduction. She's been surrounded with endless luxury during her two big pictures. Two and a half million dollars may seem like a large sum, but, as you know, it's the least possible budget for a first-class film, which this has to be or our corporation will fold. We will have to make seven and a half million to break even. The interest on our loans is enough to make your head swim. I hope she can adjust to the reality of it."

Claudia snubbed out her cigarette, angered at this newcomer's businesslike tone. She could teach him in spades. And why couldn't he give Belinda one kind word—at least compliment her talent?

"Look, Scott, I know all this," she said. "Perhaps it's just as well that creative people are not always subsidized. Maybe it's wrong for people like Belinda, and myself—when I was young—to sit under the comfortable umbrella of a corporation. Stardom with complete protection can make us feel bigger than life.

"Money can't buy everything, only more luxurious creature comforts, it certainly doesn't give us peace of mind. We have to seek our own destinies and fulfill our own talents. I took a risk a long time ago; hocked everything I owned to make a picture in England. The challenge was plasma for me. It gave me my life."

"I don't think Belinda need worry," said Scott. "She can pretty well pick and choose. Stardom has been easy for her."

Claudia was so irritated she jumped up and walked to the pool, glancing at the reflection of the stars. Then she turned to him angrily.

"Easy!" she cried. "It's never easy. What kind of man are you, Scott? You've been punishing my niece with your goddamned warped sense of morality ever since you learned about Alex!"

He half arose. She came up to him and in her wrath seemed to tower over him, as petite as she was.

She pushed him back into the chair.

"Damn it, sit down and listen to me," she said, her voice shaking. "It's time for you to stop thinking about yourself and get some perspective. I admit we were wrong not to tell you the truth, but it was an omission of love. If you don't recognize that Belinda is special and incredibly talented, then you don't deserve to even know her."

Scott stared up at her. He opened his mouth to speak.

"Just shut up and listen," said Claudia, "instead of smothering it all inside and creeping back to that suite at the Racquet Club where you cheat both yourself and Belinda by sleeping in separate rooms. You have to hear me."

She took his arm to emphasize her point.

"Belinda loves you. Yes, she was involved with a relationship that had tragic circumstances. But listen. That incredible thousands and thousands to one chance brought Alex to us.

"Belinda was too young, too afraid not to belong to the big world we thrust her into. We never allowed her to grow up. The adoration of this man, Niadas, who looked upon her as a goddess, gave her a dignity she needed desperately.

"What a fuss you are making about the most sought-after of human events—seeking, touching, reaching for the ultimate—the yearning to belong and be part of the human experience, away from the constant loneliness of humankind."

Claudia continued, her voice deep with emotion, spilling out her distress.

"Certainly we would have stopped that emotional and physical explosion if we had known about it. But after Niadas died, that poor, frightened kid didn't tell us for months. She carried the whole pregnancy with dignity and courage.

"Don't deny the living grace of Alex. Forgive the act; bless him as a perfect step forward in destiny. See the marvelous result, a human being born of a great man and a beautiful young girl. A step in our incarnate progression."

"That sounds great," said Scott, "but it's hard to live with under the circumstances."

"You're just too bullheaded to listen," said Claudia. "It's your ego—your injured feelings. I don't know what you're trying to prove. That you're first? Was she first with you? Would you forgive her more if she hadn't conceived?"

"You've made a good case for her youthful naïveté—but it's not only Niadas," said Scott. "What about that Kevin Frazier? I was the solution to her blighted romance, wasn't I?"

Claudia was about to tell him how Belinda had recently rejected Kevin, when the sliding doors opened and Belinda joined them.

"Not a word about this," said Claudia under her breath. "I'll talk to you later." She had promised Belinda she wouldn't say anything, but she had felt forced to break her word.

As soon as she could, she would tell him how Belinda had dismissed Kevin, even in her loneliness and rejection as a woman.

"Well," said Claudia brightly to Belinda, "we've been saying how soon we'll all be plunging into the picture."

"Right," said Belinda, "and that's the last of Effie's cake. Tomorrow I'll be starting training to be an undernourished little cockney." She kissed her aunt. "With your help."

Scott looked at his watch. "It's time to go," he said. "We'll be fighting the traffic back to the city in the morning."

"All right," said Claudia, "I'll come in tomorrow and bring Alex and Effie with me."

The Yorkshire, Atlas, jumped up on her lap.

"And Atlas, too," she said. "I guess during this picture he'll stay in the nursery instead of being on the set."

"Maybe," said Belinda, "but he's my good luck token." She picked him up and petted him.

They said their farewells and returned to the Racquet Club.

Scott seemed even more introspective than usual, but Belinda didn't question him.

With a sad heart she prepared for bed. She could hear him in the other room. Both of them turned out the lights, separated by six inches of wall and a lifetime of emotional barriers.

31

Nothing is more depressing than a sanatorium around Christmastime. Those patients who could still relate to the world thought about other times, other places, and other faces, while the imitation trees on dresser tables whispered a sad, small refrain of past family festivities.

Those who could not remember stared like children at the decorations that had been left as halfhearted penances by some relative, friend, or nurse. The vacant stares at the reflection of red and green tinsel against light, or fake cellophane fir, seemed a denial of the true celebration of a Christmas tree.

Sometimes palsied hands fumbled with gifts, and busy relatives and friends, irritated at the waste of time, finished opening packages. The usual fuzzy bed jackets and long-sleeved nightgowns, or washable robes and sensible pajamas bespoke the unfortunate reality that there was little to be given or used in what was left of life.

The richer the patients, the more concerned the nurses were about the room decoration. For they knew that their image of tender and loving care would pay off in bountiful presents, guilt payments for the fact that the dear one had been shunted off into paid care to await the day when a sigh of relief would signal the end of the fading trail.

In the case of Esther Moses, there was an exception. She was the best-natured patient in Las Cruces, and by a strange quirk of fate she had kept an incandescent beauty. Among the dour, lost souls in her wing of the home, she had the unique characteristics of a sunny disposition, a smile, and an eagerness to greet each day.

The fact that her conversation was rare and inchoate did not bother the nurses. She was their baby doll, to be

477

fussed over, to have her hair curled and ribboned, to be dressed in a large selection of expensive gowns and negligees. They could enjoy any program on her expensive television set or play music on her record machine or look at the magazines that were ordered for her. She thought it was all fine.

Her husband, Fergus Austin, belonged to the type of visitor the nurses secretly called "the guilties." He visited as regularly as clockwork on Saturdays, brought things that had obviously been ordered by secretaries, and overtipped, which made every nurse in the sanatorium hope to be involved in Esther's care.

On the other hand, her handsome son, David Austin, was in and out, for he traveled a great deal. Sometimes his picture was in *Tattler*, the *Queen*, or *Town and Country*, and his studio activities were eagerly read in the newspapers.

But his quiet affection for his mother and her reaction to him were unique among the inhabitants of this particular slice of unwanted life.

Whenever Esther saw him, her face lighted up. She abandoned her dreams and came back to earth. Her thin transparent hands lifted up almost in prayer, and her face was illuminated.

"She looks like a madonna," whispered one nurse, watching them.

When David came to see Esther the morning of Christmas Eve, he immediately asked for privacy. The staff agreed, being deeply impressed by him and the nature of his gifts, for he was generous in thought as well as practicality when it came to his mother.

This morning was early for his visit, but he had to go over to Belinda's set—the company would break midafternoon. And, of course, his mother had no idea of time.

There was one reason he always saw Esther alone. And that had been a sinful secret which he had kept with her, especially during recent years.

She thought he was Jeffrey Barstow.

At first he had tried to dissuade her from this fantasy, but he realized it was impossible, so he went along with it.

Sometimes he was so shaken after leaving her that he had to sit in his car a few moments before he braved the freeway back to Hollywood. It was startling to be considered the father he had never really known. Often he thought his masquerade was as mad as she was, but seeing the joy in her face was not the only reason he allowed it.

He wondered if he would ever find the wellspring of her love, the reason, and the meaning that had brought him into this world. As much as he was comforting her, he was also seeking the secret of his own existence.

This day especially, he wanted to get some sign of the love that sustained her. He brought her pearl earrings, perfume, bath powder, a silk gown, and a white lace robe, everything he would have liked to shower on a woman who could look at him the way she did.

· Once the gifts had all been opened, he looked into her eyes and saw that she was alive, alert, out of her trauma.

"Oh, Jeffrey," she said. "It's a wonderful Christmas with you here!"

She bent her head and glanced up at him, sidelong, her eyes glistening with a look that hurt him, it was so intense.

"You know," she whispered, "the world began when I looked into your eyes, Jeffrey . . . How strange that we only loved once . . . But that was enough to last forever."

David felt he was listening to a secret he should not know. In his own desperate unhappiness, and his dilemma about Laura, he was seeking consolation and nourishment from an insane woman. It was wrong. It was immoral.

But his mother took his hand and clasped it with both of hers, bending to kiss it. He could not pull away; it would have been cruel.

She touched the white lace robe.

"You know," she whispered, "I wanted to wear white and be a virgin for you. Nothing that happened to me before mattered. It was a nightmare. But you gave me my dream—you got me with child . . ."

David started to rise. He couldn't bear it.

She suddenly panicked and pulled him back. Seeing the fear in her eyes, he sat by her bed again.

"Oh!" she cried. "Don't pull away from me—God is not angry with me. He is laughing because I got my wish —Oh, Jeffrey, let us go away and be joyous again."

Her face lighted up. "Remember how you read to me, 'Sweet is thy voice, and thy countenance is comely.'?"

She leaned back. Already the veils were beginning to lower. She closed her eyes.

" 'Thy countenance is comely . . .' "

She clasped his hand gently, and in a few moments she released it. She was asleep.

The white robe slid to the floor. He picked it up and laid it gently over her. Strangely, it did look like a white wedding dress. And she looked pure and virginal.

The lights on the little Christmas tree flickered. He looked at her peaceful face, and he felt like a little boy. He wanted to cry, and then he pulled himself short.

Cry—for what? She was the happiest woman he knew.

Crossing the Pasadena bridge, the stream of traffic against him like a moving necklace, all people going to join family Christmas celebrations, he thought of what she'd said.

"Nothing that happened to me before mattered . . ."

He increased his speed. The gloom that had been encompassing him lately seemed to be lifting. Life was a series of decisions, priorities. What came first to the heart and found a home was all that mattered.

Belinda had settled into a stoic frame of mind about her picture, *The Promise*. At first she had envied the splendor surrounding Martha Ralston's ascendancy as Titan's queen bee. She had watched the chauffeur-driven Silver Cloud enter the studio and had caught glimpses of the woman framed with a small crystal vase with a white orchid in it, always at her car window.

She had overheard a comment of one of the carpenters as she stood by the entrance to the commissary.

"With all her fine airs, that broad acts more and more like a little old lady from Pasadena. What's she trying to prove? We knew her when."

Belinda cherished the remark. It was doubly delightful to her that Fergus was involved with this unpopular personality, for Belinda was building up a case against him, thinking of what Kevin had told her about their being sabotaged. A man who did that was capable of any deceit.

The first businesslike gesture Belinda made as a corporate partner was to inform the wardrobe department that Peggy Rush was not to be her wardrobe woman. The second was to try to get Laura West on her picture handling publicity.

Her final decision, which not only made her a name around the studio, but garnered her more admiration than she could have had any other way, was to say that she wanted a trailer dressing room. As long as her family dressing room had been preempted and ripped apart, she wanted no part of any other. Wherever she located, a trailer would be her quarters, whether they were on the back lot or on a sound stage with indoor sets.

David had been irked at the way Fergus had taken over the Barstow dressing room, and he decided that Belinda was not going to be penalized. After all, her company was of value to Titan—with use of its laboratories, space rentals, and distribution bringing in a tidy sum.

Using the umbrella of her successful studio relationship, David decided to give her a personal gift, to start Belinda Productions off with a flair.

Glancing through *Holiday* magazine he saw an estate sale advertisement for a pleasure bus.

It had been custom-built for a Texas millionaire—with a powerful White motor, and a body by Pullman. In its thirty feet were contained an elegant sitting area with a small Franklin stove. David ordered a dressing room complete with makeup lights built into one of its two private sleeping compartments. It contained a bathroom with shower, a small galley, and a built-in sound system, telephones, and wardrobe closets. A mirrored wall was installed near the dining area, and orchid plants were set on the observation platform.

Memorabilia from the dressing rooms of Jeffrey and Claudia were stylishly assembled.

A portable awning and garden furnishings could be brought out of one of the property trucks to assemble an outdoor sitting area.

The vehicle was so stunning and unusual that it became a passionate point of interest to studio personnel who were rooting for Belinda to upstage Miss Moneybags Ralston. It was photographed for many magazines and referred to as Shangri-La on wheels.

Belinda embraced David when he showed it to her.

"I can't believe it," she said, staring in amazement. "David, I want to live in it the rest of my life."

"Hope you will," he said. "We can't let that silly bitch one-up us, can we?"

He stood for a moment, looking at the gold-framed pictures of Jeffrey.

Belinda was moved to tears. How much they looked alike.

He turned to her. "Well, here we are. Isn't it great to know it!"

They put their arms about each other, savoring their intimacy and kinship.

When Martha Ralston heard about it, she was furious at Fergus.

"Why didn't you find this for *me*? After all, it was advertised in a national magazine!"

"Well," said Fergus, "considering that you have such a large dressing room, it didn't enter my mind."

God, he thought, how can I cope with this madwoman?

"You'd better get around and take a look at it," she continued, "and we'll see what we can do to improve on it."

He nodded dumbly, and took refuge in his cigarette to hide his shaking hand.

Belinda's picture, as scheduled, began its first sequence on the London street on the back lot. During the holidays, the company had become a snug unit. The presence of Belinda was a time for rejoicing as far as the company was concerned. There were at least four old character actors and two wardrobe people who were Barstow buffs. Claudia, with her mimicry of cockney, was an enchantment to the old-timers, and they were delighted to see Belinda, with her British stage family background, in coster finery.

Frederick Winston, a director from London, was engaged for the film. He was slender, slightly bald, scholarly, and meticulous, the sort of man who had to be called Frederick, never Fred.

He had a habit of reading a scene with the principals, being enthusiastic and witty, and then deliberately allowing himself to be called away, observing their attack by themselves before he came back and whetted their appetites anew.

He suited Belinda. He combined Max's scholarliness with a younger, brasher enthusiasm and a keen knowledge of

England and the cockney scene. He laced his rehearsals with amusing anecdotes about London which set her at ease and put her into the mood for her character; this was the first comedy role she had attempted.

Claudia and he hit it off from the first word. The set was a pleasant, efficient unit, even in the midst of the scramble of back lot shooting.

The usual holdups because of traffic noises and occasional jet streams from the nearby airport were standard, but expected.

The sounds and sights of the traffic beyond were somewhat smothered by a berm that Titan gardeners had grown over the years. The thick, leafy trees hid the adjacent front lot, and the set was placed so that the enormous Titan water tank—the source of water for use in not only sprinkler systems but the rivers and ponds that dotted the back lot—could not be seen.

Claudia looked up at the hulking tower. "All my working life," she said, "we've been ducking this monster in our cameras. In the old days it was a real landmark. We thought Fergus was crazy when he said we needed 300,000 gallons of water for the studio. But look at it, it practically waters a city."

"What happens if an earthquake hits?"

"It's been through that; it just sloshes its water a lot," said Claudia, smiling. "Just hope those spidery legs keep on holding."

When the tank made its shadow on Belinda's trailer, she looked up at it and thought of what changes had come to the area since it had been put up so long ago, before the city water system took over some of the load. It seemed out of date, an antediluvian grotesquerie.

After dark, a red light flashed on it as if it were a peril to some antique low-flying plane. Belinda wondered what would happen to it with the encroachment of David's city plan. It would probably have to be dismantled.

But now, even as she drove to the studio (she had insisted there was to be no chauffeur and car on their budget), and she sometimes fought the dawn on her way, the tower stuck up in the distance like a beacon, showing her the way to her work. That seemed to be all there was of her life these days—work. Often she did not even see Scott when she went off to her job.

Effie, as she had all her life, gave her breakfast and packed her a lunch, and she kissed a sleeping Alex and drove away in her car, often accompanied by the Yorkshire, who cuddled up against her and slept.

Sometimes, as she kissed Alex in the precious moments they had before she went to work, she grieved a little because she had lost so much of him, not only as a working mother, but as a secret mother. But these days were golden. Having him live with her in her own house was not only tender, but they were both growing. They had always been close—seeking and enjoying each other naturally.

Now, as he always should have been, he was the focal point in her life. She was beginning to realize that she might know many men; they could come and go—husbands or lovers—but there was only one Alex, the blood of her blood, the child of her body, and he would belong to her no matter what, as long as she lived.

It was a comfort, and yet poignant. She knew she would fight Scott or anyone else who tried to interfere with this vital and wonderful part of her life.

As she drove to work, her mind was full of the scene she was to play, thoughts about the actors she would work with, and problems to discuss with Frederick Winston.

Claudia, who was staying at the Beverly Crest Hotel, would meet her, coffee in hand, at the door of the big bus, which had become, in a sense, her real home. The two would discuss dialogue and characterization while the makeup man and hairdresser prepared Belinda for the day. The set slowly came alive as cast and staff assembled and gathered around the coffee wagon, the doughnuts laid out for a cheerful start to a grueling day.

It was a pleasant, fulfilling routine and the most nourishing part of her life.

This day, the day before Christmas, Belinda was happy on the set. Packages of all sizes had been placed on the shelves of her trailer. The weather was mild, so her awning had been put up, and she had coffee, tea, sandwiches, and Christmas cakes set out to celebrate.

Claudia and Penny had shopped for her, and packages were wrapped for the party that was planned after the last shot in midafternoon. Liquor had been banned on Christmas, as a gesture to the families who would wait for their members to get home. Guards were posted to keep studio personnel from joining the company's private celebration.

Belinda was expecting Laura West. She had bought her an elegant patent leather briefcase. Scott was arriving with Penny and Harry. Penny had become her dear friend. And to crown it all, David had promised to come by in the afternoon.

For a moment Belinda thought of the warmth she had felt at Elderberry when the largesse of the villagers had been put at her feet. Again she felt the same feeling. Those around her cared for her in work; they, too, were a village; friends.

Everything would have been perfect, she thought, if Scott had been coming to take her home to a happy Christmas celebration.

Effie had trimmed the tree, and although it would be a wonderful holiday with Alex, it was not what it might have been; that dream still remained with her.

She tried not to think of it. She was surrounded with love; she had made many friends, she was happy with the first few days' rushes, and she felt that this modest picture was a step forward for her, even after the multimillion-dollar superproductions—the real meaning of being an actress, the legitimate unfolding of a good story, well told, with honest characterizations, a web of fine comedy overlaying it. It might be what the industry called a "sleeper." A picture that could surprisingly become a big smash without those many millions behind it.

She wondered if Scott had any idea of what a promising beginning their company had.

She was beginning to look upon her co-workers with a different eye.

Even the unit manager, Matt Perkins, who had been on the Borgia film, told her that, since she had become a co-owner, her whole attitude had changed. She was right on the spot, ready for any rehearsal or scene, she did not complain or fuss about wardrobe or sets, and she seemed content with a smaller focus of the production and staff than she had known before.

She laughed. "It's true. I'm going to be a female Simon Legree. You'd better watch out!"

She began to play a game. Every time she heard of one

of the scandalous extravagances of Martha Ralston, she did something in counterpoint to prove that such a display was not necessary.

The company and the enthusiasm of all involved began to be discussed in the studio and even in the industry.

On this special day Belinda had gathered personal tokens around her, perhaps to compensate for her sadness when she saw Scott or heard his name. It was strange to be a bride and wait for a phone call from him, or see him coming on the set on business, her heart leaping at the sight of him, and then being crushed. She looked for the eye-to-eye contact, the smile, or the vestige of warmth that would reveal that he was beginning to trust her, and that the long thaw was not endless.

How bitterly strange it was to be so in love with a man she could not have—her own husband.

On her dressing table was the talisman from her father, the chunk of amber that had sat among his own pots and paints throughout his life. Now, whenever she did an important scene, she touched it for luck. And in his little wicker basket was the Yorkshire, Atlas, given her by David so long ago in Greece. Atlas was used to sets and constant attention, but he preferred to sit at his mistress's feet. Claudia sat by comfortably, the script in her lap.

An establishing shot was being lighted for the parade of costers on their way to the Lord Mayor's tea.

The "boomer boys," a husky team of handsome men, were setting the giant camera crane on its tracks, arranging the weights to adjust to the load of cameraman and operator who would swing aloft to record the panorama; it would glide steadily from a close shot of Belinda's surrey, to pull back and reveal the whole bustling London street scene. Someone had gaily perched a miniature Christmas tree atop the camera. A wind blew in the treetops and through the adjacent standing sets. It set plumes and banners dancing.

The flash of sharp exterior lights had already begun, and the director was perched on the crane seat, having a last look at what the camera would reveal, the cinematographer and his operator standing by, ready to take over.

Gaffers in their thick gloves, the "muscle" of the set, worked busily, and the sound man with his earphones and dials at hand was adjusting the controls. It was all the solid mechanics of make-believe getting into action to sell reality.

Wranglers were placing horses and carriages in position; assistants were busy with extras and bit people; the flower girls were set up in their stalls, the street vendors and the hawkers organizing their props.

Belinda saw Penny and Harry and Scott coming down the end of the lane.

Penny was wide-eyed, and she carried a large box with her. "First brownies of the season," she said, kissing Belinda. "I baked a batch for your crew." She smiled.

"You act like a country girl, not high society," said Belinda fondly.

"High society!" mocked Penny. "Where do you think a lot of us come from? In my case, it's Broken Arrow, Oklahoma."

Harry set down a magnum of champagne and kissed Belinda.

"I don't always get a chance to pay tribute to a movie star," he said. "Gad, I guess we'll have to get a bigger yacht!"

Belinda smiled. She took her white-plumed hat from a hat rack and set it on her head, waving the ever-ready wardrobe woman away, pinning it on herself with hairpins.

Scott stood watching. "Things are going well, aren't they?" he said.

An assistant knocked at the open door and handed her a folded paper.

"Fine," Belinda said to him. "Will you excuse me?"

She opened the note. It was from Kevin.

"Where is he?" she asked the assistant.

"Mr. Frazier's at the set entrance. Says he has a present for you and would like to see you."

Belinda could feel Scott stiffen.

"Tell him the set is closed," she said, dropping the note in the wastebasket.

"Well," said Penny, "if someone has a present for you, don't you see him?"

"Not this one," said Belinda.

"Okay, Miss Barstow," said the assistant, "we're ready."

"You'll have to excuse me," she said. "This is a long shot; no big makeup problem. Stick around."

She started out the door. She had to smile at Penny, peering out like a child at a circus.

"It's really work," Belinda assured her as she left them.

She was halfway to the carriage when a man blocked her path. She looked up, for her mind was already on the scene. Who could be interfering?

It was Fergus.

He shifted his cigarette to his left hand and put his hand out.

"Belinda," he said, "happy holidays. I came to ask you a little favor."

She was startled. It was the first time she had seen him since Kevin told her of his duplicity.

"A favor?" she asked.

"It's just that I'd like to take a look at your elegant motor coach. And, of course, to wish you a Merry Christmas," he said lamely.

"Why do you want to see my motor coach?" she said acidly. "Don't tell me Martha Ralston wants one of those, too."

"Well, yes," said Fergus, taken aback. "Everyone's talking about it."

Belinda stared at him. She felt the red flush of anger rising in her face must be visible through her makeup.

"Listen, Fergus, I think you have your bloody nerve. You preempted and ruined my family dressing room. You interfered with my personal life when it meant everything to me. I don't like two-faced people, and you aren't my friend. I don't want you, your bedmate Peggy Rush, or your business partner, that rotten Martha Ralston, to come near me again. Ever."

Fergus stared. His face paled. He opened his mouth. No words came out.

"Ready, Miss Barstow," called out an assistant.

"And furthermore," said Belinda, "don't get the idea that I'm jealous. In spite of all the money you have to back you, all the privileges that can be bought in this studio, you're not going to make it. We may be on a budget, and this picture is small potatoes compared to what you're doing, but what has your picture got?" She let out a low chortle. "Martha Ralston."

She waited a moment, then decided to give him the

coup de grace. "And on this side, we have the Barstows: Claudia, myself—," she paused a moment, "and *David*."

She was gone with a toss of her hat, and Fergus stood there staring as she was helped into the waiting surrey.

He stood for a moment in shock, and then, seeing that Claudia was at the door of the trailer, hand raised ready to greet him, he decided to retreat.

He left the set and cut through the stand of trees— pine and cypress and the eucalyptus windbreak against the fences were rustling in the warm Santa Ana wind. Pushing the spiny branches aside in annoyance, he wanted to flee to the privacy of his office.

He was shocked by Belinda's outburst and shattered by the fact that there were no secrets about his life, but he also was shaken by what lay in the back of his mind. It was up to him to make a star property out of a woman who was, to say the most, a mature beauty, and—to say the least—not a gifted actress. He wanted to pour himself a stiff drink and simmer down. He felt as if his blood pressure was rising.

How outrageous that this girl, whom he had protected from a misalliance, as well as from public knowledge of her youthful mishaps, could turn on him. He felt he had done everything he could to protect her as well as defend the economy of Titan studio. If he had done anything against popular opinion, it was only because the studio was his life and meant more to him than anything or anyone.

A pine branch scraped his face. Angrily he pushed it aside, dropping his cigarette. He left the thicket of trees, many of them planted at his order forty years before, and found his way along the jungle path.

Old Whitey was at his kiosk, keeping unwanted visitors off the London street set. He greeted Fergus warmly.

Fergus brushed the greeting aside with a gesture and strode briskly up the road to the gate of the main lot. All he wanted was to be alone. As he neared the studio portals, he heard the whistle that signified all quiet for exterior action.

He could see the wind whipping the American flag on the Titan flagpole. It would be a stormy Christmas; he could imagine street ornaments sailing in the wind.

He looked back toward the set, wondering if the wind-storm would affect shooting.

And as he turned, he saw a wall of orange flame literally explode in the air. It rose to a height of four stories or so, topped by a great rolling cloud of white smoke billowing upward. The pines became torches, the natural draft pulling the fire into the sky like a giant chimney.

He heard what sounded like another explosion as currents fanned the fire and dropped glowing hot sparks on the old African set. Bone-dry, the set crackled and roared as it passed its fiery cargo on to the western street adjacent.

A wave of heat hit him on the face.

He rushed back to Whitey's kiosk.

The old guard stood paralyzed. The vertical sets—unlike fires enclosed within four walls—fanned by the wind, burst into instant flame.

Fergus snatched the wall phone in the kiosk.

The roar and crackle was so loud he had to scream into the phone. "Get me the fire department!" he cried. "The back lot's on fire! Call our fire department! Call the city fire department! Alert the police!"

The fire was as quick and as deadly as a serpent. Even as he heard the sirens of the studio fire engines as they rushed into action, there was another explosion.

The holocaust had hit the gasoline and oil storage tanks on the back lot at the adjacent street: a freak circumstance. Burning oil was running along the street, clouds of rolling, black oil smoke whirled into the sky. The London set was surrounded in spite of the precautions that had been made for avenues of entrance and exit. Eucalyptus crackled, the branches curling as they became tall torches.

Fergus automatically reached for his cigarette. He paused, his hand in midair. My God—he realized, my cigarette—the pines. I did it! *I* did it!

He tried to make his way back to the set, but a sheet of flame halted him from the false-fronted New York streets, wedges of buildings built together, a compact barricade of fire.

There were hydrants and water systems on the lot, but first the firemen would have to hose their way into the inferno using a fine spray of water to smother the heat and push away the killing smoke.

The ceiling sprinkler systems that protected the sound stages were of no use in the back lot.

In the distance he could hear screams and cries of panic. Oh God! That whole company's trapped in there, he thought. They could be incinerated!

Whitey came to him, shaking. "They could get out the back wire fence," he said, "if they could cut through it."

The studio fire trucks pulled up. The men hooked up to the in-plant storage system of the Titan tower. Ninety pounds of pressure pumping 150 gallons a minute came from the tank. A godsend! Much more pressure than the city water, and the local firemen would augment this.

But as fast as one spot was battled, another set burst into flame. The fire wind, as well as the rising "Santa Ana," blew across the acreage like a breath from Hades.

It seemed an eternity, but in a few moments he heard the screaming sirens and clarions of the rigs; reinforcements rushing from neighboring fire stations.

Fergus skirted around to the side street, but flames from the ruptured oil tank halted him. Burning sparks as large as his fist were raining down, and one of them set his coat on fire. He had to stamp it out with his hand.

"My God. My God!" he cried, realizing again that he had done this himself.

Then he was accosted by what seemed a nightmare. A snake, a squirrel, several rabbits, and a singed cat carrying a kitten rushed out of the smoke, longtime inhabitants of the nooks and crannies of the make-believe realm blindly finding their way across the road to safety in the city street. As he looked down, several rats ran across his feet, and a bird, its feathers aflame, dropped near him, gasping and dying.

More rigs pulled in from adjacent stations, the hoses and equipment put into immediate use. Police cars and ambulances filled the street.

Fergus stood blinded and sick at heart, his whole life falling in flames about him.

The sound and the heat were terrifying. Cries of terror, the deafening roar and crackle of the flames, more sirens. Men were calling out orders, rushing into the melee with hoses, some with masks and asbestos suits.

Someone called out, "The copper underground wires

have melted; there's no more communication! Get the walkie-talkies!"

The stench of tar and creosote, paint, several dead animals, and fake grass with its plastic snapping incineration was heavy in the smoke-filled air. Fergus knew that smoke inhalation was as deadly as heat. He clawed at a wire gate and the skin came off his hands; the metal was red-hot.

On the set, Belinda had barely made the first walk-through when she looked up to see a tower of flame where the berm had protected her trailer.

Everyone on the set had stood in shock for a moment. Three natural entrances to the set had been blocked off. The fourth was against the fence where eucalyptus flamed and burning oil poured down the street. Along one side of the set, a high, wire-mesh fence prevented escape.

Belinda jumped out of the surrey and started blindly for the motor coach. As she did so, a long burning branch fell and the outside awning was set aflame.

She had one thought. Her dog was in there and the amber—oh God—the chunk of amber! Her talisman.

She rushed to the coach. Everyone was in a panic. Scott headed for her and grabbed her arm.

"Stay here," he called.

"No!" she said, "get Claudia. I'm all right."

Pulling away from him with all her strength, she rushed past him. Claudia was immobilized against the doorway.

Belinda rushed in. She couldn't see Atlas, but she could hear him choking. She blindly gathered him up, and with her free hand snatched the lump of amber from the table and rushed out.

Claudia was ahead of her, pulled into the clearing near the street by Scott.

Next to the set a southern mansion had gone up in volatile, searing flame. And in the distance, a sheet of red rose up into the sky in a crazy dance. Above it the sky was filled with rolling, blackened clouds.

Before Belinda could move, the white plumes on her hat had ignited. Someone snatched the hat from her head, and she looked up to see who it was. It was Scott. He pressed her head against his chest, brushing the sparks from her hair.

She held his hand tightly, and he took hers. In her hand was an object. She put it in his. Unthinking, he grasped it.

One of the boomer boys rushed up.

"Here, Belinda!" he yelled. "You and Claudia come here!"

Before she knew what had happened, the great camera boom had been moved on its tracks. Scott led her to it. She and Claudia were perched on the camera seat, and the machine lifted them high over the hot wire fence. Belinda, in a panic, looked down at the burning terrain, the holocaust, a dozen sets all going up at once. She saw Scott looking up at her, distressed and loving at the same time. And she saw Penny and Harry clinging to each other. Oh—she thought, those darling people! Why them!

She couldn't let go of Claudia or the dog, but she twisted around as much as she dared to catch a last glimpse of Scott. The smoke blotted him out. Clouds of ashes fell on them like snow. The rising heat was stifling.

Scott! Scott! . . . How would he get out?

"Oh, God," said Claudia, "I'm going to fall!"

"No you're not," said Belinda. "Hang on to me. Close your eyes!"

She clutched Claudia and the dog, and after a panicked moment the crane veered upward crazily. Another blast of heat hit them like a slap from a great devilish hand. The little Christmas tree so joyously lashed onto the camera a few moments before burst into flame.

Oh, dear God, help us, prayed Belinda as they wobbled crazily in the sky. What will happen to Alex if Claudia and I should die? Please, God, it's not a cop-out, but let me live. I'll do my best for Alex—and Scott!

The crane had reached the peak of its parabola; it seemed to halt as if frozen a moment, and then it slowly set them down outside the fence. Pictures were being taken of their escape. It was mad, in the middle of all this, to see photographers doing such an inconsequential thing when help was needed for more important things.

But people had already gathered, standing ankle-deep in water, held back by a cordon of police.

A cheer arose as she and Claudia descended from the crane. The silly little Christmas tree was still flaming on top of the camera.

The machine reared up like a crazy dragon, the loss of their weight taking it off-balance.

Belinda was revolted at the ovation; people on the other side of that fence could be dying. Oh, Scott! Scott!

On the set, seeing that Belinda was safe, Scott looked in his hand. Belinda had handed him the chunk of amber. He put it in his pocket.

He turned back to the trailer. The snap-on awning was in flames. He rushed over to it to pull it off and stood staring at the gigantic machine.

As he ripped off the awning and stamped the fire out, he looked through the drifts of smoke to some crewmen who were cutting away at the fence with metal cutters. Their gloves were singeing; the fence was too hot to touch.

"The motor coach," said Scott, seeing Barney, one of the drivers. "Run Belinda's coach through the fence!"

Barney stared at him, and then at the motor coach. There was a leeway of about two hundred feet to the fence.

He looked at Scott. "How do we get momentum?"

"What's to lose?" said Scott. "We'll have to back up as far as we dare."

Killing clouds of smoke were blowing onto the set. Everyone was coughing, and several men were lying on the ground overcome by the heat and smoke. In the distance a building crashed, a heat wave spawned from it, and a fountain of golden sparks fell like meteors in the white smoke and moved onward to new targets.

Barney and Scott ran for the motor coach. They would have to use the heavy machine as a juggernaut to break down the fence. And if it crashed and didn't go over, it would be deadly.

Scott jumped into the truck; he couldn't ask Barney to risk his life alone.

Barney started the engine, daring to back it into the burning embers of the berm to get more momentum, and with a jerk got the massive vehicle into gear and plunged forward.

For a terrifying moment, the coach smashed into the wire barricade. Both men were thrown into the windshield. But with the engine in low gear, the machine kept going, plowing the fence down. One side of the motor coach ripped open, furniture and clothing tumbling out, but it moved on into the street, sundering the wire.

They were free.

There was a cheer behind them as men and women poured into the street.

Protected by fine sprays of water, the company walked through the gap, out of hell, into life.

Scott crawled out of the coach. His forehead was cut, but he staggered out, taking a deep breath, away from the smoke.

Belinda rushed to him, clinging, holding, touching. Her face was streaked with soot, her hair hung in singed, blackened strands down her face.

"Oh, Scott!" was all she could say. "Oh, Scott!"

He looked down at her as she lifted her hand up and brushed the blood away.

"You're hurt!" she said.

An ambulance stood by and an attendant stepped out.

"We'd better patch you up," he said. "Come along."

Belinda clung to Scott.

"He's my husband," she said. "I'll stay with him."

As she walked with him to the first aid station, she thought, all this time I've had such dreams of us getting together, romantically. And look at us now!

He put his arm around her shoulder and as he looked into her eyes she saw what she had been waiting for.

As David drove off the freeway, he could see the smoke scattering a cloud over Hollywood. What a big fire, he thought; why do these things have to happen on Christmas? Some Christmas tree probably started it . . .

As he approached the environs of the studio, he realized it could well be Titan's back lot.

Ten blocks from the studio, he was stopped by the police. He could see citizens in the small houses nearby on their roofs, watering down their property to keep any random embers from setting them on fire.

He identified himself to a busy fire chief and was allowed to enter the area. Firemen were crawling all over the streets and penetrating the back lot with their gear. A path had been chopped through the smoldering ruins. Hoses, tangled like snakes, from the private hydrants of Titan were disgorging their powerful jets of water—fed by the old water tank.

A fine fog of water and chemicals had smothered the oily street conflagration.

David saw Belinda's motor coach, its side ripped open, the furnishings and clothes soaking and stained on the street, tilted along the twisted fence.

The broken fence looked as terrible as a torn freeway divider after a dreadful accident. It must have taken some power and guts to drive that bus through the barricade, he thought.

He turned in horror to a nearby man. It was Whitey, the guard, whom David had known since boyhood.

"Whitey! What happened?"

"It's okay, Mr. Austin," Whitey said, "they're all safe. The crew got out with several minor burn cases and some smoke inhalation, but believe it or not, nobody's hurt bad. They were all released to go home to their families."

The old man shook his head. "Those Santa Ana winds. They pull all sorts of devilish tricks. One spark from a generator, you've had it."

A reporter came up. "Hey, mister, heard you were on duty. Tell us all about it."

As Whitey opened up, glorious in his importance, David moved behind a fire truck. This was a time he did not wish to be identified by the press.

He heard Whitey rambling on.

"And you know," Whitey said, "it was like a movie. Mr. Scott himself with Barney crashing that truck through the fence. And Miss Claudia and Belinda and that little dog like birds up on that crane, rescued by the boomer boys. It was like an old-time serial. Pearl White should have thought up that one. A real thriller."

David followed the soggy path. Men were monitoring the hot embers, which could still burst into flames, although the fire was completely contained.

He looked up at the blackened tank. The Titan logo was blistered and smoked half away. He knew that Titan's fire protection and the tank's pressure power had undoubtedly been a primary factor in saving the main lot sound stages and offices, for the city hydrants were weak by comparison.

He heard Whitey going on. The old boy would never run down. He was spewing out enough information for the evening papers and ten fan magazines.

"Yes, sir," he said, "they've all gone home. Miss Belinda and her husband, and Miss Claudia with them. Mr. Ziska came in from Palm Springs just in time to pick them up in his hired car. It will sure be some Christmas Eve over at their house tonight."

Well, thought David, that takes cares of them. I don't have to worry.

He moved on into the wet never-never land that had been his playground and his work ground, the land that had been owned and built by his family, which he had always accepted as his small kingdom, as much as he denied it, and had traveled everywhere in the world to escape it.

This was the African set. The black, oily mass of water, with debris floating in it, had once been the placid river.

And the jungle surrounding it. A few trunks of trees, now burned stumps, still signified the place where leaves and blossoms had been so real to thousands and thousands of people, young and old.

It flashed in his mind that, even if things had worked out with Laura, now they would never have that picnic. Their dream, or at least his, for most possibly she had never had it, would never come true.

It was a lonely scene, and he walked away from it. There was nothing he could do now. It would all come later. Insurance; postponement of production; quick rebuilding of current sets. He'd try to find Fergus. He realized that Fergus alone had the key to the complicated inner workings of Titan. Fergus had dealt with a thousand crises over the years—and undoubtedly he had the answer in his files to make order out of this chaos.

David wended his way past the confusion; there must have been at least eleven or twelve rigs that had come in from various stations. There would be many people to thank. Thank God no one had been seriously hurt.

More people were crowding the streets. Traffic had been stopped. Newsreel camera crews were gathering their gear to go home. The drama was ended. At least for now. Strangely, he'd probably witness the whole disaster on evening newscasts.

He got in his car, slowed down by crowds. Several people, studio personnel who were standing by, waved at him, recognizing their boss and owner.

One clown yelled, "Merry Christmas!"

He drove past the cluster of firemen, police, and spectators. Cars lined the streets, some of them double-parked.

As he turned the corner, he saw a Rolls Royce parked there.

He pulled into the curb.

Laura was sitting at the wheel. Her head was bowed; she was crying.

He jumped out of his car. She did not look up. He opened the door and got in next to her.

He noticed that her shoes and stockings were filthy with soot. She, too, had gone to the ruins. He saw that she had pulled off her white, soot-blackened glove. It lay on the seat of the car. Her hand was up to her face as she wiped her tears. He saw the left hand; the ring finger missing.

She glanced up at him, startled, and then, without attempting to hide her hand, wiped her eyes with a tissue.

"Our jungle's gone," she sobbed. "It's gone. All the magic."

He saw the first emotion he had ever seen on her face, the pain, the bewilderment, the vulnerable child making a last cry in the ravaged life of an adult.

He took his handkerchief out of his pocket and wiped her cheek.

"No," he said, "the magic isn't gone. Look, Laura, it's only lath and plaster that went up in flame. The world is on stilts—people are marching like Paul Bunyan in their minds, striding over continents. Those old relics out there were outmoded—they belong to an innocent age that is long gone. We don't need them anymore. Let them go. Forget them—"

She looked at him, swallowing, still weeping.

"Forget the whole past. It's done."

She opened her eyes wide, wondering if he knew about her now that Abe Moses was dead. After all, David was the trustee. Was it possible that what he was saying was personal? She couldn't speak.

"I'm driving you home," he said. "You're not fit to drive."

She slid over to give him her place behind the wheel. It was the first time in her life she had surrendered to a man because she wanted to, because it was natural.

As he moved behind the steering wheel he picked up the glove.

"You dropped your glove," he said, throwing it out the window.

Instinctively, she covered her damaged hand with the other. But he took it before she could realize what he was doing, and he kissed it.

Christmas Day was bright and sharp. The wind had died. The house in Beverly Hills had settled into peace.

Scott and Belinda were asleep in each other's arms.

Alex and Effie were having early Christmas breakfast in the breakfast room, Atlas cuddled up, bedraggled, sooty, and waiting for what he knew was likely—a bath.

Max was still sleeping.

Claudia came in to join Effie. She wore slacks and walking boots, and she carried a sweater.

"You know, Effie," she said, "you'll think I'm crazy, but I'm going to run over to the studio and take a look at the back lot."

Effie put orange juice in front of her and poured her coffee.

"Good," she said, "I want to hear all about it." She handed her the morning *Times*.

"You and Belinda are all over the front page, perched like birds on that crane, and Atlas hanging his tongue out like he was after a lollipop. And that crazy burning Christmas tree on the camera above you! What a Christmas picture! I took the liberty of taking the phone off the hook. It was ringin' its head off. After all, everybody that matters is under this roof, so what difference does it make?"

Claudia nodded, taking the paper. "Yes, I guess so. Except I wonder where Fergus is, and if he's had a fit—Oh, my God, look at my hair! What a dreadful picture."

The drama of the shot failed to impress her. Effie grinned. An actress; a star to the last ditch.

Claudia gulped down her coffee.

"I'll be back in a couple of hours. They'll probably all be still snoring."

Thank God, she thought, smiling to herself that Belinda was with Scott in their own bedroom at last . . . Married and tucked away . . . *pax vobiscum* . . .

After a fire at a studio, the earth has to be tilled as if for a new harvest.

Fergus was already walking through the desolation. Christmas meant little to him. Like many tycoons, it was only a day without work, an empty void with expenses ballooning. Later in the day he would pay his ceremonial visit to Las Cruces Sanatorium and visit Esther, but since she paid him little heed, it meant nothing. The fact that there had to be action going on in the back lot, a cleanup crew working to protect the property from further fire damage, gave him an excuse to go to the studio.

He walked, planning roadways, figuring how many builders and dump trucks would be needed later. His fingers wore bandages where they had been burned touching the hot fence, but he seemed impervious to that. His mind was elsewhere.

Fragments of forgotten streets would have to be plowed under. It was amazing how large the acreage seemed without the fretwork of buildings and crooked streets that had been built over a span of thirty years. One or two remnants of former glories still remained.

Men on duty were hosing down piles of embers. Little bursts of flame revealed the last strength of the holocaust of the day before.

Fergus had spent the early hours of the morning going over the policies of Bayly, Martin, and Fay, Inc., the insurance company that carried the massive studio account.

He was calculating the value of sets that had been built twenty or thirty years ago and had amortized themselves. Originally, they might have cost ten thousand dollars, but they carried no value on the books. Yet fortunately they were heavily insured. A quick figure, based on the estimates he heard from other studios (including Warner Brothers, famous for the many fires that garnered them a large profit), assured him that this Titan scrap heap would finally net close to a million and a half dollars.

The money would be used to upgrade assets. New sets charged off to new productions would bring in more money. Amortization could start all over again on a grander scale.

Thinking of how cleverly he had managed the studio's insurance, he wondered how Titan would get along without his expertise. If David asked him, he might jettison Martha Ralston after one picture and get back to running the studio properly; no one else cared, or knew how to do it.

In the euphoric excitement of massive profit, he forgot that he had actually started the fire.

As he poked among the ruins, he did not see Claudia in the distance. The studio police on duty knew her and waved her a greeting. Just like old-timers, they remarked, to want to see what was left.

Claudia's throat was dry from the smoke, or was it a perverse lump of sentimentality choking her up?

Here she saw a little plaster Roman cornice. How noble the scowling warrior Jeffrey had looked in his laurel wreath as he rode past the camera in a chariot, and she had laughed with the rest of the company. It was a silent shot and he was beefing his head off because his toga was too drafty.

A few yards away was a little section of a cobblestone Paris courtyard. She remembered herself playing a young midinette carrying a hatbox in a scene with Leslie Charles. He had loaded it with bricks just before the take for a gag. When she picked it up, the still cameraman had caught the startled expression on her face.

Here a plastic African idol; over there, a fragment of a Mexican pyramid.

Yes, and this little fretwork was off a western saloon where they shot Jesse James. And this—must be an iron piece off that troika Jeffrey rode on borax snow when he played a prince and she a princess. How they had argued when Fergus tried to make them husband and wife in the movies. No incest, they had insisted hotly. The public won't stand for a famous brother and sister making it in a film. So they had changed the cast. And each found a lover in the new casting.

Oh, how memory can go on!

Her reverie was disturbed. From one of the small houses across the way a radio echoed out across the silent reaches of the ashes. It seemed as if the flattened, encrusted earth was a sounding board for all the neighborhood noises previously smothered by the many buildings and trees. She wished they would turn the damned music off; she wanted to be alone with her memories.

Look at the part of that Renaissance bridge where Belinda so recently rode her palfrey in the Borgia film. And dear Max, worrying about her being so hot in the summer sun in those medieval velvets—all the bridge, castle, medieval street burned, scorched, gone to ash.

Perhaps there was a stray cinder settling in her eyes. She had to wipe them.

She glanced up. There was Fergus, loping over some fallen beams, coming to her.

"Are you crazy?" he said. "What in God's name are you doing here?"

"The same as you," she said. "Thinking about it all before it gets leveled off."

"And about that," he said, pointing upward. "Remember when Simon Moses called it Fergus's folly?"

He smiled almost cockily, as if he were putting something over on Simon these many years gone.

The water tower was blistered, and the Titan logo had been burned away. The great tank stood firm on its spindly legs. They could hear the gush of water as it was being refilled.

"Ready to perform its function, if and when needed," said Claudia.

Like myself, she thought, or Fergus.

The distant radio was playing, "*I'll Be Seeing You in All the Old Familiar Places.*" It made Claudia shiver.

A bulldozer pushed over a part of the Main Street facade. Where was Claudia, a young dance hall girl in scarlet sequins, laughing as she came out the swinging doors? The set toppled, crumbled, and fell, raising a cloud of ashes.

The destruction distressed Claudia. The distant music was smothered. I must remember, she said to herself, it's not real, it's only a front.

"Well," said Fergus cheerily, "everything has its sunny side. This back lot was falling to pieces. I figure we'll get over a million and a half in insurance."

Claudia wanted to hit him.

"You're a bastard!" she said.

"No," he said, smiling faintly, "just a survivor—like you."

ABOUT THE AUTHOR

MARY LOOS is the third generation of her family to write
for the motion picture industry. Her grandfather wrote
silent film titles for Famous Players Lasky (now Paramount). Her aunt Anita Loos is the well-known screen
writer and author of *Gentlemen Prefer Blondes*. The
author's own career has been quite varied; she has done
publicity for MGM, collaborated with her former husband
as a writing team on over fifteen films and was associate
producer and screenwriter of *Gentlemen Marry Brunettes*,
which was filmed in London, Paris and Monte Carlo.
She has been under contract to Twentieth Century Fox
Studio, RKO where she collaborated on *The French Line*
for Howard Hughes, Columbia Studio, and Republic
Studio. She has also been highly successful in the television world. With Richard Sale she co-produced and
co-wrote the series *Yancy Derringer*. Together they also
wrote segments for *The Wackiest Ship in the Army*,
Please Don't Eat the Daisies, and *Bewitched*. She was
Literary Executive to M. J. Frankovich Productions at
Columbia Studio, and resigned to write her novels, *The
Beggars Are Coming*, *Belinda*, and the current *Barstow
Legend*. She lives in Santa Monica, and is now at work
on her fourth book.

A Special Preview of
the opening pages of the first
novel, which traces the beginnings
of the glamorous Barstow family.

The Beggars Are Coming

by *Mary Loos*

Author of BELINDA
and
THE BARSTOW LEGEND

It all started with this blazing book, in which
the passionate, talented members of this acting family became part of the wild and bold
pioneer days of the motion picture industry.

1

The neighborhood would never be the same again. It was Saturday night and the East Bronx was astir.

The dazzling marquee of the new movie house, the Little Diamond, signaled that bright lights were coming to ordinary people. The first neighborhood nondenominational meeting place was opening.

Simon Moses fastened the blue satin ribbon that stretched across the lobby of his pristine theater. The brass fittings on his plate glass doors were polished to gold. Two potted palms rested in elegant jardinieres on the turkey-red carpeting. A fancy No Smoking sign stood on an easel in the lobby. Simon stepped back to admire the display sheets, then walked outside to make sure that all the light bulbs were on. The thought of the light bill made him a little sick.

He had come a long way in his thirty-eight years to own a three-hundred-seat palace like this. He had parlayed the profits from a secondhand furniture store and a furniture factory into four neighborhood movie houses. This newest one was a far reach from the first—a nickelodeon, created from an empty store and some repossessed funeral-parlor chairs.

The last workman had just left. It was incredible that the whole thing had come together. The auditorium still smelled of sawdust and paint; he'd barely had time to get his hair trimmed and his face steamed and shaved at Tony Cuneo's barbershop. Half the men there were dandying themselves up for the event and had congratulated him.

He had stopped at the tailors, picked up his tuxedo, rushed home, and dressed hurriedly, without even enough time to enjoy his reflection. He relished the fact that women said he was the handsomest man in the Bronx; he used his looks to bring glamour to his business, but now he seemed to present only a harassed face.

He had rushed from the apartment, leaving his two pretty daughters in the kitchen, excitedly pressing the flounces and sashes of their dresses. Esther, seventeen, was fair-haired like her mother; Martha, the youngest, had curly black hair like his.

His wife Rebecca was folding paper cuffs to protect her crushed-velvet sleeves while she handled the ticket booth. David, his son, the middle one, slender and scholarly, was brushing his Saturday jacket.

Simon took a gift box of cigars to hand out to dignitaries. After all, he figured, as he dashed around the corner to his new theater, tonight's the night. The sky's the limit! Eggs all in one basket! Sink or swim!

His brother, Abe, was in the auditorium smoking a cigar. He wore a checkered vest, and he looked rich. This burned Simon.

"Don't you believe in signs?" said Simon. "You know that film's in the booth already. You want to blow up the place? Why ain't you in front? It's about time for the trade."

"Why don't you relax?" said Abe. Twelve years younger, he was the smart aleck of the family. About to take his bar examination, he was also, naturally, the family snob, while being supported by his brother.

"So join up. The whole family's in on it. Why not you?" said Simon. "Esther's working the piano here along with Martha. Mother's handling the ticket booth, and David is helping your Uncle Sid run the film. Now, after you finish spieling in front, you'd better help at the door."

"You could hire some cheap help," said Abe. "How'm I gonna handle your legal problems if I don't get my degree?"

"Listen to me for a change," said Simon, "instead of thinking me, me, me like you always do. Even with this classy showhouse that's costing me my life's earnings, the Motion Picture Patent Company gives me rotten film. I gotta pay a fee each week for every one of my projectors. Rent, rent, rent, I never can buy, and half a cent a foot for lousy second-rate footage. And if I try to get a better class of picture from an independent maker, the Trust's goon squads come in and wreck my movie house. And if that happens, then who carries the whole family on their shoulders?"

"Well, if you have to make money, why do you play this trash? What's wrong with good movies like *Quo Vadis?*"

"I own the Astor?" said Simon. "Could I get a dollar fifty a ticket in this nebbish neighborhood? Fifteen cents will be tough enough, with kids free, and they all got six!"

Simon looked at his critical young brother. His nose quivered.

"These things you wouldn't remember. How our pappa who couldn't read struggled to keep us in school, with only a lousy barrow on Doyer Street to do it with. And how I worked to educate you better than me when he went. You know how much I've invested in your law education?"

"You'll get paid, you'll get paid, I'm not worried about your economy," said Abe wearily, having heard it a hundred times. "You know how to save a buck. You think I don't know about the bicycling of film between your picture houses?"

Simon clenched his teeth with rage and looked around to be sure no one heard.

"So ruin me!" he said. "That's gratitude!"

"Gratitude!" snorted Abe. "Who's been drawing up your contracts for free? Who works for you like a slave for nothing? I ought to give you a kick in the pants!"

"What?" said Simon, looking down at the kid's neatly shod feet, "with my shoes?"

He turned abruptly and strode away.

A fivesome stood staring through the elegant doors. Simon's anger choked in his throat, but he controlled himself. Martha was dressed in canary yellow, and her hair was curled up on her head above her snapping black eyes. David burst the door open and rushed in, full of enthusiasm. He knew why. A new projection machine to David was like every holiday in one.

Esther smiled, and he paused, as always, to smile back, for she was his favorite. Her pink dress cast a glow on her face. Her fair hair was folded in smooth plaits around her head, and she had pinned on a candy-striped ribbon which stood out on each side like wings. Her father knew how pretty she'd look sitting at the piano, her back straight as a rod, playing away at the action on the screen while the audience cheered and groaned.

He gestured, and the young people ducked under the barrier. Following the girls, Mike Cuneo, the barber's son, held open the door. His curly black hair was greased, and his broad face was wreathed in a grin.

Fergus Austin followed at the rear, ducking awkwardly under the ribbon. At seventeen, he was tall and skinny. He had red hair, pale skin, and blue eyes that seemed almost purple as he glanced through his thick red lashes. Like most boys of his age, he wore black-ribbed stockings and high shoes with knots in the laces. He had on thin pants and a tight-buttoned jacket, short in the sleeve and slick at the elbows. Simon remembered that when he came to visit, he always smelled of wool, urine, and cubebs.

Everything about Fergus rankled Simon Moses. He knew Fergus was enamored of his darling, Esther, and the idea revolted him. To him, the kid was a walking tract of righteous Catholic poverty. Simon detested the public drunkenness and misbehavior of Fergus's father, and the poor-mouth obsequiousness of his mother, who ran a boardinghouse.

If Simon had known that this night would link his destiny with Fergus, he probably wouldn't have opened his theater at all.

Fergus stuck out a bony hand and wrist. "Hi, Mr. Moses. Good luck."

Simon shook as brusquely as he could and pulled his hand away.

A man brought in a horseshoe of stock and asparagus fern from the office entrance. Gold letters on a ribbon read Good Luck.

"Nice," said Simon, reading the card. "It's from Bernie's Delicatessen across the street. They ought to. We'll do them nothing but good. Girls, you'd better go read the program and look at the posters, so you can decide what music to play."

They left, twittering about their project.

He turned to David. "You collect tickets, son. After they're all in, you can go to the projection booth. Can you handle splicing already?"

"Oh, sure, sure, pappa," said Dave, his face alight with pleasure.

"And check the signs," said Simon. "If they start to clap, check to see if the sprockets are off. And if a doctor is called, use the Dr. Blank Is Wanted at Once sign! Fill the doc's name in with grease pencil before you slide it. Okay?"

"Okay," said Dave. He rubbed his hands, testing their cleanliness.

Simon turned to Mike. "And now, neighbor, Eyetalians are supposed to be good at music. Live it up. Spiel. And run the Gramophone out front."

"Gee, me?" said Mike. "Me?" He clasped his head with pleasure.

"It's a snap," Simon said. "March up and down with your fingers in your vest like a big shot."

"I ain't got a vest," said Mike.

"Act like you got one," said Simon. "Throw out that golden voice of yours. Tell 'em it's the greatest laugh carnival in town. Yell, Mabel Normand, John Bunny, Bronco Billy Anderson."

"It says so out in front," said Mike.

"Since when can everybody read?" said Simon. "Wind up the machine. Sing a little. Laugh. Kid the goils. Big shots are gonna be here. Fifty cents okay?"

Mike looked delighted. In a minute he had his thumbs under his armpits, and he strode up and down grinning.

"And now," said Simon, "I left the hardest job for the smartest. Fergie, boy, this is very important. I'm gonna be busy with the honored guests. I got a bicycle with a basket on the handlebars out by the alley. When the *Bronco Billy* picture is finished, you take the can of film over to the Ruby. Pick up *Sailor's Honeymoon* and bring it back quick. Then as soon as you do that, you pop over to the Electric Theater and pick up *Gertie Learns to Swim*. Bring that back here, Fergie." Simon pulled out his turnip watch. "I'm depending on you, kid. The show must go on. Then you take *Bronco Billy* from the Ruby and take it to the Pearl—"

Fergus scratched his head. "Gee, Mr. Moses, I'm all mixed up. Why couldn't Dave—"

Simon waved his hand. "Dave understands splicing film. And they gave me such lousy, patched prints. I need him. Don't worry," he bent forward confidentially. "Don't tell Mike, but you're going to make a dollar. It's a higher class of work!"

Simon slapped his back. "You're a smart kid, this is a new business. You oughta go in it with me. I'll give you the card with the schedule."

When the first reel was finished, Fergus wheeled down the alley, and crossed the street, wobbling, as his bike skidded. Saturday night the whitewings couldn't keep up with the horses and buggies that thronged the streets.

Damned if I'll end up with horseshit on my good suit, Fergus thought, as he brought the bicycle under control. He began to wonder if Mr. Moses hadn't given him the dirty end of the stick. He stuck out his chin. I gotta be smarter than him, he thought. Seems something's fishy about jockeying these cans like this.

He got *Bronco Billy* to the Ruby. Esther's Aunt Hannah was just finishing playing "Alexander's Ragtime Band." A claque of ruffians was beginning to stomp and clap in unison. In the projection booth, the operator dimmed the lights, flashed on the No Stomping Please slide, and took the film from Fergus. He handed him *Sailor's Honeymoon,* and Fergus got it on the bike and raced back to the Little Diamond. Simon was standing nervously by the side door. He grabbed the film, slapping Fergus on the back.

"Great Fergie, just great, now get going to the Electric, pick up *Gertie Learns to Swim,* and haul it back fast."

Fergus, sweating, was about to complain, when he saw that Mr. Moses had slammed the door, which locked from the inside so no freeloaders could get in. He got on his machine, moved along the street in the wake of a Chinese laundry wagon, peeled off by the alley, and was surprised but pleased to see that old Uncle Irving Moses was standing by the door, one foot in the opening. Irving handed him *Gertie Learns to Swim* and slammed the door quickly. A little annoyed, Fergus moved down the street, got cussed at for splashing mud on a couple as he skidded to a halt, and then scooted down the alley.

Nobody was in sight. He must have been pretty fast. He bent over to unload the basket, and as he did so he was belted on the side of the head.

For a moment he was stunned. His teeth felt shaken loose; he almost felt the bones grate in his head. He slowly fell and heard his pants rip as his bony knee hit the ground.

This can't be happening to me, he thought. He pulled himself to his feet. Three toughs were staring at him. He'd never seen them before. Two moved forward, grabbed him.

"Bicycling, Bud?" the third one asked.

"Whata ya mean?" asked Fergus. He put his hand to his head which felt bigger than a balloon.

The man held the can of film up to the streetlight. Fergus tried to move, but the other two men held him.

"Now ain't that funny?" said the man. "This here can says, *Gertie Learns to Swim*. That ain't right, because it's not booked here at the Little Diamond. My boss says it's booked up the street at the Electric." His eyes were hard.

"Who you working for?"

"I don't know," said Fergus, surprised that he could even talk. "I'm just delivering."

"Just imagine, he don't know!" said the man. He reached forward and with calculated precision punched Fergus on the nose with a swift, hard jab.

Fergus felt a bone crack in his nose. After the flash of light, he felt the salt taste of blood on his lips.

"Memory better?" asked the man.

Fergus shook his head, trying to shake the pain away. He didn't know what to do. Suddenly he heard Esther playing *William Tell* on the piano inside. It meant that somebody had opened that door a crack. He cried out as loud as he could. "I don't know. And I won't ever know, because you'll kill me."

His stomach clenched in a knot of fear, for the door closed, and the piano was muffled.

The man hit him in the eye. Fergus hoped he'd pass out, but his torturer was too experienced.

"You won't be such a stupid mick next time," he said, "workin' for these mocky bastards. And when I get through breaking your legs, you ain't gonna be able to bicycle illegal film no more."

The man moved forward to hit him again. Fergus thought for a moment he must have passed out and died, for a shower of flowers fell over the man's head and shoulders. The horseshoe of stock and fern, in its thick wire frame, sent to Mr. Moses from Bernie's Delicatessen, was being used as a weapon. The banner fell across the man's face, its Good Luck in gold letters bandaging his eyes.

The whole staff of the Little Diamond Theater erupted into the alley. Mr. Moses, Dave, Uncle Sid, Abe, and Mike were all wide-eyed scared, but they had every weapon they could get hold of, from pop bottles to the ceremonial scissors. Esther was still pounding away at the piano, and the movie was running.

Fergus's three assailants tore themselves free of the flowers and got out of the alley in a hurry.

When David Moses and Mike Cuneo brought Fergus home, mom put a beefsteak on his eye, packed his bruises with soda compresses, and tried to get him out of shock by giving him some hot broth. He threw up the broth.

His old man, alterted at Gertie's Parlor House that his son had been half killed in a brawl in an alley, got dressed, came home, and prescribed a medicinal shot of brandy. Fergus threw up the brandy.

A young intern from Germany, "Doc" Wolfrum, who lived in the Austin boardinghouse, gave him a sedative. He looked him over, checked his bones for breaks, his groin and belly for hernia, and then violating all rules, looked at his nose, took hold of the swollen bridge, and gave it a pull, which caused it to snap. Fergus fainted.

"Otherwise he will a crooked nose have. The patient will live."

When Fergus came to, the doc gave him a painkiller, taped his nose, and told everyone to clear out until the next day. "Let him sleep," said the doctor, "that is best."

David and Mike sat around. They wouldn't leave until he was resting easily.

"Who the heck hit me?" Fergus asked woozily, waiting for the pill to take effect.

"It was the film trust hoodlums," said David. "That Motion Picture Patent Company. Pappa says they're a rotten monopoly. If we don't pay them rent for every piece of equipment and every foot of film we show in every house, they strong-arm us. We can't operate, nobody can, without a license from them. They're robbers!"

"Now you tell me, you son of a—"

The pill was beginning to take effect. Fergus felt he was falling into a vortex. The shadowy face of David hung over him, a concerned look on his face.

"Jeez, Ferg, I'm sorry. They never raided us before. Pappa pays too much for his license the way it is. Why should he pay several times for the same film just because he has several movie houses? You can't even operate without paying the Trust off over and over."

Fergus closed his eyes and began to sink into oblivion. He heard his mother and the two boys whispering as they left. He tried to conjure up resentment against Mr. Moses, but he fell into sleep.

The morning was different. Fergus awoke in

pain, sore, and seeing slightly double. The pain-killer made him feel thick, and his mouth tasted the way a chemistry set smells. He tried to figure out what had happened. Something was very screwy. And it all went back to Mr. Moses.

About ten o'clock, Mom opened the door. "Mr. Moses wants to see you, dear."

Fergus knew now something was fishy. His mother put another pillow behind him and straightened out the bedclothes.

"I don't feel so good," said Fergus. "My nose must be busted, my ear hurts, and I can't see out of one eye."

"Oh, my God," said Simon, staring at him. Fergus knew he was scared. "I—I'm sorry, Fergie—"

He stopped. Fergus looked up out of his good eye. "My name is Fergus," he said.

"I'll do right by you, Ferg—Fergus." Simon took a handkerchief out of his pocket. "It's that movie trust. They hire bullies. It was the goon squad was after you. They should go to prison for beating up a kid."

"That won't fix my face or help my busted ear-drum," said Fergus. "You didn't send Dave. You didn't send your brother Abe, or Mike. You didn't let me know you were trying to save money. I was the goat."

That made Mr. Moses more agitated.

"Look, boy, I had no idea. So everybody bi-cycles films back and forth. My four houses may be closed. The Trust may boycott me. Never rent me no more film. Take my cameras. Close me up!"

"Tough titty," said Fergus.

"Fergus!" said his mother.

Simon turned. "Look, Mrs. Austin, let me see the boy. You go out and talk to Abe."

As Mrs. Austin opened the door, Fergus saw Abe, all slicked up, standing by the door, bowing smartly to his mother. He wondered why the hell Abe should be so polite to his ma. Nobody was polite to ma.

"Fergie—Fergus—" Simon corrected, "I got problems." His eyes brimmed.

Fergus sat up. Nobody had ever put on a show like this for him. And he knew Mr. Moses had no use for him.

"Fergus," said Simon, "I need your help."

"Mine?" said Fergus. "What could I do? Get beat up again? Rip my other pants?"

He had Mr. Moses on a skewer. He winced. "I'll buy you a new suit, boy, even two pairs of pants. I'll do anything." He gave it a thought. "Reasonable," he added.

Fergus had never been one up on an adult before. It was a powerful feeling.

"Fergus," said Simon, "when you get better, you gotta help me. I need someone who can think big."

"What's wong with Dave and Abe?"

Simon looked hurt. "Could I ask you if I didn't need help. Me—who am to blame for you lying there, covered with blood."

Fergus put his hand up to his nose. Was he bleeding again? He decided it was a figure of speech. He shifted slightly in bed.

"Don't move," said Simon, leaning forward to straighten the blanket. "Don't move. Just get well. Do you know what a big world this is? The opportunity. Oh, I wish I had your youth." He put his hands out. "I'd grab it, and I'd eat it with both hands."

Fergus was puzzled.

"This film business," he went on, "they're gonna break that Moving Picture Patent Company. No more Trust. No more monopolies and back-breaking rentals. They've had us by the shorts. But they can't get away with it. Everybody's gonna look at more and more movies. And make more. Nobody can stop it. It's a gold rush, son, a gold rush all over again!"

"What has this got to do with me?" said Fergus.

"I need somebody can use his wits. We gotta find all the outlaw companies. We gotta find free-lance movies. We gotta get a product that doesn't break our back. Why, we might even make our own. Just think, Ferg—us, moviemakers. Actresses. Travel. You're gonna work for me."

"With you, Mr. Moses," said Fergus.

"With me," echoed Simon, surprised. "You gotta get around. Go to Fort Lee—Biograph. See how they work. I can't."

Of course he can't, thought Fergus, with a flash of intuition. He's an exhibitor. He's known. But a kid could find out a lot about free-lance films and all.

"I'd have to be on a salary right away," said Fergus, "to spend the time. I'd have to give up my newspaper corner, and helping mom. That is, after my doctors get paid for."

Simon looked at him and grinned. "Say, Fergus," he said, "are you sure you're a goy? Are you sure we ain't related?"

Fergus managed a small grin. "How about it?"

"Well—how about two dollars a week?"

Fergus couldn't raise his eyebrows because his face hurt. It was a good thing.

"And I'll pay the doctors, and you get a new suit."

"I'll be in bed awhile," said Fergus. "You'd better have Dave or Esther or somebody bring me all the newspapers, reviews, and *Film Index* and *Motion Picture Story Magazine*. I'll study."

Simon looked at him with respect. "I'll have Esther bring them. We gotta think big."

He got up and took out his wallet. "Here's two dollars for the first week, partner."

"And a dollar you owe me for bicycling last night."

Simon didn't miss a beat. He took another dollar out and gave it to Fergus. "Think big," he said, flashing a false smile.

For a moment, Fergus lay back, trying to analyze his good fortune. His mother came in happily, disturbing his reverie.

"Did you have a nice visit?" she asked.

"Okay," said Fergus.

"You know," she said, pulling the curtains, "they're really nice people. Mr. Moses is so well mannered and handsome and open. I didn't know that Abe was such a nice young man."

"He ain't," said Fergus, looking at her suspiciously. "Why?"

She held up a paper. "Just for signing this little paper while you were visiting with Mr. Moses, he gave me a check for ten dollars. Imagine. That's quite a nest egg."

Fergus snatched the paper. She had signed a release on any injuries sustained by her son, Fergus Austin, in return for compensation. He looked at her with despair.

"We could have got a hundred dollars," he said. "Old man Moses never wanted any of this to be in court. He's in deep trouble with the film Trust. Why didn't you ask me?"

She looked at him, hurt. "Why, he's your friend."

That dirty old bastard, thought Fergus. Simon Moses is not my friend. He's my partner.

And so a few men parlayed the East Bronx movie house into a multi-million-dollar film studio. This dazzling business attracted and developed stars like Claudia and Jeffrey Barstow, whose lives were transformed overnight. Be sure to read the complete book as well as the sequel, BELINDA. They are both now available wherever Bantam Books are sold.

RELAX!
SIT DOWN
and Catch Up On Your Reading!

☐	11877	**HOLOCAUST** by Gerald Green	$2.25
☐	11260	**THE CHANCELOR MANUSCRIPT** by Robert Ludlum	$2.25
☐	10077	**TRINITY** by Leon Uris	$2.75
☐	2300	**THE MONEYCHANGERS** by Arthur Hailey	$1.95
☐	12550	**THE MEDITERRANEAN CAPER** by Clive Cussler	$2.25
☐	2500	**THE EAGLE HAS LANDED** by Jack Higgins	$1.95
☐	2600	**RAGTIME** by E. L. Doctorow	$2.25
☐	10888	**RAISE THE TITANIC!** by Clive Cussler	$2.25
☐	11966	**THE ODESSA FILE** by Frederick Forsyth	$2.25
☐	11770	**ONCE IS NOT ENOUGH** by Jacqueline Susann	$2.25
☐	11708	**JAWS 2** by Hank Searls	$2.25
☐	12490	**TINKER, TAILOR, SOLDIER, SPY** by John Le Carre	$2.50
☐	11929	**THE DOGS OF WAR** by Frederick Forsyth	$2.25
☐	10526	**INDIA ALLEN** by Elizabeth B. Coker	$1.95
☐	12489	**THE HARRAD EXPERIMENT** by Robert Rimmer	$2.25
☐	10422	**THE DEEP** by Peter Benchley	$2.25
☐	10500	**DOLORES** by Jacqueline Susann	$1.95
☐	11601	**THE LOVE MACHINE** by Jacqueline Susann	$2.25
☐	10600	**BURR** by Gore Vidal	$2.25
☐	10857	**THE DAY OF THE JACKAL** by Frederick Forsyth	$1.95
☐	11952	**DRAGONARD** by Rupert Gilchrist	$1.95
☐	2491	**ASPEN** by Burt Hirschfeld	$1.95
☐	11330	**THE BEGGARS ARE COMING** by Mary Loos	$1.95

Buy them at your local bookstore or use this handy coupon for ordering:

DON'T MISS
THESE CURRENT
Bantam Bestsellers

☐	11708	**JAWS 2** Hank Searls	$2.25
☐	11150	**THE BOOK OF LISTS** Wallechinsky & Wallace	$2.50
☐	11001	**DR. ATKINS DIET REVOLUTION**	$2.25
☐	11161	**CHANGING** Liv Ullmann	$2.25
☐	10970	**HOW TO SPEAK SOUTHERN** Mitchell & Rawls	$1.25
☐	10077	**TRINITY** Leon Uris	$2.75
☐	12250	**ALL CREATURES GREAT AND SMALL** James Herriot	$2.50
☐	12256	**ALL THINGS BRIGHT AND BEAUTIFUL** James Herriot	$2.50
☐	11770	**ONCE IS NOT ENOUGH** Jacqueline Susann	$2.25
☐	11699	**THE LAST CHANCE DIET** Dr. Robert Linn	$2.25
☐	10150	**FUTURE SHOCK** Alvin Toffler	$2.25
☐	12196	**PASSAGES** Gail Sheehy	$2.75
☐	11255	**THE GUINNESS BOOK OF WORLD RECORDS 16th Ed.** The McWhirters	$2.25
☐	12220	**LIFE AFTER LIFE** Raymond Moody, Jr.	$2.25
☐	11917	**LINDA GOODMAN'S SUN SIGNS**	$2.50
☐	10310	**ZEN AND THE ART OF MOTORCYCLE MAINTENANCE** Pirsig	$2.50
☐	10888	**RAISE THE TITANIC!** Clive Cussler	$2.25
☐	2491	**ASPEN** Burt Hirschfeld	$1.95
☐	2222	**HELTER SKELTER** Vincent Bugliosi	$1.95

Buy them at your local bookstore or use this handy coupon for ordering: